THE VEIL
OF
ILLUSION

Also by Rebecca Ryman

OLIVIA AND JAI

REBECCA RYMAN

THE VEIL
OF
ILLUSION

A NOVEL

St. Martin's Press ✹ *New York*

Library of Congress Cataloging-in-Publication Data
Ryman, Rebecca.
    The veil of illusion   /   Rebecca Ryman.
      p. cm.
    ISBN 0-312-13200-X
    1. India—History—19th century—Fiction.   I. Title.
PR9499.3.R9V45   1995
823—dc20   95-16218
                                               CIP

First Edition: August 1995

10 9 8 7 6 5 4 3 2 1

In loving memory of my husband

Gone but always near

AUTHOR'S NOTE

I have to express my warm thanks to the many dear friends and relations whose good nature and affection I have once again blatantly exploited to produce this sequel to the story of *Olivia and Jai*. Having pestered them endlessly for their comments and criticism—and no doubt bored and irritated them in equal measure—I marvel that their patience never flagged even though, I daresay, their energies frequently did. Being one of those to whom the mysteries of electronics are always likely to remain so, I am also greatly indebted to my computer-enlightened gurus, who were always on hand with their magic mantras and waving wands to counter unwitting calamities. Admirably tolerant of my ignorance, they helped me to understand at least some of the bewildering esoterica of artificial intelligence.

I would also like to thank my agent, Robert I. Ducas, for his unfailing encouragement, and George Witte of St. Martin's Press for his forbearance with missed deadlines and his patient and perceptive editing. Finally, my gratitude to all those whose meticulous labours behind the scenes have combined to fashion this book and steer it through the complexities of publication.

A FOREST CLEARING NEAR CAWNPORE, NORTHERN INDIA

JULY 1857

PROLOGUE

A N ENGLISH ARMY CAPTAIN in his early thirties sits writing at an improvised desk in a dilapidated shed. His uniform is torn, the heavily stained jacket unbuttoned carelessly down the front. Below his ginger hair, matted and unkempt, his face is drawn, showing signs of immense fatigue. Trapped underneath the seasonal cover of swollen monsoon clouds, the still, turgid air is oppressive, made even more so by the persistent swarms of flies. Another English army officer, a lieutenant and equally bedraggled, enters through a jagged hole in the brickwork which comprises the doorway. He walks to the upturned wooden crate at which his superior officer sits writing. His gaze skims over the untidy assortment of papers and objects heaped on a corner of the crate. Idly, he flicks through the scraps of papers, reading one or two. He picks up an object, a penknife in a wooden casing with the words "Paradise, Christmas 1854" carved into it. Next, he examines the silver pocket watch and chain, opening the back flap of the watch and studying the initials engraved within: "J.R." He smiles to himself, replaces that too, and clears his throat as a means of requesting attention. The captain ignores him and continues to write.

"Sir . . . ?" The junior officer ventures an interruption. A comment is forming in his mind but he hesitates to voice it.

For a moment the unspoken words hang between them, palpable, quivering. Then, with a quizzical look, the captain tilts his head to one side.

"Well, had a good look?"

"Yes, sir."

"And *is* it?"

"Without a doubt, sir. I am absolutely certain." The lieutenant's confirmation comes without hesitation.

"There is no question of error?"

"No, sir."

The captain smiles and picks up his pen. The junior officer is silent, his expression thoughtful. After a while he again clears his throat.

"Shall I have it taken down, sir?"

"No." The captain does not look up. "Let it be."

"It will be difficult to keep the scavengers away tonight, sir. And the mood of the crowd is turning ugly."

"Don't keep them away. Let them have their fill."

The junior officer stares, shocked, then swallows hard as if fighting nausea. "And the crowd, sir?"

The captain shrugs. "Their mood is immaterial. Let them have their fill too." He continues to write.

The lieutenant debates silently for a moment, then, arriving at a decision, puts both hands on the desk, palms down. "But surely, sir, the point is already made. What do we gain by this . . . unnecessarily provocative display?" He waits for a reaction; receiving none, he doggedly carries on. "The feeling even among our own men, sir, with all due respects, is that enough is enough. After all, we don't want another rebellion on our hands. If you ask my advice, sir, I. . . ."

"I don't ask your advice, Tom. Leave it where it is."

The lieutenant flushes at the rebuke and snaps his mouth shut. The captain pays him no further attention, again immersed in his work. The lieutenant shrugs, walks up to what might once have been a window and stands staring out in sullen silence. Finally, it is the captain who breaks the silence, his tone noticeably less brusque.

"You are not long out of England, are you, Tom?"

The junior officer turns. "No, sir, eight months."

"Sandhurst, if I remember correctly?"

"Yes, sir."

The captain chuckles. "I take it, how to fight rapists and killers of women and children in a mutiny of savages wasn't part of your curriculum, was it, Tom?"

The lieutenant chews on a lip but says nothing.

"Well, there are many more unorthodox lessons yet to be learned in this God-rotting country, Tom. Especially the cardinal rule for survival—when among beasts, *live* like one." He lays down his pen, carefully blots the ink dry and starts to collate the sheaf of papers. "I assume that you are not unaware of the Bibighar? Or of General Neill's orders?"

There is sarcasm in the question and the lieutenant lowers his eyes. "I am aware of them, sir."

"A salutary example is to be made, Tom. The bigger the fish, the more salutary the example."

The lieutenant's chin rises in a gesture of mild defiance. He opens his mouth to say something, but then, thinking better of it, shuts it again.

The captain resumes his work, his pen poised to make occasional corrections to what he has written. The young lieutenant heaves a long, audible sigh, as if in resignation, and walks back to the window. Finally, the captain finishes the review of his report and gets up. He stretches his limbs, yawns, and strolls over to join the lieutenant.

Outside, in the litter-strewn forest clearing, a sparse crowd of peasants sits in silence on the sun-baked ground at the base of a spreading peepul tree. In between, a few sepoys walk about, aimlessly brandishing swords. Their faces, dull and dirt-stained, show no expression, but in their darting eyes there is confusion and, perhaps, something else not easily definable. Green and lush and cool-looking, the giant tree presents a sharp contrast to the arid landscape visible beyond the edge of the thicket. The crowd is quiet, but the hushed silence is deceptive and charged with tension. All eyes are turned upwards, riveted to the tree.

From one of its branches hangs the body of a man.

Urged by sporadic breezes, the near-naked corpse swings gently to and fro in the lap of the breeze, glassy eyes in a barely discernible face staring stupidly at nothing. At the foot of the improvised gallows, vaguely standing guard, are two more sepoys, as weary and apathetic as their counterparts. A pack of stray dogs prances and whines beneath the carcass, snapping hungrily at the swinging heels just beyond reach. A family of wild pigs sniffs the air and restlessly awaits its turn from a safe distance. Above the extensive peepul, against the metallic grey of the monsoon sky, circles a cloud of shrieking, long-necked vultures, impatient to swoop for their own share of the bounty.

A whiff of something putrid carries on the wind and reaches the window. The captain grimaces, and almost retching, the lieutenant hastily takes out a soiled handkerchief and clamps it to his nose. Out in the compound, one of the sepoys flourishes his sword and makes a move towards the carcass, as if to cut it down. He pauses, then glances uncertainly over his shoulder at the window where the two men stand. Pointedly, the captain's right hand moves to the holster of the pistol strapped to his waist and remains there. The sepoy has a moment of uncertainty, then he lowers his sword and retreats, but reluctantly and with obvious resentment.

For a while the two Englishmen continue to stare in silence at the scene outside. Then, still without speaking, the captain walks back to his seat, gropes beneath the wooden crate and takes out a bottle. He raises it to the window in a mockery of a toast, smiles, and takes a swig. Wiping his mouth with the back of his hand, he nods his head at the lieutenant. The latter hesitates, but then, as the captain makes a gesture of impatience, unhooks a flask from his belt and drinks from it greedily. It is only rough country liquor, but he gulps it down in huge, thirsty swallows. Continuing to smile, the captain extracts a crumpled cheroot from his pocket, lights up and inhales with obvious pleasure. He stares again at the scene outside, abstractedly and without emotion.

"Are you frightened, Tom? Concerned about reprimands? Reprisals, perhaps?"

The lieutenant runs the tip of his tongue over his cracked lips. "Well, sir, he is believed to have had considerable influence with the Nana Sahib. . . ."

5

"There will be no reprimands, Tom, no reprisals. His influence, such as it was, is no longer of importance. The black beggars are already on the run. Naturally, the Nana Sahib leads the rat pack." He chuckles, but the sound is devoid of humour. "They say he plans to drown himself."

The lieutenant stares at the body hanging from the tree and continues to look troubled. "I know, sir, but it's still a mystery, isn't it?"

"Not so much a mystery, Tom, as a *miracle*. You might even say, manna from heaven!" He laughs, but then, swiftly, wipes the amusement off his face. His eyes narrow. "As far as we are concerned, Tom, he was captured fairly, entirely in accordance with prevailing orders. This is still war, my conscience-stricken friend, make no mistake about that! Indeed, from now on, it will *always* be war in this accursed country—in case you suffer any pious delusions to the contrary." He pauses for breath and his tone hardens. "He was the arch-fiend behind the massacres. For that alone, the punishment and the price on his head are justified."

The lieutenant remains troubled. "You intend to . . . claim that reward, sir?"

"Not *you*, Tom," the captain amends softly, "*we*." He allows himself another small smile, pleasurably savouring the other man's discomfiture. "Five thousand pounds, even halved, is hardly an inconsiderable sum—wouldn't you agree, Tom? More than adequate, shall we say, to override even the most tiresome of consciences?" The younger man cannot conceal the involuntary glint that leaps into his eyes. Catching it, the captain laughs under his breath, walks over and places a paternal hand on his shoulder. "This has been a bloody, bloody war, Tom, hasn't it?" His tone now is smooth, conciliatory. Tears he can no longer control start to stream down the lieutenant's cheeks. The captain pats his back comfortingly and takes another long draught from the bottle. "If you must shed tears, my boy, shed them for those deserving of your compassion, the pitiable, innocent band of victims at Satichowra Ghat, and in that monstrous well outside the Bibighar. Cry for *them*, Tom, our own flesh and blood, our kith and kin, not for this"—his features twist with hate as he spits loudly out of the window—"this *mongrel!*" With an effort he brings himself again under control. "He was an enemy, Tom, the Nana Sahib's flunkey, his brother in crime. It was his malignant brain that devised all this evil, Tom—have you forgotten that so soon?"

The lieutenant lifts his head and stares, biting hard on his lip to pull himself together. "No, sir." He averts his face.

The captain strokes his unshaven chin, plucking at it, his eyes slitted with malice. "One way or another, they are all part of Satichowra Ghat, and those abominations at the Bibighar! Never forget that, Tom, not for an instant. Do you think even one of these allegedly loyal black bastards out there," he cocks his head contemptuously at the window, "would hesitate to run a knife through your gut, or mine, given the chance?"

The junior officer stares down at his feet and shuffles them, still uncertain. "Perhaps not, sir, but Samuels said that at the Bibighar. . . ."

"Samuels is dead, Tom."

The lieutenant's eyes again fill with tears. "I know, sir. But he was my friend, sir. He. . . ."

"Samuels was touched with the tarbrush, Tom," the captain breathes with vicious softness, "hardly a worthy friend for someone of *your* calibre, Tom—or was he?" It is with great difficulty that the captain restrains his temper. "Do I need to repeat what we, the English, think of those touched with the tarbrush, Tom?" His blazing eyes pin down the lieutenant's gaze so that the younger man is unable to look away. "The half-caste is by nature sly, devious, wholly unworthy of the white man's trust. You would do well to remember that too, my friend. The Englishman has *abhorrence* for the half-caste, Tom, especially one who has, shall we say," his voice slips into a silken purr, "*lied* for the sake of his own miserable advancement?"

Slowly, the lieutenant's expression changes; where there was uncertainty, now there is fear. He runs the tip of his tongue nervously over drying lips. "I . . . wouldn't know, sir." His whisper is scarcely audible.

"Wouldn't you, Tom?" The captain does not raise his voice, but it is still sharp, like a whiplash, as he points out of the window. "He was one of those five butchers at the Bibighar, Lieutenant. And it is to *us* that the hand of Providence, in all its glorious unpredictability, has chosen to deliver him. Beyond that, you need not be concerned." The thin lips are tight with anger. "It's all in my report, *our* report, Tom. I suggest you commit every word of that report to memory *very, very* thoroughly. Should you be tempted to resort to convenient amnesia while deposing before any inquiry committee, it would not bode well for your future in the British Army. Do I make my meaning clear?"

The lieutenant squeezes his eyes shut, his face white, his hands clenched tight by his sides. A spasm runs through his body. Unable to speak, he merely nods.

"Good." The captain takes another gulp of his drink. For a long time there is silence between the two men as they stand at the window gazing out, each lost in his own thoughts. Then the captain pulls in a long, shuddering breath. His eyes are far away, focussed dreamily on something remote, something perhaps in another dimension.

"She was only nineteen, you know."

It is a private thought murmured aloud. The lieutenant makes no response.

"We were to be married in six months."

The lieutenant gulps and wipes the sweat off his forehead, relieved at the change of topic. "So I've heard, sir."

"Oh?"

"Well. . . . Samuels did talk about it in the barracks, sir."

The captain's face is expressionless. "What else did Samuels talk about in the barracks, Tom?"

"It was just idle g-gossip, sir." The lieutenant's fingers pluck nervously at each other.

"What did the idle gossip suggest, Tom?" the captain persists. The younger man's expression is again fearful as he struggles to contain his panic. "Well?"

"That . . . that it all happened a long time ago, sir," he mumbles. "In Calcutta."

"A long time ago?" the captain frowns. "No, the gossip is wrong, Tom. It happened *yesterday*." The lieutenant looks bewildered, his glances alternating between the impassive face of his companion and the gruesome sight outside in the compound. "You don't entirely understand, do you, Tom?"

"No, sir."

"No matter, Tom, no matter. One day, when you have been in this hellbound country as long as I have, you will. As you will understand all this for what it really is." He waves his hand at the window. "Biblical justice, Tom, no more, no less." He drains the bottle and tosses it out of the window. It hits the hard, sun-baked earth with a clatter. He throws his shoulders back and pulls himself up to his full height, his voice brisk and his manner businesslike. "Let him swing tonight, Tom. At dawn, if these bloody beggars are still there, let them have him. If not, feed him to the pigs." About to dismiss the matter with a gesture, he halts and holds up a forefinger. "Except for the head, of course. Mutilated or not, the authorities will need to see the damnable bastard's *face!*"

CALCUTTA

1 8 7 1

THROUGH THE WIRE MESH at the kitchen house window, Maya Raventhorne gazed thoughtfully across the back garden. Beyond, the river gleamed like a milky opal, thick with drowse and sheened with diffident gold from the slowly rising sun. The water's surface was dawn smooth, polished; its movement so delicate in its languid undulations as to be almost imperceptible. The hesitant winds, poised between night cool and morning incandescence, sat motionless for the moment, silently plotting diurnal battle strategy. The morning was still defiantly crisp, the embankment still alive with people muttering their morning mantras as they hurried to finish ablutions before the sun attacked in all its thermal majesty. Like a huntsman, the deceptively soft buttercup yellow spread lazily across the eastern horizon, stalking the apricot blush of dawn with predatory relish. Very soon, all memory of the morning cool would vanish; only the familiar brassy gold would remain, promising an early spring day of punishing warmth.

As she stared out of the window, however, Maya's thoughts dwelt neither on the slowly awakening Hooghly nor on whatever murderous plans the sun might be devising for the hapless denizens of the city. What absorbed her totally was the thought of English muffins.

No, she conceded sadly, turning her gaze back to the sorry mess spreadeagled across the baking tray; her very first attempt at English muffins had not been an unqualified success. The one she had sampled had tasted very definitely of mouldy cardboard; there was no reason to hope the rest would be any better. It was, of course, the fault of that flour she had foolishly allowed herself to be talked into buying from the wretched local bania. She should never have listened to Ah Ling, concerned only with saving himself a long run into town. She should have trusted her own instincts and despatched Sheba to Mr. Barton's grocery where, if one paid a few pice more, one was at least assured of the finest imported English quality.

"So, what do you two think we ought to do?" she asked the pair of handsome black, white and tan English setters hunched in the back door-way watching her with puzzled, frowning eyes. "We can't *possibly* serve up these disasters to Christian Pendlebury, can we? What on earth would he *think* of me, of us all?"

The dogs whimpered and shuffled their front paws but vouchshafed no decipherable opinion. Maya sighed, feeling the first stirrings of an unchar-acteristic panic; somehow the situation had to be redeemed before the afternoon. Fortunately, there was still time enough for remedial action. Had Mother been home and in a receptive frame of mind, she might well have come up with some acceptable solution with her usual resourceful-ness. But since she had left for Clive Street unusually early this morning, and since Anthony, the confectionery cook, was still not well enough to resume his duties, there was no alternative but to fall back on the advice of Sheba, their housekeeper, well meaning but probably inadequate in a sit-uation of such extreme delicacy.

Resolutely suppressing her brief spell of panic and ignoring Ah Ling's covert amusement and the scullion's rather more cheeky sniggers, Maya walked out of the kitchen house in search of the housekeeper, followed by Sugar and Spice jostling each other with excited yelps in the hope of some proper exercise around the paddocks.

As always recently at almost any given time of the day—and sometimes night—Sheba would no doubt be found in the dhobi house beyond the stables at the back of the servants' quarters. As she skirted the paddock and caught sight of Abdul Mian entering the stable house, Maya's foot-steps faltered. For a moment she stood debating whether she should make a quick detour to inquire about Cavalcade's condition, but then she decided against it. Abdul Mian was an experienced groom; he would have already done whatever was necessary by way of treatment. Cavalcade could wait; the muffins definitely could not.

As she resumed her journey towards the dhobi house, Maya guessed exactly the scene that would greet her in the large, stone-flagged shed that was the collection point of the mountainous daily household wash. Nor was she wrong. However, a stranger chancing upon the shed might be for-given for mistaking the dhobi house for a highly sacrosanct place of wor-ship within which some profoundly religious ritual was in progress. A captivated audience crammed the large shed to capacity, all eyes fixed in awe upon a small clearing in the middle of the room.

Present were the dhobi with his assistant and their combined families, both the ayahs, the chief bearer, the water-carriers, the gardener's entire family, all three day punka-wallahs en route to their duties inside the main house, a large contingent of assorted children, most of the servants from the neighbouring homes on either side, some with their families, and for good measure, a few stragglers from the embankment curious to see what the fuss was all about. In silent reverence, they gazed upon the centrepiece of the room: a squat, ugly, wooden barrel-shaped object open at the top, standing on four metal legs. Across the opening of the barrel were affixed two parallel rollers, one above the other, with a common handle. Sheba stood next to the barrel vigorously turning the handle to the accompaniment of a diligent, if somewhat breathless, commentary. Her manner, as she explained the process and purpose of her labour, was that of an evangelist exhibiting some divine device guaranteed to provide a lifetime of bliss.

The home washing machine and wringer, arrived only last month from New York and the first such apparatus in Calcutta, was the current passion of Sheba's life and, inevitably, the wonder of the White Town neighbourhood. Even the la-di-dah Mrs. and Misses Anderson next door—quite capable of publicly cutting dead the family in other circumstances—had been driven to request permission to witness a demonstration of the miracle machine proclaimed to be sounding the death knell of washboard drudgery in thousands of households across the American continent.

"Well yes, it *does* take the drudgery out of washing clothes, I grant you," Mrs. Anderson had reluctantly admitted to a tongue-tied Sheba overwhelmed by the honour of the visit, "but if one banishes *all* drudgery from one's life, pray, what is one to give one's horde of servants to do? They're idle enough as it is." Privately, however, Mrs. Anderson had been much put out. She had lost no time in writing off to her sister in Boston to purchase the miracle device for instant despatch to Calcutta aboard the very next steamship sailing. As she put it to her husband, "Of course, one *expects* ill-bred ostentation from *that* family." She paused and sniffed pointedly in case he missed the import of her italics. "But isn't it imperative that the station's pukka *English* households not let down their own side? It is, after all, a matter of national honour!"

"Well, *hardly*, my dear!" Buried within the pages of his copy of the *Times of India* fresh from Bombay, Lucas Anderson took care to keep his own italics mild. "If Britain's honour is to be contingent on imported American whimsicalities, one might as well pack up the blasted Empire and go home!"

"That's not the point, Lucas!" his wife retorted warmly. "Why, the natives might think we English can't *afford* to import a simple American clothes washer!" Her husband wasn't sure the natives wouldn't be right, but with great wisdom he refrained from saying so.

Understandably, the only members of the Raventhorne staff rather less than enthusiastic about the imported novelty were the two dhobis whose domain the newfangled invention had invaded and irredeemably annexed. Sensing a threat to their livelihood and comfortable existence in the Raventhorne household, they had adamantly refused to have anything to do with the intruder save stand and watch its daily performance from a disdainful distance. "The day *he* cleans collars better than I do," the senior dhobi had challenged darkly, "I will give up washing clothes and take to street sweeping."

Reluctant to be dragged away from her enchanting plaything in the wash house, Sheba nevertheless gave in to Maya's insistent pleadings and followed her back to the kitchen house. She surveyed the untidy baking tray with its unappetising load, cluck-clucked and shook her head in disapproval at all three—the disastrous muffins, the grinning cook, and the still sniggering scullion boy. Breaking off a piece of dough, she chewed on it.

"Well?" Maya asked anxiously. "What do you think?"

"They may not *all* be bad," the housekeeper finally pronounced with supreme optimism. "Maybe we could select a few, cover them with layers of honey and cream and chopped walnuts, and serve them up as Indian trifle pudding?"

"No, we could not!" Maya said crossly. "Christian Pendlebury's probably used to the finest, most elaborate trifles made by their own cooks in their own kitchens in England. We don't want him to think us unsophisticated *fools,* that too on his very first social engagement in station."

The housekeeper conceded the point with a solemn nod. "In that case, we could order a box of Mrs. Watkins's strawberry jam tartlets. They're always fresh; even the pukka memsahibs say so."

"Perhaps." Maya remained dubious. "But then she'll want to know who's coming to tea and why and from where, and she'll ask a thousand questions. You know what the old cat's like. Besides," she turned away with a faint heightening of colour, "I'd like Mr. Pendlebury to be served something he does not expect, something that reminds him of home, something *English,* to show we're not all monkeys just off the trees!"

Sheba was tempted to point out that strawberry jam tartlets were every bit as English as muffins, but she restrained herself. When the child got something into her head it was useless to argue. It was obvious she had worked herself into a rare pet, which, for this quiet, secretive girl, was curious. "Maybe if you asked Madam, she would agree to bake something American for you, apple turnovers, perhaps?"

"Goodness knows when Mother will be back from the office. Besides, considering how unpredictable her moods can be, it would be *fatal* to depend on her for help. Oh, blast Anthony and his hives! Couldn't he have had them next week?"

Since that was a question to which there was no answer, Sheba offered none. However, after much discussion it was decided that the most sensible option would be to attempt a second batch of muffins with fresh flour, the best quality English available from Mr. Barton's.

"And if these go wrong as well?" Maya asked, far from satisfied. "What if it wasn't bad flour that ruined the first batch but something else?"

"Then we will just have to fall back on Mrs. Watkins's jam tartlets," Sheba said firmly. "And if by then she's out of them, maybe a pot of rasgollahs will have to do."

"No, *not* rasgollahs, for heaven's sake! He's only just arrived. He knows nothing of native sweets. And even if he does, he probably hates them. Most pukka people think they're over-sweet and gooey and dreadfully unhealthy. And they are, of course." She made a face to mark her own distaste. "Now, about the savouries. I've drawn up a tentative list of what could be considered. We have to have cucumber sandwiches, of course, cut very, very thin. Ah Ling does those quite well so we can leave them to him, and then there's a choice between potted shrimps and tuna fishcakes, or maybe both. I'll ask Mother if I can take some imported provisions out of the storeroom. We've still got those tinned oysters Grandma Sally sent out last Christmas. Maybe we could. . . ." She paused and frowned. "No. On second thought, we'd better not. Not everyone likes oysters. Samir had them over Christmas and was almost sick, remember? So, what we could serve instead might be. . . ." Still thinking aloud, she turned on her heel and strode out into the compound. Sheba followed more slowly, starting to look decidedly troubled.

It was a good hour later, when the vital high tea menu had eventually been decided following many revisions and much active debate, that Sheba decided to voice a hitherto unasked question. No matter how much it might anger the child, she felt she had to say something. "Inviting Mr. Pendlebury is all very well," she remarked quietly, "but do you think he will really . . . come?"

Maya stood still, her face expressionless. Then she smiled, a small, private smile. "Yes, he'll come," she breathed. "I know he will." For an instant, just an instant, a strange light shone in her startlingly blue eyes, and then it was gone.

"These pukkas say many things they don't mean, dearie," Sheba persisted, noticing the momentary sparkle. "Besides, I don't think your brother is likely to approve."

"Amos is out of town," Maya said shortly. "He's not expected back until the day after. Besides, whether or not he approves is of no interest to me. *Mother* has no objections since I've also asked Samir, tiresome as he is, and of course, Grace." She suddenly clenched her hands and flew into a temper. "Oh, what a *damned* fuss about nothing at all! It's only a silly old tea party, not a state banquet for the Viceroy!" In the act of flouncing out of the room, she stopped. "And *don't* call me 'dearie'—it's common and chichi and you know I *hate* it!" Very close to tears, she ran out of the room.

Not surprised by the sudden outburst but startled at the depth of the girl's feelings, Sheba ached with compassion. Poor child, poor confused, unhappy child—how unfair that she should have to go through all this with none of it her own fault! Sheba had been with the Raventhornes since Amos was two and Maya yet to be born. She had nurtured them, protected and cherished them both as her very own. She had shared in all their sufferings, all their tragic emotional upheavals over the years, first in Hawaii, then back here in Calcutta. She had watched them grow in their divergent ways, taken pride in their development into adults, into individuals in their own right. Much as she loved Amos, it was to Maya that she was totally devoted. She understood the girl, perhaps even better than her own mother did. That she should now be so torn, so utterly lost, pained Sheba more than she had the capacity to express. But she thanked the Lord that it would not be long now before they whisked the child away from here into the safe arms of her grandma. Once she was in California, everything would change. Things were different in America, *people* were different.

Sheba shook her head one last time. Then, remembering her unfinished demonstration, she brightened. Galvanised into action by thoughts of the mountains of unwashed clothes and an admiring audience, she hurried across the back lawn in the direction of the dhobi house.

"Ten thousand spindles and a hundred looms would constitute a great responsibility," Ranjan Moitra said, a frown creasing his usually smooth forehead. "The financial burden will be heavy, the risks very pronounced. On the other hand, whoever makes the highest bid at the auction would certainly have the privilege of owning the first upcountry cotton weaving mill in India." He paused to pick up a folded Bengali newspaper and successfully swatted a fat black fly hovering over the rim of his teacup on the desk. "The expansion *could* possibly serve Trident well. Or it could be a mistake of the highest order." He paused again, this time a whit longer, to wait for her response. When it did not appear to be forthcoming, he fell silent, leant back in his chair and stared out of the window in the direction of the jetty where the *Ganga* was unloading. He realised that he no longer had her attention. He waited a moment or two, then, still not receiving any response, called softly, "Mrs. Raventhorne . . . ?"

Moitra had to repeat her name twice before Olivia appeared to hear him. She blinked and raised a smile of apology. "Oh, I'm so sorry, Ranjan Babu, I seem to have let myself wander off again." She forced a rueful laugh, took a few sips from the teacup at her elbow, and leaned forward on the desk. "Ten thousand spindles and a hundred looms, did you say?" She made an effort to appear interested. "Yes, that does sound an awful lot. Would anyone be able actually to utilise all that capacity and still make a good profit?"

Moitra spread his hands across his desk. "Who can tell? Master Amos appears to believe that, with more efficient management and an importation of skilled technicians, *we* could."

"But you yourself are not certain?"

He pondered before replying. "No. I regret that I myself am far from certain. Our experience is with steam navigation, warehousing, the export of tea from our estates. In all these areas we are still acknowledged pioneers—despite past difficulties." He allowed himself a small smile of forgivable pride. "Therefore, I am not convinced that we can successfully diversify into cotton milling—and that too in Cawnpore." He gave her an oblique look. "Perhaps if Madam would talk to Master Amos . . . ?"

Olivia shook her head. "No, Ranjan Babu. That would not be right. Amos is no longer a child. He has worked with you long enough to have acquired the wherewithal to make independent judgements. He appears to have thought over the matter of the mill very seriously. If it is a mistake, then it will be *his* mistake. He must be allowed the chance to make it."

"The mistake could cost us dear, Madam, very dear."

Olivia smiled privately at the familiar conservatism. "In that case, we must hope that he will learn well from it," she said gently. "Children must be given the freedom to grow in their own way, at their own pace, Ranjan Babu. It is a principle my father and my husband both held dear. As for possible losses," she shrugged, "we can afford them. One can never put too high a price on lessons learned through mistakes." She rose and went to stand by the window, gazing out onto the Trident jetty and the controlled confusion of the wharfside below. For a while she stood in silence, absently waving the palm-leaf fan in front of her face.

She asked, "Are you seriously considering selling the *Ganga*, Ranjan Babu?"

He pulled in a deep breath of resignation; she was no longer interested in the matter of the cotton mill. Indeed, she appeared to have entirely forgotten that it was to discuss precisely that that she had summoned him to the Trident office so early this morning. They had talked of it before Master Amos had left for Cawnpore, of course, but he was not certain how much she remembered. She had a habit of forgetting everything these days. Understandable, perhaps, but also sad. There was a time during her days with the Farrowsham Agency House when she was considered unique, the shrewdest, most courageous, certainly the most adventurous businesswoman in Calcutta. But then, so much had happened since, so much! For the moment, he decided to let the subject of the cotton mill lapse.

"We are wondering if it might not be the most practical thing to do, Madam," he said, answering her question with care. "The ship now shows her age, she is no longer economical to run, and maintenance costs rise every day." He coughed as if in apology. "She is, after all, twenty-three years old—a year older than Master Amos! One can no longer deny that she has outlived her usefulness."

"We?"

"Master Amos and myself."

"I see."

Amos too? *Outlived her usefulness.* In silent pain, Olivia turned over in her mind the phrase with which, in all innocence, he had dismissed so vital a slice of her life.

Would you have agreed with that verdict, Jai? Would you have ever considered discarding this marvel of her times you once called "poetry in motion," this dearly beloved vessel, silent witness to so much of our complex destinies . . . ?

Sensing something of what passed through her mind, almost feeling her pain, Moitra rose quickly and went to stand beside her at the window. "It is not heartlessness that prompts us, Madam," he said, his voice low and distressed. "The *Ganga* is a proud symbol of our past, but a past that can never return or be relived, except in memory. Now we must attempt to arrive at a point from which we cease to look back, a point at which the present and the future begin. Now we must begin to *accept*."

She turned wounded eyes towards him, wondering if he knew how much she was beginning to detest that word she had heard so often. "And this magical point, Ranjan Babu, have you yourself succeeded in arriving at it yet? Can you ever *accept*, knowing everything that has happened?"

Filled with emotion, for a while he could not speak. No, he wanted to tell her—unable to bear that she might be disappointed in him, question his loyalty after all these years—there was not a day, not a moment of a day, when he did not think of the Sarkar and burn with rage at the gross injustice perpetrated on him by the white usurpers. How could he not? It was the Sarkar who had given him the dignity of this high seat of office in Trident, extended to him his hand in friendship and brotherly love, made him into a man. Wisely, however, Moitra restrained his impulse and kept his thoughts to himself; he could not, *would* not, encourage her to brood over the past. Instead, he pointed out as emphatically as he dared, "But it *has* happened, Madam! Our histories can never now be undone. This it is surely foolishly stubborn and self-defeating not to accept!"

He stopped, again wondering if he had exceeded his limits. In all these years that she had been back, fighting valiantly to undo that very history that could not be undone, he had never ventured to speak to her with quite so much bluntness. But he saw that he worried needlessly; once again she had stopped listening and drifted away. For some reason, she was in an unusually melancholy mood this morning. He wondered why. There had been occasions when she had seemed so much better lately, so much more ready for reality. But then, there was often no logic to her moods: they went up and down each day like the tides in the river, and with far less reason.

With a sigh, Ranjan Moitra returned to his seat and let his eyes skim across the glass-entombed models of the Trident steamships that adorned his personal office. Normally the sight never failed to produce in him a tingle, a thrill, even after all these years. They had had many steamships since the *Ganga*, designed and built by America's most acclaimed nautical architects. The Trident fleet was still considered the finest, the swiftest, the most modern and most efficient east of the Suez Canal, even by competitors. But suddenly, somehow, Moitra too felt unaccountably dejected, the thought of past successes failing to revive his good humour.

In all honesty but privately, he sympathized with her feelings about the ship. The *Ganga* had been the Sarkar's very first American clipper, Calcutta's very first steam-propelled commercial vessel, way back in 'forty-eight. The Sarkar had loved it, been fiercely proud of it, had sailed in it with his family to the New World in those strange, desperate years of the early fifties. However uneconomical, the *Ganga* would always be a reminder of the Sarkar's spectacular triumph in beating the English at their own game. No, the *Ganga* could never be replaced. Sentiment and commerce do not mix, the Sarkar had always impressed upon him; nevertheless, Moitra could not help feeling ashamed of his own callous appraisal of the ageing clipper.

For a while longer he sat in patient silence, watching Olivia as she continued to stare through the window with that same somnolent, faraway look in her eyes that indicated she had once more lost touch with present reality and retreated within herself. At forty-five she was still a beautiful woman, her chestnut hair touched only very delicately with grey. Her tall, lithe figure was still youthful, the smooth oval of her face belying the terrible tragedies of her life. What was lost—sadly and perhaps irrevocably—was the core, the substance, that astonishing vitality that had once shone with such fierceness out of her luminescent golden eyes. Yes, she had changed much in these past years, Moitra concluded sorrowfully; but then, how could she not have? She who had suffered so grievously, battled so hard, lost so much and so many! With a shuddering little breath, he leaned forward, folded his hands on his desk and impatiently cast aside his futile regrets. Regardless of consequences and her displeasure, he felt he must now complete what he had started to say. Sooner or later it had to be said; better now when he had the courage than later when he might not.

But before he could speak, Olivia did. "Perhaps you are right, Ranjan Babu," she conceded, surprising him. Returning to the desk, she again seated herself opposite him. "It appears that history refuses to be undone after all." She rummaged within her handbag to pull out an envelope, the back flap of which, Moitra noticed, bore the Viceroy's seal of office. "This was delivered to me yesterday morning. You will be pleased to note that Lord Mayo agrees entirely with your thinking."

He was wounded by the bitterness in her voice, even though he could guess what news the Viceroy's communication would bear. Nevertheless he made a show of reading the letter with attention. Submerged in lengthy official rhetoric, the gist of the letter was brief, impersonal, and precisely what he had expected. The signature it bore was of some minion in the viceregal Secretariat who begged to inform Mrs. Olivia Raventhorne that His Excellency had considered very carefully the request made by her in her petition of 30 January 1871. However, since no new, relevant and irrefutable facts had been presented in the matter pertaining to the case of Mr. Jai Raventhorne (deceased), Her Majesty's Government in India regretted that no justifiable reason could be found to reopen the case for review. Mrs. Olivia Raventhorne was therefore advised to take it as final that the above-numbered file was now irrevocably closed, and that no further petitions relating to this matter would be entertained.

Moitra folded the letter neatly and replaced it within the envelope. So *that* was why she was so excessively depressed this morning! He felt a surge of anger at the cold-blooded tone of the letter, a sense of disappointment as cutting as hers. She deserved better, far better, this strange, deep American woman he had been privileged to serve for two decades and whom he had grown to love like a sister. But then, if even her own karma had never played her fair, never, from the very beginning, why should the uncaring British Crown? The sahibs had always hated the Sarkar, more so since the Mutiny. Why should they not continue to do so now when so many vile official falsehoods had been propagated to justify that hatred? Seething with resentment, he nonetheless considered it prudent to remain silent rather than add to her sorrow with meaningless platitudes.

Olivia ran the back of her hand across her eyes wearily, too defeated even for tears. "A fitting memorial for your Sarkar, would you say, Ranjan Babu? A dehumanised file, a *closed* file, left to decay in perpetuity on some dusty shelf." She laughed, a hollow, despairing sound. "But you are right, I cannot fight any more. I am sucked dry of energy, defeated at last. And tired, very tired. . . ."

He was profoundly moved at seeing her so devastated, so without hope. "I am truly sorry," he started, then stopped.

No, he was not sorry at all! At least, he must *force* himself not to feel sorry. What he must now feel was relief—relief at the arrival of this cold, arrogant letter that had closed forever the final door of appeal and so ended her unbearable suspense. Sometimes it was necessary to be cruel to be kind, and thirteen years were long enough to have battled against events that could never now be reversed, however mutilated their consequences. He would miss her greatly when she sailed for America; she was as vital, as indispensable a part of his life as had been his beloved Sarkar. But regardless of his own sentiments, for her sake he was glad. It was time she buried the past and all its wretchedness and started to live again in her own country, with her own people, at least for the sake of her children.

Her children. . . .

Ranjan Moitra gave a small start as he suddenly remembered his conversation with Mr. William Donaldson's head clerk yesterday during a routine visit to the Farrowsham Agency House. He wondered—should he inform her of the current rumour circulating around the Farrowsham offices? But then he decided against it. She was dejected enough as it was; it would be heartless to add to her troubles in this state of intense depression, and in any case, she would find out for herself soon enough. In silence, Moitra rose to escort Olivia out of the door of his office and through the cool, spacious halls of the main Trident workrooms down into Clive Street, where her carriage awaited.

The thoroughfare was beginning to come to life with its customary morning traffic of carriages and horses, bearing Calcutta's merchants to their places of work in the ever-expanding commercial district. Familiar confusion prevailed everywhere: two handcart pullers, their carts entangled and their bundles of cargo scattered, argued vociferously while an indolent constable stood by and grinned. Although, understandably, it was English presence that dominated Calcutta's foreign population, the seat of Britain's Eastern Empire was a remarkably cosmopolitan city. Apart from several thousand residents from other Asian countries, Calcutta boasted an affluent European contingent representative of many nations on the Continent, energetically engaged in social and commercial pursuits. A scattering of beggars now scurried after the pedestrians, many in their colourful traditional wear: Armenians, Chinese, Burmese, Jews, Parsis, Afghans and Pathans, Arabs, Europeans, English and, of course,

Bengalis. Hands outstretched, the mendicants—some of them children—solicited alms in thin, reedy voices, patting their bare stomachs like hollow drums, latching on to those who appeared less likely to send them packing with a flea in their ear. Quickly, Olivia opened her purse and thrust a handful of coins at a lame boy who hobbled forward to open the carriage door for her, much to her coachman's annoyance. Had it not been for her patronage of him, he would certainly have given the boy a mouthful.

European passers-by gave Olivia curious looks accompanied by fleeting smiles and then, embarrassed, looked away. One or two even doffed their hats but then hastily strode away, hoping that the gesture of greeting had passed unnoticed by their peers. Some Bengali merchants, however, looking somewhat odd in their knee-high socks and English shoes below crisp white dhotis, stopped and bowed with folded hands in the traditional mark of respect.

Whether Olivia was even aware of all this, Moitra could not tell, for once again her thoughts seemed far away. He stood and watched her departing carriage, his expression pensive and troubled. Should the rumour circulating about Farrowsham be true, how would she react to it, he wondered.

More to the point—how would Master Amos?

Quietly, Maya tiptoed through the doorway. In spite of the blazing day outside—or perhaps because of it—the heavy curtains were drawn tightly across the bay window and the bedroom was bathed in gloom. In the silence, the rhythmic creak of the punka sounded like the mournful chirp of a starling stranded somewhere among the rafters. Despite the valiant endeavours of the punka-wallah, crouched sleepily in a corner behind the door of the balcony, the air was sluggish, suffocating in its humidity. Why her mother had refused to instal a thermantidote in one of the windows as in the other bedrooms, Maya had never been able to understand. She made a sound of exasperation; striding to the window, she resolutely swept aside the heavy green velvet curtains she disliked so much and threw open the shutters. Instantly, the room flooded with gusts of air, warm but fresh, and middle afternoon sunlight. The sleeping figure on the fourposter, however, still did not stir.

For a moment Maya stood surveying the room. Clothes lay scattered everywhere; peeping from under the bed was a pair of sandals, tossed off carelessly. The rolltop desk stood open, an array of brown, faded photographs in ornate silver frames ranged on its top shelf. Family groups on a distant, forgotten beach—carefree, smiling faces unaware of future disasters, frozen forever in a moment of indestructible happiness. One face in particular held her gaze and would not let go: an arrogant, handsome face, Amos and yet not Amos, alien and yet remembered, dead and yet ever alive. She wrenched her gaze away from the unmoving, silverfish eyes and laid the picture flat, face down. On top of a clutter of old newspapers was an issue of *Equality*. The initial sentences of the editorial on the front page caught her eye: "The Eurasian situation in India can best be explained with the help of a piano keyboard. Neither black nor white, Eurasians are the spaces that lie between the keys. This vacancy, this absence of shape and form, this amorphous *nothingness* if you like, is the essence of the Eurasian trapped between the cultural duality that is India."

The editorial incensed Maya. With an exclamation of disgust, she swept the periodical off the desk into the wastepaper basket. The movement raised a cloud of dust; she coughed, then vented her silent irritation on her mother's ayah, snoring away outside the door. Again the wretched woman was neglecting to dust the room twice daily as instructed—oh, if only Mother would start taking an interest in her household and staff! She lingered at the desk for a moment, then shrugged, retrieved the magazine from the wastepaper basket, and grudgingly replaced it on the desk.

Walking up to the large bed, Maya leaned over the motionless mound shrouded in a white cotton sheet. Her eyes clouded; in silence she stood and observed the sleeping face. Her mother had appeared so much better, so much more at peace, before that wretched letter arrived, almost her normal self again. Normal self? The words brought a sour smile to Maya's lips; what *was* her mother's normal self, anyway? *She* had never known her to be any different! And now, given the excuse of that letter, she would again turn inwards, sitting and brooding for hours on those infernal steps by the river, regressing deeper and deeper into the past.

"Mother?" she called in a whisper. Receiving no answer, she laid a light hand on the cloud of chestnut hair, so much like her own, spilling across the pillow; it was damp with perspiration. Her eyes softened. *Rapunzel, Rapunzel, let down your golden hair. . . .* In the much loved bedtime story, to her, her mother had always been the beautiful princess whose hair the prince climbed up each night to woo her in her castle cell. Remembering, savouring again flickering images of a long-ago childhood memory, Maya inadvertently smiled. Hesitantly, she skimmed the palm of a hand across the tangled denseness. Olivia woke with a start, half sat up and stared around her with dazed, fearful eyes. "Yes? Wh-what's happened?"

Maya pressed a reassuring hand down on her shoulder. "Nothing's happened, Mother. I'm sorry if I startled you." Quickly, she rearranged her features into their customary impassivity. "It's almost four o'clock— aren't you going to get up and change?"

Olivia struggled up further, still entangled in the meshes of the dream that stretched across her consciousness like a giant cobweb. Reaching back into the crevices of her mind, behind closed eyes, she sat invoking the gossamer visions, reliving them one by one, reluctant to let them go. . . .

The Hawaiian sand was warm beneath their feet, sparkling white like fine sugar; the sea was blue and green and malignant gold and treacherous, for she knew it was about to betray her. In the distance, far away beyond the green hills and the sandalwood forests and the sweet scent of fruit, she heard the drums and the bugles and the cannon, and she was screaming to be heard above the din—the world doesn't need any more heroes, Jai, the world can do without you! And he

was smiling and smiling and shaking his head and speaking in those silken, sooth-
ing, persuasive tones she had learned to fear so much. Yes it can, I know it can, he
was saying, but I have to silence the drums and the bugles and the cannon. I have
to go, I have to go, I have to go. . . . And he walked backwards into the sea, and she
watched him melt into the spray and become one with the sky and the sun and the
winds, knowing that he was no longer hers, knowing that they would never now
return him to her. . . .

The dream was so vivid in her mind that, for a moment, she remained as she was, swaying back and forth, perched precariously on the rim of sleep, skin wet with fear, wet with the salt of that evil sea.

"Mother?"

"Yes," she murmured, without opening her eyes. "Yes, I'm awake, darling. I had no idea it was so late."

"You took another dose of laudanum?"

Olivia picked up a corner of the sheet, wiped her dripping face and nodded.

"You promised you wouldn't, not in the middle of the day!"

"Yes, I know. But I couldn't sleep and I was so tired, so *tired, . . .*" She lowered her face and buried it between the folds of the sheet.

Maya let it go; what was the use anyway? For a split second she had an overpowering urge to cry. Oh God, when will it all end? *Will* it ever end? Biting savagely on a lip, she swallowed her despair and, instead, walked away from the bed to the other side of the room towards her mother's large, double-fronted mahogany almirah. "They'll be here soon. I think you should get up and change." Olivia yawned and opened her eyes, trying to regroup her scattered wits. For a moment she sat gazing vacantly at her daughter, standing motionless before the full-length mirror on the almirah door surveying herself. "Do you think this is all right, Mother? Not too fussy for the occasion?"

With an effort, Olivia slid off the bed and fumbled her feet into her thonged leather slippers. "*Is* it an occasion, darling?" she asked vaguely, suppressing another yawn with difficulty. "No, it's very pretty, dear, very nice," she added without waiting for an answer to a question she had already forgotten.

"*Nice!*" Maya barred her way as Olivia padded heavily towards the bathroom, still not quite steady on her feet. "*Look* at me, Mother!" she cried, clutching both her mother's arms and shaking her. "Don't just mumble the first thing that comes into your mind—you haven't even noticed what I'm wearing!"

Taken by surprise, Olivia sat down heavily on the dressing-table stool. "Well, of course I have. . . ." She broke off and blinked rapidly several times, still leaden-headed with the drug and the dream. With an effort she focussed on her daughter and tried to concentrate, shading her eyes against the glare from the window. "I don't remember having seen that blue organdie before—it is blue, isn't it?"

"Yes, it's blue. The twins made it up for me last year. I've worn it twice before, once to the Seva Sangh annual concert. Don't you *remember?*"

23

"Of course I remember!" Olivia turned on the stool and, rubbing her forehead with two fingertips, scrutinised herself in the dressing-table mirror. Her eyes were puffy, her hair knotted and lifeless; she looked dreadful. "Did you say you met him at the wharf yesterday?"

"Yes. He arrived on the *Ganga*. I told you that last night."

"So you did." Picking up a comb, Olivia ran it slowly through her long, tangled tresses, wincing a little as she did so. "And you were with Grace, weren't you?"

"*Yes*, Mother! We had gone for an evening stroll on the Strand, Grace and I, and chanced upon Mr. Twining. He was there to receive Mr. Pendlebury. When the budgerow arrived at the wharf, he introduced us both to him."

Watching Maya in the mirror, for the first time and with some surprise, Olivia took in the heightened pinkness of her cheeks, the nervous twitching of her fingers, the rare animation in her intensely private blue eyes, so secretive, so intolerant of intrusion. And again that excessive use of talcum on her face! Within herself, Olivia sighed. "Clarence Twining knows the Pendlebury family, does he?"

"He knows *of* them, yes. An Inspector-General of Police is paid to know everything about everyone who arrives, he says. He had been requested by Lord Mayo's office to offer assistance to Mr. Pendlebury on his arrival. Evidently, Mr. Pendlebury's father is a baronet and a member of the Council of India in London. They have an estate in Buckinghamshire and a town house in Berkeley Square. His mother is a highly regarded hostess—Christian Pendlebury's mother, that is—and an active patroness of the arts. Invitations to her musical and literary soirées, Mr. Twining says, are very anxiously sought." If there was a ring of pride in her voice, Maya was not aware of it.

"Is that what impressed you about him?" Olivia asked before she could stop herself, and regretted it instantly.

Maya flushed. "No, of course it didn't *impress* me! I was merely repeating to you what Mr. Twining said about his family."

"I see. Is he in India on holiday?"

"No. He's a competition-wallah. After he's completed his various courses, he expects to be posted somewhere in the Mofussil." Anticipating her mother's next question, she added with a touch of sarcasm, "There was time to discover all this because Mr. Pendlebury's traps had been misplaced and it took Mr. Twining quite a while to find them."

"So, he's a competition-wallah." Olivia's tone was markedly flat.

"You say that as if you disapproved."

"One can hardly disapprove of the cream of England's youth, darling," Olivia pointed out drily. "Quite the contrary. Those able to pass the Civil Service examinations are judged to be exceptionally clever." *And exceptionally eligible.* She did not voice the thought. "Is that how he struck you?"

Maya shrugged, irritated by the subtle questioning, even more so by the reason for it. "He was pleasant. He talked well, seemed excited about his language studies at Fort William College and his prospects in the Civil Service. He said he hardly had any acquaintances in Calcutta but was eager to meet people, so I thought. . . ." She stopped and made a gesture of exasperation.

"Oh, I'm *pleased* you asked him to tea, dear! It's everyone's duty to be hospitable to newcomers." Carefully coiling her hair into a chignon, Olivia pinned it to the back of her head, then inserted a comb underneath to keep it in place. "What is today—Wednesday?"

"Yes."

"Kyle said he would come to collect some papers Amos had promised to let him have. He needs to take them with him to Lucknow."

"Kyle?" A small chill travelled up Maya's spine. *Oh God, not Kyle, not today!*

Olivia stared at her in the mirror. "He's only coming to collect some papers, dear," she pointed out gently.

"You'll have to put him off, or send the papers to him. I couldn't *bear* it if he . . . if they. . . ." She faltered, clasping and unclasping her hands in agitation.

Olivia pulled in a deep breath. "Very well, dear." For a moment she concentrated on arranging her hair to her satisfaction, then asked casually, too casually, "Might it not have been more prudent to give Mr. Pendlebury time to settle down before inviting him here?"

Spinning on her heel, Maya walked away towards the bay window. Down in the front garden, the mali was busy sprinkling water over the herbaceous borders and arcing great, cool sprays across the jade green lawn. Against the far wall, at right angles to the embankment, the brilliant yellow laburnums were beginning to burst into blossom. "Why?" she asked quietly. "To give him a chance to hear all the town gossip about us?"

"He's bound to hear it sooner or later."

Maya crossed her arms and faced her mother with cold, resentful eyes. "Then *that* is when we will truly learn Mr. Pendlebury's calibre, won't we, Mother?"

Olivia's heart twisted at the bitterness that couldn't quite be concealed. "Darling, all I want is for you not to. . . ."

"Don't read into it more than there is," Maya interrupted sharply. "I asked him merely because he knows no one in station. And because, somehow, he seemed . . . different."

Impulsively Olivia rose, went to her and pulled her into her arms. "You mustn't mind my questions, darling," she whispered. "I ask only because I care so very, very much." Overwhelmed with love, filled with pity and remorse and sadness, enjoying on her cheek the smooth touch of youth in all its freshness, all its hope and yearning, Olivia pressed her close.

For a fraction of a moment, Maya responded. Against her mother's shoulder, her chin quivered; she squeezed her eyes shut and clamped her teeth on her underlip to force back her tears.

Tightening her embrace, Olivia stroked her hair. "Everything will be all right once we sail for America, my darling, you'll see, *everything!*" Her eyes brimmed. She laid her cheek against her daughter's and stifled a sob. "Had your father been here, our lives would have been so different, so different! He would have. . . ."

"But he *is* here!" Violently, Maya tried to pull away. "He'll *always* be here. No matter where we are, he will always be with us, won't he, Mother!"

Olivia clung to her, refusing to let her go. "In that case we must be grateful," she cried, anguished. "We must cherish his presence as a blessing, as a source of strength, as an inspiration, yes, an *inspiration!* Your father *loved* us, Maya! He gave us everything we have, made us everything we are—you must never forget that, darling, *never!* We. . . ."

"And what exactly *are* we, Mother?" Resolutely, Maya disengaged herself and stepped back out of Olivia's reach, once again cold and impersonal. "Besides pariahs?" Her lips set in a thin, hard line. "Do you know? Does any one of us? *Will* we ever find out who and what we are?" Without waiting for her mother's reply, she walked out of the room. Olivia tried to call out to her but no sound came. In any case, there were no answers to Maya's questions.

Olivia stared at the door as it closed, her eyes clouded with despair. With a small sigh she sank back on the stool and hid her face in her hands.

Yes, Amos is right—she will have a better chance in America. We took away her childhood, Jai, we stole her innocence, forced upon her a past that is not hers, that she cannot understand. Will she ever forgive us, you and me, Jai? Can she? Protect her, my beloved one, wherever you are, whatever you are. She's so lost, so bruised, so ready for disaster. . . .

"Well, I told her she was wrong, *quite* wrong, to expect a charitable institution to pay for her bunions! It's not as if she's destitute, is it?" Marianne Lubbock's swarthy, well-rounded cheeks gleamed red with indignation, almost matching her pyramid of heavily rinsed hair. "There's a very competent chiropodist on the Chitpore Road almost next to our Home, and his charges, I happen to know because I took the trouble to find out, are *perfectly* reasonable."

"Yes, well, maybe we can discuss that at our next meeting," Olivia said, a little embarrassed. She made a sign to Francis, the chief bearer, to again pass around the savouries. "Maybe she does need some extra finances. Now. . . ."

"Extra finances?" Marianne snorted. "Well, if Joycie Crum needs extra finances, considering all that she managed to extort from that. . . ."

"We'll talk about it later, dear!" Olivia cut in firmly, throwing an anxious glance at Maya. Marianne had a heart of the proverbial gold but, unfortunately, also a foot that made a habit of finding its way into her mouth with the most extraordinary accuracy and at the most inopportune of moments. "I'm sure neither Mr. Pendlebury nor Samir is interested in the mundane affairs of our little Seva Sangh. Another sandwich, Samir? I notice you've only tasted one and I know you like cucumber, especially with French mustard."

The shy young Bengali sitting by himself in a corner, trying to hide behind his outsized gold-rimmed glasses, blushed. "Oh yes, I . . . thank you. . . ." He hastily picked up a sandwich from the plate Francis offered and devoted himself to its consumption with the dedication of a soldier obeying a military command.

Surprisingly at ease—if uncomfortably hot—in the company of strangers in a strange house on his second day in a strange country, Christian Pendlebury dragged his eyes away from Maya with visible effort. As discreetly as he could, he patted his sweat-beaded forehead with a folded handkerchief and helped himself to a tuna fishcake from the plate Sheba proffered. He inched forward in his seat. "On the contrary, Mrs. Raventhorne," he protested with a smile of considerable charm, "I'm greatly interested in anything to do with Calcutta and its activities, truly I am. I know so little, you see. Er, what exactly is a . . . Seva Sangh?"

Sitting on the window seat next to Grace Lubbock in the formal drawing room that opened out into the back garden, Maya allowed herself a moment of cautious pride. No, she had not been mistaken in her first, indeed instant, impressions of Christian Pendlebury. He had not only kept the appointment and proved himself to be a man of his word, but had arrived on the stroke of half past four precisely. Since then, his manner had been that of a true gentleman, courteous and considerate, with none of the false airs and graces displayed by so many of the other pukkas. If one could overlook the rather garrulous presence of Marianne Lubbock chattering away in that awfully common chi-chi accent of hers—and that dreadful, overblown dress!—the evening was proceeding very pleasantly indeed. Even Mother was making an effort. And it was certainly fortunate that Amos was still away, knowing how tiresome he could be on occasion. The thought of Kyle flashed through Maya's mind and she was briefly discomfitted; *had* Mother made arrangements to despatch the papers to him— or had she forgotten? Oh sweet Lord—she couldn't bear it if Kyle suddenly arrived while Christian Pendlebury was still on the premises!

"He's feeling terribly *hot*, you know," Grace whispered from behind her fan. "Wouldn't he be more comfortable in the garden by the river?"

Dismissing thoughts of Kyle, Maya nodded, wishing it had been she who had thought of that first. "Yes. We'll go on the embankment as soon as everyone finishes eating and Mother gives her permission." She got up and opened the window behind her. Immediately, the pale blue lace curtains billowed out and cool gusts of the southerly breeze swept through the stuffy room, supplementing the frantic efforts of the overhead punka. Christian Pendlebury smiled at her in gratitude for her thoughtfulness and Maya, pleased at the acknowledgement, smiled back.

"A Seva Sangh? Well, in our case it's a charitable society," Olivia explained, not missing the exchanged smiles. "In the broader sense of the words, *seva* means 'service' and *sangh* is a, well, 'group.' A few of us run a vocational institution for the benefit of destitute women with no means of support. Initially our inmates were all Eurasians because they are the most deprived and neglected women in India, but now we make no such restriction."

"Yours is a residential establishment, then?"

"Yes, we. . . ."

"It certainly is!" Marianne intervened, bristling with pride. "Dear Olivia has made over to our Seva Sangh her extensive premises in Chitpore. They haven't been used since . . . well. . . ." She stopped, all atwitter, and looked beseechingly at Olivia.

"Yes, we are fortunate to have the premises." Olivia covered the gap smoothly with no change in expression. "However, in work like ours one can always do with more space."

"And what skills do you teach your young ladies?" Genuinely interested, Christian leaned forward as if to listen better.

"They're not all young, of course. We teach them whatever skills might bring future gainful employment or provide a means of generating other income."

He looked surprised. "Employers in Calcutta have no reservations about employing ladies? Unfortunately, many still do in England."

"Oh, many do here too, although not the truly forward-looking." *Yes, he is different,* Olivia thought, *but he'll change. They all do. I wonder how much Clarence Twining has told him?*

"My Gracie is a qualified nurse and also secretary of our Sangh." Composure restored, Marianne Lubbock again took firm charge of the conversation. There was a determined gleam in her eye, one that no eligible bachelor worth his salt could possibly fail to recognise. "I'm sure she'd be *delighted* to take you around both our establishments some day when you can spare the time, Mr. Pendlebury. Wouldn't you, Gracie dear?"

"Yes, Mama." Grace demurely lowered her eyes. Then, not knowing if more was expected of her, she rose and bounced up and down in a curtsey aimed in Christian's direction.

"Both?" Christian asked, flushing and acknowledging Grace's curtsey with an awkward smile. "You run another charitable institution as well?"

"Oh dear no, quite the contrary!" Marianne gave a coy little laugh. Of mixed Indian and Portuguese parentage, she spoke with a slight accent and with compulsive volubility. "My husband and I have a furniture-making factory. We design and fabricate carved furniture in the Chinese style for export to Europe and America. My ancesters were European, you see, Portuguese to be precise, but my husband," she paused to let this momentous pronouncement have its proper effect, "hails from the United States of America, just as Mrs. Raventhorne does."

Inevitably, a few moments now had to be spent in satisfying Christian's curiosity about this entirely new and unexpected aspect of the Raventhornes' lives. Yes, she was born and brought up in America, Olivia conceded briefly. Where? Well, mostly in California. Mr. Twining had mentioned something about the Hawaiian Islands, Christian said—did they have connections there too? Trying not to show her dismay, Olivia merely nodded, parrying his questions as best she could, nervously watching Maya, wondering how to divert the flow. Then, ironically enough, it was Marianne who came to the rescue with an unwitting remark about Hawaiian sandalwood which allowed a smooth return to the subject of furniture making. The offer to conduct Christian Pendlebury round the Lubbock factory premises was renewed and received by him with somewhat contained enthusiasm. Noticing that Marianne still sat open-mouthed, poised on the verge of further amplifications, and that if Samir sank any lower in his chair he would soon be under it, Olivia decided to divert the conversation into entirely different channels.

"Samir's father happens to be one of the enlightened employers I mentioned, Mr. Pendlebury," she remarked with a pointed glance at the shy young man. "With his extensive commercial interests he has very generously arranged positions for several of our women. Samir's mother is one of my dearest friends and a very active member of our Sangh. Samir, on the other hand," staring hard, she pinned him down with a look he couldn't possibly avoid, "appears to prefer academics to business. Isn't that so, dear? He's a student of English literature and history at Presidency College. Samir and both my children went to school at the same Academy."

"Indeed." Christian took the excuse to again exchange smiles with Maya, then, sensitive to the hint contained in his hostess's remarks, rose to walk across the room and seat himself next to Samir. "How many years do you still have left to complete your course, Mr. Go . . . Go . . . ?"

"Goswami. Samir Charan Goswami." Samir rose and bowed, in the process almost upsetting a whatnot and the flower vase resting upon it, both of which rocked alarmingly. He watched, stricken, but then the table mercifully steadied itself and catastrophe was averted by a hair's breadth. "Er, I am in my final year," he replied in an inaudible mumble as he smoothed down the folds of his pristine white dhoti, starched to perfection. On one shoulder, over his cream-colored kurta, heavily embroidered around the neck, was draped a neatly folded tussur shawl. Next to him, propped against the side of his chair, stood a furled black umbrella. He looked exactly what he was, the epitome of enlightened Bengali nobility.

"And how many years' study does the entire course entail? I'm sorry, I'm not familiar with the Indian education system yet." Christian smiled easily, unashamed of his ignorance. "Ours at home appears to be so different in some ways. How do you manage here with so many languages?"

Samir swallowed hard but could scarcely evade the direct questions without seeming rude. "It's not so m-many. That is, we . . . er, mostly English and B-bengali. Not in all the. . . ." Hopelessly entangled, he stopped, looked at Maya for help, and then, when she callously ignored his appeal, took a deep breath and started again. "Our lessons are in English and Bengali only." Having successfully negotiated his piece, Samir hastily grabbed a buttered muffin he had no wish to eat and put it into his mouth as a deterrent not only to speech but also to further questions.

Really, he's impossible, Maya thought irritably. So terribly juvenile, so gauche! "What does he think a pukka Englishman might do?" she asked Grace in a whisper. "Fancy a bit of Bengali Brahmin for pudding?"

Grace giggled and hid her face behind her fan, but Christian remained undeterred. He immediately asked Samir another question, waiting patiently for the total demolishment of the muffin to receive an answer. By the time he had received it and had been enlightened on several other aspects of the higher education system prevailing in the city, Samir had loosened sufficiently to even risk a cautious smile.

It was later—after Grace had entertained them with English songs accompanied on the piano by Maya, and Christian Pendlebury had dutifully conversed with everyone, and after many more questions had been asked and answered in the interests of his consuming thirst for knowledge about India—that Christian fixed his attention once again on Olivia.

"Hawaii still seems part of some alien paradise to us in the British Isles," he said, smiling, "therefore I am curious about your reason for being there. Would it be an impertinence to ask why?"

Olivia heaved a silent sigh, again wishing that Maya had waited before asking him to tea. Given enough time in station, he would not have needed to ask so many questions—if he had elected to come at all! Nevertheless, she remained composed, the reluctance with which she replied barely perceptible. "Not at all. My father, my stepmother and her two sons were settled there at one time."

He nodded. "From what little I know of the islands, I understand Honolulu is now considered the most important port in the Pacific, with modern, well-equipped shipyards?"

"Yes, I believe so." Olivia matched his smile, concealing to perfection the coldness that had again started to build up within. "I'm afraid I'm rather out of touch, Mr. Pendlebury. We left Honolulu more than thirteen years ago and since my father died, my stepmother and her two boys have moved back to California."

"Thirteen years!" Marianne Lubbock gave an exaggerated gasp, a well-manicured hand pressed against her throat. "My, how time does *fly*, doesn't it? I had a joint fifth birthday party for my Gracie and your Maya the day after you disembarked because you were too . . . *oh!*" She broke off, eyes wide with dismay, and her hand flew to her mouth.

"Yes, I remember," Olivia said quickly, stepping into the breach. "It still feels like yesterday, doesn't it?"

Maya got up abruptly, her face pale, her palms starting to sweat. Silently, she set about helping Sheba to clear away the dishes.

Please God, don't let him ask about Father, not now, not yet, not ever!

But if there was sudden tension in the room, Christian seemed unaware of it. He too rose and, with perfect naturalness, started to help with the removal of the crockery. He was about to ask what might have been another unwanted question when, rather fortuitously, Sheba intervened. Running up to him, she almost snatched the jar of potted shrimps from his hand. "Oh no *please*, you must not!" she gasped in horror. "It is not to be *done!*"

Startled, Christian hurriedly took a step back. "Oh, I'm sorry, I was only trying to. . . ." Red-faced and confused, he stood apart with his hands held awkwardly by his sides.

Olivia threw a look of mild reproof at the housekeeper, then laughed to ease Christian's obvious embarrassment. "I'm afraid Sheba believes it is not the right thing to allow gentlemen to help with the housework. Needless to say, my son, Amos, heartily subscribes to her philosophy. And now," she got up from her seat and turned to Maya, "why don't you and Grace take the young gentlemen into the garden, darling? It will certainly be cooler and more agreeable by the river. And perhaps Mr. Pendlebury might like a round of the stables before it gets too dark to see the horses. Mrs. Lubbock and I have some Seva Sangh accounts to complete before Mr. Lubbock comes to fetch them."

"Horses?" Christian's eyes lit up. "Oh, indeed I would!"

"My daughter has recently started breeding horses," Olivia explained. "She has already made considerable headway in a field that, as you can imagine, is highly competitive."

"*Breeding* horses?" He was so surprised that, involuntarily, he sat down again. "How extraordinary! Yes, in that case I would most *definitely* be interested to inspect your stables, Miss Raventhorne. You see, we too breed horses at home on our farm—what an amazing coincidence!"

In Christian's astonishment there was such obvious admiration that Maya blushed. "I would be very happy to show you round my stables," she said with a touch of sudden shyness. "They are best seen in daylight, of course," she added, not entirely without motive, "but if we hurry we can still catch a glimpse or two of the horses."

On the pretext of fetching a handkerchief, however, she deliberately delayed the outing further. As a consequence, by the time they arrived at the stables, Abdul Mian was in the process of lighting the lanterns and it was far too dim to see anything much. Upon being introduced to the grizzled old groom, Christian solemnly extended his hand. Abdul Mian hesitated, examined his calloused palms dubiously, rubbed them clean on the sides of his long shirt, and accepted the handshake with considerable reluctance. Being already quite familiar with the stables and their inmates, Samir and Grace had opted to proceed to the towpath that ran alongside the river.

"How many animals do you have in all?" Christian asked, peering through the gloom, trying to discern shapes and breeds.

"Well, three sires, seven dams and three foals. I only started two years ago. I have to expand slowly. Two Arab yearlings are due to arrive next week from Bombay. Abdul Mian's son has purchased them for me at the horse auction. His cousin is a *jambaaz* from Nadj."

"A . . . what?"

"A horse dealer from a town in Arabia. They bring horses to Bombay every year for the auctions." She slipped into Cavalcade's stall, knelt down and anxiously felt his right flank. The bay gelding belonged to Amos and was his particular favourite. He was depending on her to have the ugly-looking ringworm ulcer fully healed by the time he returned from Cawnpore. Enjoying the gentle feel of her fingers, the gelding whinnied, lowered his head and nuzzled the top of hers.

Christian stood outside the stall door watching her, listening to her murmured reassurances and the gelding's gratified responses. "You certainly do have a way with horses, Miss Raventhorne," he remarked admiringly. "No wonder you chose such an . . . unusual occupation."

"Oh, I wouldn't say it's all that unusual. There are plenty of breeders in India. After all, everyone needs horses to ride."

"I meant, unusual for a . . . lady. I shouldn't imagine there could be many *women* horse breeders in India!"

"Oh, I see. No, I suppose not." She fed Cavalcade a lump of molasses, expressed herself satisfied with the healing process, and joined Christian outside the stall. "My mother used to breed horses at Grandpa's ranch in California before—when she was a young girl. I suppose I inherited my interest from her. She started these stables and taught us, my brother and me, everything we know about horses. They say she still has the best seat anyone has seen on a woman." Her chin lifted with pride.

"And your father? Is he too a lover of horses?"

Pretending not to have heard, Maya quickly turned to Abdul Mian with an impromptu instruction, then, without giving Christian time to repeat the question, ran out of the stable house. "Why don't we join the others by the river?" she called back over her shoulder. "It's too dark in here to see anything more, anyway."

Christian followed in mild puzzlement. But he did not repeat his question.

The summer evening was surprisingly benign. The river glowed with the final remnants of day painted in slashes of fading orange across the crenellated surface of the Hooghly. A few boatmen still plied slowly, sluggish after the day's arduous endeavours, as they wended their way back to their villages along the river banks; the echoing *plip-plop* of their oars sounded like hollow beats of some gigantic drum in the stillness of the evening. It was such a pleasant change from the heat of the day that for a while no one spoke, preferring to stroll along the towpath in companionable silence, drawing in huge, fresh gulps of the southerly winds sweeping up from the Bay of Bengal. Around the scattered outhouses of the Raventhorne mansion clusters of women and children from the servants' quarters stood and stared. A lone rooster, refugee from some neighbour's poultry coop, sped clucking and screeching down the embankment with Sugar and Spice in ecstatic and noisy pursuit. In the compound next door, visible over the acacia hedges, white-uniformed bearers hurried to and fro in the performance of various evening duties as the time approached for their master to return home from work. Over her shoulder, Maya glanced at the Anderson residence, their immediate neighbour. She hoped the three vixens were watching, as usual, from that first-floor bedroom window. She smiled to herself and her eyes lit up with quiet triumph.

"You have a very beautiful and gracious home, Miss Raventhorne, and the views of the river are quite enchanting." Profoundly impressed, Christian paused to survey the row of imposing mansions peeping out at them from beyond thick screens of greenery all along the embankment. "I had heard in England how well and elegantly people lived in Calcutta, indeed a city of palaces."

"Not all people, Mr. Pendlebury. Only some." No longer tongue-tied,

Samir had quite successfully quelled his earlier inhibitions. In fact, he was delighted at this opportunity to practise his English conversation with a genuine Englishman. The accents of the American and English traders and sea captains with whom his father did business, and whom he was often called upon to entertain, sounded so unfamiliar to his ears, he sometimes wondered if the language they spoke was indeed English. "There are many who remain very poor, mostly natives."

"Yes, I've heard that too," Christian said. "I believe it is the English merchant princes who are the worst offenders when it comes to ostentatious living." He paused to pluck a small white flower, inhaled its perfume and glanced at Samir. "Jasmine?"

"Yes."

Maya felt a twinge of jealousy at their sudden rapport. "Well, many of the rich Indians don't do so badly either," she remarked with a tart smile. "Some Bengali families, for instance, maintain several homes, including lavish *bagan baris*—houses with orchards. They have over a hundred servants, and no less than a dozen cooks in as many kitchens! Isn't that so, Samir?"

Through the recital Samir had slowly coloured. "That may be for reasons of tradition, not ostentation," he murmured, embarrassed but not at all offended.

"Well, at one time tradition also called for widows to be *burnt* on their husbands' funeral pyres!" Grace exclaimed, her round, rather bovine eyes wide open with shock. "Isn't that right, Maya?"

Christian laughed. "Well, at one time they used to burn so-called witches at the stake in England and America," he countered lightly, refusing to share in the shock. "Sadly enough, superstition is not the monopoly of any single society." Arriving at the stone steps leading to the river, he gave an exclamation of delight and quickly ran down them.

Loath to encourage a debate that might flaw the wonderful harmony of the evening, Maya merely shrugged and, grabbing Grace's hand, pulled her down the steps to the edge of the water. She closed her eyes, raised her face to the darkening sky, and ran her fingers lingeringly through her long, loose hair—a shining, burnished frame for her startlingly beautiful face. Silently, she thrilled to Christian's presence next to her, resisting the absurd temptation to reach out and touch his hand. He was so extraordinarily sensitive, so very appealing. His attitudes confused her; they were so strange, so unusual. But she sensed that it would please him if she used them to fashion her own when they next met—as inevitably they would! In a sudden rush of happiness, she gazed up at him from that corner of the steps that was her mother's favourite. She patted the place next to her to signal Grace to sit beside her.

"Let's talk of something else," she suggested, dazzling Christian with a rare smile. "It wouldn't do at all to bore you with tedious matters on your very first engagement in station."

His breath caught a little at the sheer perfection of her features. He had never met anyone quite as exquisite in all his life. "Nothing I see or hear in Calcutta could ever *bore* me," he breathed fervently, fighting hard to sound normal. "I find it difficult to believe anyone could actually *be* bored in a city as colourful and as complicated in its indigenous stratifications as this."

Maya caught the little gasp trying to hide in his throat; as their glances locked, she was again filled with elation, an elation so overwhelming that her own throat constricted. "Tell us something about England, Mr. Pendlebury," she said quickly, concealing her breathlessness under another brilliant smile. "Is Buckinghamshire very far from London?"

From her bedroom window on the first floor, Melody Anderson silently observed the group by the riverside and quickly reached for her opera-glasses. She peered through them for a moment and her mouth tightened. "Come and see what she's up to now, Melanie," she said to her older sister. "She's got another one in tow but I can't make out who he is—see if you can."

Melanie jumped off the bed, ran to the window and snatched the glasses out of her sister's hand. "Oh-ho! This one is even *more* presentable, isn't he? I can't remember ever having seen him before, can you? I wonder who he is, someone just arrived?"

"Probably. Do you think he's English?"

Melanie lowered the glasses and subjected her sister to a withering look. "Of *course* he's English, silly! Do you think she'd be fawning all over him if he weren't?"

Melody twirled a kiss curl around a finger and brushed it into a tight coil. "She never gives up, does she?"

Raising the glasses, Melanie focussed them again on the embankment. "Yes, *very* presentable indeed! Do you think we could make another informal call to see that washing apparatus?"

"Why bother? He's bound to be at the polo match next Sunday, especially if he is newly arrived. We'll get Mr. Illingworth to introduce us." She rearranged her fringe and carefully patted it into place. "*She* won't be there, naturally."

"Naturally!" Melanie echoed. Their eyes locked in the mirror and they laughed.

In her study in the adjoining Raventhorne house, Olivia also stood at a window gazing out thoughtfully in the direction of the river. A small frown divided her forehead.

"Maya does appear unusually animated today, doesn't she, dear?" Following Olivia's gaze and catching her mood, Marianne frowned in sympathy. "I wonder if it was *wise* to . . . ?" She left the rest unsaid and looked up at her friend, worried.

"No," Olivia murmured, her amber eyes disturbed. "It was *not* wise."

"Aw, leave the gal alone!" Hal Lubbock drawled from an easy chair at the back of the room. "What's wrong with havin' a bit of fun, eh?"

"Shut *up*, Hal!" his wife rebuked crossly. "You haven't the faintest idea what we're talking about!"

He raised his hands in a good-natured gesture of surrender and grinned quite cheerfully. "Naw, but then ah nevah do, do ah?"

It was well into late evening. Goodbyes and many words of gratitude at the Raventhornes' gracious hospitality had already been expressed in the formal drawing room. Samir had left earlier, surrendering himself reluctantly to an appointment with his tutor, and Grace and her parents had hastened away to the bedside of a sick friend. Briefly, as she saw him off at the front gate, Maya and Christian were by themselves, save for the syce holding the reins of Christian's rather unimpressive sorrel. In the few moments of unexpected privacy, Christian ventured to ask, "Do you ride every morning, Miss Raventhorne?"

"As far as possible, yes. I like to ensure the animals are exercised well and regularly."

There was a pause. Maya let it expand, knowing what was going through his mind, scarcely daring to breathe.

"I . . . er, I was wondering if. . . ."

"Yes?"

"Well . . . if some morning I might be permitted to ride with you? You see, horses are a passion with me too, Miss Raventhorne, although I have not yet purchased my own here. This one is on hire for a week."

Casually, her expression not giving away the pounding of her heart, Maya strolled up to the sorrel and stroked his nose. "Well, he seems docile enough, but if we do ride together, I think you will certainly need a better specimen than this."

"Oh, I can see that. In fact, just this morning I have concluded arrangements to purchase a rather splendid chocolate brown, fourteen hands high. Unfortunately, he will not be delivered for another week."

"Well, in the meantime perhaps you could ride one of mine," she suggested lightly. "It would be very useful to have two exercised at the same time. I prefer to ride very early, at dawn. Would that suit you?"

"Perfectly! My language classes do not start until eleven." He looked enormously pleased. "And your Arabs arrive next week?"

"Yes."

"Well, I would be privileged to have the opportunity to inspect your stables during daylight hours and to learn something about horse-breeding practices in India. Naturally," he added quickly, "I will write a formal note to ask for Mrs. Raventhorne's permission before I take the liberty of calling again. Oh, by the way"—he paused in the act of mounting—"I believe there is a native sweet, a Bengal speciality, known as the rasgollah, which many commend?"

Maya frowned. "Yes, but it's horribly rich and over-sweet," she said with a touch of frost.

"Well, since it's a speciality of the region," he called out gaily as he swung into the saddle, "I feel I am honour-bound to try it at least once, perhaps under your own expert supervision?"

Christian Pendlebury had helped himself twice to her muffins; there was no doubt that he had approved of them thoroughly. Even so, Maya was relieved that Sheba had not been present to hear his parting remark.

2

A MOS FOUND HER, as he knew he would, on the steps by the river. "What are you doing out here all on your own, Mother? It's almost midnight." He spoke softly, knowing full well what she was doing, but not wishing to startle her.

"Thinking." Olivia smiled up at him, pleased that he was back. "Just thinking."

He dropped a kiss on the top of her head and flopped tiredly on the opposite end of the step. "What about?"

"Well, I was watching the river go by, wondering why it seemed to flow so much more swiftly at night. Do you think it could be an optical illusion?"

"I don't know. I've never really thought about it." He yawned, amused. "The trouble with you, Mother, is that you think too much."

Olivia sighed. "Yes, I suppose I do. But then you mustn't grudge me my one remaining self-indulgence. We expected you would arrive by dinnertime. Have you eaten yet?"

"No. Sheba said you haven't, either. You shouldn't have waited." He stretched to shake the tiredness out of his limbs. "The train was late. There was a derailment and we had to wait until the line could be cleared." He settled back comfortably and crossed his hands behind his head. "It's astonishing how that railway line has changed everything up north, Mother. Had I not seen it for myself, I would not have believed it. Cawnpore is *transformed*, the reconstructions quite remarkable! Remember how devastated, how demoralised, it was just after the Mutiny?"

"Yes. I remember." She smiled to herself, wondering just how much he recalled of those days when he was still only a boy. But not wanting to curb his raring high spirits, she said nothing. He continued to speak, his lovely large grey eyes animated, shining in the cool, misty starlight. She shifted positions so that she could look at him better, enjoying watching him, almost tasting his excitement on her tongue.

He sits just as you did, Jai, that night we met, that first night, now vanished without trace save in the deep blue caverns of memory, here, on these very steps with these very skies and stars as witness. So much like you, Jai, cast in the mould that is the same and yet not the same. Like you, Jai, a boy without a childhood, a boy forced to become a man before his time. But he would have enchanted you, I know, he would have made you proud. . . .

"Mother? Are you listening?" Gently, he nudged her with his voice.

"Yes." She struggled to pay attention. "Tell me more about your explorations in Cawnpore. Ranjan Babu said you are well satisfied with them."

"More than satisfied, Mother, delighted!" He sat up and leaned forward, anxious that she should hear everything he had discovered. "Cawnpore is destined to become the new industrial centre of the north, I'd wager my life on it. The town is booming, Mother, positively *booming!* The mill is bound to come up for auction before the year is out. Already there are rumours of dissension among board members and almost certainly some will resign. Sutherland can't continue on his own, he will have to sell out. And in different hands it *can* be run profitably, I'm convinced of that now." He sprang up to pace restlessly across the length of the step. "You should see the mountains of cotton bales still piling up everywhere in the city! Isn't it odd that Cawnpore should owe its regeneration to the American Civil War?" He chuckled at the irony of it. "With America's cotton exports so severely impaired, Lancashire is crying out for raw stock—and suddenly the English are being forced to again look towards our Indian cotton to keep their mills rolling. Would you not call that poetic justice, eh?" He laughed again, barely able to stay still in his exhilaration. "Yes indeed, I do believe we have a gold mine in the offing."

"You will need skilled men and good managerial staff for an endeavour so out of your experience." She was careful not to let that sound like a criticism. "I know you've talked to Hal Lubbock. He was a cotton man once in Mississippi, but he hasn't worked a plantation or a mill in more than two decades."

"I *know* that, Mother! I'd be a fool not to see that I will have a great deal to learn, a great deal. After all, what do we at Trident know about the manufacture of towels and khaki drill and tents? We will have to depend on expert advice, employ good managers, perhaps import one or two from England, train our staff to work on modern looms. But," he hit his fist against his palm to emphasise the point he made, "I *want* to do it, Mother, I must! I want to do something that is my own, my very own, instead of. . . ." He stopped and averted his head, gazing out into the black distances, trembling with ambition.

She said nothing, understanding his need, sharing his fierce young dream, filled again with guilt at not sharing it more fully, still bewildered by his sudden leap into adulthood. She stared up at the night sky, seeking from it the reassurance of continuity. There, at least, nothing had changed, nothing would, year after year, millennium after millennium. She could trace out in her mind each constellation with her eyes shut, all old friends in a crowd of familiar faces. The voices and sounds of the night, the heady dankness of the river, the seductive perfume of a wild, wild queen of the night, the rustling of leaves orchestrated in harmony with the chorus of cicadas, the caress of the breezes—all these were living memories, constant and faithful, providing strength within the comforting anonymity of the womb of night. She skimmed with the tips of her fingers the water lapping at her feet; it felt cool, so wonderfully familiar, another dear friend. Amos had stopped talking, either because he too had private thoughts to think or because he knew that she had stopped listening.

She asked, "Did you remember to call on Colonel Bradbury?"

"I remembered, yes." He said nothing more.

"And?" Olivia prompted, leaning forward with attention. "Did he give you a patient hearing?"

"He refused to see me." He sat down again. "Maya told me about the letter from the Viceroy's office. There is now nothing more to be done."

"But perhaps another visit to Bithoor...?"

"Why, Mother? You know it would be futile!"

"Rationally speaking, perhaps. But," she drew a deep breath, "I cannot get over this feeling that the answer to what we seek is somehow connected with that place."

"No one remains to talk to in Bithoor, Mother," Amos reminded her patiently. "Everyone ever associated with the Nana Sahib is either dead or gone away. Not much remains of the palace, either—we both saw that with our own eyes years ago. Now Bithoor is just another dusty village like thousands of others. The Nana Sahib might have once been at the hub of the Mutiny, but few today even remember what the diabolical man looked like!"

"If he was that diabolical, why did your father ally himself with him at all? Surely, there must have been. . . ."

"Oh, Mother—let's not go into all that again!" Amos cut in with a tired groan. "Why he allied himself with the Nana Sahib no one knows, or will ever know. What counts now is how history views them both and," he added with some bitterness, "we already have the answer to that."

"You know very well that that history is incorrect," Olivia said sharply. "It will be rewritten, it must!"

"How, Mother?" He was starting to sound impatient. "How many times do we cover the same damned tracks? We've scoured every village near Cawnpore, picked the brains of every man, woman, child and official, read every scrap of paper that could possibly have any bearing on the case—and what are we left with? A pack of conflicting testimonies—and that infernal report, not one word of which we have been able to repudiate, much less disprove."

"But if we could locate those two men, talk to them *personally*, ask. . . ."

"Why?" he demanded, suddenly harsh. "What would that achieve? Do you truly think they would alter their testimonies now to suit our purpose? And say we *do* find them, then suppose. . . ." He stopped.

Her hands felt cold. "Suppose what?"

He did not reply but merely looked away.

She closed her eyes, the dull pain returning to the region of her heart. *He is not convinced yet, Jai, not yet, not even now, even he, even your Amos! Can there ever be peace for you knowing that? Can there ever be for me, for me?*

"Suppose what, Amos?" she repeated, quivering with disappointment.

"Oh, for heaven's sake, Mother," he muttered, not having the courage to say what he felt, still looking away. "We've already given it thirteen years of our lives! Isn't that enough?"

"Your father was innocent." She argued dully, purely out of a stubbornness that had now become habit. "He deserves to have that innocence established."

Inwardly, Amos sighed. They had been over the same ground so many times, he could predict almost every word that she would say. For a few silent moments he again hated his father, the man who would not go away, not even in death, the man who controlled, manipulated, dictated, distorted their every waking thought, defiled, yes *defiled* their most ordinary relationships. The man who had made untouchables of them all. But then, as always, the feeling passed and he was ashamed. "Of course he deserves it, Mother, but we can do nothing without evidence, without *proof!*"

"The proof is here, here in my heart!" she cried. "In the hearts of all those who knew and loved him! Look into your own heart, Amos. Can you *truly* believe this of the man you knew as your father?"

"In law, instincts and emotions have no validity, Mother! They cannot be taken as proof." He despaired of ever making her accept that.

"If one has faith, the proof will come. One has to *search* for it. Some day it will be found."

"We have searched for thirteen years—how much longer does one beat one's head against the wall? Faith cannot be a substitute for facts—hard, incontrovertible facts that can be substantiated by witnesses and verified by documents. Not even Arvind Singh, with all his clout, has been able to unearth more than what we have now. If there *is* any more to know, the English have made damned certain we never have access to it." He slid sideways along the step so that he sat next to her. "Let it go, Mother," he pleaded softly. "Let it go! There is still so much life left to be lived, it *cannot* be lived like this, dark and joyless under the shadow of a hope we know to be false, it must not!"

"No," she conceded, dispirited, crippled with a renewed sense of loss. "No, of course it cannot."

She leaned back against his shoulder. It felt warm and strong and loving. How could she ever make him understand that this now *was* her life, that there was none other left for her to live? He would be so wounded, so terribly betrayed.

"This Englishman who visited," Amos suddenly asked, "who was he?"

"Englishman?" For a moment she couldn't remember, but then it came back. "Oh, you mean Christian Pendlebury?"

"If that is his name, yes. Sheba just called him the English lord. Lord, ha!" he laughed sourly. "To Sheba, every Englishman is a lord."

"He's a newly arrived competition-wallah. Maya invited him for tea." She added quickly, "She also asked Samir, Marianne and Grace."

"Where did Maya meet him if he is newly arrived?"

"At the wharf. He disembarked from the *Ganga*."

"What does he want with her?" Even in the dark she could sense his disapproval.

"Apparently, his family too breeds horses in England. He appeared interested in our breeding methods here."

"Well, don't encourage him," he said shortly. "You know how Maya feels about these damned pukkas. And I certainly don't want another melodrama on our hands."

"Once he settles in, he probably won't wish to call again," Olivia remarked sadly. "In any case, we will soon be away, hopefully on the June sailing." She quickly changed the topic. "Talking about the *Ganga*, dear, do you really intend to part with her?"

"Would it upset you if we did?"

"You know it would!"

You were conceived on that ship, my precious son, on a night touched with magic, a night that diverted the course of so many lives. Do you know that, my dearest one? No, of course you don't. How can you? But then, there is so much else you don't know, perhaps never will know. . . .

He suddenly laughed, slid along the step to sit beside her, and planted a soft kiss on her cheek. "I'm sorry, I was only teasing you. No, I'm not going to sell the *Ganga*. As a matter of fact, Kyle has suggested an excellent plan to put her to good use. I'm sure you would approve of it."

Instantly her heart lifted. "Oh?"

"It's just an idea at the moment. We have to discuss it in detail once Kyle returns from Lucknow. We'd like to announce the project at the Derozio meeting." He rose and dusted his trousers. "I hope you haven't changed your plans to go to Kirtinagar before you sail?"

Kirtinagar—how reviving it would be to escape from Calcutta for a while! But how heartbreaking to have to bid farewell once again to her beloved Kinjal and Arvind Singh! Tarun's wife was expecting a second child and perhaps Tara would be there for another visit. The Maharaja, Maharani and their children were almost like her own family, her very own flesh and blood. "No," she said with a melancholy smile. "No, of course not. I couldn't think of leaving without one last visit before we sail."

He allowed a yawn to escape and blinked, his eyes heavy with fatigue. "It's late, Mother, and I'm exhausted. We'd better go in and eat before I fall asleep on my feet."

They started to walk back to the house. At the top of the steps Amos halted, his hands on his hips, his wide shoulders in bold outline against the sky.

"I have to own that mill, Mother."

Olivia's breath knotted; she could have been facing the silhouette of his father. "Yes, I know."

"I want to be known as the man who made a success of the first cotton mill in the north." There was such intense longing in his voice that Olivia's heart reached out to him, full of love.

Remember, Jai? That day in Hawaii when he was seven? I want to be the first boy on the beach to ride a full-length surfboard, Father! And you had lifted him and tossed him high up in the air with a roar of approval. You want to be first in everything like your father, eh? you laughed. And so you shall, my son, so you shall! Tomorrow you will have a man-sized surfboard all of your own!

"And so you *shall*, my son!" she breathed, her throat tight with memories. "You will be like your father—first in everything."

"Oh, Mother!" He shook his head in mild exasperation. "Why do you always think of me as an extension of Father?" The rebuke was gentle, voiced more in resignation than in resentment. "He had his methods, I have mine."

Without waiting for her response, he strode on ahead.

Over Ah Ling's excellent dinner of Amos's particular favourites, prawn curry cooked in coconut milk, and *aloo makallah*—whole potatoes deep fried into golden crispness—Amos once more waxed eloquent about Cawnpore. Olivia listened very carefully, not daring to let her attention wander. He couldn't wait to return, he informed her. There were so many further investigations needed.

"I wish I could go back immediately but I can't. I have to wait for Kyle's return so that we can chalk out a final agenda for the Derozio meeting. Unless we can suggest practical action after what has been circulated and what Kyle has written, we'll merely end up with another circus, a *tamasha*. Leonard Whitney is ready to help any way that he can. In his position in McNaughton's inner office, he's an excellent contact for us."

Olivia smiled dreamily into the night. "Sometimes he reminds me of your father, you know."

"Who, Whitney?" He looked up, surprised.

"No. Kyle." Her expression softened. "So much fire, so many unhealed wounds, so much hidden anger!"

"Sometimes not so hidden," Amos remarked drily.

She laughed. "Yes, I know. I've been reading his latest editorial. Your father would have endorsed it."

"Well, the authorities certainly don't. There are already rumours of tighter censorship rules for the press. They might even close down *Equality* if Kyle isn't more careful."

"Might they? Yes, that would be a shame," Olivia said absently. "Did I ever tell you what he once said to me? Your father, I mean—about the Englishman's bastard?"

"No," he lied, having heard it several times before.

"He said, 'In America, livestock carries its brand on its haunches. In India, what brands the Englishman's bastard forever is his face.' Isn't that an astonishing truth?"

"Yes, I suppose it is. Kyle certainly endorses that in his editorials!" He pushed away his plate and crossed his arms on the table. "You know, we agree on so much—Kyle and I—and differ on so much else. Our aims are the same but, somehow, the means we use are like chalk and cheese."

"As your father was," Olivia said softly, "Kyle is driven—a man of passions, with an obsessive need to release those passions. He *feels* for the oppressed, Amos, he feels very deeply."

"Oh, I know. I could never doubt his motives, only his methods. In fact, sometimes he . . . frightens me."

Bleary-eyed with sleep, Maya joined them in her dressing gown. In one hand she held a hairbrush. Drowsily pulling out a chair, she sat down at the table. Olivia looked at her in surprise. "I thought you had eaten, darling."

"I have eaten, thank you. I was waiting up to tell Amos about Cavalcade, but I fell asleep over a book." She cocked her head to a side, plucked a grape from the fruit bowl and sucked on it. "Don't tell me there's something that actually frightens the great Amos Raventhorne?"

"There isn't," he retorted. "We were talking about Kyle."

"Oh." Her expression chilled. She sat staring at the fruit bowl, then curled her lip. "Why should you be frightened of Kyle? He's overbearing, self-opinionated and utterly unscrupulous—but hardly frightening."

"What I meant was . . . oh, never mind." He tossed his napkin on the table and stood up. "You wouldn't understand anyway."

"Oh, I understand perfectly! Kyle wants to destroy *everything* that ever came from England, especially the English, and you only *some* things— isn't that it?"

"More than some," Amos countered pleasantly, refusing to be baited, "regardless of your propensities to the contrary. Anyway, I'm just too tired for another political argument now. So tell me, how is my horse? Is he better—or have your ministrations killed him off entirely?"

"For your information, he's almost recovered," she returned warmly. "I sat up all night last week when he was unusually tetchy—didn't I, Mother?"

"All right, all right, I was only teasing." He reached out and fondly tousled her hair. "Is he well enough to be ridden tomorrow?" He plucked a pipe from his belt and started to light it.

"No. You'll have to make do with one of the others for a few days. The ringworm is drying up nicely and a saddle might chafe it into flaring up again."

"Is Rafiq back with the Arabs?"

"Yes. Have a look at them in the morning. Maybe you'd like to try one of them out while Cavalcade is recuperating."

"Have they been thoroughly checked for spavine?"

"Yes, but I've asked Abdul Mian to. . . ."

As they relapsed into casual horse talk, Olivia observed both her children in reflective silence and smiled to herself.

You would never believe how different they are from each other, Jai, your son and your daughter. Yet, in their diverse ways, they're both so much like you, so much—although neither will admit it. . . .

The conversation between them was light; even so, Olivia sensed a sort of wariness in her daughter's manner towards her brother. It was not difficult to guess its source, but fortunately, Amos did not remember to repeat his questions about Christian Pendlebury. It was after they had eaten and were on the verandah waiting for their coffee that Amos suddenly gave an exclamation and sat up straight in his chair. "Oh, I almost forgot—I'm most dreadfully sorry."

"What's happened?" Olivia asked in alarm. As she reclined on the canework chaise-longue brushing out her hair, Maya's hand stilled.

"Nothing's happened, it's just that. . . ." He frowned. "I came across something rather curious in Cawnpore. I'm truly sorry. I should have mentioned it earlier."

"Well, mention it now, quickly, for heaven's sake," Maya said, "before we all die of suspense!"

There was an enforced silence as Francis appeared with the coffee salver and proceeded to place it on the glass-topped cane table in front of Olivia. Outside, the night air was still warm, tousling the dusty tops of the trees tipped with moonlight. Around the dimmed sconces geckos crouched, waiting for tasty bites of fluttering wings and fat, juicy bodies. Even the vast silences of the night filled with purple fragrance from the curling vines around the balustrades seemed breathless with anticipation. Finally, as the bearer left, Amos spoke.

"You remember our most recent insertion in the northern newspapers a couple of months back?"

As she started to pour the coffee, Olivia's hand jerked and a few drops of liquid splattered the glass tabletop. "Yes? Has anyone responded to it?"

He nodded. "A couple called Pickford. Apparently, they're a well-known mercantile family of Cawnpore. They specialise in the manufacture of leather goods, but they also own a general store on the Mall which is very well patronised. Anyway, Mrs. Pickford happened to see our insertion quite by chance, and rather late, and took the trouble to send a note to Kasturi Ram, our agent in Cawnpore, in whose name the advertisement had been inserted."

Olivia handed out the two cups and sat very still, with her hands tightly clasped in her lap. "You went to see them?"

"Yes, of course. I wrote and asked for an appointment for the following evening. They responded at once and very kindly invited me to their home for a glass of sherry. I met both, Mr. and Mrs. Pickford and, as it happened, also their daughter Rose. They received me very willingly and with understanding."

Olivia ran her tongue over her lips as her mouth ran dry. "And what did they have to say? Have they any news of anyone who might be a likely candidate?"

"Well, that's the strange part—they couldn't really tell. Certainly the tale they related was very bizarre indeed. I hardly knew what to make of it."

He stopped to take a few sips of his coffee. "It appears that they are acquainted with a woman, an Englishwoman, who used to come to see them every few weeks, they said. They don't know her name, her real name that is, but she called herself Sitara Begum. She told them she was married to a Pathan, a carpet tradesman. The Pickfords have no idea where she lived because she never revealed her address, but they concluded she must belong to some orthodox Muslim locality of the town because she always came clad in traditional clothes wearing a burka."

"Where did the Pickfords meet her? Do they have any information about her antecedents?" Olivia could not keep the tremble out of her voice.

"No, they know nothing of her antecedents. She was always very secretive. They first met when this Sitara Begum walked into their shop one day about a year ago to buy something for her child—oh, she has a child, by the way, this she did tell them. That morning Miss Rose Pickford also happened to be on the premises. Because they had never before had a burka-clad customer in the shop—which caters in the main to a European clientele—Miss Pickford started a conversation with her. The woman spoke English with a peculiar sing-song accent and initially declared herself to be a Eurasian. Subsequently she blurted out that she was actually English, but would not reveal more.

"After she had made her purchases, she lingered on, obviously reluctant to leave. As they continued to chat, the woman started to question Miss Pickford about their home, about how they lived and so on. Far from considering it an impertinence, Miss Pickford was rather intrigued, not only by the woman's altogether strange appearance, but more so by the longing in her voice as she asked her questions. There was, Rose Pickford told me, something rather sad and forlorn about the woman; it was as if she was lost and reaching out for something, and it touched her heart. Very curious now about the woman's history, on an impulse, Miss Pickford asked if she would care to visit them at their home. Openly delighted by the spontaneous invitation, the woman accepted eagerly and a meeting was agreed for the following week. After that, the woman took to calling upon them fairly regularly every few weeks."

"But during these visits they must have surely found out more about her background!" Olivia cried, now shivering with impatience. "What did she say? What did they talk about?" Quickly Maya rose, knelt besides Olivia's chair and placed a comforting hand on her arm. "Come on, Amos—tell us what the woman *said!*"

"Whoa, whoa—I'm coming to that. It's not what she *said* that was of significance because she never said very much that mattered—it's what she *did* that was so odd. At first she requested to see some of Miss Pickford's clothes, and then, after another visit or two, she felt bold enough to ask if she might be allowed to wear one of the dresses for the duration of her visit. Very curious to see what happened next, Miss Pickford agreed, and this became a regular feature of her subsequent visits. Clad in an English gown, giggling and looking very pleased indeed, the woman would talk quite freely about mundane, everyday matters, but she took great care

44

never to reveal anything about her history. After an hour or two she would change back into her own clothes and leave. During each visit the pattern was more or less the same."

"And that was all?"

"Apparently. Mrs. Pickford once asked her if she had any family in India. She said she did but that she had no wish to see them. And then she started to cry. Taking pity on her, they neither raised the subject again nor ever risked embarrassing her with personal questions."

"Did they think she was being kept by force wherever she was?" Maya asked.

"No. They say she appeared perfectly content, free to come and go as she wished. In fact, she talked frequently and not at all unkindly of her husband. She gave them to understand that he did good business with his carpets, and from her general appearance and conversation they deduced that she lived in reasonably comfortable circumstances."

Olivia frowned. "You say she used to visit them—does she not come any more?"

"No. Her visits stopped altogether about six months ago, as abruptly as they had started. The Pickfords have no address for her and have chosen not to make inquiries. Since she went to such lengths to preserve her anonymity, they feel they should continue to respect her need for it, whatever her reasons. The woman obviously derived some private satisfaction from her visits, and being compassionate people, the Pickfords decided to leave it at that—until Mrs. Pickford chanced upon our insertion. Anyway," he released the yawns he had been holding back and rubbed his eyes, "I've left a letter with them for her, asking her to write to you in case she does happen to contact them again. And, of course, in case she does turn out to be your cousin."

Olivia's eyes welled. "Oh, *Amos!*"

"Now, Mother," Maya warned, "don't build up your hopes again. You've been disappointed enough times as it is."

"Precisely what I was about to say!" Amos agreed emphatically with his sister. "You know perfectly well how many Englishwomen went missing during the Mutiny, never to be heard of again. Or, for all we know, this woman could be just one of those eccentrics left over from some Fishing Fleet of yesteryear living in a fantasy world that doesn't exist any more. After all, we have no way of knowing whether what little she said about herself was the truth. We'll just have to wait and see. Anyhow, I've left word with Kasturi Ram to keep in touch with Mr. and Mrs. Pickford and to send me a telegraph message if the woman does happen to make contact again." He got up and blinked his eyes. "Well, goodnight—I really *must* get to bed."

He kissed Olivia lightly on a cheek and gave his sister's backside an affectionate pat. "Oh, by the way"—he did not look at either of them—"I told the Pickfords my name was Amos Thorne. I thought it would be less of a . . . problem."

Olivia made no response. What was there to say? Maya merely stared fixedly at a gecko on the wall as it inched its way upwards towards a night insect and, with a flick of its tongue, struck unerringly. Taking a napkin, she carefully wiped the spilt coffee off the glass tabletop. Still silent, she kissed her mother goodnight, picked up the tray and carried it inside.

Late that night, seething with conjecture and hope, unable to sleep, Olivia sat down to write a letter to Kinjal:

> *Amos brings exciting news from Cawnpore; someone has answered our advertisement! An English woman who could possibly be my cousin (although the probability, I know, is thin) is living somewhere in the Cawnpore area as a Muslim. I am much too excited about this sudden revelation to consider leaving Calcutta at the present time even for a day in case further news arrives suddenly. Until I learn more about this mysterious contender, I will not be able to rest for even a minute! Therefore, I am again forced to defer my long-awaited visit to you. I am as disappointed as I know you will be, but realising the seriousness of the circumstances that force this postponement, you better than anyone will understand my compulsions and forgive me. Rest assured, my dear friend, that I will not—would not!—ever consider leaving these shores without being with you and Arvind Singh again one last time.*
>
> *Oh, Kinjal, just think! What would I not give to have my beloved Estelle returned to me after all these many, many years!*

"All right," Olivia said, resigning herself to the inevitable, "let me have a look at those bunions. Then we'll decide what to do about them."

Tall and faded, full of jutting bones, Joycie Crum hobbled forward and sat herself down heavily, her pencil-straight lips pursed into even thinner lines. Belligerently, she thrust her feet in Olivia's direction. "See? You wan I pay for all dis, ducky? You wan I end up on de rasta again?"

"No, of course we don't want you to end up on the street!" Olivia interrupted the shrill, whiny voice and ignored the snort emanating from Marianne Lubbock sitting at the desk next to hers in the Seva Sangh office. "Now, if you'll just calm down, we'll see what we can do about the treatment." Carefully, she examined the swollen, deformed and none too clean toes. "Yes, they do look rather angry, don't they?" Throwing Marianne a triumphant glance, Joycie sat back, crossed her arms against her flattened chest and glowered at the world in general. "What does our Dr. Humphries have to say about them?" Olivia asked.

Joycie gave a squawk of indignation. "You wan I let dat clumsy striplin' put a knife to my feet and *kill* me?" she cried, outraged. "You truss dat iggerant little . . . ?"

"Charles may be young, Joycie," Olivia interrupted quickly, before the trickle became a deluge, "but he's a kind and competent physician, just like his dear father was before him." Seeing Joycie's scowl darken as she opened her mouth to make an indignant retort, Olivia heaved a sigh and gave in. "All right. How much did you say that chiropodist charges?"

While they discussed the treatment and the charge that went with it,

Joycie Crum continued to glower, her skimpy brows drawn together like feathered arrows quivering to take off. She was a middle-aged spinster with pale blue eyes and lanky, butter-coloured hair which hung down her neck in straight, wispy fronds, presumably both legacies from a Caucasian father she had never known. Her skin, patchy brown and wrinkled like very old parchment, came from her mother, a Tamil seamstress from Madras. In her time, it was said, Joycie Crum was quite a coquette, long-time mistress of a wealthy nawab in the north who had promised to make her his third wife but had never quite got round to it. Instead, when Joycie returned from her annual sojourn in the Simla Hills one fine summer's day, she found a younger, more nubile contender firmly ensconced in the royal bed, and she herself relegated to the servants' quarters at the back of the palace. The nawab had died shortly thereafter, and fearful of any possible claim she might lay to his estate, his children had unceremoni-ously sent her packing without allowing her a single possession.

Destitute and heartbroken, she had eventually been brought to Calcutta by Kyle Hawkesworth, who had arranged for her to be given shelter in the Home. Because of the chequered life she had led, rumours about Joycie Crum ran rampant for a while. Some said that she had borne children, all of whom the nawab had had drowned like unwanted kittens. Others insisted that, in spite of her vociferous claims of penury, Joycie still retained a cache of jewellery given to her by the nawab, including the famous Roshanara ruby, a gem that had originally come from the Persian court. For all her irritating eccentricities, however, Joycie Crum was a remarkably clever needlewoman, having inherited the talent from her hardworking mother. Her embroidery stitches were so fine and so neat, many mistook her motifs and patterns for brushwork. Consequently, she was extremely popular with houseproud memsahibs, who provided enough regular orders for her to be able to make a modest living.

While the sensitive matter of Joycie's bunions and who was to pay for their treatment was being resolved, Abala Goswami—Samir's mother—came bustling in, trailing a small, slim Bengali girl with nervous, darting eyes and a diffident manner. "Well, she's interested, she says, but she's frightened to do it," Abala announced without preamble in a voice that reverberated against each wall in turn. "What do you think?"

Olivia sat back, folded her arms and smiled. "You've answered your own question, Abala. If she's frightened, I'd say that's a very good reason to wait."

"But surely there's no harm if she merely *walks* with our protest march, is there?" Abala sat down heavily and wiped her face with a corner of her sari, impatiently patting her thick, disobedient black hair into place. "Espe-cially since she says she approves of the aims of the organisation?"

"Personally I think we should take one step at a time, but it's really up to Sarojini. She knows the temperament of her father better than we do." Olivia turned to the young woman standing silently with her eyes low-ered. "Well, Sarojini? What do you think?"

The young woman lowered her head further, her hands fidgeting with an end of her white, borderless sari. "I will do as you both say," she mumbled inaudibly.

Olivia sighed. "You will not do as *we* say, Sarojini—you will make your own decision, my dear. If you feel strongly enough about it, of course you must participate. But do think carefully before provoking your father's temper further."

Sarojini remained silent as Abala frowned and drummed the tabletop with impatient fingertips. "Well, perhaps you are right, Olivia," she finally decided. "It would be more sensible to tackle one problem at a time, although our Brahmo Samaj—like any other social reform group—could certainly do with more women like Sarojini as supporters. Anyway," she pulled in a decisive breath, "first things must come first, I suppose. And, the first thing is, of course, not to antagonise that impossible father of yours any more than we can help.

"Now," briskly she turned again to Olivia, "shall we proceed to the annexe for inspection? The municipal surveyors have finally deigned to arrive, and if they can be persuaded to submit their report in good time, we could acquire the structure and have the roof re-tarred before the monsoons arrive and create further havoc. It's about to collapse over our heads any day now."

"Yes, of course. Let me finish here with Joycie. I'll be with you in a few moments."

But it was more than a few moments before Olivia could extricate herself from her office. As soon as Joycie Crum had been despatched to the chiropodist down the street triumphantly armed with the requisite fees, the Home's matron—known universally as "Didi" or Big Sister—arrived. The girl who repaired musical instruments had hurt her hand while tuning a *tabla* and was having difficulty completing the job. Who could they deputise as a substitute, since both likely candidates were otherwise engaged and the instruments were urgently required by the customer for a hymn-singing session?

Olivia looked at her with slight irritation. "Is Mrs. Chalcott not here today? I thought she was going to see to the matter of instrument repairs."

"No. She left you a note. Did you not get it?"

"A note? Oh, yes. Of course she did. I'm sorry, it had slipped my memory." Rummaging among the papers on her desk, Olivia found the note, read it again and smiled. "Mrs. Chalcott's gone off on another of her little jaunts, this time to the Himalayas to relive her memories of childhood. I wish I had the energy to travel *half* as much as she does! Now—what was the problem again?"

As soon as the matron left with the necessary solution, a middle-aged Assamese woman staggered in under the weight of a huge clay pot embellished with gold ribbon, sequins and painted patterns. The pot was on order for a nuptial ceremony; she asked Olivia to choose between two draft designs for a second pot, and that selection took time. Working with Grace on the Home's monthly accounts in her room next door, Marianne wanted clarifications on the allocation of a recently received donation from an anonymous benefactor: should they use it to purchase wood for another bookcase or set it aside for Dr. Humphries's use in the medical dispensary?

Almost an hour had elapsed before Olivia found herself making her way to the annexe to join Abala Goswami, and her passage was punctuated by frequent interruptions. A pretty young girl brutally maimed by a drunken father when she was only five years old limped out of a classroom to ask if her pukka sahib customer had brought the promised books for rebinding. Further down the corridor a pair of bright-eyed identical twins, with fair skin and pale brown hair, sat at a table jointly working away on an Isaac Singer treadle sewing machine, one of four imported from America last year to modernise the tailoring department. As Olivia passed they stood up, bobbed in identical curtseys and, smiling broadly, held up their work for inspection. Then, pleased with her gestures of approval, they carried on happily with their labours on a pink and white sateen confirmation dress being copied from an English pattern book.

Both girls were stone deaf and had therefore never learned to speak. Nothing was known of their history except that they were visibly of mixed parentage, and that, until brought by a well-wisher to the Home, they had survived through beggary and prostitution around the Kidderpore docks. Unable to hear, speak, read, or write, they could reveal nothing about their antecedents or relatives or, indeed, their names. Olivia had christened them Eunice and Bernice. Happy enough in their new identities and environment, they had settled down well in the Home. Being surprisingly nimble-fingered and possessed of a quick, natural intelligence, they had learned through practical example. Their two years in the Chitpore Home had turned them into expert seamstresses, able to imitate any given pattern, however complex or alien.

As always, Olivia felt a warm glow of satisfaction at the many signs of success now available at the Home. She had started the organisation at the suggestion of Abala and Kali Charan Goswami, two years after she returned to Calcutta. The Chitpore house, sad and neglected and no longer of use to anyone, had lain vacant for years, a hollow shell filled with spectral echoes of that past which could now never be again. This was the house in which Jai had once lived; like the *Ganga*, this too was a comforting friend, silent witness to many twists of their unfolding fortunes and misfortunes. Olivia couldn't bear the thought of selling off the property, but the prospect of living in it at a time when her anguish was still raw and her grief all-pervasive was equally intolerable. The suggestion to convert it into an institution in the service of destitute Eurasian women had come as an ideal solution.

Because of the increasing education and awareness of Indian women, many similar institutions had sprouted in the city over the years. Some were run by Indian social service groups, others by Christian missionary societies or Hindu reformist movements such as the Brahmo Samaj, yet others by the more enterprising women of rich Bengali families and by liberal, broad-minded Bengali rajas. There were many concerned

Englishwomen too who ran much needed charitable ventures such as soup kitchens and free dispensaries, either in independent groups or through local churches. Indeed, as a visiting Liverpool journalist had written recently—rather unkindly, Olivia thought—"The most fashionable amusement of the present age in Calcutta appears to be philanthropy."

To those who worked at the Jai Raventhorne Seva Sangh, however, the dedicated services that had made the institution what it was were neither fashionable nor an amusement. Even though space was short and the dormitories, classrooms and workshops cramped, refuge was constantly being sought by the desperate and the discarded, partly because the Home's American connections ensured the best and the most modern in training equipment, and partly because of the patience and professionalism with which that training was dispensed. Because Olivia didn't have the heart to turn away anyone in need, impoverished women of any community were somehow accommodated and taught useful skills that were marketable. Since its inception, two more storeys had been added to the sturdy structure and several outhouses put up in the compound at the rear in order to supplement existing work areas. Even so, with daily appeals for help pouring in, space was at a premium. Negotiations were presently in progress through Kali Charan Babu to acquire an adjoining derelict house as a much needed annexe.

With its many cool, high-ceilinged rooms, sprawling grounds and courtyards, its convenient location just off the Chitpore bazaar, the Seva Sangh was an inspiring place, alive with bustle and productive activity. It was well thought of in the neighbourhood, not only because of the native locality's respect for the Raventhorne family, but because many recognised the value of what the institution was trying to achieve. The once deserted rooms that had echoed with sorrow now rang with the laughter of those who had seldom known occasions to laugh. In the evenings there was music, the jingle of dancers' bells, the soothing strains of instruments lying idle for years, the rousing sound of voices born and bred never to be raised or, indeed, heard. Through its imaginative workings, the Sangh had helped to restore dignity, self-esteem and confidence in many shattered lives, lives that had, once, given up on life altogether.

Like her own. . . .

The project had become Olivia's lifeline, her most valuable avenue of escape from the realities of a harsh, punitive world at a time when, in her despair at having lost the man who was everything to her, she too was often tempted to put an end to a life she had no interest in living. Surrounded by women who, like her, had plumbed unimaginable depths of desperation, and had then, like the phoenix, risen again out of ashes, Olivia felt a sense of homecoming here. "Life shouldn't be about regrets and self-reproaches and looking back," Abala often scolded her. "It should be about a daily count of blessings."

Now, so many years later, when the sharp edges of grief had dulled into that constant ache that would be a lifelong companion, Olivia still gathered sustenance and hope from the inmates of the institution. Within these walls of a house that had once been lived in and loved by Jai, she felt his presence in every brick, in every marble slab and delicately carved pillar, in the very air that circulated through the rooms and corridors. The feeling was sometimes so strong, his presence so tangible that, involuntarily, she would glance over her shoulder, surprised not to find his smoky grey eyes gazing intently into her own. With him at her side, as he was now, as he had always been and always would be, Olivia invariably felt her aloneness lift, once more loved and protected in the comforting shelter of his shadowy embrace.

Not lost, my dearest, merely gone on ahead. . . .

It was more than a week after his visit that Christian's formal letter was delivered to Olivia. Not expecting to hear from him at all, much less so soon, she was surprised. Indeed, engrossed in visions of Estelle, affairs of the Home, and her own depressions, she had given Christian Pendlebury hardly any thought at all.

"When he was here, did he suggest he would like to call again?" she asked Maya, ashamed and guilty at having once more been so forgetful.

"Yes."

"You didn't say anything to me about that."

Maya shrugged. "If I had, would you have remembered? Besides, he mentioned it so casually, it slipped my mind."

Filled with remorse as she was, Olivia did not challenge the small white lie. For a moment she sat tapping the letter, then, on an impulse, blurted out, "Be careful, darling—he's still rather naïve, unwary of the more vicious aspects of Calcutta society. . . ."

"By that if you mean, does he know about *us*—I should imagine by now he's heard everything there is to be heard." Maya's tone was offhand, her expression closed. "In any case, his main interest is in our stables and breeding methods. His offer to help exercise the horses is merely to indulge his own passion for riding. But to come to the point—would you have any objections if he called again and rode with me in the mornings?"

"No," Olivia sighed, not having the heart to speak her mind. "But Amos might."

"Amos is not my keeper," Maya said coldly. "He leads his life as he wishes. I don't see why I should not be allowed the same privilege."

"No one is preventing you from exercising your freedom, darling. All I'm asking is that you be . . . careful."

"Careful of Christian Pendlebury?" She was vastly amused. *No,* Olivia wanted to say, *careful of your own motives!* But she didn't. "Careful of harmful, malicious tongues. He's a nice young man, Maya, a true innocent abroad. I wouldn't want him to damage his prospects through sheer ignorance of a milieu to which he is still not fully accustomed."

"His prospects are his business," Maya retorted, her colour rising. "It is for him to protect them as he wishes."

"True. But I'm also concerned that you shouldn't put yourself again in a position where you could be . . . well, disappointed. After all, there's not very much time left before we leave for America."

Anger sparked in Maya's eyes. "Don't make a mountain out of a mole-hill, Mother. The question of my being disappointed or otherwise simply does not arise." She halted at the door, one hand on the door knob. "Tell me, Mother, just as a matter of interest, did *you* ever concern yourself with such things as prospects and malicious tongues and disappointments when *you* sailed away with Father while still the wife of another man? Did Father . . . ?" Before Olivia could answer, or indeed recover from her sense of shock, Maya was gone and the door had closed behind her.

Olivia felt a rush of unaccustomed fury. How dare she bring that up, how *dare* she, the insolent little chit! In her rage, she almost ran out the door after her defiant daughter to exact well-deserved punishment. But then, all at once, the fury died and the sense of shock evaporated. The child was right; of course she was right. One can hardly devise one code of rules for oneself and expect one's children to follow another. Neither she nor Jai had ever resorted to such hypocrisy. If they had once chosen to flout public opinion, with what words could she persuade their daughter not to? But in conceding Maya's right to have answers to her questions, however impertinent and hurtful, Olivia felt even more depressed. And in her depression, oddly enough, the person who came to mind was a man she had never even met: the hot-headed, intemperate father of her hapless protégée, Sarojini. Suddenly, she felt a stab of sympathy for him in his predicament.

Oh dear God—how difficult it was to be logical when it came to one's own children!

That night, unable to put it off any longer, Olivia opened the locker in her almirah and took out the bound packet of letters Estelle had written to her fourteen years ago from Cawnpore. In the light of what Amos had related, she felt compelled to read them again, hoping to stumble across some small, unnoticed clue buried somewhere in the voluminous correspon-dence, something trivial enough to have been missed earlier. As she once again recapitulated everything that Amos had narrated, something trivial but persistent kept tapping at the back of her mind. Maddeningly, she could not trap it.

A second, thinner packet of letters bound in red ribbon brought a wrench to her heart, but she left it undisturbed. These were the last letters Jai had written to her in Hawaii from India, and the last photograph her father had taken of him before he had sailed back to Calcutta in his *Ganga* in the November of 1856. For a moment she stared at the faded picture— the beloved face thrown back in laughter, the pale, pale eyes full of confi-dence and love and hope, unaware of the whirring wings of disaster fluttering silently just over the horizon. Next to the packet of letters was a small box. From that she took out a silver pocket watch; it had been given to Jai by her father, who had had Jai's initials engraved at the back. The penknife with the wooden casing had been a Christmas gift from her one year when they sailed in the Pacific on the *Ganga*. The silver locket and chain, so cherished by Jai and her, had never been found although she had made tireless inquiries everywhere. Obviously, it had been stolen. Well, what did it matter when he was no longer there to wear it?

These sad little impromptu scraps were all she had left of her Jai, of his final thoughts in which he had shared with her his strangely compulsive aspirations, his despair, his terrible fears, his anger and his intolerable anguish. She had read the few sheets a hundred, a thousand times, attempting through the bare messages to reconstruct somehow details of that most vital part of his life that was to be its concluding phase. She had tried desperately to read between the lines, to find significance in the gaps and the blank spaces, to infuse the commonplace words with mystic, cryptic meanings. But the reconstructions remained at best skeletal, giving only shadowy impressions of his fast-ebbing life. Now the unfilled gaps would always remain so, unrevealed and unknown, lost in the wastes of an unshared past.

It seemed to Olivia a supreme irony that she who had worked so hard to know every aspect of Jai, every nuance of his tragically short, stormy life, should forever be denied knowledge of his death and of those few vital weeks preceding it. It was yet another cruel trick of a perverse, malicious fate that had allowed them to taste perfect happiness, and then snatched it away before it dared to become a habit.

Thoughts of Jai, of Estelle, of Aunt Bridget and Uncle Josh and Arthur Ransome, and Freddie—yes, even poor, dear Freddie—and of those fateful earlier years in Calcutta, came sweeping through Olivia's mind like a river in spate. She had lost them all, each one gone forever. Over the edge of the ravine of her memory, all she saw were scattered, shattered corpses, once loved and cherished and full of the vitality of life. Even Estelle was gone. In all these years that she had searched for her, there had not been even a hint to suggest that her beloved cousin could still be alive. With so many Englishwomen slaughtered in that hideous, unspeakable riverside betrayal, why should Estelle alone have survived?

Going through the pile of letters, Olivia picked out for perusal the last few she had received from her cousin as possibly the most pertinent in her present quest. Olivia had not looked at the painful, poignant correspondence in years, recoiling from the images it invoked, not insulated enough even after all these years to suffer their tragic resurrections. But now, with Amos's curious story playing havoc with her peace of mind, she steeled herself to face again her lost cousin's familiar, childish handwriting peppered with italics and exclamation marks, eloquent with the sheer joy of living. Warning herself not to rekindle hopes, keeping in the forefront of her mind her many previous searches and bitter disappointments, Olivia sat down to read once more Estelle's final messages before she too was cruelly felled for the innocent crime of being in the wrong place at the wrong time.

"My darling Coz," began the letter of January 11, 1857.

Oh, how happy we were today to see our dearest Jai returned to us after such a long, intolerable separation! He is all nut brown and healthy and simply oozing Hawaiian sunshine and sea. I sat down immediately and absolutely devoured your pile of letters with all the news about the children whom I so long to see. Your voyages aboard the Ganga around the Pacific and South Seas over the past years (which he described in pitiless detail to tease me and decimate me with envy!) I shall treasure always. As indeed I do the firsthand news he brings of your lives in Honolulu. After we had eaten luncheon, he showed us the most recent photographs that you had sent of yourself and the children and your family. They are so much more grown now and Amos, of course, is still exactly like Jai— but who, pray, has your Maya taken after? Jai says she has an angelic face (as if I can't see that for myself!) and, according to him, owes little to you save her glorious chestnut hair and (regretfully, he alleges!) your fierce wilfulness, even though she is not quite four. Her eyes, he maintains, are so blue they are almost violet in sunlight. Now who on earth could she have got those from—me or Mama? (I prefer to think it was both!) Jai tells us you and the children may join him shortly when Uncle Sean's health improves. He looks so dreadfully wan and tired in the picture and I was greatly distressed to learn that his asthma worsens and that he loses strength rapidly. I pray for his recovery and for your return! I can hardly wait, my dearly beloved Coz. Oh, how I have missed you both, especially you! Jai appears to be very preoccupied but, I hasten to add lest you worry, very content to be back and as frenetic as ever.

There followed news of *burra khanas* and of a sporting event arranged by the Cawnpore Tent Club, and details of John's work in the Magazine stocked high with artillery and ammunition, and a lot about General Wheeler, whom sepoys and officers alike apparently adored. The final paragraphs read:

In answer to your questions, yes, there are strange and unpleasant rumblings in the air. Everyone keeps talking about the disaffection among the sepoys, but John is staunch in his belief that it is merely a canard propagated by mischief makers. Thank God, his men have nothing but affection for him, which is very reassuring.

Jai has been going a great deal to Bithoor, which is about twelve miles from here, where the Nana Sahib (also called the Peshwa by some although the British have not granted him the use of the title yet, which is what makes him so churlish) has his fine Palace. He is certainly a most odd gentleman but also very generous to those to whom he happens to take a fancy. On one occasion, we hear, he distributed cashmere shawls and diamond jewellery to all the ladies present at one of his banquets! Can you imagine how these lucky ladies were envied (especially by yours truly!)?

On February 7, Estelle wrote:

Jonathan had his fifth birthday yesterday. The Red Indian headdress you sent him is very amusing and he wears it even to bed! If he could write, I know he would want to thank you himself. He looks so much like Papa that it is quite uncanny. Thank goodness he doesn't look like John's father—wouldn't that really be too awful?! I send you a photograph of the birthday party so that you can assess for yourself.

The letter of March 3 was full of excitement:

I can hardly wait to tell you, dearest Coz, that last night we too were dinner guests at one of the Nana Sahib's banquets! It was a rather eccentric but most royally lavish dinner party to which many other Europeans were invited. His palace in Bithoor looks like an auction house with all its bizarre decorations! We ate at a thirty-foot-long (at least) dinner table at which we were served in the most peculiar assortment of mismatched dishes. Soup arrived in a trifle dish, if you please, and as ladle we were expected to use a broken teacup! Instead of napkins to match the white damask tablecloth, we were given small rough towels and champagne glasses for the claret. John's beer, however (although iced to perfection), came in a tumbler fashioned out of the meanest of metals! Alas, no cashmere shawls or diamonds for lady guests this time, more's the pity—but, in his great kindness, the Nana Sahib has offered a carriage and the use of a suite in his Palace to a newly wed English couple for a royal honeymoon. Isn't that splendid?

In spite of John's optimism, I sense there is something brewing somewhere. Jai, of course, is as infuriating as ever and will not reveal anything. I have the suspicion that he is more involved than he would have us believe. You know how he has always hated British presence in India. There is still a great deal of fuss about these wretched new Enfield rifles that are being given to the soldiers. They say the cartridges are greased with pig and cow fat, so neither the Muslims nor the Hindus are prepared to touch, much less use them. However, many feel the rifles are being used merely as an excuse. The real reason for the discontent, people say, is the annexation of the state of Oudh last year by our General Outram, and the summary removal of its ruler. All his palaces and property in his capital, Lucknow, have been confiscated and all his thousands of family retainers thrown out on their ears with no means of sustenance. Apparently, the majority of our sepoys come from Oudh, and the annexation has made them lose face and status among their peers. Rumours of an uprising instigated by these sepoys are still rampant and the assault could come at any time.

Nevertheless, John still remains sanguine, although there's talk of nothing else at burra khanas and it's becoming such a bore! Jai disagrees with John and there are violent arguments between them. Jai wants me to move out of Cawnpore with Jonathan and go to Calcutta, but John just laughs and pooh-poohs the idea. He says Jai is unduly alarmist and no dissatisfaction prevails or can possibly be envisaged to prevail in our heavenly and peaceful Cawnpore! But I am not so sure; I had once hated Cawnpore, remember? Perhaps it was my instinct then that warned me of hideous things to come. We shall see.

Estelle's letters of March and April, although written in the same light vein, contained undertones of her festering anxiety. Then, on May 12, she wrote:

We have dreadful news from Meerut—the Mutiny, they say, has begun! On April 24, I believe, eighty-five sepoys of the 3rd Light Cavalry refused to use the new cartridges and so were stripped of their uniforms, shackled and taken to jail. To avenge this humiliation, it is said, day before yesterday, Sunday, all the native infantry, light cavalry, horse and foot artillery, even the 6th Dragoon Guards, all rose to take up arms against their officers! There has been terrible carnage and pillaging and torching. The rebels now march to Delhi, we hear, but no one believes they intend to attack Cawnpore. Nevertheless, I am so frightened, Olivia. . . .

"Today it is our Queen's birthday," the letter of May 24 began on a more cheerful note.

There is to be only a token entertainment. Cawnpore station is much excited and so, I confess, am I. You know how dreary life has been for us just lately with so many sepoy regiments having already risen. The entertainment this evening will at least divert our thoughts for a while. However, there are to be no pealing church bells and no gun salutes. General Wheeler has absolutely forbidden any such displays in case they are misunderstood. Wouldn't it be too dreadful if the sepoys thought we were attacking and opened fire just as we were at our kebabs and curries? Think what that might do to our combined nerves, to say nothing of the hapless hostess's soufflés!

Jai came for a few moments in the dead of night. He is insistent that Jonathan and I leave for Calcutta immediately, but John still will not hear of it. There was quite an argument! I have to admit that now I am again uneasy, as are most in station. No one knows what is about to happen. Meerut has been devastated, we hear, but so far there is no physical sign of rebellion in Cawnpore. How long will this uncertainty last? . . .

Estelle's letter of May 26 seethed with disquiet. Finally convinced of imminent danger, General Hugh Wheeler had belatedly ordered work to begin on an entrenchment where endangered civilians and army families could take refuge in the event of a siege. "But at the *same* time," she wrote:

The General relies heavily on the Nana Sahib to provide protection for the treasury, which contains enormous sums of revenue collections! Now even John is shocked and disturbed, but both General Wheeler (whose Indian wife is said to be of the same caste as the Nana Sahib) and

Mr. Hillersden, our magistrate, appear to trust the Nana Sahib com-
pletely. Is that not a foolish thing to do when the man is not yet fully an
ally? I now suspect that even Jai is disenchanted with the Nana Sahib.
He has not said so in words, but knowing him as I do, I can sense his
disappointment and anger. . . .

Estelle's letter of May 29 began with a chilling announcement:

The British have put a price on Jai's head! *They are willing to pay*
fifty thousand rupees *to anyone who can capture him, dead or alive—*
isn't that dreadful? *Cawnpore is very tense and it is the* silence *that is*
now extremely *hard to bear, waiting, waiting,* waiting *for something to*
happen! John makes reassuring sounds but he can no longer hide his own
gathering apprehensions. Everyone knows *now that Jai is with the muti-*
neers—oh, Olivia, I am so terribly, terribly afraid *for him, and so is*
John! I know *there is a Judas hidden in* every *sepoy regiment, greedy for*
easy loot at the cost of dispensable loyalty, because John meets these rene-
gades every day. Our government is trying to seize Trident and the ships
and all Jai's property in Calcutta, but Ranjan Moitra is fighting them
tooth and nail. Jai only laughs and says not to worry as if I am still a
child—and it's oh so infuriating! Jai came again, which makes it twice
in as many days. He now comes only at night *so as not to embarrass*
John (being on opposite sides, I mean—isn't that a hoot?*). He said he*
had come to take us away, Jonathan and me, but despite his fears John
remains adamant that we will not be parted. There is now a look about Jai
that is very strange and really quite demented—*he seems obsessed, as if*
in a terrible rage! *I don't know what to make of it but in spite of every-*
thing I still love him dearly—*half or full, he is the only brother I will*
ever have. How can I not *cherish him? Oh, darling Coz, I sometimes fear*
that the world has gone quite, quite mad! *. . .*

Estelle's second to last letter was dated May 31. It began on a note that
was deceptively lighthearted:

I am writing to you from the entrenchment. We have now been ordered
to remain here day and night, *which is really rather discomfitting. Can*
you imagine all the men, women and children sleeping together higgledy-
piggledy on an open verandah with not a vestige of privacy? *If our*
predicament weren't so serious, *it would really be very* funny. *Old Mr.*
Martin from the Post Office insists on wearing his nightcap and long
johns even as he patrols at night with his rifle by his side! Our poor, dear
chaplain, Mr. Turner, has gone raving mad *with anxiety and parades*
all day long without a stitch *on, but so strange has become our situation*
that no one gives him a second glance any more, not even Miss Pomfrey,
who under normal circumstances would have first brained him with her
umbrella and then fainted. And Mrs. Nightingale, our celebrated merry
widow (I wrote about her last year, remember?), can no longer *hide*

what we have always suspected—that she wears, you know, artificial aids *to make herself more buxom! Isn't that a* scream?

In Lucknow as in Meerut, all the European bungalows have been burnt down. *I wonder, darling Coz, if we will ever meet again? Some* still *believe that our only hope is the Nana Sahib, whose troops guard the Magazine in alliance with General Wheeler. Many are convinced (although John isn't) that he is* truly *our friend and ally (the Nana Sahib, I mean, not the General, who is a* dear!), *but* many *continue to distrust him. If he were not trustworthy, Jai would* never *have thrown in his lot with him. But then, Jai is also with the sepoys, the rebels! Oh, I can't understand* anything, *Olivia, it's all so* confusing! *We have very little food and water and it is* stiflingly *hot. It is difficult to sleep at night and Jonathan cries* all the time. *Thank God John is posted in the entrenchment for our protection and so we are at least together. Am I a coward to be so* frightened? *Is* this *how our world is destined to end?* Whatever *our fate, my dearest Coz, I hope that your frightened little star can* bear *it. . . .*

And then, for many agonising months, silence.

Estelle's final message did not reach Olivia until almost a year later, delivered with Jai's paltry belongings. It was a largely incoherent note, written in an almost illegible scribble on a torn fragment of paper, and it was undated. In the light of subsequent events, however, it was calculated to have been written on, or just before, 26 June 1857, very possibly the last message to be sent out of the entrenchment before it was evacuated. If the contents of the note—addressed not to her but to Jai—were searingly painful, the tortuous means by which it had eventually come to Olivia were even more so. She had been able to decipher the garbled, grimy, badly defaced little scrap only because what had transpired later was now part of tragic history. Why had Jai not responded to his sister's cry for help? *Had* he been there, or had he *not*?

"At last, repr . . . !", the note began abruptly.

> . . . *surrender . . . greed. Siege to . . . tomorrow. . . . na Sahib . . . liberation! Too la . . . . . . , too . . . God, Jai . . . come . . . please, I beg . . . John is dea. . . . pray for us . . . Jai, please,* come. . . .

Olivia laid down the letter, unable to go on. Estelle's pathetic situation, her consuming fears, her mounting despair and unanswered pleas for help, rose from the lifeless paper like palpable entities, filling Olivia's nostrils with the cloying fumes of death. In her remorseless and cruelly perceptive mind's eye, she again saw the Bibighar, the steps of Satichowra Ghat and the river, red and shining and oily with blood.

Oh dear God—how could they ever believe that you were part of all that putrefaction, Jai?

She thought she was going to be sick. With shaking fingers she picked up the faded, sepia photograph that had fallen out of the folds of one letter. It was a group picture of the three of them—John, Estelle and

Jonathan—against a table laid with birthday fare in a room alive with balloons and streamers and happy smiles. The faces were indistinct, but what the reality lacked was made up by the imagination. She saw her cousin, plump and pretty and irrepressibly saucy, with mischief spilling out of her violet-blue eyes, and in her ears she heard Estelle's interminable giggles, so spontaneous, so full of merriment, so joyously and gloriously *alive!*

Olivia's eyes blurred; her hands went cold, as if packed in ice. Blindly, she thrust the pile of earlier letters back into the almirah. She stumbled out of the room and down the stairs of the silent, sleeping house, out of the back door and onto the embankment, devastated once more by grief, weighted down again by the intolerable burdens of memory. She stopped running only when she reached the steps and folded over the metal rails, gasping and panting to regain her breath. Then she collapsed onto the step, put her head down on her knees, and wept as if her heart had broken all over again.

Later, much later, when the owls had gone to sleep and the frogs and the cicadas had fallen silent and her own grief had expended itself and been replaced by healing numbness, Olivia leaned back against the wall, exhausted. Above her, the sequinned arc of night seemed to revolve almost visibly; once again, its cool, velvet-smooth embrace gave her solace and its caressing breezes hummed a faint lullaby in her ear. She felt drowsy and was almost asleep when, suddenly, she jerked upright, startled and wide awake. A flash of memory brought back something small but significant contained in Estelle's penultimate letter; like a sharp little needlepoint, this was what had been pricking away at the back of her brain ever since Amos's return from Cawnpore.

Shaken and now totally awake, Olivia sat for a moment reflecting silently on the extraordinary coincidence. The full implication of her discovery hit her and she started to tremble. She hated and dreaded the prospect of a return to Cawnpore; but she saw now that there was no way she could avoid it.

"To Cawnpore?" When she told him of her decision the next morning at breakfast, Amos was aghast. "To *Cawnpore?* Mother, do you know what you are saying?"

"Yes. I have to go. I *must!* I now feel very strongly that this strange Englishwoman *is* my cousin Estelle."

He stared, even more astonished. "But on what basis, Mother? She said or did nothing that could possibly lead to such a conclusion!"

"She didn't need to. She gave herself away quite inadvertently, not to them but to me." Olivia's golden eyes shone with a rare, rare sparkle, such as Amos had not seen in years. "Don't you see—*Sitara* in Urdu means a 'star,' a literal translation of 'Estelle'!"

He started to laugh. "Oh, *Mother!* And is that all you have to go by?"

"No. She called herself 'your frightened little star' in her last letter to me. She was referring to a silly private joke we had once shared a long, long time ago."

Amos was by no mean convinced. "Well, I still think your logic is preposterous. But even if we accept that this woman, by some extraordinary coincidence, *is* Aunt Estelle—why then has she never made contact with you through all these years? From all you've told me, you were very attached to each other."

Olivia shook her head. "I don't know. Or maybe I do. For the moment, all we can presume is that Estelle—if she is Estelle—has good reasons for her silence. Either way I have to learn the truth, Amos!"

"Yes, but just as long as you are fully prepared for yet another disappointment."

"Of course. It would be foolish not to be."

"In any case, I can't leave until next month after the Derozio meeting. There are too many vital issues at stake."

"Next *month?*" She was dismayed. "Oh, Amos, how will I be able to wait that long? I want to leave now, *today!*"

"*Do* try and be reasonable, Mother, you know I can hardly leave station now. With so much dependent on this meeting, it's unthinkable that I should not be present. In fact, it's out of the question."

"For you, yes, but not for me. I'm perfectly capable of going on my own."

"On your own?" He was horrified. "To Cawnpore?"

She had known that he would be shocked and that there would be an argument. But despite his fierce protestations, her persuasions eventually prevailed and they compromised. She would go to Cawnpore without Amos, provided she agreed to an escort of Francis, the chief bearer, her ayah, and Hari Babu, Amos's confidential assistant from the office. While in Cawnpore she was to permit their agent there, Kasturi Ram, and Hari Babu to accompany her on all her errands at all times. Meekly, Olivia agreed to all his conditions. Amos was not to know that she had no intention of honouring any one of them.

"Don't stay a day longer than you need to," he pleaded.

"No."

"If this woman isn't your cousin, come back at once."

"Yes."

"I would still much rather you waited, Mother."

"I know, darling, but I can't. I have to go, I *must!* I owe it to Estelle. More than that, I owe it to your father."

CHAPTER

3

THERE ARE SOME DAYS in one's life, Christian Pendlebury was to reflect later, that one simply cannot forget. Not because they are exceptional in the usual sense of the word, but because, in some curious way, they linger in the memory as patterns in time touched with magic. That first glorious morning he rode with Maya, he sensed instinctively, was to become part of his life's mythology. In years to come, no matter with what plots and ploys fate awaited, it would stand out like a beacon in his Indian destiny, a morning born to immortality.

They had ridden side by side for miles, way beyond the city and its environs, flying across fields and forests and embankments on the wings of an infant, lavender wind to the forlorn cries of strange tropical birds he had never seen before. He had spent the week thinking of the many things that he would say to her, many more that he had a need to ask. But when the time came and they sat, panting and drenched with perspiration and satiated with fatigue, under a flaming gulmohar in a forest alight with sunrise, all he could offer were meaningless banalities. Oddly tongue-tied, content merely to watch her from under lowered lashes, he reclined opposite her balanced on one elbow, giddy with the sheer fulfilment of having her near. He had never before met a woman with whom it was so comfortable to be silent.

It suddenly seemed to him as he lay, monosyllabic and filled with wonder, that nothing was real any more. He was encapsulated in a dreamscape, a still, somnolent world of soothing silences peopled by two. He felt disoriented but at the same time, paradoxically, marvellously alive, all his senses honed to an extraordinary pitch of sharpness. The carpeted jade of the grass had never been so green, so vibrant, nor morning birdsong so piercingly eloquent. He could segregate in his mind's eye the formation of every blade, of every petal of every wild flower as it opened joyously to welcome the sun. The sky exploded with rainbows, their luminosity such that, fearing blindness, he shut his eyes and in his foolishness smiled at himself. The hum of honeybees, the whir of butterflies' wings, the lightning swift *whoosh!* of the blue-breasted kingfisher as it swooped into the grass for an insect, the chittering antics of a troupe of monkeys—all sounded like angelic choirs resounding and reverberating in his ears, paeons to the awakening forest and to the nymph with whom he shared it. And in his nostrils he could discern with astonishing clarity each of the fragile, pale pink perfumes that radiated the air of this mint-cool, memorable summer's morning that would remain with him forever.

But sweetest wonder of all, *sweetest* of all, he could trace with his eyes shut every aspect of her lovely, fine-boned oval face, from the sun-kissed, wind-blown strands of opulent hair that framed it, to the smooth alabaster of her long, long neck, held high with such regal arrogance, giving her the look of a swan. Without opening his eyes he could reproduce in his mind the pattern of glistening sweat droplets on her forehead, the brilliant, blinding violet of her eyes—heavy-lidded and strangely watchful, waiting, ever waiting, for something! If there was anything about her that offended him, it was the forbidding aloofness of those eyes, with their impenetrable grill of lashes, and the skill with which she guarded her innermost secrets from invaders. He felt excluded, not entirely accepted. Ravaged by the delicious torment of uncertainty, with a sigh Christian again closed his eyes, contenting himself with mental revocations of the coral contours of her lips, the subtle curves of her lithe, slender body, the exquisitely moulded ivory of her tapering fingers. Yes, she had the look of a swan, all fluid grace and shining hauteur and a sort of grave, frozen beauty.

And, of course, she rode magnificently! She sat on her Arab astride, like a man, her slim, coltish figure daringly clad in britches and a scarlet riding jacket. Initially, Christian had to admit to himself, he had been startled; he had never before seen a woman dressed like a man, except perhaps in a stage comedy. But then as he got used to the idea, he was amused and enchanted. It made her even more exciting and somehow—oddly enough—even more feminine in his eyes.

"Be careful, my innocent, uninformed friend," Lytton Prescott had warned with a superior smile. "She had her sharp little talons into an army bloke from the Forty-Ninth called Maynard. Lost his marbles because of her, they say. Starting drinking, got into bad company—and a confounded mess!—poor devil. It was a *hell* of a business, I might tell you. He was almost cashiered out of the army for no fault of his own. Fortunately for him, Maynard had an uncle who was an admiral. Pulled strings to have him transferred to the garrison at the Penal Colony in the Andamans instead without loss of rank." He pulled down the corners of his mouth in a grimace. "She's not known to conform to standards, yours or mine, or for that matter native. But then, neither did her mother—to say nothing of her scoundrel of a father. And remember, old boy—quite apart from anything else—she's Eurasian. *Strictly* non grata!"

That last bit, of course, had come as more of a shock than all the rest. Not having known then what he did now about her extraordinary antecedents, he had been, frankly, shaken. She certainly didn't *look* Eurasian—but then how did Eurasians look? Never having met any in England, Christian couldn't tell. For a while he was discomfited, not only by Maya's history but, even more so, by what he had learned about her father. No wonder she had recoiled at the mention of his name that afternoon. But then, superseding all of Lytton's distressing revelations, his own magical recollections of her came surging back—and the delicious prospect of another morning ride with her by his side—and instantly, every other consideration was forgotten. Suddenly, all Christian could remember was how she had looked at him at that wharf, and her shy, oblique smile on those river steps that evening with her face turning golden in the setting sun. Even thinking of it, his knees felt weak and his breath ran shallow. Quickly he turned away in case Lytton noticed his loss of composure. It was then, precisely at that instant, that Christian saw with absolute clarity that whatever Maya Raventhorne might or might not be, the prospect of not seeing her again was one he simply could not endure.

Now, totally lost in his thoughts, trying to grapple with this morning of astonishing self-revelations, Christian again sighed.

"Shall we return?" Maya asked, stirring for the first time as she lay chewing idly on a twig, long legs stretched carelessly, watching a plump little black spider spin a lacy curtain in the branches above. "Perhaps you would care to join me at breakfast after you've inspected the stables?" Delighted as he was at this unexpected invitation, Christian nevertheless hesitated. "Had she been here, Mother would have welcomed you," Maya added quickly, recognising the reason for his hesitation. "But she left yesterday for Cawnpore."

He rose and brushed a blade of grass off his britches. "In that case, I accept most willingly. I look forward to the pleasure of meeting your brother. I would like to compliment him on the excellent services offered to passengers on the *Ganga*."

Maya smiled and said nothing, content in the knowledge that Amos had spent the night on the ship in order to navigate her to the shipyard this morning for repairs. Throwing Christian a tantalising glance over her shoulder, she mounted her dapple grey mare, nudged it gently with her spurs, and sped away down the meandering forest path.

When they reached it, breathless and sheened with perspiration, the red brick stable house was ablaze with early morning sunlight. Outside, in the larger of the paddocks, two of the foals frolicked and gambolled, their spindly legs kicking up tufts of grass as they bucked back and forth in joyous abandon. Some of the horses grazed on the lush green verges of the river, and in a smaller paddock enclosed behind a white picket fence, a syce lad gave a young stallion practice in lunging.

Glasses of iced sherbet arrived from the main house with remarkable dispatch. Maya tossed her cap on the ground and shook out her hair. It tumbled down her back in a cascade, a shimmering waterfall magically released by the flick of a wrist. Tired but marvellously exhilarated,

Christian sat on an upturned bucket, drinking thirstily in huge, grateful gulps, listening to her converse in Hindustani with Rafiq Mian, the head groom's son, recently returned from Bombay. In two adjoining stalls stood the newly arrived Arabians—one a magnificent grey and the other a strawberry mare—flicking away the flies with their long, whiplike tails, their nostrils twitching nervously in their new surroundings. The strawberry mare gave a hollow cough; Maya opened a cupboard and pulled out a tin box. From it she abstracted something and fed it to the horse.

"I don't like the sound of that cough," she said over her shoulder. "I think she has a slight chill. The train from Bombay takes forever to reach here and the horse-boxes are notorious for coal dust and draughts."

"Homemade cough balls?"

"Yes. One of Mother's old recipes from Sacramento. Four ounces of asafoetida, two ounces of nitre and two ounces of raw sugar. It never fails."

Squatting on the ground and pointing to the mare's hoofs, Abdul Mian made a comment.

"What did he say?" Christian asked fascinated, wanting to know everything.

"He says the toes turn neither inwards nor outwards, which is as it should be. Some Arabs arrive with a defective action of the forehand which is not immediately noticeable. Fortunately, Rafiq is as careful a buyer as his father, so special horseshoes will not be necessary."

Christian stood up to observe the grizzled old groom use his hand as a tool to rub down the animal, moving his fingers with such expertise that the mare gave a soft neigh of pleasure.

"You do not have proper grooming kits available in India?" he asked. "In England we use a whole range of furry combs, body brushes, sponges, wisps, leather, broom, pitchfork and towel flicks for the daily rubdown."

Maya threw him a complacent smile. "Abdul Mian believes in manual massage. He feels it's a much better way of increasing circulation, and as you can see, the horses enjoy the feel of his fingers. He says in Arabia no one uses all this fancy stuff you have in England."

Christian accepted the explanation with a nod, much too content to think of presenting an argument in defence of the more sophisticated English methods. Certainly, the animals all appeared to be in excellent condition and faultlessly groomed. "These auctions in Bombay—do they offer opportunities to buy really first-class stock?"

"Oh yes. One can be cheated, of course, if one is not careful, but the variety available allows one ample choice."

"You yourself have been to these auctions?"

"Once. Mother made arrangements for me to travel to Bombay last year in the charge of a very good friend, Mr. Lubbock, Grace's father. We came back with three very fine specimens." She thrust her chin forward. "As a matter of fact, one of them recently won the very first Ballygunge Steeplechase."

"You *race* your horses?" he asked, surprised.

Maya shrugged. "Once in a while. I'm really not much of a gambler, although prize money does come in useful. I prefer to sell to others who race and so will look after the animals well. Mother believes that the stables should now start to earn their keep."

"And do they?"

"I would have made the stables self-supporting this coming year had I not been going away."

"Going away?" he echoed, dismayed. "Going away where?"

"To America, to my grandmother in California."

"For *good?*"

"Perhaps." She gave a careless shrug. "If I like it there."

The words sank in and he was devastated. It seemed to him that if she went away, with her she would take the light of the whole world. "When do you sail?"

She smiled, enjoying his dismay, revelling in the disappointment he simply could not hide. "Not until June."

"Oh." He took a deep breath of relief; a great deal could be achieved in the remaining months! Once again he was full of confidence, so much so that he almost asked her about Chester Maynard, but then thought better of it. He did not know her well enough yet; she would consider him brash and unforgivably presumptuous.

He got up to stroll down the aisles, noticing the clean, well-swept stalls, the attention to good cross-ventilation, the care with which she devised and implemented dietary charts. "How does one tell whether or not a horse will be a good racer when buying at these auctions?" he asked, not because he particularly cared, but because he liked to hear the lilt of her accent, quaint and delightfully different. Lytton had said Eurasians talked with what he called a "chi-chi" accent—but if this was chi-chi, then more power to her tongue! "At Doncaster and Newmarket, every horse on sale has a pedigree."

She was immediately on the offensive. "Yes, but even with all those long fancy pedigrees, only about three in two *thousand* thoroughbreds turn out to be champions—that too if one is lucky."

"Well, yes. I agree that there's always an element of chance involved in the making of a racer, but surely even more so when there is no known pedigree at all?"

"These horses may not have *written* pedigrees," Maya contested warmly, "but the Byculla auctions are the largest in Asia and they are held out in the open. There aren't any dark corners which will hide defective animals. Every horse is fully visible and one can browse to one's heart's content."

"Browse?" He raised a sceptical eyebrow. "And you can pick a winner merely by browsing?"

"No, of *course* not!" She was very cross indeed. "They have riding boys who trot, canter and gallop the horses if one wishes. Serious buyers are even permitted to ride the mount themselves before the bargain is completed." Proudly she patted the snout of a black and white mare. "Scheherazade, for instance, clocked a mile in just one minute and fifty-four seconds when I put her through her paces in Bombay last year. In fact, she's being sold next week to the Aga Khan's stables. They plan to race her here and then in Poona and Bangalore." She arched a contemptuous eyebrow. "So much for pedigree!"

Enjoying the argument that had brought such rich colour to her cheeks, Christian laughed and teased her further. "But, as you yourself just admitted, isn't that more a matter of luck rather than sound, scientific breeding?"

She fielded that with an impatient question of her own. "Surely one can be as wrong about an Arab as one can about the most carefully engineered thoroughbred?"

"Perhaps." Christian deliberately prolonged the exchange by continuing to look dubious. He sauntered into a stall and critically surveyed one of her new acquisitions. "In so small a breed, wouldn't you say the chances of producing a winner are essentially reduced?"

"Not in the slightest!" Maya returned, indignant. "I see that you *do* have a great deal yet to learn about the Arabian horse, Mr. Pendlebury!" She pushed back a stray strand of hair in an unconscious gesture Christian found utterly entrancing. "They might be small, but they are amazingly sturdy and have enormous powers of endurance. Why, only recently a Persian troop horse, although only fourteen hands and three inches at the withers, was ridden by a private of the Eighteenth Hussars over eight hundred miles, including a river crossing, carrying equipment that weighed *twenty-two and a half stone*! Wouldn't you call that something of a record?" Hands on hips, she faced him with flashing eyes, challenging him to refute her contention.

"Maybe." He was pointedly offhanded. "There are always exceptions to every rule." She threw her hands up in exasperation and turned away, now truly angry. "But seriously, Miss Raventhorne," he said, persisting in his little game, delighted that at last he had found a weapon with which to prise open at least a chink in those maddeningly frustrating barricades, "do you *really* believe the Arabian's virtues can match those of our own thoroughbreds? There are some in England who consider Arabs to be, well"—he shrugged and smiled apologetically to show that these were not necessarily his own views—"no more than bad . . . hacks."

"And there are many who *don't*! I have read testimonials in your equestrian journals that place the Arabian between the very good and the positively matchless! After all, it's purely a matter of individual preference, isn't it?"

This he could hardly deny, but before he could express his agreement, Sheba materialised at the door. "It's time for breakfast, Missy Maya," she said reproachfully. "You want the poor Lord sahib to go hungry?"

Over kippers and bacon and eggs and large breakfast cups of freshly ground Brazilian coffee, Christian wanted to ply her with more questions, but Maya laughed and shook her head. "All we appear to have talked about is horses! If you exhaust all your questions now, what will we have to talk about the next time?"

"I cannot ever imagine a situation in which we would have nothing to talk about!" he exclaimed fervently. "I know so little and I want to know so much about"—he almost said "you"—"well, *everything.*"

"Nevertheless," she said firmly, "I've been terribly rude in not asking the questions that I should be asking you about, for instance, your living arrangements. Have you settled in well? Are you comfortable where you are?"

He shrugged as he attacked his heaped plate, obviously ravenous, and Maya was pleased she had taken the trouble to make arrangements beforehand for a truly English breakfast. "Fairly. I share a chummery with two other competition-wallahs. I can't honestly say that at the moment our lives are of an especially exalted quality. We appear to have so little to do that is of any consequence."

"Oh? But surely your language classes and your studies arising from them must keep you more than adequately busy?"

"Hardly." He looked quite disgusted. "In fact, our daily routine is so puerile, I am positively ashamed to repeat it. However, I'm told this is the regimen all competition-wallahs are expected to follow while they prepare for examinations in language, law and procedures." She served him a second helping of scrambled eggs, happy that he ate well, deriving pleasure from his healthy appetite, quietly admiring the aquiline sharpness of his well-proportioned features, his clear, inquiring eyes so innocent of guile. He was about to confide in her his daily routine, his living habits; there was an odd sort of intimacy subsumed in the confidence, and a thrill of anticipation made the back of her neck tingle.

"Well, we rise fairly early, at five or so. Then, still in our dressing gowns and slippers, we drink tea on a balcony overlooking Bow Bazaar Street, each served by his personal *khidmutgar.* Mine happens to be a frisky one-eyed fellow called Karamat, who must surely be the most resourceful scamp in station! In fact, it was he who arranged the purchase of my horse, no doubt at great profit to himself. Karamat considers it his bounden duty to help me bath, dress, undress, put on and take off my shoes, shampoo my hair, brush the inside of my finger and toe nails. Indeed, if I were to allow it, he would even shave me in bed so that I am spared the trouble." With a sheepish grin, he tossed his hands in the air. "I have to confess that I am thoroughly ashamed at how dreadfully *cosseted* I have been even in these few weeks that I have been here!"

"Well, as an English civil servant of some standing, it is only right that you should be," Maya replied.

Christian gave her a sidelong glance, not certain if she teased, but he saw that she was perfectly serious. "Incidentally, while I think of it"—he paused, laden fork suspended in mid-air, suddenly remembering one of the questions he had wanted to ask her—"would you have allowed me to purchase a horse from your stables had I mentioned it earlier?"

Her answer came without hesitation. "No. I don't believe in selling to friends." She coloured. "That is, at least, I *hope* we will be friends."

The dazzling, unblinking violet gaze, as she blushed pink, unnerved him totally. "Oh, most *d-definitely!*" he breathed, speaking with difficulty. "I, ah, would be *honoured* to be known as your friend, Miss Raventhorne."

In his elation he almost reached for her hand resting casually on the table, but pulled back in time. The Eurasian housekeeper, he could see, was hovering in a corner of the breakfast room by the window, the stern expression on her chocolate brown face defying him to overstep his bounds. To precipitate a situation that would be an embarrassment to them all at this early juncture would be not only uncouth but self-defeating. Hastily, he thrust his fork into his mouth, chewed for a moment, then, with a rueful grimace, returned to the account of his daily doings.

"Anyway . . . following morning tea and a rather desultory look at the newspaper, we ride at six, either together or individually with companions of our choosing." He stopped and smiled and downed several gulps of coffee. "After we have shaved, bathed and dressed for the day, friends and colleagues usually drop in, which gives us a welcome excuse to drink *more* tea and dawdle over breakfast. We sit smoking and chatting and exchanging notes and reading the newspapers until about ten. We start our language studies at eleven and they last for about two hours. Then we call on various families—I am still in the process of being introduced around, of course—and an invitation to stay for luncheon might follow. This midday meal, I find, is so vast that without an afternoon siesta there is imminent danger of expiry, either from the heat outside or the weight of the food within, or both. In the evenings we loll about the Club, playing cards or billiards, or propping up the bar drinking iced beer and exchanging idle gossip. If we feel particularly energetic, we indulge in a strenuous stroll along the Strand, where the exercise of doffing one's hat every five minutes for the benefit of passing ladies is especially exhausting. By the time the sun sets it is time for another change of clothes and, of course, for *another* vast meal, probably at yet one more *burra khana*, possibly the fourth or fifth of the week, which precludes all post-prandial activity save bed.

"And on Sundays," he went on, "it's even worse—if such a prospect is conceivable." He made a gesture of self-deprecation. "It is mandatory, we are instructed, to show our faces at Church either at morning or evening service so as to Set a Good Example." He rolled his eyes heavenwards. "Through the rest of the Sabbath we are permitted to sin like mad with a game of cricket or polo on the Maidan, or by bending elbows at the Club bar. If we wish to conserve our energies for the labours of the coming week, however, we just lie around in our beds laying wagers on whatever grabs our fancy.

"Oh, I almost forgot!" He held up a forefinger. "In between all this frenetic activity, there is also the incidental matter of tutorials in governance, but not many appear to take all that *too* seriously." He gave a somewhat humourless grin and looked glum. "So you see, I am not exactly the most *energetic* of men, Miss Raventhorne, and now you have every right to scoff if you wish." Christian made the offer lightly enough, but he knew that if she did, he would be mortified.

She did not scoff. Indeed, she listened with rapt attention, fascinated by these intimate details of a colonial life that she could only observe from a

68

distance. "You might not be fully occupied yet," she said, unsmiling, "but I imagine you will have all the physical and mental activity you crave once you are posted to your rural duties in far less hospitable circumstances. And then, I'm sure, you will look back on these days of leisure with very definite regret."

His eyes lit up. "To tell you the truth, Miss Raventhorne, I can't *wait* to be posted! So much needs doing in the Mofussil, I can scarcely contain my impatience to be off and away rather than bogged down in idle. . . ." He stopped abruptly. Suddenly aware of the implications of a posting away from Calcutta, he felt his eagerness fade and fell into an uneasy silence. However dreary and lugubrious his life at the moment, he was at least within easy reach of Maya Raventhorne. Once he was posted, she would be off to America and they would never see each other again. It seemed such a hollow end to a glorious interlude so full of rich promise that for a moment he was utterly desolated.

In the forlorn silence that followed, Maya picked up his unspoken thoughts and, within herself, watched them expand and form into questions of her own. Where would he be posted? When? Would she ever see him again? Would some young pukka mem suddenly divert his attention and remove him from her forever? Had she *already* done so, during those introductory social calls, those jolly *burra khanas* and cricket matches and polo chukkers from which she herself was so irrevocably excluded? Or was he in the process of succumbing to some forward little chit's flirtatious overtures on those ambling constitutionals along the Strand, where warm, wet breezes whipped mild dalliance into passion and passion into inadvertent commitment? Sitting opposite him, watching patches of sunlight move in spasms across the gleaming mahogany surface of the breakfast table, Maya wrenched with jealousy and anger and despair, already rejected, already abandoned. Silently, she luxuriated in hating the nameless, faceless, anonymous rivals who would steal away from her his fevered thoughts, his love-laden sidelong glances, his nascent confidences, his unspoken dreams and hopes and confused, undefined longings.

Tears welled in her eyes. Unable to contain them, she rose and left the room under the pretext of fetching a book that she felt he might enjoy reading. By the time she returned with a fat volume on the Arab horse, the absurd fantasy was over, the panic controlled and the barriers once more securely in place. If Christian had noticed her distress, he made no mention of it.

Neither did he question or comment upon Amos's absence.

What he did mention, however, was the subject Maya dreaded most. But it was with customary thoughtfulness, and not until the very last moment of parting. "I know about your father," he said quietly. "I am truly sorry. I want you to know that . . . it doesn't matter."

Just that, nothing more. Then he was gone.

Cawnpore.

City of death.

Graveyard of her life, her love, her all. . . .

"Promise me you won't go to the entrenchment, Mother," Amos had insisted as he saw her off at the railway station.

"Yes."

"Nor seek an audience with Colonel Bradbury or any other British official in Cawnpore," he had persisted.

"Yes. I promise."

"And promise me you won't venture anywhere near the Ghat or the Bibighar or that clearing. More than anything else, Mother, promise me that, *promise* me that!"

She had nodded, moved by his concern for her. Silly boy—did he really think that she *could?*

Considerate as always, he had made sure that Francis carried enough drinking water and food for the journey, that the stationmaster had not neglected to put a tub of ice in the compartment to bring down the temperature, that an adequate supply of fresh fruits had been procured, and that the ayah had not left behind the pile of reading material he had gathered for his mother's diversion during the long hours of travel.

Despite her loathing of Cawnpore, etched forever in her memory as a purveyor of nightmares, at her first sight of the renovated town, Olivia could not help but marvel. The physical reconstructions were admirable, astonishingly thorough in their contempt of history. Gone forever were the endless rows of gutted houses with gaping, smoke-blackened windows staring out like kohl-lined skeletal sockets; in their place had again risen neat English homes with pretty cottage gardens seemingly transported intact from Kent or Devon or suburban London. Thirteen years ago, the Assembly Rooms, the Magazine, the theatre, Christ Church, the Masonic Lodge and many other familiar landmarks were all in ruins. Scarcely a bridge was to be seen standing; railway property was destroyed with abandon. During the darkest hours of the uprising, the gullies and alleys of the town were littered with European goods plundered from English shops and homes. For many months following the Mutiny, the body and spirit of the town were to lie broken and buried under its blood-drenched soil, ravished, it would seem, beyond redemption.

But, miraculously, Cawnpore had reincarnated itself. Out of the broken fragments of its corporate existence it had somehow extracted new courage with which to fashion new lives, new aspirations and enterprises. The vistas now were of remodelled buildings, neatly trimmed hedges and landscaped greenery, re-paved and newly laid roads, refurbished and restocked shops, throbbing marketplaces carved out of shattered bazaars. Under the determined supervision of an imaginative Collector, hygienic abattoirs and a new grain market at Collectorganj had been built. A pioneering conservancy department had organised efficient clearance of garbage and night soil, public latrines were now in evidence, and three brick-lined main sewers transported Cawnpore's effluents far away from the city. Parks and playgrounds abounded.

Indeed, everywhere there were symbols of prosperity and modernisation and ambitious plans for the future. Now, if European goods were to be seen in profusion, it was again on the shelves of thriving shops bustling with customers. Once more the boast of the town was that young English brides had little need to write home for their trousseaux and household goods; few items or services required by well-appointed English homes were not available in station. The town's enviable communication network provided steam transport on the Ganges to Allahabad and along the canals; on the Grand Trunk Road from Calcutta, frequent and regular dak gharries plied, carrying mail to the capital and elsewhere. The miracle of the electric telegraph had brought the town closer to the main urban centres of the country and Cawnpore's commercial lifeline now was, of course, the East Indian Railway.

It was as if Cawnpore had excised the terrifying holocaust out of its collective memory. It was as if the midsummer of 1857 had never been.

Olivia felt a blinding sense of envy, of bitterness. One way or another, they were all survivors of the Sepoy Mutiny; but whereas others had been given the right to survive with honour, she and her children had not. *Why not?*

"Cawnpore is especially famous for its fruit," David Pickford said, as his wife and daughter dispensed generous hospitality over tea. "Indeed, our guavas, custard-apples and melons are to be found in many markets of the country, surely even in Calcutta?"

"Of course," Olivia agreed politely. "In fact, I am particularly partial to your lychees—so much larger and juicier than those grown in our own region."

Adelaide Pickford sighed. "Our much battered town has truly been born again, Mrs. Thorne. There is a great deal we must thank the good Lord for."

"Yes. I can see that."

They had not yet discovered that her real name was not Thorne. . . .

David Pickford rose to proffer a plate of sandwiches and insisted that she take one. "In little more than a decade we have become the largest centre in the country for the leather trade," he informed her, his broad, florid face alive with pride. He did not add that it was he who was at the helm of this trade—as Olivia had been informed by Kasturi Ram. "I think your young lad, Amos, has absolutely the right idea. Given a few more years, Cawnpore will also be the cotton capital of India, second only to Bombay." He tucked his thumbs in the armholes of his waistcoat and beamed.

The Pickfords had received her as warmly as they had Amos; nervous and uncertain, Olivia was grateful for the informality. It was obvious that they had taken her problem very much to heart, generously offering whatever assistance she might require in her search for her missing cousin.

She had brought them packets of prime tea from the Raventhorne estate in the hills of Assam, a gift received with far more pleasure and exclamations of delight than she considered it merited. Orders were immediately given for the tea to be brewed, its aromatic flavour and richness of colour endorsed with much enthusiasm and many compliments. During their conversation over several cups in the cosy little parlour overlooking a serene, well-ordered lawn arranged with symmetrical flower beds around a lily pond, Olivia learned something about the family. David and Adelaide Pickford were both country-born, their families having lived in northern India for three generations. Mr. Pickford's grandfather had been a purser in the East India Company's Maritime Service, his father a Quarter Master-general in the Delhi Field Force of the British Army. Mrs. Pickford's family, on the other hand, had been in business with an active trade in borax, safflower and tallow, which one of her brothers still maintained in Lucknow. Contrary to the prevailing custom among English families, they had chosen not to send their children home to England for schooling. Their daughter, Rose, had studied in a Lucknow convent, and their two sons at La Martinière. Whether out of politeness or abridged foreknowledge acquired from Amos, they asked mercifully few personal questions. They were, Olivia could see, a fine, forthright family; it would have pained her to have to lie to them.

Obviously responding to some discreet signal by his mistress, the bearer came in with yet another pot of tea and fresh cups. "Now, Mrs. Thorne," Adelaide Pickford said briskly, adding a spoonful of sugar to the teapot and stirring vigorously to bring out the full flavour of the brew, "I have no doubt you are impatient to get down to the *real* purpose of your visit. Therefore, we will waste no more time in social chitchat." She turned to her husband. "David, dear, didn't I hear you say you had promised Archie Bainbridge a game at five?"

David Pickford quickly pulled out his pocket watch and muttered an exclamation. "Bless you, dear—so you did, so you did!" He stood up quickly. "Well, since I am obviously *de trop* among you ladies, I take it I am only too willingly excused?" A big, barrel-chested man with a hearty manner and clear, good-natured eyes, he gave a bellow of a laugh, not in the least offended by his wife's peremptory dismissal. "Archie Bainbridge happens to be our doctor, Mrs. Thorne. If I don't let him win once a week at backgammon, he retaliates by sending me the most hideously exaggerated medical bills." He chuckled a little, then again turned solemn. "I sincerely hope we will see you again, Mrs. Thorne. Whether or not you require our further assistance in this particular matter is immaterial—whatever your needs, we are entirely at your disposal. I wish you God-speed in the fulfilment of your sad quest."

Touched by the offer, Olivia thanked him accordingly, thinking to herself should Amos ever need good friends in Cawnpore, as no doubt he would some day, there could be none better qualified than this genuinely hospitable family.

As soon as her husband had left, Adelaide Pickford came and sat next to Olivia on the settee. "David is really quite a dear," she said, her eyes full of conspiratorial twinkles, "but men can be *such* a nuisance in certain situations, can't they?"

She was a buxom woman with a rather plain face, made extremely appealing by the unexpected radiance of a lovely smile. Her daughter

Rose, a pale, delicate girl with finely spun flaxen hair and grave eyes, placed a fresh cup of tea at Olivia's elbow and pulled up a chair opposite so that they sat facing each other. Mrs. Pickford took Olivia's hands in hers and gave them a squeeze.

"It was Rose who spent the most time with Sitara Begum during those visits, Mrs. Thorne," she explained. "Therefore I think it would be best if she related to you the sequence of events right from the beginning. I'm sure your son has already told you everything he heard from us, but it is possible that he inadvertently omitted to mention some minor fact that might provide a useful lead."

"Yes, I would appreciate that," Olivia responded eagerly. "What I'm looking for is as much detail as you can recall, Miss Pickford."

Helped occasionally by her mother, Rose delivered her account with painstaking effort. In her thoughtfulness she had committed several points to paper. Olivia listened with close attention, interrupting only to ask pertinent questions as and when they occurred to her. Much to her disappointment, however, nothing new of any great significance emerged from Rose Pickford's recital. There were no startling revelations, no forgotten minutiae or hidden clues to jog latent memory, nothing that made Olivia any the wiser about the true identity of Sitara Begum. The mysterious woman had remained deliberately circumspect in her conversations, revealing only what she had wished to be known. And that, Olivia saw ruefully, was not much more than what Amos had already told her.

Concealing her disappointment, Olivia extracted from her handbag the photograph Estelle had sent her of Jonathan's fifth birthday party. The images were now faint, the outlines blurred, the faces obscure. "I'm not sure if this will serve any purpose, but did this Sitara Begum look anything like this? Is it possible to discern any likeness at all from a photograph that is so inadequate? Sadly, it is the only one I have of my cousin."

Mother and daughter peered closely at the rather confused sepia print. "It's difficult to say," Mrs. Pickford finally decided with a frown. "The faces are so diffuse that I am reluctant to commit myself. What do you think, dear?"

Rose carried the photograph to the window to scan it better by natural light and immediately shook her head. "I'm sorry," she said with absolutely no hesitation, "I can't seem to see any resemblance at all. Of course, Sitara Begum was a much older woman, also far more plump, and her hair was arranged differently. When was this photograph taken?"

"About fourteen years ago, a few weeks before they moved into the entrenchment."

Rose spread her hands as a sign of her helplessness, and with a sympathetic smile returned the picture to Olivia. "In all your years in Cawnpore, Mrs. Pickford," Olivia asked, trying yet another avenue, "did you never happen to encounter anyone by the name of Sturges? John was a Major with the First Native Infantry posted here when . . . when it all happened. His wife, my cousin, used to be Estelle Templewood. Their son, the little boy in the photograph, was called Jonathan."

Mrs. Pickford shook her head sadly. "No, I'm sorry. Your son mentioned those names, but they didn't ring any bells. You see, we only moved to Cawnpore from Lucknow almost a year after the main uprising. There was still considerable confusion in town—whatever was left of it— and no one quite knew where *anyone* was any more. Constant additions were being made to the army's list of fatalities, and with rumour and gossip buzzing about like swarms of mosquitoes, it was impossible to separate fact from fiction. Also, since most of the English officers and civilians had been. . . ." She stopped for a moment, overcome, then left the rest unsaid. "In fact, it was *because* Cawnpore so badly needed able-bodied men that David decided we must do our bit for a town with such a ruthlessly depleted population." For a moment she sat in silence, then asked, "So, like many others, your hapless cousin and her family also sought refuge in the entrenchment?"

"Yes." Olivia could not bring herself to elaborate, but her voice, deliberately matter-of-fact, remained well controlled.

"What kind of monster *was* this man, this Nana Sahib?" Adelaide Pickford suddenly cried, her fists clenched with emotion. "How could he, how could *anyone*, even in so *brutal* a war, indulge in acts of such savagery?"

There was, of course, no answer to that question, nor perhaps would there ever be. But Olivia felt a small chill travel up her spine in case the matter of the riverside massacres was also mentioned as a natural corollary. To avoid the contingency, she quickly asked, "Did Sitara Begum never bring her son with her when she came to visit?"

"No, never. But, as I've already told you, she referred to the child as Munna. I'm certain she never said anything about anyone called Jonathan."

"Did you form any idea of how old this Munna might be? Jonathan, if he is alive, would be about nineteen now."

"Oh, the child she talked about was *much* younger! In fact, the very first time she came into our shop, she told us it was to buy him a stuffed English toy."

"And she *never* talked of an earlier home or family?" They were going round and round in circles, Olivia knew, but she just could not let go.

"No. We asked her about them once, as we related to you, but she became so agitated and distressed that we never questioned her again," Rose said.

"You say Estelle Sturges was your cousin?" Adelaide Pickford asked.

"Yes."

"But you were born and brought up in America, your son mentioned. Presumably your parents were English?"

"Well, my mother was. She and Estelle's mother, Lady Bridget Templewood, were sisters. My father was Irish. It was Estelle's parents who invited me to India." Olivia stared bleakly into her cup. "Estelle and I were very close. Although she is four years younger than I, we were more like sisters than cousins. We . . . we shared a very vital part of our lives. . . ." She broke off before she could relapse into futile sentimentality. "I appreciate that Sitara Begum does not want her true identity to be revealed. Whatever her reasons, I'm sure *she* considers them valid, and I have no wish to disturb her life but, you see"—in spite of her efforts, her eyes brimmed—"I must know, I *must* know one way or the other. How can I rest until I do?"

Moved, Adelaide Pickford again took Olivia's hands in hers and Rose, equally sympathetic, came and sat on her other side. "Let us not forget that Sitara Begum sought our company for a reason," Rose pointed out gently, "and that was plain and simple nostalgia. It was evident that she had started to miss the life she once knew, the clothes she once wore, the language she once spoke." Her large eyes, deeply brown like her mother's, were very earnest. "Who knows—perhaps Sitara Begum now does wish to be discovered, *does* want her life to be disturbed!"

"Then all she has to do is write to me!" Olivia cried. "Why has she not done so? And why has she stopped coming to see you altogether? There must be reasons for that!"

"I can't answer your second question," Adelaide Pickford said without looking at her, "but the answer to the first could be—and in your own interests you must never lose sight of this—that she is *not* your cousin."

Startled by the reminder, Olivia frowned and then turned morose. "Yes, of course I must not," she agreed sadly. "In my eagerness to find Estelle I do keep forgetting that, alas, only too real possibility."

"On the other hand, if she is Estelle," Rose suggested, "her silence could be due to inhibitions that have become a habit. Having refused contact with you all these years, she doesn't know how to break the ice. As for not visiting us any more, have you considered that they might have simply moved away from Cawnpore and returned to Peshawar? Or, perhaps, settled in another town?"

Olivia nodded her head in agreement and then smiled at Rose. There was something about the girl that was very fetching. Her voice was clear-toned and sweet, like a village church bell. Even after being questioned so closely for so long, she gave no hint of impatience. Yes, indeed, there was something about this grave, soft-spoken girl that was greatly appealing.

"Yes, There are still options left, I know." Olivia sighed. "After all, there are so many whose fates are not known to this day, perhaps never will be known. Estelle's name does not appear in any list that positively identifies the dead, although it has been established that she too was at the Ghat. It is all this uncertainty surrounding her fate that gives me some semblance of hope."

They had run the subject dry; there was now no more to be said. After a few minutes more of conversation and many expressions of gratitude, Olivia rose to leave, promising to visit again. Outside, Hari Babu and Kasturi Ram, her loyal watchdogs, waited in the carriage that had been hired for the duration of her stay.

A wild goose chase? An exercise in futility? Perhaps.

Even so, Olivia felt strangely animated, more so than she had known herself to be in years. What she now faced was a challenge that shouted to be met, a riddle that demanded to be solved. She made a silent vow to herself. She was not yet defeated, no, not yet! She would not leave Cawnpore until she had unravelled the mystery of this woman who called herself Sitara Begum—wherever or whatever or whoever she might be!

The inner office behind the Raventhorne stables was a pleasantly furnished room full of colour and brightness and comfortably cushioned chairs, with green-painted slatted bamboo blinds at the windows to fend off the glare of the afternoon sun. A glass-fronted bookcase contained an impressive array of books on the horse and its care; clean, whitewashed walls held neat arrangements of photographs of various racing champions, panoramic views of the snow-capped peaks of the Himalayas, and a group picture of two women and some children in which Christian recognised an infant Maya on her mother's lap against a background of sea beach. A young boy beside them with dark, curly hair and pale, staring eyes he deduced to be Amos. As he had suspected, there were no pictures of anyone who might have been identified as Jai Raventhorne.

A beautifully fashioned French escritoire held piles of spiked papers, some ledgers and a huge bunch of yellow summer roses in a polished brass vase. He could tell that a good deal of Maya's time was spent in here. And indeed it was, she confirmed later. This was where she met prospective customers, prepared and filed her paperwork, held discussions with the grooms about each of her charges. And daydreamed.

"What about?" he asked, ravenous for her inner thoughts.

But she merely smiled, shook her head and wouldn't tell him. "Oh, just this and that, nothing important."

He flicked through the records she presented for his perusal and observed that they were in immaculate order, set out with admirable professionalism. Clearly listed were dates, times, vital statistics, diet sheets, special characteristics, medical records, sales records, foaling and stud information, exercise charts and a wealth of incidental detail with a tidy system of cross references. Christian was impressed; she was diligent and she took her work seriously, and that pleased him. Not one of the many young Englishwomen he had met since he had arrived in Calcutta did much more than gossip and languish in cloistered boudoirs bemoaning the climate and her own witting or unwitting incarceration in a country which she, like all her peers, considered almost entirely devoid of virtue.

As they sat opposite each other on chairs covered in chintz with soothing patterns of ice blue flowers and cool, sage green leaves, Maya gave him careful, painstaking answers to his many questions, asking some of her own, as hungry to know him as he was her. He listened attentively and answered with apparently matching care, but his true concentration was elsewhere. She would be furious, Christian thought ruefully, if she knew how superficially he absorbed her conscientious explanations and how haphazardly he answered her interminable questions about England

and his life there. There was about her an aura, a *magical* aura, that seemed to carry him off into realms of fantasy and played havoc with his awareness of reality. He was just beginning to sound foolish and incoherent when, with fortuitous timing, Rafiq Mian walked in with some routine remark or question, and Christian was saved from himself.

On their way out of the stablehouse, he halted in the aisle in front of one of the stalls. "What on *earth* is he doing?" he exclaimed, the curious sight returning him to mundane, manageable reality.

Abdul Mian was squatting on the floor of a stall, his hands on the back legs of the newly arrived stallion. He sat rock still with his eyes closed. Only his fingers moved, playing the animal's knee joint as if it were a musical instrument.

"He's comparing the hocks of the two hind legs to see if the animal is spavined. Rafiq has already checked him out thoroughly, of course, but his father just wants to make sure."

"He can diagnose spavine merely by feel?"

"Yes. His fingertips are sensitive enough to discern any unnatural bone growth on either joint. His father was even more of an expert, Abdul Mian says, although he was totally blind." Christian didn't believe her, of course, but he said nothing and merely smiled.

Out near the paddock in which the foals roistered and two mares grazed, a bearer served them tall glasses of sweet, frothy buttermilk tinkling with ice. A faintly damp river breeze stirred the grasses, scattering the rich, mysterious fragrances of an Indian spring. There was something pastoral and placid about the colourful patchwork of the embankment, the deep-pile velvety olive green grass in the paddocks, the groves of mango trees starting to sprout infant fruit, and the clumps of sweet-smelling jasmine bushes round the stables. Christian could not remember when he had felt so utterly at peace.

"Do you also have a river running alongside your property in Buckinghamshire?" Maya asked, noticing his look of pleasure.

"Well, not exactly a river, but we do have a sort of stream that forms one of the boundaries."

"Do you swim in it?"

He smiled. "Most of the year it's too cold to swim, but if we're lucky there are some days in summer when the sun is sufficiently warm to allow for a dip or two."

"I swim in the river even in winter," she said with a touch of scorn. "But only at night when no one can see me."

"Do you really!" He was full of admiration, considering the width and depth of the Hooghly. "Well, our English winters are very much more severe than yours here in Bengal. Many of the waterways are iced over for months."

"Oh, how frightful!" She gave a little shiver. "But then, English country homes have huge log fires burning in enormous stone fireplaces for much of the year, don't they?"

"Yes, I daresay they do."

"Fires around which you all sit and roast chestnuts and marshmallows and tell ghost stories?"

He laughed. "Sometimes."

"It must be strange to have four kinds of contrasting countryside in a year, with all your changes of season."

He was amused and enchanted by the innocence of her questions, her romantic visions of England. "I suppose so. I've never really thought about it. Visible changes in season are so much a part of English life."

She rose and started to stroll, tossing sticks for the dogs to pursue and fetch. "Talking of seasons, isn't summer supposed to be *the* London season? I mean as far as coming-out balls and concerts and theatre, are concerned? I've read about it in magazines and novels. That's when London society *really* comes to life, they say."

He shrugged. "I suppose so. For those who like that sort of thing."

"Don't you?" she asked, astonished.

He drained his glass, wiped the line of frothy white off his upper lip, bent down and plucked a handful of lucerne grass. Leaning on the picket fence, he held his hand out to the mare. She gave him a suspicious look, put her head down and neighed, then came up to him at a trot and nibbled the succulent blades out of his palm.

"Not especially," he said in answer to Maya's question. "Our *burra khanas* at home are as much of an infernal bore as they are here, I assure you. Unfortunately, I'm still too much of a griffen in station to refuse invitations without causing offence, but at home I avoid these jollifications like the plague."

"Even the dinner parties hosted by your parents?" Maya exclaimed, her eyes alive with awe and envy.

"Well, no." He threw her a rueful grin. "Those are the exceptions I'm forced to make in deference to my mother. If I stayed away from those, she'd throw a fit."

"Yes, I can understand that," she murmured as he walked up to join her at the water's edge.

"Don't tell me an exceptionally intelligent girl like you can find any redeeming virtue in this endless succession of parties in station?" he asked, without thinking.

She tilted her head to one side, letting the river breeze ruffle her loose hair, and combed her fingers through it in slow, languid caresses. "I wouldn't know one way or the other," she said, gazing across the expanse of the Hooghly. "You see, I haven't been invited to any."

He was devastated by his faux pas. For a moment he stood stricken, desperate to make restitution but not knowing with what words. Then she herself redeemed the situation. "But if they are as dreadful as you contend," she added with a light, bright smile, "perhaps I haven't missed very much."

He heaved a deep sigh of relief, frantically devising some impersonal question with which to stop himself from plunging headlong into some other imbecilic indiscretion. He worked hard for a few minutes to repair the mood of easy companionship, and then it was time for him to leave.

This morning he was not invited to breakfast. Was it because she was offended by his stupid, unthinking remark, or because her brother was still in the house? She seemed determined that he should not meet Amos Raventhorne. Not for the first time, Christian wondered why.

Most carpet dealers in the north, Olivia learned, were either Kashmiris or Pathans or had active connections with those communities hailing from the north-west provinces where carpet weaving was a traditional industry. Over the next few days, she despatched Kasturi Ram and Hari Babu to all the known carpet dealers in Cawnpore to make inquiries about any carpet merchant who happened to have a European wife known as Sitara Begum. Both returned empty-handed. However, both returned with strong suspicions that although the name of Sitara Begum appeared to be known to those questioned, for some reason no one was willing to dispense any information either about her or her husband and family. In fact, Kasturi Ram told Olivia, the moment the name was mentioned, those questioned not only clammed up but turned visibly hostile. One dealer, a highly aggrieved Hari Babu reported, had had him physically removed from the premises without giving him a chance to even attempt an explanation. Consequently, they had not dared to set foot in those *mohollas*, neighbourhoods, known to be dominated by Kashmiri Muslims and Pathans, for fear of provoking even more alarming reactions.

Olivia was disappointed but not altogether surprised; the reason for the hostility was understandable. It was known that during the Mutiny several Englishwomen had been openly carried away by the Peshwa's horsemen. Some of these women had been defiled and killed, and their mutilated bodies subsequently recovered and identified. Others had never been traced, their fates unknown even to this day. A few had willingly assimilated with the families of their abductors, too ashamed to return to their own. Still others, rejected by society everywhere, had turned to prostitution; and some, unable to bear the horror of their experiences, had simply put an end to their lives by whatever means available.

It had later been announced by the British military authorities that anyone found restraining a white woman in his house against her will would be arrested and summarily executed. The Mutiny was long over, but the brutality of the rebels in slaying women and children, and the vicious, equally brutal revenge subsequently exacted by the British, were far from forgotten by either side. Fears among the innocent civilian population of official retribution obviously still persisted.

It was as Olivia sat in her hotel room examining the various options now left to her that she received a note from Adelaide Pickford.

Outside, it was a bright, sunny morning, the piercingly blue sky embroidered with frothy white clouds fashioned into ever-changing shapes by warm, playful breezes. Beyond the hotel wall below Olivia's window, a pair of honey-coloured monkeys with cunning, lively eyes were performing somersaults for the benefit of a few stragglers to the beat of a small drum being thumped by their keeper. Should she, Olivia considered in gathering desperation, request police help as a last resort? Or should she herself (suitably disguised under a burka) set about visiting the Kashmiri and Pathan *mohollas* and make door-to-door inquiries? The first option she rejected immediately. Indians, especially those of the lower middle classes, had an innate mistrust of any English uniform, more so since the Mutiny. To unleash a brash, insensitive posse on an Indian bazaar would be to incur the wrath of the entire locality, and perhaps defeat her very purpose. On the other hand, door-to-door inquiries by her in crowded, claustrophobic gullies and alleys would not only be physically exhausting but might eventually provoke those very suspicions and hostilities she was so anxious to avoid. Finally, after much introspection, Olivia arrived at a decision. If the only practical option now open to her was to personally investigate each bazaar, well, she would take it—and to hell with the consequences! Faced at last with the prospect of some positive activity, her spirits started to soar.

It was at this point that Francis entered the suite to announce the arrival of the Pickfords' bearer with a letter.

"Dear Mrs. Thorne—at last, at *last* a morsel of luck!" the note began.

> *Our bearer, Aziz Rasool, has remembered something which we feel he* must *communicate to you immediately. The tiresome man only mentioned it this morning, otherwise I would have sent him to you much, much earlier and, no doubt, saved you a great deal of trouble.*
>
> *Do let us know, whenever you can spare the time, the results (if any) of Aziz Rasool's sudden resurgence of memory. My husband, Rose and I pray for your success and most earnestly hope that the information the bearer brings will be of use to you in concluding your long search.*
>
> *With our warm regards and all good wishes to you. I do apologise for this hurried, scrappy note, but I am so impatient to have the man on his way to you!*
>
> Yours sincerely,
> Adelaide Pickford

Ceremonially dressed for what he considered an important occasion, the bearer stood waiting patiently while Olivia read through the note twice. "I believe you have something to tell me, Aziz Rasool?" she asked then, her mouth dry with anticipation.

"Yes, memsahib." The bearer sprang to attention and once more made his salaams.

"Well?"

The old man coughed. "Memsahib will kindly forgive my impertinence, but the other afternoon I could not help overhearing part of your conversation with my missy sahib and memsahib." He cleared his throat, stroked his greying beard and stared politely at the floor. "About this lady, Sitara Begum. . . ."

"Yes?"

"Well, the honourable memsahib will not know—although my *own* memsahib and missy sahib now remember well—that on the final occasion Sitara Begum sahiba visited the house, the tonga that she usually retained had mysteriously disappeared and the mali had to be sent off to fetch her another."

Olivia waited, not daring to interrupt in case she broke the old man's thread of thought. He was trying so hard to recall every detail of that afternoon.

"Well, as it happened the *second* tonga-wallah turned out to be one of my relatives, my son's first wife's second cousin on her mother's side. He has only recently returned from Agra, where his paternal uncle runs a hair-cutting establishment near the big vegetable market." Olivia waited in an agony of impatience while Aziz Rasool unhurriedly went through his son's first wife's second cousin's family tree and business successes, before returning to the subject in hand.

"Well, it is *he* who reached Sitara Begum home that afternoon, memsahib. Therefore, it is my deduction that he must also know where she lives!" His eyes shone with triumph. "If granted leave for an hour or so now, memsahib, I could easily find out her address from him. But if he is out with his tonga, then I will have to wait until he returns. He lives about five miles beyond the old Magazine on the way to Bithoor."

It really was an extraordinary stroke of luck!

"Yes, *yes*, Aziz Rasool, *wherever* he lives, take my carriage and please go!" Olivia could scarcely hide her excitement. "Hari Babu will accompany you, but please, oh please, *do* return as *fast* as you can!"

Escorted by Hari Babu amid much chatter and enthusiasm, the old bearer was instantly despatched by carriage to locate his son's first wife's second cousin on her mother's side, and in celebration, Olivia ordered herself a bottle of the best possible sherry from the hotel's cellars. The rich Spanish wine helped considerably to fortify her nerves and loosen their agonising tensions. By the time Aziz Rasool returned, true to his word within the hour, she was not only much more at ease but positively buoyant.

As further good luck would have it, Aziz Rasool's son's first wife's second cousin had developed a septic boil on his buttock, a condition that made it temporarily impossible for him to ply a trade so essentially sedentary. He was, therefore, to be found at home lying on his stomach, groaning with pain and being fussed over by the women of the household. Gory details of the boil and its successful treatment followed as a substantial part of Aziz Rasool's recital. The young man did not know the actual address at which the begum sahiba lived, the bearer informed Olivia, but the house appeared to be somewhere within the labyrinth of the native city. At Sitara Begum's request, the tonga-wallah had taken her to the junction of Cowrie Bazaar and the main Allahabad Road, and she had specifically asked to be deposited at a corner distinguished by an attar shop run by a bearded perfumier.

"It's not much," Aziz Rasool admitted, "but that is all that my son's first wife's second cousin has been able to tell us." Seeing her expression, he added, "I hope that the memsahib is not too disappointed?"

Olivia assured him that she was not and, deeply obliged to the old man for his trouble, pressed into his hand a generous baksheesh which he received with much protestation and many expressions of gratitude. But after he had left, once again her spirits plummetted. Of what possible use could such an imprecise address be in a bewilderingly populous native locality?

4

I T WAS WITH CONSIDERABLE SURPRISE—and no small degree of suspicion—that Amos received Christian Pendlebury's letter requesting
an appointment.

"Why the devil should he suddenly want to see me?" Amos muttered as
he sat in his Clive Street office waiting for Pendlebury to arrive. "I can't
think of any aspect of our lives that we might have in common."

Kyle Hawkesworth raised an amused eyebrow. "Can't you?"

Amos coloured and said nothing.

There was, of course, a very pertinent area of mutual concern, but this
Amos could not bring himself to discuss just yet even with Kyle—not that
Kyle, of all people, didn't already know exactly what was going on. By
now the whole town, white, native and Eurasian, was starting to rumble
with gossip about Maya Raventhorne and the competition-wallah newly
arrived from England. Amos was aware that Maya spent considerable
time each day with Christian Pendlebury. They rode every morning,
passed long hours in the stables allegedly discussing horses, frequently
strolled on the embankment or in the banyan forest at Shibpore across the
Hooghly. Inevitably, tongues had started to wag and that rankled Amos—
as did the fact that Maya had deliberately avoided introducing Pendlebury to him. But with customary patience, he had refrained from a
confrontation with Maya while their mother was away.

However annoyed he might be by his sister's habitual secretiveness,
past experience had taught Amos that once Maya set a path for herself,
she would not be easily diverted from it. Nor would she have learned any
lessons from the previous disaster. It was precisely this refusal to learn
that disturbed Amos the most. He had nothing personal against Christian
Pendlebury, he admitted quite honestly. In the light of what he had

learned of the man's personal and educational background, he had no doubt Pendlebury was a perfect gentleman. But he was also a pukka, member of a relentless colonial society, an uninformed stranger to Calcutta with motives yet to be revealed. Amos trusted neither the pukkas nor their motives—any more than he trusted his sister's fragile emotional balances.

"Pendlebury," Kyle murmured as he stroked his chin thoughtfully. "A man to be reckoned with."

"You've already met Christian Pendlebury?" Amos asked in some surprise.

"No. I refer to his father. An erstwhile director of the East India Company, now a member of the Council of India. At one time, an Assistant Commissioner in the state of Oudh."

"Oudh? You mean, he was posted in Lucknow during the Mutiny?"

"Yes." A sickle smile curved Kyle's lips as he contemplated an indefinable middle distance. "Jasper Montague Pendlebury," he mused. "Man of many, many parts. . . ."

There was something in his tone, a mere inflection, that roused Amos's interest. "You knew him?"

"Knew him?" Kyle stretched his long legs to rest them across a low coffee table and tugged at a pipe tucked in his belt. "Yes, I suppose you could say that. But then, in those days everybody in Lucknow knew Jasper Pendlebury, if not personally then by repute. Among other things, he was known for his passion for Indian classical arts—and his violent dislike of the non-white Press. On one occasion he personally took the whip to the editor of an Urdu newspaper who had dared to make an allegation Pendlebury considered insolent." He struck a match against the sole of his shoe, took a moment to light the pipe and breathed out a thin ribbon of smoke. "A week later, a mysterious fire gutted the newspaper's offices. No one was ever charged with the crime."

"Well, in that case," Amos said with a grim smile, "be thankful that the man is seven seas away in London, safely out of firing range as far as you are concerned—or should we say vice versa?"

"Gratitude at this juncture might be a little premature, my friend," Kyle remarked drily. "Rumours are, Pendlebury has been offered a seat on the Viceroy's Executive Council. If he accepts—and I can hardly see him refusing—he could be well within firing range sooner than you think."

"And that worries you?"

Kyle considered. "No," he said after a minimal pause. "Not unduly."

Amos did not think to question the accuracy of Kyle's information. His informants, like octopus tentacles, reached out in many directions, not the least being the recently opened Red Sea telegraph office that now provided direct governmental and private communication between Calcutta and London. And Leonard Whitney, of course, was firmly installed in the inner sanctum of the Lieutenant-Governor of Bengal.

"Well, I just wish his wretched son weren't coming to see me," Amos grumbled. "I'd rather not have anything to do with the fellow—surely he must sense that?"

Uncoiling his tall, wide-shouldered frame from the couch, Kyle rose and tapped out his pipe bowl against the wall of a large circular ashtray. "Don't worry, maybe he's merely raising funds for one of their charities," he suggested sarcastically as he started to collect some papers scattered over Amos's desk. "The pukkas know Trident can be generous with deserving causes. And the colour of money, at least, is all the same to the Englishman."

Amos dismissed the suggestion with a muttered curse, his mood souring further.

"Well, I must be away." Kyle put the papers back into the folder. "The Muse beckons—as do the compositors and the creditors. That ass Grinstead has again made a hash of the political cartoons on the back page and I'm faced with an entire afternoon of rectifications."

Amos's heart sank as he watched Kyle prepare to leave. He hesitated a moment, then arrived at an impulsive decision. "Kyle . . . ?"

"No." Kyle pre-empted his question. "I have work to do and my presence here is hardly likely to help matters—whatever they might be."

"How do you know? It might."

Kyle threw him a sceptical look. "However touched I might be by your faith in my ability to resolve domestic crises, I fear it is, alas, misplaced. I wouldn't have the foggiest idea how to deal with the situation—if indeed it *is* a situation. Having been mercifully spared the cross of familial involvements myself, I see no reason why I should bear somebody else's. Even yours."

"Well, I'd still appreciate it if you stayed," Amos muttered, "if only for moral support."

Halfway through the door, Kyle stopped. For a moment he stood without moving, immersed in silent thought. Then, with characteristic suddenness, he closed the door and walked back into the room. "Very well. Since you insist. On second thought, it might even be educative to listen to what the man has to say. But I warn you, I have little stomach for the Pendleburys of this world, as you already know."

"Yes, I know." Amos was visibly relieved. "Nonetheless, I would be grateful if you could just be on hand." His usually clear, pale grey eyes again clouded over. "If the fellow mentions, even *mentions,* my sister, I might just be tempted to knock his teeth down his throat—and that would be most inadvisable, don't you think?"

As it happened, Amos need not have worried; Christian Pendlebury did not mention Maya. Indeed, his visit had nothing to do with her at all. At least, not directly.

"I understand that you are the founder president of the Henry Derozio East Indian Educational Society?" Christian asked, after the introductions and the social formalities were over.

Amos's eyes widened; he could not have been more taken aback. Even Kyle's expression of studied indifference turned watchful. "Yes, that is so."

"The Society has been formed with a view to improving the employment prospects of Eurasian youth, am I right?"

"Yes." Amos exchanged a puzzled glance with Kyle. Standing

arrogantly away from them by the window, Kyle persisted in silence, not making any effort to participate in the conversation although he now listened with attention.

"From the newsletter that has been circulated, I understand some important future programmes of the Society are to be discussed at the meeting?"

"Yes," Amos said for the third time, even more perplexed. He leaned forward on his desk. "May I ask where you happened to see this circular, Mr. Pendlebury? I shouldn't imagine you choose to move in social circles that are likely to have received it."

Pendlebury sidestepped the barb. "It was shown to me by one of our Eurasian tutors at Fort William, Cecil Trevors, and I was most interested to read it." He paused as a uniformed attendant entered bearing a tray of tea and refreshments. However unwelcome the visitor, etiquette decreed that time-honoured rules of hospitality be observed. The peon poured out cups of pale gold Orange Pekoe, handed them round and then offered a plate of shortbread biscuits which Christian refused.

Finally, after the trivialities were over, Christian continued. "I have come to ask if I might be permitted to attend the meeting of your Society next Saturday."

Amos concealed his further astonishment. "Why?" he asked bluntly, his expression openly suspicious. "What precisely would your interest be in a Society meant for Eurasians?"

"My interest is purely academic. Having learned something about the subject since my arrival, I am appalled at my own ignorance about a community that we, the British and the Europeans, have helped to create and perpetuate in your country. I am anxious to dispel that ignorance, that is all."

Pendlebury's manner was open, courteous and, barring a certain formality, perfectly natural. But perhaps because his visitor was so much at ease and he himself was not, Amos's resentment compounded. In fact, he felt a quick stab of anger. Academic interest? Like hell! It was the man's infatuation with Maya, naturally, that was at the crux of this sudden concern for Eurasians.

Nevertheless, Amos refrained from voicing his indignant observation. It would be foolish to drag his sister's name into a discussion that might not call for it at all. However, before he could say anything, Kyle did.

"In other words, your sudden thirst for knowledge springs from the need to salvage the white man's collective conscience, does it?" He strolled back from the window with his hands dug deep in his pockets and joined them at the table.

Again Christian fielded the taunt. "If you wish," he agreed equably. "Whatever the impetus, I would genuinely like to learn more about your community. Listening to people air their grievances at the meeting, and to the solutions that might emerge, will be as good a starting point as any." He sat up and alternated anxious glances between them. "Look, I can understand that you resent my saying all this; in your place, perhaps I would too. But the fact remains that what I have told you is the truth. I have no ulterior motive in requesting permission to be present at your meeting."

Sensing Kyle's gathering antagonism and knowing with what ease his temper could ignite, Amos swallowed his own suspicions and said smoothly, "I appreciate your interest, Mr. Pendlebury, but I regret that, for various reasons, attendance at our meetings is restricted to members." It was not the strict truth but it was an adequate excuse. If the fellow had enough sensitivity, he would recognise it as such.

Either Christian failed to notice the hint or he deliberately refused to acknowledge it. "Well, could I not be accommodated as a guest? Or as a neutral, interested observer? Surely there will be others present who are not members? Indian sympathisers and friends, for instance?"

Which was, of course, perfectly true.

"Sympathisers and friends, yes, but not pukkas, Mr. Pendlebury," Kyle cut in coldly before Amos could relent. "If we make one exception, it will set a precedent. For obvious reasons, that must be avoided."

"You don't believe that any pukka—as you call the English—can also be a sympathiser or a friend?" Christian asked quietly.

"It is not the *capability* that is in question," Kyle returned with a look of marked hostility. "It is the motive."

Still refusing to take umbrage, Christian smiled. "All right. Point taken. But in that case, what would it require for me to become a member of your Society?"

Kyle's eyebrows shot up in astonishment and Amos was frankly startled. "Become a member of a blackie-white society, Mr. Pendlebury?" Kyle's dark, saturnine eyes simulated shock. "Tut, tut! What *would* your compatriots have to say about that, I wonder?"

This time the taunt struck home and Christian flushed. Amos sat back with an inward sigh of resignation; the conversation was slipping out of his hands, as it usually did when Kyle was aroused. He started to feel almost sorry for the Englishman, so passionately earnest, so naïve, so totally out of his depth. . . .

Red-faced and uncomfortable, Christian sat in silence for a moment. His thoughts raced back to earlier in the day.

"Attend a meeting of the blackie-whites?" Patrick Illingworth, a batchmate at the chummery, had thrown up his hands in mock horror as they lounged on their balcony in the early morning enjoying their *chota hazris*. "Isn't that stretching the cause of true love a shade *too* far, old boy? What do you want to do, dammit, bring the wrath of the gods on *all* our bloody heads?"

Lytton had added his sixpence worth with his usual supercilious sneer. "Granted she's melted your heart, my wilting Lothario—and why not? After all, brushed with the tar or not, she *is* a lovely piece of baggage. But do you have to let her get to your head and addle your brains as well?"

"I'd like to know how they think," Christian had persisted doggedly, sorry now that he had mentioned the subject at all. "We made them what they are, shouldn't we shoulder *some* responsibility for their welfare?"

"Oh, don't be so damned sanctimonious!" Patrick had not bothered to conceal his disgust. "What makes you think they're looking to us for their welfare, anyway? Besides, it takes two to make them, my friend, and the female of the darkie species is not known to be exactly averse to open her legs to. . . ."

"That's a crude, malicious, *obnoxious* thing to say!" He had been intolerably incensed. "You mean, they're good enough to be bedded, but not to be *wedded*, eh?" He had stormed out of the room in a huff, leaving Patrick staring in genuine amazement. Of course, he hadn't intended to put it quite like that, Christian realised ruefully, but it was too late to retract the remark.

Now, recalling the conversation, he was again enraged but he kept his temper to himself. "Yes, I realise they would not approve," he agreed quite frankly. "There are many amongst us who *are* coarse and ill-informed and prejudiced, but there are also many who are not. Not all Englishmen are callous fiends, you know, nor is prejudice an inalienable preserve of the English. But to return to what I was saying," he continued quickly before the remark could be used as an excuse for more debate, "what would be the qualifications needed to acquire membership of your Society?"

Kyle tilted his head to a side. "Do you really want to know, Mr. Pendlebury?"

"Yes, of course I do."

"Well, as a first requisite, you would need to arrange to be reborn. As a second—preferably on the wrong side of the blanket."

This time Christian reacted strongly. In fact, he went quite pale. For a few seconds he said nothing. Then, still not having lost his dignity, still magnanimous in his acceptance of the insult, he stood up. "I have greatly admired your editorials in *Equality*, Mr. Hawkesworth," he said, his voice low and shaky. "I have considered you an extraordinarily clever man, certainly clever enough to be able to distinguish between friends and enemies—of whatever colour. It would disappoint me to learn that my assessment has been hasty. I thank you for having given me your time." He bowed to each in turn and, without proffering his hand to either, walked out.

As soon as the door closed behind him, Amos cradled his head in his hands and groaned. "Was it necessary to be quite so abrasive, Kyle?"

Kyle shrugged, got up and retrieved his folder from the couch. "He was patronising and condescending. I found that intolerable."

"On the contrary, the man was perfectly reasonable and courteous, and obviously well meaning."

"God save us all from those with good intentions," Kyle sneered, his anger rising. "I'd rather tackle wolves than Englishmen masquerading as damned sheep! The man is a fool."

"Perhaps, but that was no reason to demolish him!" Amos looked at him closely. "What on earth got into you all of a sudden?"

Kyle pulled in a sharp breath, on the verge of another scathing remark.

But then, suddenly, he loosened. His brow cleared and, throwing back his head, he laughed. It was something he did so rarely that the flash of humour illuminated his face and brought to his hard, craggy features a charm that was utterly unexpected. It was an aspect of Kyle Hawkesworth even Amos, his best friend, saw but seldom.

"Oh, all right, all right!" Kyle combed his fingers through his thick, unkempt hair. Dense and dark, the brown was rather oddly interwoven with lighter wheat-coloured strands, giving it an unusual and not unattractive look. "I concede that I behaved badly. I warned you that I might. But there's something about these pious, mealy-mouthed, eternally equanimous, pure-hearted do-gooders that sticks in the craw. I find them indigestible."

Amos got up and, joining his friend at the window, put his arm about his shoulder. "What we both find indigestible has nothing to do with his request to attend the meeting."

"No?" Kyle's scowl was once more back in place. "That's *all* it has to do with, my friend, nothing else." His shoulders lifted in a gesture of indifference. "But have it your own way. It's of no consequence to me one way or the other."

Amos folded his arms against his chest. "Maybe you're right. But what harm is there if he does attend the meeting?"

"None whatsoever, except that you might encourage hordes of arrogant young pukkas to barge into future meetings with the sole purpose of disruption."

"I think we can afford to take that chance," Amos said. "We have enough muscle-power of our own."

Kyle merely shrugged, having lost interest in the subject. "Well, it's up to you, Amos. I won't be at the meeting anyway."

Amos sighed. "You won't change your mind about that?"

"No. We've drawn up a fairly comprehensive plan for the educational project. We'll fill in the remaining details when the time comes. Listening to a lot of gutless gas-bags moan and whine and wallow in self-pity will only make me more foul-tempered than I usually am, you know that."

"I was hoping you might address the meeting, Kyle, perhaps make some mention of the other project we've been discussing."

"No!" There was such sharpness in the monosyllabic reaction that Amos was immediately silenced. "That will have to remain between you, Whitney and me. I have undertaken to raise the necessary funds for the project. There's no point in making it public before we have at least part of what is required."

"But exactly *how* do you propose to collect all these huge amounts of money, Kyle?"

"The how is my concern. For the moment, let it rest at that."

Amos did not press him further; he knew there would be no point in doing so. Thoughtfully, he considered the ungiving face, the veiled eyes behind which lay impenetrable depths. He knew the emotional seclusion in which Kyle Hawkesworth preferred to live, and he respected it. However intimate their relationship, he had learned to walk on eggshells as far as Kyle was concerned. For instance, he had never questioned Kyle about his part in that dreadful Maynard affair, although he had always suspected that Kyle knew more about it than he had cared to reveal. Nor had he ever tried to probe into Kyle's curious dislike of Maya—or, for that matter, into why she returned the compliment with such matching fervour.

"Well, how do you think Maya will react when she finds out Pendlebury has asked to attend the meeting?" Worried, he voiced the question that had been in the forefront of his mind ever since Christian Pendlebury had made his strange request.

Kyle stopped in his tracks; his expression turned cool. "I have no idea. And, with all due respect, I don't particularly care. Your sister's actions and reactions are of absolutely no consequence to me." Then he thought for a second or two and the hard line of his jaw relaxed in a shadow of a smile. "Come to think of it, Amos," he said slowly, "I really have no objection to Christian Pendlebury being present at the meeting. As a matter of fact, I consider it to be an excellent idea. He could prove rather useful as a catalyst."

Amos stood staring at the door behind which Kyle vanished, rubbing his chin in perplexity at the sudden volte-face. *Catalyst?* Now what the devil did he mean by that? Amos knew little about the motivations that turned the wheels of Kyle's curiously closeted mind; but he knew enough about his methods to feel vaguely uneasy.

However meagre the snippet of information Aziz Rasool had brought back with him, Olivia saw that it needed to be investigated. She doubted that such sparse indication would be enough to locate Sitara Begum's house in the rabbit warren that was Cowrie Bazaar, but as it transpired, she was to be most pleasantly surprised. The old bearer's information turned out to be more than adequate for her purposes.

"First lane to the right after Jamir Ahmed's haberdashery shop. Fourth house on the left. It has a green door. You can't miss it." The bearded attar shopowner at the corner of Cowrie Bazaar whom Olivia addressed in Hindustani from behind the embroidered lattice of a nondescript black burka surveyed the anonymous figure with only minimal curiosity. "But alas, no longer a *wife*, begum sahiba," he added rather sadly. "Azhar Khan became dear to Allah last October."

So, that was why Estelle (it had to be Estelle, it *had* to be!) had stopped visiting the Pickfords. How strange that, despite their long separation, their destinies should have run on such similar lines—they had both been widowed twice! With each step Olivia took towards that green door deep in the entrails of Cowrie Bazaar, she felt more and more convinced that this time her quest was not to be in vain, that this Sitara Begum and her cousin Estelle were indeed one and the same person.

The corner of the lane into which Olivia now had to turn was packed with people. A troupe of acrobats was in the middle of a performance with a sword-swallower commanding centre stage. Holding a lethal-looking weapon by its hilt, he inserted the point into his mouth and then proceeded to push it slowly down his throat. With every inch that he swallowed, he presented himself for inspection to the front row of the encircling crowd to show that there was no trompe d'oeil. Ready to scream with impatience, Olivia was compelled to wait on the fringe of the crowd, unable to get past. At last, the man withdrew the sword from his throat and embarked on a final round of the audience to demonstrate with open-mouthed triumph that he had suffered no visible damage. The audience applauded in boisterous appreciation and the air rang with cries of *"Wah, wah!"* A few of the spectators started to move on. Before the performer could be persuaded to embark on an encore, Olivia hastily slipped through a gap and turned into the lane in which was her destination.

The fourth house down the lane indeed had a green front door, and it stood ajar. The house itself was a neat, triple-storeyed brick structure off the main bazaar street in, as she had guessed, a predominantly Muslim neighbourhood. Once again Olivia was glad she had decided to venture forth on her own. Kasturi Ram and Hari Babu had protested, of course, but this time she had stood firm. Strange male presence in a conservative locality where the women were all *purdah-nasheen* would have certainly attracted unsavoury suspicions. She knew Amos would be annoyed by her solitary sortie, but far too excited now that she was so close to her quarry, Olivia thrust the thought aside and decided to worry about it later. Heart pounding, she stood for a while on the steps outside the house gathering together her courage, once more riddled with doubts. What if Sitara Begum was not Estelle and she made a fool of herself? What if her expedition was taking her down yet another blind alley leading nowhere?

She knocked and waited. There was no response. Deafened perhaps by the tumult of the acrobatic performance at the corner, no one had heard the knock. Flattening her palm against the door, Olivia slapped it hard a few times. Then, when there was still silence from within, she peered round the edge of the door and boldly stepped inside.

As were most traditional Indian houses, this too was built round an open brick-paved courtyard. For the moment Olivia noticed little except that the courtyard was cool, there were slatted bamboo curtains at the upper windows, in one of which hung a large brass parrot cage with a splash of brilliant green against the bars, and a crude string cot stood propped up against one of the walls of the courtyard in which she stood.

From a corner staircase, suddenly, a man descended. He was dressed in loose white cotton pyjamas, a knee-length checked shirt and a maroon turban. His well-trimmed goatee beard was tinged with henna and he appeared to be in his forties. Seeing the stranger, he stopped short in surprise. In a reflex action, his hand rose to touch his forehead.

"Us-salaam-alaikum."

"Wah-laikum-salaam." Olivia returned the greeting without raising the flap of her burka off her face. "I am looking for a lady known as Sitara

Begum, widow of Azhar Khan, carpet merchant. I believe she lives in this house?" she said in Hindustani.

Even though her speech was fluent, her accent was recognisably foreign. Instantly, his look of casual curiosity turned to one of suspicion. "Who is it that wishes to see her and on what business?"

"I am a friend from Calcutta."

"And your business?"

"My business is private."

His expression chilled. "I regret that you have come to the wrong house. There is no Sitara Begum here."

"But I was told. . . ."

"You were misinformed."

"I don't think so. My sources are unimpeachable." Olivia felt her temper rise. "I *insist* on seeing Sitara Begum who, I believe, is being held here against her wishes."

"Against her wishes?" His eyes widened more in surprise than in alarm at her impromptu accusation. "Who has told you such lies?"

"That is unimportant. What is important is that if you prevent me from seeing the begum sahiba, I will be forced to lodge a complaint at the police station."

At the mention of the police, he paled. Nervously, he licked his lips. "The police? What has the police to do with Sitara Begum? She is not restrained against her. . . ." He stopped, realising too late the trap into which he had fallen. By this time, their raised voices and the argument had attracted the attention of the other inmates of the household, of whom there appeared to be many. All around in the first-floor balconies Olivia was aware of peering eyes, bobbing heads, whispered exclamations. "Anyway," the man continued angrily, pulling himself together, "this is *my* house. I will not permit. . . ."

"Oh, don't be so *tiresome*, Mazhar—you know it's not for you to permit or forbid!" The interruption came from the direction of the stairs. "It might be your house, but it is I who run it!" The voice approached and a woman came into view. "Of course Sitara Begum lives here and *of course* she will see the honoured visitor from Calcutta."

And then, before Olivia could recover from her surprise, in front of her stood the woman she had sought so assiduously and for so long. Eyes wide and incredulous, she could only stare in stunned silence, numbed by the sudden appearance. The man said something, but impatiently the woman waved him away with a few sharp words of reprimand. His expression turned sulky; without further argument he slunk out into the lane through the green door.

The woman approached. She was clad in a loose black caftan with a black veil wound tightly around her head, obscuring all but her essential features and a few tendrils of orange hair. For a moment she stood watching Olivia, her face expressionless, the piercingly blue eyes blank. Then she spoke, and it was still in Urdu.

"You won't need this now." She came up to Olivia and slid the burka off her head and shoulders. "There is no other adult male in the house." A servant boy materialised from somewhere carrying a chair and placed it at Olivia's disposal. The woman issued a silent command; he fetched the string cot and arranged it close to the chair. From a clothes-line stretched across a corner of the courtyard, he retrieved a striped black and white rug with tasselled edges and threw it over the string cot. The woman neither spoke nor smiled, but when all was ready, she indicated with a sign that Olivia should seat herself. Still not out of shock, Olivia sank into the chair just as her knees almost buckled beneath her. The woman settled herself down on the cot, her legs crossed Indian fashion, and the strings squeaked under her weight. It was all so bizarre, so much like one of her incredible dreams, that Olivia could not quite grasp the reality.

"Estelle . . . ?" Her trembling voice could not rise above a whisper.

The woman smiled, a strange smile, sly and full of mockery. She made no response to the whispered question. Instead, continuing in what was very good Urdu rather than the more colloquial Hindustani favoured by the English, she called out to someone over her shoulder to fetch cups of cardamom tea and palm-leaf fans, berating them soundly for not having thought of it themselves.

"Munna?" she summoned a shy young lad of about twelve hiding behind a pillar. "Come and kiss your darling *khala* from Calcutta. She is your only aunt from your Amma's side, you know. I *told* you she would come to see you one day, didn't I?"

As the boy stepped forward stiffly and laid a perfunctory peck on Olivia's cheek, from behind him, eyes dark and apprehensive, emerged a little girl of about eight. She stood before Olivia, staring at the floor, tongue-tied with fright.

"And this is my little Razia." Pulling the child to her, the woman gave her a hug. "Her mother, my sister-in-law, became dear to Allah about four years ago of smallpox, so I've adopted her as my own. Come my little pet, give this beautiful lady at least a smile. No?" She laughed and patted the child fondly on the cheek. "Where *is* everybody?" She clucked and looked upwards at the balconies. "Miriam *appa*? Fatima? Hamid, oh Hamid! Hai Allah, where are you all? And where are your manners, huh? Come on down this instant! Shame on you! Is this the way to treat an honoured guest who has come all the way from Calcutta to see us?"

Slowly, amid much shuffling of feet and many muffled whispers and giggles, a veritable crowd of people descended noisily from above. Old women, young girls, children, a snivelling babe in arms, one or two gangling youths, all dressed in bright, gaudy clothes. The crowd fanned out around them in semicircular formation, eyes puckered with curiosity, breathing raucous, hands twitching against mouths in an effort to quell nervous laughter. Introductions were made with lighthearted informality, names rattled off, incomprehensible relationships explained. Someone handed Olivia a cup of tea, another a plate of sticky brown sweets smothered in sesame seeds, a third fanned her from behind. A little boy made to climb on to her lap and was given a sound box on the ear by an older relative. Holding his head, he started to howl and was whisked away by a young girl with thick, oily plaits, grumbling under her breath.

Mesmerised, Olivia gazed fixedly at the woman on the string cot, not feeling or seeing or hearing anything. Mechanically, she raised the cup to her lips and, without registering any taste, drank thirstily. The servant boy returned with an ornamental silver casket stuffed with betel leaves, and placed it on the cot at the woman's feet. The casket was heavily engraved on the outside and the inside was divided into several compartments to contain various spices. Some ingredient appeared to be missing: as she carefully prepared a betel cone stuffed with some of the spices, the woman showered curses on the boy and his ancestry. Then, with a sigh of anticipation, she thrust the cone deep inside her mouth and revolved her jaws around it with little gurgles of pleasure.

Through much of this activity, she subjected Olivia to a steady flow of chatter. Without looking in her direction, she droned on in a high-pitched, sing-song voice about people and events that held neither meaning nor interest for Olivia. The fast-flowing words tumbled out of the betel-stained mouth without a break, buzzing about Olivia's ears like an army of wasps. The faces around Olivia started to blur; her head swirled in the claustrophobic courtyard and thick bile crawled up the inside of her throat. She started to feel sick.

Who were all these bewildering people, these incongruous children? What was Estelle, *her* Estelle, doing here, in this house, among all these alien faces? No, this was *not* Estelle! How could she ever equate Estelle Templewood Sturges with this grotesque, overweight, middle-aged woman, with her beringed fingers and fat feet, her henna-tinged hair and folds of bulging flesh and betel juice stains on ugly, grinning lips?

Olivia's nostrils filled with smells—oh, God the smells!—of mutton curry and saffron, attar and sweat and jasmine oil, open drains and overpowering, extrinsic humanity . . . she was overwhelmed with revulsion, almost fainting with the horror of it all, and her eyes ceased to focus. Panic-stricken, she opened her mouth to say something, but before she could speak the woman did.

"Go home, Olivia." This time the woman spoke in English, and suddenly the voice was chillingly familiar, exactly as it had been more than two long decades ago, down to the last inflection. But the tone was dismissive, riddled with contempt. "And take with you the answer to your question. No, I am *not* Estelle! Nor ever will be again. I am Sitara Begum."

If the unrecognisable physical appearance of her cousin had come to Olivia as a shock, the incongruous sound of the well-remembered, well-loved voice that emerged from the corpulent figure was like an icy slap in the face. She gasped and staggered to her feet, almost falling over with the effort. Someone's hand clutched at her arm to steady her, but she shook it off with a jerk. "I'm . . . sorry . . . I . . . !" Incoherent and unaware of what she said, she started to splutter, consumed by the need to escape. *"I'm sorry. . . ."*

Estelle also rose to her feet, her brilliant blue eyes filmed over with frost. "Why did you come, Olivia?" she asked coldly. "You should not have."

Grabbing her burka, Olivia somehow made her way to the green door. She stopped for a last horrified look over her shoulder. The same sly, mocking smile had reappeared on Estelle's streaky paan-red lips. Working her cheeks so that the betel juice gathered in her mouth, she turned and spat expertly into an open drain, her eyes never leaving Olivia's face. Then she touched her forehead with a hand and made a low, exaggerated salaam. "*Khuda hafiz*, my dearest Coz. May Allah forever be your protector."

Almost fainting from the rising nausea within, Olivia turned and fled.

The meeting of the newly formed Henry Derozio East Indian Educational Society was crowded, so much so that they had run short of hired chairs. Many stood on the sidelines, and still they continued to arrive, singly, in couples, in groups and with families.

Amos was surprised and gratified by the response to his appeal, even more so by the calibre of those who attended. In the hired school hall, packed to capacity, he recognised many well-known Eurasian faces: engineers from the East Indian Railway, river pilots and officials of the Port Trust, a group from the telegraph office, railway station personnel, a former Deputy Collector of Calcutta, highly placed municipal personnel, some employees of Trident, schoolteachers, private tutors, Customs officials, a scattering of journalists and men of letters, and a large contingent of students from various institutions. There was also a healthy sprinkling of women from the Home, including Joycie Crum, resplendent in a pink bonnet. In a front row he was pleased to see Kali Charan Goswami with his wife and son; the Lubbocks; a professor of Sanskrit from Presidency College; two of Trident's Bengali suppliers; and, surprisingly, an accomplished herbalist the company sometimes used for its staff's medical problems, Dayananda Babu.

Christian Pendlebury was also surprised by the strength of the audience, although he was still too much of a stranger in station to be able to assess its qualitative importance. From his Eurasian tutor, Cecil Trevors (sitting in the second row from the front without having noticed him), Christian had learned that Henry Derozio, after whom the Society was named, was a greatly revered Eurasian poet, journalist and educationist of an earlier decade, also known as a reformer and tireless crusader for the benefit of his community.

Sitting in a far corner of the hall, Christian tried to make himself as unobtrusive as possible, anxious not to become an object of curiosity. From the front row someone stood up and waved at him; he recognised her as Grace Lubbock. She had come to the meeting with her parents, whose acquaintance also he had made during his initial visit to the Raventhorne home. With a self-conscious blush, he waved back, hoping they would not draw attention to him by approaching him now before the meeting had a chance to get under way.

He looked around with interest. Was he the only pukka present?

Christian smiled to himself; how quickly he was becoming accustomed to the local jargon! By the look of faces surrounding him it seemed improbable. Yet he knew that it was often difficult to tell pure Europeans from those of mixed blood, and in this gathering it was well nigh impossible. Although, in the main, faces were dark and dusky, there were many others that were fair-complexioned, with light hair and eyes that could pass unnoticed in any European gathering—or so one might have thought. However, by now Christian was aware that in Calcutta's segregated and highly pigment-conscious colonial society there operated a remarkably efficient sort of "nostril brigade" where Eurasians were concerned. These olfactory experts, it was said, could sniff out the faintest whiff of the tarbrush in even the most deceptively Nordic of appearances. Once detected, imposters were given no quarter and retribution was swift and merciless. It was a situation Christian deplored, but there was little he could do about it save fume in private.

Which was why he had been so awfully pleased to receive Amos's note this morning. It was brief to the point of curtness, but eminently adequate: if he still wished to attend the meeting of the Derozio Society, Amos wrote, he was welcome to do so. Christian had liked Amos Raventhorne. They were fairly close in age and he was, after all, Maya's brother. Given other circumstances, Christian wondered wistfully, might they not have been friends? Once again he had a moment of unease at what Maya's reaction might be to his forwardness in instigating a meeting with her brother without her knowledge, but then he dismissed his qualms. The meeting would have come sooner or later; at whose instigation and under what conditions were surely immaterial.

As far as Kyle Hawkesworth was concerned, Christian had some reservations. Nevertheless, he had to admit that there was something about the man—regardless of his overt antagonism and appalling lack of courtesy— that he had found strangely fascinating. It could be, of course, that his impressions were fashioned by what he had read in *Equality*. The potency of Hawkesworth's language was such that his personality and intellect positively shone through the pages. Christian could see that, liked or disliked, Kyle Hawkesworth was a man impossible to ignore. He felt instinctively that their paths would cross again, but why and in what circumstances he simply could not imagine. Whatever the reasons, the prospect of meeting Kyle Hawkesworth again was one that Christian found oddly exhilarating.

Cecil Trevors was also Christian's source of whatever additional information he had acquired about Hawkesworth. Like many others, Eurasians and Indians alike, Hawkesworth despised the English presence in India, as was abundantly clear in his writings (and as Christian had already discovered to his cost). The cause closest to Hawkesworth's heart, however, was the betterment of the sizeable Eurasian community, and it was towards this end that all his efforts and energies were directed. As to his outward lifestyle, Trevors said, it was capricious, open to view, uncaring of public opinion. But, paradoxically, Hawkesworth was not a man who revealed his inner self easily. Little was known of his background except that he had come to Calcutta from Lucknow some years ago to study at Presidency College for a university degree in economics and English literature, and had remained here ever since. Rumours about his beginnings in Lucknow proliferated, but he had not chosen to dignify any with either confirmation or denial. In any case, it was of little consequence. Among Eurasians there were many like Kyle Hawkesworth, their parentage unknown, their backgrounds obscure, a floating, amorphous people existing in the twilight zones between two cultures, with no clearly defined identity in either. As Trevors had once remarked to Christian with bitter humour, "At least we don't have to worry about pedigrees, like dogs and horses!"

Was Hawkesworth to be one of the speakers this evening? The possibility brought a flush of pleasurable anticipation to Christian's cheeks. However abrasive and hostile, the man was magnetic, an impassioned writer with an instinctive feel for words. What he might have to say would no doubt be vitriolic and outrageous, but it would also be stimulating. Christian craned his neck and had a good look around, but so far there appeared to be no sign of Kyle Hawkesworth in the hall. Then the first speaker, a retired railway stationmaster called Sidney Tavistock, was announced by someone named Leonard Whitney, and there was no more time for conjecture.

"To listen to people talk," Mr. Tavistock began in a dry, tired voice heavy with sarcasm, "one would think that we East Indians—or Eurasians, if you prefer—are a newly arrived phenomenon on this subcontinent. Sizeable numbers of Eurasians have existed here since the time of Alexander the Great and his Greeks. Indeed, it might come as a surprise to some that not so long ago, before the opening of the overland route and the Suez Canal augmented the white population in India, there were more of us in this country than of those who deny us in the hope that, if ignored sufficiently, one day we will quietly fade away and conveniently vanish from this subcontinent." The remark elicited a few titters, which Mr. Tavistock received without reaction. He continued, "I would like to remind you that there was a time when inter-race marriages were not uncommon, when the progeny of such unions did not need to be born out of wedlock, when Eurasians were not stigmatised by that seven-letter word *bastard* that is today thrown at them with such contempt. But since those early years of colonial presence, attitudes have changed, the injustices against our community have increased and continue to increase unabated. In our own century, especially since the Sepoy Mutiny, these atrocities have exceeded all bounds of humanity. Why? For what possible reason?" His voice gained strength.

"Over the years we have fought shoulder to shoulder with the Englishman against his enemies. We have thrown our considerable weight behind him in his disasters, especially those of 1857, when this subcontinent was torn apart with hate and discord. We have shared in his hopes and aspirations and endeavours and also in his greed to amass more and more wealth—yes, even in that!" He stopped to thump the table. "We built the Englishman's markets, we augmented his armies when he faced imminent defeat. It is with *our* labour that the English government in India has made roads, expanded river navigation, railway networks, mapped perilous terrain for laying postal routes, telegraph lines, and it is with *our* manpower that he now runs his ports and harbours and railways and telegraph and Customs offices. We were the first teachers of his language in Indian schools, the first—perhaps only!—volunteers for dirty, dangerous work in remote corners of the country where neither the English nor the Indian cared or dared to tread. And what have we today to show for our loyalty, our labours, our efforts, our endeavours, our blood, sweat and tears?"

"Nothing, nothing!" the audience roared in unison, stamping the floor with its collective feet. Christian joined in the applause, listening to the litany of charges with rising indignation.

Of the many speakers who followed, some were vociferous, others apologetic, still others merely melodramatic and repetitive and full of personal grievances. Some launched vitriolic tirades against the Indians, even more callous in their caste-ridden bigotry, even less subtle in their rejection of the Eurasian than the English. Others were shamelessly sycophantic, suggesting that salvation for the Eurasian lay only in unquestioning obedience and deference to the superior white-skinned races that controlled their collective destiny with every justification.

From all that was said Christian was appalled to learn that Eurasians were forbidden commissions in the British Army and relegated only to very basic duties in the service, prohibited by order from sending orphans of the community to England to study in case they mixed blood with the English and so defiled the master race. However, no such prohibition existed for Indian orphans. Because they followed unquestioningly in the footsteps of their fathers, known and unknown, most Eurasians considered themselves Christians. Neither the Hindu nor the Mohammedan civil laws applied to them, and they had none of their own. No laws regulated their marriages, defined the legitimacy or otherwise of their children, related to their inheritance of property, entitled them to bequeath their property by the instrument of a will, defined inheritance in case of intestacy. They were forced to suffer the disabilities of both countries, India and England, without being allowed the advantages of either.

A timid, middle-aged civil servant with the municipality suggested sending another petition to Lord Mayo, the Viceroy, and to Westminster, so that it would reach the Queen. Someone pressed for schools and colleges exclusively for Eurasians. Others, mostly young hotheads, were for insurgency, an open show of non-cooperation with their English rulers, and deliberate or covert destruction of those nefarious institutions from which Eurasians were excluded. But whatever remedies they suggested, all the speakers agreed that there was a wicked conspiracy afoot to deprive the hardworking, loyal Eurasian community of honourable means of earning a living. There were many who had managed to rise above the twin barriers of prejudice and persecution, but they had had to struggle long and hard against formidable odds.

"England is our fatherland and India our motherland," the penultimate speaker thundered in an address Christian found particularly distressing. "We have cousins, half-brothers and half-sisters on two continents, but are denied by both. It is indeed a foul plot mounted against us by this unholy alliance of the European and the native. In his alleged quest for fairness and justice, it is to the *native* that the Englishman allots those choice jobs that he does not want for himself; it is towards the *native* that the English-man's thoughts turn when there is need for representation in the seats of government, or when the post of a magistrate falls vacant, or when he wants to investigate Indian opinion. Are we then not Indians, children of this soil, of this country? It has in recent years become the norm for us and our wretched mothers to be denied even by our own fathers—nay, not denied, *abandoned*—left to scratch for survival on rubbish dumps like mon-grel pups, without benefit of shelter or sustenance or education as a means of future livelihood. The supreme paradox of his society is that in public the Englishman must be seen to despise all women not the same colour as his mother or wife or sister, but in private—as all of us here know only too well—he is free to reverse that ruling with impunity! If the English-man abhors the very thought of a native woman at his table, why then is he not similarly revolted by the prospect of a native woman in his bed? Is that not the ultimate hypocrisy? And it is we, the unfortunate conse-quences of this hypocritical dualism, who are the innocent victims. To hide his own shame, the Englishman thinks nothing of leaving us naked—naked and defenceless against the fury of two societies embarrassed by our existence, both of which would frankly have us dead."

Christian shared heartily and rousingly in the anger the speech pro-voked throughout the hall. The audience cheered and booed and clapped lustily, and he with them. For the very first time in his life he felt some-thing he had never felt before: a sense of shame, of deep mortification, at being a passive contributor to this appalling state of affairs. It was an alien, uneasy feeling, and in some strange way it made him feel personally defiled.

It was now, at the very end of the meeting, that Amos Raventhorne finally rose to speak. Christian had looked forward enormously to his address, sensing that in tone, intent, and content it would be very different to the enflamed rhetoric that had gone before. As scion of Calcutta's first Eurasian family, Amos received respect as a matter of course. Over and above that, he was admired and looked up to for his balanced opinions, his maturity of judgement, his innate decency as a human being. If Jai Raventhorne had once been a pillar of support to his community, his son was no less. And if injustice was the theme for this evening, well, no one had suffered more grossly at the hands of the English than the tragic Raventhorne family. As Amos rose to speak, a hush descended over the room. Sensing that this was to be the focal point of the meeting, no one wanted to miss a single word of what was about to be said.

Amos began with a quotation from an address given by a Dr. Alexan-der Duff to the Assembly of Edinburgh six years ago: " 'The East Indian community, we have been told, is in a very backward and deteriorated condition. Be it so. Is that a reason why it should continue so? Place the same community in more genial circumstances and the whole of the lamentable process and state of things may at once be reversed'." Having said that, he laid down his sheet of paper and continued verbatim.

"The operative phrase here, as far as I am concerned, is 'in more genial circumstances.' This, in a nutshell, is what the aims of our Society are all about. If the English have done nothing for us over three centuries, why do we expect them to do anything for us now? Why do we not ourselves do something to compensate for what the English have left undone? I have no intention of denigrating the splendid efforts that the community has put into formulating our existing educational and charitable institutions, nor the personal and professional achievements of those of you who have risen above meagre beginnings to reach positions of responsibility and skill. But when we consider the generally pitiable conditions in which the Eurasian community in India lives, we find no room for complacency. We have to concede that these efforts have just not been enough!

"What we still need badly is *practical* education, vocational guidance and training so that our young men and women can acquire skills and subsequently secure jobs commensurate with these skills. We need more mechanical, agricultural, industrial colleges, not merely institutions that teach the three R's without guarantee of subsequent decent employment. Therefore, as an initial project, our Society has devised a scheme we hope will help to ameliorate, if not entirely remedy, the deplorable situation that persists in our community today.

"Some of our older members," he continued, "may remember that in 1828 the government and the East India Company drew up a plan to establish a Marine School on the Hooghly aboard an East India Company ship called the *Princess Charlotte of Wales*. They may also recall that, for one reason or another, the scheme remained unimplemented and was finally abandoned, even though several marine insurance companies of that time had promised financial support. Well," he paused and pulled in a deep breath, "we who have founded this Society now think it is time to restart the scheme and to ensure that this time it *is* implemented." A murmur of interest rippled across the hall but there were no interruptions.

"On behalf of Trident and with the full support of my family, I propose to start a fund to revive this project to provide practical navigational training to young Eurasians. Trident's initial contribution towards this fund will be two hundred thousand rupees. Several mercantile houses, both European and Indian, with whom we do business have promised support for the project, either in cash or in kind." The murmurs expanded and one or two voices cheered.

Amos held up a hand. "Our marine school will have a staff of highly qualified instructors, including one from the Royal College of Engineering at Cooper's Hill in England, and three from American universities and industrial firms. The majority will be locally recruited from our own engineering institutions. We aim to provide the finest equipment needed for practical instruction, and this we are in the process of importing from America at our own expense." He paused; it was obvious there was more to come. "Many of you must be puzzled as to how we can possibly envisage the establishment of a marine school without that most basic of essentials, a *ship!*

"Well, I am happy to announce that Trident intends to donate its steamship *Ganga* to the project." There were gasps from the audience and some spontaneous claps and cheers, but Amos quietened them with a gesture. "Some of you may know that the *Ganga* was a pioneer of steam navigation in this country, the first clipper out of an Indian port to be fitted with a coal engine way back in 1848. The vessel was designed by America's leading naval architect of the time, Willis Hall Griffiths, under commission from my late father. The training centre and marine school will be established aboard the *Ganga*. We are grateful to the Calcutta Port Trust for having sanctioned us a permanent mooring berth on the Hooghly for this purpose." He stopped to sip from a glass of water and mop his forehead, for it was becoming uncomfortably hot and close in the tightly packed hall. This time no one disturbed the silence as they waited avidly for the rest.

"I would like to remind you," Amos resumed, "that if this project is today feasible at all, it is because of my late father. It is towards him that all credit must be directed. It was his pioneering spirit, his courage, his ceaseless endeavours for our community, his spectacular success against overwhelming odds, that have given Trident the proud privilege to be a benefactor of our community. I stand before you merely as my father's emissary, and I speak only in his name. To do honour to a man who was never ashamed of his penurious beginnings on the streets of this city, a man proud to be called Eurasian, a man whose life was cruelly snatched away from him in a grotesque travesty of justice, and a man whose name will always remain a shameful blot on the red, white and blue flag of our imperial rulers, I hand over this ship to the Eurasians of Calcutta and proudly rename it the S.S. *Jai Raventhorne.*"

The audience exploded! Thunderous applause, wholehearted and spontaneous, reverberated through the hall in a tidal wave of jubilation. For a few moments pandemonium reigned, but no one made the slightest effort to restore order. Profoundly impressed, emotionally stirred and genuinely exhilarated, Christian Pendlebury joined enthusiastically in the displays of approval. What a noble gesture, what a fine example of service to the community! He had never before witnessed a scene of such inspiration, such solidarity. How glad he was to have come—and how grateful he was to Amos Raventhorne for having made his presence possible!

The audience was now rising, some to crowd round the dais at the front of the hall, others to make for the exits. Fearing a crush at the doors, Christian rose and, his head lowered, slowly made his way out, anxious to avoid encounters with acquaintances. At the gates of the school, however, he found Grace and her parents standing in wait for him. Before the fact had even registered fully, his hand was engulfed by an enormously strong paw and he received a thump on the back that almost sent him flying face downward.

"Ah'm *maghty* pleased to renew your acquaintance, mah boy!" Hal

Lubbock wrung his hand until Christian felt he would surely lose it. "Ah've heard a *great* deal moah abaht yuh from mah wahfe and dawter, but we shure are surprised to see yuh heah, Mr. Pennelberry—wudden'ave thought *yuh'd* be innerested in a bunch of Yewrashuns, eh?"

His wife and daughter nodded, and as they all waited for him to come forth with an explanation, Christian flushed. He started to attempt an answer, but his few muttered words were fortunately cut off almost immediately by Lubbock. A hearty offer of dinner and a tour around the furniture factory, "anytahme, mah lad, anytahme," were voiced with such effusiveness and at such length that Christian found there was no need for further explanation. In the several weeks that Christian had been in Calcutta, he had learned much. However, his most salutary lesson (imparted feelingly by other unattached bachelors) was to recognise at the very earliest a certain glint in the eyes of determined mothers of unmarried daughters. Christian had no difficulty in identifying that glint now in Marianne Lubbock's eyes. Much alarmed, he decided that, no matter how pressing the invitations, he would have to avoid the Lubbocks as fervently as he would bubonic plague. Thanking them profusely and stammering vague assurances about arranging an imminent visit, he effected a hasty escape.

Christian's mind was in a turmoil, whirling with information and indignation. He needed to be alone in order to clarify his conflicting impressions. There was much that had distressed him, so much else that he had not been able to understand. Deep in thought, he made his way to a secluded riverside spot to sit and cogitate at length. He had received a great deal of food for thought; there was now an urgent need to absorb it. There was no doubt in his mind that his time that day had indeed been well and profitably spent.

In her room at the hotel Olivia sat and stared out of the window all night, cocooned by the dark, wide-eyed and sleepless. She did not hear the hourly cries of *khabardar! khabardar!* from the night-watchman as he perambulated the hotel premises, nor the desolate howl of jackals foraging for food in the dense jungles along the banks of the Ganges. Unheeding of the changing patterns of the night sky as it revolved silently towards the dawn of another day, she sat dry-eyed with grief, absorbing the darkness, trying to come to terms with her inexplicable behaviour.

What had possessed her to be so cruel, so unforgivably offensive to Estelle?

She had been forewarned by the Pickfords; she had known what to expect of "Sitara Begum." Nothing that she had seen had come as a total surprise. Yet, after all these years of searching for her beloved Estelle, she had ended by turning her back on her! What she had done was monstrous, despicable. She had rejected her cousin; she had passed judgement even before the hearing. And for that she could never forgive herself. Bewildered by her extraordinary reactions, seething with guilt and remorse, Olivia cried out silently to her beloved cousin for forgiveness, praying that her words would somehow reach her, *somehow*. . . .

As midnight struck, Olivia punished herself further. Unlocking her trunk, she pulled out from under her clothes a folder. It was thick and dog-eared, and it bore an official stamp on the cover. She had not opened the folder for many years, not since her last visit to Cawnpore. She had not needed to: each word contained in the documents it held was etched in her brain in acid, indelible and unforgettable. Yet, even remembering every syllable, she flagellated herself by reading it all again, from the first document to the last.

Later, as the mauve fingers of dawn pushed aside the indigo shrouds of night, she replaced the folder in her trunk, bathed, changed into a fresh linen dress and ordered herself a light breakfast of melon slices, lychees and coffee. Before either Kasturi Ram or Hari Babu could arrive to invade her privacy and thwart her plans for the day, she wrote out a brief note for them and left it with the hotel manageress downstairs. Ignoring her hired carriage and the questioning looks of Francis and her ayah, she ordered herself a tonga from the bazaar.

Then she proceeded to do precisely what she had promised Amos she would not. She set out for the entrenchment.

It was an astonishingly breezy day, the gusting winds still damp with the remains of a night rain she had not noticed. In a pale blue sky a lemon sun flickered diffidently behind banks of ash-tinged clouds that promised more rain during the day—"mango showers," in picturesque local termi-nology. The dusty streets were momentarily washed clean; swollen-bellied children splashed boisterously in the gushing open gutters that car-ried loads of bobbing flotsam and jetsam to the river. A wayside barber sat on his haunches twirling lethal-looking instruments inside the ear of a customer, his concentration so deep as to be almost a meditation. Fruit and vegetable and gaudy sweet sellers haggled with customers striking bar-gains in a flurry of rising voices and extravagant gestures. The tonga jogged happily along the main Allahabad Road, its youthful, curly-haired driver singing a joyful song of love and summer rains and sugarcane fields in rhythm with the *clip-clop* of the little brown hack.

The pitiable ruins of the entrenchment, mutilated and abandoned and hideously ugly, looked even more decrepit than they had thirteen years ago, a meagre mausoleum for some of the many who had sought sanctu-ary within. Pockmarked with cannon holes, battered beyond redemption by the relentless assaults of a twenty-one-day siege, the structure remained a mute testimony of the brave but sadly inadequate role it had played in the Mutiny. Rubble lay strewn everywhere, each broken brick a tomb-stone. On what was once a verandah, jagged arches looked like toothless open mouths left yawning in some hideous surprise. A pack of stray dogs, scrounging for forgotten scraps amid the debris, eyed Olivia with growl-ing resentment and then, tails between their legs, slunk away without a bark, as if sensing her need to be alone. From a distance, leaning indolently against a wheel, the youthful tonga-wallah watched with crossed arms, wondering what on earth it was that the memsahib sought among this disgusting heap of rubble.

What *was* it that she sought? Olivia could not tell. She had travelled this route only once, many years ago. To travel it again was intolerable, but she knew she must, no matter how sharp the pain, how cutting the grief, how remorseless the demands of memory. As part of the penance she had devised for herself, this too had to be borne. Strolling in and out of the crumbling archways of the verandah, trying in vain to identify one among many—a punitive, purposeless exercise!—Olivia knelt down and picked up a forgotten metal shell from under a mess of stones. In her mind's eye, the walls of the cavernous ruins were plastered with images, frieze upon frieze of frozen phantoms petrified until eternity. Some had voices that echoed silently in the hollows of her brain, voices known and loved and now forever stilled.

Major John Sturges was standing on the verandah of the Pukka Barracks under an arch talking to his wife when he was disembowelled by a round shot. He fell at her feet and died at once.

The rest of the official reports and eyewitness accounts unfolded in her mind, graven letters never to be erased or forgotten. For a long while Olivia stood, silently remembering their every word, tormenting herself with the gruesome litany of death and destruction. Then, still not punished enough, she remounted her tonga and asked to be taken to another favourite foraging place of her nightmares.

The tonga-wallah looked at her in surprise. "Satichowra Ghat? But there is no one there, memsahib, nothing to see except the dhobis!"

She frowned in genuine puzzlement. "No one there?" she echoed, not knowing if she had spoken aloud. "Oh no, you are mistaken—there is *everyone* there, *everything* to see."

He shrugged and started up his tonga with a flick of the whip and a series of clicks of his tongue. Privately he decided that, like so many of these strange mems, she was deranged—fortunately for him! Why else would she have agreed to pay him three times what anyone else would have?

Following lengthy negotiations about the terms and conditions of surrender, the siege of the entrenchment was lifted. A treaty to provide conveyance to the Ghat, riverworthy and provisioned boats and safe passage to Allahabad for the survivors of the siege was signed by the Nana Sahib on 26 June 1857.

From the entrenchment it was not difficult to follow the path of the ill-starred procession of elephants and *palkees* and hackeries and horses, and of limping, stumbling men, women and children, their clothes bloodstained and in tatters, their eyes dull but full of hope at the promised reprieve. Among the pathetic survivors Olivia saw Estelle—adored, pampered, wilful, vivacious, utterly enchanting Estelle, born to love and luxury—her enormous blue eyes wild with terror, one hand clutching that of her son Jonathan as they staggered towards the mirage of salvation.

At the Ghat, a large crowd had assembled to watch the procession arrive from the entrenchment. As the survivors waded through the shallow waters of the river and started to climb onto the bamboo boats, the boatmen were seen to set fire to the thatched roofs of the boats. Within seconds, the fragile structures were ablaze. Those with strength enough to jump into the river did so; the wounded and helpless perished in the flames. The blaze appeared to be a signal to the troops gathered on either side of the river. The first to open fire were men of the 2nd Cavalry who had provided safe escort for the survivors up to the river. Four guns now opened on the forty boats and the massacre began. When it was over, not a single British man was left alive. Among the first to fall were General Wheeler and his family, hacked to death by his own men. About eighty women and children survived the slaughter. With some others, they were taken and imprisoned in a house known as the Bibighar, not far from Satichowra Ghat.

Entombed in the icy wastes of her memory, her mind forbidden to feel or think or question, Olivia stepped out of herself and back in time to watch the grotesque passing parades that had once been. These then were the inhabitants of her dreamscapes, the evil creatures of her nights. Absorbed in her terrifying revocations, yet detached and removed from them, she strolled unhurriedly down the embankment towards that ultimate horror of her night thoughts: the Bibighar.

The survivors of the river slaughter and some others, 206 women and children in all, were kept imprisoned in the Bibighar for thirteen days. They were attended to by a woman called the Begum, given one meal a day of dal and chappatis and made to sleep on the floor on coarse bamboo matting. Nearby, at Mohammed's Hotel, the Nana Sahib and his henchman, Azimullah Khan, maintained their headquarters, from which daily instructions were issued about the fate of the Bibighar prisoners.

On the twelfth day of the imprisonment, the Nana Sahib received news of the imminent arrival of General Havelock's relief force. The next morning the Begum conveyed his orders to the guards at the Bibighar, men of the 6th Native Infantry and some of the 1st Regiment: all the women and children were to be killed. Appalled, the guards refused to obey the orders. The Begum returned later with five outsiders, one a Eurasian later identified by name by two eyewitnesses. They entered the Bibighar with swords upraised. Behind closed doors all the women and children were slain, their bodies—some still with signs of life—thrown either into the well or the river.

Now, almost fourteen years later, the well had been filled in and covered, the spot commemorated by a cross and a pretty marble statue of the

Angel of the Well. The Memorial Well Gardens, as the sixty-acre surroundings were now called, appeared a haven of colour and peace, tranquillity and enormous spreading trees, no evidence remaining of the
brutal tragedies once enacted here. But behind and beneath and far, far
beyond the fragrance of spring flowers and freshly cut grass and sinuous,
shiny mulberries hanging from leafy branches, there still lingered the cloying smell of death, never to be eradicated from these cursed grounds fertilised into greening with the blood and decaying bones of children.

*A male child answering to the description of Jonathan Joshua Sturges
but not confirmed to be he was seen to have been impaled by a swordsman outside the Bibighar, his arms sliced off and his body, still alive and
writhing, thrown into the well with those of all the others.*

*The fate of his mother, Mrs. Estelle Sturges, remains unresolved. It is
presumed that she was killed at the Ghat or in the Bibighar. Witnesses
depose that a few women, including General Wheeler's youngest daughter, were seen to be abducted by horse-borne troops of the Nana Sahib. It
has not been established beyond all reasonable doubt that Mrs. Estelle
Sturges was one of them.*

Something within Olivia stirred and swelled, an ache, a shaft of pain, a
torrent of anguish. With a cry, she put her hands up against her ears to shut
out the sounds of the shrieks and wails and pleas for mercy that crashed
against the hard, smooth walls of her skull. Eyes squeezed tight to blot out
the bloody images hounding her from all sides, she ran out of the Gardens
like one demented, neither knowing nor caring in which direction.

Save for a group of washermen and a few village children playing a
stick and ball game, the river embankment was deserted in the clammy
heat of the noonday sun. She ran back towards the welcome seclusion of
the flight of stone steps leading down to the water's edge, hardly aware
of other human presence. The air above the river was calm and embalmed,
cool and untainted; the wavelets made soft, lyrical music as they rippled
gaily along their way. Overhead, the lush neem and peepul trees spread
their branches generously like an umbrella, or perhaps a compassionate
shroud. A long, narrow punt, a punter at either end, skimmed swiftly
across the water. One of the boatmen salaamed and called out to ask if she
was looking for a boat ride. She did not reply. He laughed and floated his
punt away, still laughing. How serene it all was, how deceptively innocent and unaware, as if the steps and the guileless, green, murmuring
waters and the trees and the Ghat had never been witness to that unspeakable day fourteen years ago.

*Oh dear God—how could they have thought that you could ever be a perpetra-
tor of all this evil, Jai, a part of this unholy carnage . . . ?*

The floodgates swung open; the shored-up currents swished and
swirled and thundered down the choked waterways of Olivia's body. She
doubled over with pain. Watched by the nonplussed tonga-wallah and the
washermen and the village children standing with puzzled, sombre

expressions on a wall of the Ghat, Olivia crouched against the stone sides of the steps and wept. She wept for all those who would never be again, for all those who were and would rather not be, and for those, like her cherished Estelle, now banished from their own world, balanced precariously for their survival on the knife edge of another.

Later, when the western horizons prepared to abandon their last streaks of orange, as the sunlight slipped away and the skies darkened to deep blue and the first splashes of a relieving rain started to fall, Olivia bathed her face in river water and refreshed herself. Her punitive incursion into the past had corrected the tilt of her balance; by walking again side by side with Estelle on her last tortured journey, by sharing once more in her agony, she had retrieved a fine edge of her own sanity and regained her perspective. In so cruelly rejecting Estelle, she had allowed herself to forget much; she would not make that mistake again. Drained and spent and wrung out of emotion, Olivia once more felt very close to her cousin. And with that sense of closeness came a healing, a catharsis, a bursting deliverance.

At the hotel waiting for her were a highly agitated Kasturi Ram and Hari Babu. Also a telegraph message from Amos. She read it and her eyes filled with tears; he had done the *Ganga* and his father proud. He had not disappointed her after all. Mollifying the patiently waiting men with a harmless fabrication of her day's activities, she refused dinner and hastened up to her room. Tonight her sleep would be long and peaceful and dreamless.

Tomorrow, she knew, would be another painful day. But, God willing, it would also bring rich and long-awaited rewards.

CHAPTER

5

T HE BOY COULD NOT HAVE BEEN more than eleven or twelve. In one hand he held a crude, obviously homemade firecracker, and in the other an impromptu torch of a length of coir rope, its tip a menacingly glowing red. Beside him a goat stood tethered to an iron stump grouted in the stony, uneven ground. The goat, a male, with large, mournful eyes and a matted pelt of dirty grey with brown splashes, was held firmly by the neck by another boy of about the same age. The firecracker was lit amid great merriment and chatter; the boy holding the goat inserted his hands into either side of the animal's mouth and forced it wide open. By the drain outside the grocery shop opposite in the narrow lane a shopkeeper squatted brushing his teeth with a neem twig, watching the boys disinterestedly and at the same time keeping a sharp eye open for customers. The bazaar was starting to fill with morning shoppers and passers-by hurrying towards some appointment or the other. No one spared a glance for the two lads, or indeed a thought for what terrible mischief they were about to perpetrate on the wretched animal.

Just as the boy prepared to push the hissing firecracker down the goat's throat, the thin black leather thong of a riding whip snaked out and curled about his wrist, halting it with a jerk.

"Stop that at once! How *dare* you inflict such cruelty on a dumb beast that cannot defend itself!"

The boy jolted back, his eyes wide and startled as he stared up at the veiled figure of the memsahib in whose hand the riding whip was held and who spoke in such fluent Hindustani. Temporarily forgotten, the firecracker that he held between his fingers exploded suddenly in a series of staccato bursts, belching forth a cloud of black smoke and a strong smell of chemicals. With a cry of pain the boy let it drop, but not before it had singed the palm of his hand. The device spluttered and crackled and spat viciously at his feet until, finally, it fell into the open drain and died with a last defiant whimper. All the while the terrified goat thrashed about from side to side, trying to break free and making piteous noises but unable to detach itself from its shackles. The boy hid his face in his palms, his wrist still gripped by the whip. The second boy, grabbing his chance, made good his escape and vanished round a corner.

After a split second of surprised silence, there was pandemonium in the street. No one knew exactly what had happened. The boy started to howl, pressing his injured palm against his chest, and a man and a woman came running out from a doorway amid a cacophony of screams and wails and curses. Some passers-by, reluctant to become involved in trouble that didn't concern them, lowered their heads and rushed on regardless; others, curious to know what the fuss was all about, lingered. Within the twinkling of an eye, as always on an Indian street, a crowd gathered and surrounded the boy and the goat and the anonymous black-veiled memsahib.

Calmly, Maya uncoiled the end of her whip from the boy's wrist. Ignoring the crowd and the angry screams of the man and the woman, presumably the boy's parents, she took the boy's hand and examined the blistering palm. "What has happened to your hand would have happened inside the goat's stomach," she said angrily. "You will live but the goat would have died in agony. Is this the kind of savage game that gives you pleasure?"

The boy snatched his hand away from hers, gave her a venomous look, and ran back into the house, still howling. The man, a sturdy specimen clothed only in a *lungi*, his broad, hairy chest bare, advanced towards Maya with his hands on his hips. Behind him, his wife continued to wail and moan and spew curses. As the man came closer with the obvious intention of confrontation, a strong smell of raw alcohol assailed Maya's nostrils.

"You had no right to hit my child, memsahib," he slurred, his bloodshot eyes trying to locate her face behind the veil. "He had not done you any harm."

The crowd, nervous of the man's drunkenness and what it might urge him to do, stepped back a little. Maya, however, firmly held her ground. "I did not hit him," she said coldly. "I merely stopped him from causing the intolerably cruel death of an innocent animal."

"It was *my* goat. . . ."

"That does not give you the right to torture it!" She turned and tossed a contemptuous glance at the crowd. "Wasn't there a single man among you to come forward and prevent such an atrocity? If these people and their children are heartless, surely not every one of you is?" There were a few murmurs from the crowd and some shamefaced looks, but no one came forward to speak. She turned her attention back to the drunk. "I come this way often. If I ever see your son indulging in an act of such barbarity again, I will set the police upon him *and* on you. Is that clearly understood?"

"Are you threatening me, memsahib?" he asked softly, his red-veined eyes starting to gleam as he took a half step towards her. *"Nobody threatens Barkat Khan, memsahib, not even a white-skinned pukka!"*

"Array, she's not a pukka mem, you fool," the watching grocer called out, getting up and joining the fray from the front line of the crowd, "she's only a half and half!"

A wave of derisory laughter rippled through the crowd and the drunk, emboldened, took another unsteady step forward. Maya went rigid; beneath the veil a film of crimson crawled up her cheeks and her hand again tightened round the handle of her whip. Ignoring the drunk, she spun on her heel towards the man who had made the insolent remark. "I'm sorry but I didn't quite hear what you said," she remarked with lethal calm. "Would you care to repeat it?" To drive home her intent, she slowly raised her whip, preparing to lash out the minute the man dared to open his mouth again.

"No!"

The single syllable rang out from behind Maya with the force of a gun-shot. Before she could react, a hard hand clamped itself around her wrist in a vice grip, and another captured her elbow. Caught off guard, she gasped and whirled around to find herself staring into the grim face of Kyle Hawkesworth.

"What the devil are you trying to do?" he hissed, "start a riot?" Tightening his grip on her wrist, he made an effort to pull her away.

Furious, Maya tried to jerk her arm free. "This man said. . . ."

"I heard what he said. Now come on before you get into more trouble than even a spoilt brat like you deserves."

"No! I have to teach this foul-mouthed lout a few. . . ."

"Don't make more of a damn fool of yourself than you already have!" he snapped, anger starting to spill over his angular face. Whisking the whip out of her hand, he pulled her back and away from the crowd. Then, strengthening his hold on her wrist, he spun her around so that she faced him. "If you want to be beaten up, why don't you just ask them point blank? I daresay they would be happy to oblige. I know I would."

"Let go of me, Kyle!" she breathed from behind clenched teeth. "How *dare* you interfere in something that is not your business!"

"If that drunk had even touched you, the repercussions would have been everybody's business including, unfortunately, mine." He spun her around again, forced her away from the crowd by placing the palm of a hand flat against the middle of her back and pushing hard. "Don't you know this bazaar is a hive of opium dens and illicit distillers, utterly unsafe for a woman on her own? What the hell are you doing here anyway?"

"What I'm doing here has nothing to do with you," she retorted, still furious and red-faced, but aware that struggling in public against a physical strength she did not have the resources to match might be even more mortifying. Sinking into sullen silence, she allowed herself to be propelled away without further protest.

He didn't bother to speak again as they left behind one bazaar to enter another, a dank, foetid lane seething with sweaty humanity, mange-ridden dogs, heaps of putrid vegetable matter covered with flies, cockroaches and rats, and blinkered on both sides by tall, decrepit structures that blotted out all vestiges of sunlight. Had she been in her senses, Maya would have been repulsed, but simmering with anger, totally preoccupied with the debasing circumstances of her situation, she barely noticed the unsavoury surroundings.

It was obvious that he knew the area well, considering the number of side streets they negotiated before arriving at Manik Babu's Ghat on the main embankment road. Still fuming, Maya paid scant attention to where they were going until Kyle turned into one final side street and halted in front of a gate leading on to a short driveway. As he reached out to unlatch the gate, he let go of her arm. She snapped out of her trance and, for the first time, took stock of her surroundings.

A small shock rippled through her as her consciousness registered the utter unfamiliarity of the locality and—in all its unpleasant implications— the identity of her escort. Maya felt a stab of alarm; she was goodness knows where with someone she disliked and distrusted intensely. Having stayed clear of this dangerous man for so long, she had absolutely no wish to be with him now or, indeed, ever.

"Wh . . . where are we?" she asked nervously, her alarm superseding all other emotions.

"Where do you think?" he countered with obvious ill grace. "This is where I live. You might as well wait here while I send someone to summon your carriage. I presume you did have the good sense to come part of the way by carriage?"

She gave him a frosty look. "Naturally. I left it at the corner of Harinath Dewan Street."

"Is it waiting there now?"

"Yes, but I can find it quite easily on my own."

"Through more bazaars—those nasty native bazaars that you despise so much?"

"I . . . can look after myself," she muttered with a touch of defiance.

"Yes, so I've noticed." He swung open the gate and stood aside for her to pass. She still hesitated and he cursed under his breath. "Get *inside*, damn it! I don't have all day to stand about awaiting your pleasure. Frankly, I don't give a tinker's cuss what happens to you, but I do owe something to your brother."

Burning with resentment, Maya scanned him in silence. He was insufferable but, unfortunately, he was also right; she could hardly wait outside on the street for her carriage, and the very thought of walking through the filth of another bazaar made her sick. Much as she loathed the prospect, under the circumstances she had no option but to accept his hospitality. Pulling in a deep breath and without another word of protest, she swept past him into the driveway of the house.

However composed Maya appeared outwardly, privately she was taken aback. Somehow, she had never imagined a nomad, a rootless nowhere man like Kyle Hawkesworth living in an ordinary, normal house such as ordinary, normal people inhabited. Indeed, to her it seemed inconceivable that Kyle Hawkesworth could subscribe to *any* of the ordinary, normal standards followed by average human beings. There was about him an arcane, unearthly dimension that set him apart from the rest. It was almost as if he possessed that mythical third eye of Hindu belief which gifted certain people with the power to transcend material barriers and probe deep into human minds. He was, she knew only too well, a man of relentless extremes, devious and vindictive, without a single redeeming feature to his name.

"All right, now tell me. What were you doing by yourself in that bazaar?"

They sat in a sort of parlour, sparsely furnished with the bare necessities of everyday living. A side window afforded a distant glimpse of the river across the embankment. There was obviously more accommodation at the back because two doors, both closed, were set in a far wall of the room. A manservant had been despatched to summon the carriage from Harinath Dewan Street and Kyle's temper had mellowed sufficiently for him to mount at least a pretence of civilised behaviour. She had not been alone with Kyle for many years, in fact, not since that devastating incident on the *Ganga.* Indeed, it was because of that incident that she had vowed never to be alone with him again. As for his more recent machinations . . . well, for those she could never even consider forgiving him!

She regarded him with wariness, massaging the wrist of her right hand with her fingertips. "I told you, it's not your. . . ." She stopped and shrugged. What did it matter anyway? "I had business with the saddler in Simly Bazaar. He makes the best riding halters in Calcutta."

Unnoticed by her, someone had placed at her elbow a cup of steaming coffee. She now observed a young lad of about twenty, with pale eyes and honey-coloured hair, standing in a far corner awaiting further orders. Near the spot where he stood lay a red wooden toy cart with a string attached, a pear-shaped spinning top and two well-used rag dolls with untidy black hair. Maya was vaguely surprised; the toys seemed such an incongruity in that spartan whitewashed room, and more particularly in the proximity of a man such as Kyle. For a moment or two she couldn't help staring, her curiosity obvious.

"Drink it before it gets cold," Kyle commanded shortly. He made an almost imperceptible gesture to the attendant; it was a gesture of annoyance. The boy quickly gathered up the toys and left the room.

Sitting stiffly in her straight-backed chair, Maya picked up the cup and sipped. "Is this where your press is too?" she asked, not because she was in the least interested but because it was a means of filling the yawning silence. She had never been comfortable in Kyle's presence, nor was she now.

"Yes." He volunteered no other information.

Her eyes crinkled with distaste. "Why do you write such seditious editorials in your journal?"

"Seditious?" He raised an eyebrow. "Sedition depends on which side of the fence you happen to be."

"I'm not on any side!"

"No?"

"No!" She was angered by his look of appraisal. "I'm on my *own* side, and I find the foul innuendos that are your stock in trade juvenile and offensive."

"That is your privilege." He gave an indifferent shrug, then leaned forward and asked, quite irrelevantly, "Do you remember what I once told you almost five years ago?"

"No."

He smiled, knowing full well that she did, knowing full well that she had not been able to erase it from her memory however much she might have tried. In fact, it was on that day that she had first learned to fear Kyle Hawkesworth—although she would rather have cut off her tongue than admit it to anyone, least of all Amos.

"Anyway," with characteristic abruptness, he reverted to the previous subject, "do you always walk down streets waving a horsewhip?"

"I wasn't *waving* it! I was taking it to the saddlery to have the thong replaced."

"And are you in the habit of conducting all this business with the saddlery on your own?"

"No, of course not! But Abdul Mian was out buying fodder and his son had to attend to. . . ." She stopped in mid-sentence, wondering why she should allow him to subject her to this demeaning inquisition. After all, she owed him no explanations. Indeed, it was he who owed her an apology for his many misdemeanours, past and present. But, impaled by his piercing, compelling gaze, she could not drag her eyes away. "I . . . I needed those halters . . . ," she mumbled, once again thrown off balance.

"Well, if you must go through these bazaars unescorted, I suggest you take the trouble to learn at least the rudiments of self-control."

With a determined effort, she disentangled her gaze from his. "What was I supposed to do?" she demanded, staring past him out of the window, "Let them torture that animal and abandon it to a living death?"

"Yes. A communal riot might have caused many more deaths—and not of animals, either."

"It's a matter of humanity."

"It's a matter of opting for the lesser evil."

"That man abused me!" she grated, setting her cup down hard and forcing herself to face him again. "Did you expect me to tolerate that without any retaliation?"

"He didn't abuse you, he spoke the truth. In his colloquial terminology, you are a half and half."

"He had no right to . . . ," she began, then faltered. Slowly, like air in a deflating balloon, her rage evaporated and her shoulders fell. All at once she was at a loss for words. To her horror, her eyes started to brim. She got up and walked quickly to the window to stand with her back towards Kyle. She would rather have died than let him see her tears. "He had no

113

right to *say* it," she whispered, overcome by despair. Squeezing her eyes shut, she stood in silence for a moment, her hands clenched by her sides. "Oh God, how I *hate* this damned country!" Her throat was tight with passion. "It's subhuman and heartless and utterly . . . barbaric!"

He made no response, but somehow he managed to fill even his silence with contempt—as she knew he would. Appalled by her impulsive outburst, Maya dug her teeth in her underlip, refusing to turn and look at him. But she could feel his hateful, all-knowing eyes boring through her back into her innermost thoughts, into her most intimate hopes and fears and apprehensions. It was a frightening invasion of her privacy, and as always in Kyle's presence, she felt exposed, denuded. Crossing her arms, she shivered, cursing her coachman for the delay in bringing the carriage that would take her away from the odious purview of Kyle Hawkesworth's magnetic eyes.

It was unlikely that he would allow her indiscretion to pass without some sneering comment. Nor did he. He laughed, a sound rife with mockery. "And where do you consider your deliverance from this barbaric country lies?" he asked softly, walking up to join her at the window. "In America—or in the arms of Christian Pendlebury?"

She almost lashed out with an open palm to strike the sneer off his mouth, but then controlled herself; to reveal more would be to play into his waiting hands. Quelling the wave of outrage that threatened to swamp her reason, she moved away from him, returned to her chair and sat down. She countered his impertinence boldly, even managing a casual little smile. "Whatever my options, they are hardly any of your concern."

"As luck would have it, they are. *Especially* Christian Pendlebury."

Especially . . . ?

A cold hand closed around Maya's heart; there was in his emphasis some impious significance, and she felt a chilling sense of *déjà vu*. "Why should you be concerned about Christian Pendlebury?" she asked, fighting to keep the minimal tremble out of her voice. "After all, he belongs to a breed I believe you detest heartily."

"You believe wrong. I don't detest the breed, only some specimens of it. There are others whose presence in our midst I applaud with unqualified enthusiasm."

She gave a hoot of derision.

"You don't believe me? Unlikely as it may sound, there are some Englishmen who have a most *salutary* function to perform in our society." He suddenly smiled, a twisted little smile full of foxy cunning. "Not the Chester Maynards of this world, of course, but certainly many others."

At the mention of the name, Maya's cheeks went hot with colour. She was aghast at the direction the conversation had taken, aghast that she should have allowed it to drift into this particular preserve she had guarded against trespass for so long. Over all these months she had deliberately avoided Kyle, knowing that even if she forced herself to resist a confrontation, in his immense perversity he would somehow provoke it. And in any battle of words with him, it was she who would emerge the loser and stand demeaned. He would not only deny all culpability, indeed all knowledge of his blatant villainy, but, in the process, decimate her with that special brand of scorn of which he was so skilful a dispenser. Fiercely, therefore, she clung to her control, determined not to let him see it slip again. She made one tactical error; she should have let pass that last remark. Carried away by her anger, she didn't.

"Chester was more of a gentleman than you will ever be, Kyle!" she said sharply before she could stop herself.

"Gentleman? Hah!" He chuckled, genuinely amused. "Is *that* what they call petty thieves and chisellers these days?"

"You drove him to steal that money to repay Mooljee!"

The words came flying out of her mouth in an involuntary reaction to his taunt, irreversibly opening that very Pandora's box she had vowed to leave tightly lidded. But now, as they stood face to face, with battle lines starting to emerge with unmistakable clarity, she suddenly ceased to care. Now it seemed imperative to have that confrontation after all, and force him to confess to his contemptible participation in the shoddy affair.

"Drove him?" Kyle's expression of surprise was as false as it was infuriating. "Come, come, Maya—not even a truly heartbroken Juliet on the point of swallowing that fatal poison—which, by Christ, you are not—could possibly fool herself into believing *that*, considering the circumstances."

"But you created that nefarious set of circumstances to trap Chester, didn't you?"

He lifted a caustic eyebrow. "One could hardly call your Chester a circus ape trained to perform cartwheels at the crack of a whip! If he was rash enough to turn a lakh, it was through his own cupidity."

"You dismiss a loss of a lakh, one hundred thousand rupees, as if it were a mere trifle?" Even knowing him for what he was, she was shocked by his callousness. "He turned a lakh because *you* played on his weaknesses, egged him on with hypocritical assurances."

"Maynard gambled for only one reason—he wanted to."

"He gambled because *you* made certain he did! You introduced him to those Bow Bazaar dens, you encouraged him to borrow from bloodsucking moneylenders like Mooljee, and then you. . . ."

"Every man eventually finds his own level," Kyle interposed smoothly, leaning his back on the window sill and crossing his arms against his chest. "Maynard's level just happened to be lower than that of most men."

"Not quite as low as *yours*, Kyle!" she spat out viciously.

He merely shrugged, bored with the debate.

Maya's breath came in loud, rapid rasps as she looked at him with bitter dislike. Nevertheless, one vital question remained to be asked. "Tell me," she demanded, compelling herself to ignore his conceit, "what *was* the motive behind all these loathsome tricks you devised to ruin Chester's career in India?"

His eyebrows shot upwards. "I devised? Surely you flatter me! Alas, I am undeserving of both the praise and the illusions of ingenuity that prompted it."

"Chester was weak, yes, but. . . ."

"Chester was an opportunist and a scoundrel." He still spoke without heat, almost pleasantly. "What is more, you knew it."

"Everyone blames me for what happened, but it was *you* who set out deliberately to destroy him. Well, I want to know why!"

"Chester Maynard destroyed himself—and he got what he deserved." With a small gesture of contempt, he dismissed the man and turned on her, starting to show anger. "What you cannot forgive is not the ruination of Chester's career—about which you couldn't care tuppence—but of your own grandiose aspirations. You really think he would have married you?"

"Yes!" she cried, too outraged and mortified to be cautious. "Yes, yes, *yes!*"

He relapsed into brief silence as he stood staring at her with narrowed, unrelenting eyes. "In that case, I stand corrected. You both got what you deserved!" His eyes slitted further. "Chester Maynard would not have married you any more than Christian Pendlebury will."

She gasped. "How dare you presume . . . !"

"I don't presume. I know. But"—he gave her no chance to respond as he raised an audacious forefinger—"I grant you, your Christian Pendlebury does appear to be more of a decent sort than Maynard ever was."

Maya felt a frisson of fear as the implications of that remark became obvious. "You've met Christian Pendlebury?"

"Yes."

He turned to the window, pulled the bamboo blind aside, and glanced out with ill-concealed impatience to see if her carriage had arrived, obviously tired of both her presence and the debate. There was no sign of the carriage and she heard him curse softly under his breath.

She gulped, forced to ask, "Where?"

"In your brother's office."

For a long Maya stood unspeaking, almost unbreathing, all thoughts of Chester Maynard forgotten. She felt sick at heart. Christian had gone to meet Amos behind her back? On the verge of asking more, she faltered, unable to bring herself to invite another spate of taunts. Her trapped breath exhaled in a gush, but kept in check through sheer willpower, her face showed no reaction.

"I see."

From the street outside, at last, came a timely rumble of carriage wheels and Maya almost fainted with relief. His final morsel of information had dismayed her, and she had a horribly uneasy feeling that he guessed just how much. She longed to know the circumstances of the encounter, but loath to spend a single moment more in the company of a man so totally devoid of moral fibre, she flew through the front door towards the gate outside which the phaeton awaited. Hands clasped behind his back, Kyle followed more slowly.

Standing at the gate, he subjected her to a look of injured innocence. "Not even a word of thanks for an act of unsolicited heroism that arguably saved your pretty little neck?"

She paused in the act of mounting the carriage steps and responded with a poisonous glare. "Not even a word of apology," she retorted with matching sarcasm, "for the unarguably diabolical frauds you perpetrated on Chester Maynard—and on me?"

"Apology? For what was essentially another act of unsolicited heroism? Chester Maynard was an unscrupled adventurer, and you know it!"

"And you, Kyle, are a presumptuous, unprincipled *bastard!* The trouble is that you *don't* know it!"

"Oh?" He laughed. "Well, despite that, we do have a great deal in common."

"In common? You and me, Kyle?" Her involuntary burst of laughter rang with derision. "You cannot be serious!"

"Oh, but I am." He no longer smiled. Leaning against the gatepost, he crossed his ankles and pinned her down with a look filled with unreadable nuances. "After all, we *both* have a vested interest in Christian Pendlebury."

This time the green door was closed. Olivia knocked twice but there was no response from within. She was suddenly apprehensive that there was no one at home, that they had all gone away, that she would never be able to make restitution to Estelle, never beg her forgiveness or tell her how much she was still loved.

Never ask her that one question that had been gnawing away at her life for almost a decade and a half.

But then there was the grating sound of a latch being lowered and the door opened wide to admit her. Without comment, a female figure stood aside to let her pass into the small antechamber that led inside. In the centre of the courtyard, dappled by an early morning sun pouring through an eastern window covered with wire mesh, Estelle sat cross-legged on the same string cot with her betel-leaf casket in front of her. It was almost as if she had not moved at all since they had last met. Olivia went limp with relief, limp with love and gratitude. Slowly, Estelle uncrossed her legs and rose to her feet. There was no sign of surprise on her face.

For a moment they stood and stared at each other in silence. Then, with little cries, they fell into each other's arms and hugged.

"I knew you would return." Enclosed in Olivia's embrace, Estelle trembled. "I was waiting for you."

Olivia pressed her cheek against her cousin's and burst into tears. "Forgive me, my darling Estelle, oh, *forgive* me!"

"There is nothing to forgive."

"But there is! I was. . . ."

"Hush. We will have time to talk later."

"Oh, Estelle, you can never know how I have missed you, *how* I have needed you!"

"And I you, my dearest Coz," Estelle said sadly, letting the tears flow unchecked, "and I you."

They clung to each other, weeping silently, overwhelmed by the reunion, trying to grapple with the reality of being together again, crushed beneath the weight of rusty memories that suddenly condensed twenty turbulent years into a single, vibrant here and now. Quietly they sobbed until their tear ducts rebelled and dried and refused to oblige any longer, until there were no more tears to be shed. All around them, in respectful silence, stood Estelle's family, solemn-faced, with quivering lips, their own cheeks damp. Finally, the cousins stood back and looked at each other again and smiled and then laughed and wiped away each other's tears. Laughing and breathless, they collapsed onto the string cot to sit side by side with their fingers entwined, their hearts briefly unburdened, their sorrows jettisoned for the moment.

Seeing that the sadness was over, Estelle's family members burst into smiles as they crowded round the cot, jabbering and giggling and hugely excited. Once more Estelle made a round of introductions and once more Olivia found herself overwhelmed by the effusiveness of their hospitality—no longer in bewilderment and revulsion but in gratefulness that they should have forgiven her and welcomed her back so readily.

She had brought packets of imported toffees and jujubes and colourful bundles of lollipops for the children, photographs of the family, a whole range of English toilet articles for Estelle, and an intriguing assortment of token novelties for all members of the very large family. A servant lad was despatched to bring in the parcels from the tonga waiting at the head of the lane under the watchful eye of the attar shop owner. As the lad returned staggering under the weight of his load, he was received with exclamations of surprise and squeals of delight.

After the gifts had been unwrapped and admired, the family photographs scrutinised with much curiosity and comment, and the sticky mouths and fingers of the children scrubbed clean despite loud wails of protest, the women of the family settled down on their haunches in a semicircle on the floor around the cot. Glasses of iced sherbet of green mango and khus-khus arrived, and amid much good-natured giggling and bantering they plied Olivia with uninhibited questions about the strange world from which she came. One asked if America was bigger than Cawnpore, another if it was further away than Peshawar. Someone wanted to know why the Angrez sahibs refused to wash every day like Indians did; another asked how they could eat as foul a creature as the pig and not die of disease, and a young girl begged, very shyly, to see Olivia's legs since she had heard that white mems didn't have any. Olivia laughed and pulled up her dress to her knees; the women first stared in awe and then rolled about holding their stomachs, shrieking with merriment. They remarked enviously on the elegance of her pale blue linen dress underneath the burka, her high-heeled sandals, her surprisingly good grasp of Hindustani, the texture of her hair and its glossy colour even without the use of henna.

"Now, now, that's *enough!*" Estelle finally decreed, laughing as she stuffed yet another betel-leaf cone into her mouth and sprayed herself lavishly with the English lavender water Olivia had brought for her. With a firm hand she shooed away the children crawling all over the cot. "Are we going to give our beloved guest something worthwhile to eat, Miriam Bibi, so that she will remember us—or are we going to let her starve to death?"

A dessicated, grey-haired woman rose with an exclamation of horror at the very idea and rushed inside, followed by several others. There was no sign anywhere, Olivia observed, of Estelle's brother-in-law, Mazhar Khan, probably banished again from the house for the duration of her visit.

Olivia noted with some surprise that although the women considered her a foreigner in their country, they accepted Estelle unquestioningly as one of their own. As they fussed and fetched, seeing to their comfort and entertainment, obeying Estelle's every wish as if it were a command, Olivia also realised that it was indeed her cousin who ruled the roost as the matriarch of the family, and it was to her that they looked for guidance in making decisions about even the most trivial of domestic matters.

Sitting cross-legged on the floor on rush mats and cushions, they lunched very fully on fluffy chicken biryani, spit-roasted lamp chops smothered with spices, and sweet vermicelli, waited on hand and foot by the women; the children did their mite by vigorously wielding hand-held fans. While they ate, Estelle talked exclusively about immediate family matters. She related without overt emotion the accident on the railway lines that had claimed her husband's life some months ago. A young nephew's wedding was due as soon as the mourning period of a year was over. It was she who had arranged the match, she informed Olivia proudly, and it was she who would bear financial responsibility for the nuptial ceremonies and festivities. She revealed her concern over her son's poor performance at school, about Razia's chronic stomach problems and about her brother-in-law's congenital antipathy to any kind of work. It was because of this last that she had been forced to take over the business herself and conduct it from behind her purdah as best she could.

In all her conversation Estelle made no mention of her earlier life, neither did she ask in any detail about Olivia's circumstances in Calcutta. Listening in silence to her cousin's preoccupations—expressed entirely in Urdu—Olivia again felt the dangerous onset of unreality. Try as she might, she could not equate this Estelle with the Estelle she had known in Calcutta. It was as if someone bearing a strong resemblance to her cousin masqueraded before her in fancy dress, or perhaps rehearsed for a part in some droll melodrama. However, remembering with chilling clarity every one of the terrible tragedies of her poor cousin's life, Olivia held her tongue and was content to remain a listener.

It was after luncheon, over tiny cups of deliciously pungent Turkish coffee, that suddenly, Estelle reverted to English. "Come," she said. "Let us now go to the riverside where we will be undisturbed. There is so much, so *much* we have to talk about." Seeing the immediate relief on her cousin's face, Estelle leaned forward and kissed her. "Everything is not always as it seems, Olivia," she said quietly. "Sometimes one has to create illusions in order to survive."

119

Along a stretch of the river far from the town, they rented a rowboat, took it some distance from the shore, and sat facing each other with their burkas forgotten and their fingertips trailing idly in the leaf green water. Hamid, their male escort, a shy young boy of about twelve who was Mazhar Khan's son by a previous wife, awaited their return on the river-bank together with Olivia's tonga-wallah. It was a languorous afternoon, heavy with earthy scents and warm, fitful breezes. For a while, it was easy to pretend that the past twenty years had never been, that they were still young and untouched and unscarred. For a while.

Perhaps because she was away from the constraints of a conservative family, Estelle had lapsed very naturally into English. Olivia started in a trivial vein with talk of mutual friends dear to them both, of *burra khanas* once so popular with her cousin, and especially of the spectacular coming-of-age ball with which Estelle's parents had commemorated their only child's passage into adulthood. She recalled fond memories of Estelle's parents, of Arthur Ransome buried these many years, according to his last wishes, in a North Bengal jungle beside his dear friend Joshua Temple-wood, of the Maharaja and Maharani of Kirtinagar, and of the vivacious gaggle of girls who had been Estelle's own contemporaries in Calcutta and from whom she had once been inseparable.

She moved on to more serious matters by telling Estelle of her years in Hawaii after she had sailed away in the *Ganga* with Jai and Amos and Sheba in 1851, filling in details too trivial or too copious to have been included in letters. Tight-throated with nostalgia, she related to Estelle their consuming, carefree happiness away from the tensions and turbu-lences of India, her father's and Sally's unquestioning acceptance of Jai and of their unconventional relationship outside marriage, their great delight and pride in Amos, their first grandchild. She talked of her life since her return, of the wounding social ostracism they faced, of Amos and Maya, of the difficult years of their growing up in Calcutta, and of how surprisingly different her two children were from each other.

"In their own ways they've both taken a great deal from Jai, but they resent being told that. Amos is tall and compelling, as you saw in the pho-tographs. With his jet black hair and pale grey eyes, he's the physical image of Jai—as you always said he would be, remember? But his person-ality is very much like that of my father—soft-spoken, thoughtful, even-tempered. As for Maya"—Olivia paused and sighed—"well, as you must have noticed from the photograph, Maya doesn't look like either of us. She's very much an individual, her own person. You asked me in one of your letters from whom she got those deep violet eyes; now that I look into yours again, I'm inclined to agree that it must be you!" She laughed and Estelle contributed a smile. "Temperamentally she has taken some-thing from me, but even more, much more, from Jai. Sometimes she's so much like him that it alarms me—unorthodox, rebellious, obsessively secretive and totally unforgiving."

But if by her enthusiastic narrations and revocations Olivia had hoped to provoke some positive responses in her cousin, she was disappointed. Estelle listened attentively enough but made little attempt to participate in the flow apart from a casual remark or question. No matter what the subject, her brow remained furrowed, her manner distant, her eyes strangely watchful, even faintly puzzled. It was as if she were trying hard to place the people and places and events Olivia talked of, as if they were not truly part of her own realities.

Estelle had asked few pertinent questions, but one she now asked, in puzzlement, was, "Why did you come back to India?"

"Why? To find Jai," Olivia answered simply. "I had no idea what had . . . happened to him until the day we returned in 1858, many months after the start of the Mutiny. I had not heard from him since the previous July, nor had Arvind Singh or Kinjal or Uncle Arthur. I was panic-stricken, so dreadfully frightened. Yes, I *hated* to return, but I felt I must. I felt Jai needed me." Her throat constricted with bitterness. "As it happened he was beyond help, mine and everyone else's."

For a moment she sat with her eyes closed, reliving those agonisingly empty days of learning to be without him, those nightmare nights of scything regrets about all the things she would never now say to him, all the unseen sights, the unfelt caresses, the unlived tomorrows they would never share. He would never see his children grow, never savour through them those small, piercing joys of childhood he himself had been denied. And now he was gone, his life snuffed out like a candle flame pinched between two fingers. All that remained was a wispy spiral of smoky memories to see her through the years ahead. He had gone and she was left behind, trapped in the straitjacket of an existence for which she had no use without him. It seemed to her one of the most grotesque ironies of their lives that Jai should have lived for so few years, but would be dead for so long, for forever, through eternity and till the end of all time. . . .

"And having returned, you have chosen to remain," Estelle murmured, not as a question but as a wondering comment.

Olivia opened her eyes with a start and her breath escaped in a sigh. "No. I have not *chosen* to remain," she said with flaring resentment. "As always in my life, it has been chosen for me by my circumstances. There were loose ends that needed to be tied . . . there still are. I remain also because my children are of two worlds. I have no right to deprive them of their Indian inheritance from their father. I owe that to Jai." That this "inheritance" was slowly tearing her daughter apart, that those damned loose ends would now never be tied, Olivia did not feel it necessary to add. Estelle would not have been interested anyway.

It was, of course, impossible not to talk also of Freddie Birkhurst. Through all these years Olivia had never been able to think of Freddie and their sad, abortive marriage without feelings of consuming guilt. "Freddie gave me his love, his protection. It was I who could never give him anything in return."

Something struck a chord, at last, and Estelle became marginally animated. "You gave him something very few women would have, Olivia."

"Yes, but it wasn't enough, Estelle," Olivia said sorrowfully, "it wasn't enough!"

She was rewarded by one of Estelle's rare smiles. "Is Lady B still alive?

Do you hear from her? Do you remember what an *extraordinary* appetite she had?" It was years since Estelle had first dubbed Freddie's mother "Lady B." As she recalled it, Estelle giggled, a well-remembered, well-loved, desperately missed sound that brought tears to Olivia's eyes.

"Yes, I do hear from her occasionally," she said, blinking back the tears. "She is now almost into her eighties, but I believe still very much in command of herself and her Farrowsham. They've had a bumper crop of barley, she writes, and the dairy farm thrives. She absolutely loathes the English winters and would dearly love to return to tropical warmth, but though her spirit is still strong, she says, the strength that remains in her body cannot match it." A blue-breasted kingfisher dived into the water not far from their boat and flew up again with a wriggling morsel held triumphantly in his beak. "Freddie was already dead when Jai and I sailed for Hawaii but we didn't know it."

"Oh?" Estelle looked vaguely surprised. "You never wrote and told me that in any of your letters, did you?"

"No. What was the point? Lady Birkhurst's letter informing me of his passing away chased us halfway round the world before it reached us in Honolulu a year later." She gave a small, sour laugh. "Another of those ironies of my life, wouldn't you say? Jai and I were free to marry a year before we eventually did. I need not have made the grand gesture of sacrificing my respectability after all!"

Estelle looked at her curiously. "Do you regret having made it?"

"No! That never, *never!* Had I not made it I would have had him for one year less—and that would have been even more intolerable."

"I've often thought of your children, Olivia," Estelle said with a first trace of wistfulness. "I've never seen Maya, and Amos was only two when I left for England with. . . ." She stopped and, for the first time, looked flustered.

"With Alistair?" Olivia smiled. "You see? I can even say his name without flinching." She shook her head, chin thrust upwards. "I vowed that Alistair would never be part of my life, Estelle, and he isn't. Nor will ever be."

Restless in her mushrooming memories, Olivia picked up the oars and started to row with strong, energetic strokes. The little boat jerked up as if in surprise and headed swiftly towards the opposite bank. When it was midstream, she let the oars drop and sat back, breathing hard with the exercise. For a moment they sat in silence, each lost within her own inner world. Then Olivia took a deep breath and resolutely turned her thoughts in another direction. Estelle owed her an explanation; it was time to claim it.

"Over all these years, why did you not get in touch with me, Estelle?" she asked quietly.

Estelle turned away, her face crumpled with bitter lines. She took a moment to formulate a reply. "I would have thought the answer to that would have been obvious to you after your first visit," she said, her tone harsh. "I couldn't bear the thought of being rejected by you—by you of all people—and you did reject me instinctively, didn't you?"

122

With an anguished cry, Olivia slid onto the wooden seat next to her cousin and hugged her. "Stupidly, I was caught unawares, not as fully prepared as I should have been . . . I can *never* forgive myself any more than you can!" Lashed again by waves of shame, she held Estelle close. "But you must know that you are very, very dear to me, Estelle, that I have missed you as much as I would an amputated limb, that I truly don't give a damn about anything so long as you are alive, so long as you are well and happy and so long as we can be together again." She pulled back to look deeply into her cousin's eyes. "And you *are* happy, Estelle, aren't you? Really happy?"

"Happy?" Estelle looked perplexed, mulling over the word as if it were one she had not heard before. "I don't know. Truly I don't. Happy, sad, love, hate"—she shrugged—"these words hold no meaning for me any more, so I cannot answer your question. But if you ask me if I am unhappy, the answer is no. I am not unhappy—why should I be?" Briefly, her eyes flashed defiance. She lowered them quickly, concentrating on smoothing the folds of her black caftan with slow, careful strokes as if performing an act of vital importance. "I have a home, a family, children, an identity. I belong to a world in which I have self-respect, in which I am *accepted*. I am grateful that I wake up every morning in the security of my own house, go to sleep every night knowing that I am protected. I have much to be thankful for, I owe a great deal to the grace of Allah." She shook her head, her blue eyes as bright and clear and matter-of-fact as her voice. "No, Olivia, I am not unhappy. I am content."

The placid announcement hurt Olivia. "If you are content, then why did you repeatedly visit the Pickfords?" she demanded bluntly. "Was it not because you had started to miss the way of life to which you *truly* belonged, missed your own kind?"

"So it *was* through the Pickfords that you found me!"

"Yes."

Estelle threw her a sidelong glance, a worried, nervous little glance, but did not hold her gaze. Having made the comment, she again relapsed into private thought, her plump fingers plucking at each other in her lap, her eyes remote.

"Why did I visit the Pickfords?" she finally repeated Olivia's question. "I don't really know, although I've often wondered. Yes, perhaps it is as you say; I surrendered to an impulse, to a sudden hunger for a familiar taste. It felt good to be with them occasionally—if only to indulge one of my illusions. I really can't explain it. I haven't thought about it much." With impatient, shaking fingers, she took out the small silver box she carried in a cloth pouch, opened it and thrust another betel-leaf cone into her mouth, as if to reinforce the trappings of an identity suddenly turned fragile.

Olivia let the matter lapse. What did it matter why as long as they had found each other again! Once more she picked up the oars and started to row, this time back towards the shore from which they had embarked. The brassy glare of afternoon had mellowed with the approach of evening, softening the harsh contours of the mudbanks and the dry, brown flats on both sides of the river. Along both banks a handful of strollers took their evening constitutionals. Under a flame-tipped gulmohar a solitary musician sat and coaxed melancholy tunes out of a crude wooden flute. A warm, indolent breeze stirred the dense leaves of the riverside trees into a sort of whispered, rhythmic chorus. In the bronze light of evening, everything looked rosy, deceptively idyllic. A grassy verge alongside the bank where they disembarked presented a pleasant vista. Arm in arm the cousins walked along it, towards a verdant thicket that promised more privacy than the open river bank. They settled themselves comfortably on two adjoining tree stumps.

It was time to fill yet another gap, the most painful one of all. It was time to harden the heart and talk of the one subject Olivia had not yet had the courage to broach, the one subject that *had* to be broached, no matter what the emotional damage to them both.

It was time to talk of the Bibighar.

"They hanged him, you know." Olivia picked up a long twig to doodle idly on the ground. "They hanged Jai in July 1857. They said he was a traitor, an accomplice of the Nana Sahib. They held him responsible for the massacre at the Bibighar." Her face was waxen white, her eyes firmly fixed to a patch of ochre sun lapping at her feet.

"Yes."

"You were at the Bibighar."

"Yes."

"You were there for thirteen days."

"Yes." Estelle's voice had steadily lowered; now it was no more than a whisper.

A creeping sense of dread brought a tremble to Olivia's hands. For so many years she had lived in expectation of this moment, but now that it was here she was struck with terror at what it might bring. Curling her hands into tight little balls, she finally asked the question she had waited so many lifetimes to ask.

"Was Jai at the Bibighar?"

Estelle's skin had turned ashen, the colour of grey putty; her eyes were glazed, a brilliant blue deadness. "I don't remember."

Olivia clasped her cousin's hands in both of hers. "I've waited *so long* to find you, Estelle, to ask you this, this one most vital question of my life! You are the only survivor of the Bibighar that I know of, the only one who can give me an answer. Please, my dearest, *please* help me!" Her throat was tight with hope, with despair, the words spewing out in short, breathless jerks. "They said in their report that Jai was identified as the Eurasian at the Bibighar, one of those butchers who"—her voice quivered with horror but she forced herself to go on—"who slaughtered those women and children. Tell me it isn't true, Estelle, *tell me!*" In her frenzy Olivia gripped Estelle's hands so tight that her nails bit into her cousin's flesh, drawing a hairline of blood.

Without any change of expression and with great concentration, Estelle prised open Olivia's fingers one by one and withdrew her hands into her lap. "I don't remember anything about . . . that place." In the parrot-like repetition, her voice was as lifeless as her eyes.

Olivia's arms dropped. With a cry of frustration she buried her face in her hands. "Forgive me, my poor unfortunate cousin, for reopening your wounds, for being so unforgivably cruel! But you are the *only* hope I have left now of clearing Jai's name. It was *you* who spent time with him over the last few months of his life, it was in *you* that he confided his last thoughts, his final fears, his ultimate intentions. The letters he wrote to me were so pitifully inadequate, so threadbare of news. I didn't know what he was truly thinking or doing, perhaps because he did not wish to alarm me. Legitimate or otherwise, he was your half-brother, you shared a father with him, you loved him as much as he loved you!" She caught Estelle's shoulders and forced her to look at her. "For your brother's sake, for the sake of his two children, Estelle, try and remember!"

"I . . . *can't!*" Recoiling at her touch, Estelle started to shiver and jerked back out of reach.

"Over those thirteen days, Estelle," Olivia continued relentlessly, "did Jai ever visit you, try to rescue you from a massacre they say he himself had planned? If he had planned it, would he not have made some attempt to save at least you, a cherished sister, someone he had tried to warn again and again earlier? *Tell* me, Estelle, did you see him at the Bibighar? *Was he there at all?*"

"I am not Estelle!" She cowered further back, the huge, porcelain eyes distended and fearful. "I am Sitara Begum. . . ."

"*Listen* to me!"

"*No!*" Estelle sprang to her feet with lightning agility, her face a mask of naked terror. "*I don't know anything!*" she screamed. "What happened there happened to Estelle. . . . I am *Sitara Begum!* Let Estelle mourn for John Sturges, for Jonathan—why should I? They meant nothing to me." She flailed her chest with her flattened palms, wild with hysteria, her eyes glassy and dilated, her breath surging forth from a twisted mouth in loud, tortured gasps. "Estelle *died* in that entrenchment, Estelle *died* that day in the Bibighar—*can't you understand that yet?*" Bursting into loud, uncontrollable sobs, she spun around and ran away from Olivia into a curtain of hanging banyan roots at the far end of the thicket.

Shocked by the sheer violence of Estelle's reaction, Olivia sat transfixed, not knowing what to do. Then, fearful for her cousin, she galvanised into action and ran into the banyan tendrils after her. Estelle stood at the base of the massive parent tree, her outstretched arms flung about its trunk, her face pressed against the rough bark, her body wrenched with silent sobs. For a moment or two Olivia stood and watched in utter helplessness, overwhelmed with pity, yearning to gather her tormented cousin in her arms, but knowing that at this moment she was beyond her reach. Sick at heart, she walked slowly back to her impromptu seat in the clearing, sank down on it, and waited miserably for the anguish to dissipate.

The scream and raised voices had brought the few evening strollers along the river bank to a startled halt as they cast anxious glances in the direction of the thicket. But now that the diversion was over, they laughed and shrugged and continued with their constitutionals, dismissing it as a domestic tiff between women. Olivia sat in disconsolate silence, staring blindly at the solitary flautist on the opposite bank of the river. It broke her heart to think that she should have so unwittingly caused the resurgence of her cousin's pain. Unwittingly? No, not unwittingly, deliberately! But then, oh sweet Lord, *how else was she ever to have the answer to that damnable question?*

Eventually, Estelle's storm subsided. Quietly, she returned to where Olivia was sitting, and with a deep shudder, sank down on the grass beside her with her knees propped under her chin. Her cheeks were wet with tears but her face bore no other trace of the emotional storm that had ravaged her only a little while ago. For a time they sat in silence; then Estelle spoke.

"You have taken so much trouble to find me, Olivia. I feel that you have earned the right to know at least something about what has transpired in my life." Her tone was as flat as the expression on her face. She did not turn to look at her. "I am a reincarnation. That day on the river bank Estelle died, and Sitara Begum was born. Azhar Khan was a sepoy in the Second Cavalry, one of those sent to slaughter us at the Ghat. It was he who rescued me, although I was scarcely aware of it at the time. I owe him my life, my everything." She finally turned, the face a void, the eyes glazed like polished pebbles. "Of the . . . Bibighar I have no memory. I cannot help you. I am sorry."

Crushed under disappointment almost too acute to bear, Olivia could think of nothing to say. She would now never know the answer to her question; it was doomed to remain unanswered, doomed to fester forever in her brain like a maggot that would neither die nor go away. She would now never be able to lay at rest her children's doubts, never be able to tell them with certainty that their father was innocent. Her own doubts? She had never had any.

In one last attempt to redeem hope she pleaded, "Come back with me to Calcutta, Estelle, at least for a while."

Estelle appeared not to have heard her. "It was Azhar Khan who tended my wounds," she continued in the same impersonal monotone. "It was he who healed me, forced me to live again. He took me to Peshawar, to his village in the mountains, where we lived for two years. During that time he and his old parents, even his first two wives, treated me with kindness. They helped me to regain my self-respect, they gave me a new identity, a new way of life, a new faith in which to pray. A whole new *world.* Then Azhar brought me back to Cawnpore and resumed his carpet trade and I have lived here ever since." She turned her large, saucer eyes towards Olivia. "This is the only world that I know now, the only world in which I can ever be comfortable."

"Then we can never be together again," Olivia said bitterly. "Is that what you are trying to tell me?"

"Yes. We can never be together again, not in the sense that you mean. You confuse me, Olivia, you force me to recall forgotten remnants from a previous life, a life I have left behind, so far behind that sometimes I wonder if it even existed. Our worlds have separate orbits, Olivia. They cannot touch. They have nothing in common."

"They have in common our love for each other!" Olivia cried, immeasurably wounded. "Are you going to deny me even that?"

Estelle's eyes shone with tears. "No! That you will always have, *always*. Don't you see, Olivia," she became briefly animated, "I can never return. You might take me back, but will others? 'My own kind,' as you call them?" She shook her head and dabbed her eyes dry with a corner of her veil. "These people are my own kind now. With them I am at home. With them I have no need to pretend."

"Only to create illusions," Olivia reminded her, still bitter, still inconsolably bereaved.

"Yes. But my illusions, as the Pickfords must have told you, are harmless. When I need them, they serve me well."

"And this is where you will spend the rest of your life?"

Estelle shrugged. "Yes. My brother-in-law wants me to marry him."

"And you have agreed to?"

"Mazhar is childish and indolent but he is a good man. He will also be kind to me. That's all that matters now, kindness. Yes, next year I will marry him."

She smiled suddenly, a smile of simple trust, of tranquillity, of hope and acceptance, of contentment in that acceptance. It was a smile that said many things, a smile of such eloquence and innocence that it took Olivia's breath away.

Olivia had always admired her cousin's resilience, her extraordinary gift to take in her stride life's most unwanted surprises. Unlike herself, Estelle had always had the capacity to adapt, to compromise, to rationalise, to make the best of the worst, to look ahead, not back. Even now, despite how close to the surface her hideous tragedy still lay, she had evolved for herself an effective mechanism of defence, a protective covering, a means of survival. Unable to live with the past, she had merely sliced it off with mental surgery as surely as that swordsman had sliced off her son's arms. As far as she had been able to, Estelle had tamed her demons, laid to rest her private ghosts. If some sudden provocation tempted them into rising again, they were swiftly, expertly, repelled, like a migraine with a tablet of aspirin.

Olivia sat back on her heels and stared at her cousin in sudden wonderment. Yes, it was truly as Estelle said, a rebirth, a reincarnation, a new beginning fashioned out of a diabolical end. And in that moment of revelation, Olivia was overwhelmed with envy.

"Will you see the Pickfords again?" she asked, heavy-hearted and forlorn, as they were about to part where their separate tongas awaited.

"No . . . perhaps. I don't know." In her uncertainty, Estelle coloured. "But when . . . when you see them again, please give them my warmest regards and good wishes. I am grateful to them for their hospitality. And for bringing you to me."

"Will I see you again?"

Estelle looked away. "Would you want to?"

"Yes, I would want to—you should know better than to even ask such a hurtful question!"

For a long moment Estelle did not speak. Then she flung her arms around Olivia and embraced her one last time. "I will never again come to Calcutta," she whispered in her ear. "I cannot!"

Olivia sighed. "Well, will you at least write to me?"

"If you would truly like me to."

"Yes, I would truly like you to!"

Estelle gave her a slow, serious look. "All else notwithstanding," she said solemnly, "I want you to remember that I will always be here for you, my beloved Coz, *always*."

Even that little scrap Olivia accepted with gratitude. She knew that, at least for the moment, Estelle could not give her more.

It was unthinkable for Olivia to leave Cawnpore without a final visit to the Pickfords. Kind and compassionate as they were, it was still difficult to decide how much to tell them. Their lives were simple and uncomplicated. And they were, after all, English! Would they be able to assimilate the sordid, outlandish twists and turns of the life that had been Estelle's karma?

David Pickford was at work the morning Olivia called, but his wife and daughter received her warmly. They were greatly excited by the news she brought, delighted at the success of her mission, even more so by the part they considered themselves fortunate to have been able to play in it. As they escorted her onto the lawn where a table had been set in the shade of spilling laburnums beside the fragrant lily pond, Olivia conveyed to them Estelle's greetings and good wishes.

"Of course, your cousin was surprised to see you," Rose Pickford remarked, "but we have been praying that she would not also be, well, disturbed in any way. Did she receive you as well as you had hoped?"

"Oh yes, she received me very well indeed," Olivia assured them. "We spent many hours together and so could talk to our hearts' content. Estelle's extended family was as welcoming as she was. Sadly, her husband, Azhar Khan the carpet merchant, passed away some months ago."

"Oh dear, how terribly tragic for her!" Adelaide Pickford looked genuinely distressed. "During our conversations we had the impression that she was truly fond of him."

Aziz Rasool, the bearer, came out bearing a salver of mid-morning coffee and plates of *petit fours*. Considering how vitally instrumental he had been in finding Estelle, it was only right that he too should share the happy news of Sitara Begum's re-emergence. He beamed, declared himself grateful to Allah, and executed many sweeping salaams. He delivered a message to Rose, who excused herself and went into the house.

"The Vicar is arranging a charity fête next Sunday," Mrs. Pickford explained. "Apparently, he's sent his curate to collect some old clothes Rose had promised him for one of the stalls."

"Estelle is in mourning," Olivia continued, picking up the thread of the earlier conversation. "This is why her visits to you stopped so abruptly." Not knowing how to word all the other explanations that needed to be made to these kind-hearted, God-fearing people, Olivia decided to leave them for later.

Adelaide Pickford busied herself with pouring the coffee and allowed the silence to enlarge. It was only after her duties as hostess were completed that she returned to sit down and placed a gentle hand on Olivia's arm. "You need make no more painful explanations, my dear. We guessed in the beginning the reason for your cousin's reluctance to contact her erstwhile family—isn't that what you were about to clarify? We did not voice our deductions to you earlier because it would have been unforgivably presumptuous on our part to have done so before you had your own confirmation." Olivia stared at her, surprised that her mind should have been read with such accuracy. Mrs. Pickford smiled at her expression. She bent down and lifted a half-completed dark blue bonnet out of the knitting basket resting at her feet. "My dear Mrs. Thorne, there is little that shocks those who have lived through the Mutiny. In those dark days of unspeakable destruction and bestiality, when one's life depended on hairsprings, when to reach another dawn one lived through several eternities, we all had our own compulsions and desperations in the name of survival."

"Yes, I can understand that."

"Can you?" Adelaide Pickford laid her knitting aside for a moment. "Just before we were all besieged in the Residency in Lucknow during the Mutiny, one day a group of men came to our bungalow to attack me and then set fire to the house. As happened frequently in those days when danger threatened, the servants had all vanished without trace, and as luck would have it, David and our two young boys were not at home. There were just Rose and myself in the house. Without our knowing it, Rose had seen her father once put away his pistol in the desk drawer in his study. She had never before touched a firearm, much less used one. When she saw the leader of the group march up the front steps and threaten me, she ran to the study unnoticed and abstracted the pistol."

Olivia showed her astonishment. "She managed to frighten him away?"

"Oh dear no!" Mrs. Pickford again took up her knitting. "She pulled the trigger and shot him dead, right in the middle of the forehead. The others all ran away. At the time Rose was only six years old." She lifted a plate and extended it in Olivia's direction. "Another almond pastry, Mrs. Thorne?" Apart from a slight tremble in the hand holding the plate, she appeared to be untroubled by the gruesome memory. "You see, Mrs. Thorne, we believed then that it was not for us to sit in judgement, any more than it is now."

Olivia remained silent for a very long moment, nibbling at the almond pastry and sipping the tasteful South Indian coffee brewed to perfection. In the small but beautifully structured rose garden, a mali sat on his haunches weeding a plot. The serried rose bushes were heavy with blossom, vibrant and rich in their myriad colours. If one alerted one's senses, one could almost taste the sweetly subtle fragrance wafting about the nostrils, and hear the harmonic hum of the bumblebees as they buzzed about their business.

"In that case there is something that I feel you should know about me, Mrs. Pickford," Olivia said, arriving at an impulsive decision. "My name is not Thorne, it is Raventhorne. Possibly you are familiar with the name. I am told it was heard often enough during the Mutiny. I am Jai Raventhorne's widow. Amos is our son. On his first meeting with you Amos decided to use the pseudonym in case, like many others, you too found the real name abhorrent." She recited her piece without hesitation or inflection. If there was a touch of bitterness in her tone, it was controlled. She picked up her bag and prepared to take her leave. "You will have to forgive us for the subterfuge, Mrs. Pickford. It makes me ashamed to have resorted to it, especially since you have been kindness itself in extending so willing a hand in friendship and support."

Adelaide Pickford received her announcement in silence. For a while she appeared to be totally engrossed in her knitting. Then she laid it on the table and crossed her hands in her lap.

"We know who you are, Mrs. Raventhorne."

Olivia went still. "You . . . know?"

"Goodness me, yes! You see, David was rather impressed with your son on that first occasion. He decided to learn more about him and your family through our agents in Calcutta. Well, it wasn't difficult to arrive at the truth. Yours is indeed a very well known name, and certainly not only for the reason that you fear." She gave a half laugh. "So you see, since there was equal subterfuge on both sides, we can both dispense with the apologies!"

Olivia was very taken aback, not only because they had known her true identity all along but because of the ease with which they appeared to have accepted it. "I . . . I hardly know what to say," she stammered, greatly unburdened and also very moved.

"Oh, my dear, you don't need to say anything." Adelaide Pickford leaned across and clasped Olivia's hands in hers. "I meant what I said—it is not for us to sit and decide right and wrong and pass sentence on *anyone*."

Olivia's vision blurred. "As God is my witness, Mrs. Pickford," she said, overcome with emotion, "I know that my husband was innocent."

Mrs. Pickford's grip on her hands tightened. "Oh my dear—how dreadfully, *dreadfully* you must be suffering!" Her features softened in shared pain. "Innocence, like light under a bushel, cannot and will not remain hidden, Mrs. Raventhorne. The truth of what happened is known to the Almighty, of course, but also, I can see, to your own heart. The Almighty speaks in strange tongues not always comprehensible to us." She smiled and her generous brown eyes twinkled. "I suggest that you retain your faith in the language of your heart. There will be less scope for misinterpretation."

Olivia laughed. In a sudden impulse, she leaned forward and kissed Adelaide Pickford on the cheek. She was blessed to have this fine family as her friends. People like the Pickfords were indeed the salt of the earth; she felt dreadfully ashamed at how grossly she had underestimated the extent of their understanding.

6

HER UNSOLICITED ENCOUNTER with Kyle had disturbed Maya more than she cared to admit. In fact, she could not stop thinking about it. As a rule, tired out by domestic demands and her onerous daily labours in the stables, she had no trouble sleeping through the nights with gratifying soundness. But on the night following the encounter, maddeningly, sleep continued to elude her no matter how assiduously she courted it. Outside, the mottled skies rumbled with the remains of a seasonal nor'wester; a hesitant half moon beat a hasty retreat behind a dense pall of cloud, plunging the room into blackness. In the compounded dark the casual, unplanned meeting seemed to assume even more sinister overtones; Maya's imagination ran wild with conjecture and her thoughts churned around her brain like the wheels of a paddle-boat steamer. Eventually, tired of tossing about between the sheets, irritated by the cloying humidity and the steady drone of mosquitoes outside the protective netting, she got up, splashed her face with cold water and went down to the pantry to revive herself with a cup of lemon grass tea.

What was Kyle's interest in Christian Pendlebury . . . ?

In the pantry next to the breakfast room she put on the kettle and went out onto the back verandah. In a far corner, leashed for the night, Spice and Sugar lay tangled in an untidy embrace, snoring peacefully. At the creak of the wire-mesh door they jerked awake, stretched lazily and whined in supplication. She gave each an affectionate hug, undid their chains, and squealing with delight, they sped off into the garden. The eerie pre-dawn hush that covered the earth like a silent black shroud was starting to lift; the gently gusting air was mint-fresh and cool, washed clean by nocturnal showers. In another hour it would be light and time for her morning ride with Christian. The kettle whistled and she returned to the pantry.

Cupping the hot mug between her palms, Maya sipped as she absorbed the darkness and restlessly paced the verandah. Trivial details from her previous day's adventure tumbled out of her memory, distorted and mis-shapen and totally out of perspective. She seemed unable to shake off the after-effects of that encounter, unable to rid herself of a persisting feeling of apprehension. And, of course, it was that one solitary question more than any other that gnawed away at her brain with the persistence of a vulture at carrion.

What could Kyle possibly want from Christian . . . ?

It was a question that revived very strongly her latent fear of Kyle Hawkesworth. Kyle was a subverter, a man to whom anarchy and des-truction came naturally. Despite his prevarications, she was convinced that it was he who had meticulously plotted Chester Maynard's downfall with-out any justifiable reason, other than sheer cussedness. Now, with just as little reason, he appeared to be turning his manipulative attentions towards Christian. Why? However great her brother's admiration for the man, she herself had never understood Kyle, never been able to plumb those viscous depths inside his cloistered mind. She doubted if Kyle ever did anything without a carefully planned motive, a self-benefitting motive. What, therefore, was the motive behind that "vested interest" he had con-fessed in Christian?

The dogs returned with a flourish; shaking their dripping pelts all over the floor, both flopped down at her feet, once again content. She patted their heads, and resting her own against the back of a chair, inhaled deeply of the wonderfully refreshing fragrances of wet earth. There were other little fragments of memory that now returned to nag her; idly, Maya won-dered about them too. Those children's playthings, for instance. Not that it was any business of hers, of course, not that Kyle and his peccadillos were of the slightest interest to her, but that fleeting look of annoyance on his face that she should have seen the toys fanned her curiosity. It intrigued her to think that there might be a secret, rather more human side to the personality of Kyle Hawkesworth, that his life too might have dark cor-ners and crevices he would rather leave unrevealed to the world. How-ever minimal her interest in Kyle, she could not deny that the prospect of discovering those unilluminated niches was, suddenly, enticing.

The morning-room clock chimed once for the half hour after four. Soon, the flickers of first light would appear in the east. This morning the venue for her rendezvous with Christian was the bridge over the Tolly Nullah. He had expressed a desire to explore the environs of the gracious estate of Tippu Sultan's descendants in Tollygunge and, if they could bribe some of the watchmen, also the extensive and beautifully verdant forests within the boundary wall. Thoughts of Christian brought a frown to her forehead and a flush to her cheeks.

She had calculated that Christian had visited Amos in his office at least a week ago. Since then, she had ridden with him every morning; had he intended to, he had had plenty of opportunity to tell her about the visit. Why had he not? And why hadn't Amos? It had further dismayed her to learn from Grace Lubbock that Christian had been at the Derozio meeting. Of that also neither he nor Amos had chosen to make any mention to her. Were the two events connected? She found it difficult to believe that they might be. Why on earth should Christian want to attend a meeting of people with whom he could have absolutely nothing in common?

Christian's unexpected duplicity injured rather than incensed Maya. But it also worried her—why had he needed to meet her brother at all? Was it because of his interest in the Derozio Society, or could the reason have something to do with her? That Kyle should have been a witness to the meeting was an additional cause for concern. So much so that, by the time dawn spilled across the eastern skies and the man arrived from the cowshed with the morning supply of milk for the stirring household, Maya had worked herself up into even more of a lather. She decided to have it out with Christian this very morning.

As it happened, Christian noticed her bad humour the moment she cantered up and dismounted at the base of the Tolly Bridge. Her expression was stiff with hauteur, her eyes cold. He guessed why, of course, and his heart sank. As a matter of fact, his own conscience had not been entirely quiescent over the past week. Indeed, it had been particularly troublesome. Now that he recognised the imminent moment of reckoning, with strategic cunning he decided to grab the offensive before she could force him into a position of defensiveness.

"Oh, by the way, I've been meaning to tell you," he began with rather overdone nonchalance as soon as the essential pleasantries were over. "I happened to meet your brother last week."

Maya's expression chilled further. "*Happened* to?"

Pinned down by her accusing gaze, Christian coloured. "Actually, no," he confessed sheepishly, unable to sustain the pretence. "I wrote to him requesting an appointment in his office. I wanted permission to attend the meeting of the Derozio Society last Saturday."

She breathed freely again; her half guess had not been wrong. Nevertheless, she saw no reason to let him off quite so easily. "And all these days you've been meaning to tell me?"

"Well, yes." He stopped. "If you want the bald truth, no! In fact, I had been meaning *not* to tell you! I sensed that, for whatever reason, you were not keen for us to meet."

"Then why are you telling me now?"

"Foolishly, I had overlooked the obvious—if I didn't tell you, Amos certainly would. And I see that he has."

She did not correct his assumption.

"I . . . I hope I haven't offended you in any way, Miss Raventhorne . . . Maya." With sudden daring he grasped her hand and carried it to his lips. "I concede that I might be unthinking on occasion but I could never, never wound you intentionally!"

He looked so anxious, so crestfallen and repentant, that she forgave him instantly, charmed once more by his essential innocence. "No. I was not offended, merely curious. And perhaps a little puzzled." She released her hand from his, thrilled at the promise contained in this first touch. "What is it about the Derozio Society that could possibly be of interest to you, I wonder?"

"Oh, a great deal," he replied earnestly, his eyes still worried as they searched hers. "A great deal! People like your brother need to be commended for their efforts on behalf of the less fortunate of a community that should be *our* responsibility. I admire those efforts—your brother's and, of course, Kyle Hawkesworth's."

"Really!" She strolled away to the stream's edge, standing with her back towards him. Raising her whip, she flicked it lightly across the tall grasses. A cloud of dandelion petals wafted up with the breeze and disappeared against the pale sky like a disintegrating feather duster. "Was Kyle one of the speakers?"

"Unfortunately not. I had been looking forward to what he might have to say, but he was not present at the meeting."

In a momentary impulse, she almost blurted out a few words of caution, but she stopped herself in time. Whatever Kyle's intentions, they were still unclear; an uninvited comment from her now would be premature and might even be construed as presumptuous. She asked instead, "The proceedings of the meeting as a whole—did they come up to your expectations?"

"Oh, indeed they did! I was especially impressed with the scheme your brother initiated in the name of your fa . . .—in the name of your Trident company."

"You mean the marine school aboard the *Ganga?*"

"Yes. It's an imaginative, pragmatic project that will benefit many, don't you think?"

Maya shrugged. "Yes, I daresay it will. My mother will certainly be relieved that the ship is to be put to good use." From her seat on a large stone at the water's edge, she stared hard into the depths of the green-slimed nullah. "Eurasians believe the world *owes* them something," she said scornfully, "not because they deserve it but merely because they are what they are."

Her use of "they" rather than "we" surprised Christian. It also sounded a warning bell in his brain. To pursue the subject, he concluded, would be to tread again on thin ice. Rather than risk further disfavour, he withdrew gracefully with an offhanded "Well, let's just say the world owes them at least the means to make a decent livelihood."

"As much as it owes anyone anything, I suppose." Their time together was so short and there was much else to talk about. She dismissed the subject with a grimace of distaste. Remounting the strawberry mare she was exercising this morning, she urged him to follow her. "If I had known you were so keen to meet Amos," she called out gaily over her shoulder as she spurred the mare and cantered away towards Tollygunge, "I would have introduced you to him long ago."

As all of Christian's mornings with Maya, this too was perfect. The guards at the Tippu Sultan estate proved to be very accommodating indeed. Consequent to a generous baksheesh, the two were allowed to wander at will through the lush greenery on the estate, suitably concealed by its denseness from the main house and its present occupants.

The subject of the Derozio meeting was not raised again.

Later in the morning, sprawled on the grass by the paddocks near the Raventhorne stables, relaxed and at ease, he purposely started to banter with her about the subject that brought such rich colour to her flawless complexion.

"All right, all right, I concede that the Arabs are the best horse breeders in the world," Christian said in answer to a remark by Maya, "but this book that you lent me the other morning contends that they are obsessive about blood purity. In other words, they don't like the idea of cross-breeding to improve stock."

"No. They don't."

"Do you?" He pressed the frosted glass of deliciously sweet melon juice to his temple, enjoying the feel of it against his skin in the rising heat of the morning.

She pondered a moment. "Yes, definitely. I approve of experimentation, of trying to achieve something unexpected, perhaps unique. I believe finer, faster horses *can* eventually be produced by cross-breeding selected regional species with known foundation breeds. The Australian Waler, for instance, which is almost as popular in India as the Arab, has been very successfully crossed with Indian breeds." She frowned and then made a face. "But you're right, of course. Abdul Mian doesn't approve at all of cross-breeding. It's the only issue on which we disagree thoroughly. He genuinely believes that the blood line is all that matters and must, at all costs, be kept pure."

Christian drained his glass and brushed the line of pink froth off his upper lip, lay back and crossed his hands beneath his head. "Well, in England too there are opposing schools of thought about that," he acknowledged. "My father, for instance, agrees with the Arabs. To give him his due, he has achieved very gratifying results with his short-horned cattle and Leicester sheep through inbreeding."

"But you don't agree with him?"

"As a matter of fact, no. In the last century greyhounds were crossed with bulldogs to produce extraordinary breeds. I know people who continue with the practice even today and the results are equally remarkable."

Maya tilted her face up to the sky and closed her eyes. A sudden whirlwind travelling from the river tousled her hair and she pressed down the heavy strands with hands held on either side of her head. "Then you yourself approve of interbreeding rather than inbreeding?" she called out over the breeze.

"Oh, absolutely! I think it's ridiculous, the excessive importance we in England give to what we arrogantly decide is pure blood! Like you, I consider interbreeding does make for better stock. In fact, I . . . ." He was about to expand on his theme when he stopped abruptly. There had appeared in Maya's eyes a look that was deep and intense and challenging, a look that pinned him down like a stake, so that he could not tear his eyes away. All at once it occurred to Christian that perhaps the subject of their debate was no longer horses.

"Even in human beings?"

She had spoken the words softly, so softly that they instantly scattered in the wind. But, befuddled as he was, far away from reality, Christian picked them up with an unerring sixth sense and gathered them close to his heart. "Yes," he gasped, hopelessly dazzled, "oh *yes*, a thousand times, yes!"

There were many in the service of the Government of India who welcomed the opening of the submarine Red Sea Telegraph between London and Calcutta. Sir Bruce McNaughton was not among them. On the contrary, as Lieutenant-Governor of Bengal he found he had ample and justifiable reason to heartily curse the newfangled invention several times a day. Since the opening last year of the telegraph line—and in 1869 of that infernal example of French cunning, the Suez Canal—not a day passed without his desk being bombarded with sheaves of messages about the most asinine, frivolous matters imaginable from pompous cretins in Whitehall who fancied themselves India experts. It appeared that the sheer novelty of an electrified communications system that allowed a message from London to Calcutta via Teheran to be transmitted in less than two hours had swept Whitehall off its collective feet. And in the process, it had made him and other long-suffering officers of Her Majesty's Eastern Empire victims of a particularly pernicious form of bureaucratic verbosity.

In the earlier days, however irritating, Whitehall's autocratic demands had not been entirely intolerable. It had taken comfortable weeks for communications to arrive to and fro. When confronted with an order one had no intention of obeying, it was possible to send back long, complex questions, content in the knowledge that several months would elapse before the replies could return to one's desk. Following receipt of the replies, more questions could be devised to prolong the matter further. By the time a year or two had passed—and if one played one's cards right—either the order would be forgotten or the instigating member safely dead.

As an old India hand trained at Haileybury, the East India Company's establishment in England, Sir Bruce had started his own long association with the country as a writer in the service of the Company (known in India as John Company). Privately, Sir Bruce rued the passing of the East India Company. He might have manipulated his appointment as the youngest director ever appointed to the board of the largest, most successful trading establishment the world had ever known (or, by gad, would ever know!), but he had bloody well deserved the honour! He had served faithfully in many desolate Mofussil regions where others, less dedicated, were loath to tread. Wherever he had been, he had converted necessity into virtue with a skill that sometimes surprised even himself. Yes, he had enjoyed his work with the Company; the lucrative opportunities that went with his elevated positions he had enjoyed even more.

The legislation that had dissolved John Company, and almost overnight deprived Sir Bruce of an extremely comfortable lifestyle with many rich perquisites and pickings, had come as a blow from which he had never recovered. It was, he was convinced, an act of petty vengeance, a personal insult to loyal officers of the Company, and it had left him angry and embittered. The subsequent series of sops offered, including his present high office, had done little to soothe a deeply injured sense of pride.

Nevertheless, until last year Sir Bruce had not been entirely discontented with his job. As Lieutenant-Governor he still enjoyed many purely material benefits. His wife revelled in the unique social status his position afforded her as First Lady of Bengal, second only to the Vicereine. It was on the strength of that status that his only daughter Arabella—a sadly plain girl well past her prime, whom marriage had so far eluded—was at last on the brink of forging a most desirable alliance that would bring her a title, an estate in Glamorganshire and a handsome personal allowance. Oh yes, before that damned Canal and telegraph line had conspired to destroy the equilibrium of his life, there had still been many fringe benefits to be savoured.

But now that direct communication had brought Whitehall virtually onto Calcutta's doorstep, Parliament's grip around them had tightened into a stranglehold. He was at the moment engaged in a fierce battle with the Law member on the Viceroy's Executive Council, currently on a visit to England. Whereas he, Sir Bruce, strongly advised the total disregard of native opinion in matters of governance, the Law member disagreed. "At present, it is unfortunate that it is only through the views of the Babus that we are aware of native political opinion," the Law member wrote from England in a wordy, pompous seven-page communication that arrived over the telegraph line in what Sir Bruce considered blatant misuse of the taxpayer's money.

> These Babus are, at best, inadequately educated and, perhaps for that very reason, given to writing semi-seditious rubbish in the native Press. It is the considered opinion of the Hon'ble Secretary of State for India and of his colleagues on the Council, that those native intellectuals educated in English, as well as the native English language Press, be encouraged to adopt the English point of view to help us spread the salutary message of the tremendous benefits to the native of English rule and civilised English law.

Rereading the communication—laid on his desk with other such rubbish by his personal assistant Leonard Whitney—Sir Bruce resisted the temptation to pitch the whole lot into his wastepaper basket. Instead, he sat back, lit a cheroot and scowled.

The Law member's reference to "semi-seditious" articles had again touched in him a nerve end that was, even after all these years, especially raw. He rummaged among his papers and found a copy of the latest issue of *Equality*. Laying it flat on the desk, he scanned the article on the front page once more, his mouth crimped with distaste. He read through it swiftly, as if swallowing a dose of bitter medicine in a single gulp to reduce its foulness to the palate. The general drift of the article was of no great interest to him, the impertinent drivel about tarnished British justice even more tedious than usual. The final few paragraphs, however, stuck firmly in Sir Bruce's throat, refusing to go down smoothly.

Imagine if you will, a cold winter's morning in a town in a district of Sind sometime before the sepoy uprising. A man, a weaver, stands before a magistrate, charged with various cases of fraud to the tune of several thousand pounds. The man has already submitted a detailed written confession admitting all the charges. The trial, therefore, is perfunctory and swift. He is sentenced to fifteen years' rigorous imprisonment. As it happened, the condemned weaver did not complete his term; he died in prison two years later. His death, as insignificant as his life, remained unnoticed and unmourned—except, perhaps, by his family.

The weaver's story is unremarkable, a routine, commonplace process of colonial law taking its course. There have been hundreds of convictions like this before and, no doubt, hundreds are yet to follow. With the man charged, tried and sentenced, to all intents and purposes, the cause of British justice was once again fully and faithfully served.

Or *would* have been were it not for one irksome little detail: the man given such brutal punishment was innocent of the crimes with which he had been charged, the confession the result of trickery. In the conveniently pliable annals of officialdom, however, his innocence remains unrecorded to this day.

How was such deliberate mutilation of the legal process in the Englishman's Utopia allowed to escape unnoticed and unremedied? Could it be that the blindfold across the eyes of British justice is not *quite* as securely tied as reputed, the scales in her hand not *quite* as evenly balanced as believed? Or is it that those who pass through the hallowed precincts of power in this country are exempted from the observance of those very laws they themselves have framed for the alleged benefit of their subjects?

Sir Bruce sat back, inhaled deeply of the fragrant weed, stared up towards the ceiling and cogitated. He could not deny that he was shaken. Why, after all these years? No, not why, *how!*

On the other hand, could it be that his reaction to those few paragraphs was excessive, that he was merely being over-fanciful? Yet the man's phraseology was curious, very curious indeed. Precincts of power . . . at whom was the insolent pup daring to point a finger, and why the italics? And a *weaver?* Was that merely an unfortunate coincidence? Sir Bruce rose to stand by the window, absently admiring the neat geometry of his extensive lawns and the affluence they indicated, his hands clasped against his generous paunch in a posture of deep introspection.

He had to find out what this damned fellow meant. Had it not been for that garrulous ass of a Law member, he would have banned the scandal-sheet long ago, when it had first reared its ugly head. Bloody rabble-rouser, rumourmonger! How *dare* he take it upon himself to vilify noble English people with his filthy insinuations! For a while Sir Bruce burned with silent outrage, but then his anger subsided somewhat. The matter was one of irritating triviality, an utter waste of time. Nevertheless, he had to find out why Hawkesworth had chosen to bring up the subject now, after all these years. He would not be able to rest until he did. But how? He was certainly not prepared to lower himself by actually asking outright for the God-rotting varmint's presence in his office! He had to think of an excuse, a credible excuse. Perhaps he could use that blasted report about the contract system prevailing in the indigo trade in North Bengal that had been gathering dust for months awaiting translation. . . .

Returning to his desk, he shoved the copy of *Equality* under a pile of correspondence and jabbed furiously at his bell. Almost immediately the door to his office opened and his personal assistant appeared.

"Oh, Whitney." Sir Bruce was somewhat taken aback by the speed with which the man responded to his summons. To cover his confusion, he picked up the first piece of paper that came to his hand. "I have been going through these latest infantile telegraphs and have absolutely no idea what the devil they mean. This one for instance," he waved the paper he held and attempted to read it aloud. "Kddly infm ef goddn rich bongloo rddy fro pandalbr." He pierced Whitney with a gimlet eye. "I fear that in its unholy enthusiasm to pander to native sentiment, Whitehall has taken to communicating in local lingos. This curious dearth of vowels, for instance, could it be in deference to some esoteric native belief in the sanctity of consonants? Or should we take the telegraph, perhaps, to be in endorsement of a newly formed Spelling Reform League?"

Leonard Whitney showed no reaction to the sarcasm. Two years in Sir Bruce's office had helped him to refine the impassive face into an art form. Now he was well used to both, the bitingly acerbic tongue and the easily ignited temper. He merely coughed politely. "Neither, sir. The spelling errors are due to the inexperience of our own telegraphists, still not fully conversant with the new system of electrically sent messages."

"Oh, is that it! Well, in that case I wonder if you would be kind enough to translate it for me? It appears that my own knowledge of English is woefully inadequate for the purpose."

Without comment, Whitney took the paper Sir Bruce proffered and obliged. "The message concerns the bungalow at Garden Reach allocated as the residence of the new Finance member on the Council, Sir Jasper Pendlebury. Someone in Whitehall wishes to know if the premises have been made ready for occupation. As we know, Sir Jasper's arrival in station is imminent."

Sir Bruce smiled sourly. "I see. So now, quite apart from collecting land revenues to make the Crown's coffers even fatter, I'm also expected to discharge the duties of a bloody housekeeper, am I? What the hell is Lord Mayo's overstaffed Secretariat paid for, I wonder?"

Whitney's expression remained prim. "I am not aware of what might constitute their duties, Sir Bruce, but I could easily find out if so ordered."

Sir Bruce examined the remark—and Leonard Whitney's bland face—with marked suspicion. There seemed to be a touch of insolence hidden somewhere in the comment, but he could not put his finger on it. Personally, he disliked Leonard Whitney. He had always wondered how anyone as black as the inside of a coal-scuttle could possibly have the impertinence to call himself by such exalted English names. Unfortunately, the half-caste was a highly competent accountant and unusually adept in the use of the English language, due to an excellent education imparted by Irish Jesuits. Had it not been so, the presence of a wretched Eurasian would never have been tolerated in any Lieutenant-Governor's inner office. Sir Bruce himself made no secret of the fact that he despised and distrusted Eurasians; they owed allegiance to neither side while pandering to both. Besides, the darker the face, Sir Bruce firmly believed, the blacker the heart.

"Well? Have you yourself inspected the bungalow?"

"Yes, sir. It is in good order and ready for occupation. The painting of the interiors and the exterior was completed last week and the upholsterer is in the process of putting up the new curtains. The plumbing has been modernised with English fittings, and thermantidotes have been installed in all the main living rooms. A suitable staff is in the process of being hired. Also, a grand piano has been purchased."

"A grand piano?"

"Yes, sir. If you will recall an earlier communication, Lady Pendlebury has specially requested a grand piano. I believe her ladyship intends to continue hostessing musical soirées during her sojourn here. She is, of course, an extremely gifted pianist herself."

Sir Bruce stared. "How in heaven's name did you come to know all this?"

"Through those, sir." Whitney pointed accusingly at the pile of unread messages on Sir Bruce's desk. "And, of course, gossip below the stairs at the Government House, sir."

"Indeed! In that case, make certain the bill for the purchase of the grand piano goes personally to Lady Pendlebury. I don't see why the government should be made to pay for the social whims and fancies of every Tom, Dick and Jasper's blasted wives, what?"

"Yes, sir. As you wish, sir." Whitney bowed and turned to leave.

"Oh, one more thing, Whitney."

The assistant paused in the doorway. "Yes, sir?"

"Come in, man, come in—I can't talk to you across the length of a bloody polo field, can I?" He waited until Whitney had closed the door and come back again to stand by the desk. "I find that I need some very good quality translations made from Bengali into English," he began briskly. "I don't trust the language capabilities of these half-baked Babus we have on the staff. Can you suggest someone who might be equally fluent in both languages?"

Whitney gave it a moment's thought. "Well, sir, there is a professor at the Presidency College who. . . ."

"Spare me these academics, Whitney. I want a translation everyone can understand, not a goddamned thesis!"

"Yes, sir." He stood steeped in more thought. "Well, sir, I could make inquiries if granted a week or so."

"I can't *afford* to wait a week!" Sir Bruce tapped a folder with a forceful forefinger. "These are urgent, highly confidential government documents. I want the work to commence *immediately*."

"Immediately?" Whitney echoed. "Sir, I doubt if. . . ."

Sir Bruce steepled his fingers and half closed his eyes, as if in thought. From behind clenched teeth, he egged Whitney on. "Come on, man, *think*. Can't you suggest someone unusually literate? Someone well used to writing in English and, of course, Bengali? Let's say a"—he clenched his teeth and took the plunge—"a journalist perhaps?"

Whitney again relapsed into thought, and suddenly his frown lifted. "Well, sir, there *is* one name that springs to mind." Then he hesitated, a more deeply etched frown appeared, and he looked extremely uncomfortable.

"Oh?" Sir Bruce's eyes gleamed. "Whose?"

Whitney shifted his weight from one foot to the other. "I regret to say that it is not a name that would be considered with favour, sir."

"*I'll* be the judge of that, Whitney, just give me the name, will you?"

"Well, sir, it's . . . Kyle Hawkesworth, sir." He flashed a weak, apologetic smile, as if having said a word not to be mentioned in decent company.

"Hawkesworth, Hawkesworth. . . ." Brow furrowed, eyes closed, Sir Bruce made a show of tickling his memory. "The name is certainly familiar but. . . ."

"He is the editor of a weekly periodical, sir."

Sir Bruce pulled his thick brows together and feigned annoyance. "Oh, *Hawkesworth!* You mean the scalawag who writes all that arrant rubbish in that dreadful rag—now what is it called? That insolent half-caste bastard? Sorry, Whitney, no offence meant."

"None taken, sir," Whitney replied a trifle coldly. "It's called *Equality*, sir. If I'm not mistaken, there's a copy of it right in front of you on the desk underneath the Archaeological Survey correspondence." Excusing himself, he leaned across the desk and abstracted the magazine. "I'm truly sorry to have brought up the name, sir. In any case, I doubt if Mr. Hawkesworth would consider undertaking such an assignment."

Sir Bruce stared thoughtfully at the inkstand. "Is he any good?"

"The very best, sir. He holds first-class degrees in both English and Bengali from Calcutta University. Also, he. . . ."

"Be that as it may," Sir Bruce cut in severely, "under no circumstances should we consider giving encouragement to a man who makes a profession of anarchy and sedition, now should we, Whitney?"

"Oh no, sir!" Whitney looked shocked.

"It goes utterly and totally against the grain."

"Precisely, sir. In that case, I will try to find. . . ."

Sir Bruce held up a stern finger and stopped him in mid-sentence, "However . . . I feel it would be entirely unethical for me to allow my personal principles to interfere with the execution of my professional duties to the best of my ability."

"Er, quite so, sir," Whitney remarked, puzzled.

"Fetch him."

Whitney looked bewildered. "Fetch Kyle Hawkesworth, sir?"

"Yes, yes. *Fetch* him. I will see him at ten o'clock on Monday morning here in my office. Make sure he's not late. If there's one thing I cannot abide, as you know, it is unpunctuality." Still surprised, Whitney turned to go. "Oh, and Whitney?"

He stopped. "Yes, sir?"

"About that grand piano . . . on second thoughts, don't send the bill to Lady Pendlebury. Jasper is a hard, intractable, even vengeful man. I don't think it would serve the cause of diplomacy well to rub him up the wrong way."

"As you wish, sir." Whitney bowed, opened the door and went out into the corridor.

Once alone, however, his expression of controlled reverence changed and he smiled to himself. Kyle was right—as he usually was. The devious old fart had swallowed the bait hook, line and sinker!

"I can no longer reach her, Kinjal," Olivia said sadly. "She has passed into another world."

"Estelle is not the first Englishwoman to be married to an Indian!" the Maharani exclaimed. "Nor the last, I daresay. Surely the worlds are not mutually exclusive?"

"It is Estelle who has decided that they should be." Still submerged in melancholy she had been unable to shake off since she left Cawnpore, Olivia remained disconsolate. "Far more than the fact of the marriage, it is its circumstances that have fashioned Estelle's present attitudes. But then, perhaps she is right after all. Can you imagine Calcutta's English society ever accepting her back in view of everything that has happened—especially now, after the Mutiny, when both sides have turned so utterly intolerant of each other?" It was a rhetorical question; Kinjal did not attempt a reply. Remembering her final conversation with her cousin, Olivia was again overwhelmed with envy. "Estelle has made her peace with her destiny. Perhaps some day I can too."

Despite the wounding sorrow of her parting with Estelle, it was immensely comforting for Olivia to be back in Kirtinagar with Arvind

Singh and Kinjal. From Cawnpore she had returned to Calcutta, but only stayed long enough to give news of her discoveries to Amos and Maya. Then, restless and impatient, she had fled to this little pocket of serenity to seek comfort from the healing company of those who had, over these past two decades, remained her dearest friends.

"So, Sitara Begum *was* Aunt Estelle, after all!" Amos had shaken his head in wonder as if still not entirely convinced. "I have to admit I was far less hopeful than you, but I am pleased that I was wrong."

"Will she be returning to Calcutta?" Maya had asked.

"No."

"Oh? She wants to stay on in Cawnpore? In those conditions, with those people?" Maya had made no secret of her astonishment.

"The conditions appear to suit her and it is those people that she now considers to be her own. Estelle seems content in her new life, in her new family."

Maya had shuddered but made no further comment.

No matter how great their relief that their missing aunt had been found, Estelle's decision was not something Olivia could expect her children to understand. In any case, Estelle Templewood Sturges was to both essentially a spectral figure from the recesses of their mother's past, confused with too many other unknown images. To Maya, who had never seen her, Estelle was even less, merely a name. Both knew, of course, that their father was the illegitimate son, by an Assamese tribal girl, of Estelle's father, Sir Joshua Templewood. In the strong conviction that they had a right to the knowledge, Olivia had told her children the unvarnished truth about their father's curious beginnings and strange early life when they were still at school. Amos had asked a few questions, then, satisfied, taken the information in his stride. Maya had shown little reaction at the time but secretly she had been thrilled that, however misguided her father might have been, *his* father should have been a titled pukka. Since then the subject had not been discussed much in the household.

Olivia's halt in Calcutta had been brief. She did not question Maya about Christian Pendlebury. However, what she learned from Amos had left her even more uneasy.

Now, once more in Kirtinagar, Olivia sat with Kinjal in their favourite arbour in the Maharani's private garden, regaled by aromas from the surrounding jasmine bushes and a thriving herb garden. Before them lay the lake, covered with huge lotus leaves bearing giant pink and white buds of tightly coiled waxen petals, and a dazzling array of pale mauve water hyacinth. By the side of the lake stood Kinjal's private temple, crowned with a glittering metal trident and draped in the sinuous tendrils of an ancient banyan, where she offered daily worship to the Mother Goddess Durga. Outside the unadorned, whitewashed structure, on a low, brick platform, a retinue of skilled palace maidservants sat around the pedestal of a sacred tulsi plant preparing offerings for the deity. Deft fingers flew across trays of flowers and fruit, oil lamps and round balls of sweets dusted with crushed cardamom that would be blessed by the goddess and later distributed among the servants' children. Around the spreading lawns, hemmed in by tall, trim casuarina hedges and dotted with groves of neem and fiery gulmohar in full bloom, peacocks strutted with majestic arrogance, their raucous cries utterly mismatched with the breathtaking beauty of their spectacular raiment.

It was only here, in Kirtinagar, that Olivia felt exposed to the true spirit and soul of India. Here the wellsprings were clear and undisturbed, the threads of the fabric delicately woven yet quietly strong and resilient and well defined. Here there was a continuity of culture, an orchestration of natural elements that played gentle melodies in beautiful harmony. Here, in contrast to Calcutta and other urban manifestations of an alien presence, there was a tranquillity that blended everything together in a fine, soothing mesh. The cycles of life sprang from the soil, without artifice, and fell naturally into pleasing patterns. If there was any place in India where Olivia always felt marvellously at ease, it was here. In this little kingdom, tucked away among green, forested hills and placid, prolific plains, comforting human warmth and compassionate nature combined to heal and elevate and enrich.

They exchanged news of each other's children. Tarun, heir to Arvind Singh's throne, was currently on a tour of a remote, hilly part of the state where there had been some illegal and alarming deforestation. His wife was at her parents' home in western India near Bombay, awaiting the birth of a second child. Tara, mother of two daughters, was due in Kirtinagar from her husband's state in the north within a month. Olivia told Kinjal about Amos's Derozio Society, formed for the benefit of the Eurasian community, of his imaginative project to use the *Ganga* as an educational institution, and of his passionate ambition to own the first cotton mill in northern India.

"How quickly they grow and how quickly the years pass by!" Kinjal exclaimed with a laugh. "It seems like yesterday that we were waiting for them to be born!"

"It is only because time does pass so quickly that we manage to survive, Kinjal. Can you imagine what our fate might be if each day turned out to be an eternity?"

Kinjal's sensitive ears, so well attuned to the nuances of her friend's moods, picked up an undertone of bitterness, and it saddened her. "Oh well, it will not be long now before you and Maya sail for California," she reminded Olivia lightly with an attempt at cheerfulness. "How many weeks before you depart?"

"The intention is to leave at the end of June."

"It must be a relief for you to be finally shaking off the dust of this heartless land, my dear. It is what you have always wanted, is it not?"

Olivia heaved a small sigh. "Yes. It is what I have always wanted."

"To be with Sally, her sons and their families will be good for you, Olivia. It will wipe away the tears, wash away the bitterness. Most important of all, it will give Maya a chance of a new life in a new environment." Her dark eyes softened with compassion. "I can understand her frustrations, her sense of humiliation. I'm not surprised that she too wants to escape from the hypocrisies of a dual society that gives her even less than it has given you. America will unfold fresh horizons for her. For her it will, quite literally, be a new world."

Olivia lay back on the soft, cool grass and stared up into the opalescent sky screened with gossamer clouds. Visions of California floated before her mind's eye, making her weak-kneed with familiar longings. *Oh dear God, what would she not give to be in Sacramento, to be home!*

"Yes, perhaps it will."

"Perhaps?"

Olivia remained silent.

Kinjal frowned and leant forward. "I sense that you still have reservations and I simply cannot imagine what they could be. With Amos firmly on his feet, well able to fashion his own destiny, and Maya as impatient to leave as you, what is there to keep you here now?"

Olivia sat up and wrapped her arms about her knees. "I have a feeling, an intuition if you like, that it is *Maya* who will elect not to go after all."

"Oh?" Kinjal was surprised. "The last time she was here, she told me she would do anything to escape from Calcutta!"

"Yes, but since then there has been an unforeseen development."

She told Kinjal about the advent of Christian Pendlebury.

There had never been any secrets between her and Kinjal. Just as Arvind Singh had been Jai's closest friend, Kinjal had been hers for more than twenty years, ever since she had first arrived in Calcutta. Their hearts, and their palatial home in the princely state of Kirtinagar over which Arvind Singh ruled, were always open to her just as they had been to Jai. Through all the emotional undulations of Olivia's curious life, the bond of friendship had never slackened; no matter how desperate her circumstances, they had never deserted her, had always remained steadfast in their support and their affection.

When she had become pregnant with Amos before she and Jai could be married, it was to Kinjal that she had turned, panic-stricken and frightened. It was in Kirtinagar, away from the vicious scandalmongers of Calcutta, that Amos had been born during her brief, ill-starred marriage to Freddie Birkhurst. In Hawaii, it was through them that she and Jai received pertinent political news of India and its dangerously boiling cauldrons. And it was to Kirtinagar that she had flown with her two bewildered children, broken-winged and lost and shattered in spirit, upon learning the truth about her beloved Jai on the day of her return to Calcutta thirteen years ago. Had it not been for these selfless, accommodating friends, Olivia often wondered, would she have been able to survive at all in this diabolical country that had brought her so much grief and heartbreak?

"This young Englishman," Kinjal asked, "what kind of a man is he?"

"The most perfect kind!" Olivia's reply came without hesitation. "He is charming, well mannered, comes from a politically renowned family of wealth and style, and has a first-class degree from Oxford. He passed the

Civil Service entrance competition in London with flying colours. I have no doubt he has a brilliant future ahead of him in India. Amos tells me his father has recently been appointed Finance member in the Viceroy's Executive Council."

Kinjal studied Olivia's stony face in perplexity. "But, my dear, all that makes him sound far more eligible than even Mr. Maynard!"

"That," Olivia agreed grimly, "is precisely the problem."

A maidservant hurried up with her long, full skirt swishing about her ankles and her glass bangles tinkling. Word had been received from His Highness's personal attendant that His Highness had just returned from the durbar hall and would be joining them by the lake within the half hour. Immediately maidservants went scurrying to fetch more rugs and cushions and bolsters. A bowl of charcoal was sprinkled with aromatic resin to produce incense that would keep away the mosquitoes, and paraffin lamps were lit behind bushes to cast soft, shadowed light on their secluded arbour. Arvind Singh's personal attendant arrived bearing a salver with crystal decanters of sherry and Glenmorangie—the Maharaja's favourite Scotch whisky—a silver bucket of ice and the Maharaja's hookah with all its many accoutrements. The rest of the conversation had perforce to be postponed as Kinjal excused herself and hurried to the temple to complete her evening rituals before her husband arrived to join them.

A few minutes later, Arvind Singh came strolling across the lawn, looking refreshed and at ease in a fresh white cotton kurta and dhoti, both beautifully starched and crimped according to style and tradition. As Olivia knew well, he was a man of astonishingly few pretensions to whom vulgar ostentation and displays of wealth were anathema. Even in his informal, simple apparel, however, his bearing was regal, the air of authority subsumed in his manner of a man born to rule. His working life was dedicated to the welfare of his state's people, to modernising public utilities in Kirtinagar, to working the coal mine so that it provided maximum benefit for all his citizens. Arvind Singh's long, tireless hours of endeavour were well rewarded; it was well known in Calcutta that Kirtinagar was one of the best administered princely states in eastern India, which, for more reason than one, the British considered advisable to leave well alone.

While the whisky was poured and the charcoal in the hookah-chillum fanned to just the right temperature, the Maharaja regaled Olivia with tales of the curious dilemmas he faced in his daily durbar. For instance, a farmer in one of the state's outer villages had bartered his wife for two cows, one of which turned out to be diseased. He now wanted his wife back and the cows returned, but the other man was refusing to oblige. Then again, in one of the new shafts of the coal mine they had discovered the labyrinthine burrow of a magnificent king cobra. Some miners wanted the pit closed and the burrow protected; others, less superstitious and sentimental, scoffed and insisted that the snake and its family be destroyed so that work could proceed as planned.

Olivia laughed. "My goodness, how are you ever going to resolve these disputes that call for the wisdom of Solomon?"

"Obviously with the wisdom of Solomon," he returned drily, handing her a glass of sherry. "Or with what I have learned from you over the years—good, solid, homespun American common sense." They joined in a laugh, comfortable and relaxed and content for the moment in small talk. Other matters that needed to be raised and discussed they postponed until later with tacit, mutual understanding.

It was after Kinjal had finished her rituals and rejoined them on the rugs that Olivia stirred the subject that had been simmering beneath the surface. "Lord Mayo has refused to review Jai's case. He will not entertain any more appeals. Since my petition was conveyed to him through you, I presume that you too have received a communication to that effect?"

"Yes." Arvind Singh's expression remained impassive as he sucked at the silver mouthpiece of his serpentine hookah coil and it gurgled gently. For a while he said nothing more, then he sighed deeply. "This Viceroy feels that in the absence of any concrete evidence pointing to Jai's innocence, his hands are tied." He grimaced. "I doubt if even our coal can be used as a bargaining lever any more."

"That is what I too fear." Had Olivia not given up already—accepted, as Ranjan Moitra had suggested—she would have been dispirited by his assessment. But now, worn out, all she felt was a strange sort of relief that it was over, even though she had lost. No, not she, *they*.

Because of the enormous importance of his coal mine to the railways and to steam navigation, over the years Arvind Singh had developed considerable clout with the British authorities. Ever hungry for more coal than the Raniganj collieries could provide, the government treated Arvind Singh with velvet gloves, grateful for whatever quantity of the precious fuel he agreed to release since much of it he reserved for use in his own state's nascent industry. The clout he had earned, Arvind Singh put to particularly good use during the administrative chaos immediately following the Mutiny. Unashamedly brandishing his coal as the carrot, he had demanded and secured access to confidential and voluminous army records and reports that poured forth in the aftermath of the uprising. As obsessed as Olivia with the need to prove Jai's innocence, to expose the gross miscarriage of justice that had so humiliatingly terminated his dear friend's life, the Maharaja had sent spies and emissaries to Bithoor to ferret out and interrogate the absconding Nana Sahib's palace staff, arranged appointments with elusive, secretive army generals, directed Olivia's many desperate petitions to pertinent high officials, and indeed, personally conveyed her final letter of appeal into the hands of the present Viceroy.

During the precarious days of the uprising when all of northern India exploded with volcanic fury, even knowing that there was a price on Jai's head, that he was as wanted a man as the Nana Sahib himself, Arvind Singh had never abandoned his friend. Whenever necessary he had offered him protection in Kirtinagar where the British had no jurisdiction. Both Arvind Singh and Kinjal supported Olivia passionately in the conviction that Jai was innocent of the crimes for which he was hanged. That his ceaseless efforts had met with such scanty success was to Arvind Singh a source of bitter disappointment and sorrow. Nevertheless, even now, when the Mutiny was little more than history relegated to dusty files in locked cupboards and so much had been forgotten, Arvind Singh soldiered on in his attempts to unravel the mystery of the last days of Jai Raventhorne's life, knowing that, if at all, it was here that the answers lay. Today was the first time in all these years that Olivia had seen him so obviously without hope, so palpably defeated, so ready to give up the fight.

It was Kinjal who suddenly broke the long, shared silence. "Isn't it ironical," she remarked with a sad little laugh, "that Jai's death should be as much of a mystery as was once his life?"

"No, not as much," Olivia amended, her throat tight, "even more so! Jai's life, at least, we could unravel, like an onion, layer by layer. But here there seem to be neither layers nor core, just blankness whichever way we turn."

So many unlived years, so much undeserved death. So many diseased destinies. What had been the purpose of it all? Olivia felt immeasurably depressed.

Arvind Singh savoured his whisky in slow, delicate sips. "There are reports of yet another one of them," he remarked with such abruptness that both Olivia and Kinjal were startled.

"Another one of whom?" Olivia asked.

A maidservant, face covered by her veil, arrived with a plate of freshly roasted chickpeas. Arvind Singh took a handful, threw back his head and tossed them into his mouth. "Another man has appeared claiming to be the Nana Sahib."

"Oh?" In the act of taking a handful herself, Olivia shivered. An icy tingle travelled up her spine. For a moment she could scarcely breathe.

It was generally believed that the Nana Sahib had died from swamp fever in the jungles of Nepal in September of 1859, more than two years after the Mutiny. However, no one so far had been able to establish the fact of his death beyond all reasonable doubt. Consequently, several men had surfaced during the past decade and a half since the Mutiny claiming to be the Nana Sahib, the erstwhile Raja of Bithoor, one of the lynchpins of the Mutiny. Not willing to let pass any chance, however remote, that might give them more information about Jai Raventhorne, Arvind Singh had had interviews with each one of these claimants. Disappointingly, they had all turned out to be imposters.

"Another hoax, do you think?" Kinjal asked.

"Or another one of those unemployed doubles!"

Olivia looked at him, intrigued. "Oh yes, I had forgotten about those. He had several look-alikes on his staff, hadn't he?"

"Every ruler has," Arvind Singh replied.

Olivia sat up in surprise. "Even you?"

"Certainly! What makes you believe some of my allegedly loyal subjects wouldn't be only too happy to despatch me upwards, given a workable chance!"

Knowing how much Arvind Singh enjoyed teasing her, Olivia laughed. "I refuse to believe you could ever find anyone handsome enough to impersonate you with any credibility!"

"Much as the compliment is appreciated, I regret to say that it is undeserved." Arvind Singh chuckled. "Do you remember our Dassera procession here last year?"

"Yes, of course. We rode two elephants behind you." She frowned in recollection. "There was some sort of a commotion on the way. One of the elephants bolted, I think."

"Because someone shot an arrow at it, mistaking it to be mine."

"And it wasn't?"

"Well, the elephant was mine, but I was not on it."

"Of course you were! I waved to you and you waved back. You even. . . ." She stopped. "Good heavens! Are you telling me that that was not *you*?"

"It wasn't." Delighted at having confounded her so thoroughly, he roared with laughter. "We had information that a disgruntled tribal with an imagined grievance would try to kill me during the Dassera celebrations. I was advised not to risk riding in a street procession amidst uncontrollable crowds and, reluctantly, I agreed to the suggestion." His eyes twinkled. "So you see, it is surprising how often the eyes perceive, not what actually is but what is expected to be."

Quite astonished, Olivia looked at Kinjal for confirmation and the Maharani nodded. "And what about the poor men who impersonate you?" Olivia asked Arvind Singh severely. "Do they consider the job worth getting killed for?"

"Their wives certainly do, considering the money they make; to say nothing of their widows, who fare even better!"

"Well, seeing how lightly you take it," Olivia said drily, "I should imagine a stable of handy doubles is a very wise precaution indeed."

The lighthearted banter continued for a while. It was not until later that they returned to the subject still gnawing away at Olivia's mind. "But you do believe that the Nana Sahib *is* truly dead, don't you?" Olivia asked seriously.

"Yes, I believe he is dead."

Kinjal caught the minimal uncertainty in her husband's tone. "But . . . ?"

Arvind Singh shook his head. "I think we have distressed Olivia enough."

"No," Olivia reached out and touched his hand. "I *want* to know these thoughts that passed through your mind just now."

"They are not new thoughts, Olivia," he said gently, "merely old ones that have returned to haunt. I am convinced the Nana Sahib is dead, but I keep thinking of how he eventually died and where." He picked up another handful of chickpeas. "And of that most mysterious file, that closed file. I keep thinking of not what it contained but what it did *not* contain. More than anything else," his voice dropped into a murmur, "I wonder why, in all these voluminous annals of the Mutiny, there is not one single record which tells us where the body of my friend Jai Raventhorne lies buried."

"And what is *your* business, young man?" the American asked, then held up a hand. "No, let me guess. Tea? Jute?" He thrust his hirsute face across the dinner table and squinted his eyes. "I'd say tea. Definitely, tea. To me, you have the unmistakable look of a newly recruited tea planter."

Christian laughed. "Actually, I'm a civil servant," he said with an air of apology. "Or at least will be when I am posted shortly in the Mofussil."

The American's eyes showed surprise. "By George, will you now! Well, shiver me timbers, sir—as you might say in Merrie England—I'd never've believed it!" He guffawed and slapped his thigh, not at all fazed that his guess had proved so wide off the mark. "He looks far too much of a greenhorn to carry the weight of the Empire on those delicate young shoulders, eh, Goswami?"

Christian blushed, not sure whether to take that as a compliment or not.

From the head of the long dinner table Kali Charan Goswami, their host, beamed. "Mr. Pendlebury is a competition-wallah, not so long ago arrived from England," he explained to the American, a business associate and ship's captain out of Philadelphia. "He is a friend of my son. Isn't that so, Samir?"

Sitting next to his mother at the other end of the table, arranged in Western style with white Irish linen napery, English bone china, carved silver cutlery and exquisite Waterford cut-glass goblets, Samir blushed and nodded shyly. His two sisters, Minali and Barnali, seated halfway up the table opposite each other, put their napkins over their mouths and giggled at his embarrassment, and their mother frowned in disapproval.

Presiding over the splendid table, Kali Charan Goswami surveyed his guests with pride and decided that the evening was definitely a success. He was greatly pleased with his wife, two daughters and enormous staff, whose combined endeavours had made it so. The table was immaculately laid, the service competent and smooth, and the food—of which his guests had partaken with gratifying lack of restraint—varied, only moderately spiced and quite delicious. Kali Charan Goswami prided himself on being a cosmopolite. He was aware that he was much envied in the city's commercial district and among his Bengali community for having achieved a status that allowed him to mingle socially on an equal footing with white foreigners. That, and the fact that he enjoyed the reputation of being a generous host of refinement and good taste, were to him matters of considerable personal satisfaction. As was, indeed, the current rumour that the Government of India was considering for him an appointment to the Central Legislative Assembly.

The highly successful family business, an agency house, had been established by Kali Charan Babu's grandfather in the last century. It specialised in trade with America and acted as agent to several American businessmen, some of whom were among his dinner guests tonight. Other guests included local dignitaries, two lawyers, a Eurasian municipal commissioner and a few visitors from the Mofussil. Apart from Abala Goswami and her two daughters, there was only one other lady among the gathering, the rather mousy wife of one of the American captains, who spoke little but made a point of giving a shrill whinny of a laugh each time her husband made a remark, whether or not it was deserving of merriment.

Wealthy and successful, Kali Charan Babu was also a man of liberal views with a strong belief in the necessity of social reform. He actively supported such radical concepts as widow remarriage, female education and equal rights for sons and daughters in matters of inheritance. His father, a man of similar views, had counted among his personal friends forward-thinking Bengali reformers like Vidyasagar, Rammohun Roy and Keshub Chandra Sen, and had enthusiastically endorsed the formation of the Brahmo Samaj, a movement aimed at modernising those Hindu practices and beliefs that many like-minded liberals considered outdated.

Sometimes it troubled Kali Charan Babu that the older and more conservative members of his joint family household should be so vehemently opposed to his modernism. His older sister, Sarala, for instance, tragically widowed in childhood and so expected to know better, was one of his most vociferous opponents, and this hurt him greatly. However, in spite of strong opposition in the home, he had stubbornly refused to place any restrictions on the activities of his wife, Abala. Indeed, he was enormously proud that she should be considered a pioneer among Bengali women. Admired by some, strongly condemned by others, she was nevertheless universally envied from behind closed shutters by those less fortunate women forced to remain incarcerated in their homes by authoritarian husbands, fathers and brothers.

As a young unmarried girl, Abala had been permitted by an unusually far-sighted father to study with boys at their family school. Her husband, as forward-looking as her father, had continued with her education, and she had been the first woman allowed by the Calcutta University Senate to sit for an entrance examination. Ever supportive of his wife's academic aspirations, Kali Charan Babu had encouraged her to actually write a book about herself and her family. Outraging not only many of his own family members but also traditional Bengali society at large, he also encouraged her to mingle freely with his men friends and business associates, to entertain and be entertained, to eat food cooked by non-Brahmins and to disregard the traditional prejudice against the consumption of meat. Their two daughters, Minali and Barnali, were being educated in English-language schools and were as comfortable in mixed, cosmopolitan society as was their energetic mother.

Having learned much of this family history from Samir when the shy young Bengali had arrived at the chummery to proffer an invitation for this evening's lavish *burra khana*, Christian had been excited at the prospect of meeting the vastly emancipated Goswami family. Maya, on the other hand, had chosen to decline Samir's invitation. "I've been to their dinner parties before with Amos and Mother," she remarked disdainfully, "and they're all dreary as ditchwater, with the most tedious collection of guests one can imagine. The Americans are all fat and coarse and loud and the Indians preen themselves like peacocks in broadcloth tailcoats and sporty cravats, looking quite ridiculous." Christian had considered Maya's comments rather unkind but had resolved not to allow them to tarnish his own enthusiasm for the coming occasion.

This was Christian's first visit to a Bengali home. Although he would never dream of saying so to Samir, he was quite taken aback at the Goswami's very Western style of entertaining. Privately, he had looked forward to the rather romantic prospect of sitting cross-legged on the floor and eating in the traditional manner with his fingers off metal plates, or, even more exotic, off disposable banana leaves, as was customary at native feasts, he'd heard. The cuisine, however—apart from a few European dishes—was gratifyingly Bengali, with plenty of fish cooked in strong-tasting mustard oil and an array of strange spices. It was pungent and unfamiliar, but he had enjoyed it thoroughly. Having never mingled socially with Indian women, he was greatly impressed by Samir's articulate mother and sisters, and by the ease with which they conversed in both English and Bengali about topics currently fashionable abroad.

Christian was particularly disappointed that the evening's festivities were confined to that portion of the vast Goswami mansion that was appointed with essentially English and Continental furnishings and fittings. He had read about traditional Indian furniture, Benaresi silks and brocades, artefacts of carved ivory and silver and spectacular blinds made of peacock feathers. The rooms in which they were being entertained, however, displayed a somewhat bewildering mixture of French tapestries, Belgian glass chandeliers, Chippendale and Regency-style furniture, elaborate Italian marble statuary and nondescript English oil and water-colour landscapes by mediocre artists, all thrown together in a sort of confusion that was neither European nor Indian. He saw, however, that Samir and his family were extremely proud of their home, so naturally he was suitably lavish in his vocal approval and took care not to make any comment that might injure their pride.

"What now?" he whispered to Samir as the meal concluded and everyone rose from the table.

"Why, it is time to bring on the nautch girls!" Samir answered gaily with a very mysterious smile.

"Nautch girls?" Christian's expression of astonishment provoked a loud burst of laughter, and rather self-consciously, Christian joined in the merriment. "Oh, I say, how very *jolly*, what?"

They removed their shoes at the door of the hall in which the entertainment was to be held and seated themselves on mattresses draped with sparkling white sheets, leaning their backs against fat velvet bolsters. The centre of the hall, covered with exquisite silken Persian carpets, was left free for the performers. Christian was grateful for the presence of Samir and his younger sister, Barnali, by his side since he knew no one else in the gathering. Nevertheless, he felt a thrill of anticipation as they waited for the entertainment to commence.

"I have to explain," Samir whispered with a sidelong glance at his sister, "that ladies are never allowed to be present at a *real* nautch. This is merely a casual performance arranged by my father solely for the benefit of our foreign guests."

"Oh? Well, what happens at a real nautch then?" Christian asked. Samir blushed and lowered his eyes, and Christian laughed.

Barefooted, uniformed attendants now made the rounds of the room, serving small cups of Turkish coffee, European liqueurs, Havana cigars, and triangular cones of betel leaf covered with silver and gold tissue. The air started to fill with ghostly spirals of fragrant cigar smoke and incense; from one of the adjoining chambers, curtained off with gold gauze, came the preparatory tinkle of dancing bells and the sounds of musical instruments being tuned.

A hush settled upon the audience. Presently, from behind the gauze curtain emerged a succession of musicians carrying various string, percussion and wind instruments. They ranged themselves in front of the curtain and struck up a soft tune, which Christian presumed to be a sort of overture. Finally, a nautch girl, the star of the evening, came floating through a doorway with the lightness of a water-sprite, dressed in dazzling crimson and gold gossamer finery such as Christian had never seen before. She bowed low and, maintaining that body position, wafted round the room greeting her audience with graceful salaams and a tantalising, coquettish smile. She then settled herself on a cushion in the centre of the carpeted space and started to sing in a sweet, melancholy voice to the accompaniment of languid, liquid gestures, her shapely hands heavily adorned with gold jewelry and dark saffron patterns in henna.

Despite his growing familiarity with Hindustani, Christian found he had considerable difficulty understanding the words of her songs. Seated next to him, Barnali offered whispered translations and explained that these were *ghazals*, passionate songs of love, composed by one of India's most famous Urdu poets, the last of the Moghul emperors, Bahadur Shah Zafar, deposed and exiled to Burma by the British after the Mutiny. As the performance progressed, Christian was much surprised to see that the audience applauded and interrupted constantly, obviously in approval of some neat turn of phrase or a particularly complex effort on the singer's part. He couldn't help smiling to himself; if anyone dared to indulge in such behaviour at one of his mother's musical soirées, he thought wryly, she would not only have hysterics but instantly order the culprit thrown out of the house on his ear, never to darken her doorstep again.

The singing was followed by several energetic dances by two other girls performing in harmony to a rousing, complicated, ever-accelerating beat on a pair of drums. Even though Christian understood little of the intricate footwork and sweeping arm movements of the dance form, he could not help responding to the infectious rhythms and the atmosphere of abandon and sensuality that the entertainers created by the sheer vigour of their performance. The dance concluded with a series of dizzying twirls and pirouettes. There was a final burst of applause, in which Christian joined with gusto, and a veritable shower of currency notes, gold coins and even some pieces of jewellery descended upon the nautch girls and musicians as the ultimate expression of approbation. His legs somewhat painful with cramp after hours of sitting on the floor, Christian staggered to his feet and, not wishing to be the odd man out, quickly tossed his own comparatively modest contribution of one gold guinea into the arena.

By now, it was almost three o'clock in the morning. Much as he had enjoyed what he had seen and heard, Christian could not help feeling rather relieved that it was time to go home and so to bed. The air in the room had turned thick and stale with cigar smoke; some of the guests were unduly noisy and boisterous, hardly surprising considering the vast quantities of alcohol consumed. A few had given up the ghost to pass out quietly and lay sprawled all over the mattresses in ungainly postures. Heavily intoxicated as he was with the spirit of the evening, Christian was only vaguely shocked to learn that the singer and the dancing girls had been whisked off by the hirsute American captain so as to continue the revelries on board one of the visiting vessels. All in all, it had been a marvellous evening. Even though the incessant assault on his senses had made his temples throb and his lungs cry out for fresh air, Christian felt lightheaded and full of lambent pleasure.

At Samir's insistence, he agreed to a nightcap of Irish coffee upstairs on the open verandah outside Samir's bedroom. The welcome brew was heady and reviving. Very mellow now and at peace with himself and the world, Christian sipped slowly and swallowed deep, reviving breaths of night air, laying his head back against the soft cushions of the cane chair on which he sat with his legs stretched out before him.

"Maya is very fond of you."

The sudden remark from Samir came without warning. Taken utterly by surprise, Christian jerked up in his chair and turned scarlet. "Oh, er . . . really? Well, I . . . er. . . ." Not knowing how to respond, he had started to stammer.

"Yes. I hope that you will reciprocate that fondness, Christian," Samir continued with the same unsmiling gravity. "I would not like to see Maya wounded again. She does not deserve it."

Profoundly embarrassed by a conversation so acutely personal, Christian groped awkwardly for words. "Er, no, of course not." He coughed, feeling inadequate, yet pleased and embarrassed at the same time. "I . . . I know she is a, ah, *good* friend of yours. . . ."

"She is not a friend," Samir said simply. "She is my *life*."

He moved and a shaft of moonlight caught his face; it was ravaged with despair.

CHAPTER

7

THE HANDSOME MARQUETRY LONG-CASE in Sir Bruce Mc-
Naughton's office chimed ten. Just as the echo of the final chime
faded, there was a knock on the door and Leonard Whitney
appeared.

"Mr. Kyle Hawkesworth, sir."

Sir Bruce, not immediately discernible amid the heavy furniture in the
room, was leaning over a side table in a far corner slowly and carefully
winding one of the many clocks that adorned almost all the flat surfaces in
the room. The one that occupied Sir Bruce's attention currently was an
ornate gilded bronze orrery. Immersed in his labours, he gave Kyle only a
cursory glance. With a single gesture he dismissed Whitney and waved
the visitor in the general direction of the bay window that overlooked the
garden.

As Whitney bowed and left the room, Kyle walked over toward the
window indicated and sank into the springs of a generously upholstered
couch. He placed his folder on the coffee table in front of him, crossed his
long legs comfortably and waited. A small smile played on his mouth.

"Devil of a business remembering to wind all these on the right days,"
Sir Bruce remarked presently.

"Yes, sir."

"But one soldiers on, you know. Mustn't let the rust get into the entrails
as it does into everything else in this damned climate, what?"

"Precisely."

"Know anything about clocks?"

"No."

"This one's French." There was the pride of the collector in his voice,
slightly offhand, slightly patronising. "Early century. It has a month-

striking movement, spring detent escapement and the orrery shows the relative positions of the sun, moon and earth through the year with an annual calendar and days of the week on the dial." He straightened and jabbed a finger at four gilded figures at the base of the clock. "The Four Seasons, you know. Beautiful piece. Beautiful."

Kyle Hawkesworth made no comment; he knew he was not expected to. The elaborate explanation was merely a device to give Sir Bruce time to size him up. He also knew that behind the bluff, expansive manner, Sir Bruce was nervous. Picking up the English morning newspaper that lay on the coffee table, Kyle opened it and behind its pages allowed his smile to widen.

It promised to be an interesting morning.

His task completed, Sir Bruce wiped each one of his podgy fingers with a white handkerchief and carefully dabbed his brow, across which small droplets of sweat were beginning to form. Walking over to a bell-rope beside a door at the opposite end of the room, he gave it a vigorous tug. A bearer, obviously positioned directly behind the door, appeared with remarkable despatch.

"Tell those damned punka-wallahs to go chop, chop, *juldee, juldee,* or I'll have their black guts for garters, *thik hai?*" The bearer salaamed and waited in case there were further instructions. On the point of ordering iced lemonades, Sir Bruce remembered the purpose of his summons to Kyle Hawkesworth and waved away the bearer. The more one fussed over these half-caste upstarts, the easier one made it for them to forget their place.

As the Lieutenant-Governor—rendered somewhat breathless by all these strenuous exertions—walked towards him, Kyle rose politely. He waited until Sir Bruce dropped heavily into a chair opposite before he resumed his own seat. Pulling his bushy brows together, Sir Bruce subjected him to a look of cold disapproval.

"Before we start, Hawkesworth, I have to tell you that I consider your paper bilge, pure *bilge*—not that I would ever dignify it by reading it myself, of course. Indeed, were it not for the sacred reverence in which I hold the freedom of the Press, even in this benighted country, I would have shut it down months ago."

Kyle acknowledged the remarks with a slight inclination of the head. He opened his folder, withdrew a copy of the latest issue of *Equality* and laid it on the coffee table. "In view of this reverence, sir, perhaps you might be kind enough to dignify it just this once? It has much that could be of personal interest to you."

Sir Bruce's button eyes buried in folds of red-veined flesh widened briefly and he felt a touch of dryness inside his mouth. He studiously avoided looking at the periodical. "Did Whitney say anything to you about why you have been summoned?"

"No, sir."

"I have an assignment in mind for you. A highly confidential assignment." He threw Kyle an oblique glance but did not look at him directly.

"Regardless of the subversive claptrap with which you fill your rag, Whitney has given me a most a favourable assessment of your expertise in the use of both the English and the Bengali languages. He recommends you highly as a translator—which is the only reason, of course, why you are here."

"Whitney is most kind," Kyle murmured from behind an expression of suitable humility as he surveyed the tips of his boots. "There is, however, a small problem, sir."

"Yes?"

"At present I am not in a position to undertake assignments."

Sir Bruce studied him for a long moment, vaguely nonplussed, not quite knowing how to subtly broach the subject that needs must be broached. "This would be a highly prestigious commission, Hawkesworth," he barked, watching him closely. "You should be honoured to have been summoned."

"Indeed I am, sir," Kyle assured him with a rueful smile. "However, I regret that at the moment I am fully committed to another, ah, *project* which requires a great deal of endeavour since the research involved is copious."

Sir Bruce stared at an icon on the wall to his right and used his peripheral vision to thoughtfully scan the man opposite. Was it his imagination, or was there something in Hawkesworth's tone that sounded rather . . . sinister? He hesitated a fraction before asking bluntly, "A *writing* project?"

"Yes."

"For your rag?"

"No."

Sir Bruce loosened and raised a smile of polite interest, his beady eyes wary. "May I inquire as to the subject of this writing project?" His palms itched to knock the smile off the arrogant face, itched to physically toss the half-breed pup out on his ear, knowing full well that at the moment he could do neither. Not yet, not until he had some indication as to the extent of the man's information.

Kyle sat back and examined his nails. "The pamphlet I am in the process of preparing is an investigation into the clandestine gem trade that flourished before the Mutiny between a certain district of Sind and the diamond mines in the princely state of Panna."

Sir Bruce's chest tightened. It was only with supreme effort that he could restrain a gasp. Somehow he managed to ask casually, "On what particular *aspect* of this trade might you be focussing your endeavours?"

Kyle rose, sauntered across to a tall, narrow stand and inspected with great curiosity the rather strange-looking clock on top of it. It was in the shape of a golden globe balanced on a pedestal with an arrow piercing the globe. "Ah, of American origin, I see. Quite modern, I take it?"

"Yes. The movement is inside the globe," the Lieutenant-Governor answered mechanically, the constriction in his throat interfering with the clarity of his speech.

"And the key?"

"It's wound by turning the arrow." Sir Bruce felt his stomach lurch as he struggled to sit up straight. "What particular asp. . . ?"

"Is it? How extraordinary! Who would have thought the crass Americans capable of such subtlety." Kyle shook his head in silent admiration, then, unhurriedly, returned to his seat and sat down once more. "Forgive me, Sir Bruce—what was that question again? Oh, what particular aspect? Well, I find I am rather intrigued by the manner in which the diamonds, legally the property of the Maharaja, found their way into various unauthorised pockets at the time." He frowned as if suddenly having remembered something. "If I am not mistaken, Sir Bruce, I believe you yourself were posted as Collector of that particular district in the early fifties?"

Very slowly the colour started to fade from the Lieutenant-Governor's bloodshot face. His palms felt hot and clammy; he could not find his voice. With clumsy fingers he fumbled for a cheroot he did not want because it gave him something to do with his hands, and took his time lighting it. He inhaled deeply and in the process managed to locate a voice.

"Yes."

"In that case, perhaps you could add to my research into the subject?" Kyle suggested brightly. "Considering your direct involvement in these processes, your recollections would be of the *utmost* importance to me."

Sir Bruce's face was like hewn stone, but behind the facade his brain galloped. The man was groping, he knew nothing, *nothing!* How could he? Foolishly, he almost asked if Hawkesworth had any particular transaction in mind, but bit back the disastrous question before it could trip off his tongue. Swallowing his agitation, he assumed an expression of disinterest. "I certainly had no involvement in these processes," he said stiffly, "but as far as I recall, those who dabbled in the diamond business were mostly Gujaratis from Surat. I could never tell one merchant from the other because, to be quite frank, to me all natives look alike."

"Yes, of course." Kyle smiled. "But perhaps this might help to refresh your memory?" He pulled out an envelope from his folder and laid it on the coffee table.

Nervously, Sir Bruce stretched forward, took the envelope and from within pulled out the photograph of a fair-skinned boy gazing apprehensively into the camera lens. For a moment, Sir Bruce stared at the picture in silent shock. It *couldn't* be . . . could it? Running the tip of his fat pink tongue over his lips, he looked sharply at Kyle. "Who . . . who the devil *is* this?"

Kyle eased himself back on the couch without removing his eyes from Sir Bruce's face. Then he leant forward, took the photograph from Sir Bruce's fingers, replaced it in the envelope and the envelope back in the folder. "The boy is Martin Weaver, son of Daniel Weaver, a Eurasian sentenced to serve fifteen years' rigorous imprisonment in 1856 in your district, for crimes he did not commit."

Sir Bruce squeezed his eyes shut and a low shudder rippled through his corpulent frame.

Hawkesworth knew!

With a mighty effort he heaved his enormous frame out of his chair and went to stand by the window. The view of the lush gardens and rolling green acreage of Belvedere House, official residence of Bengal's Lieutenant-Governors, usually filled him with immense pride and pleasure. Today they left him unimpressed. In fact, he hardly saw them as, with quivering fingers, he pushed open a window and gulped in several lungfuls of fresh air. No, he consoled himself bravely, Hawkesworth did not know, he merely *suspected*—a very different matter altogether!

"Where is the boy now?"

"In a place where he cannot be easily found."

In a sudden burst of fury, Sir Bruce spun on his heel and muttered a hoarse oath under his breath. "You can bloody well go to *hell*, Hawkesworth!" he hissed, frantically dabbing a dripping brow. "Do you think anyone is likely to believe these blatant fabrications after all these years? Weaver had a fair trial. You have no proof to the contrary—least of all the imaginings of his wretched family!"

"So, you do remember the family!" Kyle laughed under his breath and then sobered again. "Yes, I have no proof. But there are effective substitutes for proof, as you would know better than anyone else, Sir Bruce." He crossed his legs languidly. "For instance, seeds of suspicion sprinkled in the right soil, then irrigated and fertilised by Calcutta's formidable rumour machines. . . ?" Allowing his voice to trail away on a questioning note, he rose to stroll across the room.

"Bah! I have a perfectly legitimate bill of sale . . . ," the Lieutenant-Governor began angrily, then stopped. Why the devil should he be on the defensive? He owed no damned explanations to this infamous specimen of lowlife!

Kyle appeared to pay no attention to the abortive explanation, indeed, hardly noticed it. Instead, he strolled up to the large bay window. "You have a most imaginatively planned garden, Sir Bruce," he commented conversationally as he stood gazing out at the expanse of vibrant colour. "I think it is the delightful Miss Arabella who personally supervises its maintenance, is it not?"

Sir Bruce felt a fresh surge of panic within his hollow stomach at the unexpected reference to his daughter. Not trusting himself to speak, he merely glared malevolently at an exquisite gulmohar outside the window—and waited.

Kyle walked over to an artistic arrangement of framed pictures on a wall and stood taking particular note of a Daniell aquatint of Chowringhee Road in the late eighteenth century, framed in gold against a mount of bright red silk. "I believe Lady McNaughton has eventually succeeded in negotiating Miss Arabella's nuptial alliance after several unsuccessful earlier attempts." He bowed with ironic deference. "Allow me to be the first to offer congratulations. I sincerely hope that no nasty, unforeseen clouds will suddenly appear in the blue skies of marital bliss to mar the young couple's future happiness."

Every muscle of Sir Bruce's body turned taut, each individual hair at the back of his neck stood up and tingled. He seemed unable to expel the air entrapped in his capacious lungs except in short, painful gasps. It would be calamitous for Arabella if scandal touched his name at this crucial juncture! And what would Clementine have to say if anything went wrong now with this alliance she had forged with such conscientious effort? He almost convulsed at the prospect of the dual disaster. "For God's sake, come to the point, Hawkesworth!" he commanded, enraged and at the same time horribly frightened. "Enough of these bloody innuendos. What the hell *is* it that you are trying to tell me?"

"Two things, Sir Bruce." Kyle gave him an amused stare. "First, I wonder if your future son-in-law and his parents would consider Miss Arabella's generous portion adequate compensation for the fact that the bride is not nineteen years old, as shown in that amended birth certificate, but almost twenty-seven, to the groom's tender twenty-three?"

"Good grief! How in the name of . . . ?"

"And second"—Kyle ignored the gasp of an interruption—"I have in hand the testimony of the Indian broker through whom you have regularly and illegally transmitted funds to London to the bank account of a certain married lady of hitherto irreproachable reputation living in Eaton Square."

Sir Bruce felt sick to the stomach. He made a valiant attempt to throw his shoulders back and regain control of himself, but didn't quite succeed. Instead, he merely stood gaping out of the window in heaving silence. When he finally spoke, it was in an undertone that was flat and barely audible. "Should you consider undertaking these . . . translations I intend to offer you, I would be prepared to make handsome payment for them."

"Ah!" A subtle change came over Kyle's face as he surveyed that of the Lieutenant-Governor. The amusement and the affable manner disappeared and his expression steeled. The aquiline features once again settled into their characteristic mould of intransigence. "How handsome?" he asked coldly.

Slowly, Sir Bruce walked back and again sank down in the upholstery, battling inwardly for a moment to suppress the surge of rage and hate that rose within him. "A thousand pounds."

Kyle laughed, his eyes rife with contempt. "A thousand pounds! You must think me a fool, Sir Bruce. You drove far more lucrative bargains with the ill-fated Daniel Weaver in Jacobabad. *Five* thousand!"

Sir Bruce went white with outrage. "God *damn* you, man!"

"You consider the price too high for, ah, *translations* that have already proved astonishingly lucrative for you?"

Unable to speak, Sir Bruce merely spluttered.

"Should the money be forthcoming, it will lay to rest once and for all the matter of Daniel Weaver's diamonds. As it will any risk to the virtue of that good lady who still resides in Eaton Square."

Sir Bruce gave a strangled cry and leapt out of his chair with an agility of which one would not have thought him capable. "Get out!" he screamed, his control suddenly snapping. *"Get out!"*

Kyle shrugged. "Certainly. If that is what you wish." Without undue hurry, he picked up his folder and walked to the door. "Daniel Weaver and his family paid a heavy price for his association with you, Sir Bruce," he said pleasantly enough as he paused with a hand on the door knob. "Ideally, I would simply twist your rotten neck for the suffering you have caused them, but being essentially a pragmatist, I am willing to settle for monetary compensation." The shadow of a smile faded and his eyes became ominous slits. "You leave on furlough in October for your daughter's marriage, due to take place in the second week of November in England. That gives you enough time to change your mind. However, should you choose not to, I assure you that that wedding will never take place because I will personally tear every aspect of your murky, worthless life apart, seam by seam. That much I promise. Good day."

The door slammed shut after Kyle and Sir Bruce fell back in his seat with a howl of impotent rage. The cunning bastard, bloody half-caste *vermin!* He groaned and covered his face with his hands, his huge, over-indulged body full of trembles. He should have killed that bloody woman when he had the chance!

Outside, in the corridor, Leonard Whitney awaited Kyle.

"Well?"

"Five thousand." His tone remained impassive.

"He agreed?"

Kyle's eyes glittered. "Not yet, but he will. By Christ, he will!"

It was a Sunday morning, two days after the Goswamis' *burra khana*. Anxious to discover in some detail Christian's reaction to the evening, Samir intercepted him at the Raventhorne house early, well aware that he and Maya were in the habit of riding together at dawn every day. If Christian still felt the lingering remnants of embarrassment at their final conversation that night of the entertainment, Samir displayed no such awkwardness. As always, he looked tranquil and composed, and his eyes, as they met Christian's, shone clear and unconfused.

Knowing that Amos had already left for Cawnpore and that her mother was not expected back from Kirtinagar until the following day, Maya had ushered Christian confidently into the downstairs parlour for breakfast. Somewhat put out by Samir's sudden and uninvited appearance just as they were preparing to sit down to fresh coffee and American-style pancakes with maple syrup, she had no option but to ask Samir to join them with as much grace as she could summon. Pleased just to be near her, Samir accepted immediately.

For a while the conversation remained casual as they exchanged pleasantries about the *burra khana* and took turns to regale Maya with various amusing incidents. Then Christian laid down his knife and fork and leaned his elbows on the table. "Would you mind if I put to you a question you might consider impertinent?" he asked.

Samir shook his head, all attention. "Not at all, please do."

"Well, I couldn't help noticing that night that in spite of the very liberal views your parents hold, your mother and sisters were the only family ladies who joined us at table for dinner."

Samir considered Christian's question as carefully as he considered everything. "Well . . . there are certain dietary taboos that some women of our family still observe."

"Oh yes, that day we first met, you started to tell me about these taboos but we could not finish the conversation. If I remember correctly, you were explaining to me the need for multiple kitchens."

Samir remembered the conversation well and was flattered that Christian should too, but aware of how much Maya disliked the subject, he glanced at her anxiously. "Is it not too early in the day yet for such a serious conversation?" he asked with a nervous smile. "Perhaps some other time when we're. . . ."

"No, I don't think it's too early in the day," Christian insisted. "What better time for serious talk than when the mind is sharp and in clear focus, isn't that so, Maya?" Without waiting for her response, he resumed his knife and fork and dug into a pancake. "Well?"

With an apologetic glance in Maya's direction, Samir plunged only too happily into his explanations. "It is for reasons of these traditional taboos that more than one kitchen is needed. You see, the male members of a Hindu family might eat flesh, but the female members might not. Therefore, food for different members must be cooked separately in separate kitchens. The cook for the male members could possibly be a Mussulman because he prepares meat dishes well, but for the vegetarian ladies food must be prepared by Hindu cooks, as also for orthodox visitors and other members of the household. Then, for the family widows. . . ." he faltered.

"For the family widows?" Christian prodded, ignoring Maya's very pronounced look of boredom.

"Well, for the widowed ladies of the family and the orthodox old retainers my father has to support, there must be only Brahmin cooks who prepare special dishes for days of fasting and as offerings to the family deity."

"Food for days of fasting?" Christian was quite amused. "Isn't that a contradiction in terms?"

"No, you see, on *ekadashi*, the first day of the Hindu lunar month, it is decreed that Hindu widows will eat only traditional foods." He stopped, looking thoroughly uncomfortable.

Maya was quick to pounce on the opening he offered. "In India, Mr. Pendlebury," she interrupted with scathing scorn, "it is the menfolk who *force* the widows of their family, whether young or old, to fast on every *ekadashi*. It's wicked, just a cruel superstition to punish them further for not having husbands. As if it's *their* fault that their husbands are dead!"

"No, that is not quite true!" Samir rejoined with sudden spirit. "I concede that many of our customs are harsh to women, but there are people who do not approve of these customs. You know very well, Maya, that we don't. It is the widows themselves who insist on keeping the barbaric practices alive. Aunt Sarala, for instance." He turned impassioned eyes towards Christian, anxious that he should be made to comprehend fully. "She is my father's oldest sister, only sixteen years of age when her husband died of cholera. Had my father not restrained her forcibly, she would have thrown herself on her husband's funeral pyre and happily burned herself to death. To this day she has not forgiven him for having interfered with what she considers to be her glorification as a suttee!"

The animated debate continued for a while, until, with pronounced reluctance, Samir announced that he had to leave for his tutor's house for a private lesson in English prosody. Conscious of Maya's gathering sulkiness and rather puzzled by it, Christian set about clearing the air as soon as they were on their own. "I appear to have done something to displease you," he ventured, subdued and penitent. "I can think of no offence that I have committed knowingly, but if there is one that I have committed unknowingly, I beg to be forgiven."

She turned on him in exasperation. "Why do you pretend this excessive interest in all things Indian? It's so forced, so . . . so hypocritical and pretentious!"

"Pretend?" Christian was astonished and hurt. "I *am* interested! Is it unnatural to show interest in all aspects of whatever environment one happens to be in, especially one that is essentially alien?"

"Yes, it is unnatural! None of the other puk . . . English care a fig for the wretched environment, why should you?"

"That's not strictly true," Christian protested. "I know many Englishmen who are genuinely interested in India. Like me, they feel that if they are to spend the rest of their lives in a country, the least they can do is try to learn something about it."

"The rest of their lives?" Maya looked blank. "You plan to spend the rest of your life in India?"

He was nonplussed by the question. "Well, naturally—that's what it means to be in the Indian Civil Service." Seeing how taken aback she looked, he hastened to give further justifications. "One opts to sit for the competition because one has made a considered choice to live and work in India to the best of one's ability."

Maya continued to stare at him in dismay. It was an aspect of Christian Pendlebury's career that, incomprehensibly enough, she had not considered before, although she now saw that she should have. "You would leave England to live and work in India?" she inquired slowly.

"Well . . . yes. I already have." He gave a small laugh and, in an effort to lighten the atmosphere, assumed an air of flippancy. "So would you in my place, I assure you! The weather is execrable and English food is like, well, pig slop! Believe me, I'm lucky to have escaped."

"Oh."

Maya made no further comment but she was horribly shaken. Somehow, she had overlooked the fact that a Civil Service job was indeed a lifetime commitment. At the same time she saw that her inadvertent reaction had been presumptuous and uncalled for, and she was suddenly ashamed of her behaviour. Why should she be concerned *where* Christian Pendle-bury chose to spend the rest of his life? To hide her belated embarrass-ment, she quickly blurted out the first idea that came into her mind as a diversion. Would he care to look through her photograph album?

Christian was delighted to accept, relieved that the storm had passed without wreaking irreparable damage, and brightening at the prospect of being allowed intimate glimpses into the lives of the Raventhorne family members. Would she also talk of her father, show him pictures of him. . . ?

Fetching the album, Maya settled down next to him on the window seat overlooking the back garden, with the open book stretched across her lap. Dazzled by her sudden proximity, Christian dismissed the earlier debate entirely from his mind, as indeed he did every other matter. In order to explain each of the photographs, she had to sit closer to him than she had ever had occasion to before. Whiffs of her perfume regaled his nostrils each time she moved; if he shifted an inch or two more to his left, his bare arm would have brushed hers. Listening to her, feeling the soft, warm gusts of her breath on his cheek, their heads nearly touching as they pored over the neatly arranged pictures, he felt his heartbeat quicken and his palms turn damp and cold with perspiration.

With supreme effort he forced himself to concentrate on her narrative. This was Grandma Sally, her grandfather's second wife, with her two sons, Dane and Dirk, their wives and children; that was Bucktooth, a retired rodeo man who had taught her mother how to ride and look after horses, now so old that he had to be confined to a wheelchair. And this was the farmhouse in Sacramento where her Grandpa O'Rourke had lived, where her mother had been brought up and where, when they finally departed for America, they too would live. There were pictures of fields and paddocks and holidays and picnics with local friends, and many explanations with each. The family litany continued for a while with the turning of the pages, but there was no mention of Jai Raventhorne. Nor did her personal memorabilia contain any photographs of him. Even in his state of dislocation, Christian was disappointed. He was puzzled by her obvious antipathy towards her dead father. Was it only because of his notoriety as a traitor to the English cause—or was it because he was Eurasian? Naturally, this was not a question Christian could raise the courage to ask just yet, although he bristled with curiosity.

"So you still plan to go to America?" he inquired, crestfallen, as they arrived at the final page of the album. "You mentioned once that you might."

"Yes." Maya closed the album and rose to replace it in its place on her bookshelf. "Why ever should I not?"

"No reason at all," he muttered, even more downcast. He had not been as close to her as this before and her intention to leave India made her intolerably desirable. Within him rose an alarming urge to abandon cau-tion, to take her in his arms and kiss her to his heart's content, until she begged for mercy. Even the thought of his lips on hers made him tremble, but of course, he did no such thing. What if she took offence, as she had every right to? What if she sent him packing and refused to see him ever again? He bit back a frustrated groan as the effort to control his baser urges sent the blood careening to his head and made him feel dizzy.

He still could not understand why in her presence he should become so utterly befuddled, so removed from reality. He could not imagine that he had had a life before he met her; indeed, he could hardly remember the faces of his parents! He felt drugged, his intellectual faculties numbed by some mysterious opiate, but at the same time he felt his physical senses honed to an incredible pitch of sharpness. She was so different from any-one he had ever known that he could not yet quite assimilate her as a per-son, could not quite iron out the many contradictions in a personality so contrary, so incomprehensible, so bewitching.

To retain a hold on his sanity, he wrenched his thoughts away from her and launched into more impassioned justifications of his decision to remain in India, sensing that she disapproved, anxious to redeem himself in her eyes.

"I want to *understand* the people of this country," he said fervently, "to help to wipe out some of the bitterness left by the Mutiny, to show people in the villages that all Englishmen are not ogres. I want to serve India, in the noble tradition established by so many others before me."

"Yes, I understand," she murmured, not understanding at all. She was bewildered by the extent and quality of commitment of this Englishman whom she so desperately wanted to know in all his aspects, an English-man so different from any other she had met. "But civil servants in the Mofussil have duties that are arduous and exhausting, don't they, with very few luxuries to make living comfortable?"

"I don't want luxuries!" Emphatically, he dismissed the very idea with a contemptuous wave. "What I want is to be allowed to do something by which I will be remembered, like Henry Lawrence and Bartle Frere and Gordon Lumsdale, especially Gordon Lumsdale, and . . . and my father." His pink complexion shone bright, as if with an inner light. "I want to build railway lines and canals and hygienic dak bungalows, schools and hospitals and post offices. I want to plant forests and dig clean water wells and make roads safe for travellers. I want to be an English official people can actually trust as a friend and a well-wisher." Breathless with effort, he paused and stared at her with a sort of despairing defiance. "I want to be exercised to my fullest capacity, I want to be *challenged!*"

Maya sat up and stared at him, taken aback by the sheer ferocity with which he voiced his ambitions. "My goodness, you want to do all that in one lifetime?"

"Why not?" His eyes burned with the fire of missionary zeal as he pre-pared to take on the world. "Others did!"

"But I hear the duties involved in a first posting are unbelievably dull and routine," she cried, partly amused and partly alarmed by his extraor-dinary flights of fancy.

Brought down to earth with a crash, he sighed. "Yes," he said in a small voice, "but, if one is lucky, not for long."

Knowing that the thought depressed him, she continued eagerly with her dissuasions. "All you will have to do, they say, is compose endless reports, go jolting from village to dusty village settling trivial disputes out in the heat, interminably measure landholdings and haggle about revenues and mortgages. And then at night, whatever few energies you have left you will have to spend in battle with mosquitoes and those horrible creepy-crawlies that make their homes in squeaky camp cots and leaky tents out in the bogs. *Ugh!*" Her lip curled and she shuddered.

Returned once again to reality, Christian's mouth drooped further. "In the beginning, yes, I suppose so. However, as one starts to go up the ladder, the prospects do improve considerably."

"But to reach the top of that ladder could take *years*, couldn't it?"

He exhaled another, deeper sigh. "Yes," he conceded sadly. "One simply has to learn to be patient."

They had been together since he had come to fetch her for the morning ride and now it was almost lunchtime. With great reluctance, Christian decided that it was time for him to go. As it was, he had already offended the Andersons greatly by declining their invitation to accompany them to morning service at St. John's. If they happened to see him on the Raventhorne property next door to theirs, there would be all hell to pay later, and Patrick, who was sweet on Melody Anderson, would be furious with him. In any case, he had promised Lytton a game of croquet at the Club and there was also that matter of the Hindustani sentences to be prepared for the morning's tutorial.

"There is an entertainment at the Star Theatre next Saturday evening," Maya said in a sudden impulse as she saw him off at the front gate, as reluctant to let him go as he was to leave. "An English travelling company is putting on a musical revue and a friend of Mother's, Mrs. Edna Chalcott, has been kind enough to secure tickets." She lowered her eyes and blushed. "Would you be free to accompany us to the entertainment?"

She had never before suggested that they should be seen together in a public place, any more than Christian had. She was shocked and yet excited by her own daring. But with Mrs. Chalcott as chaperone, there was no risk of inviting unmanageable displeasure later, either from Amos or from her mother. And with the Anderson family no doubt also present in the audience, the evening could turn out to be doubly rewarding.

"Oh, I . . . I would have been d-delighted to," Christian stammered, flushing with pleasure and dismay at the same time, "delighted, but I have promised to spend next Saturday evening with Mr. Hawkesworth."

Maya's head jerked up. "With Kyle?"

"Yes. He sent me a chitty inviting me to inspect his press and to have high tea with him later at his home. Apparently, he has no other evening available but Saturday and I have already accepted."

She felt a stab of apprehension. "At his . . . home?"

"Yes. I had mentioned to Mr. Hawkesworth in your brother's office that I admired his writings. It is kind of him to have remembered and to invite me to tea and to inspect his press." His expression was one of remorse. "Had I but known. . . ."

166

"Oh, it doesn't matter at all." Maya put on a brave face and smiled. "There will be other occasions."

After Christian had left, however, she stood on the front steps in grim silence. She felt a sudden chill in the pit of her stomach and hugged herself, although the midday sun was blazingly hot. Kyle was going out of his way to cultivate Christian Pendlebury.

What *was* his vested interest in Christian?

"Kussowlee would be *divine* were it not for those blasted leeches!" Edna Chalcott grumbled. "Each time we returned after gypsying in the hills, we had to spend simply *hours* picking the revolting creatures off our bodies and clothing. But the climate was glorious and the hillsides covered with walnut trees and wild flowers. Regardless of leeches, we were out doors all day without the *slightest* risk of heat stroke, even at the height of summer."

"You stayed at the school?" Meeting Edna for the first time since her return from Kirtinagar, Olivia was fascinated by Edna's account of yet another indefatigable journey. This time her wanderlust had taken her on a sentimental pilgrimage to the northern Simla Hills where, many years ago, she had taught at the famous residential educational institution started by Henry Lawrence.

"Oh yes. I wouldn't dream of staying anywhere else." Edna nodded her tousled head with positive satisfaction. "It's expanded *greatly* since my day, of course. They now have over four hundred children, a chapel of pointed Gothic architecture in grey stone with cedar-pine furniture, and a separate house for the girls, also of grey stone. And Simla is, of course, as blissful as ever—except for those *dreadful* F sharps and B flats."

Olivia laughed. It was years since she had heard fleas and bedbugs described in the graphic colloquial. "I wish I could travel as easily as you, Edna," she said with a deep sigh of envy. "You've seen so much more of India than I have."

"This country has been kinder to me, perhaps, than it has to you, my dear," Edna said gently. "But why not come with me next time?" She burst into smiles and her happy blue eyes twinkled. "Winter, they say, is the *perfect* season for a holiday in the Nilgiris. We can have a really good *chutti*, eh?"

"Yes, I *would* like a holiday with you," Olivia said with a touch of wistfulness. "Well, who knows, perhaps next year—that is, if I ever return from America."

"What you really mean," Edna corrected her with a cheerful laugh, "is if you ever go at all!"

Olivia sighed. "Yes, that too."

Edna was about to say something else when the Home's Bengali matron, Didi, came hurrying in. "That man is here again," she whispered, gesticulating nervously towards the door.

"Which man?" Olivia asked.

"Sarojini's father."

"Oh dear." Olivia's heart sank. "I'm afraid that means trouble."

"Say you're out," Edna advised. "Or ask Abala to deal with him. She's good at putting people in their places."

"I can't say I'm out for a second time! He came once before I went to Cawnpore. He'll turn even more suspicious and unpleasant." Olivia made a face. "I suppose I'll have to confront him sooner or later. It might as well be now." She turned to Didi. "Has Mrs. Goswami finished with her classes?" The matron nodded. "Very well then, please show the gentleman into the front parlour and ask Mrs. Goswami and Sarojini if they would be kind enough to join us there."

"Well, good luck, dear. I too must get back to my class." Edna picked up the patchwork cloth bag without which she never went anywhere and clasped Olivia's hand in a gesture of sympathy. "I'm sorry Maya has decided against coming with me to the revue on Saturday. I'm told it's all very jolly, although rather naughty in parts." She hesitated before adding, "I should tell you that Maya asked my permission to invite her young man too on my behalf."

"Christian Pendlebury?"

"Yes. I said she could. You were still in Kirtinagar and I was sure you wouldn't mind as long as she was suitably chaperoned."

Olivia laid down her pen and shook her head. "There's not much point in minding about something the whole town is talking about," she remarked drily. "Did he accept the invitation?"

"No. It seems he has other plans for the evening, which is why Maya too has declined."

"Oh?" Olivia's smile tightened. "Cold feet, do you think?"

Edna frowned. "No. No, I wouldn't say so. If he hasn't shied away yet considering all the gossip, I shouldn't imagine a public appearance together would make much difference to him." She gave Olivia a considered look. "As I've told her many times already, Maya needs to have more friends of her age, you know. As far as I can tell, she hardly sees anyone except Grace and that too not often."

"Yes, I know." Olivia stacked her papers neatly and withdrew a comb from her handbag. "But Maya is not given to taking advice, Edna. I need hardly tell you that. She does as she pleases." She ran the comb lightly through her hair, then patted it into place and grimaced at herself in the mirror.

"I suppose it's the age," Edna said with a sigh. "They get such odd notions when they're that age, don't they?"

"With Maya it is not the age," Olivia replied slowly. "Like Jai, she too has a canker in her soul. I fear that canker will not go without exacting what it considers is its due."

Edna gave a delicate shiver. "Thank God and all my lucky stars I'm not young any more!"

Shaking off her depression, Olivia laughed. "Well, I'll certainly second that!"

There was something cosy and comforting and infectiously cheerful about Edna Chalcott, which was why she was one of the most popular workers at the Home in Chitpore. She had come to India as a child with her Welsh parents when her father had accepted an appointment in the Indian Customs Service. Contrary to prevailing practice among the colonials, she had been educated in India and had subsequently married a man who held a high position with John Company. Tragically widowed almost twenty years ago while still in her early thirties when her husband perished in a boating accident, she had chosen to stay on in India although her parents were dead and her brothers and sisters long returned to England. A man of private means, her husband had left her fairly comfortable, with an adequate income and a double-storeyed house on Dharamtala Street. She let out rooms to boarders to augment what she called her "escape fund," which allowed her to indulge her lust for travel. Edna had volunteered her services at the Chitpore Home even before it was fully operational and had remained ever since. She had become a close and dear friend of Olivia and, in her own words, "godmother emeritus" to Maya and Amos. It was sad that she had no children of her own; Edna Chalcott was one of those women born to be a mother.

With a final wave in Edna's direction, Olivia cast aside the troublesome matter of her daughter and quickly made her way downstairs. She had not yet met Sarojini's father, but from what she had heard she gathered that he was mean-tempered, self-opinionated and extremely stubborn. It was a great relief that Abala was still on the premises to provide badly needed moral and physical support.

The man awaiting her with ill-concealed impatience in the front parlour where visitors were received was well built, immaculately dressed and of patrician appearance. Olivia was surprised; she had expected someone far less sophisticated. Her courage slipped a little further.

"I am Nalini Chandra Ganguly, Sarojini's father, by profession a lawyer." He introduced himself curtly but politely enough with folded hands. "I have come to take my daughter home." He fixed an unwavering gaze on the young girl who crept in through the doorway fearfully behind Olivia and positioned herself in a corner with her eyes lowered.

"Certainly." Motioning him into a chair, Olivia made a signal to the girl to come and sit beside her on the settee, hoping that Abala would join them soon. In sensitive matters involving caste or religious customs and social traditions which the Home came up against from time to time, Abala Goswami, with her emancipated beliefs and outspoken manner, was an invaluable ally. "If Sarojini wishes to return, she is quite free to do so."

The visitor had addressed her in English. If he was surprised that Olivia chose to reply in Bengali, he did not show it. Nevertheless, he too switched to the regional language. "*Wishes* to return?" He smiled and raised an eyebrow. "Sarojini's wishes, surely, have little to do with the matter. I am her father. Do I not have the right to take my child home when I wish?"

"Sarojini is hardly a child, Nalini Babu," Olivia pointed out, but taking good care to match his show of cordiality. "She is of age and competent to make her own decisions."

A faint spark of anger kindled in his dark, arrogant eyes. "And how do you conclude that someone who has never made even a simple decision for herself in her life is suddenly competent to assume full charge of her destiny?"

To Olivia's great relief, Samir's mother arrived just then, preventing her from making an unnecessarily tart response. A moment or two was taken up with introductions. Nalini Chandra, it transpired, was acquainted with Kali Charan Goswami, and declared himself a great admirer of a man gifted with remarkable entrepreneurial skills, a leader among the Indian merchant community. Abala acknowledged the compliment with an impatient nod of her head, after which the conversation returned to the subject of Sarojini.

Turning to the girl, Abala asked without further preamble, "Do you wish to return to your parents' home, Sarojini?" After only brief hesitation and without raising her eyes, the girl shook her head.

Visibly angered by her response, her father struggled to contain a clearly volatile temper. Adroitly, Abala used the hiatus to her own advantage. "Sarojini has come to us of her own free will, Nalini Babu," she said rather more gently. "As you are aware, the life she has been forced to lead as the sixth—or is it seventh?—wife of a man more than twice her age has been quite wretched."

"She has shamed her family and her community by running away from a home to which she has been committed," he answered coldly, emphasising each word with a tap on the floor with his stick.

"The commitment was made by you, Nalini Babu, not by her," Abala pointed out, a small glint appearing in her own eyes. "And that too without her consent, when she was not even fifteen. If she was driven to run away and seek asylum with us, it was because she was not certain of being accepted back by her own kith and kin."

He rose and went to stand by the window, his back towards them. "Do you deny then that a Hindu wife's duty lies with her husband's family?"

"Her husband is dead. She has no children. As a widow, she has been subjected to gross ill-treatment by her late husband's other wives and her in-laws. She ran away because she was being beaten and had actually started to fear for her life."

"It is her karma. . . ."

"To live like a slave and eventually be beaten to death?" He did not reply and Abala again changed her tactics to turn persuasive. "Surely you love your daughter enough to wish to see her happy, Nalini Babu? She has already suffered eleven years of misery which she did not deserve. Fortunately, Sarojini is still young enough to. . . ."

"No!" He spun around, his expression one of outrage. "I have been hearing rumours that your Home is bent upon encouraging some vile, abhorrent practices. I came here today hoping to find that these rumours are inaccurate. I now suspect strongly that they are not." He turned away again and, in an effort to control his fury, crossed his arms and tucked his hands under his armpits. "Sarojini is a Hindu Brahmin widow. She cannot and *will* not be permitted to remarry. I would rather she had plunged into her husband's funeral pyre and become suttee than bring shame and calumny to her community with a sinful second marriage."

Behind his intractable back heaving with anger, Olivia and Abala exchanged glances. "Sarojini is twenty-six years old," Olivia re-entered the argument. "If she so wishes, she now has a legal right to remarry. As a lawyer, you must surely be aware of that. If she has not so far made decisions for herself, it is simply because she has never been permitted to."

He turned to subject her to an enraged, insolent stare. "There is a great difference between your Christian customs and our orthodox Hindu beliefs, Mrs. Raventhorne," he said with glacial scorn. "I consider it inadvisable for a foreigner to interfere in the way we choose to live in our own country."

"The Widows' Remarriage Act was passed in 1856 at the behest of Indian reformers."

"Indian reformers, bah! We God-fearing Brahmins do not. . . ."

"I am as much a Brahmin as you are, Nalini Babu," Abala cut in acidly. "Wherever they might originate, beliefs that accept the exploitation and denigration of women are to me, and surely to every decent human being, obnoxious. I am disappointed that a man belonging to the legal profession, a highly educated *bhadralok* such as you, should profess to believe otherwise."

He flushed with angry colour at the reprimand. "It is *because* I am a highly educated gentleman that I am aghast, scandalised at your intentions!" He was about to say more, but then, suddenly tiring of the argument, he dismissed it with a gesture of contempt. "However, let us come to the point instead of wasting time in futile debate. I have my beliefs, you have yours. What concerns me now is this conspiracy to involve my family in a practice we consider utterly insupportable!"

"Hardly a conspiracy," Olivia retorted, taking the girl's trembling hand in hers and pressing it in reassurance. "The decision to remarry, this time the man of her choice, is Sarojini's own, without any interference from us. Indeed, you arranged her first marriage, she tells us, with the sole intention of separating her from this man to whom she had formed an early attachment."

Ignoring Olivia, he strode furiously towards the settee and, for the first time, addressed his daughter directly. "Is this true, Sarojini?" he thundered.

Once again Olivia squeezed the terrified girl's hand and, without raising her head, the girl nodded.

"How can you *think* of belittling us, your own people, in the eyes of our community, you selfish, brazen hussy?" He was beside himself with rage. "That scoundrel is not even of our caste! He is nothing but *dirt*, a . . . a base, low-down opportunist!" Choking on his own rage, he started to splutter.

Olivia glanced at Abala. A signal passed between them and they both rose. "I think, in all fairness, your father should have the opportunity to speak to you alone, Sarojini," Olivia said. White-faced with fright, the girl pleaded silently with her eyes, but Olivia shook her head. "No, my dear, if you have a conviction, you must also have the courage to act upon it. You owe it to your family to at least be honest with them." She turned to Nalini Chandra, her expression grim. "It would be wise and compassionate of you to accede to your daughter's wishes and willingly participate in her decision, Nalini Babu. However," her tone hardened, "if you attempt to intimidate her in any way whatsoever, or try to remove her by force, we will have no option left but to lodge a complaint on her behalf with the appropriate authorities."

Outside in the compound where a handsome fountain sprayed cool, pale green water on the surrounds, Olivia leaned against a pillar and gulped to lubricate her dry mouth, relieved that the unpleasant confrontation was over, at least for the moment. Her gaze, nevertheless, remained fixed to the door of the front parlour in case the girl called for help. For all his pretensions to education and respectability, she knew that Nalini Chandra Ganguly would not be above using violence against his daughter to force his own will upon her.

"I fear we will have to send Sarojini away to some safe place if he threatens more trouble," Abala said, worried. "He has considerable clout in his community, and most orthodox Hindus do feel very strongly against widow remarriage."

"Well, perhaps it is understandable," Olivia replied with a sigh. "One cannot wipe away the beliefs of centuries through mere paper legislation. Maybe his natural love for his daughter will eventually overcome his prejudices," she added, but without much conviction.

"I don't trust this man," Abala said. "The law, after all, is a double-edged sword. When it comes to religious emotions, even magistrates fight shy of pronouncing judgements they privately consider radical and subversive. If we do have to send the girl away, have you any thoughts as to where she might be kept safely?"

"Yes. We could send her to Kirtinagar. I have already spoken to the Maharani. She will be discreet and understanding of the girl's problem. She will ensure that Sarojini is well protected."

Anger still glowed in Abala Goswami's stormy eyes. "Why do people make their children victims of their own wretched bigotry?" she cried fiercely, thumping a clenched fist against her palm. "Oh, how I hate all this hypocrisy that makes us exploit tradition as a convenient camouflage for our own cowardice!"

The press, situated in a high-ceilinged, cavernous structure of mature years, had once, Kyle Hawkesworth informed Christian, been a *nilkothi*— an indigo planter's premises. The walls and flagstone floor still carried a sort of patchwork of faded blue stains, even though they had no doubt been scrubbed and scoured many times during the past several decades.

Indeed, a blue-tinged haze seemed to hang permanently in the atmosphere of the hall, giving it an air that was rather sepulchral, although by no means unpleasant.

As he escorted Christian Pendlebury around his premises, Kyle made detailed explanations about the many time-consuming processes that went into producing a periodical on a virtual shoestring. Several times he asked for Christian's opinion and listened attentively to his replies, his dark eyes intent, his forehead creased with concentration. Christian could not deny that he was flattered by the attention Kyle lavished on him, by the importance he appeared to give to his opinions. With an inward smile he put down the attentiveness—and, indeed, the invitation to tea—to his host's desire to make reparation for his excessive rudeness during their initial encounter. Privately, Christian applauded the effort as a generous gesture. Nevertheless he remained wary, prepared for the sudden taunt, the pointed barb. However, apart from some excusable causticisms about Christian's English compatriots and the general asininity of the British bureaucracy they subscribed to, there were none. Kyle's mood was mellow, his manner expansive and comparatively courteous.

With much evidence of the financial constraints under which it operated, the printing establishment was essentially modest. Yet it appeared to Christian to have subtle undertones of a dynamism that could not be missed. This he saw in the eager faces of the workers, in their confident, well-coordinated movements, and in the energy and silent industry with which they applied themselves to their separate duties, oblivious of the presence of a visitor. In his imagination he sensed behind the commonplace exterior a determined force, a power unseen but still very tangible. A stringently run journal, challenging and radical, dedicated to a cause as distasteful to the formidable British establishment as the Eurasian situation, seemed to Christian a symbol of something noble that reached far beyond four bare walls and outmoded printing machinery.

"We use the stereotype system of printing." Kyle pointed to a ponderous machine that clattered and clacked with rattling regularity. "As you can see, the plates are fixed onto these cylinders for continuous printing." He had, he confided, been lucky to be able to buy the unit and its accessories from a Danish missionary's printing shop in Serampore. The man had imported a newer European model and so disposed of the old one at a very reasonable discounted price.

In an area behind a wooden partition, two foundrymen fashioned typefaces to compensate for frequent breakages. Nearby, a compositor worked with his sectioned box of metal pieces placed on a sloping pedestal, his left hand holding the composing stick, his right picking out and positioning in it the required typefaces. Christian watched with interest as the man's fingers flew back and forth, brows furrowed and eyes unwavering in their concentration. There were altogether about six or seven workers, and all of them, Christian observed, bore varying physiognomic indications of mixed blood, their complexions ranging between the very fair and the swarthy.

"It's an irritatingly slow method of typesetting," Kyle was saying, "but the only one available at present. Abroad they're experimenting with linotypes, automatic typecasting machines, but who knows when they will become available to us here." He shrugged, obviously not particularly concerned with purely mechanical improvements. Engrossed in his own thoughts, Christian nodded absently, only half listening to the technical explanations. With his gaze fixed on the compositor, through a corner of his eye he observed his host with great intensity, trying to assess to his own satisfaction the enigmatic man through whom he hoped to learn more fully the "mind" of that Eurasian India that weighed so heavily upon his conscience.

Hawkesworth ran his magazine, Christian had learned from Trevors, with his own money. In his determined bid to remain independent, he refused to accept contributions from anyone, even his best friend, Amos Raventhorne. Where he got his funds was a mystery, for it was well known that Hawkesworth himself was not a man of grand means and printing a magazine, however modest, was a highly expensive occupation.

They had come to the end of their tour of inspection. As they stepped into the brightly sunlit compound that separated the press from the residence, Christian made some flippant remark about the eeriness of the huge space occupied by the printing machinery and equipment.

"Well, it is believed to be haunted," Kyle said. "The spirit of the indigo planter, a Dutchman, returns periodically, they say, to take inventory of his invisible indigo stocks. This is why we haven't been able to get rid of those stains on the walls and floor."

"Oh, really?" Christian did not hide his amusement. "Have you yourself ever encountered the worthy gent?"

"No, but some of my workers have."

There was something in Kyle's tone that arrested Christian's flippancy. "You believe in ghosts, Mr. Hawkesworth?" he asked with an uncertain smile.

Kyle remained grave and unsmiling. "Oh yes. Absolutely. Don't you?"

Christian was taken aback by the question, only half convinced that he was being teased. "Well, I don't really know."

"You should," Kyle said, still quite serious. "Ghosts are very much a living part of our daily realities, Mr. Pendlebury. In India, especially, spirits enjoy a fundamental right to return and walk freely in order to settle old scores whenever so inclined." While Christian was still trying to digest this extraordinary pronouncement, Kyle pointed to the floor and tapped it lightly with the heel of his knee boot. "Underneath this at one time lay a secret tunnel that connected the warehouse to the Hooghly. It was allegedly excavated in the eighteenth century by a smuggler who used it to store his contraband."

"Have you explored the tunnel?" Christian asked, a little breathless with all this exotica.

"No. It is now completely blocked and unpassable. Come," he placed a light hand on Christian's arm, "let us go to the house and continue our conversation over a cup of tea. There is much that we have to talk about."

Ghosts, secret tunnels, smugglers, contraband! Ye gods, what next? Christian's head whirled with the romantic esoterica, but none of it surprised him. Indeed, he was thoroughly enjoying every moment of it. The nonconformity of Kyle's premises seemed to fit in perfectly with the eccentric personality of the man himself. It was not a personality that Christian could grasp yet—a mask behind a mask. But in time, he had no doubt that he would, and he was exhilarated at the prospect. That the man was a rebel and a defiant radical bothered Christian not at all. In the generally dreary panorama of Calcutta's stilted colonial society that he had seen so far, Kyle Hawkesworth seemed to stand out like a basilisk, sharp and tall and incisive, and Christian looked forward enormously to a relationship that would be all the more stimulating for its unorthodoxy.

The sumptuous high tea consisting of a dozen aromatic Indian delicacies, still unfamiliar to Christian, was served in a room he presumed to be Kyle's study. Like the front parlour they had passed through, this too was sparsely furnished, its predominant features an oversized mahogany desk littered with papers, folders and open books, and glass-fronted bookcases that lined two walls from floor to ceiling. In one corner there was a cursory but adequate seating arrangement of some cane chairs around a marble-topped table with ornate wrought-iron legs. As they made themselves comfortable, servants appeared bearing plates of far more food than could possibly be consumed by two people.

Although the appearance of the room was spartan, the austerity was somewhat compensated for by its extreme neatness. Apart from the littered desk, everything else was arranged with an almost feminine instinct for order. This surprised Christian. He would not have thought of Kyle as a particularly tidy man. In fact, his clothes were carelessly worn, chosen obviously out of habit for comfort and practicality rather than in deference to any sartorial dictates. Dark brown cotton cord trousers encased his long legs; a matching jacket, slightly threadbare at the elbows, was carelessly thrown over a striped shirt with a buttoned-down collar. The bright red silk cravat was, Christian felt, a concession to the occasion, and in a small way he was flattered. Kyle's unusual hair colouring reminded Christian of some exotic geological stratification in a rockface, its dark brown blending well with streaks of several lighter tones. Christian had not seen hair like that on anyone before; it added to the man's general air of unconventionality. Usually tousled, more used to being combed with impatient fingers than with any implement devised for the purpose, it was today smooth and brushed well back from a high, pale forehead, to curl neatly at the nape, perhaps another polite concession to Christian's presence.

A dozen questions of a strictly personal nature sprang to Christian's mind, but naturally he did not voice them. According to Trevors, Kyle Hawkesworth was a bachelor who lived alone but was well attended to by a host of young Eurasian boys of poor means for whom he provided work and sanctuary. Being a flamboyant, volatile and attractive man, he was certainly not celibate, although he scoffed at the idea of becoming, as he put it, a pet husband on the leash of some diabolical mother and daughter combination. Understandably, he was admired by ladies of every hue—black, white, yellow, brown and brindle—not caring to conceal his frequent liaisons, even less bothered by how they were dissected or disseminated by wagging tongues. It was hardly surprising that his affairs should be common knowledge in this imperial city with the mentality of a village, where inquisitiveness was considered a necessary virtue in the cause of social survival.

The scattered touches of feminine care in Kyle's home nevertheless intrigued Christian. A small bowl of magenta flowers embellished a window sill; an obviously homemade rag and tinsel puppet hung from a shining brass curtain rail; in the bookcases, volumes had been arranged in neat formation according to size and height. Whiffs of rose attar assailed the nostrils occasionally, and the room itself was spotlessly clean. Either Kyle was fortunate to have exceptionally gifted servants, or there was some lady in residence resolutely priming a future "pet husband" for a leash already woven and waiting somewhere behind the scenes. The thought brought a smile to Christian's lips, which he quickly concealed behind a hand.

A servant approached: discarding his introspections, Christian eagerly helped himself to another samosa. He was beginning to feel relaxed and comfortable, responding visibly to the warmth of such generous hospitality.

"Is this where you write your features?" he asked, realising with a small thrill that those scribbled notes lying scattered across the desk probably contained the makings of another incendiary editorial. Like all of Kyle's writings, this one too would probably be received with equal parts of outrage and approval by various communities, the subject of hot debate at clubs and sundry *burra khanas*. At a recent Sunday cricket match on the Maidan in which Christian had scored an impressive century as an opening batsman for a Fort William eleven, two young spectators had almost come to blows over the editorial and had had to be forcibly escorted off the grounds.

"Here and everywhere," Kyle said in response to his question. "One writes with the mind, not necessarily with pen in hand."

"Yes, of course." Christian pondered a moment, then asked with studied caution, "Do you consider that you can achieve through your magazine what your bannerhead suggests?"

"Equality?" Kyle shrugged. "The name of the game is surely effort, is it not?"

"But the establishment will not relent easily, no matter how great the effort. At least, that is what I deduced from all the shocking facts revealed at the Derozio meeting."

"Even a wall, however extensive or thick or tall, is composed only of individual bricks."

Christian was surprised at Kyle's mild responses, the offhandedness of his manner. "Meaning?"

"Meaning that every massive entity has individual components that are less massive."

"But from what I gathered at the meeting," Christian said earnestly, "it is the law that is at fault in its perpetuation of injustice. The changes needed to remedy the situation are surely draconian."

"Precisely. Therefore it is towards the lawmakers that our efforts must be directed."

"How?"

Kyle laughed. "Have you ever seen how they trap a tiger in the jungle at a shikar?"

"No."

"They beat drums around it to drive it into a corner of their choice and then shoot it."

"And you believe you can beat them into a corner with *words?*" Christian asked with an astonished laugh.

"What else?" Kyle spread his hands. "I have no other weapons to wield." He paused before adding, "Except perhaps. . . ." He did not complete the sentence.

Something in Kyle's tone intrigued Christian as he nibbled at a savoury biscuit. "Except perhaps—what?"

Kyle leant forward. "I wonder that you didn't gather something else at the Derozio meeting, a rather curious paradox."

Brows knitted, Christian remained silent as he waited for more.

Making a pyramid of his fingers against his chest, Kyle stared at the ceiling. "Consider this, my friend: the Eurasian hates the Anglo-Saxon, yet it is with precisely this race that he is obsessed. However much he raves and rants and curses and implores, whether he is angry or accusing or apologetic or admiring or merely proselytising, it is this very Anglo-Saxon who remains at the focal point of his existence. Does that not strike you as curious?"

"Well yes, now that you mention it. But is this obsession not self-defeating?" Christian asked, confused.

Kyle swung forward in his chair, his ebony eyes glittering. "Never underestimate the value of an obsession, my friend," he said softly. "It is an emotional navigational aid, a *beacon,* if you like, that gives direction to one's life, one of the few things that is entirely one's own. To a Eurasian, it is a life force without which he would be lost, aimless and adrift and entirely rudderless. It is this obsession that is his greatest strength, and perhaps, in the final analysis, also his greatest weakness." He sat back and smiled. "Now, have I not succeeded in confusing you thoroughly?"

"Thoroughly!" Christian shook his head and joined in the smile. "Tell me, were you always good with words? I mean, even when you were a child?"

Kyle shrugged. "Who knows? I never really had occasion to find out."

"But your parents must have noticed?"

"Parents?" Kyle interposed, genuinely amused. "These days Eurasians can't always take even one parent for granted, my friend. To claim two would be an unforgivable exercise in cupidity! You might even say that some of us are the only truly immaculate conceptions of this world."

Christian gulped. "F-forgive me, I am so dreadfully sorry. . . ." He was as distressed by his unthinking faux pas as he was by Kyle's corroding cynicism.

"Don't apologise." Kyle waved a dismissive hand and held out a plate of sweet white cakes made of thickened milk and nuts which were quite delicious. "It must be difficult for you to envisage a situation you have never met. Anyway, talking of parents *per se*," he cocked his head to one side, "it must please you that your own are soon to be with you in Calcutta?"

Relieved at the change of subject, Christian did not ask how Kyle had come by information still not fully public. According to Trevors, although Hawkesworth disdained politics and professed contempt for politicians, he had ready means of knowing everything that went on in government circles.

"Yes."

If there was marked lack of enthusiasm in Christian's response, Kyle made the concession of appearing not to notice it. Instead, he lifted the teapot off a tray the servant had placed before him and engrossed himself in the business of pouring out two cups of tea. There was an incongruity in the act that amused Christian, but Kyle performed it with meticulous attention, brows drawn together, eyes unmoving. When the milk and sugar had been added in accordance with their respective tastes and the tea satisfactorily stirred, he daintily dabbed a napkin over two brown drops that had spilled onto the white marble-topped table. Explaining that the aromatic brew came from the mountainsides of Darjeeling where a planter friend was experimenting with tea cultivation, he handed Christian a cup. The matter of Christian's imminent reunion with his parents seemed to have been forgotten for the moment.

"What made you choose the Indian Civil Service as a career?"

Christian sipped and gave a nod of appreciation. "Well, my father was in India during the fifties. I was fascinated with the stories he brought home with him. They seemed so . . . otherworldly, so removed from our own bovine existence in all its parochial predictability. When I was older, I used to sit and absolutely devour the newspapers that arrived for him from here. To explore the tantalising esoterica of India, to comprehend its ancient civilisation, to . . . to be in tune with its *heartbeat*—this became my obsession and it remains with me still." He sat back laughing shyly, embarrassed at having given such free rein to his enthusiasm.

Kyle smiled, possibly at his young guest's luminescent sincerity. "And your parents approved of your choice of career?"

The corners of Christian's mouth turned noticeably downward as he stared into his cup. "Well, my father did, but my mother had set her heart on my acceptance of an appointment in Whitehall, possibly in the India Secretariat."

"And that didn't appeal to you?"

"No, it did *not*," Christian said very emphatically. "I wanted to be here in person, not a blasted pen-pushing cipher ten thousand miles away composing official gobbledegook in triplicate!"

Kyle laughed. "You never had occasion to visit India while your father was here? Or even later, after he had left?"

"No. There was nothing I would have liked better, but Mama refused to allow my education to be disrupted, either at Eton or later at Oxford. She believed, quite wrongly of course, that I was too young to be subjected to the rigours of tropical living. She still does." He made a wry face. "I think you better than anyone must be aware of the ignorance and prejudice that form the cornerstone of English attitudes as far as this subcontinent is concerned—even more so since the Mutiny."

Kyle's eyebrow rose a fraction but he said nothing.

For a moment Christian brooded darkly over what he had just said, then added to it. "I can still remember how shocked I was when I was finally old enough to read what had been printed in the English-language newspapers both at home and here about the Mutiny. Some of the accounts, especially of the Cawnpore massacre, put to shame even the savage journals of Herbert and Marat written at the time of the French Revolution. Yet they were accepted as gospel by many of us. I've read blatantly inflammatory exhortations inciting white colonials to murder every Hindu and Muslim as a rebel and a potential traitor, as if—as Trevelyan pointed out—India had but one neck and all the hemp in the country could be twisted into but one rope with which to hang it." His face glowed red with the warmth of righteous indignation. "And they have the nerve to call your editorials seditious?"

Kyle nodded, the smile lingering on his lips and his manner still surprisingly mild. "But what you read obviously did not weaken your own determination to come to India?"

"No." Christian's jaw firmed. "On the contrary, it reinforced it."

Kyle nodded again, his eyes solemn. "But then there are canards perpetrated by both sides in every war of attrition."

"Yes, but. . . ."

Holding up a finger, Kyle cut him off before the argument could proceed. "There are also men of rare courage who sometimes come forward to *expose* these fictions. Men like"—breaking off, he rose, walked to a bookcase, and after a moment's search, returned with a slim volume which he tossed on the table in front of Christian—"Edward Leckey."

Christian picked up the book and examined the title: *Fictions Connected with the Indian Outbreak of 1857 Exposed.* The date of publication was 1859. "Who was Leckey, a Eurasian?"

"No. He was English, obviously an intrepid man of conscience. He demolishes mischief-makers on both sides, many of them his own countrymen. One compatriot Lecky exposes rather mercilessly is the venerable Earl of Shaftesbury."

"I say, does he really? The same Shaftesbury who crusaded so ardently for the poor in England?"

"The same."

Christian chuckled. "Well, then, how the devil was Leckey allowed to get away with such barefaced *lèse-majesté?*"

"He wasn't. The poor man eventually paid the ultimate price English justice could exact."

"My God, they hanged him?" Christian was outraged.

"No. They had him blackballed by his Club."

Christian threw back his head and roared with laughter. But then, determined not to abandon the debate, he quickly sobered and returned to the subject of the Mutiny. "All right, I concede that there were canards and atrocities on both sides. I also accept that there were, no doubt, many Englishmen and many natives who retained their sense of perspective and remained sane and clearheaded. But you can't deny that what really triggered off the violence was not sepoy malcontent but *our* provocative policies."

"Oh?"

The inflection of the single syllable seemed to call for an amplification and, flattered, Christian was only too eager to provide it. "Those Enfield rifles, for example, the insufferable arrogance of many British officers and, in the final analysis, the disastrous annexation of Oudh." He broke off, suddenly uncomfortable, as if having said something he had not intended to. "Well . . . there was a series of blunders committed at the time, wasn't there?" he muttered, his cheeks again pink. Replacing his cup, he took his time to wipe clean the corners of his mouth with his napkin. Then he leant forward in his seat. "There is something that I have been wanting to ask you."

"Yes?"

"I would like to learn more about Jai Raventhorne."

"Ah, I was wondering when we would come to that! Well, what would you like to know?"

"According to the records of the Military Department of the Government of India, he was hanged for his . . . complicity in the Cawnpore massacre."

"Let's just say that he was hanged, yes."

Christian pondered a moment. "Tell me honestly. In your opinion, was he guilty as charged?"

"He was never charged. Nor tried, for that matter. He was simply lynched." Shocked at the use of the word, Christian blanched. "Was he guilty?" Kyle's tone changed; it was no longer mild and unprovocative and his eyes shone with inner fire. "If it is treason to want an alien plunderer out of your country, then yes, Jai Raventhorne was guilty. If not, he was a man of exceptional conviction and courage, a true martyr who eventually laid down his life for his beliefs."

Christian was taken aback by the depth of Kyle's passion. "You admire what Jai Raventhorne did?"

"I admire what Jai Raventhorne *was*, more than any other man, before or since."

"But the Nana Sahib was a monster, an inhuman fiend!" Christian spoke with equal feeling. "And Raventhorne is alleged to have supported him to the hilt. How do you explain that?"

"I don't. Neither do others. Therein lies the great enigma of Jai Raventhorne, my friend. The day that mystery is resolved will be the day that the innocence of Jai Raventhorne is established."

"You are convinced that he *was* innocent of that massacre?"

"Absolutely! There are thousands of other Indians, even many of your own countrymen, who believe that Raventhorne was incapable of committing a crime so heinous, so utterly out of character. Indeed, it is not only the Raventhorne family who have been battling to have his innocence acknowledged, it is his entire community, a community that still reveres him as a hero of the people. There are many who would give almost anything to see Jai Raventhorne proven innocent."

"Would you?"

"Yes." Kyle's answer came without hesitation. "I would lay down my life for it."

Christian regarded him curiously. "You knew him personally?"

"No. But I saw him several times in Lucknow and I knew of his reputation. Hardly anyone of Eurasian and British extraction did not or, for that matter, does not today. And, of course, I have known Amos and his family for several years."

Christian stared intently at his feet and shuffled a little in his chair. "Some people . . . ah, close to Jai Raventhorne refuse to believe in his innocence," he mumbled, refusing to meet Kyle's eyes.

Kyle made no effort to hide his amusement. "If by 'some people' you mean Maya Raventhorne," he commented drily, "yes, she subscribes openly to the theory that her father was guilty."

Blushing furiously, Christian continued, "But *why*, if, as you say, he was not, could not have been guilty?"

"The British believed that he was," Kyle replied with cutting scorn, "and there are many, including Raventhorne's daughter, who consider British justice to be sacred, as inviolate as a virgin's chastity-belt."

"But you still cannot deny that Raventhorne was in sympathy with the Nana Sahib, any more than you can deny the testimony of those two army officers who captured and then executed him near the Ghat, a testimony that is on record?"

"Jai Raventhorne was a patriot," Kyle retorted with a return of the sharpness. "He did what he believed to be right." He swung forward to pincer Christian with a look that was suddenly very alert. "*Exactly* as your father did in Oudh!"

Christian straightened with an involuntary jerk and his eyes widened. For a moment he said nothing, then he remarked stiffly, "I may not see eye to eye with my father on many political issues, Mr. Hawkesworth, but nonetheless I admire him as a man of undiluted single-mindedness and implicit honesty. I have never known my father to perform *any* act that could be called dishonourable. He participated with General Outram in the deposition of the King of Oudh because he believed that it was his duty to do as commanded."

"But my dear fellow, of course!" Kyle cried, throwing his hands up in the air with another lightning change of mood. "Your father is renowned as a man of unimpeachable integrity! Whatever reservations one might have about the annexation of the state of Oudh and the summary dismissal of its ruler, no one would deny that, as an Assistant Commissioner, your father fulfilled his duties with exemplary dedication."

Thrown off balance by the unexpected compliments, Christian again looked uncertain. "Well, I have always chosen to believe so, however miscalculated the deed. . . ."

Kyle lifted the teapot to refresh Christian's cup, waving aside his pleas of sufficiency. "As a matter of fact, I personally hold your father in great esteem, Christian—I may call you that, may I not? His thirst for learning, I believe, was unquenchable, perhaps still is. During his posting in Lucknow, I was told, he became a scholar of Oriental philosophy and taught himself Sanskrit and Persian in order to better pursue his studies in the original languages." He picked up a bowl of sweets and extended it in Christian's direction. "One more Lady Canning, perhaps?"

Christian debated for a moment, then decided to accept the offer. "Lady Canning!" he laughed. "Isn't that rather an odd name for a sweetmeat?"

"I suppose it is. It was devised by an enterprising Bengali chef when she was Vicereine during and just after the Mutiny."

There was a momentary silence as Christian munched with relish, enjoying the succulence of the delicacy. "I don't agree that they are over-rich and too sweet," he mused, recalling Maya's comment, "I think they are quite perfect. Anyway, you were saying?"

"I was remarking on the commendable diversity of your father's unusual accomplishments. Apart from his scholarship, he was well known in Lucknow's intellectual circles for his appreciation of the Indian arts. I'm told he was a frequent guest at performances of classical music and dance at the court of Oudh. Before Nawab Wajid Ali Shah was sent packing, of course."

Christian was surprised but by no means displeased. "How do you know so much about my father?"

Kyle spread his hands and smiled. "Your father was a gifted public figure, as well known in Lucknow as were General James Outram and, later, Henry Lawrence. There must have been few in the Oudh capital who had not heard of Jasper Montague Pendlebury, the elegant, urbane and rather dashing officer of the East India Company." He rose to fetch a brass box from his desk, opened it and offered Christian a cheroot. Christian declined politely. Taking one himself, Kyle sat down again. "Your father is a man who has earned the admiration of many, including myself."

Christian stared. "But I thought you considered all Englishmen to be invaders and intruders as a matter of principle."

Kyle lit his cheroot and inhaled deeply. "My dear fellow, you are invaders and intruders, make no mistake about that! No matter what justification you attempt, British presence in this country is an invasion, an intrusion. As such, I heartily endorse people like Jai Raventhorne who gave up their lives to try to rid India of the white scourge. Certainly there is much about your compatriots that I do despise fervently, but at the same time, despite all that is to be abhorred about your race, there is still much that one cannot help but admire. The English have so much that we ourselves lack—a genetic sense of discipline, a flair for meticulous documentation, a practical reverence for antiquity, passionate devotion to order and—as long as it does not hurt one of their own—fair play. It is their collective thirst for self-expression that has made the English language graphic and receptive, a language capable of producing the most exquisite and matchless treasury of literature in the world. And it is, after all, the English who, with a skill amounting to genius, have refined into a perfect art form the pursuit and process of enlightened self-interest." Tilting his head to one side, Kyle surveyed Christian through a haze of blue smoke. "All these can scarcely go unapplauded, my friend, even by the most ardent of nationalists."

"And where does my father fit into all this?" Christian cried, fascinated by the rhetoric.

Kyle laid his head back against the chair rest and released a succession of smoke rings into the air, adding to the blue haze. They floated upwards like spectral ballerinas, then shivered away into nothingness. "In the midst of the crass and the mediocre and the deplorably pedestrian, Christian, there stands out a small breed of Englishmen that has succeeded in breaking through the constraints of blinkered prejudice, that has striven to rise above the humdrum and cast off the yoke of the socially trivial, the offensively conventional and the trite. I consider your father to be one of this rare breed, a pukka and a gentleman."

Christian was overwhelmed, so much so that for a moment or two he could say nothing. Then to cover his embarrassment at such lavish compliments to his father, he asked quickly, "Tell me, Kyle, what precisely is the meaning of this word *pukka* that I hear everywhere? I have had so many explanations that I am really quite confused."

Kyle chuckled. "Precisely, it is difficult to define the word. It's an elusive little fellow, impossible to pin down. But imprecisely, there are many interpretations. Literally, *pukka* means 'ripe,' as a fruit might be. Also 'strong' or 'firm'—for example, a concrete structure as opposed to a thatched hut. For the rest, I suppose you could translate it as 'thorough' or 'complete' or, loosely speaking, even 'perfect.' "

"And this is why many call Englishmen pukkas?" Christian asked in astonishment.

"Regretfully no." Kyle's eyes twinkled briefly. "When used for Englishmen, the word starts to play tricks. Originally it is a contraction of *pukka sahib,* a pure *firanghi* as opposed to a Eurasian. Nowadays, *pukka* tends to be a little less than complimentary, one of those terms that, through sheer colloquial usage, has turned derogatory without logical explanation." He got up. "If I started to give you a lesson in the vagaries of Indian English, my friend, I fear that you would have to spare me a good six months, time that neither you nor I can afford."

Seeing that he was being dismissed, Christian hastily rose to leave, although reluctant to abandon so stimulating an evening. He cast a last look at the book by Edward Leckey still lying open on the table.

"Take it, if you wish." Kyle said. "I think you will enjoy it." He waved his hand at his well-filled bookcases. "Are there any others you would like to borrow?"

It was not an offer Christian could refuse.

Presently, his arms laden with a selection of volumes, Christian reluctantly took leave of his host with many expressions of gratitude. "I would be delighted to come again, if I may, whenever you find time for another afternoon of discussion. And, since you express such admiration for my father, would you care to be introduced to him when he arrives?"

"There is nothing that I would like better," Kyle answered softly, "believe me!" Then, cocking his head to one side, he murmured something that Christian found very strange indeed. "Be careful, my friend. You tread a slippery path and you are inadequately shod."

As he walked slowly up the embankment on his way back to the chummery, Christian repeated the curious parting remark to himself several times, but he could not quite grasp its meaning. Then he shrugged and cast it out of his mind. The truth was that his brain swirled with a flurry of *bon mots*, lingering phrases and fragments from his extensive conversations with Kyle. It had been a marvellously entertaining and invigorating afternoon, and he had enjoyed it greatly. More than anything else, however, he was hugely pleased with Kyle's high praise of his father. The imminent advent of his parents in the city at this delicate juncture of his life did not particularly inspire Christian. Nevertheless, he fiercely admired and loved his father. Despite their often divergent views on colonial politics, in Christian's eyes Jasper Pendlebury remained a paragon of every virtue he would like to see in himself as a civil servant—and one day hoped to. Kyle's generous endorsements of his father pleased him greatly. He accepted them at face value.

Christian was not to realise until much later that he should not have done so.

8

T HEIR FIRST SIGHT of the Suez Canal was truly awesome. Even Sir Jasper, man of few words and fewer emotions, fell into a deep, respectful silence as the *Greenock Belle,* escorted by pilot-boats on either side, slipped into the Canal opening between Egypt and the Sinai with the effortlessness of a warm knife slicing through a tub of lard. Behind them lay Europe, the Mediterranean, Port Said; ahead, Ismailia, Port Suez and then the Red Sea, gateway to the East, flowing into the mighty swells of the Indian Ocean. How magical to arrive from the West into the Orient almost overnight at the mere billow of a sail!

It was not long past dawn; the streaky pink and layered clouds of the eastern skies were yet to give indication of their intentions for the coming day. On either side of the Canal stretched endless sheets of glittering sand embroidered with squat date palms, their fronds waving in the gusty cool of the early morning desert breezes as if in a salute to the passing clipper. Astonished villagers, still not quite used to the engineering miracle of the artificial waterway that allowed ships to sail virtually across the sands from one sea into another, stood in long flowing robes gesticulating tumultuous welcomes and adieus.

Constance Pendlebury took a deep breath and closed her eyes, savouring the taste of salt on her tongue, allowing the tangy freshness of the morning air to flow freely through her lungs. It was the talk of music circles all over Europe that Giuseppe Verdi had been commissioned by the Khedive of Egypt to compose an opera for the glory of his country. The inaugural performance was to be at the Cairo Opera House at the end of the year. Sailing through this cradle of civilisation, through these regions of wild and desolate beauty, repository of biblical history, Constance Pendlebury thrilled at the thought of Verdi's musical majesty in the desert, this very desert! Behind closed eyes she heard every note of the music perhaps not yet even written, as it thundered across the ancient dunes paying homage to the glorious remembrances of the past.

"If for this alone," she breathed, deeply moved, "I will consider the journey to India worthwhile." So vivid was her vision of the scene, so overwhelmingly real Verdi's nascent arias in her ears, that her eyes filled with tears.

"Oh, come, come, my dear!" Standing not far away at the rails, Sir Jasper overheard her impassioned whisper and offered a light reproof. "India will have a great deal more to offer. You can't dismiss her as casually as all that! Remember, my dear, I speak from personal experience. Am I not right, Captain Carthew?" This last to the portly master of the ship, who now approached to join them at the rails to offer his morning respects and ascertain that all was to the satisfaction of the most important passengers on board his ship.

"India? Oh aye." The Captain nodded in vigorous agreement, squinting his eyes eastwards and tugging at his flourishing moustache. "She be me second love, all right—and a right frisky jade, full of surprises at that!" He chuckled with hearty humour. "When I'm done with the sea, I aim to buy meself a cottage in some far fold of them Downs in the Nilgiris and give meself up to sublime contentment in the bosom of Mother Nature, that's what I aim!" He heaved a gusty sigh of pleasure, as if the future prospect was already a reality.

"And what might be your first love, Captain, if that isn't an impertinent question?" Lady Pendlebury inquired with some amusement.

"Why me ship, of course, ma'am!" He thumped the sparkling brass rail on which rested his beefy, heavily tattooed forearms. "Me ole darlin' *Belle*—the best of the tea clipper fleet."

"Oh yes." Sir Jasper nodded as he extracted a pair of heavy binoculars from a fine hand-tooled leather box. "It was your vessel that won the Great Tea Race last year against five contestants, was it not?"

"Yes, sir! Ninety-seven days out of Foochow straight home to London with jest o'er fifteen hundred tons of tea—the season's first and finest." He gave a complacent grunt, his sea-dog eyes proudly scanning the gleaming pine board decks of the nine-hundred-ton Scottish clipper holystoned daily into pristine perfection by hordes of Lascars. "*And* a prize of five hundred guineas from the owners of the cargo in Mincin' Lane for bein' first with the new teas in the markets of Liverpool!"

"Oh? Well, that must have fetched them a pretty penny." Sir Jasper slowly skimmed the binoculars over the countryside for a closer view of a scene he found altogether charming.

"To be sure! Sixpence a pound more than the nearest competitor—no one can do better than that!"

"I hear the Tea Races are to be stopped after this year?" Sir Jasper remarked conversationally as the butler set about arranging the breakfast table under the canvas awning stretched above the private deck outside the owner's stateroom which the Pendleburys occupied.

"Aye, so I hear, more's the pity. It's this God-rottin' Canal—beggin' yer pardon, ma'am—that's ringin' the death knell of the old windjammers. Not havin' to watch every ruddy pound of coal burned any more, and what with time and money becomin' the same in current commercial parlance, steamships have the 'vantage, and no two ways about it."

"A great shame indeed," Sir Jasper commiserated. "I shall miss these old windjammers, as you call them, just as much as you, Captain. It pains me to see the romance of the seas relegated to the clumsy devices of a bunch of soulless greasers, what?"

"Oh, it sure does, sir!" The Captain nodded in fervent agreement. "I couldn' have put it better meself."

"Won't you please join us for breakfast, Captain Carthew?" Lady Pendlebury asked. "There's more than enough to go around, I assure you."

It was an invitation not to be declined and Captain Carthew certainly had no thought to do so. He accepted eagerly. As on the majority of passenger ships between Great Britain and the Orient, food on the *Belle* left a great deal to be desired. Rather than trust the indifferent fare and service normally provided, Lady Pendlebury had insisted on bringing with her their French chef and English butler (who also served as a valet), together with a sizeable stock of dry provisions, vintage wines, crockery, cutlery and napery to ensure that there was no fall in those standards to which the Pendleburys were accustomed. As a consequence, their table on board the vessel was far better than anything the Captain could hope for below deck in the common dining room.

He eyed with undisguised relish the array of dishes being ranged on the breakfast table by the somewhat intimidating English butler. As soon as Sir Jasper invited him to be seated and Lady Pendlebury started to pour out cups of tea, he attacked the food with gusto: chicken pie, crumbed filets of fresh sea fish, scrambled eggs atop rashers of best back bacon, tinned peaches with custard, English marmalade, toast, butter, a superb Stilton, tea, coffee, and fresh coconut water and fruit purchased from the last port of call.

It was after breakfast, when a happily sated Captain Carthew had left them to resume his designated position on the bridge, and Sir Jasper had settled down once more with his sheaf of official despatches, that Lady Pendlebury ventured to revive the worrisome subject uppermost in her mind.

"I have asked for another telegraph to be sent to Calcutta, Jasper."

"Good." For all the attention he paid, she might just as well have informed him that the ship was about to sink.

Lady Constance reached for her basket of tatting materials. "What if it *is* true, Jasper?"

Head bowed over his papers as he sat at his desk in the master cabin, Sir Jasper made a small sign of irritation. "If *what* is true, Constance?"

"What Clementine McNaughton told us on her way up to Glamorgan with Arabella. About Christian and this girl. The Eurasian girl."

Sir Jasper dipped his quill in the inkstand and started to write. "We will cross that bridge when we come to it, m'dear."

"Would it not be wise to decide how to tackle the situation *before* we come to the bridge?" Lady Pendlebury suggested, her tranquil grey eyes and composed tone of voice giving little indication of the consuming anxiety within.

Engrossed in his paperwork, it was a moment or two before Sir Jasper replied. "No. It would be unwise to jump to a conclusion without all the facts in hand." He allowed himself a dry little smile. "A crop of wild oats is an occupational hazard with young men sent out to the colonies. I presume Christian is as eager as any to enjoy his allotted ration before the opportunity passes."

A look of alarm briefly marred the serenity of Lady Pendlebury's features. "How can you be so . . . *uncaring* about it, Jasper! What if he's been naïve enough to get himself irretrievably involved?"

"Oh, for goodness' sake, Constance, I was speaking in jest!" Seeing that his flippancy had not been received in the spirit in which it was delivered, he attempted vague reparation. "In any case, I refuse to give credence to old biddy gossip at these infernal Women's Institutes. In India, one learns to live with that sort of thing."

The summary dismissal failed to convince Lady Pendlebury. "Clementine and Arabella came to us directly from Calcutta. They said Christian's cavortings with this girl were the talk of the town. Even Bruce knew about them and they said that he too, like everyone else, was scandalised. If these were mere *rumours,* would the McNaughtons have paid them the attention they appeared to?"

Sir Jasper laid down his pen sharply with a show of exasperation. "Clementine McNaughton is a desiccated old witch with a forked tongue, and Bruce is a scoundrel as well as an ass!" He mouthed an oath, rose and stretched his aching back with ill-concealed impatience. "There's absolutely no point in getting worked up now when the actual story is so totally out of our reach. For heaven's sake, leave it alone for the time being, Constance. In any case, Christian is old enough to be credited with adequate sense to know what he is doing."

Lady Pendlebury's hands stilled for a moment as she gazed through an open porthole pouring sunbeams into the cabin. "I hope so, Jasper," she sighed. "Oh, I do hope so!"

"And now I really *must* get on with these papers." With a determined shake of his head, he reseated himself and picked up his pen. "The Opposition at home is baying for the government's blood because they insist that the finances of India are unsound. To counter the charge I must be entirely conversant with these budget estimates, confident of all facts when I discuss them with Benjamin Ingersoll, a diplomat but also a finance man. He wants a meeting the day after we disembark, and he will certainly. . . ."

"Ingersoll? One of the Devonshire Ingersolls?"

"No, dear. *Viscount* Ingersoll, eldest son of the Earl."

"*Harriet* Ingersoll's husband?" she asked with sudden interest.

"Yes, he. . . ."

"Harriet's husband is one of your colleagues on the Viceroy's Executive Council?"

"A colleague, yes, but not on the Executive Council. He's just been appointed Foreign Secretary—a position that enjoys even greater importance. Apart from anything else, he has an astonishing facility with figures." Seeing that his wife was about to ask yet another question, his tone sharpened. "Why don't you go up to the bridge, Constance? Carthew would be only too pleased to point out all the passing landmarks on both sides of the Canal. He's done the voyage enough times to know each of the date palms by name, I'm sure."

Knowing only too well her husband's tolerance level, Lady Pendlebury gathered up her tatting materials and, with a sigh of resignation, did as she was bid.

Following dinner that night, however, as they sat on deck enjoying a final glass of Cognac and a well-deserved respite from the heat of the day, Sir Jasper suddenly made a somewhat oblique reference to the subject of his son. "You know very well, Constance," he said, his mood mellowed by the excellent entrée and wines he was in the process of digesting, "that I have never tolerated anything that might compromise either my career or my reputation." His cheeks hollowed as he sucked contentedly at his cigar, his eyes turned up towards the stars that hung like clusters of shining grapes in a satin black sky. "But you must see that it is futile to ruminate and speculate upon rumours that are, as they stand now, entirely unsubstantiated. Once we disembark and find that the reality is, indeed, what you suspect, then such action as might be deemed necessary will be taken to protect what we consider to be our priorities. That much I do promise." He leaned forward and patted her hand in reassurance. "Now, does that satisfy you, m'dear?"

It did not. But for the time being Constance Pendlebury had no option but to declare herself content.

At approximately the time the *Greenock Belle* was leaving the Red Sea behind and preparing to enter the waters of the Indian Ocean, Christian Pendlebury was with Maya deep in the banyan forest at Shibpore, celebrating the birth of yet another day full of rich promise.

They sat in the cool, sheltered womb of the great banyan, glittering with the dews of dawn. The silence above them was immense, like a canopy, touching the early morning gossamer vapours with enchantment. Out of the shimmering mists the day came rolling with delicate slowness, lifting the gloom of the forest as it tipped each leaf in turn with light. Christian plucked idly at a tendril reaching far down into the earth, the nascent trunk of yet another banyan clone. His forehead was creased and there was discontent in his eyes.

The truth was that this morning his mood was far from celebratory. Whatever promises other days might have held, this morning appeared to him singularly bleak and broody. Hunched on an impromptu seat of gnarled roots, he sat in ruminative quiet, his thoughts in some other distant sphere, his manner abstracted. Nearby, Maya reclined on one elbow, a frown dividing her forehead as her own thoughts raced along a rut increasingly disturbing. The silence that reigned between them today was far from comfortable. In their gathering rapport, their easy companionship, Christian usually felt at peace, uplifted even. This morning, however, he could not shake off his depression; he felt restless and out of sorts.

He had received yet another telegraph from his mother via the Viceroy's office—the third so far—and his mind heaved with conflicting emotions. On the one hand, he knew that the time had come to declare himself to Maya, to make a clearly spoken commitment; on the other, the prospect of his parents' imminent arrival loomed ahead, seriously eroding his confidence. Out of the corner of his eyes he observed Maya, silent and introspective, cocooned in her own world. It seemed to him that she was once more detached, scarcely aware of his presence, and he felt a sudden aching resentment.

"Why don't you ever share with me what you're *really* thinking?" he asked petulantly, his mood souring further.

She was instantly contrite. "I was not aware that my thoughts were of such importance to you, but if they are I will share them willingly."

"Well, what *were* you thinking just now when you frowned?"

She rose and came to sit closer to him. "Just an idle thought that happened to pass through my mind, nothing of any significance. I was thinking of your meeting with Kyle."

"Oh?"

"I was wondering, what did he want to talk to you about?"

Maya had waited all morning to ask the question that had been picking away at her brain over the past few days. So far she had exercised enormous restraint, waiting to see if Christian stirred the topic first. He did not. However profuse he might have been in his apologies for having declined her invitation to the musical review, he had given no indication of having regretted the choice that he had made.

He shrugged. "Oh, this and that. Many things. He gave me some books to read and, of course, he showed me around his press."

The studied lack of detail irked Maya, but she swallowed a sound of impatience and persisted. "And that's all?"

"Well, no. We conversed in general about my career, the Mutiny, colonial politics, books," he made a vague gesture, "that sort of thing. Kyle is astonishingly well informed, you know. He can give one a pretty good argument from either side of just about any fence." Her expression indicated that she was not yet satisfied, that she waited for more. He smiled. "Oh yes, he told me about his private ghosts and smugglers' tunnels. He has them all, you know, right there on his premises."

"Really!"

He added a few more details to the frivolous trivia and summarised the gist of one or two of their more casual conversations. He did not elucidate on their discussions about the Mutiny and mentioned nothing of the dialogue concerning her father. He knew that she would not approve of either. "Kyle was curious about my family. Well, mostly about my father." On the point of saying something else, he changed his mind and looked away.

"Your father?" Slowly Maya sat up. "Why?"

"Kyle knows of the reputation my father earned in Lucknow during the fifties. He said he had always been one of his most avid admirers." He got up and made an effort to divert the course of the conversation. "Shall we ride on towards the crossing near the Fort?"

She remained seated and ignored his suggestion. "Kyle said he *admired* your father?"

"Yes." Christian felt a flash of annoyance at her look of disbelief. "Well, why ever not? My father is still remembered in this country for his services to Oudh. There are many who *do* admire him, and with very good reason, too! Why does it come as a surprise that Kyle should be one of them?"

In the uncharacteristic sharpness of his tone, Maya froze. "Because I know Kyle," she said coldly. She stood up, dusted her britches and made to remount her horse. "Anyway, let's drop the subject since it evidently displeases you to discuss it."

"No, wait!" Devastated at having vented his bad humour on her, he grabbed her hand and kissed it fervently. "I . . . I'm sorry. . . ." Dismayed and tongue-tied, he pressed her palm to his lips and held it there, his own hand quivering, his eyes moist with sudden tears.

Startled, Maya scanned him for a moment, thrown off balance by the intensity of his reaction. She did not withdraw her hand, but all at once her legs felt shaky and she folded onto the ground, pulling him down with her. For a moment she could not speak.

Overwhelmed, almost bewildered by this initial impulsive step he had taken towards commitment, Christian squeezed his eyes shut and said the first thing that came to his mind. "This . . . Chester Maynard. Who was he?" Having blurted it out, he released her hand and turned away, desperately unhappy.

Maya's face went blank. "No one."

"Nobody is no one," he said, distraught. "If he was human, he must have been *someone!*" He wrenched a blade of grass from the ground and chewed on it glumly.

"I mean, no one of any consequence."

"They say. . . ."

"Who are 'they'?"

"It doesn't matter who, *they,* everyone at the chummery, everyone in Calcutta"—battling with his emotions, he waved his hands wildly—"they say that you were in love with him. Were you . . . *are* you still?"

Taken entirely unawares by the impassioned onslaught, Maya sought his eyes, but sullenly, he refused to meet them. "No. He was just a . . . friend."

"They say you wanted to marry him!"

Yes. But he never asked me. . . .

"No," she said quietly. "I never wanted to marry him."

"Why was he nearly cashiered?"

"Because he ran up a gambling debt he did not have the means to pay."

"Is that the only reason he was transferred out of station?"

"Yes."

Christian frowned and toyed with his riding crop. "But then, why. . . ?"

"Why, why, why!" So far she had answered him with patience, stone-faced and dispassionate. But now she leapt to her feet and turned on him in sudden fury. "Why do you need to ask so many damned questions? For all I care, Chester Maynard could be *dead!*" Hot tears stung the back of her eyelids but she refused to let them fall. "Is there no one in *your* life you have ever loved before?"

His shoulders slumped. "So you *did* love him!"

She stamped her foot. "No, I did not! But answer my question—is there no one?"

He lowered his head between his knees and shook it. "No. Tell me about him, Maya, I have a need to know. What was there between you?"

"There was nothing between us, nothing! How *could* there be?" Her taunt was savage, her eyes filled with pain and hate. "Do you still not know what it means to bear the cursed name of Raventhorne? To be the daughter of the man who slaughtered English women and children and was hanged as a traitor? To carry the brand of the half-caste? No, it was *not* the only reason he was transferred! Now, does that satisfy your curiosity?"

Reduced to shocked silence by her outburst, Christian sat stock still as, breathing hard, she stared at him for a moment with something very close to contempt. Then, all at once, her anger subsided. She regained control of herself as swiftly as she had lost it. "The veterinary surgeon has promised to call this morning," she said, again calm and blank-faced. "One of the mares is almost ready to foal."

The prospect of parting on a note of such bitterness galvanised him once more into action. "Oh God don't go, *please* don't!" He leapt up, frustrated by his inability to control any situation with her. It was the first time they had exchanged such harsh words and he was crippled with regrets. She made to walk away, but before she could, he enfolded her in his arms. Within the sudden embrace she stiffened and struggled briefly, but he would not release her. Pressing her head against his chest, he ran quivering fingers through her hair, muttering passionate apologies, trying to soothe her with frantic caresses.

"Forgive me," he whispered, sick at heart, "I should not have asked such hurtful questions." In case she again resisted, he tightened his hold on her. "If you only knew how wretched, how terribly *tormented* I've been with jealousy. I don't give tuppence *whose* damned daughter you are! All I want is that you should feel about me as I do about you." His voice caught in a sob. Holding her away from him, he looked at her with ravaged eyes. "You must know by now how desperately I am in love with you, Maya— my God, you *must!*"

With her palms pressed against his heaving chest, Maya stood motion-less, her gaze fixed on the brass buttons of his riding tunic. His trembling fingers cut deep into her shoulders but she was not aware of the pain. She raised her eyes to look into his stricken face; his cheeks were wet, streaked with tears.

Her trapped breath escaped in a sigh. Wearily, she leaned her forehead against his chest. "Yes," she murmured, forgiving him everything, numbed by the depth of his feelings. "Yes, I know."

He surrendered to a fresh surge of emotion so powerful that his body seemed a woefully inadequate receptacle to contain it. Her face remained buried in his tunic; in feverish silence, her brain battled to absorb his sud-den expressions of love. One by one, the words seeped into her con-sciousness; she raised her face and, slowly, her mouth curved in a smile. Watching her every nuance of expression, Christian sensed acceptance in the smile and, with a small cry, he again pressed her close to him. He filled with longing, hungry for her, desperate to taste the sweetness promised by her smile. Whispering her name over and over again, he closed his eyes, rapturous that she no longer resisted. Softly, hesitantly, he kissed a corner of her smiling mouth.

"I am a cad, a heartless nincompoop, for having wounded you! I didn't mean to—but I cannot *bear* the thought of you belonging to anyone else. It's been driving me out of my bloody wits!"

Still shaky, she balanced herself on the tip of her toes and daringly kissed the dimple in his chin as a sign of her forgiveness. He gasped with delighted surprise. The touch of her lips was soft, cool, on his skin, yet it made him burn as if he were on fire. He shuddered with joy, absurdly happy, and returned her kiss, but suddenly clumsy in his eagerness. He was again seventeen, unsure and gauche, full of angles and rough-hewn edges. He cupped her lovely face between unsteady palms and kissed her on each eyelid, carefully, reverently, as if performing an act of worship. Her fragrance filled his nose, his mouth, his entire being, and he kissed her again, this time more boldly, experimenting delicately with the tip of his tongue. She neither recoiled nor pushed him away. With fleeting aston-ishment, her eyes sprang open, then closed again with a sigh. Cushioned against the alabaster paleness of her cheek, her long, dark lashes looked like fragile brushwork from the hand of a master painter. Christian's breath turned ragged; it was a full moment before he could untangle the knot of words that formed to collect in his mouth.

"T-tell me you love me too, my d-dearest," he stammered against her cheek. "I . . . I would *die* if you were to turn me away now."

She remained silent, contenting herself with tremulous, featherlight fin-gers along his cheek, his jawline, the back of his neck, making his head reel. For Christian, the world slipped into eclipse. Reality began and ended with the curve of her cheek, the violet sparkles in her eyes, the contours and corners and crevices of her mouth. A small cry of agony rose in the depths of his throat.

"Tell me, Maya, for pity's sake *tell* me!"

"Yes," she finally murmured. "Yes, I do."

He gave a yell, insane with triumph, covering her face with tiny kisses, bursting with relief. Not knowing how else to expend his jubilation, he threw back his head and laughed out long and loud. Shyly, she joined in his laugh, sharing in his exhilaration, still astonished and incredulous and bewildered. Hand in hand, fingers entwined, they ambled towards their horses, reluctant to abandon such a secluded haven, yet knowing that they must. They did not mount immediately but continued to stroll so as to sustain physical contact with their hands, their well-trained horses following with trailing reins.

"What does *Maya* mean?" Christian asked suddenly, intoxicated with the wonders of a morning he had actually considered bleak.

She returned the pressure of his fingers around hers, still floating in her impossible dream. "It means an illusion."

He stopped, lifted her hand and kissed each fingertip in turn. "You mean, something that doesn't exist?" he teased, lightheaded with her nearness, not really caring a hoot. "Like a mirage?"

"Yes. I suppose so. Like a mirage. The Hindus believe. . . ."

"You mean you are here but not really here?" he interrupted with a laugh.

"You're teasing me," she pouted, "You don't really want to know!"

"No. I don't care what it means, but tell me anyway."

"Well, the Hindus believe that the world, our existence, all things material, are mere illusions created for transient pleasure. Therefore, we must not become attached to them. The name they give to these illusory pleasures is *maya*."

He stopped walking, not listening at all. "Tell me you will marry me."

"What?" Maya's footsteps too halted in their tracks.

He was deeply serious. "I am asking you to be my wife."

The colour from her face drained. She stood rooted, staring at him with confused, disbelieving eyes. Her face was like a mask, every muscle frozen. The silence between them expanded; speechless, both struggled to assimilate the enormity of the irreversible commitment he had just made. A pair of large grey- and black-striped squirrels crashed down from a branch screeching, and the spell binding them in mutual wordlessness was broken. Maya's eyes, wide and frightened, filled with suspicion.

"Don't say anything you don't mean, Christian," she whispered, starting to tremble. He tried to take her in his arms again but she stepped back out of his reach, her face colourless, her expression once more closed.

"Of *course* I mean it!" His protest was immediate and vehement. "Dammit, what kind of a cad do you take me to be?" She tried to turn away, but he would not let her. "Give me an answer, Maya, say something, *anything*. . . anything. . . ," he pleaded, crippled with suspense.

"Are you sure that is what you really want?" she asked, resolutely solemn and unsmiling. "To marry me?"

"Isn't that what *you* want?" he cried, immensely wounded.

She studied him for a long moment before she gave him her answer. "Yes," she said calmly. "Yes. That is what I want."

In Christian's ears, the rustling leaves of the forest became a concert of heavenly music; there was a taste of wine in the air. Moving in lacy patterns through the foliage, the light came from the wings of smiling angels and the skies exploded with rainbows. He was ecstatic. Unable to speak, he merely bent forward and placed a small, chaste kiss on her forehead, choking with wonderment and gratitude. "I . . . I am *honoured,*" was all he could say.

Once again hand in hand, submerged in unreality and marvellous contentment, they resumed their stroll through the meandering paths of the forest. From a distance came the sound of horses' hooves and then of loud human voices, coarse and raucous. Instantly the realm of fantasy they shared faded and the real world slipped back into focus. A posse of early morning riders thundered by, defiling the quietude and destroying the magical peace of the precious moments. Quickly and in tacitly mutual consent, they remounted and began the long ride back to the ferry that would return them to the English Town across the river.

At the front gate of the Raventhorne mansion, they stood tongue-tied, gazing at each other, untouching and wonder-filled. Still dazed, they were suddenly awkward and shy for having shared a morning so momentous as to have changed their perception of the world, yet not knowing with what words to part.

"Until tomorrow then, my darling," Christian murmured, blushing and glancing around and over his shoulder to make certain there were no eavesdroppers about.

"Yes."

For a moment he stood shuffling his feet, frowning and uncomfortable, wanting to say something but not knowing how. "I was wondering. . . ."

"Yes?"

"I was wondering if it might not be more . . . prudent to . . . to. . . ." He stopped, flustered.

Maya looked away from him across the river. "Don't worry. There is no need to make any announcements yet if you would rather wait."

His colour deepened. "You know I don't mean. . . ," he began unhappily.

"I know you don't, but yes, it would be wiser to keep this to ourselves for the present."

Mortified that she should find him so transparent, that she should have guessed his thoughts with such ease, yet visibly relieved at her instant understanding, he hastened to change the topic. "You wanted to know about the other afternoon."

"Yes?" She was immediately alert, knowing instinctively to which afternoon he referred.

"I remember now, I suddenly had the most curious feeling while we were sitting in Kyle's study."

"Oh?"

"I sensed a, well, a female presence somewhere in the house."

"A female presence? You mean a maidservant?"

Recalling the vague impressions of that afternoon, he gave an uncertain laugh. "I can't be sure, but my impression was not one of a maidservant. I just had this very strong, very fleeting awareness of a woman's hand running the household. It could have been because of the perfume in the air or the prettily arranged bowl of flowers or," he shook his head, "more likely, just a figment of my imagination."

"You didn't meet her, then?"

"No. It was just an impression I had."

"You had the impression that she was actually *living* on the premises?"

He coloured again, embarrassed by the implications of her question. "Well, I don't really know, but, well, yes." He stopped and shrugged, sorry now that he had mentioned the matter at all. "It was just a momentary impression, rather foolish, I suppose. In any case, it's none of our business."

Our business!

His casual, unpremeditated use of the pronoun in the plural sent an odd kind of thrill coursing through Maya's veins. Such a mundane word, such a common, nondescript word, yet suddenly made so significant, so magical! It seemed to bind them in a mutual identity, a commonality, as if she were indeed part of his world. Tears sprang into Maya's eyes; repeating the word to herself, she held it close to her heart and hugged it. Before Christian could even grasp what she was doing, she laid a kiss on her palm and blew it in his direction, uncaring of who might be watching—but if anyone was, she hoped it would be the Anderson sisters!

Christian Pendlebury *was* going to marry her. So much for Kyle Hawkesworth and his black tongue!

Listening to Maya's laugh follow her down the drive like a bridal train, Christian suddenly remembered something and coloured with guilt. He had entirely forgotten to tell her about the imminent arrival of his parents!

"Five thousand pounds!" Amos exclaimed, astounded.

"Yes."

"You extracted five thousand pounds out of McNaughton?"

"Yes."

"How in heaven's name did you manage that?"

They were waiting at the end of the Trident wharf, watching the unloading of one of the clippers returned that morning from Boston. Further down the jetty at the centre of a knot of workers stood Ranjan Moitra, gesticulating energetically as he argued with a pair of English Customs officials and the Bengali receiving agents for whom the shipment was intended. In the blazing heat of the afternoon the ebony black skins of the coolies glistened as if sheened with a patina of oil. Bent double with the weight, they carried ashore mountainous cargoes of brimstone, pine boards, rosin, mahogany and bales of machine-loomed cloth from Lancashire's mills. Sitting on the jetty with his legs over the side, Kyle Hawkesworth leant back against a bollard and squinted up at Amos through the blinding glare of the noonday sun.

"With disappointing ease, really." Kyle spoke almost with regret as he stroked his chin between a thumb and a finger. "I tinkled a few skeletons in his cupboard with promise of a full-blooded rattle to follow. Rather than face the resultant music, he agreed."

"He agreed willingly?"

"Willingly?" A half smile played on Kyle's lips. "No, I wouldn't go *quite* as far as that. But he certainly agreed more swiftly than Whitney and I had bargained for."

Amos gave him a long, worried look. "You used blackmail to get that money from McNaughton!"

"Of course, how else?" Kyle looked surprised. "If that is the word you choose to use."

"What word would *you* choose to use?"

Kyle reflected. "Bargaining power? Persuasion? Or why not simply quid pro quo?" Shading his eyes with a hand, he looked up at Amos. "You find that difficult to accept?"

Amos shook his head in some confusion. "I don't know . . . I really don't know."

Kyle whipped the smile off his mouth. "McNaughton is a freebooting, avaricious wretch and a yellow-bellied coward, a man who has made a practice of cheating his government and the public alike throughout his long, unrelievedly tainted career. He was shaking like a half-set blancmange when I left him, frightened enough to have happily parted with *twice* the amount just to salvage his miserable skin—and, of course, the marriage of that hideous daughter of his."

Still troubled, Amos sat down heavily on the jetty next to Kyle, the documents held in his hand forgotten for the moment. "But a Lieutenant-Governor, Kyle! I'm at a complete loss for words. I hardly know what to say."

"Whatever my reservations about British presence in India," Kyle continued with a hardening of his tone, "I do not deny that there are many fine men in their Civil Service. However, Bruce McNaughton is one of their worst. Wherever he has been posted, he has left behind a trail of dirty dealings. At the very inception of his career with the Company, he made a fraudulent attempt to evade signing of the mandatory covenant whereby Company servants promise not to accept valuable gifts from Indians. While battling with the Council of Directors about this, he proceeded to amass enormous wealth through graft and corruption. Concurrently, he entered into clandestine partnership with a series of dubious individuals to trade with great profit in several commodities, especially stolen diamonds from the Panna mines in Bundelkhand."

Amos grimaced, then shook his head. "I accept that the man is a thoroughgoing scoundrel, Kyle, but *blackmail?* Was that really necessary or, for that matter, wise?"

"You don't consider it necessary and wise to secure compensation for those McNaughton has most grievously wronged?"

"Compensation?"

Kyle rose and started to pace. "In one of his earlier postings as a Collector in Sind, McNaughton had regular dealings with a petty trader named Daniel Weaver, a Eurasian. Weaver was a drunken lout, illiterate and uncouth, but perhaps more stupid than sly. When Weaver arrived one day with a cache of unusually pure white diamonds which he had managed to secure cheaply from the mines and which he had had faceted in Surat, McNaughton's greed got the better of him. He plied the foolishly trusting Weaver with drink one evening, and when the man was too intoxicated to know what he was doing, secured his thumbprint on a bill of sale and on some other paper purporting to be an innocent letter. In fact, the second document was a detailed confession admitting to various criminal escapades. McNaughton pocketed the gemstones and had the befuddled Weaver arrested, tried and convicted, all in a single day, on the strength of that confession.

"Weaver was clapped in jail for fifteen years the next evening," Kyle went on. "He died long before his sentence could be completed, still vehemently protesting his innocence. Except for his wife, no one believed him. With the bill of sale in hand, McNaughton was free to sell the diamonds, and did so with considerable profit. In fact, I believe this was the single most profitable transaction he made during his tenure in Sind."

Shocked into silence, Amos suddenly remembered Kyle's mysterious editorial of a few weeks ago. He could think of nothing to say.

"Weaver's destitute wife ran from pillar to post with her story, but with no success. Eventually, McNaughton threatened to have her physically silenced, and terrified, she fled to Karachi with her son and two daughters."

"How do you know all this?"

"McNaughton finally lost touch with the Weavers," Kyle continued, ignoring the question, "but he was always worried in case they surfaced again and embarrassed him. Two years ago, Mrs. Weaver died in Karachi. On her deathbed, she related the story to an Irish priest who administered the last rites to her. The priest happens to be an acquaintance of mine. After making a few inquiries to verify the facts, he gave the Weaver boy, Martin, some money and sent him on to me in case I could help."

"Sent him here where McNaughton is Lieutenant-Governor?" Amos exclaimed in surprise.

"Because he is Lieutenant-Governor!" Kyle amended. "Wisely, my clergyman friend calculated that the time had come for the matter to be settled through direct confrontation with the man—and settled it has been."

"What happened to Weaver's daughters?"

"With no other means of livelihood, the two impoverished girls resorted to prostitution and beggary on the streets of Karachi. Martin himself eked out a meagre living as a pickpocket, a rather accomplished one, I might add, but the pickings were lean. Last year, unable to bear the degradation and the disease resulting from her trade, one of his sisters eventually took her life. The other still survives in Karachi, but only just."

It was a dreadful story and Amos was appalled. "Are you convinced that the boy is telling the truth about what happened?"

"I wasn't—until McNaughton nibbled at the bait I dangled in that editorial. The article meant little to most people, but McNaughton immediately recognised the name 'Weaver' and panicked. The last thing he wants at this juncture, when his daughter is on the verge of marriage and he himself on that of retirement, is even the whiff of a scandal. He sent for me through Whitney with some fabricated excuse. I showed McNaughton a photograph of Martin. Because he knew exactly what I was talking about, he sensed the boy's identity rather than recognised his face." He shrugged. "After that, it was easy."

"You have no doubts about McNaughton's guilt?"

"None."

Amos again relapsed into an uneasy silence. "Well, I can't say the old swine doesn't deserve it," he said finally, "but I'm not sure blackmail was the only means of doing this."

"Name another."

Unable to do so, Amos merely spread his hands.

"As a matter of fact, I disagree that McNaughton got what he deserved," Kyle remarked grimly, tight lines of anger appearing at the sides of his mouth. "What McNaughton deserves is to be publicly flogged and his invidious career in the Civil Service brought to a timely end. Unfortunately," his shoulders lifted in a frustrated shrug, "it is not within my powers to give him his justifiable comeuppance. I can only hope that someday someone will. For the moment, all I have at my disposal is blackmail, and by Christ, I'm grateful for that!"

"Even so, perhaps he does have a better side that. . . ."

"Hah!" Kyle cut him off with a raucous laugh. "Are you trying to tell me that a man who is a thief, who deliberately has an innocent man condemned and then relentlessly hounds his poverty-stricken family, is likely to have a better side?"

"Well, perhaps I put it badly, but. . . ."

"You were born into wealth, Amos," Kyle again interrupted him, this time with sudden harshness. "You can afford the luxury of principles, the extravagance of ethics and these fine splurges of conscience. If you rub your magic lamp, you can even invoke this genie called the Law to grant you at least a hearing in the mighty edifices of colonial power. For other Eurasians, the wretched Weavers of our twilit limbo, there can only be street justice—that too if they are lucky." He gave a caustic little smile. "There's a lot to be said for blackmail, Amos. It's cheap, it's efficient, and it saves a hell of a lot of time."

"It is also dangerous, Kyle."

"Perhaps. That is a chance I am prepared to take." His shoulders lifted in a shrug. "How does one gain if one doesn't venture? Ironically enough," he added bitterly, "the one who has gained most in this case remains McNaughton. He has already made his pile with those stones, the rightful inheritance of Weaver's family."

With the best will in the world Amos found it difficult to counter the argument. "You believe that the end justifies the means?" he asked, subdued.

"Yes! In this instance, absolutely."

Amos sucked in his underlip, then nodded in grudging agreement. "Well, I suppose you're right, but for heaven's sake be careful. You already have the money?"

"Yes. Three quarters will be divided equally between Martin and his surviving sister."

"And the remaining quarter?"

"That is already in the bank paving the way for our other project—with Martin's sanction."

Amos was about to voice an objection when, catching Kyle's ungiving expression, he changed his mind. "Where is this Martin Weaver now?"

"With me. I've given him a job of sorts for the time being so that he can keep body and soul together. He leaves within the week for Lahore. With the money from McNaughton, the boy hopes to move his sister there too, buy a house and settle down to some sort of decent existence, perhaps even arrange a marriage for her—if her stars are in the right configuration. Being not entirely unlettered, Martin himself wants to train to be a draughtsman."

A spark of involuntary admiration shone in Amos's clouded grey eyes, but before he could say anything, Ranjan Moitra came hurrying up. An unexpected problem had cropped up with regard to the excise levies due on the consignment and it took some time to resolve. Eventually, leaving Moitra to deal with the situation, they started to stroll back along the jetty towards Clive Street.

"I've finally persuaded Ranjan Babu to risk a visit to Cawnpore with me," Amos remarked with a laugh. "He's dead against this project, as you know. He thinks it's too much of a financial gamble. I'm hoping that once he actually sees the mill, he will be persuaded to change his opinion."

"Have they announced the date for the auction yet?" Kyle asked.

"No, not yet. I'm impatient to get started, of course, but I suppose I'll have to bide my time."

They continued to discuss the ambitious plans Amos had for the revival of the mill and the innovations he planned once the unit became his, but despite his underlying excitement, Amos's manner remained abstracted. As they arrived at the main entrance of the Trident building, he stopped and turned to Kyle.

"All right, you've brought McNaughton partly to book," he said, once more worried. "Maybe the man deserved more than he got, and maybe the cause of what you call street justice has been served as well as it could have been. But—and this is a very big but, Kyle—I have to confess that I still have reservations about your methods. You know that I always have."

"Why? You don't think those who have violated all norms of decency for their own ends should be forced to make retribution to the helpless victims they have damaged and abandoned?"

"You know I didn't mean that. I'm only disputing the *means* used to enforce that retribution."

"*Any* means that produce results are to be commended!" Kyle retorted.

"My means have been productive with McNaughton. They will also be with. . . ." He broke off and then threw his hands up in the air.

"Also be with . . . whom?" Amos asked with a sharp intake of breath, pinning him down with questioning eyes.

Kyle's gaze was steady. "With anyone else who's ever ruined innocent lives," he said easily.

Amos knew that that was not what Kyle had almost said, but he also knew that he would not explain further. "You plan to hunt out every man who has ever exploited a Eurasian?"

"No." His eyes twinkled briefly. "Only those that I hear of."

"But there must surely be other ways of achieving the same end, Kyle," Amos repeated helplessly.

Kyle tilted his head to a side, once again unsmiling. "Well, when you find one, my friend, be sure to let me know." Spinning on a heel, he stalked away without another word.

For a moment, Amos stood and watched the tall, striding figure until it disappeared among the crowds thronging Clive Street. He knew Kyle as well as anyone ever would, but the man's cynicism bothered him. He sensed now that something new brewed in the dark, unreachable recesses of Kyle's brain. This was a man so intensely private that, perhaps, he didn't even know himself fully. In that moment Amos would have given a great deal to learn what Kyle Hawkesworth had in mind.

No, not what, *who!*

Not for the first time Amos was relieved that they fought on the same side for the same cause. He would have hated to have had Kyle Hawkesworth as an enemy.

Maya's loud and persistent knocks on the door were answered by the boy with the honey-coloured hair and light, nervous eyes who had served her coffee on the previous occasion. This time, however, he studied her with marked suspicion. He did not invite her in. In fact, he shut the door quickly in her face, keeping open just a narrow chink through which he asked her what she wanted.

"I wish to see Mr. Hawkesworth," she said, much put out, sounding as imperious as she could.

"Mr. Hawkesworth is not at home."

The boy narrowed the chink in the door even further. No, he said in answer to her second question, he did not know where his master had gone or when he was likely to be back. Did he think Mr. Hawkesworth would be late in returning? To this, the boy made a noncommittal grunt that could have meant anything. Well, in that case, Maya announced firmly, determined not to let the effort of her journey go to waste however distasteful the process, she would take a chance and wait for his return. Wait? For a moment the boy was visibly disconcerted. Even without being able to see his face fully, Maya felt his alarm at the unexpected prospect. In the silence that followed she sensed that he cast furtive glances over his shoulder, and vaguely, she wondered at whom. Another moment or two elapsed before he suddenly arrived at a decision. With a vigorous nod, he threw open the door, and without any explanation, gestured for her to enter.

Maya had not imagined there could ever be an occasion when she would actually be impatient to seek out Kyle Hawkesworth. What little she had learned from Christian, however, confirmed her instinctive suspicion that Kyle was cultivating him for a purpose. To protect Christian—and her own future—from whatever evil machinations this unscrupulous man devised, she needed to learn that purpose. And it was because of this nagging need that she had swallowed the bitter pill of her pride to pay Kyle Hawkesworth a visit the day after Christian had proposed marriage.

The honey-haired lad, still nervous but now all smiles and bows, ushered Maya into the same parlour in which she had sat the last time she had been in Kyle's home. While she stood and waited, the boy dusted an armchair with such energy and diligence that she wondered if he would ever stop. Once she was seated, he pulled down the bamboo blinds to cut the glare of the afternoon sun and inquired very courteously if she would care for a cup of tea or a glass of lime juice sherbet. Maya declined both. She scrutinised the lad with a mixture of amusement and curiosity. His face was flushed; a spray of perspiration speckled his forehead. She concluded that, for whatever reason, he was disturbed by her presence, and again she wondered what that reason could possibly be.

For want of anything better to occupy her mind, Maya continued to ponder the boy's strange behaviour after he had left the room. Then a small chord stirred in her memory. Could his odd manner have something to do with the presence of that mysterious woman Christian had sensed the other day? And could it be that the servant boy had been instructed to keep that presence a secret from unwelcome, uninvited visitors?

The thought brought to Maya's mind an impromptu vision of Kyle in a frenzy of passion making violent love to yet another voluptuous mistress. Indeed, so shockingly explicit were the images that rose in her imagination that her heart turned a somersault and she felt her mouth run dry. But then, outraged by her fantasies, she gave an exclamation of self-disgust and got up quickly to look for other mental diversions.

There was plenty of scattered reading material in the room—periodicals, daily newspapers and a shelf of books—but she found that none of them held her attention. She sauntered towards a glass cupboard that contained some ornamental bric-à-brac. For a while she stood and examined each nondescript item with a thoroughness scarcely merited by its value, still not able to leash fully her wildly perambulating thoughts. To her dismay, try as she might, she simply could not suppress another unwanted revocation. A succession of images started to unwind in the repository of her brain, as strong and clear as the reality had been that night almost five years ago.

It was her fourteenth birthday. She was on the *Ganga* with Amos, her mother, the Lubbocks, Edna Chalcott, Ranjan Babu and a small group from the Home. With great aplomb, Amos—only recently graduated from the Academy—had arranged a high tea party aboard the clipper to celebrate the occasion. She had never had a proper birthday party before, not since she was five, when the Lubbocks had arranged a joint celebration for her and Grace soon after they had landed in Calcutta. With her heartbroken mother engrossed in the hopeless hunt for the truth about their father, there had never been a truly happy celebration of the day. Shadowed in gloom, birthdays in the Raventhorne household tended to be desultory occasions within the narrow confines of the home, acknowledged with a few presents, a hastily remembered sponge cake produced by Anthony, and a string of tired melodies thumped out on a tuneless piano with forced gaiety by Edna and Sheba.

This fourteenth birthday, therefore, was truly an occasion and Maya was over the moon with excitement. Apart from the splendid new dress, the lavish presents and the elaborate menu planned by her brother, what thrilled her was the fact that for the first time she was in a position to invite some of her friends from the Academy to her birthday party. The special friends she had chosen to ask were two pukka sisters and a brother, children of an English missionary couple called Shingleton, who had not been able to afford to send them to England for schooling. Maya was proud of her friendship with the Shingletons; it gave her status with her peers because the Shingletons did not care to fraternise with everyone. She had cultivated their friendship very carefully over many months, sharing with them the elaborate tiffin her mother sent to school, giving them rides in her carriage when their hired palanquins failed to arrive on time, purchasing as presents books they themselves could ill afford to buy.

Inexplicably, her mother had not been in favour of the invitation to the Shingleton children. Maya had considered her mother's attitude harsh and unreasonable, and had waged a fierce battle to get her own way. Eventually, worn down by days of argument and tears, her mother had capitulated. The invitations to the Shingleton children had been duly sent and, much to Maya's joy, accepted.

On the evening of the party, however, although Maya waited late into the night for them to arrive, not one of the Shingleton children put in an appearance. Nor did they bother to send explanations and apologies, let alone gifts.

Heartbroken and humiliated, Maya eventually fled from the lavishly decorated stateroom aboard the *Ganga* to the deserted quarterdeck to sob out her misery in solitude. As she stood crying softly, pounding the brass rails with fists clenched in impotent rage, she was unaware that she was being watched. It was after the sobs had subsided and the anger spent that a figure slipped out of the silver dark to stand quietly beside her at the rails. It was Kyle Hawkesworth.

She had met Kyle before, of course. Even though six years older than Amos and in his final year at the University, he had struck up a close friendship with her brother. As she did all of Amos's friends, she considered Kyle self-opinionated and conceited even then, but secretly, she had been quite taken by his undeniable good looks and rather flamboyant manner. In fact, in the privacy of her room at night, she often found herself weaving outrageous fantasies around Kyle, surprising herself with the wanton fecundity of her imagination. Now, as he stood beside her at the ship's rail, unspeaking and contained, she realised that he had been watching her for some time and she blushed. In his unexpected nearness, her heartbeat quickened; recalling some of her more febrile nocturnal imaginings, she felt waves of heat rise up her neck and into her face. She was greatly relieved that it was dark.

He offered her a handkerchief. "Clean your face."

Too intimidated to refuse, she obeyed without argument.

"Why were you crying?"

Another sob rose in her throat but she bit it back. "You know why," she mumbled.

A mosquito buzzed around them. Raising his hands, he clapped and then spread his palms for her to examine. The mosquito had escaped. "You see? My hands are larger and stronger than this miserable speck, but still it survived. Even the meanest of God's creatures has *some* means of self-defence. Do you understand what I am trying to say?"

"No." She wondered if he mocked her, but the sidelong glance she ventured indicated no signs of levity in his face.

"Creatures like us also need mechanisms of self-defence, even more so."

"Creatures like us . . . ?" She only half listened. The cold, white light of the moon sharpened his profile. Straight and tall and confident, he appeared to her like a winged god, an Apollo, his unusual, dark hair blowing in the wind, his deep, deep eyes smouldering with those inner fires around which she had constructed such fascinating myths.

"Yes. Creatures of the night that hang upside down, like bats, in the crevices between two mismatched worlds."

She felt a stab of unaccountable fear, hating the analogy and refusing to acknowledge it. With a small shiver she shut her eyes, again close to tears. "I thought the Shingletons were my f-friends," she whispered, angry and unforgiving. "They *promised* they would come!"

"The Shingletons of this world will never be your friends."

She bunched a fist against her quivering lips. "I'd like to go out and shoot them all!" she cried. *"That's* what I'd like to do!"

"Then why don't you?"

He spoke with considered gravity and she was momentarily taken aback. "You mean with a gun?"

"There are other weapons of destruction, equally effective."

In spite of herself, she was intrigued. "Like what?"

He shrugged. "We all have to devise our own."

"You too?"

"Yes."

She looked, but he didn't appear to be wearing a gun belt. "You carry your weapon on your person?"

"Always!"

"Where?"

"You cannot see it because it is invisible."

Had anyone else made such a ridiculous contention, she would have hooted with laughter. But there was something about Kyle that demanded to be taken seriously. She neither understood what he meant nor much liked what he said, and once again the intensity with which he spoke made her nervous. The light that the moon now cast on his features made them look unfamiliar and his mood was strange. Giving her no warning of his intention, he suddenly reached down and took her hand, stroking the back of it lightly with the ball of his thumb. He stared deep into her eyes, pinning them down so that she could not look away.

"Your skin is very soft."

In the fitful river breezes, the murmur of his voice sounded dreamy and distant, as if borne on the winds from far, far away. But in her sudden surge of excitement, she scarcely heard what he said.

It was the first time that he had touched her. She was utterly unprepared for the involuntary responses that unexpected contact provoked in her body. Like a drop of dew in the first rays of the sun, she felt herself dissolve, slowly, languorously, into nothingness. Her breath vaporised; the blood in her temples hummed and sizzled, making her head seem light and weightless. There was a weakness in the region of her knees that made her legs feel oddly liquid. If she had not clung to the rails with her free hand, she would have fallen. For a moment she swayed precariously, mindless and bewildered. Eyes riveted to his, head swimming, she felt herself swept along on the crest of a mountainous, unfamiliar wave. And her body, no longer hers, no longer within her control, filled with a rapture more insane, more exquisite than any she had ever imagined. Time stood suspended. She thought that she had died, merged forever with eternity.

"Too soft!" He dropped her hand with an exclamation of disgust.

"What?" Still in a dream, she stared at him stupidly.

"To survive, you need to harden it." He glared at her, suddenly angered. "Don't you know, you silly girl, what the most effective weapon is of self-defence?"

She shook her head, dumb and uncomprehending.

"Information!"

She wondered if he had gone mad.

"Aimed well, it destroys without a trace of blood. Remember that. Some day it will come in useful."

He was gone, devoured by the shadows.

Limp and quite befuddled, Maya clutched the rails with both hands, still savouring the residual sensations that lingered in the secret niches of her body. She had never known such sensations before, not even in the course of her most daring imaginary excesses. She did not understand what she had experienced, nor why it should have brought with it a torment that was so unbelievably delicious. But, instinctively, she also felt ashamed, as if he had perpetrated on her some vile act that had left her degraded. It seemed to her that he had conspired with her body to betray her, urged it to develop a will of its own, and the fact that he could do this without her consent left her badly frightened.

Had Kyle sensed her reactions?

The very idea of it made her cringe with shame. She could not rid herself of the conviction that he had actually *foraged* inside her mind, explored and identified all her thoughts, violated her most sacred privacy. For that trespass, imagined or otherwise, she had never been able to forgive him. Appalled that she could ever have woven such abandoned fantasies around him, that day she had vowed that she would banish him entirely from her life. It was easier said than done, of course; all she had succeeded in doing over the years was to see as little of Kyle Hawkesworth as possible and try not to think of him at all.

Information. . . .

That enigmatic word that he had thrown at her with such suddenness, however, Maya thought about a great deal. During the night following her disastrous birthday party, she lay awake for hours wondering how something as inoffensive as mere information could possibly be turned into a weapon. Her wonderings were so intense, conducted with such single-minded concentration, that by the time dawn arrived she could actually see the first glimmerings of an answer.

"Mama and Papa don't want us to have anything to do with you and your brother," Andrew Shingleton informed her at school the next morning with a self-righteous smirk when she tearfully questioned him. "You're not nice to know, so there!"

"Your father was a blackie-white guttersnipe, Mama says," his sister added with a toss of her abundant curls. "And everyone knows he was a bas. . . . a *you know what*, as well!"

"And your mother was a . . . a . . . what the Bible says Mary Magdalene was," the other sister informed her with a malicious laugh. "She never even married your father!"

The following morning Maya put to the test the lesson she had learned from Kyle Hawkesworth. Francis, the Raventhornes' Goan bearer, was said to be sweet on the Shingletons' ayah, who had once confided to him something that was, she said, the most closely guarded secret of the Shingleton family. Very early in the morning, in the deserted classroom, Maya scrawled the information on the blackboard in large, bold, capital letters:

ANDREW SHINGLETON WETS HIS BED EVERY NIGHT.

Later, cold-eyed and triumphant, she sat silently at the back of the classroom reaping the sweet, sweet fruits of her revenge. Andrew Shingleton crouched in a corner blubbering, his nose running all over his blotchy red face. In another corner, his two sisters clutched each other in a fit of hysterics, watched by a shocked and embarrassed class. Hastily summoned, their parents arrived promising hellfire and brimstone to all and sundry, until persuaded to remove their brood from the premises. That was the last anyone ever saw of the Shingletons. The children never returned to the Academy. Subsequently it was heard that the family had packed up and moved upcountry to some unknown parish in the Mofussil.

Kyle's weapon had passed its inaugural test with flying colours. However much she might distrust him, some day she would have to return his favour. . . .

So intense was Maya's concentration as she relived that graphic memory of five years ago that, for a while, she lost contact with all reality, forgetting where she happened to be. The glass-fronted cupboard in Kyle's front parlour into which she stood staring unseeingly as vivid sounds and images from the past flashed across her mind was positioned near a curtained doorway leading to an inner room. All of a sudden, her nose picked up a strong fragrance of attar-of-roses, and with a jolt, she snapped out of her trance. Her face was filmed over with cold sweat, as were the palms of her hands. To bring herself under control, she breathed in deeply several times and, suddenly attentive, listened. From the next room came a faint sound, distant but clear. Maya stood unmoving, her ears sharp and alert. The sound came again, closer and louder. This time she had no trouble identifying it.

It was the unmistakable tinkle of glass bangles nudging each other on a woman's wrist!

The sound appeared to come from the far end of the inner room. Cautiously, Maya lifted a corner of the curtain and peered within. She was just in time to see a flash of bright scarlet disappear around a door at the far end of the room leading out into a courtyard. There was no one about; the young lad seemed to have disappeared. As far as she could make out, she was alone in this part of the house. Without giving herself time to think, she slipped through the doorway and ran across the inner room out into the courtyard in pursuit of the fleeting fragment of colour. Even as she indulged her sudden impulse, she was shocked at her daring, but her rampaging curiosity simply refused to be contained.

The courtyard was deserted.

Maya frowned. For a moment she stood rooted, confused and at a loss. She looked around. The brick-paved space, quadrangular in shape, was surrounded by a stone wall far too high for anyone to scale in a hurry, especially a woman. Along the length of one wall was a sort of low shrubbery, unkempt and overgrown and spilling all over the brick paving. There was a door in the wall opposite to where she stood, but it was shut and she could see a large brass lock dangling on the latch that secured it. It was out of the question for anyone to have unlocked the door, gone out in the blink of an eyelid, and performed the impossible task of replacing the brass lock in the hook from the outside. As far as she could see, there was no other exit from or entrance to the yard save the one in which she herself stood. If there had been someone there—and she was convinced that there was—where had that someone gone?

She suddenly recalled something Christian had said: Kyle's house was said to be haunted! Despite her instant scepticism, Maya shivered. Much to her annoyance, everything within her turned cold. Her skin erupted with goose pimples. Was it a ghost that she had seen? If not, who else could have possibly vanished into thin air in an enclosed courtyard from which there were no means of escape?

Hurriedly she returned to the parlour and sat down, trembling. There was still no sign of Kyle and it was fast turning dark. If he returned while she was still here, she would be no match for him in her present sorry condition; he would walk all over her with comfortable ease. Remembrance of that strange evening so many years ago revived in her that nervousness she still felt in his presence. There was something about Kyle that was uniquely and incomprehensibly his own, and her fears, however illogical they might be to her reason, were still very real to her. No, Maya decided, there was absolutely no way that she could face Kyle at this moment. However vital her business with him, the confrontation would have to wait until another day.

Muttering incoherent excuses to the surprised servant boy who appeared just as she returned to the parlour, she ran out of the front door as if pursued by the hounds of hell.

CHAPTER

9

BEING ESSENTIALLY a creature of habit, Ranjan Moitra disliked Cawnpore. Transported away from his natural habitat, he felt insecure and entirely at sea. The people looked different, the food tasted not only different but vile, and he found himself utterly defeated by the upcountry nuances of Hindi, a language he considered vastly inferior to his native Bengali. On a more painful level, he had spent long periods of time in the region during the sepoy uprising after the *firanghis* had murdered his beloved Sarkar. He had not forgotten those days, nor their terrible trauma. Cawnpore to him would always remain a tainted, evil town; no matter how diligent its pretensions to change, for him the transformations remained superficial.

He had agreed to make the trip with Amos for only one reason: he felt that, in all fairness, he should experience at least once the resurrected city with which his young master was so enamoured, before making a final bid to dissuade him from embarking on a project he himself considered impractical, speculative and foolhardy. Privately Ranjan Babu had wondered if, after seeing the renovated town and the cotton mill in question, he himself might not be tempted to change his opinion. But he had not been tempted. For all its cosmetic reconstructions, his memories of Cawnpore were as acute as ever and he had not been impressed. Consequently, he remained strongly opposed to the idea of diversifying into a highly capital-intensive field of manufacture about which they knew next to nothing.

"If it is textiles that you have set your heart upon," Ranjan Babu suggested as they sat in their hotel sipping ice-cold fruit juices after an exhausting inspection of the cotton mill and its twenty-acre grounds that had left his feet sore and his head aching, "why don't you consider going

into the manufacture of tussur silk? The advantages would be manifold."
He winced a little as the salted warm water in which he sat soaking his
throbbing feet touched a particularly tender spot.

"Perhaps. But silk manufacture does not interest me," Amos replied.
"What interests me is this challenge to make a success of the first cotton
mill in northern India."

"But challenge and profit exist also in the tussur business," Ranjan Babu
pressed home his point. "First, we would not have to venture out of Bengal, which is the home of tussur, therefore the capital outlay and the losses,
if any, would be much reduced. Then, these silkworms that produce the
tussur fibre do not require special mulberry trees to feed upon, they can be
bred in any forest on any trees. Third—and most important—tussur silk
has great potential as a commodity for exportation. I'm told that the
demand for it increases every day in England and the Continent. As you
might know, the English are. . . ."

"Yes, I know, I know. They're designing special machinery to weave
tussur into fabrics suitable for European wear." Amos drained his glass
and picked up a palm-leaf fan to ward off the crackling dry summer heat
of the afternoon. "Nevertheless, the fact remains that silk, however specially and carefully manufactured and marketed, can never match the popularity of cotton, Ranjan Babu. And you heard what the special officer of
the Cotton Supply Association in England had to say when we met him
last month. The government is increasing its subsidies to cotton manufacturers to urge them to lengthen Indian short staple further and make it
even more suitable for Lancashire."

"Yes, but despite these inducements, our indigenous long staple has met
with only limited success." Ranjan Babu allowed himself a small smile of
triumph, then paused to summon an attendant and order a fresh tub of
salted warm water for his feet. "During the American Civil War, yes, there
was a cotton boom, but you know as well as I do that that boom is now
almost over. The increase in demand has gone down. Exportations now
are less than they were two years ago."

"But more than they were before the Civil War. We export about four
million hundredweight of raw cotton annually and the figures are going
up each year—haven't you seen the warehouses here bursting with cotton bales piled right up to the ceiling?"

Ranjan Babu refused to be convinced. "There are already fifty-three
spinning and weaving mills, about ten thousand looms and a million and
a half spindles in India."

"But none in northern India," Amos retorted, becoming irritated by the
argument. "And thereby precisely hangs the challenge! If Bombay's textile mills continue to thrive, why shouldn't ours in Cawnpore?"

"Well, for one, the mill is not ours until the judge declares our bid to be
the highest at the auction," Ranjan Babu reminded Amos coldly. "And for
another, to make a defunct and badly mismanaged mill actually thrive . . .
well, do not let us forget that there is many a slip between the cup and the
mouth," he ended primly.

"Oh don't be such a pessimist, Ranjan Babu." Amos laughed and shook his head. "Look at what we stand to gain if our bid is successful: twenty acres of prime land with several sturdy constructions, good, solid, almost new English machinery imported six years ago from Platt Brothers in Old-ham, and a basically sound cotton mill with ten thousand spindles and a hundred looms, probably at a fraction of their true cost."

"*If* our bid is successful."

Amos frowned. "If? Why should there be any doubt? The population is not exactly queuing up to acquire a liquidated cotton mill that couldn't survive its teething problems. As far as my information goes, we are likely to be the only bidders."

Ranjan Babu lowered his gaze to give his full attention to an angry blis-ter forming on his right big toe. "There are rumours of other . . . interested buyers."

The information came as a surprise to Amos. "Other interested buyers? Who?"

Ranjan Babu shrugged. "So far I have not been able to ascertain their identity, but I am making all endeavours to do so." He could not bring himself to look up and meet Amos's anxious eyes.

"Well, try harder, Ranjan Babu," Amos said with unusual sharpness, too put out to notice his manager's furtive manner. "If there are other interested buyers, I want to know who they are, and as soon as possible. I will not let anyone or, for that matter, anything stand between Trident and that cotton mill, Ranjan Babu. Do I make myself clear?" He balled a fist and struck it hard against his palm to drive home his point.

"Yes," Ranjan Babu replied sadly. "As always, I will do my best."

"How much time will we have once the auction notices are posted?"

"Several weeks, I would say."

"Very well. In that case, from now until then, I want to know the name of every single person interested in acquiring the Sutherland Cotton Spin-ning and Weaving Mill, anyone who has made any inquiries, casual or otherwise. I want that well understood, Ranjan Babu!"

"Yes. It is well understood." Ranjan Babu's face fell further. He had sel-dom seen Amos Raventhorne so disturbed, so close to losing control. He hastily asked a trivial question to change the prickly subject. "Tonight you dine again with Mr. and Mrs. Pickford, is it not? Will you require the car-riage or shall I dismiss it for the day?"

With an effort, Amos pulled himself together. The reminder of the evening that lay ahead was undoubtedly pleasing, and as his mind dwelt upon it, an inadvertent smile started to replace the sour droop of his mouth. He had dined with the Pickfords thrice since he had arrived in Cawnpore, but he had not yet had occasion to discuss fully with David Pickford the subject of the cotton mill upon which he had set his heart. He had decided to do so this evening after dinner, and the prospect was immensely bracing. During the peak of the cotton boom, he had learned, David Pickford had been one of the founder members of the Cotton Coun-cil formed to start the mill for the purpose of weaving the yarn locally rather than having to send it as far afield as Calcutta or Bombay. On a rather more frivolous level, Amos looked forward to another delicious home-cooked meal that would make a blessed change from the infernal "Sudden Death" chicken curry and glutinous balls of rice that appeared to be the tediously persistent specialities of the hotel cook.

And over and above everything else, there was the prospect of seeing Miss Rose Pickford again. It was a prospect Amos was beginning to find more and more appealing.

"No, I shall not need the carriage this evening," he answered, feeling decidedly uplifted. "Mrs. Pickford was kind enough to offer to send theirs to fetch me." He glanced up at the wall clock. "I am expected there at six. That gives me just enough time for a bath and a shave." Unmistakably elated, he walked out of the room with a decided spring in his step.

Full of sorrow, Ranjan Moitra's thoughts returned to the true reason for his dislike for this project. He had hoped against hope that the situation would not come to this. Yet at the same time, in some small, faraway corner of his heart, was tucked away the premonition that some day it would indeed, inevitably, come to this. Like all the other ironies that had dogged the footsteps of the unfortunate Raventhornes, this too seemed ordained; already the writing had started to appear on the wall. Ranjan Moitra knew only too well that, for all his outward gentleness, Amos was very much his father's son. Given a fitting trigger, he too was capable of irrational rage when thwarted, of a terrible thirst for vengeance. In his desire to acquire the cotton mill, Amos had devised for himself a passionate purpose; no matter how urgent and earnest his own persuasions, the boy would not now be diverted from that purpose. It was in this grim realisation that Ranjan Moitra hung his head down in unhappy defeat. He had tried his best, he could do no more.

The rest lay in the lap of the gods.

"I hear you came looking for me yesterday?"

It was mid-morning. Maya stood at the palings of the Calcutta race course on the Maidan watching one of her newer acquisitions being put through its paces. She had named her new grey Morning Mist and today he was being given a trial run by Hassan Shooter, the racing circuit's leading jockey, who often helped her to assess the racing potential of her horses. Stopwatch in one hand, binoculars in the other held close to her eyes, Maya was deeply engrossed when she was startled by the sudden question in her ear, even more so by the unexpected appearance of Kyle Hawkesworth at her side. Not expecting an intrusion, certainly not from Kyle, she was momentarily flustered. Without taking her eyes off Morning Mist, she merely nodded.

"May I ask to what I might have owed the highly unexpected pleasure?" Kyle inquired with customary sarcasm, uncaring of her preoccupation. "Not pursued again by the hordes of Simly Bazaar, I sincerely hope?"

Using the binoculars as a shield behind which to think, Maya did not reply immediately. Outwardly she appeared cool, but within, a strange kind of turmoil brewed, part excitement, part panic. Since her rather impulsive, ill-advised visit to Kyle's house yesterday, she had had second thoughts about the confrontation she courted with such impatience. Yesterday she had almost plunged headlong into unknown waters, unarmed and open to attack. Had Kyle been at home, he would have lacerated her with scorn, mocked her right out of the door. She would have had nothing in her armoury with which to give a fitting retort and would have merely made a fool of herself. It was her great good fortune that Kyle had been out. It was precisely because of this felicitous circumstance that she had discovered a potential source of ammunition that had changed her situation quite dramatically.

She had stumbled upon something Kyle wished to keep secret!

But *had* she? Maya couldn't be sure of that yet. The facts were nebulous, the circumstances decidedly weird. Nevertheless, she had every intention of investigating further at the earliest possible opportunity. Kyle was a man known for his arrogant disregard for public opinion. He was a man who unashamedly indulged his eccentricities, formulated his own arbitrary rules of personal conduct. It was an open secret that he had frequent involvements with misguided women who went to quite absurd lengths to curry his favours. The intriguing question was, why then should he suddenly turn coy about *one* mistress in a succession of many? But fortunately for Maya, he had—for whatever reason—and therein, she sensed, might well lie the core of her newfound firepower. Kyle Hawkesworth had ruined her relationship with Chester Maynard; he had now turned his vile attentions on Christian Pendlebury to the same end. Well, she was damned if she was going to let him get away with it this time! If she trod carefully, Kyle Hawkesworth would be hoist with his own petard—and it was she who would do the hoisting! The prospect was utterly delicious. It was all Maya could do not to smile.

Her expression, however, gave away nothing. "Yes, I did," she answered easily. "I wanted to talk to you."

He arched an eyebrow. "About?"

"About an Armenian gentleman from whom I've had a remarkably good offer for Morning Mist—that grey being put through his paces now by Hassan—a gentleman called Nicholas."

"Aaron Nicholas?"

"Yes. I have a suspicion that Mr. Nicholas will not be able to pay for the purchase, however good his offer." She threw him a look of great charm. "And I simply cannot risk acquiring another bad debt. I've had two already."

"I presume all this does have something to do with me?" His fingers drummed an impatient tattoo on the fence.

She struggled to retain her smile. "Well, since you are so well informed about everyone, I felt sure you would have the most accurate information about the man's financial status."

Whether or not he accepted her lie, he chose not to challenge it, at least not for the moment. Only his eyes narrowed a little. "Yes. Aaron Nicholas is in dire financial straits. I wouldn't advise selling him a horseshoe, much less a horse."

"Well, that's what I've heard," she said. "I would have asked Amos or Ranjan Babu for advice on the matter but both are away, as you know, and I didn't know where else to turn."

"Didn't you?" He leaned an elbow on the wooden paling and half turned to face her. There was faint, very faint, puzzlement in the questioning eyes that were usually so knowing. "That's surprising. You could have got Nicholas's financial status from just about any shop in the municipal market. He owes the whole world and its brother, including, as it happens, me. In fact, the only thing that separates Nicholas from the bankruptcy court is the skin of his rotten teeth—and his long-standing association with the Lieutenant-Governor. Apart from everything else, he's a thoroughly nasty bit of work. Why the devil should he suddenly need to buy another horse?"

Maya shrugged. "I have absolutely no idea. Maybe he intends to make a third attempt to win the Calcutta Derby Sweep this winter to cut some of his losses. After all, it does carry a pool of more than fifty thousand and, as you can see, Morning Mist is proving to be a remarkably swift runner."

She realised, of course, that her impromptu choice of excuse was highly implausible, especially to someone as sharp as Kyle. Aaron Nicholas, an occasional businessman and race horse owner, was indeed notorious for failing to pay bills and repay debts. In any case, she had never intended to sell him a horse as fine and as promising as Morning Mist, although it was true that he had, indeed, made a flattering offer for it. Just before Kyle arrived, she had noticed Nicholas standing at the grandstand end of the course arguing with some of the Stewards of the Turf Club, and she had used him as an excuse because it was the first one that sprang to mind. She met Kyle's sceptical gaze without wavering.

"Martin said that you waited almost an hour for me. Somehow"—his voice turned soft and, it seemed to her, slightly menacing—"I find it difficult to believe all that effort was for information you could have picked up at any street corner in town."

"Martin?"

"The boy who let you in."

"Oh." She made a sound of irritation. "Yes, of course I could have approached someone else. But, as it happens, nobody's information is as reliable as yours, Kyle. After all," she added with a hard, sweet smile, "you make a profession out of knowing everything about everyone, don't you?"

"Not about you!" His voice turned even softer, even more menacing. "In fact, at this moment I would give a great deal to know what lies behind those cool, calculating, deceptively innocent eyes you use with such admirable skill." He stared deep into them, his own cold and suspicious. "I could have sworn your visit had nothing to do with the convenient Mr. Nicholas, but everything to do with our mutual vested interest."

Maya felt the heat rise into her cheeks but defiantly held his gaze. "Well, it didn't," she snapped. "And now, if you will excuse me, I. . . ." She was about to walk away when Hassan Shooter galloped up and she was forced to stop.

Crouching low in the saddle, the jockey brought the horse to the other side of the fence as close as he could get and pulled the reins tight. The magnificent grey reared up on his hind legs with a ferocious neigh of protest, kicking up a spray of grassy tufts behind him. Shooter laughed, patted the horse's neck and then tipped his cap to them both.

"Wot brings you aht 'ere to this den of iniquity then, eh Mr. 'awkesworth? Didn't know you was a racin' man?"

Kyle shuddered. "Perish the thought! I merely came to find something interesting for the racing supplement next week."

"You pay fer hinformation, eh?"

Kyle laughed. "What an incorrigibly mercenary rascal you are, Shooter! I do, as a matter of fact. For something worthwhile, I might even stretch myself to a few pints of beer this evening."

"Can't complain abaht that then," Shooter acknowledged promptly with a cheeky grin. "Well, it's jest an amusin' lickle snippet abaht our fox-huntin' Irishman."

"The Viceroy?"

" 'Oo else? As you know, me cousin William is 'is lordship's pers'nal valet. Any'ow, everyone's well aware that our burra-most sahib's a sturdy racin' man, as fond of the 'orses as 'e is of the 'ounds. Well, you wouldn't believe wot he *reelly* thinks of the bobbery pack they keep at that pukka chummery dahn in Bow Bazaar!"

Maya's smile cooled. The chummery to which Hassan referred was the one where Christian lived. She was aware that he too subscribed to the maintenance of the pack of dogs used to run jackals to earth in fox-hunting style up in Barrackpore. "Lord Mayo attends the meets organised by the chummery very regularly," she said sharply. "He is a very keen supporter of the bobbery pack."

"Not any more 'e isn't," Shooter insisted. " 'E says it's more like chasin' an old woman's cat rahnd a village than fox 'untin'." Shooter threw back his head and roared. "Cross me 'eart, m'am—William 'eard 'im last night at dinner as clear as a bleedin' bell." He looked at her with mischief spilling out of his humourous eyes. "Beggin' yer pardon, m'am, seein' as it's Mr. Pendlebury's pack, too."

"Well, it doesn't really matter," Maya said frostily, annoyed that he should have mentioned Christian at all in Kyle's presence. "Let those whose pack it is worry about it. I have other things to do."

Unfazed and still grinning, the irrepressible jockey now tackled Kyle. "So, 'ave I earned them pints then, guv'nor?"

"With that bit of nonsense? You should be ashamed even to ask." Kyle looked at him severely. "But come to the house anyway. Maybe a brew of crushed hops will lubricate your memory further. Seven o'clock. One moment earlier and I'll have your hide."

The jockey's mouth split wide open with a happy grin. "Rightio, guv'nor. Seven sharp it is, then." Very pleased with himself, he twitched the horse's ears and then scratched his own. " 'E's a fine one this one, Miss Raventhorne. My watch sez three minutes fifty-one over the two miles. And I swear 'e can do better. Mind you, 'e's got a Roman nose and curby 'ocks and 'ardly any racin' points at all, but 'e's got good eyes, a brave look and an easy creepin' style of runnin' comin' from 'ere, a strong loin and quarter." Vigorously he thumped the horse's right flank and his eyes lit up. "I'd be pleased to ride 'im fer you in the Viceroy's Cup this comin' season, m'am. I'd bet me last penny 'e'd run two races of an afternoon with-aht sheddin' a drop of bleedin' sweat."

Maya looked immensely pleased, but before she could say anything, Kyle intervened with a sly, pointed look in her direction. "Miss Raven-thorne isn't planning to be here next racing season, Shooter," he com-mented blandly. "If she's racing horses at all, it will probably be at Newmarket."

Shooter's face fell. "It's not true, is it, Miss Raventhorne? I was 'opin' to ride a few under yer colours this winter, seein' as you've now got together some decent racin' stock."

"No, it isn't true!" Maya hissed, livid, glaring at Kyle. "As usual, Mr. Hawkesworth is busy manufacturing rumours, which is, of course, how he makes his living." With a haughty toss of her head, she moved away a few paces. "In any case, Hassan, I'm thinking of selling Morning Mist. A good performance at trials will help me fetch a better price. Maybe you can ride him for whoever the new owner will be."

Someone called from the other end of the course and Shooter waved back. "If you want the others tried, m'am, I'm at yer service. It's always a pleasure to do business with you and yer brother." He half stood up in the saddle and managed a bow, then dug his spurs in the horse's side and can-tered off, calling over his shoulder, "Mebbe I could tell yer a think or two abaht a certain racin' gent over those crushed 'ops this evenin' Mr. 'awkesworth!"

They watched as he galloped away, his small, wiry body glued to the saddle, almost making rider and horse one. The popular jockey was a half-caste, the legitimate son of a Bihari Muslim mother and a Cockney shippie father. From modest beginnings, he had risen to become a professional rider of immense skill and experience, and had ridden successfully for the Maharaja of Patiala, Sheikh Ibrahim and the Aga Khan. A funny little man, shrivelled and much like an oversized prune, as a jockey Shooter was said to be without peer. Of late he had taken to writing angry letters to *Equal-ity*—all of which Kyle had published—complaining bitterly about the unfairness of giving white jockeys eighty rupees for a winning ride and forty for a losing one, while native jockeys—who included Eurasians—had to be satisfied with fifty and twenty-five, respectively. That apart, he was a man with an impudent, endearing sense of Cockney humour and stories about him were legion. Since native jockeys could claim three pounds in weight, it was said he had once confounded the Clerk of the Scales before a race by asking if, by the same token, Eurasians could claim one and a half pounds. Hassan—and the Clerk—had dined off that story for days.

Unwilling to spend another moment in the company of Kyle Hawkesworth, Maya turned to go as soon as Shooter cantered off. But before she could take a step, she heard her name being called out with frantic urgency as a rather portly figure approached with rapid strides. She was dismayed to see that it was Aaron Nicholas.

"Good day to you, Miss Raventhorne." Huffing and puffing, he swept a shower of perspiration off his dripping forehead with the back of his hand. "Beastly hot, isn't it? Why and how we tolerate such abominable weather when we could escape to Darjeeling, I really don't know."

"Good day, Mr. Nicholas. We were just talking about you." Maya said, not at all pleased at the new arrival. "You do know Mr. Hawkesworth, I take it?"

The smile on Nicholas's face turned sour. "Of course! Who doesn't?" He thrust out a hand and again brushed his forehead with his palm. "Ever heard of racing in the middle of the blasted afternoon with the sun straight in the eyes from the grandstand? Either move the grandstand, I say, or move racing to the mornings—now doesn't that make sense? Of course it does! But do you think those pig-headed Stewards will agree?" He grumbled for a moment, cursing the Stewards and every other official of the Turf Club, then remembered what he had come for. "Well, now to business." He turned to Maya. "I've been watching the trials of your grey. As I told you earlier, despite all his faults I like him and I'd be willing to go up to three thousand. Send your man in the evening to collect the bank draft."

"I'm afraid not, Mr. Nicholas," Maya said very firmly, annoyed at his presumptuousness. "For one, my terms are strictly cash, paid in advance of delivery. For another, I've been offered a higher price since you made your offer and I've already made a commitment to another buyer."

"Another buyer?" His bushy beetle eyebrows came together with an almost audible crash. "Who? That ass Mordecai Ben Elias?"

"No," Maya replied. "Not Mr. Ben Elias."

"But the grey was promised to me!" he shouted, gesticulating angrily. "I consider your refusal to sell a breach of promise. I could take you to court for that!"

"It was never promised, Mr. Nicholas," Maya returned warmly. "I said I would *consider* your offer and I have. I find it is not acceptable to me."

"Well, then, I demand to know the identity of the other buyer," the man raged, not willing to accept defeat. "I'll break his bloody neck for having sneaked in behind my back!"

A little alarmed now by the open show of belligerence, Maya quickly moved back a step or two. "Whoever it is, Mr. Nicholas, I don't think it is any of your business!"

Nicholas sneered at her, fists balled and expression ugly. "You've been listening to all those rumours about me, haven't you? Well, you had no right. . . ."

"I have every right to do what I wish. After all, the horse is my property!"

217

During the heated argument, Kyle had stood pointedly apart, listening with amused but cursory interest. Now, as Nicholas glowered and bunched his fists in a threatening gesture, he strolled up and casually positioned himself between the two. "Well, if you must know, Nicholas," he said quite pleasantly, "Miss Raventhorne has sold the grey to me. Believe it or not, I can even pay for it."

"You?" Nicholas was first taken aback, then his face turned purple. Raising his fists in front of his face, he made prancing little movements with his feet. "And you think I can't? Why, you low-down, scandalmongering. . . ."

He got no further. Without seeming to move at all, Kyle's fist shot out and, all at once, Nicholas became horizontal, one hand held to a bleeding nose, the other still bunched. His expression was one of astonishment. There was a momentary silence as Nicholas lay still, then, slowly, he started to stagger to his feet. He groaned, swayed a little, one eye still distended in surprise, the other closing rapidly. Speechless at the unexpected turn of events, Maya stood and watched in horror.

"Some day you'll be sorry for this, Hawkesworth!" Nicholas breathed, glaring venomously at Kyle. "Some day I'll get you—if it's the last bloody thing I do. By God, I'll get you!"

He spun on a heel and loped off unsteadily in the direction of the grandstand, muttering foul imprecations and vowing salutary revenge.

Kyle gave a snort of disgust as he massaged a bruised knuckle. "I'm becoming a little tired of having to play Sir Galahad every damn time we happen to meet." He scowled with the return of his habitual ill humour. "Gallantry is not one of my prime virtues, thank God."

"Well, I didn't ask you to be gallant," Maya returned with spirit. "I could have managed quite nicely on my own, thank you very much."

Wincing as he flexed his fingers, he mumbled an oath or two and withered her with a look of severe disapproval. "That's the kind of lowlife from whom you have to take insults when you choose to poke fingers in a man's world. Couldn't you think of a more feminine vocation like piano teaching or pastry making?"

Maya regarded him with cold dislike. "Not all lowlife is restricted to racing circles! My vocation is for me to choose. I couldn't care a broken penny whether you approve or not!"

"Well, just as long as you don't expect me to actually *buy* your wretched animal," he grumbled. "There's a limit to nobility, especially mine. All right," he ruffled his hair and again pincered her with a look, "now tell me the truth . . . why did you come to see me yesterday?"

"I've already told you. It was to find out about Nicholas."

He grasped her upper arm, his hold painfully tight. "Well, I don't believe you," he breathed in a vicious whisper. "Martin said he heard you prowling around. Why?"

All at once, there was something so dark and unpleasant about his expression that Maya recoiled. Somehow she stilled her involuntary shudder. "Prowling around?" she asked with a nervous laugh. "Why, what an utterly absurd idea!"

For a moment she thought he was going to fly into a real temper, but then, without warning, he dropped her arm and the spark of fury in his eyes subsided. "It's all the same to me whom you choose to fraternise with in pursuit of your business," he said with another swift change of direction. "It might not be to others. For instance, Sir Jasper and Lady Pendlebury."

She stared. "Sir Jasper and Lady Pendlebury?"

"Presumably, you *do* want to make a good impression on them."

She continued to stare, uncomprehending.

"Tut, tut." He shook his head in simulated regret. "You mean, Christian hasn't told you that they arrive next week?"

"During your previous visits, Mr. Raventhorne," Rose said as they sat down to dinner, "you did not tell us very much about your splendid tea garden in Assam. Being so far removed from the north-eastern hills ourselves, we would love to hear more about it, especially as we now know that your teas are to be so highly commended."

"Yes, indeed." Tucking his serviette into the rim of his starched collar, David Pickford endorsed his daughter's suggestion. "Considering Indian black tea plantations have only recently come into their own, how is it that yours is already so well established?"

Sitting at the Pickfords' table this evening again enjoying their unqualified hospitality, Amos felt a familiar flash of guilt. The uneasy fact was that, following his initial encounter with the family during his previous visit to Cawnpore, he had been frankly suspicious of their show of cordiality. It was no secret that English families abhorred the idea of interaction with Eurasians and Indians, particularly in a social context. For one bearing the name of Raventhorne—a fact the Pickfords had discovered prior to his mother's visit—the abhorrence would have normally been even more pronounced. Why, then, Amos had wondered, should the Pickfords choose to be so different from their compatriots? Either there was an ulterior motive hidden behind the effusiveness (regardless of anything else, the Raventhornes were, after all, extremely wealthy and also influential in the mercantile world of Calcutta), or the Pickfords were not true pukkas but of mixed blood, hence arguably given to fewer prejudices than the English. It was a demeaning—but certainly not uncommon—practice among some of the fairer Eurasians to try to pass themselves off as Europeans. No matter how remote or unknown the darker side of their ancestry, many often went to extraordinary lengths to conceal it, even resorting to fraud and perjury in the process.

Suppressing an innate sense of embarrassment, Amos had finally approached Kyle with his suspicions about the Pickfords. Even the most meticulous inquiries over these past few weeks, however, conducted with commendable discretion and thoroughness by Kyle's Eurasian contacts in Cawnpore, Lucknow and Allahabad, had failed to reveal any traces of Indian blood in the Pickford genealogy. They were, it seemed, of purely

English descent, although many of the younger generation were country-born. David and Adelaide Pickford's two sons were now both settled in England. One was a general medical practitioner in Manchester and the other an engineer with a public works department in the west of England. Both had married English girls and the Pickfords were grandparents three times over.

Deeply ashamed now when he thought of his initial mistrust of these fine and pure-hearted people, Amos was relieved that his suspicions should have proved to be so thoroughly unfounded. He felt small to think that he could ever have doubted the motives of such an open and God-fearing family merely because they were unafflicted by the all too common scourge of racial prejudice. On this visit to Cawnpore, therefore, he had lost no time in presenting himself at the Pickford bungalow laden with offerings to indicate his genuine appreciation of the family's hospitality and to make amends to his own satisfaction for his unworthy thoughts—thoughts about which, mercifully, they remained unaware. David Pickford, Amos now knew, was a leader of Cawnpore's commercial contingent, highly regarded for his integrity and his astuteness in business. There was no doubt that he himself could benefit greatly from his host's advice and opinions regarding the intricacies of running a manufacturing enterprise in the northern region.

Quite apart from David Pickford's business perceptions and his wife's warmth as a hostess, however, there was the matter of Amos's growing attraction to Rose Pickford. If he was charmed by the parents, he was beginning to be frankly captivated by the daughter. She possessed a combination of virtues that he had rarely met in a woman: a delicacy of manner, a dignity of bearing and a quiet intelligence that he found difficult to resist. When she spoke, she chose her words with care, pronouncing perceptive and well-substantiated opinions with feminine softness; when she listened, which was far more often, it was with meticulous concentration. Armed with Mr. and Mrs. Pickford's assurances that he was always welcome in their home, Amos had had occasion to spend time with Rose alone once or twice when he had called without having made a previous appointment and her parents had happened to be out. He had enjoyed their conversations greatly, and her presence even more, surprised at the quiet grasp she appeared to have acquired of the finer points of commercial practices in Cawnpore. He had confided in her his ambitions about the Sutherland Cotton Mill and she had evinced gratifying interest in his plans, pointing out difficulties, offering suggestions, urging him to discuss the matter frankly and fully with her father.

Now, as the soup was being served and Rose voiced her question about the tea garden, Amos turned to look at her. As his gaze met her eloquent brown eyes and took in her shy half smile, he felt a familiar thrill course through his body and he blushed rather more profusely than he would have wished.

"Well, the tea trees grown on our plantation are extremely old," he said quickly, willing the heat in his cheeks to subside and reddening even more in the process. "The Assamese have been brewing tea traditionally as a beverage for many decades, although it was only early in this century that the British became aware that the tea plant is indigenous to north-east India."

"And who runs this tea garden for you?" Adelaide Pickford asked.

"Our tribe." Wondering privately how this family connection would be received, Amos again felt his colour deepen. The subject of Jai Raventhorne and his background had naturally not been broached during his earlier visits to the Pickford home. But now that they knew his true identity and the topic had been stirred, he saw no reason for prevarication. "My paternal grandmother belonged to one of the hill tribes of Assam," he explained, not mentioning his English grandfather and keeping his eyes fixed on his bowl of mulligatawny soup. "The land under tea cultivation is the property of the tribe as a whole. It was during his early journeys to China that my father first learned about the cultivation and commercial profitability of tea. He introduced these modern methods to his tribesmen in the early forties and the results have been gratifying."

During his recital, David Pickford nodded his head several times as if in appreciation. Mrs. Pickford and Rose continued to eat their soup and listened with equal attention. As far as Amos could see, there were no signs of either surprise or shock on any of their faces. They appeared to accept the fact of his partially tribal ancestry with perfect equanimity, raising no questions as to how the illegitimate son of an English baronet called Templewood had acquired the name of Raventhorne. In fact, the name had been that of a Boston shopkeeper with whom his father had been employed many years ago. Having become attached to the kindly old man who had taught him so much about trade and commerce, Jai Raventhorne had decided to adopt it as his own. However, all this Amos saw no reason to clarify at this juncture.

"And are the tea leaves processed up in Assam?" Mr. Pickford asked.

"Oh yes." There was a flash of pride in Amos's dove grey eyes. "It is the women of the tribe who do the picking; the drying and roasting are in the hands of men my father trained. Packaging and labelling for exportation to the east coast of America we prefer to do in our Calcutta warehouses. Now most trading houses pack their teas in smaller, more convenient packets, of course, but the innovation was first introduced by my father and has proved immensely successful."

"You don't find financial management a problem, considering the distance between your headquarters and the plantation?" Mr. Pickford inquired.

"No. Profits are shared equally between our company, Trident, and the tribe. The arrangement works extremely well since tribals generally pride themselves on being scrupulously honest and highly industrious."

"In that case, I would say you are extremely fortunate!" Mr. Pickford exclaimed. "I hear that many government-run tea plantations are constantly plagued by labour problems."

Rose listened with quiet fascination, her fingers interwoven under her chin. "From what little I've read of the north-eastern hills," she now put in, "it appears that they are quite the most beautiful region God has ever created."

Amos smiled. "Well, I wouldn't lay claim to that, but yes, the country-side up there is unspoilt, occasionally even spectacular, and the air is pure. The hillsides are covered with wild flowers. We have over a hundred vari-eties of orchids on our plantation alone."

"You go up to Assam often?" Rose asked.

Amos made a rueful face. "Alas, not as often as I would like." The bear-ers started to serve the fish course and Amos took an appreciative sip of the excellent wine. "The constraints of time and work allow me a trip only once every three months."

"And Mrs. Raventhorne and your sister?"

"Mother accompanies me once in a while, but Maya. . . ." He hesitated. "Well, Maya is very preoccupied with the running and maintenance of her stables. Since she has started making good sales, she prefers to remain in Calcutta."

It was, as always, an evening of comfortable informality, during the course of which they talked of many things. Since Amos was the only guest, the conversation tended to be freer and more frank than it might have been had there been others present. Nevertheless, the one subject everyone appeared to avoid, except by inference, was that of the Mutiny. Rose inquired if he intended to call upon his aunt, the former Estelle Sturges, now that she had been so happily found alive.

Amos shook his head. "No. Mother has advised against it, unless Aunt Estelle makes the first move. I merely get Kasturi Ram to deliver the letters and gifts Mother sends. Although my aunt receives them and always re-ciprocates with a letter in return, so far she has given no indication that she would like to meet me. Naturally, I have no wish to intrude upon her privacy unless she invites me to do so."

Adelaide Pickford heaved a deep sigh. "Well, as long as she is content in this new world she has fashioned around her, I suppose it is best to leave it undisturbed with past memories."

It was after the meal was over—while they were enjoying their glasses of port and the gentlemen had taken to their cigars and the ladies to their embroidery frames in David Pickford's study—that the conversation sud-denly took an unexpected turn. Wondering when and how to broach the subject of the cotton mill, since to discuss business in the presence of the ladies would be considered unforgivably rude, Amos sauntered across to a side table and absently picked up a rather lovely marble statuette of the Madonna and Child. For a moment or two he stood peering at it closely, although his thoughts were elsewhere. He was trying to formulate in his mind all the questions he would like to ask his host about the Sutherland Cotton Mill.

Mistaking his concentration for interest in the object, Adelaide Pickford explained, "That was given to David by the Nana Sahib as a memento of a most strange evening, remember, dear?"

Despite his preoccupation with other thoughts, Amos was surprised. "You knew him when he was in Bithoor?"

"Well, I can't say we knew him," David Pickford said, stroking the luxuriant moustache of which, obviously, he was very proud. "He didn't move much from his Bithoor palace, but once, when he was on a visit to Lucknow, we happened to meet him. For some reason that we have never been able to establish, he asked us to be his guests at dinner in Bithoor the following week. During the course of the evening, quite casually, I happened to admire this little statuette displayed in a glass cupboard in the palace dining room. We were astonished when it was delivered to us by a messenger the very next day. We protested, of course, but His Highness refused to take it back." He added quickly, "I realise all this sounds quite outrageous in the light of subsequent events, but at that time, you must understand, my boy, the Raja was generally considered to be a, well, fairly decent chap. Eccentric, perhaps, and not too high on sophistication or morals, but nevertheless an ally and a good sort."

His wife shivered. "In those days, long before . . . everything happened, that was the impression he gave everybody. Later, of course, the government put a price on his head of ten thousand pounds—not that he was ever caught."

Amos could not deny that he was intrigued. One way or another, the Nana Sahib, Raja of Bithoor, had been a very significant component of his life, a sinister, shadowy figure destined to haunt his early memory. He had grown up with the spectre of the man lurking somewhere in the background of his mind. Being too young while his mother conducted her desperate inquiries in Bithoor after the Mutiny, he had not thought deeply about the man at the time. But later, as he grew older, partly out of necessity, partly because of curiosity, he had made it a point to read everything that he could find about him. As an adult, however, he had never had occasion actually to talk to anyone who had had personal contact with him. The subject of the ruler of Bithoor, the arch villain of the Mutiny—at least in British eyes—was so close to the role his own father had played in the uprising that it always made him uncomfortable.

"Do you believe these current newspaper reports alleging that he has again surfaced?" Amos asked, his curiosity getting the better of his disquiet.

Pickford blew a cloud of blue smoke into the air and his eyes followed it up to the ceiling. "Sometimes I wonder. The man was a cunning old beggar, you know, rather like the cat with nine lives." He turned to his wife. "Do you remember all that commotion about his alleged suicide, dear?"

"Yes, of course. It was the talk of the town for days!" She turned to Amos. "Do you know of the incident, Mr. Raventhorne?"

Amos did, of course, but seeing how much Mrs. Pickford looked forward to relating it to him, he decided not to spoil her enjoyment. "Yes, but only vaguely. I read about it so long ago that now most of the salient details are forgotten."

Adelaide Pickford laid down her knitting so as to concentrate better. "This was at the height of the Mutiny, soon after those two massacres at the riverside . . . sometime in July of that year." She threw an anxious glance at Amos, but his expression was one of curiosity, nothing more, a measure of how comfortable he was beginning to feel in the company of this family. "As you know, the Nana Sahib vehemently denied any involvement in those killings. But there was such a horrified public out-cry against him that he was forced to flee to his palace in Bithoor. Knowing that it was only a matter of days before General Havelock attacked and that the attack would be virulent, the Nana Sahib quickly announced that he intended to sacrifice his life to the mother Ganges and drown himself as a sign of his surrender. Watched by massive crowds, he set off two nights after the Bibighar incident in this rather rough boat with various members of his family. When the boat reached mid-stream, its lamps were extin-guished. This was the signal to the multitude that their Raja had jumped into the water and drowned."

Rose gave a small laugh. "Surely he didn't expect anyone to believe such a silly charade, did he?"

"No, but it achieved what he intended that it should. He knew that the British would not attack until they were certain that the suicide *was* a fake, that they would wait for the man's body to be washed ashore and identi-fied. This gave the Nana Sahib's generals three or four very precious days in which to regroup their forces and plan further battle strategy. Naturally, his dead body never turned up, but the live one soon did!"

"And has continued to do so ever since," her husband remarked drily. "I wouldn't be surprised if the genuine article really did resurrect itself one of these fine days."

"Oh, don't be absurd, dear," his wife scoffed. "Everyone now accepts that the man finally died of swamp fever in the Terai jungles of Nepal more than two years after the uprising."

"Not everyone, dear. There is still considerable mystery surrounding that widely reported death. After all, there were no eyewitnesses who came forward to give testimony—which is what encourages the contro-versy to survive. Anyway, enough of the misbegotten rogue." He got up to refresh their glasses. "Now tell me, young man, how goes that cotton mill business you mentioned to me once or twice?"

It was the opening Amos had been hoping for and he grasped it eagerly. He inched forward in his chair. "I'm not sure if it is going," he remarked with a wry laugh. "We are still waiting for the auction notices to be posted."

"Well, I happened to be with Judge Hoskins the night before last. As no doubt you already know, Guy Sutherland is on furlough in England. The good judge tells me the notices will not be posted until he returns to sta-tion."

"You know Mr. Sutherland well, sir?"

"Yes, extremely well. I've known him over many years, as I have the other directors." He looked at Amos hard. "Are you serious about mak-ing this bid for the mill?"

"Perfectly, sir."

"Even though cotton manufacture has not hitherto been within your field of operations?"

"Perhaps because of that. I believe strongly that upcountry textile manufacture is an inevitable industrial development of the future and I simply cannot resist the challenge." Amos stood up and started to pace. "I understand you were one of the committee formed in the sixties that decided to manufacture the cotton here in Cawnpore rather than send it to Calcutta and Bombay?"

"Yes, that is correct. Because of the unexpected glut of Indian cotton then, we felt something positive had to be done, especially in Cawnpore. The more we stored, the more arrived from Bundelkhand, Rohilkhand, Oudh and the Doab, and the railways simply didn't have the capacity to carry it away. We formed this committee, drew up the requisite plans and the mill started to function in 1864. Unfortunately, my own long-term interests lay elsewhere, in the leather trade. I resigned voluntarily from the committee not long after the mill started to function."

"I also understand the sales were rather poor in the beginning?"

"That, young man, might be something of an understatement! Initially, we had to give away free cloth to persuade people to buy in the future. But then, of course, sales picked up quite well."

"And the eventual cause of the collapse of the mill?"

David Pickford shrugged. "Sadly, differences of opinion among the board members. Guy is a good man, one of the best, but he can be dictatorial, impulsive and easily led. The others objected to his high-handedness in some matters and resigned. Guy couldn't manage on his own, of course, and finally went into liquidation."

"You would advise that investment in this project would be a good proposition, sir?" Amos asked anxiously.

His host pondered for a moment, then nodded. "Definitely. With imaginative management, more qualified workers, better and more modern machinery—an excellent proposition. But one must be prepared to work hard and have the means to absorb some initial losses." He chuckled and slapped Amos on the back. "By gad, if I weren't so fully occupied with my own expansions and exportations, I'd be right in there with you, my lad. Handled properly, it's a grand opportunity, a *grand* opportunity."

It was the highest commendation Amos could have expected, and he was both delighted and relieved by this unqualified confirmation of his own assessments. They continued to discuss the matter for a while, then Adelaide Pickford made mention of some amusing sporting events organized by the Cawnpore Tent Club that they had all enjoyed greatly, and the conversation again turned general. David Pickford was, Amos knew, the secretary of the popular Club, and polo was apparently becoming as much a favourite with the British here as it was in Calcutta.

Quite unexpectedly, Mrs. Pickford made a suggestion. "Perhaps Mr. Raventhorne would like to join us at Church this Sunday for the morning service?" she said. "An American visitor, a doctor of theology from New York, will be delivering the sermon and David has been asked to introduce him."

Amos flushed, startled at the suggestion. He was not sure whether it had been made as an oversight. He knew, of course, that the Pickfords were a God-fearing family who attended church services every Sunday, but the idea that they should be seen in public with him disconcerted him, not for his sake but for theirs. Besides, churchgoing had not been a part of his upbringing in Calcutta for a very good reason. At the one and only service they had attended with their mother at St. John's when he was ten and Maya six, they had been subjected to whispers and remarks of such scathing cruelty that Olivia had vowed never to expose them again.

"I would have been most happy to join you," Amos said with great tact, "but alas, I return to Calcutta the day after tomorrow."

"Oh, that is a shame. Our services, unlike many others, are really quite jolly, you know. There's hardly a snore to be heard anywhere." Mrs. Pickford laughed and then gave him a very direct look. "Well, then, perhaps the next time you are in Cawnpore?"

Once again Amos looked uncertain, even more surprised. With the repetition, there was no doubt that the invitation was deliberate. For a few seconds he remained silent, then decided to be blunt. "It is extremely kind of you to invite me and, naturally, I would be delighted to accept. But I fear that my presence would prove to be an embarrassment to you."

There was a small, awkward silence during which David Pickford puffed steadily at his cigar, his wife sat staring at her clasped hands waiting for her husband to answer Amos's question, and Rose got up quickly to gather the soiled glasses on a tray.

Finally, his host broke the silence. "It is now many years since the Mutiny, my boy," he said quietly. "Enough blood has been spilled and enough hatred expended to satisfy everyone's lust for revenge. But there has to come a time, I believe most fervently, when one must try to look forward with hope, not backwards with anger. Grudges, however legitimate, cannot be nursed forever. And," he concluded, "what better place to start healing wounds than in the presence of God?"

Amos was moved by the sentiments, but his smile was touched with rare bitterness. "Unfortunately, there are not many who would agree with you, sir. The majority, on both sides I fear, remains determined not to let those wounds heal." His tone tempered. "Even if I were not Eurasian, the fact that I bear the name of Raventhorne would place you in an awkward position with your compatriots, and that I simply could not allow."

David Pickford stood up. "Why don't you let me take care of that, my boy?" He smiled and, surprisingly, his eyes twinkled. "Your presence in our church will be a nine-day wonder, no less, no more, something to gossip about through the dreary week. After that, someone's frisky wife will run away with her husband's head clerk and the office petty cash, and your very existence will be forgotten. None more fickle, alas, than the wagging tongue."

Amos had to laugh. "Nevertheless, sir, I regret that I cannot accept your very generous offer, although I know the kind motive that prompted it." His head rose in an unconscious gesture of pride. "Until my father can be declared innocent, the Raventhorne name cleared and the fact publicly acknowledged, I will not create circumstances that place the reputation, and perhaps business interests, of good friends in jeopardy."

David Pickford fell momentarily silent, then nodded his head in agreement. "Very well, my boy. It will be as you wish. God willing, your family's efforts to clear your father's name will some day bear deserving fruit."

Amos did not share in David Pickford's smile. He had not a shadow of a doubt that that hope was futile, that it was destined to remain forever unfulfilled.

As he stood on the doorstep waiting for the coachman to bring the carriage round to the front porch, Amos noticed that he and Rose happened to be briefly on their own. David Pickford had vanished into his study to fetch a manual on the Cawnpore cotton trade that Amos had requested to borrow, and his wife stood in the hallway, out of earshot, giving instructions to the bearer.

Suddenly, in a low voice, Rose asked, "If you do acquire this mill, Mr. Raventhorne, will you then move residence to Cawnpore?"

Amos shrugged. "Well, I must confess that I haven't given that aspect of the matter much thought, but, yes, I suppose I shall have to." He looked at her and, fleetingly, their gazes locked. Her expression was one of eager anticipation: it was not only unmistakable, it was enormously flattering. Amos's breath caught. Impulsively, and with considerable daring, he asked, "Would it . . . please you if I did?"

She met his eyes squarely and nodded. "Yes," she replied with astonishing firmness. "It would."

"In th-that c-case," he stammered, appalled at his boldness and quite taken aback by her equally bold response, "the prospect of a move becomes even more . . . appealing." He bowed stiffly, longing to say more, knowing that he must not, not yet, not for a long time yet, and feeling quite wretched in his helplessness.

As it happened the rapid exchange, the impromptu blushes and the mutually eloquent glances, did not go entirely unnoticed by Adelaide Pickford as she emerged from the hallway into the well-lit porch. It was not the first time that her acutely honed maternal instincts had intercepted similar, although unspoken, exchanges between her normally introverted daughter and this good-looking, essentially decent young man scarred by such tragic circumstances whom she and David found so eminently likeable. Was it wise of them to encourage his interest in Rose and risk her bitter disappointment, she wondered, considering Amos Raventhorne's self-enforced reticence?

As she watched Amos climb into the carriage and wave a final goodnight, the expression on Adelaide Pickford's face was touched with sadness.

"Why didn't you *tell* me, Christian?" Maya asked, close to tears, not of anger but of bitter disappointment. "How could you not want to share such an important happening with me?"

He hung down his head, ashamed, unable to meet her eyes. "I wanted to, I swear it! But I didn't have the courage. I thought you might be . . . upset."

"Why should I be upset?" Maya cried, even more wounded. "I'm happy that your parents arrive, happy that you and they are to be reunited!"

It was not the strict truth, of course, and both she and Christian were aware of it. In fact, the initial impact of the news Kyle had dropped upon her so casually had been shattering. Although she had had time to recover since, Maya was still badly shaken. Not only was she deeply hurt that Christian should have excluded her from his confidence no matter how noble his intentions, but for other, even more understandable reasons, she was filled with sudden dread.

He offered no answer to her question, save to look yet more ashamed and mumble repeated apologies. Neither did he offer any further excuses for his sin of omission. Despite his obvious remorse, throughout their time together that morning between them hung a subtle barrier, a fine mesh of unsaid thoughts and unspoken fears which nothing seemed able to dispel.

Nevertheless, determined to salvage his lost ground somehow, Christian continued to struggle valiantly all morning. He tried in every way that he could to compensate for his lapse. He was tender and thoughtful and amusing, showering Maya with expressions of love and undying devotion, overwhelming her with attention and small services. He ignored her sulks, her little displays of temper, and entertained her with childish jokes and clownish antics. Maya resisted for a while, but then, as always, she melted in the warmth of his charm, and rewarded his efforts with a small smile as an indication of her forgiveness.

Elated once more, he kissed her gently, then laid his head on her lap and, looking up at her with shining eyes, shared with her his plans for the future, their future!

"I have been summoned to the Secretariat for an interview. I think there has already been some talk about my posting."

Her heart sank. "Do you know yet where?"

"No, but College gossip has it that it might be in Champaran."

"The indigo belt?" She was aghast. "But that's dreadful! Those planters are out-and-out anarchists and murderers!"

With a wry grimace, he sat up. "Well, it's not as bad as all that, but yes, that is precisely why strong officers are needed to maintain law and order."

"But why you? There must be others, better qualified and more experienced."

"Somebody has to do the job." He made a manful attempt to contain his own disappointment. "I suppose I should be flattered that they consider me worthy of the task."

"Flattered to be a subdivisional officer?"

"Well, only as a first step."

"And you are certain you will be able to tolerate living in the Mofussil amid all those flies and dust and disease, with poverty-ridden peasants?" It was still incomprehensible to her that anyone would not only want to abandon the pastoral peace of the English countryside and the exciting hubbub of London for an existence in some desolate tropical limbo, but could actually look forward to it with such enthusiasm. To Maya it seemed the height of perversity.

He sat up. "Look, I know it's not the sort of posting I had envisaged, but there will be advantages."

She couldn't think of any and churlishly said so.

"We will have an independent bungalow, you know."

Her breath caught. "We?"

"Yes." He laughed, hugely relieved to have diverted another argument and taken her by such surprise. "You don't think I'd ever go without you, do you?" Playfully, he tweaked her nose and then kissed its deliciously upturned tip. "You will have horses and a carriage and all the servants you need at your instant command. You will come with me on every single tour that I will have to undertake of my district, exactly like Honoria Lawrence, who followed Henry Lawrence everywhere, all over the country, even to Nepal and Kashmir. Like Robinson Crusoe, we will live under cosy canvas in the open, on permanent picnic, with plenty of food and drink and," his voice turned husky, "and *love*. We will make a warm little nest for ourselves and bill and coo like a pair of turtle doves without a care in the world—that is, until the little ones arrive."

Breathless and blushing, Maya hid her warm face in the frontage of his riding shirt. "And you will take me to England with you every year when you go home on furlough?"

"Well, I doubt if I'll be allowed to go every year," he amended, "but yes, of course I'll take you with me whenever I go. And you will have roasted chestnuts to your heart's content, and mince pies at Christmas and Easter eggs at Easter. We will go to Bond Street and Westminster and Brighton beach, and especially to Buckingham Palace, so that you can wave to the Queen!"

Maya laughed, dizzy with excitement. "You promise, Christian, you *promise?*"

"Well, of course I do, you silly girl! If for no other reason, I have to take you to England to prove how superior our full-blooded thoroughbreds are to your puny little Arab hacks!"

She knew that he was teasing and she responded with spirit, tickling his stomach till he rolled about howling for mercy. They fell into each other's arms, laughing uproariously, and for the moment all other matters, including that of the lowly posting, were forgotten. Maya thought of nothing else but that he intended to keep his commitment to her, that wherever fate decreed that he spend it, his life would forever include her. She felt ashamed of her occasional doubts, her sporadic uncertainties, reassured again by these indications of his constancy and steadfastness, his determination to be with her always. Holding her arms out to him, she hugged him, filled with renewed courage. "Oh, I do love you so very much, Christian, so *very* much!"

The subject of his parents still hovered in the background, an invisible spectre by no means forgotten, but suddenly much less intimidating. If they were together, resolute and united, she felt they could overcome all obstacles, however daunting. Ravaged by curiosity, she longed to ask him about his awesome father and mother, about their daily lives, their habits, their likes and dislikes; how they were likely to receive his announcement about her. But she could not find the words. For the moment, her tumbling questions had to remained unasked.

It was as they prepared to return to the town that he said, "I . . . we might not be able to meet for a few days, my darling one." He evaded her eyes. "In the beginning, at least, I will have to spend time with my parents. They will expect it of me."

"Yes, of course." She saw that it was inevitable that she should now see less of him and, stifling her disappointment, she smiled. "You will tell them about . . . us?" With her eyes modestly lowered, her opalescent skin glowing hot with colour, she simply could not resist asking that.

"Naturally!" He looked shocked that she could have thought otherwise. "I will tell them at the very first opportunity."

"I have said nothing yet to Mother or to Amos."

"I know." He frowned. "It is for me to speak to them before you do. And I will, I promise, just as soon as. . . ." He stopped, his frown deepening. She reached out and stroked away the crease in his forehead, and he smiled and kissed the tip of her finger. "You must understand, my dearest," he said earnestly, "that it will take time to . . . to . . . bring them around to my . . . to *our* way of thinking. We will have to be discreet and, of course, tactful."

She heaved a rapturous sigh, once more enchanted by the pronouns he used, pronouns which bound them together with such finality. Whatever plans he had, she was part of them. What more proof could she want of his honourable intentions?

"Yes, I do understand."

"It will be torture for me not to see you each day," he whispered unhappily, taking her once more in his arms, "but we must be patient, that most of all." He held her close for a long time, trembling with love. "I will write to you every single day! In the end, you will see, it will be exactly as we want it. Just *trust* me!"

She looked up at him with a brave smile, and setting aside her own fears, tried to gently kiss away his anxieties. "Yes. Of course it will be, and of course I do."

"When they come to know you, they'll love you as much as I do," he insisted, reassuring her as much as he did himself. "How can they ever not?"

"Will they?" she murmured, dazed with involuntary hope. "Will they really?"

"Of *course* they will!" His voice rang loud with sudden confidence. "We will have all the *burra khanas* you want, and you will be the belle of the ball at every one of them."

She didn't believe him, of course, but just listening to him say the words was enough to bring tears to her eyes, and to her heart an ache of longing.

CHAPTER

10

B
UT WHERE ARE WE GOING?" Grace asked, for the third time.
Keeping her eyes fixed on her reflection in the mirror as she carefully arranged her rich, lustrous hair into a sophisticated roll, Maya
remained absorbed in her coiffeur. She noticed an errant strand, picked
up a bejewelled tortoise-shell comb and speared it firmly within the luxuriant denseness.

"You'll see when we get there."

"I don't hear from you for weeks," Grace complained with a pout, "and
then suddenly you send me a chitty asking me to come to your house
without even telling me why. I could have gone with Mama to White-
aways to buy trimmings for my new boater."

Maya met her eyes in the mirror. "Well, if you would rather *not* come
with me. . . ."

"Oh no, no, I didn't mean that," Grace amended hastily, loath to miss
whatever adventure might be in store during the mysterious outing. Even
when they were in school, Maya's escapades tended to be unconventional
and touched with bravura. There was a breathtaking non-conformism
about everything she did, a promise of the unexpected, that Grace decided
she would not miss for anything. Their imminent sortie, she sensed, had
something to do with Christian Pendlebury, and that, of course, made it all
the more irresistible. The whole town now was alive with gossip about
their daring romance. Smelling a whiff or two of further scandal, Grace
shivered with anticipation and swallowed all her objections.

It was late on Tuesday afternoon. Pale and unsmiling, Maya had
dressed with unusual care, although she scarcely knew why. It was
unlikely that *they* would see her—even more unlikely that she would want
them to. The aquamarine taffeta patterned in brown and yellow was frilly

and unusually feminine, with its puffed sleeves and jaunty little over-jacket, newly stitched and ironed to perfection. Somehow, it seemed appropriate for the occasion.

Maya loved Grace dearly, but on the whole, she would have much rather gone out on her own this evening. Like her mother, Grace was an inveterate gossip, genetically unable to keep anything to herself for more than five seconds. But this evening, Grace would have her uses. If some-one did happen to notice their presence in their intended location, two of them together up there were likely to excite less comment than if she were by herself. And her mother would ask fewer questions. As Maya dabbed light colour on her cheeks and touched her eyelashes one last time with Vaseline to make them curlier and glossier, her breath quickened; for all her nervousness, she felt strangely exhilarated, as if about to approach a milestone, a signpost giving direction to her life. She smiled at herself in the mirror and started to hum.

"For a sour little puss with not a smile to spare, you sound very happy today, my girl," Sheba remarked as she came into the room and set about folding scattered clothes.

"I'm always happy."

"Hah! Not so that anyone should notice," Sheba retorted. "And that colour on your cheeks, it's not rouge, is it? For all the liberties your mother allows you, I doubt if she would want you looking like a circus clown."

"No. It's not rouge." Maya stuck her tongue out at her in the mirror. "Ask Grace if you don't believe me."

Quickly and loyally, Grace provided confirmation with a shake of her head. "It's not rouge. It's just, well, excitement."

"Excitement? What about?" Receiving no reply, the housekeeper assumed a stance of belligerence, with her hands on her ample hips. "And when are you going to start packing, miss?" she demanded to know. "That letter from your grandma—you haven't even replied to it yet, now have you?"

"Oh, I will, I will!" Maya glanced up at the wall clock in impatience. "What's the hurry, anyway?"

"Hurry? We sail in eight weeks, *that's* the hurry, or had you forgotten?"

"No. I hadn't forgotten." Too elated to let anything dampen her bound-ing spirits, Maya playfully flicked her scarf under Sheba's squat little black nose and, with a light laugh, ran out of the bedroom down the stairs before the housekeeper could react. Hastily, Grace followed.

Down in the informal parlour, Olivia was arranging an enormous glass bowl of tiger-lilies from the garden. Without looking up she said, "If you're going to the Maidan again with your horses, there have been more complaints in the papers about the damage to the turf caused by all those galloping hooves. In fact, they're thinking of imposing restrictions and fines on stables training horses on the Maidan, so do tell Hassan to be careful."

"We're not going to the Maidan."

Something in Maya's tone made Olivia look up. She was taken by surprise by the fashionable dress, the very formal hairstyle and the vivid flush on her daughter's face. She laid down her secateurs and, for an instant, trembled on the verge of asking a question. But then, on second thought, she decided against it. They had had relatively few arguments lately. It would be foolish to disturb the truce and perhaps provoke another tantrum with a carelessly worded inquiry. After all, she couldn't be up to very much mischief as long as she was with Grace.

"The twins have almost completed your two day dresses," she contented herself with saying instead, "and Joycie says the embroidered cape is almost ready. They want you for fittings so that they can make any alterations you might consider necessary."

"Very well. I'll go as soon as I can."

Olivia picked up the secateurs again and snipped off the end of a fat, juicy stem. "If there is anything else you want stitched, you'll have to give them the materials now. There's not all that much time left and the twins are over-booked with orders as it is. Francis could fetch the cloth merchant tomorrow. Apparently, he's just received a fresh consignment of Irish linens, organdies and nankeen from London."

"No, not tomorrow," Maya said quickly, impatient to be away. "I have . . . other matters to attend to."

Olivia resisted the impulse to demand more explanations. What was the point? "Well, anyway, don't be too late coming home this evening. Edna will be here for supper and I rather think she would like to meet you."

Noticing that her fingers were stained, Olivia wiped them carefully on her gardening apron and refrained from saying any more. Without appearing to, she once again studied the unusually high colour on her daughter's cheeks, the restless fidget of her fingers clutching a pochette, the abnormal brightness of her eyes. Yes, these past few days there had been a visible change in Maya. She was more animated, yet at the same time she also seemed more preoccupied and broody, even less willing to share her thoughts. At table, Olivia had sometimes caught her smiling to herself, barely listening to what was being said, unable to recall the most trivial instruction, ready to snap when reprimanded. These contradictions in her daughter's behaviour worried Olivia because the symptoms of the malaise were unmistakable. Not for the first time she wondered, how far *had* matters progressed between this wilful child and Christian Pendlebury?

"You didn't go riding this morning?" she asked.

"No."

The monosyllabic answer irritated Olivia, but with great self-control she did not pursue the topic. "Anyway, you'll have to make time soon to go to the Home for those fittings, the sooner the better. Sheba was saying you haven't even started to pack yet?"

"Do we have to talk about all this now, Mother? Can't it wait until tonight?" Then, noticing that Grace was listening intently to the mild contretemps, she volunteered in a rather more amiable tone of voice, "I was thinking we might go for a drive along the river this evening."

"Oh, good!" Grace clapped her hands, hugely pleased. "There's a new ship due to dock today and we haven't been down to the Strand for absolute ages. Shall I go and ask Francis to summon the carriage?" Without waiting for an answer, she ran out of the room to do the needful before Maya, with her usual capriciousness, decided to change her mind.

Taking advantage of Grace's absence, Olivia gave her a meaningful look. "I'm sure you know that Christian Pendlebury's parents disembark this evening. Is that what this drive is about?"

Maya made a face. "The whole world seems to have known that!"

"And you didn't?" Olivia asked sharply. "Christian didn't tell you?"

"Of course he did. I've known about it for *weeks.*"

There was defiance in the kohl-lined violet eyes and a ring of impertinence in the tone, but because she knew her daughter so well, Olivia could also sense the fear, the uncertainty, the tearing tensions. Maya walked down the length of the room towards the exit and then, inexplicably, stopped. She turned to face her mother.

"He's asked me to marry him."

She made the announcement with perfect calm, but in the undertones there was triumph and defiance, as if she delivered a challenge.

Olivia's stomach lurched. For an instant, just an instant, she felt the onset of nausea, but then, just as swiftly, she rallied. "And have you accepted his proposal?" she asked evenly.

"Of course. Did you expect me not to?"

Olivia did not vouchsafe an answer. "Then you have decided not to go to America after all," she said, her tone flat.

"Yes. He will approach you formally as soon as . . . "—her voice tailed away, the rest of the sentence subsumed in the slight lift of her shoulders.

" . . . as he has spoken to his parents?" Olivia searched her daughter's ungiving face with deeply disturbed eyes. "Presumably they know nothing about this yet?"

"How can they? Christian intends to tell them at the first opportunity he has."

In a sudden impulse, Olivia walked up to her daughter and put a hand on her shoulder. "Maya, listen to me."

"Don't say anything more, Mother!" Maya shied away from her mother's touch. "No one is going to spoil this for me, *no one,* neither you nor Amos nor. . . ." Swallowing the rest, she pivoted on one heel and, without looking back, walked out of the door.

Slowly, Olivia's eyes filled with tears. And with pity. She felt a stir of cold, irrational anger.

It is because of you, Jai, that I fail so miserably as a mother, she raged silently. *You abandoned, yes, abandoned me, spurned your children, left me with this monstrous burden that has taken over my life, my soul, the very essence of my being. Even in death you are selfish, Jai! You still devise means to possess me, to force me to give you in death what rightfully belongs to the living. Wherever you are, whatever you are, tell me at least what to do about your tormented daughter. Reach out to me, damn you, help me, help me!*

As always, there was no response. And as always, overcome by despair, Olivia sat down and wept.

Calcutta's riverine port was one of the busiest in the East. Amidst the cranes and heavy machinery and piles of stacked cargo on the wharves, the whiffs of salt and the squawks of sea birds, there was always vitality, an infectious exuberance, an air of derring-do and discovery. One felt the world was one's oyster, every corner of it instantly within reach, no matter how isolated or inaccessible. It was the one place where it was difficult not to feel gloriously and zestfully alive.

As always, the surface of the Hooghly was splattered with an untidy assortment of vessels of all classes, sizes and flags, either on their way to, or just having returned from, the furthest corners of the globe. There were sloops, squareriggers, sleek, elegant steam clippers, Royal Navy coastal steam packets and men-o-war, long-masted sailing ships, short-masted cargo haulers, country rowboats and fishercraft.

The Strand, an elegant carriageway along the river with lush green verges fringed with trees, was a favourite meeting place of Calcutta's European community, especially the ladies. Incarcerated all day behind bamboo curtains well away from bright sunlight that might damage delicate English rose complexions and turn them ruddy, most of these ladies ventured out to brave the elements only at sundown. These evening sorties in the cool, fresh breeze of the river provided ample and varied entertainment. There were opportunities to chat with old friends, make new ones, inspect those newly arrived should passengers happen to be disembarking, scrutinise at close quarters the latest fashions from London in gowns and gloves, bonnets and brollies. Most rewarding of all, the evening strolls and drives allowed unfettered exchange of gossip away from the ever-listening ears of walls and servants, giving everyone the chance to discover what everyone else was doing (and with whom) and distribute the information accordingly.

Maya often drove along the Strand, either with her mother or with friends like the Lubbocks and Mrs. Chalcott, or all by herself, which was what she enjoyed most. Sitting up high in one of the splendid Raventhorne carriages, she would wistfully observe the fine ladies and gentlemen as they strolled and perambulated, laughed and gossiped with that enviable confidence that belonged exclusively to a class that commanded. No less arrogant were their pedigreed dogs, combed and cossetted and sporting fancy collars, yapping at the heels of frisky baba-log, followed by irate nannies and ayahs making impassioned pleas for obedience to which no one paid any heed.

Sitting all alone, aloof and silent in the awareness that in Calcutta she herself was a popular topic of gossip, Maya would watch the outside world go by with secret longing. Wherever she went, people stared and whispered, and some even dared to point as they wondered and shook their heads in disapproval. Often, some of the younger men flashed her furtive smiles and sidelong glances full of admiration; the women cloaked themselves in hauteur, making nasty sotto voce remarks, their telltale glances revealing their envy of her exquisite beauty and wealth and stylishly encased form. Maya had grown up with the stares of people. She was quite used to being looked at and talked about. Being a focus of gossip, true and manufactured, annoyed her occasionally. Yet, at the same time, it gave her a perverse sense of pleasure, of power, as if she were on a stage before a captivated audience forced to watch every move that she made.

This evening, however, there were few strollers along the Strand. Most of them were congregated at the landing stage where the new arrivals were to be ceremonially received. With Clarence Twining, the Inspector-General of Police, and his men out in full force, there was not a sign of the ubiquitous touts who usually infested the landing stages in the hope of persuading some gullible griffin to part with his money in exchange for this or that imaginary service. The handsome stone esplanade at the Ghat had a flight of broad steps descending into the water. The triumphal archway that led to the street was heavily festooned with garlands and paper flags of red, white and blue. To one side the Royal Navy Band stood in attendance, the white of their uniforms sparkling with starch, their brass instruments and gold-fringed epaulettes glinting in the setting sun. On the other side of a red carpet lined with flower vats ranged officials waiting to receive the Pendleburys, and among them Maya noticed Leonard Whitney. Against the pristine white uniforms and pale pink complexions of the reception committee, his unusually dark face stood out rather oddly, she thought.

The second-floor window of the Trident warehouse presented a splendid, uninterrupted view of the Ghat and was an ideal vantage point for Maya's purpose this evening, especially with neither her brother nor Ranjan Babu in station to ask tiresome questions. The warehouse nightwatchman was an old friend who had known her since she was a child; her impromptu excuses had gained them instant admission. With the help of a pair of powerful binoculars, it seemed to Maya that they too were part of the crowd below, every wart and wrinkle on each face satisfactorily enlarged.

"Why don't we go and watch from down there, where the others are?" Grace grumbled, crinkling her nose in distaste at the grime-encrusted wooden crate on which she was precariously perched. Peering out of the window through her binoculars, Maya made no response, too engrossed in watching the scene below to waste time on an answer.

"Well, what is all that fuss for, then?" Grace asked, looking over Maya's shoulder. "Some burra sahibs arriving from England?"

"Yes."

"Who?"

"The Pendleburys."

Grace gasped. "Christian's father and mother?"

"Yes."

"My goodness, how *thrilling!* What on earth are they coming here for?" Round-eyed and breathless, Grace wondered if it might be for a wedding, but knowing how touchy Maya could be about her personal life, she didn't dare risk further questions.

"Don't you know anything about what's going on?" Maya asked irritably. "Everyone knows his father is the new Finance member in the Viceroy's Council. Now do be *quiet,* Grace. I'll give you the glasses in a minute and you can look for yourself."

Beyond the welcoming crowd waiting for the arrival of the fleet of small boats that would bring passengers of the *Greenock Belle* up the river from Kedgeree, sixty-nine miles downstream, Clarence Twining mopped his beefy brow against the humidity. Sir Bruce and Lady McNaughton, seated on chairs as befitted their lofty position, looked rather bored as two punka-wallahs wielded large ornamental palm-leaf fans behind their chairs, and a host of aides, flunkeys and factotums fluttered around performing various services.

Maya swivelled the glasses as she searched for Christian. She finally spotted him in one corner of the landing stage, deep in conversation with an official she did not recognise, trying his best to look as inconspicuous as possible. He seemed hot and uncomfortable in his dark, formal suit with buttoned-up collar. Every now and then he inserted a finger to loosen it around his neck. Maya focussed on him for a long while, observing his every gesture, each nuance of his expression, her heart bursting with pride. She had never before seen him in formal attire; he looked so terribly handsome, so dashing! In a rush of elation she remembered that she was soon to be his wife and, with an impromptu laugh, she handed the field glasses to Grace. "Don't you think Christian looks absolutely splendid in his dark suit?"

Grace peered through the lenses and nodded with a touch of wistfulness. "He promised to call on us but never did. And now, with his parents here and all, I suppose he never will." Sadly, she lowered her glasses but then raised them again immediately. "Oh, look!" she squealed. "I think something's happening!"

Maya grabbed the glasses from her and focussed again. Yes, there did seem to be heightened activity among the waiting officials. Obviously, the convoy of small boats bearing the Pendleburys had been sighted; a few more minutes and they would be here! Maya's breath caught with excitement. In her impatience, she could barely sit still. With a roll of drums the band struck up a gay, nautical tune; all the officials leapt into action. Even the McNaughtons rose from their chairs and, at a sign from Twining, all his men sprang to attention, their chests thrust out like pouter pigeons.

The band completed the tune with excellent timing. Just as the final chord was struck, the leading canopied boat slid into position at the bottom of the steps. Maya's fingers tightened around the binoculars. A tingling thrill rippled up her spine, making her shiver.

Sir Bruce took up his position at the top of the steps and, as far as his enormous stomach would allow him to, leant forward to extend a hand. A white-gloved hand, small and feminine, reached out to take it with con-siderable delicacy, followed by the lady herself. Behind the tall, elegant female figure came Sir Jasper, lean and spry, declining helping hands to jump confidently onto terra firma. Lady Pendlebury and Lady Mc-Naughton gave each other crisp little pecks on the cheeks, there were smiles all round and snatches of light, lively conversation floated up on the wind as pleasantries were exchanged. Lady Pendlebury said some-thing to Bruce McNaughton and he guffawed. Heart thumping madly, Maya turned the glasses onto Christian's face. He looked even paler, his eyes darting nervously from side to side, his hands clasping and unclasp-ing behind his back. It was only after the McNaughtons had finished speaking with his parents that, with due regard to protocol, he modestly stepped forward. Very formally, he put his lips to his mother's cheek and received in return a warm kiss and an affectionate hug. Taking Christian's right hand in both of his, his father shook it vigorously, then gave him an approving pat on the back. Sir Jasper said something, Christian looked pleased, blushed and everyone laughed. Maya could see Lady Pendle-bury's lips move as she spoke, her pleasure obvious at seeing her son again. Then her cool, tranquil eyes searched her son's face, the powerful lenses of the binoculars revealing small traces of anxiety. Christian responded with a weak smile and he shook his head. A shadow of a frown appeared on his high, clear forehead.

Was his mother asking him about her? Maya trembled. What would she not have given to hear that initial exchange between Christian and his parents!

Grace snatched the glasses out of her hand, insisting that it was now her turn. "My goodness, she looks rather . . . forbidding, doesn't she?"

Privately, Maya agreed, but she was annoyed that Grace should have had the temerity to make such an observation. "Forbidding? No, I wouldn't say so at all," she said coldly. "Lady Pendlebury happens to be a woman of poise and sophistication, anyone can see that. What else would one expect of someone of her social standing?"

Having delivered a suitable reproof and put Grace in her place, Maya mulled over her own conclusions. Whether or not it came from sophisti-cation and poise, there was an air about Lady Pendlebury that was unmis-takably aloof. Dressed in a stylish, beautifully tailored *café au lait* sheath of some lacy material, she looked positively regal, an aristocrat down to the triangular points of her shining, patent leather shoes that peeped from beneath the frilled hem of her skirt. The gown, Maya guessed without knowing much about Parisian *haute couture*, was obviously of French design and cut, and that deceptively simple look had probably cost a for-tune to achieve. On the elongated, erect neck was balanced a perfectly pro-portioned head, held at just the right angle to blend hauteur with smiling charm. From whatever was visible of Lady Pendlebury's coiffeur beneath the wide brim of the hat that so faultlessly matched her gown, one could see that it was undisturbed even after a long and windy boat ride, not a single strand having dared to go astray. The heat and humidity of the waning day were crushing, yet Lady Pendlebury looked cool and collected and full of statuesque grace. The fan held in her right hand fluttered occasionally, but otherwise she showed no sign of reacting to the climate few could withstand. The frilly little umbrella swinging from her left wrist was as pretty and fragile as a doll—and about as useful, one imagined, in a monsoon downpour.

Grace relinquished the binoculars with a sigh. "Oh, what a splendid, splendid occasion! You *are* so very lucky, you know." When Maya made no response, she sighed again. "Christian Pendlebury is your . . . friend, and his parents are such . . . important people." She added daringly, "You . . . you might even be living in England one of these days."

Maya did not reply, she could not. Seeing Christian in the company of his parents, with his own kind, she felt a rush of conflicting emotions. The dread that rose side by side with the sense of pride she resolutely pushed aside, determined not to let it quench the tenuous flame of hope. Peering again through the glasses, she tried to discern Sir Jasper's features, but there was not enough light, and anyway he had turned his face in another direction. All she could make out was that he was tall, in good trim, straight-backed and walked with long, decisive strides, as if he knew exactly where he was going. Even in the dusk, he seemed compelling and forceful, effortlessly radiating strength and authority. It was difficult to see much more, and in any case, the crowd had started to disperse through the arch onto the Strand Road where a succession of carriages awaited.

Maya aimed her glasses at the queue of smartly shining carriages now starting to fill as the Pendleburys prepared to mount theirs and depart for their new home at Garden Reach. In the more modest carriages and carts behind were loaded their extensive entourage and some of their baggage, the rest no doubt to follow later with other minions. Briefly, Maya wondered if Christian would now decide to move out of the chummery; the prospect depressed and exhilarated her at the same time. They would not be able to see each other as freely as before if he chose to live with his parents. On the other hand, would he not also invite her to meet them in the exclusive portals of that splendid Garden Reach mansion?

One last time, Maya looked through the glasses at the scene below. In the gloom a few of the faces could still be recognised. One she identified instantly and with crystal clarity was that of Kyle Hawkesworth! She gave a violent start and the binoculars slipped from her fingers. Had it not been for Grace's swift retrieval, they would have crashed to the floor, beyond redemption.

"What's happened?" Grace gasped, clutching the precious glasses to her chest. "Is something wrong?"

Kyle here? How? *Why?*

Maya swallowed hard and merely shook her head, all her elation evaporating like a puff of smoke. She appropriated the binoculars from Grace and held them again to her eyes. During the few seconds that had elapsed, the Pendleburys' coachman had lit the lamps on either side of their open landau. In the buttery illumination they provided, she saw Kyle even more clearly. He stood next to Christian, being formally presented to his parents. Solemn and half smiling, he bowed, first to Lady Pendlebury, then to Sir Jasper, who offered him his hand. A few words were exchanged, a fragment or two of quiet laughter was heard, and then, with a farewell wave, the Pendleburys climbed into their open carriage. The coachman raised his whip and the team of four horses started to move away. Kyle put a casual arm about Christian's shoulders and, conversing with great intimacy, they walked away to be swallowed up by the dusk.

Slowly Maya lowered the glasses, cold with astonishment and profoundly uneasy. She sat very still, her eyes fixed on nothing in particular on the other side of the darkening river. She didn't hear any of Grace's petulant questions, nor thought to give her any replies. For a few moments she remained entirely lost within the maze of her own careening thoughts.

Kyle was starting to expand the deadly little webs in which he had entrapped Christian. She had to stop him before he went any further.

It had been projected that by the end of the decade, the total length of railway line open for traffic in India and Burma would be 8,611 miles, with proposals under consideration for an additional 1,850 miles. The capital expended on these constructions and expansions by Her Majesty's Government would have amounted by then to more than 120 million pounds sterling. A fifth of a century had elapsed since construction was started on the country's inaugural track between Bombay and Thana in western India, and twenty-three years since the comprehensive scheme had been laid out by Lord Dalhousie under the aegis of the East India Company. Undoubtedly the radiating railway network was a masterly achievement, a marvel of planning and engineering considering that every rail, girder, engine and wagon had to be sent out from England by ship over thousands of nautical miles. None of this Amos had any wish to deny as he sat slouched in a corner of a railway compartment on his way back to Calcutta. He conceded that the Indian railway companies were an admirable lot, worthy of every Indian resident's adulation and gratitude. But at the same time he wondered, with 120 million damn pounds sterling at their disposal, why the hell couldn't they have designed travelling compartments that weren't such lethal hazards to life, limb and sanity?

Since Ranjan Babu and he had entrained in Cawnpore the previous evening, he had been waging a running battle with flies. Because the window shutter was jammed and refused to shut, the wretched pests were free to swarm into the compartment without restraint from the sugar-cane fields alongside the track, giving him not a moment's respite. He must have swatted close to a hundred, hitting some, missing more, probably swallowing a few in the bargain. Furthermore, his forehead was encrusted with thick, black grime from the coal dust and sparks that blew from the engine straight into his face and eyes without let-up. Every single bone in his body seemed on the verge of imminent disintegration as the rattling bogey thundered along its allotted route with a violence not unlike an extended earthquake. Now, the morning sun poured in from the east making him even more intolerably hot and, to add insult to injury, the tub of ice they had purchased at the previous station at extortionist rates to cool the compartment had melted a full hour before the stationmaster had vowed that it would. And Allahabad, their immediate destination, was still two hours away.

Gingerly, Amos lowered his legs to the floor, and noticed a blue bruise forming on one shin. He again cursed generously. "They could have at least cushioned the damn bunks in these wooden coffins," he grumbled. "One would think we paid enough blasted taxes to deserve *some* modicum of consideration."

"Well, it is certainly better than riding a thousand miles on a horse and getting sore bottoms, or being carried in a palanquin entirely at the mercy of some coolie's tottering feet and thieving fingers."

Stretched out lazily on the opposite bunk with every indication of inner peace and outer comfort, Ranjan Babu smiled, suppressed a yawn and gurgled contentedly, without opening his eyes.

Ranjan Babu's complacency, and the fact that he had snored his way right through the night without any trouble at all, irked Amos all the more. He himself had spent a terrible night, sleepless and hot, which had left him exhausted and bad-tempered and aching all over. He considered it the height of bad form that whereas he suffered dreadfully, his manager should be absolved of all participation in that suffering.

"I'll tell you one thing, Ranjan Babu," he said grimly. "When we get this blasted mill, I'll . . ."

"*If* we get it," Ranjan Babu murmured without opening his eyes.

The interruption and the reminder gave Amos a legitimate excuse to vent his frustration. "Why do you keep saying that?" he exploded, losing his temper. "From the very beginning you've given me nothing but discouragement—and, to be frank, I'm sick and tired of all this persistent pessimism. For once in your life, Ranjan Babu, can't you be a little less damned conservative? Can't you make an exception this time and be open-minded?" In an absolute rage, he kicked the tub of erstwhile ice with a vicious foot, turned his red-hot face in the opposite direction and resolutely stared out of the window.

Startled by the outburst, Ranjan Moitra hastily sat up. "I am sorry, I did not mean to. . . ."

"Yes, you did, you *did*! You've never been in favour of this project, never, and I have to confess I just *cannot* understand your attitude. It is almost as if you try in every way you can to make me fail in my endeavour. Are you hoping that I make a fool of myself in the eyes of the commercial community, is that it?" Ranjan Moitra paled, profoundly injured. For a moment or two he merely sat staring at the floor. Then he lay down again and closed his eyes without saying a word in his own defence.

The argument had been raging for months, ever since Amos had first decided to make a bid for the cotton mill, all through their stay in

Cawnpore. He was now utterly exasperated by Ranjan Babu's extraordinary obstinacy. No, not just exasperated, puzzled and wounded. He simply could not understand the man's reasoning—if any. Much as he had tried, he simply could not. For a long while, silence reigned between them (if silence was indeed the right word considering the clamour of the rattling bogey). It was a heavy, sullen silence in which both simmered quietly. Then Amos's anger—always quicker to die than it was to rise—subsided. Involuntarily, almost with a will of their own, his thoughts raced back over the years and he started to brood.

Ever since he had left the Academy and his mother had agreed that it was time for him to be given an apprenticeship in Trident, it was Ranjan Babu who had taken him under his wing and taught him everything he knew about the administration of tea and about shipping and warehousing. The manager had been an immensely patient and understanding mentor, never too tired to explain, to amplify, to repeat as many times as necessary. Amos knew that Ranjan Babu had enormous affection for the family and that, over the decades, his loyalty and concern for them all had been beyond question. During the dark days of the Mutiny, John Company had threatened to confiscate all the Raventhorne properties and so end Trident's commercial activities, as vindictive punishment for Jai Raventhorne's alleged treachery. At that time it was Ranjan Moitra who had refused to capitulate, mounting a lone battle against this vendetta of hate. Eventually, he had taken his courage in his hands and boldly approached the Governor-General, Lord Canning. Known as a man of compassion, understanding and clemency who abhorred post-Mutiny exercises in mindless revenge, His Excellency had interceded and reversed the Company's order.

Through the six years that Amos had been with Trident, Ranjan Moitra had eagerly and selflessly shared with him his knowledge and wisdom. He had taken Amos into his confidence and, without reservation, imparted to him the considerable expertise he himself had acquired during his many years with Trident and in the cut and thrust of Calcutta's commercial arenas. If one could forgive Ranjan Babu his rather excessive traditionalism, his innate distrust of change in any shape or form, there was no denying that he was a man worth his weight in gold, the salt of the very earth, a rare friend and an absolutely trustworthy supporter.

Thinking of all this now as he sulked in his compartment corner, Amos felt ashamed of his loss of temper. But he was truly confounded by Ranjan Babu's extraordinary stubbornness. In the past, he had always assessed Amos's schemes and suggestions, however immature, with patience and a willingness to concede merit where merit was due. It hurt and bewildered Amos now to see how fiercely Ranjan Babu opposed this project at every given chance, how hostile he seemed to the very idea. This attitude of someone he loved and respected dearly, someone who was a proven well-wisher, ally and mentor, disappointed Amos more than he could say.

Nevertheless, Amos's sense of shame at his outburst and at the entirely unfair accusations he had voiced was far greater than his incomprehension of Ranjan Babu's motives. He had seldom spoken so harshly to anyone, let alone to this man to whom he and his family were so profoundly beholden. He threw an oblique glance across the compartment and saw that the manager still lay with his eyes closed, stiff and overwhelmed with dejection.

Drawing in a deep breath, Amos attempted a smile. "I'm sorry, Ranjan Babu, I shouldn't have said to you all that I did. I apologise and ask for your forgiveness." Ranjan Babu didn't look at him but merely acknowledged the apology with a slight inclination of the head. For a moment Amos studied the set, solemn face. "Tell me, Ranjan Babu," he asked quietly, with unsmiling gravity, "is there some special reason why you object so vehemently to this mill project? Is there something that you know that you are keeping from me?"

Accosted with such directness, Ranjan Babu had no option but to respond. He sat up slowly, keeping his head well lowered and started to polish his glasses. "Reason? Er, no . . . not at all. I merely. . . ."

"Tell me the truth, Ranjan Babu, *please*. I promise I won't be offended." Amos rose, went to sit next to the manager and laid a hand on the older man's arm. "If there is something troubling you, I would like to know what it is."

Ranjan Babu heaved a deep sigh and settled back in his bunk. As his head hit the wooden back rest of the bunk with a thud, he winced and rubbed the spot with a tentative finger. "I have been worried because I do not wish you to be disappointed."

"Is there any reason that I should be?"

"No, but. . . ." He faltered, then tears sprang to his eyes. "But first of all I would like you to know that at no time would I wish you in any way to fail, Master Amos! You are the son of my beloved Sarkar, his heir, and as such you are like my own son. There could never be anything that I would do to . . . to. . . ." Words failed him as he was overcome with emotion.

Watching the older man's distress, Amos filled with self-disgust, even more ashamed of himself. Impulsively, he reached out for Ranjan Moitra's hand and squeezed it hard, desperate to make amends. "All that is already understood, Ranjan Babu," he said, deeply moved. "I too consider you like a father, a very wise father at that, and once again I beg to be forgiven my unthinking outburst. But it is because of this very intimate understanding that we have always had that I feel you must be absolutely honest with me. Now tell me, what is it that troubles you about this project?"

For a moment or two Ranjan Moitra said nothing, obviously struggling within himself. Then he arrived at a decision. "Yes," he said sadly. "There *is* something that troubles me about your project." He paused and Amos tensed. "It is rumoured that the mill will not be put up for auction after all."

"Why ever not?" Amos's half laugh was incredulous. "You heard what was being discussed by the workers at the mill the day before we left."

"Yes, I heard all that, but it is also being said in Calcutta that Mr. Sutherland—who is still in England—has already made a private arrangement with an English buyer." He added quickly, "I hasten to explain that currently, this is only a rumour. Whether it will turn out to be true is difficult to tell."

"You heard the rumour in Calcutta?"

The older man did not meet his eyes. "Yes."

"Why did you never mention it to me before?"

"It is only bazaar gossip!" Ranjan Moitra protested, spreading his hands. "How can one confirm it? Nevertheless, I would like you to be prepared for disappointment. It is this that has been troubling me greatly."

Amos continued to stare, pale and shocked but not yet entirely convinced. "I don't think you are telling me everything, Ranjan Babu. How long have you known about this?"

"Well, not long. . . ."

"How long, Ranjan Babu, tell me the truth?"

The manager gave a small shudder and closed his eyes. "I have been hearing the rumour about the private sale for some time now, long before we left for Cawnpore."

Amos was flabbergasted. "Then why in heaven's name did you allow me to waste all this time and energy? Why did you never *say* anything?" Had he not been so completely mystified, he would have been furious once more.

"Would you have listened to me if I had?" Moitra cried in frustration. "Would you have accepted my advice not to return to Cawnpore on the strength of a rumour?"

Amos fell silent, a sharp pain piercing his chest. "All right, but now you can tell me the full extent of the rumour. How far *has* this sale progressed?"

For the first time, Moitra raised his eyes and levelled them with his. "Except for the paperwork, the rumour goes, the mill is as good as sold."

Amos's shoulders slumped. He sat back with his eyes closed. All this effort for nothing! All his hopes and dreams ground into dust. . . .

"Who is the buyer?"

Moitra quickly lowered his eyes again and occupied himself in brushing particles of coal off his bed-roll. "That, I am sorry, I do not know. All I have heard is that he is an Englishman."

A thought suddenly struck Amos and he sat up. "If we can discover his identity, we could make him a counter-offer. As long as we can assure him a fair profit, he might be willing to transfer the sale to us. What do you think?"

"Yes, that is always possible."

"Can we not talk to someone, a member of the outgoing board perhaps, in Cawnpore?"

"Mr. Sutherland owns eighty-five percent of the company. There is no one else in any position of authority who can give us more information. We will simply have to await his return from England."

"Or wait until this buyer turns up to claim the property." Looking decidedly brighter, Amos rubbed his hands together. "Yes, the more I think of it, the better it sounds. I see no reason why he should not be willing to sell the mill to us if he stands to make a healthy gain in the process."

"There would be no harm in trying."

Once again animated, Amos smiled with anticipation. "We will institute the process as soon as we have completed our business in Allahabad and returned to Calcutta. No, sir, all is by no means lost!"

With an expression of delicate distaste, Ranjan Moitra picked up the fly swat and aimed it at a prospective victim. He missed and the gleeful fly buzzed away out into the open. With a few choice words in Bengali in the direction of the window, he lay down again, closed his eyes and resolutely courted sleep.

He had neither the heart nor the stomach to carry the discussion further.

It was pitch dark. The embankment was deserted.

In a restless night sky curdling with anger, there was not even an apology of a moon. Remnants of an early evening nor'wester clung to the air, weighing it down with damp. Huge black rocks studded the embankment, a veritable obstacle course in the unrelenting dark. Laced around the boulders, the meandering path was slippery underfoot, hazardous and difficult to negotiate. In between its two shores the Hooghly lay low and flat, like a thick slick of oil. Cloying earth smells mingled with dank fumes rising from the river to produce a combined assault on the senses; in the receding tide the river smelled of dead fish and rotting weeds and salt carried in from the Bay to the south. In the north-west corner of the sky, lightning crackled and an army of belligerent clouds growled in instant retaliation. But otherwise, save for the natural, nightly harmonies of a tropical riverside, the night was eerily still.

Maya shivered and pulled her dark linen cape closer about her shoulders. By the uncertain light of her lantern, she picked her way carefully and cautiously between the giant boulders glistening with a skin of residual rain. A lazy wind rose in the north-west. Sporadic gusts, fresh and young, brushed her cheeks, briefly sweeping away the leaden wetness. Worriedly, Maya scanned the sky, wondering if she would have time to complete her mission before the rain came. From a dark smudge of clustered trees a jackal howled, and the cry was immediately taken up by the pack. Maya shivered again. She wished she had not chosen such a hostile night for her impetuous errand, even though, ironically enough, it was precisely because of the foul weather that she had ventured forth tonight. The route she had taken, past the docks and the wharves, was unfrequented and solitary. It was unlikely that she would be accosted. Angrily, she cast aside the momentary weakness. However uncertain the outcome, she would do what she had set out to. Throwing back her shoulders, she hardened herself against the moonless dark and pressed on.

Scrambling across the smaller boulders and the wet, grassy patches of coarse weeds and tall grasses, her alert eyes caught sight of a wavering patch of light in the distance. She halted and peered through the gloom, holding her lantern low in case it was observed. Through a thick lattice of branches, she saw the light again and recognised the point at which she stood. In her relief and impatience to proceed, she kicked and dislodged a sizeable rock. It flew down the embankment with a clatter, taking with it several others, and Maya mouthed a curse. She stopped and listened for a moment, but there were no sudden shouts of discovery and the embankment remained deserted.

She clambered over another boulder to clear her view of what lay ahead and, suddenly, the light turned into a large, solid square. A window! She felt a surge of satisfaction; yes, it was indeed a window of Kyle's press. In the intermittent flashes of lightning she could discern the outline of the hulking structure, dark and brooding like its owner, and then more squares of light, more windows. She did not dare move any closer in case someone looked out and she was observed. She would have to wait until all the lights were extinguished before she proceeded further. Damn! It was already past midnight; did Kyle never go to sleep? Selecting the large flat surface of a stone less damp than the rest, she sat down to wait in feverish anticipation.

Tonight, she would know if her deductions were right. Tonight, she would learn more about Kyle Hawkesworth's mysterious lady—if indeed she existed.

Maya had thought a great deal about her curious experience at Kyle's house. The more she thought about it, the more puzzled she became. Then, two nights ago, as she pondered and paced in an agony of impatience, a sudden spark of memory had come to her rescue: a tunnel! Wasn't that what Christian had mentioned when talking of his visit to Kyle's press? As a direct corollary to that, she had also remembered that that day at Kyle's house, while she inspected the courtyard where that ephemeral flash of colour had vanished, one trifling observation had burrowed into the back of her mind and remained there, although at the time she had not been aware of it. There was not a breath of wind that evening; even the few clothes hanging on the washing line were absolutely still. Yet, as she looked, the bushes along one side of the courtyard had shook and quivered as if buffeted by a gale.

After that, it was easy to put two and two together. What she had seen and heard that day had nothing to do with ghosts and ghouls; it was physical evidence of a very solid human presence. The bushes obviously concealed some sort of opening through which the person (surely a woman!) had vanished, an opening that led to a subterranean room or a tunnel. Maya knew from stories she had heard as a child from her mother that there had been a time when smuggling was rampant along the Hooghly and contraband was brought up the river by boat. If indeed a tunnel did run beneath Kyle's *nilkothi*, then that must have been used once to store contraband. All that was now perfectly clear. What was not clear was where exactly along the extensive embankment *was* the riverside entrance to this mysterious tunnel?

Unfortunately, there was only one way to find out.

A pair of bats making daring loops in the air just above Maya's head as they targeted insects broke her trend of thought. She glanced quickly at the press building and her heart leapt: all the lights had finally been extinguished. The huge structure, gaunt and forbidding, stood shrouded in silence and presumably deserted for the night. Quickly, Maya rose and resumed her investigations.

The mouth of the tunnel, she calculated, had to be somewhere along the embankment very near to the press, set in a vertical rather than horizontal rockface for protection from the elements. It had to be well above the highwater mark so as not to invite flooding when the tide was in. That the mouth of the tunnel would not be blocked, she was reasonably sure. Even if it had been at one time, if her theory was correct, Kyle would have certainly had it excavated to allow for the inlet of fresh air to make it suitable for human occupation. The question was, with such scant data based purely on guesswork, would she be able to find the tunnel at all?

She gazed across the deserted stretch of embankment ahead of her and her heart sank. It would take hours, maybe days (or rather, nights) to find what she was looking for. But then, what was the alternative—to give up altogether? No! Having risked her mother's wrath to steal out alone in the dead of night and come so far, she refused to abandon her mission now. Once more she gritted her teeth and resolutely swallowed her horror of spiders and scorpions, to set about the daunting task without allowing herself further mental diversions. Using a stick to probe inside tangles of undergrowth and sizeable crevices, she slowly worked her way towards the *nilkothi,* concentrating on topographical formations tall enough to accommodate a fairly large opening. At the same time she kept an alert eye open for any other indication of what she sought. Inch by painstaking inch, she worked her way forward. It was slow work, but she persevered, grateful for the intermittent flashes of lightning that supplemented the inadequate illumination provided by her lantern. Somewhere in the distance she heard a church clock chime two; she had been on the embankment since before midnight. Maya stopped and wearily wiped the sweat and grime off her face.

She had found nothing.

A fine mist of rain had started to fall; she was drenched with perspiration and exhausted. With a muted cry of frustration, she flung down the stick, feeling angry and disheartened. What if all her calculations were wrong? What if there was no tunnel, no mysterious woman at all? What if those tinkling bangles, that swift streak of colour, those quivering bushes, had just been figments of an overworked imagination? Or, perhaps, a wraith after all?

With a groan, Maya sank down on a flat rock for a brief rest, starting to feel hopeless. Somewhere a jackal howled again. Fearfully, she looked towards the huddle of trees, now alarmingly close. Then her breath caught. The sound did not seem to be coming from the direction of the trees at all, it sounded even closer. Nervously, Maya looked around. In the all-pervasive gloom, she could see nothing. She patted a pocket in her cape wherein reposed her mother's derringer, purloined earlier that evening without her mother's knowledge, and felt a renewal of courage. Letting her breath flow once more, she listened intently.

The call came again, this time louder. It was a strange sound, a sort of wail, hollow and disembodied and somehow unearthly, as if from a throat not quite human. The small hairs at the nape of her neck tingled and stiffened; her blood chilled. Had she not been so petrified with fear, she would have risen and fled, abandoning her mission without a second thought. But unable to move, she merely sat rooted, forced to listen. The wailing, which had started on a fairly low note, now rose in pitch to a crescendo, climaxing with a sharp, angry shriek. For a second or two it quivered uncertainly, then relapsed into a succession of diminishing grunts and whines. Slowly the sounds faded away altogether and once more the night was restored to silence. Maya was struck by two sudden realisations: the wailing came not from some supernatural, but from the young of some animal very much of her own environment. And it came not from the embankment at all but from *underneath* it. In the first discovery she felt relief, in the second the overwhelming thrill of victory.

She had found the location of the tunnel!

Maya sat for just a moment longer, letting the panic dispel, then, too flushed with excitement to be frightened, she once more sprang into action. All that remained now was to actually pinpoint the entrance to the tunnel, still a formidable task but no longer outside her capabilities. She set to work with renewed fervour.

Perhaps because fortune is said to favour the brave, no sooner had Maya continued with her endeavors than she came across another sudden windfall. Out of the corner of one eye, behind a feathery bush not more than ten yards from where she stood, she noticed a pale shimmer, a mere whisper of something not quite part of the natural terrain. She raised her lantern to see it better and it vanished; when she lowered the lantern, it appeared again. Her heart palpitating madly, hardly daring to breathe, she made her way towards the bush from behind which the gauzy glow appeared to emanate. A fairly narrow but quite secure ledge ran along the rockface ahead. Treading with care, Maya negotiated it without much difficulty, glad that she wore britches and stout, knee-high boots. The fernlike plant grew out of a deep crevice in a vertical rockface scored with ridges and folds. She balanced herself on her knees, and with a stick, cautiously parted the feathery stalks of the bush. Her mouth went dry with the thrill of a final discovery. There, right in front of her, was the elusive aperture!

The entrance was closer to the *nilkothi* than she had calculated, indeed, almost directly below one of the windows of the press. Man-sized, the opening was protected by an iron grille, but badly rusted, with the surrounding cement in a state of decay. A very faint light relieved the gloom inside the tunnel, which was deserted. She felt a flutter of panic—was she being watched, perhaps, by someone at the window of the press directly above where she stood? Then she cast off her trepidations as ridiculous. Kyle had no idea at all that she suspected anything, so why should anyone be keeping watch at this unearthly hour on such a cussed night? Boldly, she placed her lantern on a small ledge above her head and got down to work without wasting any more time.

Ten minutes later, the grille was loose and came away easily in her hands. She paused a moment to ensure that she had not been heard, but there was no sign of any life anywhere and the tunnel remained deserted. Far too intoxicated now with triumph to wait even a minute longer, she slid her legs through the opening and dropped soundlessly into the cavernous opening.

The passage, roughly excavated but perfectly negotiable, appeared to be in the shape of a dog's leg and not as long as she had thought. At the point at which the tunnel curved, a low-burning lantern hung on a nail in the wall—the source of the light that she had seen. The air she breathed in now was adequately fresh; possibly other vents had been made to ensure proper circulation. At the bend she halted and, taut with tension, peered round it. The passage ahead was wider, cut off with the barrier of a brick wall, an obviously recent construction that reached all the way up to the ceiling. Two large ventilators had been built into the top. Below, in the centre of the wall, was set a neat, green-painted, shuttered door.

The top half of one of the shutters was minimally open.

Maya slid her moist, clammy palms against the sides of her britches to wipe them dry. It was all she could do to force the breath in and out of her lungs. She stood for a long while wondering whether to venture further or not. Then, cautiously, she took a few steps forward. Behind the door was evidently a room, but it was shrouded in silence. Taking another few steps, Maya crept right up to the shutter and peered through the crack. All she could see was a thin, horizontal sliver of wall upon which large, grotesque shadows danced, indicating the presence of a low-burning lamp somewhere in the room. As her eyes became accustomed to the half dark, she discerned part of a string cot. Upon one end of it reposed a pair of feet—female feet!

Even in the greyness, Maya could see that they were long and slim and beautifully proportioned. One foot moved a fraction and the bed creaked; with the change of position, the silver of the woman's anklets caught the flickering flame and glinted. Next to the bed, on the other side, there was the shadow of another shape—a *cage?* With upright wooden slats along the side?

Somewhere in the near distance lightning cracked, so loudly and so suddenly that in her state of tension, Maya almost cried out in alarm. A deep, persistent roll of thunder followed. Within the narrow confines of the tunnel, briefly ablaze with the flash, the sounds grew and amplified to clamorous proportions. The quality of the air changed; it became cooler, sharper, more abundant. Outside, it was raining.

The strange wailing started up again!

Even though she was prepared for it, Maya was thrown briefly off balance and hurriedly retreated from her peephole. The cries came from within the room, but this time they were subdued, deep-throated, little whines and jerky animal-like grunts. Standing away from the door with her back pressed against the wall, Maya listened in chilled fascination. She heard a prolonged creak of the cot; obviously the woman had risen. Maya abandoned caution and again crept towards the door to peer through the crack. Part of an unmistakably female figure was bending over the cage, making cooing noises into it. Her voice, low and melodious, was full of love and concern. Lulled by the soothing sounds, the gurgles lessened and died, relapsing into steady, rhythmic breathing.

Maya pressed her face closer into the crack and, in the process, pushed the shutter open a little more. Too engrossed to notice the slight noise behind her, the woman remained where she was, her arms reaching down, one hand moving as if patting something.

Oh, sweet Lord, a *child?*

Maya almost stopped breathing—it was such an obvious answer, she wondered why it had not struck her before. A memory flashed before her eyes of a wooden cart, a top, two rag dolls, the look of annoyance on Kyle's face that she should have seen the toys. . . . yes, a child! But with such a terrifyingly inhuman cry, and whose?

Kyle's?

All was again eerily quiet. Outside, even the patter of the rain had ceased. The woman had returned to her bed and the child was silent, deep in slumber. Maya shivered; cold sweat dappled her forehead. Shaking like a leaf, she turned and ran back to the mouth of the tunnel, flung herself out into the open, and with clumsy, trembling fingers replaced the grille. Regardless of its wetness, she sank down on the edge of the shelf, quivering with shock, drenched in perspiration. She sat for a while trying to absorb what she had seen and heard, but she could make no sense of any of it. It was all so preposterous, so unbelievably bizarre.

Had she learned enough for her purpose? No. She had to know more, she had to know it all. She would not rest until she did!

CHAPTER

11

A H, TUSSUR SILK, is it not, Mr. Whitney?"
Not knowing tussur from twill, Leonard Whitney tried to look
wise and nodded.

Dubiously, Constance Pendlebury fingered the weave of the new high
curtains in the new sitting room of her new mansion at Garden Reach.
"Very fine, I grant you, but perhaps a shade—how shall I put it?—*de trop?*
Magenta doesn't really go with anything, does it, Mr. Whitney? Especially
not with Wedgwood blue, Quinling porcelain and salmon pink damask.
What we need in the tropics, I think, is subtlety, with perhaps just a soup-
con of panache. What do you say, Mr. Whitney?"

Notebook in hand, pencil poised in mid-air, Leonard Whitney stared at
her blankly. He had no idea what Lady Pendlebury was talking about. He
shuffled his feet and coughed. "Well, yes."

"Oh, I'm so glad you agree, Mr. Whitney. In that case, would you please
make a note to summon the tailors and the cloth vendor tomorrow—that
nice man with the fresh consignment from London that Mrs. Anderson so
highly recommended?" She sailed through the lofty archway into the
music room next door, followed by the hapless Whitney. "First of all, and
most important, we must have that piano tuner in *immediately.* The Stein-
way sounds like a death rattle and the less said about the harpsichord the
better. As for the portable folding music desks and the punka protectors
for the music stand, I think perhaps. . . ."

Calmly but meticulously, Lady Pendlebury rattled off instructions,
hardly pausing for breath, knowing exactly what she wanted. By the time
they had completed their tour of the enormous triple-storeyed mansion,
room by room, Whitney's head whirled and his notebook bulged with the
esoterica of silver-plated biscuit-caskets, D-shape eye-preservers against

early daylight, and wind-and punka-proof Hink's lamps with triple-action burners.

"I have a feeling there is something quite vital we have overlooked," Lady Pendlebury remarked as they finished with the banqueting hall and returned to the formal drawing room. "Do you remember what it is, Mr. Whitney?"

For a wild moment, Whitney was tempted to lie. His temples hummed with an incipient headache and he was thoroughly confused. But then he remembered that this was his first week on deputation to the all-important Pendleburys and much depended upon the diligence with which he conducted his new duties. He sighed and turned a fresh page of his notebook. "The kitchens, your ladyship."

Lady Pendlebury brightened. "Dear me! Monsieur Pierre would never forgive me if I overlooked those! Now let me see . . . oh yes, yesterday we talked about acquiring a decent oven, didn't we? I suppose the native *baburchis* are used to those hideous old monstrosities, but they simply will not do for Monsieur Pierre. As it is he's most upset, and threatens to return to Marseilles on the very first sailing—you know how terribly touchy these French chefs tend to be!"

Whitney didn't know, but he had a dreadful feeling he was about to find out. He was right. It took another two hours to complete the epicurean shopping list that revealed, in all its awesome majesty, the touchiness of the French chef. Despite the several crates of kitchen equipment that Lady Pendlebury had brought with her from England, the list ran into seven closely written pages of more ovens, double-boilers, terrines, Charlotte moulds, quenelles, soufflé timbales and an entire range of unpronounceable culinary aids Whitney had never heard of, much less seen. Renovations for the accommodation of Monsieur Pierre and Sir Jasper's English butler-cum-valet, Tremaine, took a further hour; one could hardly expect them to share the scandalous dwellings of the native staff in the servants' compound. By the end of all that, even Lady Pendlebury's formidable energies were beginning to show signs of flagging.

"Mrs. Anderson tells me there is a French widow once married to a Eurasian railway guardsman who keeps an imported stock of all that is required for Monsieur Pierre's kitchen. I believe she lives in the French territory of Chandernagore."

"I am acquainted with Madame Brigitte," Whitney interrupted wearily. "I will arrange for the necessary purchases to be made."

"Good. Oh, and just one more thing, Mr. Whitney, while I think of it. I believe there is a new type of kerosene stove available in Bentinck Street that allows fingertip control of the flame. Mrs. Anderson certainly swears by it. Two of those in Monsieur's kitchen would be absolutely perfect for the sensitive sauces and roulades and, I think, maybe another two in the pantry for morning tea and *chota hazri*. Which reminds me, Mr. Whitney, *surely* the initials on the coat fronts and turbans of the bearers' uniforms should be embroidered in red, white and blue rather than that awful sickly, lacklustre green? Mrs. Anderson tells me. . . ."

Leonard Whitney was beginning to dislike Mrs. Anderson intensely. Indeed, by the time Lady Pendlebury had finally dispensed with his services for the day, he had begun to heartily regret having accepted this assignment at all. When Sir Bruce had offered to loan him to the new Finance member for a period of three months, he had been flattered and under the impression that his duties as a personal aide to Sir Jasper would be exclusively of an official nature. He was dismayed to find that this was not so. What he appeared to be rapidly becoming during these first few days was a flunkey, a sort of general domestic factotum, at the beck and call of Lady Pendlebury—hardly a role befitting an accountant of his experience and qualifications.

But then, as he cursed his luck and simmered with quiet indignation, Whitney also remembered that Kyle had attached considerable importance to his acceptance of the offer. Whitney trusted Kyle. He knew that Kyle never did or said anything without a valid reason. Heaving a protracted sigh, Whitney bravely put his complaints behind him. For the moment, in any case, he had little choice but to try to survive Lady Pendlebury's onerous demands with as much fortitude as he could manage.

It might have given Leonard Whitney some small crumbs of comfort to know that, in actual fact, the Garden Reach mansion had taken Lady Pendlebury quite pleasantly by surprise. It was, she was forced to admit, not quite as frightful as she had presumed. Indeed, to be absolutely fair and honest, she found the mansion undeniably attractive, with enormous potential for comfort and European style entertaining. Of course, there was damp in the walls, the plumbing was mediaeval, the lighting fixtures atrocious and needing immediate replacement. And the less said about the veritable army of servants that had greeted them on arrival (sixty-three with, no doubt, twelve hundred and sixty thieving fingers between them!), the better. They made Lady Pendlebury's flesh positively crawl with alarm. Thank God she had had the good sense to bring Pierre and Tremaine out with them to ensure service of a standard that the British upper classes were used to and expected.

But petty details apart, with the house itself Lady Pendlebury was reasonably content. It was spacious, south-facing and therefore airy, and had unexpectedly elegant proportions. The surround of open, pillared verandahs gave it an almost Arcadian look, and the large portico in front enclosed a graceful sweep of long, shallow marble steps that added dignity to a handsome entrance. Each window and door had deep blue shutters, and against the pale yellow wash of the exterior walls, they looked really rather chic. The two lofty gateways that guarded the entrance and exit at either end of the driveway gave the house a distinctly imperial air, adding to its air of exclusivity.

The mansion stood in its own grounds, of course. The gardens needed tending and the malis had to be taken sternly in hand, but the back lawns rolled all the way down to the river, absolutely ideal for open-air *burra khanas*. A wooden dance floor laid on the grass under a large canopy, a moveable dais for the orchestra, some trestle tables for the buffet, scattered seating arrangements—and *voilà, c'est fait!* As Lady Pendlebury surveyed the extensive grounds, her eyes turned dreamy. Already she could hear strains of "The Blue Danube" floating across the toffee-coloured Hooghly as her guests, replete with Monsieur Pierre's gustatory delights, waltzed across a velvet-smooth lawn under swaying Japanese lanterns. Open-air festivities, however, Lady Pendlebury decided regretfully, would have to wait until after the rains when everyone returned from the hills.

The annual hot weather exodus, Lady Pendlebury had learnt, was led by the Viceroy and his imperial government. Opting for discretion over valour, they escaped each year to Simla, the summer capital in the foothills of the western Himalayas, from about April to September. Among the non-official population it was the women who headed the departing hordes, frantic to flee into the merciful coolth of various hills and dales for as long as budgets and husbands permitted.

The government's annual move had been initiated in 1864 by Sir John Lawrence, Viceroy at the time, for reasons of personal ill health, and had remained as hot a topic for debate as the weather ever since. Much as the pure mountain air and admirably English climate of Simla (to say nothing of the notorious frivolity of its Season, its surfeit of grass widows, spinsters and gay blades) might benefit European health and humour, many even in Whitehall considered the transference impractical, wasteful and an administrative absurdity. Nevertheless, the practice persisted, as much for the avowed advantage of having the government closer to the volatile north-west frontier states for at least half the year, as for the unabashed entertainment of its functionaries. Even so, many of the more senior government officials resisted the monumental upheaval, manipulating their affairs so that they could divide their time between Calcutta and Simla rather than move lock, stock and barrel to a godforsaken hill station more than a thousand miles away, no matter how rejuvenating the respite.

Constance Pendlebury herself longed to join the summer migration into the Himalayan foothills. From Charlotte Anderson's evocative descriptions of Simla, she could almost smell the fresh, pine-scented air, see the lush rhododendron forests and distant snow peaks, savour the very *Englishness* of the summer capital. Sadly, however, she knew that, whatever her husband's plans for the summer might be, she herself could not dream of abandoning Calcutta at this crucial juncture with their son poised so precariously on the precipice of self-destruction. Therefore, she decided with commendable pragmatism, what could not be cured must be endured; there was no reason why summer in this devilish plain should not be made as pleasurable as possible. As such, she had every intention of squeezing at least one formal indoor ball and (if she could find decent performers) a musical soirée or two into the monsoon social calendar to relieve the tedium of the soggy season.

Comparatively uplifted at the prospect of resuming a role she knew she played to perfection, and rather chuffed by her morning's domestic labours, Lady Pendlebury hummed under her breath as she joined her husband for luncheon in the small morning parlour adjoining their personal suite on the first floor. Yes, the household was beginning to take such shape as she wanted. Apart from the dreadful state of the main kitchen and Monsieur Pierre's determined migraines, the only cloud on this new horizon of her life remained the undeniably nagging worries about her son.

Since they had disembarked a week ago, Christian's behaviour had been decidedly odd and, for that matter, really rather wounding. Using the excuse of his studies, he had spent very little time with them, giving them no opportunity for any discussion of a serious nature. In fact, she had the distinct impression that he was avoiding them intentionally, and that distressed and alarmed her even more. Had this not been the first afternoon since he had started to attend his office that Sir Jasper had decided to return home for tiffin, and had he not been so visibly tetchy, she would have brought up the subject at the luncheon table. In view of his obvious bad humour, however, she decided to wait until the meal was over.

Sir Jasper picked up the daily menu card, neatly printed in Leonard Whitney's impeccable handwriting. "Is this what we're supposed to be having for luncheon?"

"Yes, dear. *Filets de poulet à la Saint-Germain.*"

"Where are the curry and rice?"

"Tremaine doesn't know how to make curry, dear," Lady Pendlebury pointed out patiently.

With marked annoyance, Sir Jasper cast a perfunctory glance at the silver salver Tremaine presented. "By the looks of this, he doesn't know how to make *filets de poulet à la Saint-Germain* either! Where the devil is your pet frog?"

Lady Pendlebury's mouth tightened. "I told you, he's down with a migraine."

"A fresh one—or the same he had on Monday?"

"Pierre refuses to cook until he gets his new kitchen exactly the way he likes it."

"And the dozen *baburchis* in the old kitchens already on the payroll?"

Lady Pendlebury bristled. "You know very well how utterly useless they all are, Jasper! Why, they couldn't tell a filet from a fig if their lives depended on it!"

"Good God, woman. You expect a Bengali *baburchi* to produce blasted filets de whatever when he's the best fish curry cook in the world?" He turned to his butler. "Does the *baburchi* understand English?"

Tremaine sniffed and stared haughtily at the ceiling. "Only in a manner of speaking, sir."

"Very well then, tell him in *his* manner of speaking that I want a plate of decent fish curry and boiled rice, with plenty of pickles. And chop, chop! Is that clear?"

"I didn't order any curry and rice, Jasper," his wife cried, her inviolate poise starting to display rifts.

Sir Jasper picked up his napkin, and with an anticipatory gleam in his eye, grimly tucked it into his collar. "Don't tell me there is a Calcutta household feeding a hundred damned mouths a day that cannot produce a plate of decent fish curry and rice at any given moment, Constance, because I simply will not believe it." Noticing that his butler still hovered behind his chair, he asked sharply, "Yes, Tremaine?"

"The only fish curry in the kitchens is what the native servants have prepared for themselves, sir."

"Excellent!" Sir Jasper rubbed his hands together. "Fetch me a plate of that. In fact, fetch me two plates of that—and don't forget the pickles, the green chilly garnish and the fried poppadums. By gad! I haven't had a decent poppadum since I left Lucknow."

Equally appalled, Lady Pendlebury and the butler exchanged silent glances. Then Tremaine left grudgingly to do the necessary in the native kitchen house, and in glacial silence, Lady Pendlebury resumed her lone battle with the all but inedible *filets de poulet à la Saint-Germain*.

It was only after the meal was over, when every visible smear of the spicy curry had been satisfactorily mopped up with a last chunk of bread and Sir Jasper's good humour had finally been restored, that domestic peace returned to the luncheon table. Smiling and satiated, he provided his wife with just the opening she had hoped for. "Pity Christian isn't here. By Jove, he would have enjoyed this! Hot as hell, but quite the best I've eaten since 'fifty-seven."

Lady Pendlebury signalled Tremaine to serve the pudding and took a deep breath. "Christian did call this morning but could stay only briefly. He said he had classes all day at the Fort."

"Is he joining us for dinner tonight?"

"No." She pursed her lips. "Apparently, he has lessons to prepare for his morning tutorials. He indicated that the earliest he could see us would be Sunday evening."

Digging gingerly into a rather precarious caramel custard, Sir Jasper nodded. "Well, I'm relieved that he's taking his work seriously and not playing the burra sahib—or the fool!"

A gleam appeared in his wife's eye; considering the circumstances, she considered that a singularly insensitive remark. However, keeping her main objective in view, she merely held her breath and counted up to five. "I understand the boys at Christian's chummery have planned some sort of celebration this evening." Her tone was conversational as she swallowed her chagrin and prepared the ground for the more purposeful dialogue she hoped would follow. "One of them is about to be engaged to the Anderson girl, the younger one. The older sister is almost twenty-two, with no hint of a betrothal in the offing. It must be quite a trial for parents when a younger girl is spoken for first, don't you think?" She paused to give a minimal shake to her perfectly coiffed head. "However, I believe there is a certain young Captain Harrison of the Second Native now starting to show signs of interest and everyone is really *so* relieved."

"Christian told you all that?"

"No. Clementine McNaughton. In confidence, of course."

"Well, I'll be damned!" Sir Jasper looked quite astonished. "We've been here a week and you've already got your ear glued to the station's gossip grapevine?"

"Don't be absurd, Jasper. We've had a stream of callers from the very first day we arrived. And a week is *quite* long enough to find out the bare facts about what everyone is doing." She paused and the conversational tone turned a trifle less so. "Including Christian, of course."

"Oh, of course," he murmured drily, dabbing the corners of his mouth with his napkin. Picking up that morning's *Friend of India*, the English newspaper that catered to Calcutta's British community, he excused himself from table and, rather pointedly, walked to the far end of the room to seat himself in his favourite winged chair overlooking the back lawns. Having finally managed to get her husband onto the prickly subject after weeks of futile effort, Lady Pendlebury was certainly not about to give up quite so easily. Asking for their coffees to be served in the seating alcove at the other end of the room, she joined him by the window.

"You can scoff all you want, Jasper, but it's perfectly true, you know." She gave an exasperated sigh at his look of incomprehension, assumed or otherwise. "About the girl, Jasper, the *Eurasian* girl. Christian has been running around with her, I'm told." Two spots of colour glowed bright pink on her cheeks.

"Told? Told by whom?"

"Charlotte Anderson. Mother of those two girls I've been telling you about. She came calling with them yesterday morning. Lucas Anderson is manager of the New Bengal Bank on Chowringhee Road. They have a bungalow in one of the English residential areas on the embankment."

"I see. And she called with the laudably selfless purpose of telling you what your son has been doing?"

"Of course not, Jasper," his wife returned placidly, quite used to her husband's acid tongue. "As it happened, Mrs. Anderson came by appointment to offer us lottery tickets for a race meeting being held for charity before the rains start. They're collecting funds for the English orphanage. I bought some tickets, naturally. One wants to start on the right foot by setting a good example to help worthy causes. I believe they're giving prizes of food hampers donated by the clubs and the larger stores. He's one of the Leicestershire Andersons—a second cousin, I think—the ones with the market gardens and prize pigs. They've been here for fifteen years and are socially very eminent."

"Who, the Leicestershire Andersons?"

"No, dear, the *Lucas* Andersons! She runs a busy household and was most helpful with domestic advice."

Sir Jasper merely grunted.

"Anyway. . . ." She stopped to take a toothpick out of a silver container that Tremaine presented and then continued after the butler had left the room. "Anyway, Mrs. Anderson let drop, quite by accident, of course, that they had been *most* surprised to see Christian, on the very next day after he disembarked, on the embankment outside this girl's house."

Engrossed in his newspaper, Sir Jasper's eyes remained glued to the front page. "Which girl?"

"The *Eurasian* girl, dear. Oh, I *do* wish you would pay attention, Jasper! Don't you consider this a matter of any importance at all?"

"No." He lowered his newspaper a fraction and speared her with a sharp look. "Not until we've heard what Christian has to say. I thought I had made that quite clear, Constance. You know very well how much I despise loose talk." Lady Pendlebury's breathing accelerated as, finally relinquishing her poise, she prepared for war. Recognizing the signs, Sir Jasper weighed the consequences of stretching her patience further, then cursed silently and surrendered. He folded the newspaper and put it down on the coffee table. "All right. They saw Christian with this girl. Then what happened?"

Lady Pendlebury inched forward in her chair. "As luck would have it, the Andersons' bungalow is next to that of this girl's family, and they have an unimpeded view of the adjoining back gardens from the first-floor bedroom. . . ."

"This Eurasian girl's family owns property in an English residential locality?" Sir Jasper interrupted, showing interest for the first time. "On the embankment?"

"Yes. Apparently, they're extremely wealthy. They own ships and tea gardens and warehouses along the docks, Mrs. Anderson said, and the girl herself breeds horses. They've met Christian many times since, of course— the Andersons, I mean—and they say they see him on this girl's back lawn quite often. There wasn't time for more than that because Mrs. Twining arrived just then with her niece, the one who plays the dulcimer—remember, Clarence Twining mentioned her at the Ghat when we landed?—and that put paid to the rest."

Sir Jasper helped himself to a toothpick from the silver box resting on the table before him and jabbed it in his mouth. "What did she say the girl's name was?"

"Verity Twining's niece?"

"No, no, the *Eurasian* girl!"

"Oh." With her mouth open, Lady Pendlebury waited as Tremaine re-entered the room and set about clearing the coffee table. She spoke the minute he had vanished from sight. "Raventhorne. Maya Raventhorne."

Slowly but perceptibly, Sir Jasper's expression changed. For a moment he sat staring out of the window at the river, then he rose to his feet. It was obvious that now his wife claimed his complete attention. "Raventhorne? Are you sure it was that?"

Her eyes widened slightly. "Yes dear, quite sure. Why, do you know them?"

There was a minimal pause. "No. I just thought the name sounded familiar, but I see that I am mistaken." He made a sign to Tremaine standing in the doorway and the butler again vanished. "Well, I must return to the office," he said with sudden briskness. "Whitney must be waiting with those interest figures on the floating debts."

"When Christian comes on Sunday evening, Jasper," Lady Pendlebury said, her voice low and shaking with urgency, "you must be firm with him. You must force him to tell us the truth."

"Yes. But for God's sake, Constance, don't nag the boy. If there is anything to tell, which I still strongly doubt, let him take his own time. We will have plenty of occasion to talk once he moves in here with us."

"He will not be moving in with us." Lady Pendlebury stood up and stretched herself to her full height. "He informed me this morning that he does not wish to leave the chummery." Her thin smile was tight with triumph. "Do you *still* believe there is nothing to all this gossip?"

He made no response. But, as he stood before the gilt-edged mirror adjusting his printed silk cravat and Tremaine hovered at the back holding his master's hat and despatch case, it was evident that Sir Jasper's thoughts were not entirely on the interest figures of India's floating debts.

As soon as her husband had departed, Lady Pendlebury sat back in her chair, her smile satisfied. With a slight air of boredom she picked up the folded copy of the newspaper her husband had been reading. She merely skimmed over the political news and then, as she did every day, turned to the most interesting section, the obituaries. Glancing down the column, she noticed only one familiar name, Findlater. Briefly she wondered if it might be one of the Somerset Findlaters whose second daughter eloped with their head groom last year and who pretended she was away at a finishing school in Switzerland, but then she saw that it was not. Happily, there were no other recognisable names to whose families condolence messages needed to be sent. She returned the paper to the coffee table and adjourned to her room for her afternoon siesta.

Sometime later that same day, Kyle Hawkesworth sat in his study scanning the same column in the same paper as part of his daily editorial routine. Arriving at the insertion that had briefly engaged Lady Pendlebury's attention, he jolted forward in his seat with sudden interest. He read through the cryptic announcement a second time, carefully and with concentration:

> *Findlater, Henry Tobias*, at Tunbridge Wells, England, on 7 April 1871. Late of the 1st Madras Fusiliers. Survived by his wife, Margaret.

Having read the notice twice, he leaned back again and stroked his chin, his eyes showing a rare glint of excitement. He cut out the insertion, placed it in an envelope with a hastily scribbled note and summoned the errand boy from the press.

"Deliver this to Trident to await Mr. Raventhorne's return from Cawnpore."

It was Sunday morning.

In the chummery sitting room, Lytton Prescott lay sprawled on the rather lumpy couch studying his notebook while Christian's bearer, Karamat, fussed about delivering cups of hot tea. "I say definitely Merry Meg. She's going to win, you know, I have it from the horse's mouth." He made an entry in his notebook.

"You talked to Merry Meg?" Patrick drawled, stretched out on an opposite, equally lumpy couch.

Lytton threw a cushion at him. "Lord Ulick Browne, you ass, the oracle of Calcutta racing himself. She's being ridden by Shooter."

"Merry Meg's strictly C.B. Not for me, old chap." Patrick continued to peruse his own list.

"Country-bred or not, she's a hot favourite, you know."

"What odds do you offer for Blue Opal?"

Lytton consulted his notebook. "Twenty to one. A fiver?"

"Good grief, no! Make it a rupee. And a fiver on Genghis Khan."

"On Genghis Khan? You must be mad! The damn thing can hardly stand still without toppling over."

"Melody says," Patrick blushed a rich plum, "he's definitely going to win. She says she had a dream about him."

"A dream!" Lytton snorted disgustedly. "Ye gods, spare us from besotted lovers! Anyway, it's your funeral. A hundred to one—and that's optimistic." Still grumbling, he scribbled in his book and tossed the coins Patrick offered into a small squat tin by his side. He threw a sidelong glance at Christian sitting out on the balcony, reading the morning paper and brooding. "Come on, Christian, it's all for a good cause," he called in a loud voice. "Not even an anna or two on your beloved's hack?"

"He's not a hack!" Christian called back without looking up from the paper. "He's an Arab—and a damned good one at that."

"Well then, why the coyness? A small flutter won't hurt. You could even win a food hamper with a raffle ticket, just think of it—pâté de fois gras, oysters, smoked ham, *petit fours*, tinned strawberries. . . ."

"Stop!" Patrick groaned, holding his stomach and licking his lips. "I think I'm going to be sick! Why should Christian think about food hampers with that froggie chef of theirs about?"

"Well, why don't you buy the raffle tickets, then?" Christian asked, nettled.

"I have," Patrick assured him glumly. "Dozens. Enough to paper the Great Wall of blasted China! Melody said she wouldn't speak to me again unless I did."

"Oh, come on, Christian, there's a good chap. As it is they besmirch the fair name of us wallahs as lacking in physical dash without a shred of the uplifting spirit of sportsmanship. Take a leaf out of faithful Patrick's book—a fiver on a mule that can barely stand and miles of wallpaper. All because of his beloved's command. Consider, old chap, a small wager on the Raventhorne hack might press your suit far harder than that slushy daily letter—even if it *is* being ridden by a native jock."

"All right." Stung by the sarcasm, Christian dug into his pocket and carelessly flung a shower of coins across the floor at Lytton. "Put it all on Morning Mist—and I'll double the stakes if he loses."

"Oh, hark! The gall riseth, eh?" Grinning, Lytton slipped off the couch and, on all fours, gleefully started to collect the scattered coins.

"For heaven's sake don't rile him, Prescott," Patrick warned. "Or we'll never get to any of that froggie-fodder!"

"True, true—the warmer the diplomatic relations, the closer the *crêpes suzettes*. And, by gad, there's a limit to how much of Karamat's stewed sludge one can stomach. We could be eating old rubber for all we know. Ugh!"

"We are eating old rubber! How else do you think the one-eyed rogue makes his daily whack in the bazaar?" Patrick watched with open admiration as Lytton poured the handful of coins into the tin. "My, my, such extravagance! All that even when your popsie's hack doesn't have a prayer?"

"Oh, doesn't he?" Christian retorted from the balcony, throwing down the newspaper and then striding into the room. "Not even if he's being ridden by Hassan Shooter?"

There was a moment of silence. "No he's not," Lytton said. "Hassan's riding Merry Meg. He told me so."

Christian smiled. "Well, he's had second thoughts. He's riding Morning Mist—and you can't take back your bet once it's entered. That's your rule, not mine, remember?"

Patrick opened his mouth to deliver a stinging retort but then shut it. Christian was in such a foul mood this morning that it was wiser not to tease him further. Instead, he asked, "Are you planning to spend the day with your parents?"

It was a perfectly civil question but it only angered Christian further. "Oh, do shut up!"

Lytton looked at Christian curiously. "By your angelic disposition these past few days, one can but presume that you haven't spoken to your parents yet."

"It's none of your damned business!"

"And that definitely confirms it. Aren't you leaving it a bit late, old chap, considering how much lady love must be champing at the bit?" Christian clenched his fists and Lytton hastily held up his hands. "All right, all right—I was only baiting you. Can't you take a joke any more?"

"No, I can't" Christian snarled, absolutely furious. "So keep your bloody tongue still or, by Christ, I'll knock your teeth down your God-rotting throat!"

Leaving them staring because he seldom lost his equanimity to the extent of swearing, Christian flounced across the room and stormed off towards the bathroom, shouting orders to Karamat to lay out his clothes *juldee, juldee,* or he'd have his bleeding hide off his back.

Once behind the locked door of the bathroom, however, Christian's temper collapsed. In fact, he felt rather ashamed of having vented his own tensions on the others, no matter how acute the provocation. Lowering himself into the rusty tin tub, he slowly sank into the water up to his chin and lay cogitating darkly. God, he was getting fed up with living in this soulless dump in the company of these two insensitive loons! They were crude, supercilious and bigoted, with not a fine feeling between them. They didn't give a tinker's cuss about anything except women and gambling and carousing, and to cap it all, were actually proud of their ignorance. Lytton was forever running wagers on just about everything, from cock fighting and pigeon racing to the price of fish in the market, and Melody Anderson was the third girl to whom Patrick had proposed since he had docked. Last night, not wanting to seem a bad sport, Christian had joined in the jollifications at the Golden Hind (a bachelor club better known, for obvious reasons, as the Golden Behind) and roistered until all hours. Consequently, this morning his head felt like a vibrating church bell and his tongue seemed overlaid with gravel. Privately, however, he considered Melody a silly little chit and a terrible snoop, and her mother and sister no better. He knew that they had lost no time in calling on his mother with goodness knows what embellishments to the truth. He was aware of Maya's opinion of all three of them and he agreed with it heartily.

It was all becoming unbearably tedious, Christian brooded. Were it not for the fact that his mother's inquisitions would be even more intolerable, for two pence he'd move to his parents' comfortable mansion and to hell with everything else. But then he swiftly discarded the thought. Patrick and Lytton might be coarse and frivolous, but at least they didn't interfere with his personal liberty—as his mother undoubtedly would. He pulled a deep, heavy sigh. Well, it wouldn't matter one way or the other for much longer. He would be moving out of Calcutta soon. . . .

Herbert Ludlow, the Chief Commissioner, had confirmed his posting in Champaran. They had talked of it at length yesterday. Yes, the Champaran posting was about the worst a griffin could be given. But then, it couldn't be helped. He had no doubt that Maya would rise to the occasion and somehow, together, they would manage to survive its tedium until he earned a better posting—as he undoubtedly would.

God, how he missed her! He had not seen her ever since his parents had arrived, and his sense of loss was unbearable. As promised, he had written to her every single day. He had got into the habit of sitting in the cool, deserted corridors of the Museum on Chowringhee to pen long, ardent letters in which he poured out his heart. But although thinking of her, writing to her, dreaming of her through the warm nights, all helped to relieve his heartache somewhat, mere words were pathetically inadequate. He needed to see her, to touch her, to hear her voice, to take her to meet his parents.

Oh God, how he wished it was over!

He was aware, naturally, that his parents had already heard much of the town gossip about him and Maya, but he didn't really give a damn about that. His father, with his usual admirable discretion, had said nothing to him, though his mother had tried to question him several times, subtly of course, but to no avail. He was determined not to say anything until the time and the place were right. Well, the appropriate time and place would be tonight, when he dined with his parents. Tonight would see the moment of truth, the moment he had been dreading for so long. However violently his parents might react to his announcement, he simply could not evade the issue any longer.

Christian's heart sank like a stone at the thought of his mother's emotional responses. He had always admired her composure, the great dignity with which she conducted herself under all circumstances, but he could hardly expect her to remain tranquil when confronted with the rather startling news he planned to deliver. There would be tears, implorations and accusations, hysterics even. Christian shuddered at the prospect, but accepted with grim resolve that it had to be faced. How much more pleasant it would be, he thought wistfully, if it were possible for him to talk to his father alone. His father was a much travelled man of the world, receptive, sympathetic and liberal in his attitudes. He had always had an instinctive understanding of him and his needs even when he was a boy. His father would certainly give him a patient hearing, with neither excessive emotionalism nor histrionics. . . .

There was a loud banging on the bathroom door. Startled at the intrusion, Christian almost jumped out of the tub. "You planning to be in there all damn day?" Lytton's voice thundered. "If you're not out in sixty seconds, I'm going to take that letter you gave Karamat to deliver and. . . ."

Christian was out before he could complete the threat.

As an able and experienced administrator and an old India hand, Sir Jasper was an admirable choice for Finance membership of the Viceroy's Council. He had a singularly clear vision of the country, a vision unclouded by delusions of social obligation or moral reform. In Whitehall, he was known as one of the most outspoken critics of the Crown's management of monetary policies in India and had often expressed his views in strong terms following the annual presentation in Parliament of the accounts of the Indian Empire. He was appalled that although revenues were fixed and taxation already at its limit of safety, government expenditure was uncontrolled and haphazard, and that military expenses, civil and judicial administration costs, were beyond the needs and means of the country. In other words, Sir Jasper was a pragmatist. He believed that the cornerstone of the British Empire was profit, and that the primary duty of Her Majesty's Government was not to change the social fabric of India either for better or for worse, but simply to stay solvent. And as Finance member, it was to this end that he intended to direct all his endeavours.

He tapped the sheaf of papers he had been reading at his mahogany desk in his newly allocated, capacious office on a side street just off Tank Square. "These budget estimates prove precisely my point—the fiscal inelasticity that exists in this country is appalling." He glowered, first at Leonard Whitney, standing at attention by the side of the desk, then at the mass of files and dispatches that were now his department's responsibility. "The Treasury simply cannot bear the burden. Governmental spending must be cut down. There are just no two ways about it. The question is, where?"

It was a rhetorical question. Whitney proffered no answer.

"All would be lost," Sir Jasper continued gravely, "if the equilibrium between revenue and expenditure were to be in any way disturbed further."

"Yes, sir."

Sir Jasper beat his fingers on the side of the desk in an absent rhythm. "It has been well said, has it not, that the imperial balance sheet is the *articulus stantis aut cadentis imperii?*"

"Quite so, sir."

Having made these weighty pronouncements about the matter, Sir Jasper snapped his folder shut and sat back. "Have all the arrangements for Simla been completed?"

"Yes, sir. The baggage trains start loading shortly. The secure placement of the trunks of files, documents and correspondence in the wagons reserved for the Treasury will be supervised personally by officers designated by yourself for the duty. Confidential papers pertaining to the budget estimates are already in safe keeping at your residence. Presumably, those will go to Simla as your personal luggage whenever you decide to travel up. Whatever is to remain here will, as usual, be in the charge of Burra Babu and his skeleton staff. Would you like to inspect the inventory of the . . . ?"

"No, I most certainly would not!" Sir Jasper shook his head with undue energy and added to it a graphic oath.

A great many changes had been effected since a Governor-General on holiday in the 1830s had frightened the fledgling village of Simla out of its wits by ascending upon it with an entourage of ten thousand, accompanied by nine hundred camels, one hundred and forty elephants, several hundred horses and numberless coollies, all heavily laden with official and domestic baggage.

Now, with the railhead at Umballa completed, the journey from Calcutta was undoubtedly easier and swifter, but it was still an annual migration cumbersome enough to put even Hannibal's army to shame. Sir Jasper, quite frankly, considered the entire exercise a gross wastage of personal time and public money. Despite the installation of the electric telegraph in both capitals, it irked him that the imperial government should place itself in a position of such ludicrous inaccessibility seven thousand and eighty-four feet above sea level, a subcontinent away from Calcutta. He had made his explanations to the Viceroy about his present urgent need to remain in station to continue work on the vital budget estimates. But, with the rest of the government, the Commander-in-Chief, their collective officials and most of his own department soon to be snugly ensconced in the hills for the duration of the summer, he knew that he would have to go up sooner or later. It was not a prospect that caused him any pleasure.

However, now as Sir Jasper sat in ruminative silence with his chin pressed deep into his chest, it appeared to Whitney that it was neither about Simla nor about the Indian fiscal situation that the Finance member cogitated. As a rule, his single-mindedness when they sat down to work was admirable. This afternoon he seemed strangely distracted.

Standing by the desk in dutiful silence, Whitney waited full five minutes, then glanced at the clock and coughed. "Sir, may I be permitted to . . . ?"

"Sit down, Whitney."

"Sir?" He was surprised. None of his employers had ever asked him to sit down in their presence.

"Sit down, man. I know it is time for you to leave, but I would be obliged if you could stay a few more minutes. There is a matter about which I would like you to give me some information."

"Very well, sir." Presuming some point of finance in the figures he had compiled needed to be clarified, Whitney seated himself at the edge of the chair and placed his notebook on his knees.

Obviously ill at ease, Sir Jasper now got up and started to pace. "You come to my office with the highest recommendation from Sir Bruce and from Lord Mayo, Whitney."

Surprised and gratified by this unexpected compliment, which helped to greatly reduce the sting of his degrading morning duties, Whitney inclined his head in formal acknowledgement. "Thank you, sir."

"I know therefore that you can respect a confidentiality, Whitney." He paused and for a moment stood twirling his exceedingly well-groomed moustache. "The information I now seek from you is of a personal nature, but even so, I would like you to be absolutely frank."

"Certainly, sir." More than a little puzzled, Whitney closed his notebook and replaced his pencil in his breast pocket. He waited.

"You have met my son, Christian?"

"Yes, sir. Once or twice very briefly."

"Tell me . . . is it true that he is involved with some Eurasian girl?"

Whitney's dark, gleaming face dulled with a deep pink flush. It was not a question he had either expected or anticipated. "I . . . wouldn't know, sir," he said stiffly.

"Come, come, Whitney." Sir Jasper smiled pleasantly. "From what I've heard, I believe there is not very much about which you *don't* know— down to the width of the stripes on Sir Bruce's pyjamas. I find it difficult to believe that you remain ignorant of something about which the whole town gossips."

"Be that as it may, sir, I. . . ."

"Don't let us waste time in absurd prevarications, Whitney!" he said sharply. "And, as I said, be free to speak your mind. You are an intelligent man. You must surely understand why I am forced to ask you something you quite rightly find repugnant to answer. But I can hardly go to the old bats at the Women's Institute for information of such a personal nature, although, I daresay, that is precisely where most of it originated. All I want from you are the basic facts. Well, is it true?"

Whitney continued to shuffle, desperately uncomfortable. He took considerable time to clear his throat. "I believe there are some rumours to that effect, sir. That is, I have heard it mentioned, not in specific words, of course, but. . . ."

"Be a good chap and stop dithering, Whitney! Just tell me, is it yes or no?"

Whitney sighed. "Yes, sir," he conceded unhappily.

"I see." Sir Jasper sat down again and pinned his aide's wavering eyes down with a determined look. "Who is the young lady in question?" Seeing Whitney's look of renewed apprehension, he prompted, "Is she Jai Raventhorne's daughter?"

"Yes, sir."

Sir Jasper's lips thinned. "I suppose it would be too much to hope," he remarked drily, "that there are two men of the same name and that this girl's father is *not* the one hanged as a traitor?"

At the use of the word "traitor," Whitney's eyes narrowed, although there was no change in his impassive expression. "It is the same Jai Raventhorne, sir," he replied, with a slight touch of frost.

Sir Jasper steepled his fingers and stared up at the frilled punka as it whooshed back and forth across the ceiling. "And how far exactly has this affair progressed, Whitney?"

Disliking the interrogation, but seeing that he was not to be let off the hook until Sir Jasper was satisfied, Whitney assumed an air of resignation. "One hears that it has progressed quite far, sir. They are said to ride together every morning."

"Ride together? Well, good God, that's hardly a venal sin! What else?"

Whitney was quietly outraged. "I regret, sir, that I am not privy to whatever their other . . . mutual activities might be!"

"No, no. I suppose not," Sir Jasper agreed, stroking his chin as he considered how to frame his next inquiry.

"Might not Mr. Christian himself be the best source of information, sir?" Whitney suggested hopefully, leaping into the pause.

Sir Jasper roused himself with an impatient nod. "Well, of course he is! But when I go into the lion's den, I want to go at least better briefed than Mrs. Anderson." He rose and started to fidget with some papers, ostensibly to prepare them for his portmanteau but actually to occupy his restless fingers. Finally, after much shuffling, he packed the papers in carefully and snapped down the latches on the case. Assuming with some relief that he was ready to leave, Whitney depressed the bell that summoned Sir Jasper's personal peon. It was after the man, in a splendid uniform with bright blue turban and cummerbund trimmed with gold, had taken the portmanteau and gone out to summon the carriage, that Sir Jasper suddenly reseated himself and signalled Whitney to do the same. "The girl's mother—she's American, isn't she?"

With ill-concealed disinclination, Whitney sat down again. "Yes, sir."

"If my memory serves me right, she was married before, I believe."

"Yes, sir. To Lord Frederick Birkhurst of Farrowsham."

"Ah, of course! I seem to remember someone telling me that Freddie's wife was American. Lady Pendlebury is casually acquainted with the old dowager. They have a rather enviable family seat in Suffolk, I hear. Lady Birkhurst must be eighty if she's a day, but my wife tells me her mind is still as sharp as a brass tack. How are the Agency House and the indigo plantation faring these days? Still going strong?"

"They are still going, sir, but I would not say strong. Indigo production continues to languish. The bazaar rumour is that the Birkhurst plantation is soon to be put up for sale. Likewise, the Agency House remains afloat only because of the endeavours of its manager, Mr. Willie Donaldson. But he is now old and ailing, incapable of energetic enterprise."

"Oh?" Sir Jasper picked up an eraser and rubbed a doodled mark off his blotter. "I'm sorry to hear that. Old Caleb Birkhurst used to live like a nabob on the pile he made out here from his enormous British importations into Indian markets." Having put Whitney at comparative ease with the general conversation, Sir Jasper now returned to his true purpose. "And the Raventhorne businesses—how are *they* reputed to be doing?"

"Oh, they continue to thrive, sir," Whitney said, not without a trace of satisfaction. "In fact, I believe they now plan to diversify into the cotton business."

Sir Jasper lifted an eyebrow, impressed, but without any great interest in the matter. He picked up a pencil and made another doodle on his blotter. "I have been leading up to questions you might find even less to your taste, Whitney, but I would still like you to answer as frankly as you can. Tell me, despite all that family wealth, could this Raventhorne girl be considered what the romance novellas are fond of calling a gold-digger?"

Whitney was aghast. "Oh *no*, sir! Miss Raventhorne has no need to dig gold elsewhere—there is plenty in the Trident coffers! In her own right she owns one third of all the family's assets, which are quite considerable, and she also stands to inherit a great deal from her mother, who is independently wealthy through *her* mother's side of the family."

Sir Jasper nodded, satisfied on that particular point. "All right, then. Can you, as a Eurasian who is, I'm sure, well acquainted with the family, think of any other reason why this girl should be interested in my son?"

"Perhaps she . . . loves him, sir," Whitney suggested.

The hesitation was not lost on Sir Jasper. Indeed, he pounced on it and a knowing look appeared in his shrewd, sharp eyes. "Perhaps?"

Realising his slip, Whitney took instant refuge behind his normal sense of propriety. "I am sorry, but I am not in a. . . ."

"All right, all right." Sir Jasper made a dismissive gesture. "You might not be in a position to know the girl's heart but, as a Eurasian, you know damn well what I'm talking about." His look was rapier sharp. "Both you and I would find it offensive if I had to spell it out, Whitney, but in your opinion does the girl have an ulterior motive in befriending my son? I remind you that the general gossip suggests that she does."

Whitney swallowed hard. "I have certainly met Miss Raventhorne on a number of occasions, sir, but the question you ask now is one which I could not presume to answer even with an opinion. All I can say is that the Raventhornes are a fiercely proud family and the young lady is of a highly spirited and independent nature. Regardless of the gossip, I doubt if she . . . if she. . . ." He swallowed again and stopped.

Sir Jasper didn't press the point. He pulled in a deep breath, then shrugged. "Knowing the whims and quirks of the colonial English mind, I presume the Raventhornes are strictly non grata in our social registers?"

"Unfortunately so, sir."

"And all this rather unsavoury gossip—is it, in your opinion, because of Raventhorne's political record or because he was a Eurasian, or both?"

"I would say both, sir." Whitney's chin came forward a fraction as he gave his employer an accusing look. "Prejudice has much to do with the rather salacious and unkind nature of the gossip."

"Yes, I suppose it has," Sir Jasper said a little impatiently. "But then, it always does, doesn't it?" He got up. "Anyway, keep this conversation to yourself, will you, Whitney? I am obliged to you for having given me the benefit of your information with as much frankness as could be expected. One more thing." He raised a finger in a gesture of warning. "Should my wife put to you these same questions, I would appreciate even less candour with her. Women don't see these things in quite the same light as men do, what?"

Whitney almost smiled, warming to him and undeniably flattered to be considered a confidant on such a delicate issue. "That is understood, sir."

Sir Jasper started towards the door with long, decisive strides, holding his hat in one hand and his silver-topped cane in the other. "Which reminds me, Whitney, of something that I have been meaning to ask you. Are you satisfied with your new duties?"

Taken by surprise, Whitney gave a guilty start. "Why . . . yes, sir!"

"I notice a reservation subsumed in your tone. Any complaints?"

"No, sir."

"Humph!" Sir Jasper walked down the steps of the porch, then stopped. "I have been thinking very seriously in terms of hiring a housekeeper, Whitney. A large household requires a great deal of attention to all sorts of detail, especially in a new place, and my official position here calls for frequent entertainment, a nuisance but a necessary one. If you would be good enough to suggest some likely candidates, I would be grateful."

Whitney's face lit up like a beacon. Forgetting his own rigid rules, he actually smiled. "Certainly, Sir Jasper! I will start making inquiries at once."

Sir Jasper's eyes twinkled. "I think the outrageous fiscal situation would benefit rather more from your undivided attention than might Monsieur Pierre's culinary whimsicalities."

A small spark of appreciation shone in Whitney's eyes. He could not deny that he was greatly taken by the man's charm and acerbic sense of humour. He was unlike any other Englishman he had met before—as Kyle had warned that he would be.

"This man Hawkesworth," Sir Jasper said abruptly as he was about to climb into his waiting carriage.

"Sir?" The smile whipped off Whitney's face and he stiffened at the mention of the name at the precise moment that it passed through his own thoughts. It was uncanny, almost as if Sir Jasper had read his mind.

"Is he the same young man Christian introduced to us at the Ghat when we arrived?"

"Yes, sir."

Sir Jasper pondered, one hand on the carriage door. "This periodical that I found on my table—*Equality*, I think—is this what he produces?"

"Yes, sir."

"Hm. Interesting. Do you know Hawkesworth personally?"

"Yes, sir."

"What is his background?"

"I couldn't say with any certainty, sir. Ours is not an intimate friendship." His tone implied a slight distaste for the man.

Even as he voiced the lie, Whitney wondered if Sir Jasper would believe him and kicked himself for not being better prepared. But without another word, Sir Jasper leapt into his carriage, knocked on the partition with his silver-headed cane and was away.

Standing on the front steps, Whitney stared after him with troubled eyes. Sir Jasper was a very different kettle of fish to McNaughton. McNaughton was at best a waffling idiot, at worst a crude, clumsy crook. Jasper Pendlebury, on the other hand, was neither. He was, in fact, alarmingly perceptive, a man of incisive intelligence whose sharp eyes could see far beyond the obvious. Behind the urbane charm, the easy wit and humour, Whitney searched perplexedly for the man Kyle had described in such graphic terms: hard, relentlessly ambitious, and if challenged for what he considered his territorial rights, brilliantly and devastatingly ruthless. At the moment, he could not quite equate his own impressions with these rather harsh opinions, but once again he reminded himself that his faith in Kyle was implicit and total. Even so, as the elegant brougham with its four matching greys disappeared round a bend, Leonard Whitney was filled with misgivings.

This time, Kyle might not find the going quite so easy. Nor, Whitney concluded despondently, would he—that is, if Sir Jasper allowed him to continue to serve in the Treasury at all.

Maya sat on the grass under a tree outside the smaller paddock reading Christian's latest letter, delivered half an hour ago by Karamat. She went through the closely written pages twice, her heart thumping hard, her mouth dry, as she eagerly absorbed his daily news. Finally, after she had devoured every word, she folded the letter and replaced it in the envelope. For a while she sat immersed in thought, the envelope clasped tightly in her hands. Then, with a heavy sigh, she forced her attention back to the task in hand and to Rafiq Mian in the paddock preparing to give Morning Mist a vigorous rubdown.

She tilted her head and, for the tenth time, examined the horse critically.

"Do you really think someone will not consider that the hind legs from the gaskins down present a sort of mean appearance, Rafiq?"

He smiled as if the idea was absurd and shook his head in quick refutation. "No. You worry too much, missy memsahib. He will prove the best horse of the afternoon, you will see. Hassan sahib will simply not let him fail. He will make him win both races."

"Oh, I'm not worried," she began, then broke off. "No, that's not true. I *am* worried. I know it's only a charity meet, but all the big buyers and their agents will be there. If he makes a sorry showing, I will have to lower his price." She stood up and walked up to the paddock fence, frowning. "Oh, bother Hassan!" she grumbled.

Maya had not wanted Morning Mist to participate in this unscheduled race meeting at all, but Hassan Shooter had insisted, and finally she had given in to his persuasions. Indeed, she had seldom seen the energetic little jockey quite so animated about any horse and she was flattered that Hassan should want to ride him in spite of the fierce competition for his services. Nevertheless, at this particular crucial juncture of her life, her mind was not on the race, nor on anything to do with it. She was jittery, very much on edge. Tonight, Christian was to dine with his parents (the "moment of truth," he had called it), and it was tonight that he would break to them news of his decision to marry her.

Oh, sweet Lord—what *would* their reaction be?

"Sometimes a good result does not proceed from the clear-sighted expert. And sometimes the ignorant boy hits the mark with an arrow by mistake."

"What?" Maya whirled round at the sound of the sudden voice to see Samir Goswami squatting on the grass behind her.

"I was quoting a couplet from Sa'di's *Gulistan.* Making a good race horse, like much else in life, is a matter of luck, is it not?"

"What are you doing here?" Maya asked, annoyed by the ill-timed intrusion. She hadn't seen, or indeed thought of Samir for weeks. "I presumed you were busy with your examinations."

"I am, but today is Sunday. I came to see you." His eyes were riveted to the envelope she held in her hand.

"Well, I am rather busy." She folded the envelope and thrust it inside a pocket of her riding britches. Pointedly, she walked away from him into the stable house.

Samir followed her inside. "Why are you busy?" he asked rather plaintively. "Christian and you do not ride together any longer. It is he who is busy with his parents."

"Well, I do have other work to do," she retorted coldly, replying in English, irritated by his presumptions, even more so by his customary insistence on talking to her in Bengali in spite of knowing how much she disliked it. "What makes you think I have no life apart from Christian?"

"Have you?"

She turned to him, hands on hips. "What do you want, Samir?"

He shrugged. "Nothing. I came to ask why you have not been to the orchard this year. The mangoes will soon be in full season and the crop is particularly bountiful. Ma said to tell you that you must come before the rains start and the fruit are all finished."

"Ma said—or have you just made that up?"

He left her question unanswered. "You did not come to my father's dinner party either, even though Christian was there."

He suddenly looked so forlorn that she felt somewhat ashamed of her brusqueness. What was happening in her life had nothing to do with Samir; it was unfair to make him the butt of her ill humour merely because he happened to be here.

"I really have been very busy, Samir," she said, her tone conciliatory. "Morning Mist has to be prepared for this race meeting and since I have agreed, I cannot let Hassan down by allowing him to appear improperly groomed. Between you and me, I would rather not expose the horse at all, not just yet, but Hassan will not take no for an answer."

Samir smiled, disproportionately pleased that she had shared even this trivial confidence with him, and he felt a flush of courage. "And grooming Morning Mist has taken all of your time?"

A retort sprang to her lips, but she bit it back and shrugged. "No." She sat down at her desk so that she did not have to look at him, and picked up a pen. "I have also had . . . other things on my mind."

"Yes, I know." He pulled up a chair and sat down behind her. "Christian's parents have arrived. That must be a matter of grave concern to . . . both of you."

She gave him no answer.

"Has he spoken to his father and mother yet?"

"About what?"

"About you. I am not a fool, Maya," Samir said with sudden heat. "I am aware of his feelings for you and," his voice thickened, "yours for him."

Maya had little patience with Samir's rather tiresome infatuation with her. At school she had been teased about it mercilessly. His endless devotion was exasperating, but at the same time there was about it a hopelessness, a subsumed despair, that was rather pathetic. Feeling sorry for him, she decided to answer his impertinent question without anger. After all, he only wondered what everyone else did.

"How do I know what he has or has not said to his parents?" She replied with a counter-question and an indulgent smile. "I'm not his keeper."

"He has not seen you for thirteen days now."

He had been spying on them? "He has been involved with his studies," she said sharply.

"But not too involved to meet Mr. Hawkesworth several times."

He waited for her answer and, when it did not come, asked, "It is because his parents are here and he is frightened of their disapproval that he does not see you, is it not?"

She again felt a stab of anger, but only briefly. Arguing with Samir was like colliding with a stone wall; he was so unmoveably obdurate. With a heavy sigh she sat back, weary with the weight of her tensions, and closed her eyes. A moment or two of silence elapsed, then, quietly, Samir came to stand behind her. She felt his hands on either side of her neck. In a reflex action, she stiffened her back; what was the silly boy up to now? He had never before ventured to actually touch her! His fingers stroked her shoulders, very delicately and carefully. Then, he pressed harder with his fingertips, moving them in circles across her skin, starting to smooth out the tautly knotted muscles of her back. For a few instants she remained rigid, but then, as she realised his intentions, she loosened and her tangled mind and body started to unwind. Slowly, under his surprisingly expert manipulations, the blood started to flow again. She felt the tightness of her shoulders soften; the sensations his hands produced were immensely soothing. With a small exclamation of pleasure, she relaxed further, leant to one side on the armrest and took a deep breath of relief.

"Where did you learn to massage like that?" she asked with a smile, not opening her eyes.

"From Mukti Babu. He was a wrestler once. He says wrestlers need to know how to make muscles ripple and flow like water."

"Mukti Babu was a wrestler?" Behind closed lids she saw one of the Goswamis' oldest retainers, small and shrivelled like a dehydrated brown berry, and she laughed. "I don't believe it. Why, he wouldn't stand a chance in a ring with professionals!"

"He would not now, I agree, but there was a time when he was younger when he was as strong as an ox, with limbs like tree trunks. Remember when he used to balance both of us on his arms and Amos around his neck and then run from one end of the orchard to the other?"

She laughed again. "Yes, and you fell off once and insisted on your whole leg being bandaged although you had only a few scratches to show for the fall."

"I fell off because of that hamadryad," Samir protested. "It was coiled upside down on the branch and brushed my cheek as we passed under it."

"Well, that was the excuse *you* offered, but no one believed you." She spoke softly, the gentle movements of his fingers making her too drowsy for debate.

Suddenly remembering those long, hot summers spent at the *bagan bari* among the lush mango trees and the rich, sweet smell of fruit all around, Maya felt a pang of nostalgia. There was a stream that ran alongside the orchard, and a placid pool of green water where dragonflies swirled and swooped on wispy wings over waxen white lotus. They often bathed in the pool to wash off the residue of the mangoes and to tease the darting goldfish with large, flapping fins, making the brilliant, panic-stricken swarms scatter in radiant showers like bursting firecrackers. Once they caught a carp, a huge fellow who had battled like fury, and Samir taught her how to gut it before they wrapped it in thick newspaper, roasted it on an impromptu fire and ate it with their fingers. She could still taste the incredible freshness of the white flesh as it melted in her mouth and the grave solicitude with which he picked for her the least bony pieces. Deluged by a confused cascade of long-abandoned memories, Maya filled with a strange melancholy. They had grown up together, shared so much, known each other for so long and so well.

"It all seems so far away now, Samir," she murmured, unbearably saddened. "Where has it all gone?"

His fingertips stilled for an instant. "It has not gone, Maya. It is still here. It is you who have gone."

He said it quietly but with such a feeling of loss that, for no reason at all, Maya's eyes filled with tears.

"Come next Sunday," he pleaded. "My examinations will be over and everyone will be there. My sisters and all my aunts and uncles and cousins ask after you. Especially Aunt Sarala. She is the one who has always been fondest of you, remember? And now she says that you have forgotten her entirely. She wants to know why she doesn't see you any more."

On a sudden impulse, Maya capitulated. "Yes," she said, suffused with excitement, overcome by remorse at having forgotten so much so easily. "Yes, I will. I would like to see Barnali and Minali and all of them again."

He continued to stand beside her, desolate and deserted. "I have missed you," he said in a low, trembling voice. "Nothing has been the same since . . . *he* came."

The tears gathered again and quickly she averted her eyes.

For all his gaucheness, his diffidence and lack of sophistication, there was an unobtrusive reliability about Samir that seemed to reinforce her inner resources. He was so entirely without malice or artifice, and in his constancy, his very dullness, there was a comforting sense of continuity. Riddled as she was with her own insecurities, vulnerable and easy to wound, she suddenly felt reassured by his presence. With a quick smile of apology, she reached out and touched his hand.

"No. Nothing has been the same, Samir. He. . . ." She almost told him about Christian's proposal, but then stopped. Under the circumstances it would be premature and grossly presumptuous. "He might be posted away soon."

Without intending to, Samir brightened. "Where?"

"Perhaps Champaran." She made a rueful face. "Terrible place, but Christian is quite excited about it."

"And you? Are you excited about it too? After all, Champaran is not London, is it?"

"I don't know what you're talking about!" she retorted crossly, much put out by his need to put words to everything.

The corners of his mouth dropped. "They want me to go to England."

Maya jumped out of her chair, her eyes alight with astonishment. "England! Oh, Samir, how wonderful! Are you not excited?"

"No. I want to remain here."

"Here? What on earth for? Think of all the new people to meet, the new places to see, the new life to experience!" Her eyes flamed with envy. "What is there to keep you here?"

"If I go," he asked, "will you miss me?"

"Miss you? Well, of course I'll miss you."

"No, I mean, *really* miss me!" He looked at her as he never had dared to before, yearningly, with a sort of desperation that covered his face with unhappiness. "Tell me truly, will you?"

Maya searched his troubled eyes, embarrassed by this new aspect of him, wondering with what words to wound him the least. "Yes, I will miss you, Samir," she said with sudden gentleness, realising with some surprise that she meant it. "But life changes and moves on, Samir, and we too must move and change with it. . . ." She broke off, feeling small and inadequate for fobbing him off with facile platitudes, but at a horrible loss as to what else to say.

Fortunately, there was no time for more. Olivia joined them in the stable house quite unexpectedly. "I saw you from the back verandah, Samir," she said, kissing him affectionately on the cheek, obviously pleased and making him welcome, "and I am so glad that you came. You must stay for luncheon because Anthony has made that lemon meringue pie that used to be such a favourite with you, remember?"

"Yes, do, Samir," Maya seconded with a rush of enthusiasm, much relieved by the timely interruption. "Then in the afternoon we can all have a game of croquet. It's *months* since we've played, isn't it, Mother?"

For Samir, the sun again broke through the clouds. Too overcome to be able to speak, he allowed himself to be led inside in contented silence.

12

S *EDUCED BY THE* new kerosene stove with fingertip flame control—
and by Christian's long-awaited presence at dinner—Monsieur
Pierre had decided to abandon his week-long migraine to emerge
from his monastic sulk and produce a rather splendid *darne de saumon à la
Chambord* garnished with quenelles of truffled mousseline force-meat with
a Genevoise sauce. He had complained bitterly that the salmon was not
salmon, that he had had to make scandalous compromises with the force-
meat, and that the scullions had not the faintest idea how to cut onions,
but the entrée was nevertheless delicious. The dish was a great favourite
with Christian, one that he had insisted on frequently in England. Tonight,
however, belying his usual enthusiasm as well as a normally hearty
appetite, he merely picked at his food. As the chef kept a grim watch on
the dinner table from behind a Kashmiri filigreed screen that shielded the
pantry and his new kitchen beyond from the formal dining room on the
ground floor, tears gathered in his eyes. It was the loud, vulgar spices of
this monstrous country that had conspired to deaden Monsieur Christian's
delicate tastebuds. *Mon Dieu,* how hard he would have to work to restore
that poor, mutilated palate to civilised normalcy!

"Do eat up, dear, or Monsieur Pierre will be most offended," Lady
Pendlebury whispered to her son, anxiously aware of the chef's determined presence behind the screen. "He's taken endless trouble to make
this exactly the way you prefer it."

Christian dutifully pushed in a few more mouthfuls, then laid down his
knife and fork. "I'm sorry, but I seem to have the remains of a most frightful headache. We drank rather a lot last night in celebration of Illingworth's engagement."

"Don't force the boy to eat if he doesn't want to, Constance," Sir Jasper said, giving her a significant look. "Indeed, the best remedy to restore a jaded appetite after going one over the eight might be a generous snifter of brandy, what?"

Christian nodded, but as Lady Pendlebury silently signalled one of the army of bearers scurrying about under the stern tutelage of Tremaine to remove the plate, she looked worriedly at the screen and threw it a conciliatory smile of apology.

It was evident that despite Monsieur Pierre's valiant efforts, dinner was not a noticeable success. With Christian sunk in fidgety silence and Lady Pendlebury's contributions to the conversation pointedly meagre, the meal was a stiff, uncomfortable affair riddled with unspoken tensions. Apparently unaware of the prevailing mood, it was Sir Jasper who fulfilled the need of the hour with an admirable, unruffled heartiness as, ignoring the generally monosyllabic responses, he regaled them both with anecdotes of his early days in India.

"You will *not* bring up the subject of this girl at table, Constance!" Sir Jasper had warned as they were dressing for dinner. "We will talk to the boy later without the servants hanging around. The last thing we need at the moment is more gossip."

"I've found out about this man Raventhorne," Lady Pendlebury said tightly, her face set. "I'm furious with Clementine McNaughton! She kept so much of the sordid story from me when she saw me in England."

"But the ubiquitous Mrs. Anderson didn't, obviously."

"Everyone in Calcutta—in India!—knows what this Raventhorne was. Why didn't you tell me the other day?"

"You would have thrown a fit, Constance, and I simply didn't have time to deal with that." He shrugged into his dinner jacket and flicked a speck off a lapel. "On second thought, I think it might be best if you let me talk to the boy first. A man-to-man chat at this juncture would be more productive than an emotional debate." Privately, Lady Pendlebury was relieved at the suggestion. She had never been able to reach Christian as well as his father could, even when he was a boy. She loved him dearly, of course, but she did not understand him—any more than she did her husband. For one, neither had an ear for—or the faintest interest in—good music, and this was one of the great sorrows of her life. In fact, so different was Christian's nature from hers, quite unlike that of his married older sister, that sometimes she wondered if he might not be a changeling. She was quite shocked, for instance, by the casual clothes he had chosen to wear at dinner this evening: a mean-looking calico overshirt, baggy nankeen trousers and a crumpled broadcloth jacket. Nothing convinced her more of his swift slide towards perdition than this utter disregard for the normal proprieties of civilised living.

Whether or not she understood the working of his mind, however, Lady Pendlebury had implicit faith in the judgement of her husband. She knew that, in every delicate situation, he could be trusted to say and do the right thing—and a more delicate situation than this could hardly be envisaged! She also knew that, no matter how hard she tried, she herself would not be able to accept with reasonable equanimity what Christian might have to reveal to them; in fact, she shuddered at the prospect. In spite of her best intentions, there would be a scene—and Lady Pendlebury hated scenes. They were plebeian and undignified, and they put her off her music for days. The last time there had been a contretemps, when Christian had announced his decision to enter the wretched colonial Civil Service instead of work in Whitehall or as an aide to a member of Parliament, she had absolutely ruined the Toccata and Fugue in D Minor in Church that Sunday and it had been horribly embarrassing, especially for the new Vicar.

"Well, how are the Hindustani studies progressing?" Sir Jasper asked over the peach Charlotte. "Think you could question in dialect a villager who has, say," he punctuated that with a little chuckle, "just chopped off an unfaithful wife's head?"

Christian joined in the laugh. "I hope so. I should imagine those are precisely the type of situations I will have to face in Champaran."

"Has Herbert Ludlow confirmed the posting?"

Christian pulled in a heavy breath as he made a sign for a second helping of the peach Charlotte. "Yes, I'm afraid so," he said with a lacklustre smile. "I leave as soon as all the courses are completed."

"Where is this place?" Lady Pendlebury asked, pleased that Monsieur Pierre's painstaking dessert, at least, was being suitably honoured by her son. "It sounds like the back of beyond."

"A few hundred miles north of Calcutta," Christian said. "But it's not as bad as everyone makes it out to be."

Which was not strictly true. A district notorious for lawlessness, Champaran was at the heart of indigo-growing country and a perpetual source of trouble for the authorities. Apart from the natural belligerence and contempt for government of the European indigo planters, the main bone of contention between them and local farmers was the "contract system." Planters gave these farmers advances to grow indigo under contract and then bought the crop from them. Because they insisted on buying cheaply, farmers preferred to grow other, more lucrative crops, such as rice. Those farmers who broke their contracts were mercilessly beaten up by the planters' henchmen and violent deaths were a regular feature of the region. When and if brought to trial, the culprits intimidated the magistrates and roused favourable public opinion among their compatriots in Calcutta so successfully that they often got away with a mere fine as punishment for even the most brutal slaughter. Since these indigo contracts were generally forged, one former Viceroy had gone so far as to call the entire practice "a gigantic system of fraud." Despite the fall in the demand for indigo in recent years, violence was still rampant in and around Champaran, and no one had been able to contain it.

Thinking about all this, Christian looked so downcast that, in a sudden burst of tenderness, his mother leant forward and covered his hand with hers. "Why don't you move in with us, darling?" she urged. "The food will be *so* much better and you've lost enough weight as it is. Your man, that one-eyed fellow, must be cheating you out of house and home every morning with the daily bazaar."

Christian gave her a wan smile, squeezed her hand in return, and then withdrew his. "I would like nothing better, Mama," he lied, "but I can't let the chaps down. I promised to share the rent and expenses until we were all posted."

"Can't they get someone else to take your place in the chummery?"

"I doubt it. It would be difficult for only a month and at such short notice. Besides," he dug his spoon into the mould and speared a large peach segment, "I don't want to seem privileged in my living conditions merely because of Papa's position."

Sir Jasper nodded a vigorous approval. "That's the spirit! I agree with Christian—he wants to stand on his own feet, regardless of the inconveniences. There are things far worse in life than rusty tin bath tubs and inedible food, Constance. I remember when I first went to Peshawar. . . ."

No more was said that evening about a transfer from the chummery.

As they rose from table in shared relief to repair to the study for coffee and brandy, Lady Pendlebury asked her husband, "Do you intend to indulge in that frightful contraption of yours, Jasper?"

"The hookah?" He pondered. "Yes, you know I think I will. I'm sure Christian would appreciate a puff or two of excellent Persian tobacco."

Lady Pendlebury looked very put out. "In that case," she said coldly, "you will not mind, I hope, if I join you after the puffing is over."

Visibly unburdened that he would be able to speak to his father alone after all, Christian brightened. Perhaps with rather more alacrity than was tactful, he assured his mother that he would not mind in the least.

"Any regrets about having turned down that job in Whitehall?" Sir Jasper asked, as they settled themselves comfortably in the study adjoining the banqueting hall and Tremaine poured out the brandy.

"No, sir."

"Good." Sir Jasper removed his dinner jacket and tossed it in Tremaine's direction. The butler made a signal and a native attendant hurried forward to kneel down at Sir Jasper's feet, take off his black patent leather shoes and black socks and replace them with informal carpet slippers. "One does what one does because at the time one has to. Subsequent regrets are a waste of time. Remember that."

"Yes, sir."

The study was one of the coolest and airiest rooms in the house and the huge thermantidote fitted into one of the doorways made it even more so. The marble floor was covered with a rich plum-coloured Bokhara carpet that went well with the beige-scuffed leather sofas and the Louis Quinze furniture that had come out with the Pendleburys. Some of the glass-fronted cupboards held Sir Jasper's enviable collection of vellum-bound books in Persian, Urdu and English; others displayed sporting trophies and Oriental memorabilia. Sir Jasper himself sat on a high chair with a very straight back, his slippered feet resting on a velvet-covered footstool. Christian slouched in a winged armchair opposite him, his forehead dappled with sweat despite the cool air blowing in through the thermantidote.

A young lad, the hookah-burdar, entered bearing a silver hookah on a large tray. He set it down some distance away from Sir Jasper on the marble verge of the floor and, quite expertly, started to make all the necessary adjustments. In one hand he held a small, embroidered cloth fan with which he gently coaxed the burning coal in the clay chillum into the correct glow. Christian watched the complicated rituals with some amusement, knowing with what patience and perseverence his father had trained their head groom's young son in England to duplicate the exact sequences. Finally satisfied, the boy attached the silver mouthpiece to the long air tube and offered it to Sir Jasper, carefully coiling the tube out of the way. Bowing low, he made his exit backwards from the room. Sir Jasper sucked at the mouthpiece a few times; the sound of a low gurgle filled the room. It was oddly soothing, almost melodious, not unlike the murmur of a babbling brook flowing languidly through some verdant, virginal forest. He inhaled deeply, then, with his eyes closed, exhaled slowly and at length. The air above their heads became lightly touched with the fragrance of sweet-scented Persian tobacco, exotic herbs, jaggery and heady, indefinable spices. Seeing that all was well with his master, Tremaine quietly withdrew from their presence.

"There's nothing quite like a good chillum, my boy." Sir Jasper sighed with intense pleasure. "It's one of the most difficult habits to give up, you know. Unfortunately, your mother can't abide the smell of the tobacco." He inhaled once more and then offered the mouthpiece to Christian. "Want to try a puff?"

Christian hesitated; he had not ever smoked in the presence of his father. But then, with a shy laugh, he accepted the mouthpiece. "Well, I'm not much of a smoker, Papa, but I think I will make an exception. I've always wanted to try a hubble-bubble, although not many Englishmen smoke hookahs these days." He breathed in cautiously and immediately succumbed to a paroxysm of coughing.

His father threw back his head and guffawed. "It might be a good exercise in diplomacy to get used to one of these," he advised, still chuckling. "Everywhere you go you will see villagers sitting in circles under trees sharing a quiet smoke over the day's affairs. It's a perfectly hygienic custom since most carry and use their own mouthpieces."

Christian took a gulp of brandy to clear his throat, then wiped his damp eyes dry and laughed sheepishly. "It's much too strong for me, Papa, but if I find that it might help in the pursuance of my duties, I will cultivate the habit when I get to my post."

"In that case, I will have a silver mouthpiece made for you to carry with you to Champaran." Sir Jasper sat back in the chair and squinted up at the ceiling. "I can still remember a good bit of Urdu and Persian, you know," he mused. "In those John Company days one could not fob the people off with this ridiculous half-language they appear to be teaching now. One had to know one's onions."

"That's not fair!" Christian protested. "What they teach us is Hindustani. It's what most of the people understand well."

"Well, in my time it was simply not enough. English attitudes were entirely different. A civil servant was concerned about his people, he made efforts to reach out to them so that he could. . . ." He broke off the rambling reminiscences as his eyes alighted on a small table by his side on which were stacked some periodicals. Christian noticed that right on top was a copy of *Equality*. Sir Jasper's expression changed. "This young friend of yours. . . ." he began, the previous thoughts forgotten.

"Kyle Hawkesworth?"

"Yes. I am astonished that Bruce McNaughton and the local administration have allowed him such licence." He picked up the paper and let his eyes skim across the front page, his distaste evident. "I consider this editorial inflammatory, scurrilous and, indeed, seditious."

"I disagree, Papa." Christian was quick to rise to his friend's defence. "Kyle is a Eurasian. He feels strongly about the injustices meted out to his community. I see nothing wrong in his crusade to improve conditions for them. You will agree, I'm sure, that they have been badly treated by us— *we* who have been responsible for them being here at all!"

Sir Jasper stared at him hard, visibly displeased. "The authorities are intolerant of subversives," he said shortly. "I would recommend that you discontinue an association that might prove detrimental to your interests."

Christian was about to offer a warm rebuttal but then changed his mind. However ardently he subscribed to Kyle's cause, he saw that it would be foolish at this juncture to provoke an argument that might divert him from a far more vital purpose. He decided to broach the matter burning holes in his mind while his father's comparatively mellow mood persisted. But before he could speak, his father did.

"You know, I have a strange feeling that I have met the man before somewhere. . . ."

"Who, Hawkesworth?" Christian was vaguely surprised, but impatient now to act before his nerve failed and the conversation wandered off in other directions again, he muttered something inaudible and inched forward in his seat. "Papa, there is something that I have to tell you. . . ."

Sir Jasper's attention returned to his son. There was no doubt that he had been waiting for Christian to say precisely that. He nodded. "Yes, I think that you have."

"I'm sure you have already heard all the gossip?"

"All?" Sir Jasper interposed drily. "I wouldn't say all—like hope, gossip springs eternal in the human breast. But yes, I have heard enough for an explanation to be in order."

"I presume Mama has also heard what you have?"

"I'm afraid so."

"Is she very upset?"

"Yes."

"And you, Papa?"

"I am neither upset nor otherwise until I hear what you have to tell me. Needless to say, I would appreciate absolute honesty."

Christian rose to refresh his empty snifter. Pale-faced but resolute, he sat down again. "Well, it's true," he said bluntly, seeing no reason for evasion. "I am in love with a Eurasian girl. I have asked her to marry me."

"And she has agreed to?"

"Yes."

"I see." Sir Jasper displayed no reaction as he drained his glass and held it out for a refill. "The young lady in question being Jai Raventhorne's daughter?"

"Yes." The slight edge of defiance in Christian's tone became more pronounced with the outward thrust of his chin as he handed his father the replenished snifter. "I do not consider Miss Raventhorne in any way responsible for her father's political beliefs and actions." He was immediately on the defensive.

"No, of course she is not," Sir Jasper agreed.

"What is more, from everything that I have heard," Christian ventured, further emboldened, "Jai Raventhorne was a very fine man, a man deeply committed to the welfare of his people."

"Yes. I believe he was," Sir Jasper again agreed readily enough, then returned to his hookah to gurgle away in silence.

Christian studied his father carefully, taken aback by all these concessions. "You didn't . . . know him, by any chance, did you, Papa?"

"No. But I did meet him in Lucknow during the Mutiny."

Christian's breath knotted. "Often?"

"No. Once."

He did not elaborate on the circumstances but Christian's astonishment mounted, although he wondered why this should be so. After all, his father had been an eminent Company official in Oudh at the same time that Raventhorne was active in the uprising. It was more than likely that their paths had crossed.

"What was your impression of him?" he asked with just a faint touch of insolence. "Did you also consider him a scoundrel and a traitor like the rest of the English?"

"He was hanged as a traitor!" Sir Jasper reminded him.

"But he was neither charged nor tried. He was merely lynched!"

His father did not reply immediately. Instead, he looped the hookah tube and the mouthpiece over the stand, then got up to go and stand by the window with his back to his son. "No. I don't think Jai Raventhorne was a scoundrel," he answered eventually. "He was merely an idealist and, in some ways, naïve. The miscalculation that cost him his life was to imagine that the English could so easily be dislodged from this country. But that apart, he was undeniably a man with a . . . quality. A rather memorable quality."

Christian was overwhelmed by the unexpected commendation. For a moment he could scarcely breathe, let alone speak. "May I take it then that"—he paused to swallow hard to relieve his choked throat—"that you have no objections to . . . to . . . ?"

"No, you may not!" Sir Jasper cut him off emphatically. "You may not take it that I have no objections! Indeed, I have very strong objections, but they are not what you might presume. Nevertheless they are objections that should be considered very seriously." He walked back, re-seated himself and leaned forward in his chair. "Do you expect that, even as your wife, Miss Raventhorne will ever be accepted in England?"

Bald as it was, Christian was prepared for the question. "We do not plan to live in England," he said, his voice ringing with confidence. "My life— *our* lives—will be spent here, in India, serving the people of this country."

"And is she accepted here, in this country?" Sir Jasper asked quietly. This question Christian was not prepared for. It confounded him enough to reduce him to temporary silence. "You must understand that wherever you live you will face social ostracism, either because she is Raventhorne's daughter or because she is a half-caste, most likely both." He held up a hand before his son could voice an indignant protest. "I use strong language, Christian, because that is precisely what you, your wife and your children will have to learn to live with. Would you be man enough to face all that?"

Christian's eyes flashed. "We are prepared to face whatever comes!" he said fiercely. "As long as we are together, we can weather all storms."

"Indeed." Sir Jasper's smile was small and acid. "Colonial society is brutal to those it considers renegades, Christian, as you must already know. Pious intentions and platitudes hardly constitute an adequate defence."

"They will, if reinforced with courage and determination."

"And she—an extremely wealthy young woman brought up in luxury— is prepared to live with you in places such as Champaran?"

"*Yes!*" Christian announced after fractional hesitation. If Sir Jasper noticed either the hesitation or the excessively forceful response, he chose to let it pass. "That initial, dreary posting will not last forever. There will be better opportunities later."

"Which brings me to my second objection," Sir Jasper said, unperturbed. "You must also understand that there may not be better opportunities later. Marriage to Raventhorne's daughter will certainly damage your career. You are dedicated and ambitious; you will be relegated to the backwoods and denied chances to rise. Inferior colleagues, unworthy of promotion, will overtake you, and you will end up bitter and frustrated." He sat back again and stretched his legs. "Yes. I fear that your Champaran posting may not be quite as brief as you hope."

Christian dismissed the gloomy prognosis with impatience. "Not necessarily, Papa—I prefer to place rather more faith in the judgement of the authorities. Jai Raventhorne and the Mutiny are now part of dead history. I cannot believe that political grudges will be kept alive from generation to generation. And Mrs. Raventhorne, after all, is a white American of Anglo-Irish extraction and impeccable lineage."

"But her husband was not," Sir Jasper pointed out drily. "And a touch of the tarbrush is very much an inheritable asset."

"All right then, by the same token, *his* father was a titled Englishman of unsullied pedigree."

"His mother, on the other hand," Sir Jasper said, unruffled by his son's gathering agitation, "was an Assamese tribal, a servant girl. Jai Raventhorne was brought up in the streets and gutters of Calcutta."

"As many abandoned Eurasian children are—not out of choice but because of our social hypocrisies! You can't blame them for trying to survive by any means available when they have been denied by their own fathers."

Sir Jasper regarded the hot, angry face of his son and smiled, this time acidly. "I see that your friend—what is his name?—has indoctrinated you well. However, in repeating his views with such conviction, I'm afraid you only help to reinforce my own. Tell me," his eyes narrowed, "do you intend to marry Miss Raventhorne because you truly love her, or as part of some noble, self-righteous crusade to salve the colonial conscience?"

"Of course I love her!" Christian cried. "But at the same time I realise that there are certain grey areas in our society that need to be cleansed, areas about which I feel strongly. Well, what better way to start the process than by example?"

"Oh, poppycock!" Sir Jasper laughed. "There are certain grey areas in everyone's society about which we all feel strongly! The tragedy is that the centuries pass, noble examples go unnoticed, we grow old and die, and the grey areas remain, unchanged and unchangeable. I don't begrudge you your ideals, Christian, but I urge you most sincerely to retain a sense of perspective."

Christian suddenly saw that the conversation was in danger of lapsing into generalities and irrelevancies. "Anyway, all that is neither here nor there," he said, standing up to pace in long, fevered strides, running his fingers through his hair. "I merely wanted to make the point that although I abominate racial prejudice and intend to fight it in every way that I can, the reason that I want to marry Maya Raventhorne is because I do truly love her."

Sir Jasper sighed as he surveyed his son's face, earnest and impassioned. "Be that as it may, Christian," he said ruefully, "prejudice is a spectre that will haunt you and yours all your lives. Like the biblical poor, it will be with you forever. By its very nature it is savage, immune to reason. And to fight it in one's own society when one is considered a betrayer, one has to be even less rational, even more barbaric. I am merely trying to assess if you are up to the task."

"I believe that I am, sir!" Christian said, trembling with emotion. "All I want and beg you to give me is your assent—and the pox on our society, I say, the pox on it!"

As Christian's ringing tones died away and his father made no further comment, a silence descended between them. Exhausted and tight with suspense as he awaited a reaction to his final plea, Christian sank into his chair and wiped his moist face with a handkerchief. Opposite him, Sir Jasper continued to puff away, wordless and abstracted, enjoying the last vestiges of his smoke. With a final puff he laid his mouthpiece to rest and reached for a silver bell resting on the table beside him. Almost as soon as it gave a first peal, Tremaine appeared in the doorway.

"Get that boy to make me a fresh chillum." When the door had closed behind the butler, he returned his attention to his son. "I consider that you are mentally well equipped to make your own decisions, Christian. It is not for anyone to dictate to you how you should or should not lead your life. As a father, it is my duty merely to point out to you the hazards that you risk facing should you decide to proceed with your plan to marry this girl. You—and she—will have to give up much, my son, but if you both are prepared to make these sacrifices. . . ." He shrugged and left the sentence unfinished.

Christian's heart leapt. "Then you will give your assent to our marriage . . . ?"

"You are an adult, a man in your own right. It is not for me to express assent or dissent. You no longer need my permission to do as you deem fit."

"But it would wound me immensely to marry someone you will not accept as a daughter-in-law, Papa!" Christian cried. "It would wound me as much as it would you and Mama."

Sir Jasper pondered for a moment or two. "Very well, in that case, I would like to reserve my answer, but on one condition."

He was euphoric. "Anything, Papa, anything!"

"That you do not announce your decision yet, most especially to your mother. She is, understandably, profoundly distressed by all the rumours flying about. It would be callous to upset her further. Before I give this assent that you say is important to you, I would like to be reassured that you speak not only from the heart but also from the head."

Christian was overpowered by his emotions, so much so that his eyes filled with involuntary tears. "Thank you, Papa, oh thank you!" It was all that he could manage to whisper.

The hookah-burdar arrived with the fresh chillum and the rest of the accoutrements, and for a few minutes there was no conversation. As the boy sat on his haunches performing the various rituals, his face glowing pink in the flames, Sir Jasper stared down at him absently.

"Have you spoken to the girl's mother?" he suddenly asked.

"No, sir. I was waiting to speak to you first. But now I feel it would be honourable to approach Mrs. Raventhorne too as soon as possible."

Sir Jasper nodded but at the same time held up a cautionary finger. "Remember, that far but no further yet."

"Yes, sir. I do take your point." A thought occurred to Christian and he was again briefly defiant. "I must inform you, Papa, that I will not stop seeing Miss Raventhorne no matter what—that I would like to make quite clear."

Sir Jasper raised an eyebrow. "How can I impose a restriction that has no hope of being obeyed and when I consider I have no right to do so? Yes, I'm sure you will continue to see her. But do me the favour of at least adding discretion to your ardour by not riding together and making a public spectacle of yourselves. Presumably she *does* have a home adequate enough for the purpose."

"Well, of course she does," Christian cried gaily, giddy with rapture. "But I also want you to meet her, Papa."

"In time, Christian, all in good time. If you heed my advice and refrain from rushing matters, you stand a far better chance of winning over your mother."

Christian made a face but he was far too happy to play the pettifogger. "Yes, Papa. As always, you are absolutely right."

It seemed that everything that needed to be said for the moment had been said. Once again, they relapsed into silence, this time a silence that was contented and companionable. Christian's heart was full of joy and gratitude, spilling over with love for this understanding, eminently sane and wise man whom he was blessed to have as a father. He felt ashamed that he could ever have doubted his sagacity, his integrity and fair-mindedness. Overcome with relief, it was all Christian could do not to throw his arms about this man he admired so fiercely and reward him with a hug. Of course he did no such thing; any extravagant display of emotion would be grossly embarrassing for them both. But because he simply had to release his high spirits somehow, Christian satisfied himself with a piercing, tuneless whistle.

Sir Jasper laughed. "Well, ready to test the strength of your Sicilian defence?"

By the time the second chillum was exhausted and Lady Pendlebury considered it safe to join them in the study without risking asphyxiation, father and son were entirely at peace with each other and the world, deeply engrossed in their second game of chess.

"Well?" The moment they reached the privacy of their bedroom later that night and the door closed behind them, Lady Pendlebury confronted her husband. "Is it true?"

Sir Jasper replied with a wordless nod. It was after he had washed and undressed that he presented to his wife a somewhat abridged and muted version of his conversation with Christian. Sitting on the bed, she listened with stone-faced attention, not saying a word until he had finished what he had to say.

"Then you were not firm with him, Jasper!" she exclaimed, bitterly disappointed. "You *promised* that you would be."

"You mean, why did I not lay down the law?" he asked with studied patience. "I did not because I do not consider that I am in a position to do so. Whatever we do must be done with grace."

"Grace?" his wife cried, perilously close to losing her temper. "At a time like this you talk of *grace?*"

Her husband slipped on his silken dressing gown and came to sit on the bed next to where she sat trembling. He took her hands in his. "I remind you, Constance, that our ambience here in Calcutta is very different to what we are used to in England," he said gravely. "Here, in the seat of the Empire, we have a position to secure, a certain status to maintain. The privacy that we take for granted in England is denied us here, as you have already discovered. Here we live in a fish bowl, every commission noted, every omission condemned. We, of the Viceroy's inner circle, more than any others, must always be seen to be in control, to sustain appearances, no matter what the cost. I cannot besmirch the dignity of this high office I bear with the stain of hot-headed impulsiveness, even in domestic matters. I certainly cannot be seen to indulge in the least display of prejudice. It is we who bear the prime responsibility of setting an example, Constance—and I cannot stress this strongly enough. Do you understand what I am trying to say?"

"No!" she said tearfully, still deeply distressed. "You talk in such riddles, Jasper! All I can think about at the moment is that Harriet Ingersoll arrives this week to join her husband. What kind of information do you think *she* might be inclined to send back about us and our son? Don't forget, she used to be a Lady of the Royal Bedchamber."

A hint of a frown brought Sir Jasper's beetle eyebrows minimally closer. "Lady Ingersoll is a highly intelligent woman," he said shortly. "I doubt if she would waste valuable time in sending back irresponsible gossip."

"But we know now that it is not irresponsible gossip—you say Christian has as good as admitted that it is true!"

He gave his wife's hand a fond pat and squeezed it. "It is still not long since spring, Constance." He smiled cheerfully. "We must not forget to make allowances for young men's fancies. In the meantime, you will be pleased to know that Christian has promised to come and have all his meals with us." He stood up and stretched his arms above his head with a yawn. "You will see him as often as you wish but," he again looked stern, "not a word to him about this girl, not one word, Constance! That is to be left entirely to me." He paused as a thought struck him. "By the way, have you considered the prospect of going up to the hills for a month or two? Perhaps Mussoorie or Darjeeling or even Simla where, I'm told, the Season is very jolly indeed? The change will certainly do you good."

She stared at him in disbelief. "Do you really consider I could even *think* of leaving station now, Jasper, with matters the way they are?"

"A few weeks here or there . . ."

"No, Jasper, I can't. I simply can't." Panic flickered briefly in her troubled eyes. "And you? Do you plan to travel up when your department does?"

"No, I have to remain here with my confidential papers until I have the estimates framed to my satisfaction." He clucked with annoyance. "It's damned stupid to have to cart up tons of highly sensitive paperwork and risk losing half of it in the ravines. However, I suppose I shall have to go to Simla for Council meetings. And, of course, when summoned by the Viceroy."

"And Christian?" she asked hopefully.

"I doubt if the Commissioner will allow an unposted griffin the luxury of a Himalayan sojourn!" He smiled drily, then waved aside the conversation. "Now, for heaven's sake, let us bury the subject for the moment. A lovesick son is not the only matter that demands my attention."

In their private sitting room next door, Sir Jasper reclined in his favourite armchair and abstractedly stroked his chin. Contrary to what he had said to his wife, the matter of his lovesick son was very much in the forefront of his mind. He now had a need to clarify his thoughts, to untangle the many wayward strands and then rearrange them in neat skeins that would make for easier manipulation later. Briefly, he also thought of the reminder of Lady Ingersoll's arrival, but then he set the thought aside. First matters first; there would be time to consider Lady Ingersoll later.

Sitting with his feet propped on a low table and his legs stretched out before him, Sir Jasper suddenly had a tremendous desire for another chillum. By Jove, nothing activated the thinking processes or soothed abraded nerves quite as effectively as a hookah smoke! To bring even a whisper of tobacco into the bedroom was, of course, unthinkable—Constance would have hysterics. But the craving was so strong that Sir Jasper decided to make the effort to return to his study, have Tremaine rouse the hookah-burdar and indulge himself at uninterrupted leisure. Light-footed with anticipation, humming under his breath, he walked towards the door. Halfway there, he suddenly stopped. His feet froze into immobility exactly where they were. He stood transfixed.

From her adjoining dressing room where she stood brushing out her hair, Lady Pendlebury noticed his abrupt halt in the mirror. Puzzled by her husband's strange posture, she observed him in silence. When he showed no signs of life at all, she nervously called out his name. He made no response, indeed, appeared not even to have heard her at all. Alarmed now, she quickly went to where he stood and touched him on the shoulder.

"Jasper?"

He gave a violent start, as if roused from a deep trance. For a moment he stared at her with glazed, unblinking eyes in which there was no sign of recognition. His normally ruddy complexion looked bloodless.

"*Jasper!*" she cried, horribly frightened, clutching at his shoulder. "What is it, dear? Are you not well?"

He blinked, disengaged his shoulder from her grasp and, in answer to her question, merely shook his head. He did not speak. He could not.

Sir Jasper had suddenly remembered where it was that he had first met Kyle Hawkesworth.

Monday was to be a day of unspeakable tragedy.

When Maya returned from her solitary morning ride, she was met at the front gate by a sobbing Sheba who gave her frightening news. There had been a devastating fire at the Home during the night. Her mother had left for Chitpore just after dawn, as soon as she received the message. No one yet knew the extent of the damage, but the fire carts were still there fighting the blaze. There had been casualties. . . .

Frantic with worry and shock, Maya stopped only long enough to change into a dress and then rushed to Chitpore to find the Home and everything around it in a state of chaos. The street was blocked with fire carts as red-coated firemen dashed around with their hoses and buckets, battling through throngs of local people who had rallied as soon as the alarm was sounded. Inside the Home, white-faced and frightened, a group of residents and staff—still in their night apparel—was gathered in the assembly room, some weeping softly, others stunned and silent. In the front parlour, Marianne Lubbock and Abala Goswami were comforting a hysterical matron and ayah. Hal Lubbock and Kali Charan Goswami stood in the courtyard, talking to the black-faced, visibly exhausted head fireman. Dozens of strangers, some trying to help, others merely curious, milled around everywhere. Clouds of thick, black smoke still billowed up into the morning sky behind the main house. The usually immaculate, serene premises looked an awful mess, but that, of course, was hardly the prime consideration of the moment.

Kali Charan Babu hurried into the parlour. "By the grace of Mother Durga, it has not been as grave a disaster as it could have been. There is much for which we have to be grateful." He also added, rather grimly, that from the evidence they had found in one of the gutted cowsheds, the firemen were almost certain that the blaze had not been an accident. He had taken on the responsibility to inform Clarence Twining and to lodge a written complaint with the police of suspected arson.

Apparently, the fire had started—no one knew exactly how or when—at the back of the main building in a derelict cowshed. Because of its thatched roof, the shed had been instantly consumed, and the flames had then spread rapidly to the other outhouses. The first alarm had been sounded by one of the cowherds who was sleeping in the compound outside. Had it not been for a brief drizzle that retarded the blaze, the entire main building would have been gutted with horrific loss of human life. As matters stood, two cowsheds had been entirely destroyed and four of the other outhouses partially damaged. Some cows, tethered for the night, had perished and three of the four cowherds had suffered burns during the rescue operations. The smell of burning cattle flesh was so horrendous that several people walked about with handkerchiefs tied across their faces in an effort to minimise the stench. Although many of those residing on the premises had received burns, mercifully only one was seriously injured, poor Joycie Crum, who had suffered multiple burns on much of her body and limbs.

Maya found her mother upstairs in Joycie Crum's room, together with Dr. Humphries and Edna Chalcott. Joycie lay on her string cot, very still and with her eyes closed, and her condition was truly pitiable. Somehow Maya swallowed the involuntary scream that rose in her throat, but her eyelids stung with tears. The flesh on Joycie's hands—so deft and quick with the needle and thread—was charred black right up to the wrists. The face was mutilated with huge, ugly blisters and the skin on her legs was badly shrivelled. There was not one strand of hair left anywhere on her head.

Maya felt her mother's arm about her shoulders and her tears spilled over. "Is it very bad?" she whispered, absolutely heartbroken.

It was Dr. Humphries who answered. "Well, let's say it's not good. There is a danger of further infection. We will just have to wait and see."

"And pray," Edna murmured, her cheeks stained with tears.

"Poor, dear Joycie." Maya hid her face against her mother's neck and sobbed quietly. It was her first personal experience of such terribly visible tragedy. She had never before seen anyone so badly mutilated, especially someone for whom she had always had great affection.

After Dr. Humphries had dispensed all his instructions and medicines and hurried away to tend to the other waiting casualties, Edna slumped down into a chair and buried her face in her hands. "My God, who could have perpetrated such a murderous act?"

Dazed and equally devastated, Olivia shook her head. "I don't know, I don't know. . . ," she kept on repeating helplessly. She ran the back of her hand across her eyes. "What I can't understand is, what on *earth* was Joycie doing in that abandoned cowshed in the middle of the night?"

It was a question to which no one had an answer.

One of the inmates rushed in with a message from Dr. Humphries. He urgently needed competent assistants to help in the matter of tending the injured. Could either of them, or both, be spared?

"You go," Edna said to Olivia. "Someone has to remain here with Joycie."

"You can both go. I'll stay with Joycie," Maya volunteered eagerly. "I can send for one of you in case there is an emergency."

"All right, dear. But don't touch her anywhere except on the sides of the hips," Olivia warned. "Most of the rest of her skin is raw and painful to the touch." Leaving her with some hurriedly dispensed instructions, they rushed away to attend to other equally pressing duties.

Maya pulled up a chair and sat down. She was still in a state of shock, unable to wrench her horrified eyes away from the disfigured body lying still and silent on the bed. She could scarcely believe that this was the same woman she had known for years, the woman who had with such loving care stitched and embroidered so many of her dresses and who, out of her meagre earnings, never forgot to give her a sweet or a small toy when she was a child. The room was full of the sickly sweet odour of charred human flesh, overlaid with that of noxious medicines that bit into the nostrils. Maya felt the onset of nausea. Desperate for fresh air, she got up and opened another window. Standing in front of it, gulping in lungfuls of the gusting breeze to blow away the odours, she began to revive. On the wall above Joycie's working table hung a few framed photographs. With her nausea under control, Maya inspected them for a while. Then, from behind her, came a sound, and she flew back to the bedside. Joycie's eyes were open.

"What is it, dear?" Maya whispered, longing to take the deformed, withered hands in hers but knowing that she must not. "Did you want something?"

The blistered lips moved and Maya put her face close to the mouth. " 'Livia?"

"No, it's me, Maya. Shall I call Mother?"

The head shook a little. "Come to . . . try on . . . de cape?" The question came in gasping fragments. The faded blue eyes were mere pinpoints beneath the blackness and the blisters.

Maya bit back a sob. "No, dear. The cape can wait. I came just to be with you. You know I really do love you, Joycie."

The lashless eyelids flickered and there appeared a hint of a proud smile on the misshapen mouth. "All done, y'know. . . . Very fine. . . . Wann you ter feel proud in 'Merica."

"I know I will, my dear, but I'll try it on when I come next. There's plenty of time. You just get well, Joycie, oh *please* get well soon!"

Joycie shook her head as violently as she could. "No, *now*. Not plenny of time. I wanna see. . . ."

Nervous in case her agitation increased, Maya quickly gave in. "All right, I'll try it on now if you wish. Where is it?"

For a long time Joycie didn't reply. Maya thought she was asleep or had forgotten about the cape. But then, suddenly, she opened her eyes again. "Unner de bed. Trunk. I get it. . . ." She tried to get up.

"You *can't*, Joycie!" Maya cried, holding her down as best she could by the side of her hips. "Dr. Humphries says you mustn't!"

"Yiss. *Can*. . . ." But her strength was unequal to her spirit. It ebbed fast and she fell back on the bed panting.

"Can't I get it from the trunk?" Maya pleaded, wondering if it was time to call for help. But then the panic passed as Joycie's fleeting rebellion ended.

"A'right." With a monumental effort, she lifted her hands and looked at them. Then she closed her eyes again and started to weep quietly. "No maw dresses f'you, dearie, no maw. . . ." Maya's heart wrenched with pity and her throat went tight, but she didn't know what to say. "A'right," Joycie whispered after a minute or so. "You open trunk."

Maya got up and pulled the trunk towards her from under the bed. A large lock hung open from its latch. As she started to raise the lid, she felt something wet and sticky on her hands. When she saw what it was, she again felt a rush of bile in her throat. Along the rim of the lid clung bits of flesh, burnt black and laced with fresh red blood. Incredibly, Joycie had opened the trunk *after* her hands were charred almost down to the bone! Breathing in deeply and quickly to stop herself from being sick, Maya wiped her hands thoroughly on her handkerchief and then used it to raise the lid of the trunk. On top of a mess of clothes and oddments was the cape that Joycie had been stitching for her to take to America, beautifully embroidered and neatly folded within sheets of old newspaper. For the moment, however, Maya's eyes were transfixed by something else, something so utterly unexpected that she gasped. Scattered on top of the newspaper protecting her cape, as if thrown in hurriedly, were several pieces of the most exquisite jewellery.

Maya was dumbfounded. For an instant all she could do was stare. Then her startled glance flew to the face on the bed. Joycie's eyes were as open as she could get them. She was watching her like a hawk. Maya sank back on the floor and again stared at the unbelievable sight.

"See?" Joycie whispered.

Maya nodded, her eyes riveted. So! What everyone had suspected for years was true, after all—Joycie *did* have a cache of jewellery saved from her halcyon days with her nawab lover! Another quite unbelievable thought struck her. "You had these hidden in the abandoned cowshed? Is that what you were doing down there last night?"

Joycie nodded, triumphant.

"Where?"

Her pale eyes gleamed with cunning and she made the sound of a low, satisfied cackle. "Wall. Behind de bricks. Had to geddem *out.*" All at once the voice sounded stronger, refreshed by the thought of her precious jewellery, her life's savings. "Bolt de door." Maya got up to obey the peremptory order, marvelling at the animation in Joycie's face. "Now puddem all togedder. Slowly. Don't drop any." There was a fragment of charred red velvet with the jewellery, obviously part of its erstwhile poche, but it was quite unusable. Maya rummaged in the trunk, found another piece of cloth and gathered the jewellery into it. "Now *you* take." Joycie commanded.

"What?" Maya asked, startled.

"Take, *take*, girl!" Her eyes were feverishly bright. "You take dem home. Keep for me. *Safe.*"

"No, listen, Joycie. . . ."

"No! *You* lissen. You keep. Safe. If I don die, you. . . ."

"Oh, Joycie, you're *not* going to die!" Maya cried tearfully.

"Don talk rubbish. Lissen, if I don die, you bring dem back. All."

"Keep them here in the trunk, Joycie," Maya coaxed. "You've already got a lock."

"Here?" At the well-meaning suggestion, Joycie became almost demented. Somehow she invoked the energy for a hoarse, stricken scream. "Here? With dem robbin' witches and deir thievin' hands? I save dem for *years*, now you wan I. . . ?"

"All right, all right, I'll take them," Maya assured her hastily, terrified of provoking a crisis that she would not be able to control. "I'll take them home and keep them safe for you in my cupboard. My mother. . . ."

"You tell 'Livia, no one else, *no one*, promise?" Maya nodded emphatically. "If I *don* die, I tink of new hideyhole. Mebbe in . . . never mind. But if I die"—she glared at Maya challenging her to protest. Too intimidated by the fierce determination in Joycie's eyes, Maya remained tactfully silent—"*den* you give dem to him."

Maya's underlip quivered. "To whom, Joycie?"

Defeated by the effort of speech, Joycie closed her eyes and whispered something Maya could not catch. She continued to babble under her breath, as if slipping into a delirium. There was only one mumbled fragment that Maya could decipher. "*He* know whom for to give dem, he know, for his. . . ." The last word was lost in a mumble of unintelligible sounds. Obviously, she was hallucinating.

"He? Who, Joycie?" Maya asked, softly stroking the side of her hip.

But there was no reply. Whatever little was left of Joycie's skin looked hot and flushed, and Maya's spine prickled with fear. Once again she wondered if she should call for the doctor. But then, making another gigantic effort, determined to complete her say, Joycie again found a voice and spoke very clearly.

"De man, *her* man. Wot gave her dat critter. He wanna kill dem, you know dat? It don matter now, *she* look after herself now, den a'right. I die happy. But you give dese to him. For *her!*"

"To whom, Joycie?" Maya pleaded urgently, bewildered.

The shadow of a frown appeared on her blistered forehead, as if in irritation. "To Kyle, my girl," she said, annoyed. "How many times you wan I say it? You give dem to *Kyle,* for her. . . ." Drained by the effort, her voice weakened.

Maya was so astonished that she could say nothing.

"For her . . . an' for dat devil critter. He don look after dem, he never look affer dem. . . ." Two huge tears gathered in her eyes and rolled down the blackened cheeks.

"Who is *them,* Joycie?"

"*Dem.* Her and dat devil critter chile."

"Child?" Maya's heart lurched. "Whose child, Joycie?" she asked in a shaky whisper. "Kyle's?"

"His critter chile . . . the chile wid de"—Joycie raised a feeble hand and took it to her mouth—"Dat critter chile wid de. . . ." Again she made the same gesture, indicating what seemed to be her mouth. Then her voice died away and she closed her eyes. Her breathing settled down into a slow, shallow rhythm.

Joycie slept.

Disturbed and puzzled, Maya sat immobile and deep in thought, the cloth bundle clasped between her palms. Presently, there was a series of knocks on the door. Remembering that it was bolted, she got up and released the latch. It was Edna, returned to take charge of Joycie Crum. Far too distressed by Joycie's condition to try to make sense out of her ramblings at the moment, Maya remained with Edna the whole day, helping to nurse the lonely woman who had had so little from life. She wondered if Joycie would speak again, but she did not. Deeply sedated to ease the crippling pain of her awesome injuries, she slept on through the day.

Joycie had been trying to tell her something. How much of what she had said had been spoken in delirium, Maya had no way of knowing. About one fact, however, there could be no doubt: Joycie knew a great deal about the woman and child hiding in Kyle Hawkesworth's tunnel!

"Someone up there looks upon us with favour!" Christian wrote in his brief, exultant note.

> *I did see Papa alone, after all. He will not commit himself but he seems not entirely averse to my decision. I dare to believe that the portents are*

good, far better than I imagined. I have written to your mother request-ing an appointment. I pray that she is willing to receive me. Patience, my darling one, we are almost there! More when we meet. I can hardly wait! With all my love and in great haste,

Ever yours,
Christian.

Christian's letter arrived very early in the morning the next day, and the news it bore eradicated everything else from Maya's mind. There could be only one reason for Christian's intention to call on her mother formally. Maddeningly, he gave no details, but nevertheless Maya's heart started to sing. Astonishingly, someone up there *was* looking upon them with favour, and the news was even more sweet for being so utterly unex-pected. For the time being even poor Joycie and her jewellery were for-gotten as Maya flew down the stairs in search of her mother. She found her already at breakfast in the morning room.

Olivia surveyed her daughter's flushed face in silence, well aware of the cause of the excitement and once again disturbed by it. "I suppose you already know that Christian has written to ask for an appointment to see me," she said without much enthusiasm as soon as Maya was seated.

"Yes."

"I have said I will see him this afternoon at five. The insurance people are coming to the Home in the morning to assess the extent of the dam-age and then I have to relieve Edna. She's been up all night looking after Joycie."

Some of Maya's excitement evaporated as memories of Joycie's muti-lated body came flooding back. "I'll come with you," she said quickly. "I was going to fumigate the stable house this morning, but Abdul Mian and Rafiq can do that on their own." She picked up a piece of toast and started to butter it. "Christian writes that he has spoken to his father."

"I gathered that from his request. Has he said anything to you about his father's reaction?"

Maya shook her head. "I would rather you heard that from Christian, Mother. His note to me was very brief." She bit into the toast and chewed on it slowly. "He only indicated that his father is not . . . entirely against the idea."

Olivia laid down her fork, balanced her elbows on the table and looked hard at her daughter. "Is this what you really want, Maya? To marry Christian Pendlebury?"

"Yes. I told you I have already accepted his proposal."

Olivia did not soften her look. "Even though he intends to spend the rest of his working life in India?"

Maya abandoned the toast with a grimace and poured herself a large breakfast cup of coffee. "There will be furloughs in England and, besides"— she smiled that secretive little smile that Olivia had begun to dislike so much—"he *might* change his mind and return to live there, after all."

"Is that what you intend to persuade him to do?"

"Perhaps. We will see when the time comes."

"And how do you think you will be received in England?"

Maya's eyes glinted. "As I will here, with respect," she said coolly. "Christian will make certain of that."

Olivia modified her expression. "I wouldn't take that for granted, darling," she said very, very gently. "Society repels very savagely those who dare to scale certain forbidden barriers."

"Of course, you speak from personal experience, don't you, Mother?" Maya asked insolently.

"Yes." This time Olivia was prepared for her daughter's questions, however insolent. "I have never been forgiven for the barrier that I dared to scale. I paid a heavy price for it."

"But you still scaled it—and you survived!"

"I scaled it and survived because I had an invincible ally." She forced her daughter to meet her gaze and hold it. "You see, Maya, I truly loved your father."

"And you don't think I love Christian?"

"Do you?"

Maya's gaze dropped; she did not answer the question. Instead, she countered with another. "How do you measure love, Mother?" she demanded, amused. "Is there some mechanical device that allows you to calibrate your affection for someone?"

"Yes. You measure love by what you are willing to give up for it."

"You gave up *everything* for Father," she said, her lip curled with contempt. "What did that noble sacrifice bring you except grief?"

"The joy it brought was worth that grief. It still is."

"You think I am unable to make sacrifices?" Maya asked tightly.

"To make this marriage, yes; to sustain it, perhaps not."

"Aren't they the same thing?"

"You tell me, do you honestly believe that they are?"

Maya threw down her napkin on the table and stood up, trembling. "I cannot, *will* not live in this country, Mother!" she said fiercely. "I have no place in it, I never have and I never will."

"You will have a place in America."

"You don't really know what I'm talking about, do you?" She swept aside her mother's contention with disdain. "You think to find a place is a matter of geography?" She laughed. "Why should I go anywhere as a refugee, Mother—I'm a refugee here, or hadn't you noticed? I have a need to have a *definition*, to be an identifiable component of a society, even one that repels me savagely, can't you understand that?" Anger shone out of her deep blue eyes like a flaming beacon. But then, slowly, the light died and her spirit crumpled. "No, of course you can't. How could you?" she said bitterly, with a quiet sort of despair. "You're not a half and half, you have a place!" Without finishing her breakfast, she walked out of the morning room.

Olivia felt a familiar shaft of pain. Overwhelmed with love, with compassion, she yearned to reach out to her tormented child, longed to take her in her arms and give her solace, but she knew that she would be repelled. As her father had once done, Maya lived within a shell, ferociously possessive of her inner world, unwilling to share it with anyone, not even her mother. Olivia ached for her, feeling her anguish from a distance, knowing that she could do nothing to relieve it. Just as Jai was sometimes in the habit of doing, Maya too had receded beyond her reach.

Christian arrived at ten minutes to five, very formally dressed, his face set and shining with purpose. For this most important interview, he had chosen to ride in a carriage and alighted in the front porch with great ceremony. Maya met him on the front steps, noting with private satisfaction that the two Anderson girls were in their front garden instructing the mali and could not possibly miss his arrival. Wordlessly, Christian stared at Maya, once again marvelling at her beauty, at the fact that she should love him. He had not seen her for many days now. Longing to touch her, but knowing that he must not, he merely expressed a few vapid banalities and devoured her with hungry eyes from a decent distance.

"I've missed you so frightfully," he could not resist whispering as she led him to her mother's study. She stood aside for him to enter, knowing that her mother would prefer to see him on her own.

"I missed you too."

"Will I see you after I have spoken to your mother?"

"Yes. If you wish to."

"Can you ever doubt that?"

He gave her a last lingering look as Olivia came down the stairs and, rather pointedly, Maya went out in the direction of the stable house. Then he said with genuine concern, "I was so dreadfully sorry to hear about the fire at the Home, Mrs. Raventhorne. Is it true what the rumours would have us believe, that the fire was deliberately started by miscreants?"

Olivia sighed. "Yes, I'm afraid so. It really is a most distressing business and we're still in a state of terrible shock. We do hope Clarence Twining will be able to catch the man responsible."

"You say that as if you know who he is?" Christian asked curiously.

"Well, we do have our suspicions," Olivia explained, once again thinking what a clean, uncomplicated young man Christian Pendlebury was. She had not met him since he had first called and she was struck anew by his essential sincerity. "The actual arsonists were paid criminals, of course. However, we think the person behind them might have been the disgruntled father of one of our former girls, who has sworn to avenge what he considers to be a gross misdemeanour on our part."

"Good heavens!" Christian looked horrified. "I can imagine no misdemeanour on your part that could possibly provoke such brutal retribution."

Olivia smiled. "Well, he considers that we have committed an unforgivable crime by encouraging his daughter to flout custom and remarry a man of her choice. They are Brahmins, you see, and she is a widow." Olivia shook her head sadly. "Sometimes I wonder if we did right."

"How can you say such a thing, Mrs. Raventhorne?" Christian

protested. "Aren't you pleased that the young lady has another chance at happiness?"

"Oh, of course. I didn't mean that. I mean—it is sometimes so difficult for the most logical of parents to think rationally when it comes to their own children. In some strange way I can understand the man's anger."

The significance of the last remark was not lost on Christian. As he followed Olivia into the study and the door closed behind them, he wondered if it was intended for him to take note of. But then, as they sat down in the comfortable chintz-covered sofas before a table where Sheba had laid a tray of tea with plates of *petit fours*, Olivia smiled warmly and Christian's courage revived. It seemed to be the right cue for what he had come to say. He cleared his throat and plunged in headlong.

"I will not waste much of your time, Mrs. Raventhorne. I have come to ask for your permission to marry your daughter. I love her very deeply and I believe my feelings are reciprocated. She has already accepted to become my wife."

He said it almost in one breath, and Olivia was a little winded by the directness of his approach. She did not reply immediately but instead set about pouring the tea. "Have you informed your parents of your intentions?"

"Well, yes. I spoke to my father last night."

"And what has been his reaction?"

"He has not objected to my choice of wife."

"You mean he has given his consent to the marriage?"

"I do not need his consent. What I do want most earnestly is his good-will."

She handed him a cup and a selection of dainty *petit fours*. He started to nibble nervously. "And you have that?"

"Yes, I think so. My father is a man of extraordinary perceptions, Mrs. Raventhorne," Christian assured her proudly. "Ever since I can remember, he has been my truest friend and mentor. He has never been dishonest with me, never given me false advice or fed me with platitudes. He has always treated me with respect, as an equal. I trust him implicitly." He quickly took a few sips of the tea to release the constriction in his throat. "All he has requested is that, for the moment, we be discreet. He was surprisingly sympathetic." He flushed. "I say surprising because. . . ."

"You don't need to explain, Christian," Olivia said with a gentle smile. "I understand. But what was his final opinion?"

"He refused to give one. He considered it was for me as an adult to make my own decision which," he added hastily, "I already have. All he asks is that I be certain of myself."

"I see," Olivia said thoughtfully. "And when you convey to him this certainty, he will accept it?"

"Yes. I am confident of that. His chief concern is for my career because. . . ." He again faltered.

"Because marriage to my daughter might constitute a serious impediment to it?"

He looked gratified that she had saved him the embarrassment of having to make such a humiliating statement. "Yes."

"But you believe it will not?"

Christian's chin shot forward. "No. I have faith in the innate good sense of the Covenanted Civil Service and its officers. Merit will carry its own worth, no matter what my personal circumstances. My first posting has already been decided, as Maya must have told you. It now only remains for the housing situation in Champaran to be investigated."

"You plan to marry *before* you are posted?" Olivia asked, dismayed.

Christian almost said yes, but then, seeing that that might be unrealistic, he shook his head and looked subdued. "Alas, no. I must first go to Champaran on my own to test the waters, so to speak. Apart from vetting the accommodation available, I have to make certain that all other living arrangements are also adequate. I am anxious that Maya should have as many comforts of home as I can possibly provide."

Olivia was tempted to smile but did not. How artless he was! Living arrangements, she imagined, would be the very least of his coming worries. "And your mother? Does she share in your father's liberal attitudes?"

Christian looked slightly crestfallen. "I doubt it," he admitted quite frankly. "I intend not to speak to her myself but leave it to my father to do so. He is hopeful that she will eventually come round to our way of thinking."

For a while Olivia remained silent, sipping her tea and wondering with what words to caution this earnest young man who accepted so much in his life at face value. All at once she felt immensely saddened. He had chosen to trust his weight to a precariously strung bridge across a chasm that was unbridgeable. The pity of it was that he did not see it.

"Maya is over eighteen, Christian," she finally said. "Like you, she is an adult. Rightly or wrongly, I have brought up my children to think for themselves, as my father always encouraged me to. Sometimes, I confess, I do have misgivings. But how could I have denied my own children those pleasures of freedom that I have myself enjoyed?" She broke off and reached impulsively for his hand. "Yes, of course, you do have my permission, Christian. But, as your father has done, I too would request you not to be hasty. Keep your decision to yourselves until you are both absolutely certain of your intentions."

It was all that Christian had hoped for. He was delighted.

Later, he sat on the river steps with Maya and related to her in detail what his father and her mother had said to him. He could not have been, he assured her, better satisfied. Having spent most of the day helping to nurse Joycie, now deep into unconsciousness and no longer aware of the world of which she was once a part, Maya clasped his hand and held it in her own, desperately in need of comfort. He drew her close and, very tenderly, smoothed down her hair as she laid her head on his shoulder.

"I have promised to eat more often with my parents," he said. "But I consider that a small price to pay for the fact that I can meet you whenever I like."

"Yes." She raised her head to look at him. "And Mr. Ludlow is not likely to change his mind about posting you in Champaran?"

"No. The administration needs new men, fresh blood. I can hardly protest more than I already have." He gave her a worried look. "You have not changed your mind about coming with me, have you?"

"No, of course not." The flawless smoothness of her forehead was marred by a minimal frown. "I don't suppose your father could request the Chief Commissioner to give you another posting?"

He rejected that instantly. "No. Oh no. I have to stand on my own or not at all. It would be shameful to try to invoke Papa's influence. He would be most disappointed if I even suggested such a thing." He got up, flexed his legs and stretched his arms contentedly above his head. "I have to go and return some books Kyle was good enough to lend me. He also wants to show me one of his latest acquisitions, a new dissertation on Thomas Paine."

Maya's spell of contentment snapped. Mention of Kyle brought back to mind Joycie's instructions as well as her own nagging fears. "Why do you see Kyle so often, Christian?" she blurted out. "Don't you know how . . . dangerous he can be?"

"Dangerous? Kyle?" He could not have been more amused. "He is the one good friend I have in Calcutta. I have learnt a great deal from him. I consider myself privileged to be able to talk to a man fired with such zeal and imagination."

"Nevertheless, please be careful, Christian. The man is not to be trusted."

His amusement faded. "You don't like Kyle much, do you?"

"No."

"Well, why ever not?"

"I believe his motives to be suspect. When the mood seizes, he can be rather . . . devious."

That Christian refused to accept. In fact, he was distinctly annoyed. "Do you speak from personal experience, or just repeat irresponsible gossip?"

Maya felt her anger rise. "Having been a frequent victim of it myself, I am not in the habit of dispensing gossip, irresponsible or otherwise," she said frostily. "I know Kyle, you don't. That's all there is to it."

"I consider Kyle to be a friend," he repeated, his tone as chilly as hers. "I am sorry that you happen not to like him. Of course, you are entitled to your opinion—as much as I am to mine. Let us just leave it at that."

Maya watched in dismay as Christian stalked off in a stubborn huff, and her anger against Kyle spiralled. Absent or present, knowingly or otherwise, he had already started to soil her relationship with Christian. Given more time, he would destroy it entirely.

She could not afford to wait any longer.

13

I*T WAS DUSK.* There were few people about on the rugged embankment, certainly none who paid particular attention to the dark-cloaked figure hurrying through the undergrowth. This time Maya felt no fear, either of the dark or of being observed. There was no light in the windows of the press. The latest issue of *Equality* was out yesterday and today was their weekly holiday.

This evening she was not prepared to risk Kyle's absence from the house; she had written to ask for an appointment. He had replied with a cursory, unsigned note asking her to come at seven. Maya had no doubt that the confrontation tonight would be unpleasant and acrimonious, but that had ceased to worry her. Tonight, she had come fully prepared. Indeed, she was astonished at just how confident she felt. However, before she faced Kyle at seven, there was one vital detail she had to confirm: she had to assure herself that his secret guest was still on the premises. Mere information about the woman would be useless if the woman herself had been whisked away somewhere else.

This time the door to the underground room stood wide open, although there appeared to be no one in it. There were still plenty of signs of human occupation and Maya heaved a sigh of relief. No, the woman had not been whisked off anywhere; she was very much on the premises. There were clothes on the bed, all neatly folded. In the strange, cagelike cot with the high wooden slats lay scattered the wooden toys.

The devil critter chile!

Maya wondered again what Joycie had meant by that curious description, but there was no time now to stop and ponder. A musical instrument, a *tanpoora*, stood propped against a wall next to a basket filled with ankle-bells such as dancers wore. On the window sill was a row of Urdu books. Who was this woman, a dancing girl?

As Maya stood boldly in the centre of the room, her hands on her hips, a sudden idea struck her. It was delightfully perverse, quite the sort of idea Kyle himself might have conjured up had the circumstances been reversed. Without a second thought, she crossed the deserted room and ran into the passage that was the continuation of the tunnel on the other side. She would enter the house through the courtyard! The mere thought of Kyle's shocked face as she suddenly materialised before him tickled Maya's fancy. It brought a buoyancy to her step and under her breath she laughed.

This passage was somewhat longer than the tunnel on the embankment side, but she traversed it without meeting a soul. A moment later she was at the foot of the roughly hewn stone stairs that would, she had no doubt, lead her up into the courtyard. She ran up the flight, cautiously nudged the trap-door above her head and peered out. Yes, she had guessed correctly. The trap-door was behind the bushes in the courtyard. Not far from the shrubbery a servant boy stood removing some clothes from the washing line, but he had his back to her. Maya waited until he had returned inside with the basket of clothes, then stepped out into the yard. Drawing a deep breath, she walked through the doorway into the house.

Kyle sat at his desk in his study next to the parlour. He was writing. Maya slipped into the room through the inner door as silently as a shadow and, scarcely breathing, took up position in a corner cloaked in gloom. Totally immersed in his labours, Kyle did not even glance up, unaware that he was no longer alone. For a moment Maya remained still, getting back her breath, waiting for her heartbeats to steady. She was surprised that he heard nothing; but the silence was deep and the scratch of his pen as it raced across the paper sounded abnormally loud. Leaning the back of her head against the wall, she stood and watched him.

His checked shirt was open at the neck, his sleeves rolled up to his elbows. His head was at an angle, propped up by one hand with the fingers spread in the untidy tangles of his abundant hair. On the desk, by his elbow, stood a solitary lamp, the sole source of light in the room. It threw a pool of white onto his sheets of paper and illuminated half his face. His lips, trained never to soften, never to expose an inner thought, were curved in a smile of some secret pleasure and glistened with wetness. Under the table, one leg was stretched out, the other folded with the foot balanced over his knee. Except for his right hand, which scribbled with astonishing speed, the rest of his body was unmoving.

Maya had never seen him like this before, at ease and at peace with himself, without the quivering tensions he had woven around himself like a cloak. Now, the furies he nursed were dormant, the lines of his face unmarred by anger or hate or mutilating cynicism. The wheat-coloured skin, smooth and polished and stretched taut over his gaunt features, was faintly sheened with sweat, almost metallic in the concentrated light. Without that protective veneer of arrogance, he looked alien, someone she had never known before. He had no suspicion of being watched.

Marvelling at this entirely unfamiliar aspect of a man she considered she knew well, Maya's thoughts streaked back to that strangely unforgettable evening on the *Ganga*. Then, in an involuntary rush, they dwelt on the mysterious woman in Kyle's life, a woman with whom he had shared so much of himself. For a wild moment she tried to imagine what it might be like to have Kyle on her side, to taste some of that secret softness available only to a few, a softness that he guarded with such possessive ferocity. But then she saw that this could never be; they aimed at different horizons, trod divergent paths. They were like two parallel lines that by their very definition were ordained never to meet. And in the realisation that they were so divided, Maya felt a tiny flicker of something, a twinge perhaps of regret. Without their opposing compulsions, under other suns, other skies, might they not have been less inalienably separated?

She heard him suck in a long, slow breath as he flexed both legs under the desk. Lazily, he raised his arms above his head and his eyes wandered up to the clock. A slight frown ruffled the smoothness of his forehead—and it was in that very instant that he saw her. He went rigid, his arms still raised above his head. Had it not been for the intense quiet, she would have missed the sharply indrawn breath, almost a gasp. Slowly he lowered his arms, staring eyes filled with astonishment as his brain grappled with explanations for her sudden appearance.

On her tongue Maya tasted triumph; it was sweet.

But then in a flash, darting about like quicksilver his brain resolved the mystery. If she expected that he would give her the satisfaction of enjoying his sense of shock, Maya was disappointed. He reconstituted his face with such rapidity that those satisfying seconds of incredulity and astonishment might never have been.

"You're late."

With that sole observation, he picked up his pen and continued with what he was writing. Maya looked up at the clock. It showed ten minutes past seven. She smiled; she knew that his show of unconcern was patently false, the assumed composure brittle. She sensed that her little ploy had worked extremely well, that the dart had struck exactly where she had aimed it—at a nerve end that was raw. Behind that hastily erected facade, he was shaken. And furious!

"Well, what do you want?"

The question was characteristically brusque, but Maya had anticipated that. Normally, the rage that was secreted in every crease of his body might have intimidated her. Tonight, she was untouched by it.

"What do I want?" She sauntered over to the desk and sat down in the chair on the opposite side of it, although he had not invited her to do so. "What I want is for you not to see Christian again."

He raised his eyes from the papers and cocked an eyebrow. "Oh? And why do you presume that you are in a position to make such an impertinent demand?"

"I won't insult your intelligence by responding to that, Kyle. You already have the answer."

He swung his chair back and pyramided his fingers against his chest, his eyes narrowed in speculation. She met his gaze calmly, neither nervous nor anxious. If anything, she was amused that he could have ever made her either. Tonight she was remarkably well secured.

"Merely because you've discovered the tunnel?" he asked with scarcely concealed contempt. "Well, then, that's settled easily enough. The answer is, no. Now, if that is all, get out. I have work to do." He swung forward and made a move towards his pen.

"No, that is not all!" She leaned over the desk and snatched the papers off the table before he could start writing again, unimpressed by his bravado. "You pursue Christian for a motive. I want to know what that motive is."

"We both pursue Christian for a motive."

She refused to loosen her anger. "Has it occurred to you that I might be in love with Christian Pendlebury?"

"No. That is the one possibility that has not occurred to me—any more than it has to you."

"I'm going to marry him, Kyle," she said evenly, holding on to the tail of her temper, "whatever might be my reasons. I'm not going to let you ruin *this* relationship, that much I promise."

"Presuming, of course, that I intend to?"

"Don't you?"

"You flatter yourself. I don't care a fig who you marry!"

"All right then, answer me this. You dislike Christian and yet you cultivate him. Why?"

"I don't dislike him. On the contrary, I find him amusing, well read and rather congenial company. Does that satisfy you?"

"No. You have always had contempt for so-called congenial company, and you are incapable of liking anyone." She was incensed by his hypocrisy. It amazed her that she could ever have melted towards this man, even marginally. "Christian considers you to be his friend."

"Then that, by your own assessment, is his misfortune."

He reached out for the papers she still held in her hand, but she evaded him. "For his sins, he hero-worships you, Kyle."

"Well, at least he has good taste in heroes."

His conceit was insufferable. "He also hero-worships his father," Maya added, watching him closely.

A flicker, a bare flicker, of something passed over his eyes and then vanished. "Then that, by my assessment, is his greater misfortune."

"Why?"

"I have no stomach for imperialists—you know that perfectly well."

Her fingers toyed with a pencil on his desk; she studied him from under lowered lashes. A succession of nuances flitted across his face so well illuminated by the lamplight. Some she could not decipher, others she could not mistake. But on the whole she knew that she had not been wrong. He was unsure of the extent of her discoveries. Underneath that withering insolence, Kyle Hawkesworth was desperately uneasy.

"I don't pretend to know—yet—what exactly it is that you hide, Kyle," she said softly, "but I can assure you that I will find out."

The curtain of the doorway parted and a young lad entered, the same Eurasian she had seen at the washing line. He stared at her, quite startled by her presence in the room. Kyle stood up, making no attempt to hide his churlishness, and made a sign to the boy. "Since my concentration for the evening is ruined anyway, you might as well have some damned tea."

"No, thank you, I. . . ."

Nevertheless he ordered it.

Obviously restless, he paced for a moment or two. Then, arriving at some decision, he sat down again and crossed his arms on the desk. "All right, I admit that I underestimated you. You are more resourceful than I had imagined."

Maya's heart leapt. "Leave Christian alone, Kyle," she said, not showing her elation. "Whatever little game you are playing, you merely use him as a pawn."

"Yes."

The admission came with such willingness that Maya was caught unawares. Her stomach gave a sickening lurch. "You plan to harm him!"

"I don't plan to, no."

"But you *will!*"

"Why do you presume that?"

"Because I know your perversities, because by your very nature you are vengeful and destructive!"

He gave her a piercing look, not bothering to hide his scorn. "I have no quarrel with your Christian. He is not of the slightest consequence to me."

"Yet you pursue him, making even your inconsequentialities suspect. I warn you, Kyle, I will *not* let you injure Christian or his interests in any way."

"*Your* interests!"

"All right, *my* interests, if you like. Your insinuations no longer touch me, Kyle." She turned the back of her hand upwards, pinched the skin hard and laughed. "See? You should be proud of how diligently your pupil has learned her lesson!"

He inclined his head in mocking acknowledgement of her compliment. Their glances locked; she held his gaze boldly. Finally, it was he who dropped his and turned away.

"You wouldn't like everyone to know about that tunnel, would you?" she asked with a cold, malicious smile.

He got up and walked over to the mantelpiece, standing with an elbow balanced on it. He made a face but did not allow his anger to surface. In fact, he half smiled. "No, I have to confess that I would not. Is that what you came to hear?"

"Among other things, yes." She hated that half smile, the forced non-chalance. She trusted neither. But, suddenly, she could not distinguish his mood and it worried her. In any case, it was time to give the knife another turn.

"I also know about the woman and the child. Your child."

"Ah!" He made no other comment but looked at her very strangely, as if re-examining the situation, making secret assessments, formulating what to say next. Beneath the coppery sheen he had turned a shade paler. He sat down, swung his legs up on the desk and—no doubt to give himself more time to think—started to light his pipe.

"And what exactly is it that you know?"

"I know that they come from Lucknow." Considering Joycie's background, it was not an irrational assumption.

"A lot of people come from Lucknow."

"Yes, but not to be concealed by you in that tunnel."

He considered that, then conceded the point. "No, perhaps not. What else?"

"Not much else at the moment, but I intend to find out."

"And having found out, what precisely do you plan to do with the information?"

"Do?" Maya smiled, then gave a light laugh. "I will do exactly as you advised—write it on the blackboard. It worked well once. It will work again."

Kyle shook his head and raised a forefinger. "It will not, you know," he said, almost in sorrow. "In fact, you would be astonished at how well it will not work." With that cryptic observation, he heaved his legs down again and stood up. "But if that is your intention, then allow me to be of some assistance in making your investigative endeavours a little less arduous."

He walked up to the doorway, pulled the curtain aside and made a gesture. Almost immediately a woman entered bearing a tray with two cups of tea. Obviously she had been standing outside the door waiting to be summoned.

"This is Nafisa Begum," Kyle said. "No one makes spiced tea quite like she does. In fact, she insisted on bringing the ingredients with her all the way from Lucknow. Isn't that so, Nafisa?"

The woman's forehead and eyes were draped over with a veil, so that only the lower half of her face was visible. Her lips moved in a smile but she made no audible acknowledgement of his remarks. She was tall and lissome and her limbs were imbued with the fluid grace of a feather floating gently in a lambent breeze—or would have been were it not for one impediment: she walked with a pronounced limp. As she made her way towards Maya, because of her disability her narrow hips swayed awkwardly from side to side. Despite that, one could see the grace in her movements, as if she still responded to silent rhythms available only to herself. She approached her chair and Maya was engulfed in clouds of intoxicating perfume—attar-of-roses—and her ears vibrated with the tinkle of glass bangles as they pushed against each other on finely boned wrists. Maya's startled eyes flew towards the woman's feet. Yes, they were the same—long and shapely—that she had seen that night on the string cot in the underground room. Round the slim ankles were a recognisable pair of silver anklets. What had not been obvious that night was that one leg was distinctly shorter than the other.

With infinite delicacy, the woman placed the two cups of tea on the desk between them. She smiled at Kyle, a sweetly intimate smile that was eloquent with love even in a half-concealed face. Then with another, rather more formal smile in Maya's direction, she turned and, with no sign of hurry, left the room.

Utterly taken aback by the unexpected revelation—even more so by Kyle's motive in making it—Maya continued to stare in silent bewilderment at the rippling curtains through which the woman had just passed. She could not think of anything to say. Instead, to marshall her scattered senses and regroup her resources, she got up abruptly and went to stand by the window with her back towards him. Quietly, she began to seethe with outrage. How dare he flaunt his wretched mistress—disabled or not—in her face without a shred of modesty? Did this shameless man have no finer feelings at all?

She finally located a voice. "Who is she?"

He shrugged. "A friend." He strolled across the room to join her at the window. With another lightning change of mood and no warning at all, he reached out and ran the tip of his forefinger along the line of her jaw. "Leave it alone, Maya," he said gently. "This has nothing to do with you."

She recoiled at his touch and jerked her head away out of his reach. "If it has anything to do with Christian," she said fiercely, "then it has everything to do with me!"

He shook his head. "Contrary to how you see it," he cautioned, still without heat, "this isn't a game and there aren't any rules. You will find yourself outwitted."

She gave a laugh full of spite. "No, I think not, Kyle. Whatever terminology you give your plots and plans, I will ferret them out—if it is the last thing that I do!"

"My plots and plans, as you call them, and my friendship with Christian are not your business." The tenuous composure was brittle. "Any more than your dedicated pursuit of self-interest is mine."

With supreme effort she retained her hold on herself, determined to pin down his evasions. "But you *do* admit that you exploit Christian?"

"Since it pleases you to believe that, yes."

"For what purpose?"

"For that purpose which, I regret, is no business of yours."

She felt a rush of rage, so overpowering that she clenched her fists, yearning to tear that unconcern off his ungiving face. "If you dare to interfere with his. . . ."

"Don't threaten me, Maya." There was a cold, incisive edge to his voice. "You know that I will not be coerced."

Her rage cooled and the calm returned. "I have a tactical advantage over you, Kyle. I suggest that you remember that, with special regard to that purpose which you say is no business of mine."

Suddenly, he uttered a vile oath and exploded with temper. "Why do you diminish yourself by chasing this Englishman, you blind little fool?" His face was dark and stormy, strangely anguished. "Have you not learned yet that Englishmen do not marry Eurasian girls?"

So demonic was this sudden burst of fury that, momentarily, Maya was reduced to shocked silence. Lurking somewhere in a crevice of her mind, a vision crept out and streaked across her inner eye. It was a vision of Joycie Crum. And in those fleeting seconds of silence, he dived into her mind with unerring instinct and brought the thought to the surface.

"Neither do Indian nawabs," he added flatly, his anger suddenly gone.

A plume of fear spiralled up Maya's stomach; cold fingers skimmed over her spine and she shivered. But then she forced herself to shake off the feeling and squared her shoulders. "And what about Eurasian men?" she taunted, with a sarcastic little laugh. "They don't keep mistresses, I suppose!"

He fixed her with a stare that was long and deep, and his eyes—once again unreadable—were shadowed with that same maddening strangeness that she could not fathom. "Don't try to score points over me, Maya," was all he said, and he spoke very quietly. "You are out of your depth."

"I think not. Don't forget, I am well within reach of that blackboard. If necessary, I will not hesitate to use it. That is really all that I came to say." She thrust her chin upwards and made her way to the door.

"You will regret it, Maya," he said with the same uninflected quietness, making no effort to stop her.

She smiled at him as she went through the door. "Not as much as *you* will, Kyle!"

Three days later Joycie Crum died.

A thick pall of gloom descended over the Home and all its inmates. There was not one who remained untouched by the tragedy that had brought such a cruel end to one of their very own. Despite Joycie's exasperating whims, her abrasive tongue and her interminable accusations of universal persecution, everyone recognised and accepted her for what she was—a lonely, loveless woman, humiliated and abandoned, condemned to emotional solitude in the middle years of her life. Filled with grief at her passing and compassion for the manner in which she had died, there was not one at the Home who did not mourn. Willing hands flew to needlework boxes and sewing machines and carpentry kits to labour over many tireless hours so that Joycie Crum would be given a funeral about which not even she could have complained.

No one remembered the suspected hoard of jewellery.

"Joycie wanted it given to Kyle?" Olivia asked, surprised, when Maya showed her the precious bundle and told her about Joycie's heroic bid to salvage it from the fire.

"Yes."

"For his press?"

Maya shrugged. "I don't know. Perhaps."

"They knew each other, of course," Olivia said. "In fact, it was Kyle who brought Joycie to us when he first came from Lucknow. I think that's where they first met, but I had no idea there was any great affection between them."

Maya remained silent; she did not feel the need to say more.

Despite the prospect of rain, there was a fair crowd of mourners at the graveside. Near the pit waiting to receive its eternal occupant, smothered under banks of flowers and wreaths, reposed the ornately carved rose-wood casket polished to a silken maroon finish, its sides studded with shining brass. Inside, it had been lined with quilted pink sateen embroidered with red roses, blue forget-me-nots and white arum lilies devised by multiple expert and loving fingers. At the bottom of Joycie's untidy trunk, under layers of tissue paper, had been found a length of exquisite white Brussels lace, a sequinned bridal veil and a blue garter, squirrelled away for a day that never came. Working at frenzied pitch through the few hours of night, the twins had miraculously fashioned out of these an admirable wedding ensemble. Wrapped in the frothy white folds, with her hideously charred face concealed beneath the sparkling bridal veil, Joycie looked resplendent. No one doubted that she would have approved of the effort.

On either side of her bridal form, shrivelled to the size of a child, were packed some of Joycie's most prized possessions: a Bible, a rosary, packets of letters and photographs, a much used sewing basket, a few cheap trinkets including a picture locket and pair of mother-of-pearl cuff links, a withered blossom pressed inside an old issue of the *Illustrated London News*, a strand of black, pomaded hair entwined inextricably with a once golden ringlet. . . .

Positioned between her mother and Edna Chalcott beside the open grave at the Lower Circular Road Cemetery, Maya stood unaware of the rest of the mourners, lost within herself. The impassioned orations, delivered in English by the parish priest and in Bengali by a highly emotional Abala Goswami, washed over her unheard. When the many tearful voices rose in unison to sing "Abide with Me," Joycie's favourite hymn, Maya joined in mechanically, scarcely conscious that she did so.

She knew with chilling certainty that it was Kyle who had devised the epitaph engraved on the marble tombstone provided by her mother and waiting to be grouted:

JOYCE VIOLETTA CRUM
A ROSE ON A LAPEL TILL THE BLUSH
WITHERED AND THE PERFUME FADED.
BURIED HERE ON THIS DAY
AMIDST HER MEMORIES AND ILLUSIONS.
2 JUNE 1871

The date was ironical. No one appeared to have realised that Joycie had, in fact, died a long time ago, crushed into extinction by the combined weight of what had once been and what was never to be. The tombstone bore no birthdate. With defiant vanity, Joycie had guarded the secret of her age as ferociously as she had the mementoes of her lost love.

A packet of photographs. . . .

Maya was one of the willing helpers who had gathered Joycie's pitiful things together. Apart from the few photographs displayed on her walls, there were others hidden away safely in her trunk, and these fascinated Maya. Sitting at Joycie's work table as the women of the Home washed and dressed the body, Maya could not tear her eyes away from the frozen images entombed in those photographs, so cruelly preserved for uncaring posterity. One picture in particular mesmerised her, every pitiless detail of it eloquent with mockery.

The photograph had been taken at a riverside picnic, and it was dominated by the figure of a ravishing female positioned in the foreground. The full-cheeked, smiling face was turned saucily to the camera, the head thrown coquettishly back, the laughing eyes spilling over with the warm, satisfied sparkles of love given and received in abundance. The gauzy, flowing robes were fashionable, full of liquid movement as they swirled about her well-contoured figure like a tasselled cloud suspended in time. Around the youthful oval face was a halo of clustered ringlets. From the earlobes dangled pear-drop pearls, matching a three-strand necklace nestling within a voluptuous bosom tantalisingly exposed by a plunging neckline.

Joycie Crum?

The insouciant little hat on her head sat at a jaunty angle. She looked invincible, protected by the magical devices of youth from whatever evils might lurk around the corner. Her long, ivory arms were flung up towards the skies in a celebration of life, flaunting her happiness before the heavens, challenging them to disturb it if they dared. At her feet on the grass reclined her nawab—a hearty, handsome man with a curling moustache and a dapper, pointed beard, gazing up at her with good-humored indulgence, unashamedly inviting seduction. His left hand played with the tips of her toes; the right offered her a flower, perhaps the same that now reposed among the folds of her bridal gown in the casket. In the sepia photograph, already blurred around the edges, the two forms looked immortal. And in that instant, they surely were. Across the lower half of the photograph, in a flourish of curlicues and whirls, was scrawled an inscription: *To my adored JoJo, forever and ever with love. Her devoted slave, Mansoor.*

How long was *forever and ever?*

At the base of the casket, by the charred feet, rested a small packet of letters tied with a red ribbon, possibly the only evidence left of Joycie's ugly betrayal. Devoured with curiosity and a strange kind of stupefaction, as if bound in a spell, Maya almost succumbed to the temptation of reading them. But then she did not, not because of any dictates of conscience but because she shied away from the painfully graphic word images she instinctively knew the nawab's letters would provoke and etch in her mind—extravagant promises easily made, easily broken; half-truths and transparent lies; hollow protestations of love, glibly devised excuses and evasions, the final deceit of a younger replacement when her back was turned, avowals of remorse, of helplessness . . . the brickwork of treachery! No, she had not needed to read the letters. The sordid tale they told rang loud even without words.

Now, the casket was being lowered into the hole made to receive it. Maya stared fixedly at the shining plank of wood beneath which lay the remains of what was once Joyce Violetta Crum amid the fragments of her unlived life. The receding echoes would soon be absorbed by nothingness; it would be as if she had never been. A ray of flickering sunshine bounced off the polished wood and, in an instant of insanity, it seemed to Maya that what she saw reflected in it was a mirror image of her own face. . . .

Gripped by panic, by a terrible fear that ripped through her body, Maya clutched her mother's hand and supported herself so that she would not fall. Her mother put an arm about her shoulder and said a few words of comfort, but Maya could not make out what they were. She leant her head back on her mother's shoulder and closed her eyes, filled with a crippling sense of loss. It was as if something of her own had gone with Joycie, never to return. It was as if innocence had fled, as if she had suddenly tasted the fruit of knowledge, and the flavour of it in her mouth was bitter.

When she reopened her eyes, it was to see Kyle standing on the other side of the grave watching her. For an instant their glances seemed to meet. She looked away, but then she realised that, behind her black veil, her face was not visible to him and she stared back steadily. His features were set in honeyed stone, but in the glance that she had intercepted she had caught a glimpse of something that might have been pain. It was an emotion that sat on him uneasily, like an ill-fitting garment; she was surprised that he could even feel it. The last shovelful of earth was poured. The shimmering lid of the coffin disappeared from view, dust returned to dust. When Maya looked again in Kyle's direction, he was no longer there.

A rose on a lapel. . . .

No, Maya realised, as she filled with slow, suppurating anger, it was not only for Joyce Violetta Crum that Kyle had devised that malignant epitaph.

If she were to be quite honest with herself, which she sometimes grudgingly was, it was not only the Garden Reach house that had taken Lady Pendlebury pleasantly by surprise; it was the entire city of Calcutta. She had heard firsthand accounts and seen innumerable photographs of the imperial capital, of course, but she had always chosen to take them with a pinch of salt. Now she saw that she had underestimated the architectural capabilities of her countrymen. Considering the Herculean labours involved in fashioning a distinctly British station out of a haphazard collection of native villages, the visual aspects they had achieved were undoubtedly commendable.

Clive Street could almost be Bishopsgate; some of the mammoth mansions they saw along the route looked as if they had been transported all the way from Northumberland Avenue. St. John's Church, she could see, was a replica of St. Martin in the Fields. From Tank Square to the Cathedral, the appearance was so essentially English that many of the vistas—the large shops and stores, the smart carriages and the rolling green of the parks and gardens—might actually lead one to believe that one was still in London. To be surrounded by such familiar sights was a matter of great security and satisfaction for Lady Pendlebury. They gave her the comfortable illusion of not having left home at all, making what might have been unendurable not only endurable but also eminently gratifying—provided one developed the happy facility to blot out some aspects entirely while concentrating wholly on others.

For instance, the native genius for manufacturing odours in an astonishing variety of combinations could not be missed by even the most stoical of nostrils. A walk down some of the lanes off Dharamtala was enough to turn the stomach of a costermonger, and the smells that emanated from any collection of bodies in any congregation simmering at ninety-eight degrees Fahrenheit in the shade—whether in the service of God or humanity—had to be experienced to be believed. Apart from the lethal scourges from which there was no respite when once contracted, Lady Pendlebury had learnt that most Europeans lived in constant dread of the ubiquitous dermal eruption known as "prickly heat." But at the same time, Mrs. Anderson had assured her, this particular affliction was welcomed by many others because it was said that it saved one from the greater penance of the ague and the flux and colourful arrays of heat boils in undignified places.

For six gruelling summer months the burning plains of Bengal turned into an inferno. Once the monsoons broke, the temperatures came hurtling down and the dust gave way to shining greenery, but even this blessing carried a sting in its tail. With the rains came permanently dank clothing, crippling humus that converted energy into apathy and will into mush, and armies of vengeful insects that burrowed their way into every human orifice available. She had been horrified to learn, also from Mrs. Anderson, that out of every thousand soldiers quartered in Bengal—sturdy, robust men in the prime of their lives—sixty-five died each year, not in the noble cause of Queen and Country, but from tropical sicknesses. Of their wives, forty-five in a thousand would not see their first year out, and of their children, eighty-eight in a thousand would perish annually. If the mortality was so high here where medical services were at least available, what must it be like in the Mofussil?

Lady Pendlebury feared greatly for Christian, but knowing that he would only scoff, with great difficulty she refrained from comment. If she had understood him little in England, here she understood him not at all; always strange, his notions here had turned stranger still. It was added agony for her not to be able to question him about this barefaced strumpet who had her talons enmeshed in her innocent boy, but keeping her husband's admonitions in mind, she did not. Muffling her natural inclinations as a mother, she resolutely held her tongue with as much grace as she could muster. Instead, she turned her mind to her unfailing panacea for all ailments: she decided to arrange a musical soirée.

"That is, if I can find some decent musicians to perform," she said to Christian, when he joined her for luncheon. "Verity Twining's niece hasn't the faintest idea what to do with her pizzicatos. She plucks at the strings of that dulcimer as if they were chickens being readied for the pot. And Philippa Robinson, married to that dreadful shopkeeper who slurps his tea in public, is little better on the harp."

"Well, what about Nigel Whatsisname, the music teacher?" Christian asked, not because he cared a hang about the musical shortcomings of Calcutta, but because he clung desperately to a conversational subject that presented no personal hazards. "Surely he's considered a neat hand with strings? He sings, too—at least that's what I've been told."

His mother regarded him coldly. "If Nigel Crockett were to inflict on the double bass in England what he does here, he would be run out of the country—and quite rightly so. As for his duet with Dora Humphries in the Canadian Boat Song, well it could have been two cats squabbling over a fish head." She shuddered. "I'm beginning to think it's easier for a camel to pass through a needle's eye than for a string quartet to be put together in Calcutta. Now, in *England* I would have simply. . . ."

"Well, in that case why travel at all, Mama?" Christian interrupted impatiently, tired of the litany of woes. "If all you look for is what you find at home, is it not better to stay at home?"

"It certainly is!" His mother returned with spirit. "And that is where I *would* have stayed, believe me, had your father not set his heart on this posting. Do you think I would ever have come to a country where coffee-coloured amateur choirs are made to murder Bach in cold blood every Sunday and divine Schumann melodies sound like tunes from a native nautch?" She dabbed her mouth with her napkin and leaned forward on the table, bristling with righteous indignation. "Do you know what the colloquial is here for fleas and bedbugs? I heard about it yesterday and I was shocked."

"F sharps and B flats?"

"Yes." She looked outraged. "You don't find that offensive?"

"No. I think it's rather amusing." He laughed and gave her a sudden pat of affection on the cheek. "Oh come now, Mama, don't take it all so seriously. There's a lighter side to everything! And what's happened to your sense of humour, anyway?"

She stared into her water glass without a smile, the small gesture of affection bringing a quiver to her lips. "You know what has happened to my sense of humour," she murmured, her voice low and intense. Having said it, she regretted it instantly; before Christian could react, she rustled up a smile and quickly changed the subject. "Anyway, I'm not going to abandon my musical evening, no matter what." She pressed her fingertips together and looked upwards, as if in divine supplication. "Oh, *what* would I not give for a competent accompanist!"

Taking care not to let her tongue slip again, she chatted on about her plans for her soirée, happy that Christian was at least keeping his promise to come for meals whenever he could. She was still dreadfully disturbed, of course, not only about his unsavoury involvement but also for his health once he left for the hinterland, where primitive conditions prevailed and took their toll even of the most robust constitutions.

"Is Papa not coming home for luncheon?" Christian asked, as the meal concluded and they rose from table.

"No. His peon came to fetch his tiffin to the office. I believe he had an important meeting this morning which carried on longer than anticipated."

"In that case I'll pay him a visit at the Treasury." Christian got up from the table. "Trevors has given me the afternoon off to prepare for a last paper before I leave on this trip tomorrow."

"Must you go, darling?" she asked, genuinely concerned for more than one reason. His sudden decision to go north alarmed her; she sensed there was more to the trip than he had told her and she didn't like it one bit. "Can't you wait until you actually receive your posting orders?"

His expression closed. "I just want to have a look around the district, Mama," he said with rather overdone nonchalance, but visibly uncomfortable. "I hear parts of Champaran are quite pleasant."

She could tell that he was keeping something from her, but she knew it was futile to probe more. She gave him a sidelong glance and tried another tack. "Was there anything . . . special that you wanted to see your father about?" she asked, pretending to be immersed in plucking a dead leaf out of the flower bowl on the hallway table.

"No. I haven't seen his office yet and I thought I'd also have a quick word with Leonard Whitney."

"Oh." She pulled in a long breath and gave up. "Well, in that case, would you thank Mr. Whitney for having found us Mademoiselle Corinne? She has a French mother who deals in *accoutrements de cuisine*, which makes the find all the more fortunate. The girl had a Eurasian father but she is certainly a competent housekeeper."

Christian flushed. "Why the 'but,' Mama?" he asked sharply. "Is there any reason why she should *not* be competent merely because she is Eurasian?"

"Now, Christian, you know I didn't mean . . . ," she started, but he was already gone.

Lady Pendlebury sighed. All in all, it had not been a satisfactory luncheon. She had ruffled Christian and yet learned nothing more than she already knew. Her lips set in a grim, determined line. There was a conspiracy afoot between father and son, she was sure of it. Even though her heart sank at the prospect of what she might learn, she decided to force her husband to tell her everything at the first possible opportunity that came her way.

As he headed his horse towards the Treasury near Tank Square, Christian felt equally dissatisfied. The fact that his mother was so obviously holding back her interrogation of him about Maya was certainly a matter of relief, but at the same time it made him uneasy. He realised that her reticence was a result of cautions given to her by his father. He was grateful that this was so, and he certainly had no wish to disturb the status quo, but he wished that it was over so that he could revert to being his natural self with her. He disliked having to make evasions, disliked having always to be on guard. He knew that she was well aware of all the circulating rumours—perhaps many more, by kind courtesy of that old cat Mrs. Anderson—and that made him even more edgy in his mother's company. He always seemed to be at a loss for words, waiting suspiciously for the carelessly dropped comment, the thinly disguised taunt. Today was by no means the first time his mother had made a barbed remark about Eurasians. This time he had snapped back instinctively. The next time he might react even more strongly, and the thought of a full-blooded argument at this juncture dismayed him.

Yes, apart from anything else, his sojourn in Champaran was a fortuitous escape, a very definite blessing in disguise.

Christian had not been to the Treasury before, and the extreme modesty of the structure that accommodated this nub of India's financial administration surprised him. When he made mention of it to his father, Sir Jasper laughed.

"Not quite Whitehall, is it, eh?" He chuckled a while, then sobered. "This is one of the many reasons, albeit minor, why I have been among those who advocate a shift of our imperial capital to some other place in the country. There simply aren't enough premises available here to provide adequate housing for all the ministries. However, that is another matter." He smiled and slapped his son on the back, pleased, as always, to see him. "Come into the sitting room where we can talk undisturbed. Perhaps you will join me in a liqueur?"

"In the middle of the day?" Christian asked, surprised as he followed his father into an adjoining antechamber rather sparsely furnished with chairs, some bookcases and a drinks cabinet.

"Well, why not? I have had a most successful meeting this morning. Perhaps a tot of something to celebrate is not uncalled for."

His father was certainly in an expansive mood. Christian smiled. "What was the meeting about?"

"Taxation, mostly. There are some who still consider the taxation in India unduly high. Utter poppycock, of course! We have one of the most moderate tax structures in the world."

"You believe taxes here should be increased?"

"Undoubtedly!" He handed Christian a tiny silver glass of glowing orange liquid and sipped his own appreciatively.

Christian gave a disbelieving laugh. "Even though our total revenues in India are nearly forty million pounds sterling annually? Surely you don't plan to kill the goose that lays all these golden eggs purely out of greed?"

"Our total revenues from the people are about thirty-six million," his father returned calmly, quite used to his son's radical views. "The remainder comes from China in opium dues and levies upon native states. If the thirty-six million is divided among the hundred and ninety million people in British India, it comes to no more than about three and a half shillings per head annually."

"That's really rather simplistic, Papa," Christian argued, this being one of the subjects most discussed and debated at some of their tutorials. "The real incidence of taxation gives a different picture. A landowner might pay only three to seven percent on the gross produce of his land, but if he goes into litigation—which he does frequently—he pays in stamp duty, if he drinks alcohol or smokes opium, he pays to Excise, if he buys English cloth he pays to Customs, and so on and so forth, ad infinitum. Indulging in even the most basic of activities, he ends up paying sizeable sums to the exchequer one way or another."

"True, but even so, these are optional taxes. The only two compulsory taxes—and I'm not talking about municipal taxes, which go elsewhere— are that on salt, even though seven pennies a year are unlikely to break any man's back, and the license tax traders must pay if their annual incomes are over fifty pounds. I would call that an eminently fair system of taxation, one that can certainly bear some expansion to secure additional revenues." He broke off and laughed. "Anyway, since you and I have never agreed on the matter of revenue collection, nor are likely to now, let us not waste time. I'm sure you haven't come all this way to debate taxes with me."

"No, sir," Christian said, remembering the true purpose of his visit and abandoning the argument quite willingly. "I came to tell you that I have been to see Mrs. Raventhorne. She has given her permission for me to marry her daughter."

Sir Jasper arched an eyebrow. "Did you think that she would not?"

"That's not fair, Papa! Mrs. Raventhorne is. . . ."

He held up a hand. "I meant no offence, Christian. I only meant that as a proud father I believe, as any proud father would, that my son is the pick of the bunch. As such, I cannot imagine any sensible mother denying you permission to marry her daughter."

Christian flushed; it was not often that his father handed out extravagant praise. "Thank you, Papa," he muttered, red-faced and inordinately pleased.

"She had no objections to the alliance?"

"Only those that you yourself had voiced."

"Oh?"

"She too fears that it will damage my prospects as a civil servant. Also, that we might face social ostracism and all-round unpleasantness." It was astonishing how easy he found it to express himself freely when speaking with his father.

Sir Jasper fingered his chin thoughtfully. "Well, that proves that she is an intelligent, pragmatic woman. I look forward to meeting her some

314

day—as, indeed, I do her daughter. The objections she confirmed haven't changed your feelings, have they?"

"No, of course not. If anything, they have merely strengthened them."

His father gave a rasp of a laugh. "You might be foolhardy, but at least you don't suffer from the all too common sin of inconstancy." Sir Jasper glanced at his pocket watch. "I'm afraid I have an appointment in another fifteen minutes with the Accountant-General. Are you dining with us this evening?"

"No, I'm afraid not. Patrick has asked the Andersons to supper. I have to help them to clean up the place. Our rooms are in an awful mess, and since Karamat's cuisine rather matches the surroundings, I've also promised to lend a hand with the cooking—for whatever that might be worth." He laughed, making no secret of his buoyancy. Drinking up the final vestiges of his Benedictine, he prepared to leave. "Oh, I forgot to mention that I have decided to make a reconnaissance visit to Champaran in order to investigate the amenities. I leave tomorrow. I should be away a fortnight."

"What is it that you wish to investigate?"

"Well, mainly the accommodations. The houses the Service provides are really quite abysmal, so much so that I might have to buy a property. I hear that some of the planters' bungalows have recently fallen vacant. I might be fortunate enough to be able to nab one of them. The planters believe in living well. The bungalows are said to be commodious and comfortably appointed."

Sir Jasper regarded him carefully. "Your plans to marry Miss Raventhorne accelerate, then, do they?"

"Yes, sir. I consider this coming winter season to be a suitable time for the wedding." He blushed and shuffled his feet. "Mother still doesn't. . . ."

"I will tell her," his father interrupted. "She will be fully informed about the matter. Obviously the time has come when she must be." Busy collecting some papers from his desk, his father's hands stilled. "By the way, that young friend of yours. . . ."

Christian halted in the doorway. "Who, Patrick?"

"No. The writer."

"Oh, Kyle Hawkesworth."

"Yes. I would like to meet him again."

Christian showed his astonishment. "You would? I thought you had strong reservations about him?"

"Oh, I have. But my reservations are about the contents of his writings. It is the quality of his prose that impresses. And, as you know, it has always been the policy of our government to encourage those who use the English language well. Yes, I would like to meet him again."

Christian's face lit up. "That's very good of you, sir. Should I bring him along when I return from Champaran?"

"Well, as it happens, I have some free time next week. You will not take umbrage if I see him while you are away, will you?"

"Not at all, sir. Indeed, I am delighted that you have had second thoughts about him. I have great regard for Kyle and for his efforts on behalf of his community." He gave his father a sidelong glance. "Kyle admires you enormously, Papa. He told me so several times."

"Oh? What else did he tell you about me?"

"Oh, just that he knew you by repute in Lucknow, that you were one of a rare breed of Englishmen." Christian's eyes twinkled. "I'm afraid he used too many superlatives for me to be able to repeat them without embarrassing you horribly."

"Indeed." Sir Jasper busied himself with his papers.

"Thank you for . . . everything, Papa," Christian started to say. "I don't know how to. . . ." His voice tailed away. Suddenly he was tongue-tied, the words refusing to emerge out of his mouth. He longed somehow to tell his father that he loved him, that he was grateful to him for his under-standing, that he admired him for his essential fairness, but he simply could not say more. He raised his hand in a sort of wave and quickly walked out of the door.

On the way back to the chummery, Christian decided to make a short detour. A geography test at the College had prevented him from attending Miss Crum's funeral this morning. A formal visit of sympathy to the Raventhorne family and apologies for his absence were very much in order. Apart from that, the last time he had met Maya they had parted rather acrimoniously. Silly and childish as the tiff was, the air between them still needed to be cleared and harmony restored. After all, he would not see her for the next fortnight, and he knew that each day without her would seem like an eternity.

Even if a death has been natural, there is something about the aftermath of a funeral that is as depressing as the rituals of the interment itself. How-ever beloved the deceased, however acute the sense of loss, in the ultimate analysis it is the reminder of mortality—a chilling reawareness of the fleet-ing substance of life, perhaps—that leaves one shaken and truly bereft.

And so it was in the Raventhorne household through the afternoon fol-lowing Joycie's burial. The terrible manner of poor Joycie's death contin-ued to be a shock no one had yet absorbed. Through the morning immediately following the funeral a stream of callers had arrived to offer their sympathies, but once they had left, everyone retreated into their own shells. A great hush descended upon the house; if anyone spoke at all, it was in whispers. Thoughts turned inwards to simmer in the immense silences of the mind and even minimal speech became an invasion. Some of the servants, taking their cue from the household, went about their duties with hangdog expressions; others abandoned their work for the day to sit by the riverside on their haunches bemoaning the curious vagaries of karma.

After a perfunctory lunch of kedgeree, buttermilk and fruit, Sheba retired to her room to nurse a searing headache. Maya fled to the stable house to solace herself in the company of her beloved horses, plunging into a frenzy of cleaning to keep her thoughts from dipping into a pit of depression. Dismissing Abdul Mian and the rest of her staff for the day, she sorted out the various bits into their different categories, polished the saddles, scrubbed out the water-troughs, washed all the bandages, brushed the rugs and blankets, then, still with energy left to spare, sat down and scribbled a list of instructions for the grooms for the following day.

It was late afternoon when Christian called. Maya knew already, of course, about his imminent departure for the north; even so, she clung to him as if he were about to leave for good, as if fearful that he would never return. It was obvious that their little contretemps was already forgotten.

"My goodness, what a silly little goose you are!" he exclaimed when she expressed her fears, greatly alarmed by her uncharacteristic behaviour. "Do you think I would ever be that callous?" He covered her face with kisses and held her close, comforting her as best he could, not understanding at all the cause of her anguish.

She shook her head, refusing to be consoled, refusing to answer his anxious questions. He stayed with her as long as he could, yearning to remain but committed to fulfil his obligations at the chummery for the social evening ahead. After he had reluctantly left, Maya sat in a corner of a stall and wept some more, watched only by her horses who, mercifully, asked no questions.

Olivia and Edna Chalcott spent the day in the upstairs parlour, sunk in unspeaking silence. Not even a long, chatty letter from Estelle and an accompanying basket of fruit and wedding sweetmeats delivered by a courier from Cawnpore could relieve Olivia's gloom. Ironically enough, they compounded it. Splattered with Urdu colloquialisms and inordinately detailed trivia about the family wedding that had just taken place, her cousin's letter only emphasized the divide that now separated them, not only geographically but culturally. Estelle seemed so absorbed in her own insular world, so oblivious of any other, that Olivia was shot through with sudden jealousy, again feeling bereft and excluded. Then, ashamed of her reactions, she hurried to her bureau before she could relapse into even more demeaning self-pity and sat down to compose an appropriately affectionate reply. Lounging on the settee, flicking idly through a picture magazine, Edna remained silent, unable to think of a single topic of conversation that might lighten their mutual depression.

"I should have thought to send a gift," Olivia finally murmured with a stab of guilt. "Estelle had told me about the wedding."

"Well, you still can, of course. The courier says he does not return until the morning."

Olivia nodded absently. "Perhaps the pair of emerald and diamond ear tops. I think they might suit a young bride well."

In the early evening, Abala Goswami called. "I've just come for a few minutes to tell you that my husband had a long discussion with Mr. Twining," she announced, plunging straight into the heart of the matter with her usual directness. "Mr. Twining is of the opinion that unless we can provide irrefutable proof of his complicity, we have no case against Saro-jini's father. He believes that to pursue the charge would be folly. We would only be asking for more trouble."

"You mean he is to be allowed to get away with his villainy?" Edna demanded with rising indignation.

"Unless we can produce verifiable proof of his involvement, unfortu-nately, yes."

Olivia spoke for the first time. "Well, I suppose Clarence Twining is right. After all, we don't even know for certain that it is he who is behind the arson. We only presume so because of our experience with him."

One of the ayahs brought in a tray of afternoon tea, sardine sandwiches and cupcakes. "And the fact that the man is a lawyer doesn't help," Edna remarked with a frown, as she set about pouring cups of tea. "I should imagine he already knows every trick in the book, the heartless black-guard!"

"He is also a very arrogant Brahmin," Abala reminded her. "He consid-ers it is because of us that he has lost face in his community."

"Someone has to lose face if society has to develop," Edna retorted. "Otherwise how is the world ever to change, for heaven's sake!"

"But the Brahmins have no wish to change," Abala said, starting to look worried. "I think you should also know that Nalini Chandra Ganguly summoned a meeting of his kinsmen at his house last Sunday. He made full use of the resentment already running high against us in the commu-nity because of our overt support of Sarojini's remarriage."

"It was a perfectly just cause," Edna said sharply.

"Yes, but Mr. Twining doesn't care much about that. He advises that, in the interests of our own safety and that of our inmates, we should either stop meddling (as he puts it) in matters that are socially sensitive or. . . ."

"Or?" Olivia asked as Abala stopped.

"Or disband the Home voluntarily before conservative opinion forces us to do so."

There was a moment of shocked silence. "Yes, if we are attacked again, I suppose we would have to close down," Olivia finally said.

If Abala's announcement had been shocking, Olivia's passive reaction to it was even more so. "Close down the Home?" Edna echoed, frankly incredulous. "You would actually consider that, Olivia?"

"No, of course she wouldn't!" Abala answered for Olivia with a hard glint in her eye. "Any more than any of us would. We will have to discuss our future strategy more fully when we are all in a more receptive frame of mind." She rose to her feet, abandoning her half-nibbled sandwich. "We leave for the *bagan bari* for a few days and I must reach home to make the arrangements so that. . . ." She flew out of the door in a confused rush, tak-ing the rest of the sentence with her.

As soon as Abala had gone, Edna turned on Olivia, still stunned by the apathy of her reaction. "Did you mean what you said?"

"About closing down the Home?"

"Yes."

Olivia shrugged. "I don't know. If we are to be subjected to violence, we will have no other option. It would be wrong to jeopardise more lives for the sake of some marginal social changes in a system so dangerously charged with emotionalism."

"It is not the quantitative change that is important, Olivia, it is the *principle* that matters!"

"I'm too worn out to fight for principles any more, Edna." Olivia ran the back of her hand across her forehead and closed her eyes. "Injustice is everywhere. It will always be with us, and I am too defeated, too disillusioned to try and fight it."

"*You* defeated?" Edna felt a wrench of sympathy at the fatigue and depression in her friend's voice. "Why, you were once known as a woman of courage who fought to the bitter end!"

Olivia took a protracted breath. "That was a long time ago, Edna, so long ago that sometimes I wonder if it might not have been in a previous lifetime." She shook her head, and then said with a sudden change of subject, "Christian has asked for my formal permission to marry Maya."

Edna's hand, holding a fork with a piece of chocolate cupcake at the end of it, remained suspended. "He has? With his parents' permission?"

"He doesn't need their permission, he says, only their goodwill."

"And he has that?"

"Well, he didn't quite say that. According to Christian, his father is as apprehensive about his son's future should he marry my daughter as I am. But Christian is also confident of his eventual blessing. He believes Sir Jasper is liberal and open-minded, a man who does not subscribe to common prejudice."

"And his mother?"

"Oh, Christian was very careful not to mention his mother," Olivia said with a sour smile.

Edna gave her a comforting pat on the arm. "Well, let's just hope for the best. It's a beginning, anyway."

"Of what?" Olivia cut in. "That's the real question, isn't it?" She put down her cup, lay down again and crossed her hands behind her head. "I wish I could feel happy for my child, Edna, but somehow I cannot. Sometimes I feel so . . . inadequate as a mother. I don't know what to do. I no longer remember the formalities of these delicate situations—the protocol, the social procedures. I have never met the Pendleburys, I don't know what sort of overtures would be required of me now. Do I make the first move, call on them? Will they, in time, call on me?"

"Constance Pendlebury is planning one of her famous musical evenings and she's desperate for a pianist," Edna said. "I've decided to offer my services, and I'm certain she will accept them. It might be a good opportunity to try and find out what lies in her mind."

"Perhaps." Olivia's eyes brimmed. She turned and buried her face in the pillow under her head. "I don't know how to tackle the situation, Edna, I feel so . . . incompetent, so lost." She balled a hand and thumped the pillow with it. "Oh, I just wish I could go back to America and take Maya with me now, today!" But then the reality came tumbling back and her shoulders sagged. "But, of course, I can't. It's too late for that."

"Has Maya spoken to you?"

"Oh yes. On the surface she is full of confidence, but underneath, she's frightened, unsure, although she would rather die than admit it." She brushed her eyes and stared up at the ceiling. "I can see so much of Jai in her, Edna. Like him, Maya does not forgive or forget easily. And like Jai, her reprisals can be ruthless and cruel."

"Reprisals?" Edna frowned. "Against whom?"

"Remember the incident with the Shingletons?"

"Good heavens, Maya was only a child then!"

Olivia shook her head. "Oh no, Maya has never been a child, I never allowed her that." Once more she was overcome. "I thrust upon my children memories that mean nothing to them, everything to me. I made them live *my* life, not their own. Amos has survived it well, Maya has not. Amos accepts what he is, Maya cannot. Amos considers, but Maya only *feels*. She is closed, like her father, fearful of exposure."

There was a knock on the door and Francis, the bearer, entered to announce the arrival of yet another visitor.

Olivia groaned and frantically shook her head. "I couldn't face anyone now, I simply couldn't! Who is it, Francis?"

"A young sahib. He says he does not wish to give his name." The bearer's expression made his own disapproval clear.

"Not give a name?" Olivia repeated, annoyed. "On what business has he come?"

"He refuses to say, Madam."

Olivia made a gesture of impatience. "Well then, tell him that I cannot see him today. Let him leave his card or make an appointment for. . . ."

"Shall I go and see who it is?" Edna interrupted.

Olivia touched her hand in gratitude. "Would you, dear? I feel I just cannot." She paused and frowned. "A sahib, did you say?" Francis nodded. "I wonder if this is something to do with Christian. Maya would never forgive me if it were. Where is missy memsahib?"

"Missy memsahib has gone out to ride."

"Well, in that case I suppose I'd better . . . oh damn!" Grumbling at the inconvenience, she put her feet down on the floor and slipped them into a pair of sandals. "Come with me, dear, if you like. We'll make certain he doesn't stay long."

She ran a comb through her hair and went down the stairs, still complaining about the manners of young people these days. In her day it would have been unthinkable for a caller to refuse to present a printed card to make known his identity.

The man who awaited Olivia in the formal drawing room was very young, no more than twenty or twenty-one, with curly brown hair, hazel eyes and an unmistakably regal bearing. By the cut of his expensive clothes it was obvious that he was English, smartly but conservatively

320

dressed in a light tan three-piece summer suit with velvet lapels. Although it was summer, the shirt he wore beneath his waistcoat was of silk. To the best of Olivia's knowledge, she had never seen him before. He was a total stranger.

"Yes?" she asked a little curtly. "I am Mrs. Raventhorne. I believe you wanted to see me?"

The youth made no answer. He neither bowed nor extended his hand in a gesture of common courtesy, nor, indeed, made any move at all to introduce himself. He merely stood and stared at her face.

"Would you mind telling me who you are and what it is that you want with me?" Olivia asked a little more sharply, making it clear that she was annoyed.

The young man still said nothing. He continued to stare at her face, his large, honey-coloured eyes very intense in their scrutiny. The stare had a strange quality about it, part insolence, part something that she could not define. Contempt? Anger? For just a moment, Olivia stared back, puzzled. There was something vaguely familiar about the young man's features.

He spoke for the first time, but without releasing her face from his gripping stare, a hand arrogantly placed on his hip. "You don't recognise me, do you?"

Edna made an angry move of protest at the impertinence of his tone, but Olivia stayed her with a gesture. She scanned the young face again with a frown. "I have to confess that you do look very familiar, but no, I'm sorry, I don't recognise you. Should I?"

"Familiar? Well, that's ripe, that's *very* ripe!" He threw back his head and laughed. It was not a pleasant sound, humourless and derisory, and it stopped as abruptly as it had started. The young man's lips curved, but whether in a sneer or a smile, it was difficult to say.

"Yes, you should," he said softly. "By God, you should!" He put his hand in his breast pocket, took out a leather wallet and from it extracted a visiting card. "Perhaps this will help to revive your memory."

Olivia took the card from him and looked at it; then her eyes flew back to his face. Very slowly, the pallor of her own turned white. She seemed to choke as, with a strangled cry, her hand flew to her throat. Her eyes, dilated with horror, remained transfixed on the young man's face. Before Edna knew what was happening, she swayed on her feet, the card dropped from her fingers and, with a soft moan, she sank to the floor in a faint.

Shaking off her momentary paralysis, Edna ran to the crumpled figure on the carpet. Frantically, she rang for the servants, and as an army of them led by Sheba descended on the drawing room, for a few moments confusion prevailed with everyone talking at once. At the height of the mêlée, Maya came rushing in, still in her riding habit. Terribly frightened at the sight that greeted her, she demanded to know what had happened. No one had the time to tell her as everyone ran here and there, fetching water and salts and snifters of brandy. Through all this, the young man remained exactly where he was, unconcerned and unsmiling, his expression still one of contempt. He made no effort to be of assistance, but merely stood and watched with disinterest.

"Who on earth are you?" Maya suddenly asked, noticing the stranger in their midst.

The look he returned was glacial. "Why don't you ask your mother?" he suggested as he prepared to leave. "Should she be inclined to do so," he added as a parting shot, "Mrs. Raventhorne will know where to find me."

Without a second glance at the figure lying on the floor, he walked out and slammed the door behind him.

It was as they prepared to carry a semi-conscious Olivia upstairs to her room that Maya noticed the visitor's card lying forgotten on the carpet. She picked it up. It read:

BARON BIRKHURST OF FARROWSHAM,
THE MANOR HOUSE
FARROWSHAM, SUFFOLK.

She went cold with shock.
Alistair . . . ?

CHAPTER

14

W HY, HIS EYES are just like mine . . . !
It was the only fragment of coherence that flashed through
Olivia's mind before it imploded, unequipped for the enormity
of a shock it simply could not absorb. Moaning and babbling incoheren-
cies, she was carried up and put to bed. While Edna laid iced compresses
on her forehead, a badly shaken Maya despatched a coachman to fetch Dr.
Humphries. It was only after the doctor had effectively sedated his
protesting patient for the night with a dose of bromide that everyone
heaved sighs of relief, took the weight off their feet and sat down to
recover their collective breath.

"Is she going to be all right by the morning?" Maya asked, her eyes wide
and worried.

"Good heavens, she's all right *now!*" Being the family physician—as his
father was before him—young Dr. Humphries knew the whole story, of
course, and was quick with his reassurances. "It's been a hard week for
your mother, what with one thing and another, but she's resilient, in excellent health and as strong as a beer-wagon horse. She just needs time to get
used to. . . ." He stopped, glanced at the motionless figure on the bed and
his features softened. "My father brought young Alistair into the world,
you know," he mused. "She nearly died when he was born."

Maya nodded and stared down at her feet.

"Your mother is a very remarkable woman, my girl. You should have
heard some of the tales my father had to tell about her in her youth—
enough to give you ringlets without hot tongs!" He chuckled and started
to pack his valise. "She had absolutely no idea Alistair was due?"

"No, none."

Edna dipped the compress in a bowl of freshly iced water and wrung out the excess. "Willie Donaldson must have known he was. It was wicked of him not to have warned her!"

As soon as the doctor had left, Maya laid her head back against the chair rest and closed her eyes. "She refused to see him when he was born, or even to listen to his birth cry."

"Yes. Did she tell you that?"

"No. I heard it from the Maharani. She and Aunt Estelle took care of Alistair before Aunt Estelle carried him off to England with his wet-nurse and that Chinese nanny who used to look after Amos."

Edna's eyes showed a trace of tears. "Yes. The parting nearly tore her apart, I heard. Poor darling, *how* she must have suffered!"

Maya toyed with the tassel of a cushion. "He's astonishingly like her, isn't he? I think that's what came as the worst shock."

Edna gave her a curious look. "You're not . . . upset by his sudden appearance, are you, darling?"

Maya shrugged. "I don't know . . . yet. I certainly can't think of him as a brother!" She made a face. "But I'm glad Amos isn't here. He'll be *livid!*" It was a sobering thought; she got up and absently smoothed the counterpane on her mother's bed. "He's very good-looking, isn't he, Aunt Edna?"

Edna smiled. "Better-looking than Amos?"

"No. Nobody is better-looking than Amos!" She cradled the back of her head in her palms and stared up at the ceiling. "But he's very aristocratic, every inch the English gentleman."

"She's always dreaded this, you know," Edna sighed. "And I'm not surprised, considering. . . ." She broke off, picked up the bowl and prepared to go downstairs. "Anyway, let's not talk about it any more—what will be, will be. Now, shall we settle for hot chicken broth, toast and cheese for supper? I believe Anthony is stewing some apricots for pudding." She gave a final glance at the bed. "No point in waking your mother—she won't want to eat anyway."

Over the meal they talked of many things, but by mutual consent, Alistair Birkhurst was not mentioned again that evening.

Through the night, Olivia slept the deep, healing sleep of the drugged. When she opened her eyes again, it was almost morning. Having refused to abandon her bedside vigil until Olivia awakened, Edna dozed on the settee. Quietly, without waking her, Olivia tiptoed into the bathroom, washed her face and performed a perfunctory toilet. Then she went to sit on the rocking chair by the window, silently watching the skies as dawn rimmed the eastern horizon with hesitant light. Among the dark shadows of the garden below there was secret movement, alive but unseen, as the world slowly woke to a new day. She sat and watched and rocked herself, part of her mind as crisp as winter lettuce, the rest still battling through an opacity of sleep. Gradually, within her something else stirred and yawned into wakefulness—a feeling as familiar as an old shoe. She felt the first prick of a sharp guilt long consigned to archival memory.

Alistair, scarcely remembered, yet never forgotten. . . .

Time unwound and crept up on her slyly, stabbing her from the back like death, ever expected, yet always a surprise. Alistair was one of those small, secret pockets of pain that she had tucked away into a deep, deep fold of her mind when reality had turned intolerable. Twenty-one years ago she had been confident of exorcising him from her consciousness, as if he had never existed at all, and in time, she had come to believe that she had done so. If he appeared in her memory, it was simply as yet another phantom in the gallery of phantoms who peopled her ectoplasmic world.

Now she saw that this was not so. The fold was not as deep as she had thought, the memory not as distant as she had presumed. She had not forgotten Alistair; indeed, it was as if he had never been away at all. She realised now that all these years he had remained with her, hibernating, breathing softly and silently, ever alive, still part of her, sharing of her flesh, her blood, her every heartbeat, almost as if he were still in her womb. She gave a small sigh, trying to grapple with this devastating paradox she could not yet assimilate, and inevitably, she thought of Estelle and Kinjal.

It was her beloved cousin and her dear, indispensable friend who had preserved her sanity during those days, two decades ago, when the strange drama of Alistair's birth was being enacted. It was they who had secreted her newborn son away from her hungering eyes, they who had nurtured him for three months, pumping energy into his meagre, premature flesh and strength into his dangerously supple bones. And it was they who had then planned and executed his long journey across the seas to his father and grandmother in faraway England. Looking back on their love and understanding and unquestioning endeavours, Olivia yearned to have them by her side once more now when the curtain was poised to rise on a painful extension of that long-forgotten, ever remembered drama. But that she knew was impossible. Kinjal was away on a sacred pilgrimage to Badrinath in the Himalayas, and Estelle now lived on another planet, in another dimension, lost to her forever.

A gentle hand pressed down on Olivia's shoulder; it was Edna's. Olivia reached up and clung to it, grateful for the comforting presence of this equally dear friend. "Will you stay with us for a few days, Edna? I feel I do not have the moral strength to face this on my own."

"If you need me, yes, of course I will."

Olivia closed her eyes. "I didn't recognise him, Edna," she said dully. "I didn't recognise my son."

"How could you have if you've never seen him?"

"Yet he is *exactly* as I have always known he would be. Isn't that extraordinary?"

"The heart has instincts of its own, Olivia. No, it is not extraordinary at all."

"I could have been looking at myself in a magic mirror," she marvelled, turning anxious eyes to Edna. "He *does* look like me, doesn't he?"

"Very much so." Edna patted her hand as she gave her the assurance Olivia sought. "Now that I've seen him, I feel I would have known him anywhere."

Olivia wondered, *Were it not for hindsight, would I have . . . ?*

Sheba came in wheeling a trolley with hot coffee, tea and breakfast, and behind her Maya.

"Did you sleep well?" Maya asked as she kissed her mother on the cheek, still full of concern.

Olivia nodded, searching Maya's face for signs of her inner thoughts; save for the concern and an unusually pale skin, there were none visible. No, it was not Maya about whom she needed to worry. Maya would assimilate Alistair's arrival, indeed, would welcome it.

But Amos?

She felt a sudden rise of panic. "I must send for Willie. I must see him *at once!*"

Leaving her breakfast untouched, she hurried to her desk to compose a note to Willie Donaldson. But before she could complete the chitty, Sheba hurried in to announce that the Scotsman, manager of the Farrowsham Agency House, was waiting for her downstairs and requested to see her with extreme urgency.

"It would be better if you saw him on your own," Edna suggested, laying a hand on Olivia's arm. "In any case, Maya and I have plenty to do up here."

In her confused state of mind, elated and yet nervous, Olivia scarcely heard her. Taking only enough time to refresh her morning's hasty toilet, she flew downstairs to the informal parlour where Willie Donaldson waited with considerable impatience.

"Willie! I was just writing a note to you. . . ."

"God's blood, lassie!" he thundered, not letting her speak, "Did you believe I would na think to come on my own?" He peered at her through crinkled eyes, very cross.

It brought a faint smile to Olivia's lips to see that his vocabulary was still colourful, his gravelled voice as abrasive as ever. She noticed that he balanced himself unsteadily on his cane, and quickly helped him into a chair. He looked old and frail. His whiskers were withered, like scrub in a drought-ridden wasteland, and as he continued to peer belligerently in her direction, it was obvious that his eyesight was greatly diminished. Her own eyes softened; she took his hand and kissed him on the cheek, bringing to it a streaky blush between the scored wrinkles. During these past years they had not met often, but Olivia knew that he had never stopped watching over her from a distance. Now that they were again face to face, it seemed as if they had been together yesterday, the stout support of this dear, dear man during one of the most turbulent periods of her life evergreen in her memory.

She sat opposite him with her hands folded in her lap. "Why did you not warn me, Willie?"

He did not reply immediately, but sank back into the chair and wiped his forehead with a hanky. His eyes looked opaque; he could barely see. But in them there was still that determined glint that made him a man of calibre and quality. In the wrinkled corners of his eyes, shrunk with age, she saw a wetness.

"His lordship would na let me," he said flatly. "By the blood of Christ, I wanted to, but he made me swear that I would na!" He shook his head. "He's a stubborn 'un, your ladyship." Briefly he slipped back into the past as his teeth bared in a wry grin. "He canna be blamed, puir wee lad, consid'rin' his mother was na diff'rent at his age!"

A wan little smile made her lip tremble. "I was not prepared, Willie. I needed time to *prepare!*"

"Och aye, you reck'n I dinna know that? But that's the way the lad planned it. He dinna *want* you to prepare!"

"That was cruel of him, Willie."

"Aye." He leaned forward and groped for her hand. "But I could do nowt, lass. I've eaten Birkhurst salt for nigh on fifty years." He sat back, worn out by the effort. "The bairn is tormented, your ladyship. A bairn who's na had mother nor father canna be otherwise." He took a deep, whistling breath and shook his head. "I have a letter . . . I would've giv'n it earlier 'cept that he would na let me."

With much huffing and puffing, he fumbled in the folds of his voluminous coat and finally located a pocket from which he withdrew an envelope. Olivia took the buff-coloured envelope from him. The Birkhurst crest of arms was stamped in gold on the back flap. She knew it came from the dowager Lady Birkhurst, at one time her mother-in-law. Frantic to learn its contents, she tore it open and started to read.

"My dearest Olivia," the letter began, as always, on a note of genuine warmth.

> By the time you receive this, sadly, its very purpose will be lost; you will know that Alistair is in Calcutta. He made me promise that I would not give you intimation of his coming, much as I would have wanted to. There are many reasons for his being in India, but most of all—although his fierce pride refuses to let him admit this—he hungers to see you. As such, he is adamant about completing this project of self-discovery. My dear, he is like you in more ways than are obvious to the eye!
>
> I wish I could be of better cheer, but I fear that the meeting will not be a pleasant one for you. He is bitter, Olivia, and he is confused. He does not think of you kindly. I tell you this at the risk of wounding you because, knowing you, I also know that you will not be satisfied with anything less than the truth.
>
> Alistair has always known about you, of course, but the complex circumstances surrounding his birth and his arrival in England I simply have not had the heart to relate to him in detail. There is much that I have never written to you about the boy; there is even more that I have withheld from him. Consequently, he is tormented by uncertainties that must now be resolved, that he has not the emotional resources to resolve on his own.
>
> For the past year, all of Alistair's energies have been urging him towards Calcutta—and you! He has grievances, Olivia, some imaginary, others only too real and, alas, he is like you—he will not be satisfied until he has learned the entire, unvarnished truth. He asks questions that I feel are not my province to answer, but answered they must be. I am

sure you will agree that this much is the very least due to a bewildered young man who has never seen his living mother, and who was deprived of a father when he was less than a year old.

I warn you, my dear, that your second son will bring you scant joy. On the contrary, he will hurt you deeply. Alistair bears the arrogance of immaturity. His tongue is harsh, his disposition deliberately brazen. I would be concerned except that I know that you do have the wisdom and strength to see him in the perspective of his circumstances. As such I have no doubt that, in your infinite common sense, you will recognise his harshness for what it is, an expression of pain and a cry for help. I am confident that you will not only forgive him his excesses but also recognise that with all that has happened, it could not have been otherwise.

I have done my best for my beloved grandson, Olivia, this much I promise. But now I see with great sorrow that it has not been enough. He needs something that I cannot give—what, I cannot say. But the young are resilient and you, Olivia, have always been wise beyond your years. I pray that you can somehow heal each other's wounds and derive from this encounter those mutual comforts that for all these years have been denied to you both.

It will not be easy, I warn you, but I also beg you to have patience. Perhaps the patience will bring rewards, perhaps it will not. I know that this too you will accept as you have accepted all the other cruel injustices of your young and tragically unfulfilled life. . . .

There were a few rambling paragraphs about the Farrowsham estate, her two daughters and other grandchildren, and there was frequent mention of Freddie and the terrible misfortunes of his abortive life. She ended the letter with a return to the subject of her grandson:

If the boy's visit cannot bring you happiness, I pray that at least it spares you more heartache. I worry greatly for the problems Alistair's unannounced presence will create for your family; God willing, you will devise means to contain them before they can wreak irreparable emotional damage. I wish all of you well, Olivia. You and yours have never been very far from my heart and thoughts. There is not a single night that I do not bless you in my prayers for having sacrificed your own need and given this darling boy to me, and now I return him to you full of hope that his will not have been a futile journey. May God be with you both in your endeavours. Had it been within the capacities of my aging flesh, I would have been there with Alistair to lend you support, but I am now confined to my bed and totally dependent on others. My spirit, however, is high and it will be with you always. Write to me soon, I will not be able to rest until I hear from you.

In all hope and love,

Yours,
Elizabeth Birkhurst.

328

Olivia read the letter with a tight throat. Over the decades, even after Freddie's death, her friendship with Lady Birkhurst had remained steady, unflawed by pique or recriminations. The dowager had a remarkable understanding. She had always advised her with wisdom, standing stoutly by her in a situation no other mother-in-law would have tolerated. Lost now in this unmapped forest of lush, mushrooming memories, Olivia felt she would give anything to have Lady Birkhurst again by her side, guiding her with that unerring instinct that made her a woman of such extraordinary perceptions.

Olivia folded the letter with shaking fingers and replaced it in the envelope. "It is as I suspected, Willie. He is bitter and unforgiving."

The Scotsman muttered a few words of protest but it was obvious he did so more out of loyalty than conviction.

"I know Alistair, Willie. I've never seen him but I know him already as I know myself. He is too young to understand and too old to forgive."

"Aye, it will na be easy." He repeated Lady Birkhurst's warning as he morosely conceded the point. "But then, when has it e'er been for you, eh? You're a strong lass, I 'dmired you when you were at Farrowsham because I'd na e'er met a lass with as much bleedin' nerve!"

Olivia shook her head. "I am no longer what I was, Willie. Those days have gone, the nerve you talk of is dead." Tears sprang to her eyes. "Now I'm truly played out. All I feel is the weight of weariness."

Suddenly animated, he shot forward in his seat and waved his cane in her face. "You dare cry, lass, and I'll na speak to you e'er again, e'er again!" He glared at her, furious, his cheeks puffed out like ridged, red balloons. "I ne'er saw you cry when the world lay about your ears in bleedin' ruins, and I will na noo!"

"It was different then, Willie," Olivia protested, startled by his anger. "I was younger. And yes, those days were bad but. . . ."

"Na as bloody bad as were to be—but you bore up, you bloody survived!" He cackled with disgust and shifted the wad of shag that was a permanent resident of his mouth from one side to another, chewing hard. "I have nae patience with mealy-mouthed mewlin' and whinin' and you were ne'er 'un for that, ne'er."

"Oh Willie!" She wiped her eyes with the back of a hand and managed a shaky laugh. "Tell me truly now, does he really hate me?"

This time he decided not to pull punches. "Aye, I reck'n that he does. But, if you ask me, it's na hatred like we know, 'tis somethin' else too."

"What?"

"That's for *you* to find oot, ain't it?" he snapped.

She sighed and nodded. "He wants to revive Farrowsham?"

"He wants to try."

"He will have a hard task doing that. The commercial world has changed so much since the Mutiny."

"Och aye, but na as hard as findin' a new *manager*." He allowed himself a smile of immodest complacency, then turned serious again. "He wants to sell the plantation and, perhaps, the manse." To Willie, the splendid

Birkhurst house on the esplanade was always the manse, as if there was none other in Calcutta.

"How long will he stay?"

"Till his work is done, I reck'n."

Something in the way Willie inflected that caught her attention. "But that's not all, is it?"

"T'aint." With the succinct syllable, Willie's eyes dropped. "His lordship aims to try somethin' else, to diversify."

"Diversify into what?"

"Cotton."

"Cotton?" Olivia echoed. "Oh, what a coincidence! You see, Amos too has decided to go into cot. . . ." Her voice tripped and she broke off. "Where?"

"In Cawnpore," Willie said unhappily, still not looking at her.

Cawnpore! A swift, chill wind blew across Olivia's heart. Already knowing the answer, she asked, "Where in Cawnpore?"

"His lordship has recently purchased the Sutherland Cotton Spinnin' and Weavin' Mill. The deed of sale was signed in London last month." In the silence that followed, Donaldson watched her in gathering distress. "I could na warn you about that either, lass," he explained, "but I want you to know that I was na in favour of it."

Olivia sat motionless. "Why on earth should Alistair want a cotton mill in Cawnpore?" She wondered why she asked such a futile question. She knew why!

"He does na want it," Willie said sadly. "But he does na want *Master Amos* to have it, either."

Jolting contentedly along in a first-class railway bogey on the final leg of his journey home from Allahabad, there was no way Amos could have known of all the significant events that had taken place during his absence from station. He was, of course, wildly impatient to start his new commercial adventure, but as he sat hunched in a corner of the compartment, his mind could not have been further away either from his family, or for that matter, from the Sutherland Cotton Mill.

What he thought about was Rose Pickford.

Young, good-looking and rich, Amos Raventhorne was inevitably the object of much female admiration in Calcutta. Within the Eurasian community he was naturally considered a catch of sizeable dimensions. But even among other communities, including the English, there were few young spinsters in town who did not eye him with wistful longing whenever they happened to catch a glimpse of him on the street or in the shops. In secret, away from the hawk eyes of their elders, many wove romantic fantasies around his dove grey eyes, his jet black curly hair, his strong, virile physique, and sighed as heavily at the prospect of earning his favours as others had in another age over earning those of his father.

Had the circumstances of his young, turbulent life been less brutal, Amos might have been able to identify the cause of his current inner disturbances as easily as others of his age and sex. But, given the unorthodoxy of his upbringing and his lack of romantic involvements, he simply could not assimilate his present malaise. The many betrayals and tragedies that he had witnessed in his twenty-three years had inevitably made him suspicious of the ulterior motives of men, imagined or otherwise. As far as the ladies were concerned, he could honestly say that he had seldom met one whose company he craved, or even appreciated to any great extent. Which was why the unaccountable manner in which he had reacted to Rose Pickford came to him as a disconcerting surprise. She was the only girl he had ever come across with whom he could remember being entirely comfortable, and this puzzled him.

Lying on the bunk opposite, Ranjan Moitra snorted in his sleep, turned sides and almost rolled over the edge. Had Amos not leapt up and interrupted the momentum of his body, he would have certainly crashed to the floor. Unaware of his brush with disaster, Moitra smiled beatifically in his sleep and continued undisturbed with his snoring.

Amos settled down again in his corner feeling restless, waiting impatiently for Calcutta to appear on the green horizon. This time there was little to complain about save the inevitable hassles of a normal railway journey in India. Once again he allowed his thoughts to dwell upon Rose Pickford, upon the eagerness with which she anticipated his move to Cawnpore and the expression of unmistakable sadness that had settled over her face when he had gone to bid the family farewell.

"Will you return soon?" she had whispered during their few moments alone, trying to still the quiver in her lower lip.

Much against his better judgement, he had taken her hand in his and lightly skimmed his lips over it. "As soon as I possibly can," he had replied, husky with feeling and deeply unhappy. Then, because he simply could not help himself, he had cursed his lack of moral strength and asked, "Will you write to me?"

She had nodded shyly and hastily pulled away her hand before her mother returned to the doorway.

Thinking of those last few moments with Rose, Amos sighed with a renewed sense of frustration and puzzlement. The fact was—and this he admitted to himself quite readily—that Rose Pickford was by no means a beauty. Indeed, she was what his American mother might bluntly describe as "homely." Oddly enough, it was precisely this aspect of Rose that appeared to attract him the most. Having lived with a beautiful mother and sister for so long, he was impervious to merely physical feminine assets. As a tribe—with the exception of his mother—he found good-looking women vain, capricious and self-oriented, accepting their superiority over others as a fact of nature. He shuddered at the thought of a wife as beautiful as, for instance, his sister; he would not be able to tolerate her eccentricities for more than five minutes flat. Rose, on the other hand, was placid, selfless and patient, obviously of a serious turn of mind, intelligent, perceptive and interested in the viewpoint of others. She spoke little and listened more, which in itself was a small wonder. Despite her lack of striking good looks, she had a personality that was immensely warm. She had none of the artifice he had come to accept as an integral component of the female mystique; she was demure and, at the same time, self-contained. Primarily, she gave the impression of being a homemaker and, as it had done men since the beginning of time, this pleased Amos greatly. Apart from everything else, he reminded himself not without a touch of self-satisfaction, she liked him!

He blushed and heaved an audible sigh, quite overwhelmed by this admirable array of virtues he had compiled for his own emotional gratification. "And, of course," he concluded, "she will get on splendidly with Mother."

"What, what?" Ranjan Moitra sat up with a jolt and stared at him with startled, sleep-rimmed eyes.

Amos coloured, unaware that he had spoken aloud. "Oh, I was just . . . working out something for myself."

"Are we there yet?"

"No, not yet. Go back to sleep, Ranjan Babu."

Ranjan Moitra settled down again to resume his slumber, and with a painful wrench, Amos returned to reality, abandoning thoughts of Rose Pickford. However strong his feelings for her, she could never be for him. Quite apart from the fact that she was a pukka, a dark, sinister cloud hung over the name of Raventhorne. Until it was removed—if ever!—he simply could not consider courting her. Or, for that matter, any other woman.

Morosely, Amos forced his thoughts away from the unattainable Rose Pickford and back onto familiar terrain, reviving his spirits by recapitulating the improvements and innovations he intended to put into practice once he had acquired the mill. As always, his imaginings were graphic and, to him, extremely real. So much so that by the time he arrived on his own doorstep in Calcutta, had anyone reminded him that the cotton mill was not yet his property, Amos would have been astounded.

Inevitably the initial conversations, over the dinner table, were almost entirely about the fire at the Home, the death of Joycie Crum and the funeral. Olivia had decided not to inform Amos about the tragedy while he was away, knowing that it would fulfil no purpose except to distress him and interfere with his errand. However, it was only after that sad topic had been exhausted, when everyone suddenly fell silent at once, that it suddenly occurred to Amos that there was more, and that perhaps they had not told him everything.

Despite their valiant attempts to appear and sound normal, the meal was a stiff, uncomfortable affair, with tensions in the forced smiles and eloquently ominous undertones in the brittle dinner-table chatter that followed the discussion about the fire. In an effort to lighten the atmosphere, Amos regaled them with a fund of amusing anecdotes about Ranjan Moitra's armed hostilities in Cawnpore, keeping news about his cotton mill project for after the meal, when they would be at ease and he would have their undivided attention. But sensing that something was being left unspoken, he eventually laid down his knife and fork, sat back and folded his arms across his chest.

"All right, enough. I want to know what else has happened while I've been away. I can see that something is being kept from me."

A deathly hush descended over the table. Maya sagged back with relief that it was, finally, out in the open. Olivia exchanged quick glances with Edna before she gave him an answer. "Yes, something has happened, Amos. Let us finish dinner and go outside. We'll talk about it over coffee."

It was cooler on the verandah, with gentle south winds stroking the trees and making the leaves rustle. The usual night chorus of frogs and cicadas had started up in the garden, interspersed with the shrill cries of night birds as they fulfilled parental obligations and foraged for hungry fledglings. A white owl flew out of a deodar and streaked past the verandah with a long, mournful hoot, and dazzled by the light, the usual swarms of rain insects fluttered around the sconces. As Francis laid the tray of coffee and orange and rum biscuits on the table, nobody spoke; with the need for pretence over, no one knew quite what to say. Amos alternated questioning glances between them.

"Well?"

Nervously, Maya looked at her mother. They had mutually agreed that the news of her decision to marry Christian should not be announced to Amos on the first evening of his return home; there was already enough on the family agenda to upset him. Nevertheless, Maya was apprehensive in case her mother let slip a careless word that would incite an unnecessary and premature debate. Amos had to be told, of course, but she intended to break the news to him herself at an opportune moment when he was in the right mood.

"Come on, Mother, what else has happened?"

Olivia grit her teeth and took the plunge. "Alistair is in Calcutta. He came to see me last evening."

Amos struggled with memory as he digested the information. "Alistair . . . Birkhurst?"

"Yes."

In the buttery light of the sconce, his jaw went tight. "I . . . see." For a while he said nothing more as he silently sipped his coffee and gazed into the blackness above the river. Finally he asked in a hard, metallic voice, "What is he doing here in Calcutta?"

"According to Willie Donaldson, he's come to see if he can salvage the sinking fortunes of Farrowsham."

"Sunken would be a more appropriate word," he scoffed. "Farrowsham is finished. He might as well try to flog a dead horse to life."

"He is also about to enter a new area of business," Olivia said, not looking at him.

"A new area? What?"

She told him.

For a second or two Amos gaped in incomprehension, as if she had spoken in a language alien to him. Then, as the words registered in his consciousness, his face went ashen; he looked sick. In almost unbreathing silence, he sat grappling with the shock, bearing the impact of the thunderbolt without uttering a sound. Olivia's heart cried out to him in shared pain. She wished she could think of something uplifting to say, something that would blunt the cutting edge of his bitter, bitter disappointment. But, in that moment, all she could devise were platitudes. She clutched Edna's hand under the table and remained silent.

Once more Amos's expression changed. He turned and pierced his mother with a terrible look and his lips thinned out as if in a snarl. The quiet, in that moment, was intense, eloquent in its unspoken accusations. Amos's hand trembled; the coffee cup that he held rattled against the saucer and the stillness was broken. He quickly put the cup down on the table and stood up.

"Excuse me. . . ."

His voice sounded hoarse and his eyes were blank, unable to focus. Turning on his heels, he walked off the verandah into the garden and, almost immediately, was swallowed up by the dark.

"Amos . . . !" Olivia half rose as if to follow him, but Edna's firm grip on her wrist restrained her.

"No. Let him go. He needs to be alone for a while."

Amos did not return to the house until much later that night. When she went searching for him well past midnight, Maya found him sitting by himself on the steps by the river. Silently, she sank down beside him and slipped her hand in his in a mute gesture of empathy. With a small sigh, he put an arm about her shoulders; a sob caught in Maya's throat as she felt the great devastation within him. They remained thus for a while, holding each other, unspeaking, lost in their widely divergent thoughts. Finally it was she who broke the silence.

"Morning Mist won both races at the charity show." He made no response but neither did he show any irritation, so she added, "Hassan Shooter proved as good as his word, didn't he?"

He squeezed her hand and gave her a whisper of a smile in acknowledgement of her effort to solace him.

Maya hesitated only for a second, then took a deep breath and said in a rush, "Christian Pendlebury has asked me to marry him."

Her heart in her mouth, she waited for an eruption, but none came. In fact, she was not even sure that he had heard her. His only reaction was a vague nod.

"I have said yes, Amos. I am going to marry Christian."

The significance of what she said suddenly dawned on him and he frowned. "He wants to *marry* you?"

"Yes."

Maya stiffened herself for an inquisition, but her brother appeared to have no further questions. He merely shrugged, once more lost in himself, steeped in sullen wordlessness. Her heart leapt with cautious relief—yes, she had chosen her moment well! Shattered by Alistair's arrival and submerged in examining his own blighted hopes, Amos had no inclination now to worry about anything else. No doubt there would be questions later, but for the time being at least, a nasty scene had been averted. Her brother's next remark, however, revealed that he had not taken her announcement quite as casually as his mild reaction had led her to believe. "Mother married Freddie Birkhurst for a selfish motive." His voice was heavy with contempt. "We still suffer the devilish consequences of *that* disaster."

"Mother married him for a very noble motive!" Maya made a spirited defence of their mother. "You, more than anyone, should be the first one to commend that."

"More noble than yours, anyway."

She ignored that. "If anyone has paid a truly high price for the so-called disaster, it has been Mother."

"Oh, has it?" He voiced an oath and his sudden laugh was raw and full of bitterness. "Then why the hell do I suddenly find myself having to foot the bloody bill?"

"Don't, Amos." Maya pleaded. "Things are bad enough as they are."

"Well, what do you want me to do—welcome him? Celebrate the fact that he's stolen my mill?" He turned and spat into the river. "I'll be damned if I do!"

She threw him an oblique glance and made a tentative suggestion. "You could make an offer for that mill, Amos. Alistair might. . . ."

"Have you taken leave of your senses?" His reaction was immediate, one of outrage. "Do you think I would ever stoop to seeking him out?" His teeth were clamped tight with fury. "If I ever so much as even see him, I'll rearrange his God-rotting face so that his own mother wouldn't. . . ." Realising what he had said, he stopped, banged the stone step with a bunched fist and mouthed a string of curses.

In a lightning jump he was on his feet and, before Maya was even aware that he had moved, had vaulted up the steps and into the blackness of the deserted embankment. She had never before seen him in such a violent mood. It would be futile, she knew, to pursue him while the mood persisted.

In her bedroom upstairs, Olivia fluttered about aimlessly, scarcely aware of what she did. "I cannot see Alistair again, Edna," she cried for the tenth time, looking ill and wretched, "I just *couldn't.*"

"Oh yes you could," Edna said, placid and resolute, as she measured out a dose of bromide. "And, what's more, you will."

"But Amos!"

"However upset he may be, Amos is not a fool. He would hardly expect otherwise."

"I would die if I saw Alistair again," Olivia whispered, eyes wide with dread. "I would simply *die!*"

But in her heart she knew that she would also die if she did not. . . .

"You *knew* it was he who had bought the cotton mill, didn't you?"

"Yes." Disregarding Amos's thundery face, Ranjan Moitra made the admission calmly and continued to scribble on his notepad. Now that the need for evasion was over, he should have felt greatly relieved. He did not. On the contrary, he felt even more disturbed.

"You've known it all along!"

"No, but I suspected it. My suspicions were confirmed only before we left for Cawnpore."

"Donaldson told you?"

Moitra looked shocked. "Mr. Donaldson would never betray the trust of an employer."

"Well, then, who?"

"Ram Chand."

"Mooljee? The moneylender?"

"Yes. He has agents in London who report to him periodically. They informed him of the projected sale and he informed me." He grimaced. "For a price, naturally. I had to offer him a scandalous discount on some warehousing space that he required."

"And when did you first learn that Birkhurst was expected in Calcutta?"

"Well, Mr. Donaldson's head clerk happened to overhear something to that effect, and since he is related to me through the niece of my wife's brother's first. . . ."

"*When?*" Amos thumped his desk hard, not letting him finish. One of the inkpots on the desk jumped and spilled over.

Ranjan Babu laid down his pen, surveyed with distaste the spreading pool of black on his immaculate desk and tapped his bell for the peon. "The rumor of your half-brother's visit has been circulating around the Farrowsham Agency for a few. . . ."

"Don't ever call him that!" Amos silenced him with a venomous hiss. "I acknowledge no relationship with that thieving, double-faced . . . interloper. Do you understand, Ranjan Babu?"

Moitra nodded sadly. "Only too well, Master Amos, only too well." He sighed and resumed his writing.

"You heard about it months ago. Why in damnation did you never mention it to me?"

"I do not believe in spreading rumours," Moitra said piously. "As for his lordship's subsequent interest in the mill, since I was confident of succeeding in my endeavours to dissuade you from involvement in the project, I concluded that there was no point in saying anything." He added, not without bitterness, "I see now that I was wrong on all counts."

Amos gave a snort of disgust and continued to stride up and down the length of the room. The peon entered, and pointing to the puddle of ink, Moitra tacitly issued an imperious instruction. Peeling off a few sheets from the blotter, the peon started to mop up the mess.

"But now that you know, I am glad," Moitra said with a trace of defiance. "I am also glad that we are finally forced to abandon a project about which I have had severe misgivings right from the start."

"Who said anything about abandoning the project?" Amos demanded. "Do you truly expect me to turn away now? To accept this vicious stab in the back meekly, without any form of retaliation?"

"But it is a perfectly legitimate sale!" Moitra protested in alarm. "Mr. Sutherland is as free to sell his property as your ha . . . as his lordship is to purchase it."

"That mill is *mine*, Ranjan Babu," Amos breathed softly, "and nobody is going to take it away from me."

"Mr. Sutherland's mill is no longer within your reach," Moitra pleaded, his heart pumping hard. "It is time to be realistic, to accept that."

Amos shook his head, his face stony. "No. That mill was destined for me. I mean to get it back."

"But how?"

He waved away the question. "I don't know. Yet! But I'll think of something." He sank into a chair and folded his arms against his chest. "Tell me—how much cargo do we carry annually for Farrowsham?"

"A fraction of what we did at one time. I don't recall the exact figures but they are all in our ledgers." The manager's eyes were guarded. "Why?"

"Farrowsham has always enjoyed better credit facilities than any of our other customers."

"Yes."

"And they still have a permanent lease on the bilges of any one of our clippers of their choice at rates which are even more laughable now than they were then."

"Yes," Moitra agreed again, pausing to clear his throat with a cough that was distinctly unhappy in tone. "As you well know, these concessions are part of that long-term agreement we made with Farrowsham in the days of—" this time the cough was more prolonged—"your, ah, mother's involvement with the Agency."

"Ah yes, my *mother's* involvement." Amos's lips curled with the faintest trace of a gibe. "Naturally they qualified for special terms then!" He gave a laugh, the sound of which was ugly. "The question now is, should they still?"

"It will not matter to them one way or the other," Moitra pointed out. "Now there are many shipping lines that will be happy to carry their cargo, perhaps give them better concessions than we do. Besides," his tone sharpened, "I see no justification in changing an established rate system for no reason at all."

"Well, I disagree. We have a very good reason to do so!"

"*You* have a good reason. I have none."

Amos's temper, still dangerously close to the surface, erupted again. "Had my father been here today," he raged, "he would not have hesitated a moment to teach this arrogant trickster a lesson or two! My father had guts, not a liver made out of goddamned lilies!"

Looking at Amos's hate-filled face, his clenched fists, his glittering pewter eyes half obscured by heavy lids behind which cerebral wheels churned to devise retribution for Farrowsham, Moitra could have sworn that he was once again in the presence of his Sarkar. For a moment or two he could not get rid of the uncanny feeling that the tall, wide-shouldered man with the smouldering eyes who faced him was indeed Jai Raven-thorne, their arguments about Farrowsham the same as they had been two decades ago. Ranjan Moitra had never seen Amos like this, nor had he ever hoped to. The boy's transformation into an obsessive, unreasonable avenger pained him deeply. He decided that he simply could not tolerate it.

He straightened his back and looked at Amos sternly. "If I am right in my surmises, the thoughts you harbour are dangerous, self-defeating and unworthy of a scion of this family. I beg of you to cast them out of your mind." He patted the virgin white blotter several times to drive home his point. "Yes, it is true that in your father's day many used violence and intimidation to deal with competitors. But today, Calcutta is a civilised station where all merchants, big or small, Indian or European, have the moral responsibility to behave with decorum, to follow accepted norms of business practice. If this was once a commercial jungle where barbaric laws applied, it is so no longer. Today we resolve our differences in the Chamber of Commerce, over negotiating tables or in the law courts. We have rules of conduct, a code of ethics, legal and commercial procedures. I therefore implore you not to be rash in making decisions that you might have cause to regret later."

Amos's expression showed faint traces of amusement at the older man's pompous little speech. "Well, I'm not about to go out and put a bullet through the blackguard's damned heart, if that's what you mean," he commented lightly, adding under his breath, "much as I would like to!"

Moitra looked aghast. "That you can even think of performing such a heinous act would be a matter of great pain to your dear mother, Master Amos—have you considered that? After all is said and done, he too is her son."

"I am only too well aware of that unfortunate circumstance, Ranjan Babu." Amos snapped. "You may therefore dispense with the need to give me hourly reminders of the fact. Anyway, that is neither here nor there. All I want is to think of some means to get that blasted mill out of his grubby little clutches."

"Well, as we had earlier decided, there is only one civilised way to...."

"No!" Amos stiffened. "If you think I would demean myself by approaching him, you can dismiss that notion altogether."

Ranjan Moitra sighed. "It is I who will demean myself. If you so wish, I will make an approach through Mr. Donaldson."

"You'll be wasting your time, I can tell you that before you even start."

Moitra looked rather helpless. "Then what else is there to be done?"

Amos did not reply. He tucked his hands in his armpits and started to pace again. Suddenly he stopped, thought for a moment, then strode up to Moitra's desk and flung himself in the chair opposite him. "Tell me about their indigo plantation."

Moitra looked surprised. "What is there to tell? It is more or less defunct."

"Do you have details of its finances?"

"Naturally. I have details of everyone's finances."

"Then tell me everything that you know."

It was early evening.

As she sat at her dressing table filing her nails into neat half moons preparatory to leaving for the McNaughtons' where they were to dine, Lady Pendlebury thoughtfully eyed the supine figure of her husband spread-eagled on the bed. Emitting occasional grunts and groans, Sir Jasper was indulging in what he considered to be one of the supreme pleasures of Indian life second only to the hookah: a brisk, mustard oil massage. Seeing that her husband would remain captive for at least the next half hour, Lady Pendlebury decided that this was indeed the perfect opportunity for that serious talk for which she had been waiting three whole days.

"I think it is about time you took me into your confidence, Jasper." There was a very determined glint in her eyes. "I want to know *exactly* what has been happening between you and Christian—even more, between Christian and this girl."

Wrapped in a bath towel, her husband lay entirely at her mercy. Towering above him by the bed was his personal masseur, pummelling and pounding the expanse of bare back with unconcealed gusto. Sir Jasper's only response to his wife's questions was a series of throaty barks, presumably indicative of pleasure. The masseur, also bare-chested, was a big, burly wrestler from Howrah, with bulging biceps, hairy arms and an all-pervading odour of mustard oil. He had been highly commended by several of Sir Jasper's colleagues for the expertise of his large, meaty hands. His additional virtue was that he was a deaf mute; private conversations in his presence, therefore, remained private. Lady Pendlebury turned to regard his ugly, oily torso with distaste, then continued her interrogation with grim persistence.

"Did you hear what I said, Jasper?"

He made a slight movement of his head which she took to be a nod.

"Well, I want to know the truth, Jasper. Surely you can see how concerned I am about the boy?"

Her husband's eyes, closed with rapture, did not open. "Everything is well under control, Constance. I've told you, there is nothing to be concerned about."

Relinquishing the dressing-table stool, she came to sit by him on the bed. "Christian went to see you at the Treasury office, didn't he?"

"Yes."

"And I have no doubt that he told you in some detail about this trip he has undertaken for a few days?"

"Yes."

"Well, I want to know what the true purpose is of that trip. I'm concerned about that, too—no, not concerned, alarmed! He seems to be planning something, I can *smell* it!"

"He merely wants to familiarise himself with the district to which he is being posted. What's wrong with that?"

"He's becoming sly and secretive, Jasper, and I simply will not have it. I *insist* on knowing exactly what is happening between him and this girl!"

Sir Jasper made a signal to the masseur, who attacked the back of his thighs with relish, making Sir Jasper respond with little gurgles of contentment. "I wish you would leave it alone, Constance," he mumbled through slack lips. "I assure you, the matter is being attended to very adequately." He raised enough energy to frown. "For heaven's sake, woman, don't you trust me?"

"That is not the point, Jasper. The point is, I see appalling changes in Christian since he came here. Why, at times I can hardly recognise him as my son. I have a feeling that matters have progressed far beyond what you tell me, and I want to know how far." Her lips settled into an angry line. "I'm desperately concerned about the boy, Jasper—aren't you?"

"No."

"In that case, you should be!" Her tone developed an edge, almost a touch of malice. "If Christian does marry this girl, it is not only *his* career that will be on the anvil, is it?" she asked softly.

He still did not open his eyes, but by the slight tightening of his facial muscles she knew that her shaft had struck home.

"You may not get that peerage the Prime Minister mentioned before we left England, Jasper."

"Don't be absurd, Constance."

"Nor the other high position upon which you have set your heart." The touch of malice sharpened. "I simply cannot believe that *you*, of all people, fail to see the danger to yourself—especially with the Ingersolls here."

"Danger? Balderdash!"

"Oh, how can you be so blind, Jasper?" Exasperated, she shook his shoulder hard so that he was forced to open at least one eye.

"I am neither blind nor deaf, Constance," he said, annoyed, nudging his shoulder free. "I am *fully* aware of everything that you have been kind enough to bring to my notice."

"And still you take the matter casually? How can I *not* worry? One of us must!"

For a while it seemed that he would not reply at all. She was about to make an acid comment and walk away from the bed when he decided to break his silence.

"I think it is time we planned a *burra khana.*"

Lady Pendlebury stopped in her tracks and slowly sat down again. "Don't be frivolous, Jasper," she rebuked, quite incensed. "Is this the time to think about *burra khanas?*"

"None better, m'dear, none better!"

"With half of Calcutta away in the Simla hills?"

"Well, *we're* not, neither are the Ingersolls, and the McNaughtons are already back. There are others who, for whatever reasons, suffer the enforced penance of a summer and monsoon in station and would give their eyeteeth for any social diversion." With a cheerful wave he dismissed the masseur, swung his legs to the edge of the bed and sat up. Retrieving his bottle of oil and other tools of his trade, the masseur bowed and left the room. "Well, does the idea of a party not appeal to you any more?"

"It does not," she snapped. "Not until you decide to apply your mind seriously to the mess Christian has got himself into."

He gave a throaty half laugh. "My dear, if you would only listen carefully, that is *precisely* what I am doing. Now—does it appeal to you or not?"

Closing her eyes, Lady Pendlebury prayed for patience. He was, she could see, in one of those perverse moods that never failed to drive her to distraction. She also saw that it would be utterly futile to return to the subject of Christian, at least for this evening. He would simply continue to feed her with his infuriating evasions, and they would end up having one of those undignified scenes that resolved nothing and left her fingers too numb to manage even the simplest of arpeggios.

"What made you suddenly think of a party?"

He shrugged. "We've enjoyed the hospitality of many since we arrived. I just thought it might be a good idea to return some of it." He got up from the bed and stretched his arms above his head, enjoying the feeling of physical well-being.

In spite of her frustration at her husband's strange responses, mention of a party had stirred a very positive chord in Lady Pendlebury's heart. In fact, she was not at all displeased at the suggestion. "Well, to be quite honest, Jasper, I've been thinking about that too. The house is almost ready. Pierre is well pleased with his new kitchen, even more so with M'amselle Corinne. Yes, I think a *burra khana* would be an excellent idea. I will have to postpone my soirée, of course," she gave a small sigh of regret, "but I don't suppose a week here or there will matter."

"How long would it take you to make the preparations?"

"Not long. I already have a guest list. There would be just the matter of having the invitations printed, written out and delivered."

"Are you sure you can manage dinner for, say, two hundred, without your pet frog acquiring a migraine?"

"Oh, don't be so silly, Jasper, of *course* I can and of *course* he won't!" Just talking about the preliminary arrangements made Lady Pendlebury's heart lift and her energies revive. "You have to admit that the house is beginning to look really *très chic.* Of course, we will have to contend with

341

the nuisance of the monsoons, but the banqueting hall and the ballroom can easily accommodate two hundred, perhaps more. I merely need to have the marble polished and the chandeliers put up." She took a moment off to mentally flick through her extensive wardrobe: the peach velour? No, too warm. Perhaps the rather more modish aquamarine that went so well with her opals. "We could hire the Navy Band, Jasper. They played very prettily on the embankment when we arrived, remember?"

Sir Jasper reached for a neat pile of small napkins on his bedside table and helped himself to one. "We will have to invite all the leading Indian businessmen—merchants, bankers, agents, manufacturers, and so forth."

She made a face. "Must we? Well, yes, I suppose we must. It will be a headache, of course. They have such absurd reservations about food."

"Your native *baburchis* will take care of that without you having to lift a finger, m'dear," he remarked drily. "Goodness knows they have little enough to do." He tightened his towel around his girth and started to rub the excess oil off his body with the napkin.

"The fact that everything will have to be indoors is a botheration," she continued, "but perhaps it won't really matter. It might be a good opportunity to try out those new fringed punkas I told you about. I don't really think we need to hire extra bearers, those Tremaine has been training should be enough. Their new uniforms with the red, white and blue cummerbunds and embroidered initials should have been ready last week, but do you think delivery dates mean anything to these native tailors? Then there's the problem with the downstairs thermantidote. Oh dear, I simply *must* write all this down before. . . ." Murmuring happily to herself, she got up from the bed to go to her desk. "Yes, once it's polished, the marble will be *perfect* for dancing, although I hope nobody slips and falls. You remember the dreadful time we had at home when the old duchess. . . ." She stopped, realising that her husband had said something and she had missed it. "What did you say, dear?"

"I said we will invite the Raventhornes."

The pencil dropped from Lady Pendlebury's fingers. "What?"

"We will invite Mrs. Raventhorne, Miss Raventhorne and Master Amos Raventhorne." He paused between the names, giving each pointed emphasis to make his meaning even clearer.

Lady Pendlebury looked horror-struck. She sank into the chair. "You cannot be serious, Jasper!"

"I am. Perfectly serious." He continued to wipe the residual oil off his shoulders. "As I have already told you, we cannot be seen to display the slightest prejudice in this matter. Amos Raventhorne runs the largest shipping line based in Calcutta. Every English commercial house does business with Trident. They are powerful, influential people, Constance. If they are singled out and left off the guest list, there will be even more talk than if they are not. Whether you like it or not, appearances must be maintained."

"Whether you like it or not, I refuse to maintain them! How can you even . . . ?"

342

"Nevertheless, my dear, maintain them you *will*," he repeated forcefully. Then, expansive again, he smiled. "The Indians have a saying—'The trick lies in killing the snake without breaking the stick.' "

Constance Pendlebury could not have cared less what the Indians had to say. "But what will everyone think?" she cried, distraught. "They will think that we accept this wretched half-caste as our son's future bride!"

"Yes, perhaps they will."

"We will be the laughing-stock of Calcutta, Jasper."

"I doubt it. The Raventhornes are on the guest list at every official function. That they choose not to attend any is another matter."

"Can you think of them refusing this invitation?" she demanded angrily. "On the contrary, they'll come running, *running*—especially that forward little minx of theirs."

"Be that as it may, invite them we must. It would be highly tactless of us not to do so."

"How can you possibly apply normal social niceties to our situation, Jasper?" She quivered with outrage, certain that her husband had taken leave of his senses. "I simply cannot and will not tolerate that family in my home! If that scheming little tarbrushed opportunist ever steps foot inside my door, I will throw her out, Jasper, I promise you I will!"

He stopped in the act of wiping down his forearms. "You will do no such thing, Constance," he said quietly, each word edged with ice. "You will not only receive the girl and her family well, you will make them welcome!"

She stared at him helplessly, not knowing how to react to his extraordinary attitude, wondering if this too was not part of the conspiracy hatched between father and son. "What you suggest is impossible, Jasper," she whispered, dabbing her nose and eyes, "unthinkable. . . ."

"It is neither impossible nor unthinkable. It is part of a solution, a culinary solution."

"A cul . . . ?" She looked bewildered. "Have you been drinking, Jasper?"

"Not in the least, m'dear!" he assured her lightly. "What I suggest is something your Monsieur Pierre would certainly approve of—a lesson in how to make omelettes without breaking the eggs."

She pulled herself up to her full height, her breathing hard. "Are you trying to tell me," she asked in shocked tones, "that you have *no* objections to Christian marrying this daughter of a mongrel traitor?"

He tossed the soiled napkin in a corner and patted the enviable flatness of his stomach with approval. "No. Quite to the contrary, *quite* to the contrary." He gathered his clothes off a chair and walked to the bathroom, pleased at the prospect of a leisurely, cooling bath. "What I am trying to tell you is that under no circumstances will Christian marry Jai Raventhorne's daughter. I give you my word on that."

15

T HE WALK ACROSS the vast parkland known as the "lungs of Calcutta" towards the Birkhurst mansion on the Esplanade was a familiar one for Olivia, although she had not traversed it for many years
now. She had chosen to walk because the monotonous rhythm of the exercise soothed the turbulence in her mind, gave her time to set her priorities
in order. Every step she took across the lime green grass, spongy with
morning moisture, was for her a regression into a past neither alive nor
quite dead, like a ghost that wafted out of its sepulchre every midnight to
tantalise those it had left behind. The sensations produced within her by
her involuntary re-enactments were confusing and, at the same time, intolerably acute.

It was not nostalgia that plagued her, for this had been a period of her
life that she had hated; it was guilt. Images from a luminous, verdant September of long ago came swarming upon her like a rush of locusts. She
thought of that day, twenty-one years ago, when Estelle had whisked her
son away to England. Lacerated by an inexpressible guilt, she had banished sentiment from her thoughts. There had been no tearful farewells,
no vulgar displays of emotion, just that festering pain, that crippling sense
of loss, that had slowly—oh so very slowly!—become a habit. Perforce, it
had to remain a secret habit, like a shameful addiction she could indulge
only in private.

Alistair had been the one area of her life that she had not been able to
share with Jai. Violently jealous of Freddie, her first husband, and of everything to do with him, he had felt threatened by her love for a son he had
had no part in fashioning. And so Alistair had been tucked away into a
niche of her mind like a stolen treasure, to be taken out and savoured only
in moments of deviously contrived solitude. She had never talked to Jai

about Alistair, never revealed to him the cavernous gaps left in her life by his absence. It was only within herself that she gave free rein to her thoughts of him—yearning, imagining and wondering, always wondering, as their destinies unfolded on opposite sides of the globe, neither touching nor transfusing. She had often tried to imagine what he might look like, knowing that even as they passed by on a street, they would not recognise each other, sharing flesh and blood yet forever strangers. And then, eventually, she had lulled herself into a false sense of security that had blunted the imagination, dulled the pain and buried the guilt. It had always seemed ironic to her that the single memory she had of Alistair should be one of pain—the tearing, ravaging pain of childbirth. Other than that she had nothing to remember him by—not a glimpse, not a touch, not even the whisper of a cry.

What did she want from this second son, Olivia asked herself as she walked towards the Birkhurst mansion: a look of love, a touch of the hand, merely a kind thought? So little, so very little! But that was not what he would want from her, she knew; what he would want from her was the truth, that elusive will-o'-the-wisp truth of twenty-one years ago buried under so many inseparable layers, a truth she could no longer define for herself, much less explain to him.

A hundred times in her mind, a thousand times, she had constructed an imaginary scene around an improbable day when they might finally meet. But now that the scene was upon her, she found herself filled with crippling dread. She recoiled at having to listen to his many justified accusations, none of which she was in a position to deny, and to the piercing questions he would ask to which she would have no answers—or, at least, none that he could either accept or understand.

Perversely enough, side by side with the dread she felt a wild kind of joy, an intoxication almost, a feeling quite indescribable. It filled her with happiness, dazzled her with blinding radiance, set alight the inner core of her very being as a mother. As she walked, her footsteps sometimes faltered and her mind raced, while the next moment she wanted to run and it was her mind that held her back. Her inner conflicts pulled in a dozen different directions at once, so that by the time she arrived at the splendid wrought-iron gates of the house of which she had once been the mistress, her hands felt like arctic ice and she crawled with nerves.

She lingered a moment outside, watched by an unfamiliar guard, stabilising her breath. A minute or two later she pulled at the front-door bell, her nerves forced back into submission and her rebellious senses once more on a leash. By the time Salim, Freddie's loyal old bearer, opened the door to her, she was entirely in control of herself, as she knew she must be in the interests of her own survival. Alistair had taken her by surprise once; he must not be allowed to do so again.

Salim welcomed her with a wide smile and a deep salaam. "Why, memsahib, I have not seen you for many years." His eyes filled with tears. "My heart bleeds that Allah gave you only two sons when you deserved a hundred."

Olivia found herself actually laughing. "Oh no, you could not possibly wish that upon me, Salim!" she protested in horror, not entirely feigned. "I think that even two sons are going to be far more than I can manage!"

He looked perplexed by what she said, unable to understand her apprehensions when he himself had eleven sons by four wives and had not regretted such divine bounty even for a moment. "The laat sahib will be down shortly, lady memsahib. Please to order 'freshment?"

"Thank you, Salim. I think I'll wait until my son. . . ." she broke off, startled at how naturally the term had sprung to her lips.

The bearer nodded again, salaamed and withdrew, leaving her to her own devices in a house to which he knew she was no stranger.

Olivia looked around curiously, then wandered through the downstairs rooms—the grand banqueting hall, the library, the conservatory and study, and the long, over-furnished withdrawing rooms with their gilded mirrors, ebony and walnut cabinets, brocade curtains and finely woven French tapestries. The mansion had lain vacant for two decades now, cloaked in gloom and the corrosive air of neglect. Everything looked tawdry and tired, worn away by sheer disuse. The all-pervasive smell of must and mothballs gave the final testimony to the passage of the hollow years. This sad, deserted house had once been her home; it was impossible not to feel at least a twinge of regret at its decay.

A few pleasant memories still lingered: the cheerful nursery on the second floor where Amos had spent the first two years of his life in the care of Mary Ling; the corner that had held the splendid tree Estelle had decorated one Christmas to transform the sombre mausoleum into a lively, laughter-filled home with her own special brand of magic; the conservatory to the right, off the library, where she had been solaced so often by Freddie's dear, dear mother. And upstairs on the first floor was the bedroom suite she had resentfully shared with Freddie, where Alistair was conceived when Amos was only three months old. . . .

"Good morning. I apologise for having kept you waiting."

Olivia's stomach lurched as she turned. For a split second she feared her throat would betray her, but then the feeling passed and she regained her composure. "It doesn't matter," she said with a smile. "I was occupying myself looking around the house."

He regarded her with a sceptically raised eyebrow. "Surely not nostalgia for the old days!"

"Perhaps. I suppose a certain amount of nostalgia is inevitable for any house in which one has lived."

He did not approach her, nor did he offer her a kiss or even a handshake. Standing at a distance from her, physically and emotionally removed, he merely waved towards a chair. "Do sit down, Mrs. Raventhorne. After all, we don't want to induce another fainting fit, do we? Should I order some tea, or would you prefer something cool?"

Mrs. Raventhorne!

She let it pass, indeed, hardly noticed it—or anything else. Her gaze was fixed to his face like a limpet. She could not stop staring at him, her eyes simply would not let him go. The taunts she brushed aside, unconcerned that he made them; in any case, she had come prepared to be wounded.

"Well, perhaps a fresh lime sherbet."

He got up and tugged at the bell-rope, then returned and sat down again, not next to her but in an opposite chair, so that they were divided by a table. His manner was the same as it had been the other day, cold and hostile, with more than a touch of insolence.

She heard herself speak as she inquired about his journey. He answered that it had been as comfortable as could be expected. "I was deeply sorry to learn that your grandmother is now an invalid," Olivia said. "Being so energetic and independent, she must hate to be confined."

"Yes." The monosyllabic response was still civil enough, but he spoke with neither enthusiasm nor emotion.

His eyes and hair are mine but his mouth is Freddie's, wide and generous. . . .

"Tell me, how is Mary Ling? Your grandmother wrote that she married a laundryman with his own shop in London. Do you see her at all?"

"Yes. She comes to visit us occasionally. She appears to be keeping well."

Disregarding his clipped responses, she questioned him further about the Anglo-Chinese governess she had sent with him to England, about his grandmother's health, about the Farrowsham estate which he now managed, and about his days at Oxford. She was only vaguely aware of what she asked or, indeed, of what he answered. The sheer inadequacy of the conversation produced in her a strange feeling of unreality. The words they spoke held no meaning for either of them; they merely played this foolish game to conceal their own insecurities. She started to feel disoriented, detached. It was as if she had stepped out of her body and observed him from some great remoteness where he could not see her. And in her imagined invisibility, she caressed the smoothness of his skin, the curling softness of his lovely chestnut hair, and touched his eyes—*her* eyes!—with her lips, marvelling that, never having seen him, she could still love him so totally.

He has such beautiful hands, and how gracefully he moves them, like a concert pianist, oddly enough, not unlike Amos's hands! And that sharp, aquiline nose—that too, surely, is mine?

"Having a good look at the face you failed to recognise?"

The sudden question, thrown at her like a well-primed javelin, pierced her imaginary bubble and jolted her back to reality. She saw that he matched her stare with bold arrogance and no hint of embarrassment.

"Yes." It was a question that she had been expecting. "I failed to recognise you because I had never seen you."

His lips curved in a smile of malice. "Well, what does that astonishing admission say about you as a mother?"

Without her noticing it, Salim had placed a tray at her elbow. Lifting the glass, she sipped thirstily at the iced sherbet. "It says that I was a victim of circumstances beyond my control," she answered, fighting the stupour induced by his mere presence. "I was compelled to disassociate that which I wanted to do from that which I had to."

He raised a mocking eyebrow. "And these circumstances also forced you never to learn what your second son looked like?"

Her throat was still parched; she took another sip of the refreshing drink. "Yes. I forbade your grandmother to send me photographs of you."

"Because you were confident that you would never see me!"

"No. Because I assumed that you would never want to see me."

He flushed. Then his expression cemented again and he leaned forward. "Before we go any further, Mrs. Raventhorne," he said coldly, "I think there is something that I have to clarify right at the start. I am anxious that you should not form any wrong impressions about my visit to Calcutta. This is why I was relieved when I received your note asking to come here this morning."

She said nothing and waited, untouched by his barbs, absurdly content to let the sound of his voice wash over her and satisfy yet another minuscule part of her vast hunger.

There is a sweetness in his throat. Does he sing, I wonder, like Freddie sometimes did . . . ?

"I want you to understand that I did not come to Calcutta specifically to see you, Mrs. Raventhorne. The fact that you happen to be here is of incidental value to me. I came because of the Agency and the severe problems that beset it." His face was red with the heat; he perspired profusely. He got up, mopped the sweat off his glistening forehead and loosened the collar of his thick broadcloth jacket.

Nobody advised him on what kind of clothes to wear in the tropics? Why, the poor boy will surely melt in that ridiculous coat of armour!

"But there must still be a reason why you came to see me."

"Yes, there is. Because of my strange—no, not strange, *freakish*—situation, I find that my life has certain loose ends that must be tied. They make my mind untidy, clutter up my thoughts and confuse me. Once they are tied, I can forget them. That is one of the reasons why I came to see you."

Loose ends! An involuntary smile touched her lips. *This little quirk he has definitely inherited from me!* The tiny observation gave her such insane pleasure that within herself her smile widened. She had never seen him before, and yet, instinctively, she felt she knew him as if he were herself. His mind to her was transparent, made of glass, every thought in it, every crease, every ache in it her own.

"And the other reasons?"

He stretched his legs and crossed one over the other. "A word exists in the English language for those who have unknown fathers, Mrs. Raventhorne. Considering your own experiences, I am sure you are only too familiar with the term. Unfortunately, no such word is available for those whose *mothers* are unknown. This, as you can imagine, constituted something of an anomaly in my life. I admit, therefore, that I was curious about you. I wanted to know, at least, what you looked like."

Something stabbed at her heart and drew a first pinprick of blood. She did not allow her reaction to show on her face. "It was I who requested your grandmother not to keep any photographs of me in your house, Alistair. I did not want you ever to put a face to a mental image of someone you would grow up to hate."

He laughed a little. "I can hardly be expected to hate someone I don't know, Mrs. Raventhorne! After all, at best, we are only . . . biological acquaintances."

An expression of pain, a cry for help. . . .

"I want you to know that you can ask me anything that you like, Alistair," she said quietly. "I will answer to the best of my recollections." Beneath her expressionless voice quivered an immensity of love that she could neither reveal nor conceal. In any case, he was not aware of it.

"Oh? And you will give me the truth?" His scepticism was veiled only very thinly.

"Yes. As I have perceived it."

"Give me a good reason why I should trust your perceptions, Mrs. Raventhorne!" He impaled her with a look of contempt. "Why should I expect truth from you, of all people—a woman who used and then destroyed my father?"

She tightened the clasp of her hands on each other to stop them from shaking. *How much does he already know?* she wondered in a fleeting second of panic. *How much has he learnt from his grandmother . . . ?*

"What I tell you will be the truth, Alistair. I have not been able to give you anything as a mother. Let me at least give you that."

His accusing eyes bored into her from across the room. "In that case, you admit that although my father was an alcoholic, it was not drink that killed him?"

"Yes." Her gaze did not waver. "He drank because I did not come up to his expectations. What killed him was disillusionment with me. Yes, you could say that I destroyed your father. I did not plan the destruction, but neither could I prevent it."

"Could not or *would* not?"

"Sometimes they are the same thing—or at least one convinces oneself that they are."

"You never loved him!"

"No."

"Then why in heaven's name did you marry him?" he demanded angrily. "For his money, his title?"

She drained the glass of sherbet and again entwined her fingers in her lap. Her knuckles shone white with the force of her grip but the gaze that met his was clear.

"There are certain actions in one's life, Alistair, that one takes because, in that point of time, one either believes them to be right or one has no other option."

"You mean, no selfless option!"

"Yes. If you like. The decisions one makes are prompted as much by self-interest as by compulsion of circumstances." She paused a moment, not looking at him, but knowing that he listened intently. "If one is

fortunate, those decisions sustain themselves in one's hindsight. If not. . . ."
She gave an involuntary shudder and looked away.

"You still haven't told me why you married him!"

She took a deep breath. "I married Freddie because I was carrying the child of another man, a man who had gone away. I needed a name to give to my child. Your father agreed to fulfil that need."

She heard his sharp, indrawn breath as he gasped; his cheeks suffused with hot colour. It was obvious that he had not known this, nor had he been prepared for quite such bluntness. His throat moved convulsively as he struggled to speak. He was unable to grasp the enormity of her confession.

"And this other man was Raventhorne?" he asked, stricken.

"Yes. Amos's father."

"He was not your . . . your *first* husband?"

"No. We could marry only after your father died."

Olivia watched in immense sorrow as he strode up and down trying to bring himself under control, battling to mentally fit snippets of his half knowledge into the slots she provided to form the complete, shocking picture. She marvelled that all this could have been kept from him for so long, that Lady Birkhurst could have guarded her secrets so well.

"My father agreed to this . . . this monstrous proposition of yours?"

"Yes."

"*Why?*" he cried out. "Why should any man be foolish enough to accept such obscene punishment?"

"The punishment was for the one unwitting crime he committed, Alistair," she said, for the first time truly bitter. "You see, he loved me. Your father was the kindest, most decent man that I have ever known."

"And you still exploited him, *used* him to give your unborn half-caste child his name?"

"Yes."

"And once you were his wife, socially acceptable and respected, you discarded him because he was no longer needed!" He made no effort to hide his disgust.

How crude it sounds, how cruel! How far removed from the truth, and yet how close to it . . . !

Outside the conservatory where they sat, a noisy woodpecker clung to a tree trunk and pecked voraciously at its bark. Olivia watched it for a moment, then heaved a weary sigh. "How does one apportion blame after all these years, Alistair? The truth is that we discarded each other. Freddie left me because he could no longer accept Amos as his son. I allowed him to leave because I could not reject my son."

"Could not reject your *first*-born son," he spat out viciously. "To reject the second-born, I believe, presented no such difficulty!"

"I did not reject you, Alistair."

But he no longer listened, burning with jealousy and the accumulated rage of two decades, too naïve for the art of concealment. "And this first-born son of yours continued to enjoy all the privileges of the Birkhurst name and money even after that, didn't he?"

"Only until it was necessary." She corrected him with a trace of sharpness. "When your father died and I could remarry, I took legal steps to waive all claims to the Birkhurst money and title, both for myself and for Amos."

"You were never tempted to keep the title for your first-born son," he sneered, "to make him one of the richest men in England?"

"No. There was no need to. Amos's own father had more money than Amos would know what to do with in a lifetime. Besides, you are also my son. I had no intention of depriving you of your birth rights."

"No, only of a mother!" Shocked and still dazed by her sordid revelations, he could not stop his voice from trembling. "You sent me to England because I was an encumbrance, an inconvenience that your new husband would not accept!"

"No, that is not true! I sent you to England to fulfil an obligation to your father's family, to ensure legitimate succession of the title. Freddie had lost a wife, however unworthy, whom he loved to distraction. . . ." Her voice broke a little. "I could not deprive him also of the only son he was ever likely to have." She stopped, searching wildly for words, but she could think of nothing else to say. What was there to say anyway to heal the wounds that had festered within him for so many years?

"Even *puppies* are not given away until they have been weaned." His mouth twisted with bitterness. "You, it seems, could not get rid of me soon enough!"

She looked at him in helplessness, almost touching his pain with her fingers. "If I had laid eyes on you even once, Alistair," she said dully, starting to throb with despair, "I would never have been able to part with you at all."

But he only shook his head in confusion.

No, he could never understand, nor could she ever make him. Were there any devices with which she could bridge the vast, unending chasm by which they were separated? Words only distorted and concealed and deceived; they vulgarised the emotions, defiled the truth. She could never make him see all the nuances. Even to try would be offensive. Something inside her—everything!—cried out with a renewed sense of bereavement, for a loss that could never now be redeemed. With her head bowed, she let the silence between them expand, not knowing how to fill it.

She could see that he was bewildered by such a heavy onslaught of truth, incapable in his immaturity of absorbing so much emotional brutality. His long, tapered fingers plucked at each other behind his back as he paced, full of anguish, unable to keep his feet still.

"If it is any consolation to you, Alistair," she said heavily, drained by the self-inflicted savagery of her confessional, "I never lied to your father, nor will I to you. It is not a pretty story, but you have a right to know it, such as it is." Despite all her efforts, her eyes welled. "I would have given anything to love Freddie as he deserved to be loved. But the heart has a mind of its own, Alistair. With the best will in the world, I could not." She stood up to leave.

351

He still did not look at her as he stared down at the carpet, his face wretched. "Yet you rejected this man who deserved to be loved, to run away with another, to co-habit with a half-caste street urchin, a tr . . . !"

"*Stop!*" Olivia's command rang out with the suddenness and sharpness of a gunshot and, startled, he did precisely that. "There is something that I too would like to clarify right at the start, Alistair." Her tone was granite hard, and for the first time, she showed anger. "I do not want you to labour under the misapprehension that every corner of my life is available for your inspection and evaluation. It is not. There are certain matters about which you have a right to know, but there are others that are not your concern. I am not accountable to you for the way that I have chosen to live my life, Alistair. Whether you approve or not is for you to decide, but your moral assessments are not of the slightest interest to me. Now is that clearly understood?"

He opened his mouth to voice a rejoinder, but intimidated by her unexpected temper, decided against it. Instead, he merely thrust his hands deep in his pockets and looked sullen.

"One day when you are older, perhaps you will understand that very often one has to make one's own moralities, set one's own standards, follow one's own star, regardless of the world and its rules." She waited for her breath to steady, then asked more composedly, "Now—are there any other questions that you would like me to answer?"

His lips turned down in a pout. "No."

"If there are, feel free to ask. I have always been honest with my other children." She stopped. She knew she should not have said that.

He glared at her, resentment and disillusionment written in every line of his young, wounded face. "I told you, I have no other questions!"

Even knowing the answer, she could not stifle the impulse to ask, "Will you come to see me again?"

His spine stiffened. "No. I have no desire to involve myself with your family! How in hell can you even ask me to after . . . ?" He faltered and his lips compressed; for the first time he exposed his deep unhappiness.

Olivia was overwhelmed with compassion, crushed by the weight of it. What a hideous burden she had placed on his youthful shoulders, not yet those of a fully developed man! Should she have punished him just yet with the truth? *Was* the cleansing of her conscience truly worth all his added suffering? Defeated by the inner turbulences he tried so hard to hide, engulfed by this huge shell of a house, he seemed so alone, so friendless and lost in this brittle, alien environment, the complexities of which he neither knew nor was prepared for. Her arms ached to hold him, to cocoon him with her love, to make up for all the years she had not held him, not loved him. She wanted to learn every day of every year of his life that she had missed being with him, to share with him all those millions of moments that would now never be hers to share.

But she knew she could not. It was too late for that and he would not let her.

"Very well then," Olivia said with a sigh. "Since you have no more questions, there is one that I would like to ask you."

He was instantly on his guard. "What?"

"Why did you buy the cotton mill?"

He averted his eyes, but she saw that the sullen look had returned. "Why does anyone buy anything? Because I wanted it."

"You have no interest in that mill."

"How would *you* know?" he taunted. "Two days ago you couldn't tell your second son from the damned milkman—now you know everything there is to know about his interests?"

"You have no intentions of ever working that mill, Alistair," she said gently.

He smiled a thin smile full of cunning. "But *he* has, hasn't he?"

"How did you learn of Amos's interest in it, from Guy Sutherland?"

"Obviously."

She scanned his face with anxious eyes. "Amos has set his heart on acquiring that mill, Alistair. Can you not see your way to letting your brother have his . . . ?"

He sliced off the rest with a violent gesture. "You expect me to consider your half-caste son a . . . *brother?*" He was aghast.

"Yes." She responded calmly. "Biology may not make emotional relationships, but neither can it be denied."

He began to laugh, that same hollow laugh she had heard when she first saw him. Then, swiftly, he bit back the sound and his expression turned nasty. "That mill is *mine*, Mrs. Raventhorne," he said softly, his hands fisted, "and I intend to keep it. It may rot and go to hell, but I swear that that other son of yours will never have it!"

Regardless of the fact that the tea it served in little mud bowls was difficult to distinguish from ditchwater, and its meagre menu unlikely to whet any but the most brazen of appetites, the tea shop in the narrow lane behind the University was astonishingly popular. Its coterie of loyal customers consisted of students, teachers, journalists, writers, poets and radical intellectuals, all devoted to its casual ambience and to the owner who provided it—if not to the cavalier refreshments that he served. The greasy, rickety tables framed by long wooden benches were crowded at all times of the day and much of the night, the peeling walls resounding with vociferous debate on every conceivable subject in Bengali, Hindustani or English, or a combination of all three. The owner of the café, a placid little Parsi bachelor with a passion for chess and pigeon racing, made hideous profit out of the abysmal fare he provided, but he was known for his generosity in extending unsecured loans to customers in temporary financial distress. As such, his trespasses as a host were only too readily forgiven.

It was here that Amos finally found Kyle Hawkesworth after he left his office one early evening. Even though it was not yet dark outside, the lamps had already been lit inside the café, for the air was viscous with smoke and the odour of stale food. Voices, however, rang out loud and clear as usual, and the sound of innumerable arguments was cacophonous. Through the pale brown haze Amos finally sighted Kyle at a corner table deeply engrossed in a game of chess with Nariman, the owner. Both were as oblivious of the gesticulating arms and raucous voices around them as they were of the two white fantails perched on Nariman's shoulders, cooing lovingly in his ear. Usually Amos participated in the chess and the arguments with enthusiasm, but today his mood was vile and his temper short. He had no stomach either for political debate or for complicated games of strategy. He elbowed his way through the crush and, catching Kyle's eye, made an impatient signal. With the café owner's queen and one castle already off the board, the game was all but over. A few moments later, Kyle extricated himself and joined Amos near the door, leaving Nariman sadly surveying the remains of his devastated army.

"For God's sake, let's get away from this madhouse," Amos muttered. "There is something that I need to talk to you about."

Kyle consulted his pocket watch and nodded. "Very well. I have an hour to kill before a rather tedious appointment. We can go over to the embankment."

Leading their horses by the reins, they started to walk towards the river. Neither spoke. The street was congested with pedestrians weaving through the usual complement of carriages, handcarts, horses and palanquins. Some people returned from work, others hurried towards the nearest marketplace before the stocks of fresh fish were exhausted, still others lingered by the colourful wayside stalls browsing rather than buying, enjoying the purely academic exercise of bargaining as an evening diversion. A wily vendor selling lurid pictures of Hindu gods and goddesses held a portly Sikh gentleman in thrall with his outrageously fabricated but ingeniously glib sales patter.

The riverside was comparatively deserted and peaceful. In the early evening sun, the water was ablaze with yellows and pinks, its surface sprinkled with fishing craft and dhoolie boats, their loincloth-clad oarsmen digging into the sluggish stream with visible effort as they headed homewards at the end of another hard day. By the nearside river bank a family of small white herons with long, sticklike legs stood in the water, as if on stilts, waiting hopefully for their dinner to swim by.

Kyle positioned himself on a boulder with his arms around his knees, tilted his head to a side and looked up at Amos with a knowing smile. "Alistair Birkhurst?"

Amos's mouth tightened. It was unlikely that Kyle would not have heard of Alistair's arrival. He nodded curtly.

Kyle laughed. "I would have imagined it would tickle your fancy to have a baron for a brother."

"Well, it doesn't, and he's not my brother," Amos snapped. "What it tickles is my gall. I have bile stuck in my craw up to here!"

Seeing that his friend was in no mood to be teased, Kyle shrugged aside the banter. "So, what appears to be the immediate problem?"

"It is he who has bought the cotton mill."

Kyle raised an eyebrow and whistled. "Indeed!"

"Yes, indeed! That puts a somewhat different complexion on the matter, doesn't it?"

"Only if he refuses to sell, which—judging by your mood—I presume he does?"

"Yes. Ranjan Babu went to see Donaldson this morning." He picked up a stone and tossed it hard and far into the river. "By God, I could twist his sneaky little neck for that!"

Kyle frowned. "Brawn isn't going to get you that mill, Amos."

"I know that, dammit!" He sat down on his haunches with his head between his knees. "But then what is?"

Kyle tapped his forehead. "Brains, my friend, brains!"

"I don't see how."

"You will. In time. Let us first give the matter some consideration without being hasty."

"I can't sit about doing *nothing* while he. . . ."

"You will not be doing nothing. You will be thinking." Kyle pulled a piece of closely written paper out of his pocket. "In the meanwhile, tell me what you think of this."

"Another editorial?"

"Yes."

Amos took the piece of paper and, interested, started to read aloud from it:

" 'Look down any alley, any lane of any bazaar in India. What do you see beyond the rubbish dumps and the flies? An army of half-breeds, their myriad faces a tribute to the manifold permutations and combinations that go to fashion a miscegene. The word 'army' is sinister but it is also apt. These desolate creatures that excite pity in most are, for others, the substance of nightmares, hidden enemies, hazards to name, repute and familial harmony. In one guise they are destitutes; in another, weapons poised for destruction, potential avengers, indeed, harbingers of the Apocalypse!

" 'Who is responsible for the existence of these latent destroyers? Should they suddenly decide to emerge into daylight and claim parentage, who stands to lose most through public exposure? The raunchy, transient sailor? The ragtag and bobtail of an itinerant British Army? Some mean, fly-by-night adventurer with neither compassion nor compunction nor, indeed, reputation? The annual tripper who, once gone, does not look back again?

" 'Perhaps. But there are others, more celebrated, less protected, who have for years been precariously balanced on the precipice of social and professional ruination. These are the truly terrorised, the renowned, respectable elite of our country, those whose hands rotate the mighty wheels of governance. They pontificate with sanctimony but are unable to defile with impunity. The sword that hangs above their heads by a hair's breadth swings with the persistence of a pendulum, and try as they might, they cannot still its movement.

" 'Ironically enough, those who hold many futures in the palms of their hands have none of their own. Would it not be just now to. . . .' " The scribbled sentences ended abruptly.

Amos looked up as he stopped reading. "That is not all, is it?"

"No. There is a final paragraph that I have to add."

"You plan to announce our second project?" There was a gleam of excitement in Amos's eyes.

"Perhaps."

Amos looked doubtful. "Do you think that the time is ripe, that we are prepared for so enormous an undertaking?"

"We are as prepared now as we will ever be. We have to take the plunge sometime." Kyle thrust the paper back into his pocket and returned to the original subject. "Birkhurst is adamant that he will not sell to you?"

"Yes."

"You offered a good price?"

"Almost double what he paid Sutherland for it! Apart from that, I instructed Ranjan Babu to indicate that we would be willing to consider purchase of that blasted plantation if our offer for the mill was accepted."

"Even that didn't tempt him?"

"No." Amos groaned. "Farrowsham's Indian businesses might be flagging, but the Birkhursts are among the richest landed gentry in England. He doesn't give a damn what happens to that mill and plantation."

"I see." Kyle sat in silence, pondering. Then he murmured, "It would be a very long shot. . . ."

"What would?"

"Nothing. I was merely talking to myself."

"What would be a long shot, Kyle?" Amos persisted. "You have an idea?"

"Perhaps. I have to think about it."

A spark of hope leapt into Amos's pale eyes. "What sort of an idea?"

But Kyle shook his head and refused to elucidate. "There are no other buyers for that plantation?"

"Not a single one, according to Donaldson."

"Are you sure?"

"Yes, I'm sure," Amos said impatiently.

"How many acres are there?"

"About four thousand. But the plantation is remote, inaccessible, riddled with problems and bankrupt. Nobody in his right mind would touch it with a barge pole. Anyway, how does it solve my problem that there aren't any buyers?"

Lost in his own introspection, Kyle did not vouchsafe any reply. He sat still, his eyes, crinkled at the corners, fixed on the edge of the water where the herons still patiently awaited their dinner. There was a strange expression on his face, as if he calculated something. So deep was his concentration that, irascible as he was, Amos did not venture to interrupt it.

"Yes. I have an idea, Amos." He got up so abruptly that Amos was startled. "It has to gestate for a while."

"But surely you can . . . ?"

"No I can't!" Kyle interrupted sharply. "Not yet. I will tell you more after I have been to see him."

"Who?"

"Jasper Pendlebury."

"Jasper Pendlebury!" Amos was astonished. "What on earth for?"

Kyle shrugged. "Whitney tells me that he wants to meet me." He gave a light laugh and spread his hands. "Who knows, he might even give me something to write about. After all, he *is* a pillar of Britain's Eastern Empire."

Amos continued to stare, his expression openly disbelieving. "What do you plan to write about him?"

"I don't know yet. Something will, no doubt, suggest itself." He paused to examine a queue of tiny crabs that emerged from under one stone to hurry under another. "In the meantime, let us keep this between ourselves. If anything at all is to happen, we must remain discreet."

"You are keeping something from me, aren't you, Kyle?" Amos asked uneasily.

"Yes."

"What?"

Kyle heaved a deep sigh. "A great deal, I'm afraid. But I cannot tell you anything more yet, not until I have spoken to the man."

"Be careful, Kyle." Amos looked worried.

But Kyle only smiled and shook his head. "See those herons? I'm taking a lesson out of their book to go fishing. For the moment we'll have to leave it at that." He took out his pocket watch and made a face. "I'm sorry, but I will have to leave you."

"What's so important about a tedious appointment?" Amos grumbled. "Surely you can stay a while longer."

"Nothing would please me more, but your sister would not approve."

"You have an appointment with Maya?"

"Yes."

"Why?"

Kyle shrugged. "I have no idea. She sent me a note to say that she wished to see me urgently."

Amos's brow darkened as his other persistent worry came to the forefront of his mind. "As it happens, that's another matter I wanted to talk to you about. Christian Pendlebury wants to marry her."

"Does he now!"

"Yes. So Maya tells me, and Mother has confirmed it. Apparently, Pendlebury went to the extent of seeking Mother's formal permission." He threw up his arms, greatly agitated. "Why the hell are all these pukkas suddenly meddling with our lives?"

"Christian meddles because she wants him to," Kyle reminded him with crackling dryness.

"Do you think he's serious about her?"

Kyle dusted a few slivers of stone off his trousers. "Who knows? Time will tell."

"I'm worried, Kyle. I have nothing against Christian Pendlebury personally, but I simply cannot imagine that his parents would even consider such a marriage, can you?"

Kyle's shoulders lifted in a careless shrug. "I haven't thought about it. In any case, it's no business of mine."

"You could at least give me an opinion," Amos protested. "What do you think I should do about it?"

Kyle turned to face him. "Why do you want to do anything about it?" he demanded, suddenly angry. "If she's determined to go to hell, my advice is, *let* her!" He walked to where his horse was tethered, vaulted into the saddle, and before Amos could recover from the outburst, galloped away.

Left highly dissatisfied with himself, with Kyle and their abortive discussion, Amos relieved his inner tensions by cursing volubly into the wind as he mounted his own steed and reluctantly headed for home, where other problems awaited. For the past few days he had been avoiding all but the most perfunctory encounters with his mother. He was simply not prepared to give her the opportunity to talk to him about Alistair. This evening, however, he knew that he would have to face her; she would make certain that he did.

He was not wrong. Olivia cornered him, eventually, in the stables where he had repaired directly after arriving home. On the ride back, Cavalcade had lost a shoe; he was in the process of giving Abdul Mian instructions to have the bay gelding reshod when Olivia found him.

"I went to see Alistair this morning," his mother said, without wasting time on a preamble.

Amos showed no reaction.

"There is much that we have to talk about, Amos. I thought it would be better if we met at his house."

"You are in no way accountable to me," he said with a shrug. "You are free to see whosoever you wish wheresoever you wish." He struggled with himself for a moment, then asked curtly, "Was he courteous with you?"

"Perfectly." Olivia managed to look surprised. "Why should he not be?"

"Judging from what I heard about his performance when he came here, I consider that an absurd question! Anyway, if you wanted to see him, why did you not summon him here? You have every right to."

"I thought it would be easier if. . . ."

"Easier for whom, you or him?" He snatched the reins from Abdul Mian's hands, dismissed him with a wave and started to unsaddle the horse himself. "Why do you suddenly feel that you have all these obligations to him, Mother? After all, you gave him away without even a first look, let alone a second!"

"He is still my son, Amos," she said, trying not to reveal how much he had hurt her. "It would make me so happy if you could be a little more reasonable."

"Reasonable?" His temper flared. "It is *you* who needs to be reasonable, considering what happened that first evening when he barged in here. Had I been at home, I would have whipped him from here to kingdom come and rubbed his nose in his own blood! I still will if I ever hear that he has been insolent with you again, I promise you that."

"He was not insolent with me!"

"He stole my cotton mill," Amos reminded her coldly, still smarting from the defeat, unable to stay away from the subject.

Olivia closed her eyes tiredly. "Let that mill go, Amos, please, for my sake!"

"No. I will *not* let it go! You should know me better than even to ask that, Mother. I am going to get that mill back!"

"How can you, Amos? Ranjan Babu says Alistair will not even consider selling it to you."

"Kyle will think of something."

"Kyle?" She echoed, alarmed. "Oh Amos, I beg of you, darling, don't do anything that will hurt either of you." Her throat started to throb in its tightness. "I couldn't *bear* it if you did! Whether you accept it or not, Alistair is your half-brother. . . ."

"It seems unlikely that I will ever be allowed to forget that!"

"And you both share at least my blood!"

"Whatever the relationship, I don't recognise it," Amos snapped. "All I am prepared to accept is that Alistair Birkhurst is the son of my mother by a man who was not my father. I cannot go beyond that, I *will* not!"

Without giving her a chance to say anything more, he stormed out of the stables.

It was in a mood very different to that of her last visit that Maya waited for Kyle to return home. As she sat in his parlour idly making fingertip patterns in the layer of dust on the window sill, she felt strangely depressed, almost desolate. She hated the prospect of seeing Kyle and his mistress together; hated having to listen to his taunts about Christian. Today she felt she simply did not have the energy to mount defences, or even to react to Kyle's endless sarcastic barbs. Furthermore, it was almost ten whole days since she had seen Christian; she missed him, felt nervous and insecure in his absence, longed for the reassurances his mere presence would bring. Had it not been for her promise to Joycie, she would have merely sent the jewellery on to Kyle with an explanatory letter.

But, of course, she did not; it would have been unthinkable to betray a dead friend's trust with such callous disregard. She had not been able to evict thoughts of Joycie from her mind since the day of the funeral. Her brain seemed single-mindedly devoted to visions of the brittle little body bundled into that enormous coffin, so grotesque in finery that spoke not of nuptial joy but of the cold hollowness of rejection. Apathetic and oddly tearful, Maya vowed to herself that this would be the very last visit she made to Kyle's *nilkothi*. Each time she had been here, there had been something hard and ugly revealed to disturb her equanimity. She was beginning to dislike the house intensely—and everyone to do with it.

However, she had dragged herself here not only to fulfil her promise to poor Joycie. She owed Kyle a long-pending favour that went back almost five years; her pride would not allow her to let that remain unpaid. With the safe delivery of the bequest to its rightful inheritors, she would consider that her obligation to Kyle had been finally cancelled.

The sounds of galloping hooves and of a horse being reined came from outside to announce Kyle's return. A moment later he walked into the parlour where she waited. Mumbling something inaudible, presumably an apology for having kept her waiting, he threw only a cursory glance in her direction. Then, ignoring her, he shrugged off his jacket, tossed it towards the hazel-eyed servant lad who had followed him into the room, and flung himself into a chair, obviously tired. The Eurasian servant boy—no more than about ten years old, and one whom Maya had not seen before—hurried to his side, crouched at his feet and eagerly started to pull off one of his heavy riding boots.

"No!" Kyle wrenched his foot roughly out of the boy's grasp. "You will never be a man unless you learn not to grovel at anyone's feet!" The boy sat back on his haunches and stared up at Kyle, puzzled by the rebuke. "I can remove my own boots, son," he said in a gentler tone, as he reached out and tousled the boy's hair. "Now go out and play in the compound. There is nothing more for you to do here."

Confidence restored, the boy burst into smiles and ran happily out of the room.

"Well, what is it this time?" Kyle wiped his moist forehead with a handkerchief. "Are you also having problems with your baronial sibling?"

"With Alistair?" She shook her head. "Why on earth should I have problems with Alistair?"

"Yes, why indeed," he countered sardonically. "Quite the contrary, I should imagine, considering he's a titled pukka." Balancing his foot on a knee, he started to tug off his boot.

It was not a bait to which she was prepared to rise. Too low-spirited to rustle up the energy for pointless badinage, and once again close to tears, she merely lowered her head and pretended to be immersed in her doodles on the window sill. When she saw that he had changed from his riding boots into the polished black shoes the boy had placed in readiness beneath his chair, she said calmly, "No, it is not Alistair."

"Well, what then?" He threw her a withering look. "Afterthoughts about how else to protect your Christian from big bad wolves like me?"

That too Maya ignored. Instead, in silence, she took out the neat little pink velvet pouch she had stitched to house Joycie's precious cache, and laid it on the table in front of him. He squinted up at her, showing his impatience.

"What is it?"

"Why don't you open it and see for yourself?" She returned to her seat by the window.

With a sound of irascibility, he reached for the pouch, tugged at its drawstrings and formed an aperture large enough to peer inside. He frowned and turned the pouch upside down on the table. The pieces of jewellery came cascading out to fall in a sparkling heap on the mottled marble tabletop. Kyle stared, first at the unexpected sight on the table, then at Maya's expressionless face.

"What the devil?" Amazed, he ran out of words.

"The jewellery belonged to Joycie." Maya made her explanations in measured tones, with detachment, wanting only to conclude her duty and flee. "She gave it to me for safe keeping on the day of the fire. In case of her death, she told me, it was to be delivered to you. She said you would know what to do with it."

Whatever reaction Maya had expected from Kyle, it was not what she saw now. As he digested what she had said, the change that came over him was quite startling. Without moving, he seemed to crumple within himself. His skin turned pallid; stretched taut over his high cheekbones, it seemed translucent. In his eyes, usually so full of arrogance and self-sufficiency, there was stupefaction. He sat quite still, regarding the twinkling heap before him in silent bewilderment, entirely at a loss for words.

"Joycie . . . ?" He looked up.

"Yes. She sacrificed her life to salvage this jewellery." She told him exactly how, and he listened closely, his gaze riveted to hers.

When she had finished, he allowed the silence to expand for a while, then got up and, without either comment or question, walked out of the room. He did not look at her. Even so, she caught a glimpse of his face before he averted it: it was full of grief, the wet shine in the corners of his eyes momentarily trapped in a shaft of lamplight. He was out of the room very briefly. When he returned, she saw that although he had tried to mask his raw emotions with a look of unfeeling severity, he had succeeded only partially. He was still shaken, his skin still pale; he seemed unable to cast off the pain that wrapped around him like a sheet.

He sat down, picked up the pieces of jewellery one by one and examined them with interest, but Maya could see that the interest was superficial; his mind was elsewhere. Most of the ornaments were of filigreed gold, but there was a pearl necklace and a pair of matching earrings (the ones Joycie had worn in the photograph), some rings, an emerald bracelet, three or four brooches with different stones in them, and a heart-shaped pendant set with a single ruby surrounded by sparkling diamonds. This last, in a dainty little box lined with purple satin, was an exquisite piece, obviously the prize of the collection. Both Maya and her mother had admired it for the rich brilliance of the deep red stone, the delicacy of the setting and the fineness of the gold chain through which it was threaded.

Kyle picked up the pendant and, for the first time, his eyes showed a flicker of interest. His gaze was transfixed, but it seemed to Maya that he thought about something else entirely. He sat silent for so long, she wondered if he had forgotten her presence altogether. But then he made a sign to indicate that she should come and sit closer to the table. She could not contain a certain inevitable curiosity and, obediently, she did as ordered.

"Do you know what this is?"

She shook her head.

"It is the Roshanara ruby, reputed to be of Burmese origin and flawless." He seemed awestruck, not so much by the jewel as by the astonishing act of generosity of the donor.

Maya was surprised that Joycie could have been in possession of so precious a gem, but she made no comment.

"The Roshanara had been in the nawab's family for more than two hundred years." He turned it around in his hand. It blinked and bubbled a lush, liquid red, like blood from a wound in his palm. "It was rumoured to have come from the Persian court in the seventeenth century. The nawab's great-great-grandfather acquired it, named it after his wife and gave it to her on the birth of their first son."

"And it was the great-great-grandson, Joycie's . . . friend, who gifted it to her?"

"Yes." A shadow of a smile sat upon his mouth as he twirled the long gold chain idly around his fingers. "I saw it as a child. Once or twice she even let me play with it."

Maya gave him a sharp look. He had never before talked to her of his childhood. "Where, in Lucknow?"

"Yes." He sat as if in a dream, hardly aware that he spoke, still staring at the priceless jewel in his hand. "She was like a child with it. It was what she treasured most in her life." His eyes were remote, as if watching some scene in another dimension. Maya observed him in silence, following the kaleidoscopic expressions flitting across his face in swift succession. She marvelled at how different he looked, metamorphosed into quite another being, like a butterfly fresh out of a chrysalis lost in wonder at another world. "They were all livid, of course, especially the nawab's three wives. They hunted for the pendant everywhere, secretly searched all her possessions, but they could never find it."

She leant towards him, intrigued by this unexpected glimpse into the life he guarded with such insane possessiveness. "Joycie told you all this?"

He nodded absently.

"She was clever with her hiding places," Maya remarked, saddened by the irony of her observation.

He did not hear her, deep in the recesses of long-forgotten memory. "She knew that if they did find it, they would never let her keep it. For years she stored it with. . . ." He stopped, but with such abruptness that he startled himself, roused from a dream he was not even aware that he was having.

"With?" She prompted, dazzled by the inadvertent glimpses into his cloistered life.

But he only stared past her, his face again blank. "It doesn't matter," he said shortly. "What matters is that she retained it, as was her right." He put the ruby and all the other pieces back into the pouch and set it aside, as if the jewels were of no further interest to him. He leant forward and crossed his arms on the table.

"What else did Joycie say?" His stare was so penetrating that it was Maya who was forced to lower her eyes.

"She said the jewellery was for . . . the lady."

He showed no embarrassment. "What else?"

"She was delirious. She kept mumbling about a man and a 'devil critter,' and also something that sounded like 'mouth'—I couldn't understand any of it."

He exhaled the breath that he had been holding; it made a hissing sound. "She said nothing else that made sense?"

"No. Soon after she gave me the jewellery and her instructions for it, she slipped into unconsciousness. To the best of my knowledge she never spoke again."

Once again he was filled with emotion, gazing without blinking at his entwined fingers resting on the table. When he finally looked up, it was without hostility.

"Thank you."

The two words sounded strained, as if extracted with immense effort. But even this meagre expression of gratitude caught Maya unawares, giving her a swift thrill of utterly disproportionate pleasure. "It was nothing," she said impassively. "I was glad to perform a last errand for someone who was a friend." She stood up, preparing to leave.

"Wait." Maya stopped in her tracks, startled by the peremptory command. "There is someone I would like you to meet again."

"No!" She went rigid. "It is not necessary."

"It *is* necessary!"

"Your personal life is no concern of mine, Kyle."

"Your personal life too!"

There was something about the way he said it that sent a chill down her veins. "My personal life . . . ?"

He merely shook his head, refusing to say anything further. There was no sign of mockery on his face, only a look of resignation. He got up and went to the door. Obviously the servant boy was hovering outside because Maya heard them speak, although she could not discern what was being said. He returned to stand facing her with his hands on his hips, his head tilted. "It is mandatory that you know more." He spoke with strange intensity; she felt her breath compress further. "It is no longer fair that you should not."

"No!" She clenched her fists by her sides, fighting off the creeping advance of fear. "I refuse to be involved in. . . ."

"You are already involved."

Maya opened her mouth to deliver a stinging rebuttal, but it was too late. The curtains parted and Nafisa Begum entered. This time her face was uncovered. Only a thin veil was draped over her head. She limped slowly across the room and sat down opposite Maya. Kyle and she exchanged a few words, none of which Maya heard, too enraged by this second hateful encounter into which he had forced her. Her eyes firmly fixed to the tip of her shoe, she fumed inwardly as they talked, barely listening. But with the woman sitting directly opposite her, it was impossible to avoid looking at her without revealing her own discomfiture. Seeing no other option, Maya finally raised her eyes and risked a cursory glance.

She found herself looking into soft, almond-shaped eyes the colour of a warm sea, of new spring leaves and young paddy fields. They were uncommonly large and luminous, heavily fringed with black, set in an oval face, the skin of which was as smooth and polished as pale, pale sandal paste. Maya quickly dropped her glance and found herself focusing on the hands, supple even in repose, as they rested one above the other in her lap, the hands of a dancer. There was an odd sort of tranquillity about the way the woman sat, like one used to patiently waiting for others or, perhaps, upon others.

A gust of breeze through the window rippled the woman's veil and it slipped off her head onto her shoulder. Maya's breath froze: woven into the black, glossy hair were unmistakable streaks of grey! She stared in confusion, her thoughts tumbling over each other. Then her eyes went compulsively back to the woman's face and, with a boldness born of surprise, she scrutinised it closely. Around the eyes there was a faint tracery of lines radiating outwards, as delicate as brushwork. On either side of the small, coral mouth, enclosing even white teeth, there were furrows etched into the skin. There was no doubt that at one time the face had been ravishingly beautiful, like a Moghul miniature in the classical perfection of its features. But now what it appeared to relate was a tale of sorrow: the lustrous eyes were melancholy and full of sadness, reminders perhaps of a life that had been hard and unkind and beset with struggle. Nafisa Begum was still youthful, but she was by no means young; she appeared to be well over forty.

Maya's shocked eyes turned towards Kyle as he watched her intently. She swallowed to lubricate her throat. "Who . . . who is she?"

Kyle did not answer her question. He merely turned his head to look towards the curtained doorway, and almost immediately, the boy came in, pushing before him a large perambulator containing something that, at first sight, appeared to be not quite human. As Maya's befuddled mind once more came into focus, she realised why. The creature—in that first instant of horror there was no other word she could think of to describe what she saw—that lay in the perambulator was hideously deformed. The torso was bulbous and oblong; the arms, thin and short, like twigs, were entirely out of proportion with the body. Curled up at the bottom of the perambulator was a pair of spindly legs; the feet attached at the extremities were turned inwards.

It was, however, on the face that Maya's eyes remained riveted, for it was this that was truly grotesque. Horribly misshapen, the oversized scalp was hairless, like a skinned rabbit, and merged into a sloping forehead that was high and wide. The beady little eyes, rolling about in a sea of pinkish flesh, were blank and obviously unseeing. From its mouth, slack with thick, glistening lips, several yellow teeth protruded. The top lip was slitted and the tear went right up to the base of a flat, splayed nose exposing fleshy gums underneath.

De devil chile wid de. . . .

She suddenly understood Joycie's abortive gesture and Maya's palm flew to her own mouth; she felt sick to her stomach. Eyes closed, she stood swaying on her feet, gulping in long, deep breaths to suppress the nausea. When she opened her eyes, the sick feeling had passed but the sense of horror persisted. She couldn't take her eyes off the creature, her mind numb.

"Who . . . ?"

"A person," Kyle replied calmly. Tucked somewhere in the level tones was a tiny crease of pain. "A human being."

"A child?" she whispered.

"A child. And yet not a child. Last winter he completed his fifteenth year."

Fifteen—she could scarcely believe it! The size of the torso indicated an age of no more than five! The boy opened the orifice he had for a mouth and from its corners a steady dribble emerged. The mouth opened wider and he started to wail. It was the same wolverine sound she had heard that first night on the embankment. This time she was not taken by surprise, but even so, the hair at the nape of her neck rose and her skin felt cold and prickly.

Before the woman could move, Kyle leapt towards the perambulator, knelt beside it, and very carefully wiped the dribble off the child's mouth with a white towel. Equally carefully, he dabbed dry the stained bedclothes, then patted and caressed and cajoled with hands as light as down, tender and full of love. He talked in soft, murmuring tones, soothing and comforting with sounds that obviously held meaning for the boy, for presently the wailing stopped, replaced by contented grunts and gurgles. Maya realised that the boy's eyes, blank and unseeing at first sight, were not so at all. Light green, like the woman's, they were small and deeply set and by no means pretty, but suddenly there was in them a curious shine of awareness, even of intelligence. They no longer rolled aimlessly: they were fixed on Kyle's face with very deep concentration, as if conveying mute thoughts in wordless communication. Slowly almost painfully, the deformed mouth split sideways in what could only be construed as a smile. A thin arm twitched, snaked up and reached out. Fumbling and quivering, the stubbled fingers brushed Kyle's cheek, then fell back exhausted.

It was an astonishing scene, unreal but also immensely touching in its simple expressions of love and commitment. Maya scarcely breathed, unable to take her eyes off Kyle's transformed face as she watched in abject fascination, feeling the sting of tears beneath her eyelids. It had never occurred to her that Kyle's heart could be touched by anything even remotely warm, except anger. Something within her stirred and strengthened. For an instant, a whisper in time, she felt the return of a forgotten feeling. It overwhelmed her, submerging all other emotions, sweeping away everything that lay in its path. Kyle suddenly turned and looked at her, taking her by surprise. Her momentary trance snapped. She flushed and averted her eyes, dismayed that he had already read too much in them.

"Tell me the truth, Kyle," she said, her mouth trembling. "Who *are* they?"

Kyle rose to his feet wiping his hands on a handkerchief, and came to stand next to her, unaware of his inadvertent revelations, uncaring of hers. "You mean, you haven't found out yet?" There was half-hearted sarcasm in the question, as if the very effort had tired him out.

Maya shook her head, not trusting herself to speak.

He did not answer her question, but merely walked to the table and resumed his seat. Maya was about to repeat her question and demand that he answer it when, for the first time, the woman spoke. She had so far sat in silence, almost motionless, her hands still folded in repose on her lap, her eyes as tranquil as a forest pool.

"I am Lal's mother."

"Lal?"

"The man you know as Kyle."

Silence fell in the room, then thickened and turned so intense that even the ticking of the clock sounded like an intrusion. Maya stared, first at the woman, then at Kyle, not knowing what to say. She did not know what she had expected but it was not that, although now she saw that, perhaps, it should have been.

"Your *mother?*" Maya could not stop staring at the once beautiful face, struck again by the impeccable grace, the delicate refinement.

Kyle laughed. "Why are you surprised? You don't think I'm entitled to have a mother?"

She went scarlet. "Don't be silly! I was . . . I thought. . . ." She felt foolish and the words entangled in her throat.

"I know what you thought!"

He took the pouch of jewellery sitting forgotten on the table, rose and handed it to his mother. He spoke to her softly in Urdu; Maya could not catch the words, but she knew that he was telling her about Joycie's bequest to her. Listening to him, the woman's eyes filled with tears. She turned to Maya.

"I thank you for your kindness to Joycie. She was very dear to me. When they put her out on the streets, it was to me that she turned. I was happy to take her in as one of our own." She looked at the pouch cupped in her hands and the tears rolled down her cheeks. "It was I who kept these safe for Joycie when they wanted to snatch everything away from her."

As she had done before, she spoke in the chaste Urdu spoken in and around Lucknow, capital of the erstwhile state of Oudh. The few words were said in a voice that had the quality of honey, rich and sweet and golden. Perhaps, Maya thought irrelevantly, she had also been a singer. The woman sighed, wiped her eyes with a corner of her veil and rose. She went over to the perambulator, laid a quick kiss on the forehead of the boy and wheeled him out of the room. Over her shoulder she threw a small, sad smile in Maya's direction.

Still confused, still filled with wonder at the beauty of this woman who was Kyle's mother, believing and yet incredulous, Maya slowly regained her composure. She now understood the reason for the generous bequest, the reason for the love between the dead woman and Kyle.

"You want me to know all this for a purpose, don't you?"

"Yes."

Cold sweat started to form on Maya's palms. She rubbed them hard against the sides of her skirt. Within her ribcage her heart beat like a kettle-drum; she knew that she was about to learn something terrible.

"I want to know who the boy is."

"You see no resemblance to anyone you know?"

"No!"

"Well, you obviously didn't look closely enough."

She shook her head, knowing that he mocked her, fearful of this new game that he devised.

"His name is Montague. I share a mother with him but not a father." He paused to let his words sink in, then added softly, "His father he shares with Christian Pendlebury."

She gasped. "Is this a joke, Kyle?" she asked, stiff with outrage.

He smiled. "I did tell you that Christian and I had a great deal in common."

Was he serious?

"But I don't . . . understand."

"Don't you?"

But then of course she did and, for a moment, she thought she would faint. She clutched at the chairback to steady herself, too stupefied to think of sitting down. As the significance of what he said sank in with all its ugliness, she was suddenly furious.

"I don't believe you!" she spat out fiercely. "How dare you make up such reprehensible lies, how *dare* you!"

Kyle shrugged, untouched by her temper. "I felt it was my duty to inform you of the truth. To believe or not is your privilege."

"It's simply another one of your fabrications," she whispered weakly, trembling, hardly knowing what she said. "A monstrous lie. . . ." Her voice tailed away, her instinct telling her that it was not. There was the terrible ring of truth in Kyle's voice, the clean look of truth on his face. Even though every fibre in her body rebelled at accepting such a horror, she knew that he did not lie. Her anger evaporated in a surge of despair. "Sir Jasper fathered this . . . child?"

"Yes."

"When? *Where?*"

"When he was an Assistant Commissioner in Lucknow before and during the Mutiny. My mother was a dancer at the court of the king, Wajid Ali Shah, before he was deposed. A courtesan, if you like." He spoke easily and with dispassion. "The rest is not your business."

"Anything to do with Christian is my business!"

"This isn't his business either. It is between Jasper Pendlebury, my mother and me."

"Does he know that they are . . . here?"

"Sir Jasper?" Kyle smiled. "Not yet."

Her legs suddenly gave way and she sat down, the fear expanding. "Does *Christian* know?"

"No."

"Are you going to tell him?"

"Don't you think that I should?"

Her numbed brain sprang to life. "No, oh *no!*"

"Why not? Don't you consider it is his right to know?"

"Christian adores his father, Kyle," she whispered, "he *worships* him."

"All the more reason for him to know."

"You admitted it wasn't his business." She fluttered with panic, her throat parched with it.

"It isn't." He gave her a sly smile. "Do you still want to blazon it on that blackboard?"

The rest of her protests died in her throat. How easily he had outwitted her. How he must have laughed at her earnest endeavours, her lofty claims and threats. How cleverly he had made it *her* secret rather than his, knowing that in her own interests, she would be compelled to guard it with her life!

"Christian will be devastated," she said helplessly, the terrible scene already vivid in her imagination.

"In what way does that concern me?"

"It concerns *me*, Kyle! If Christian ever. . . ." She stopped. She was beginning to plead, to humiliate herself, and she despised herself for it. Kyle would not bend, this she knew. But then, she decided, neither would she. "I recommend that you do not tell Christian," she said coldly, once again gripped by that special fury she had never felt against anyone but him. "If you do, you will regret it."

He considered her with amusement. "Oh? Well, if not a blackboard, then what is your weapon to be this time?"

"A Colt revolver, Kyle," she said calmly. "You see, if you ever tell Christian, I will kill you."

CHAPTER

16

W HEN IN 1813 THE CROWN revised the charter of the East India Company to abolish all monopolies save those of tea and
opium, one of the very first Englishmen to jump onto the golden
bandwagon of opportunity was Caleb Birkhurst, Alistair's grandfather.
Disdaining involvement in the thriving but hazardous China Coast trade,
Caleb Birkhurst established the Farrowsham Agency House soon after the
revision of the charter. A canny, silver-tongued salesman, he made mid-
dlemanship into an art form, matching supply with demand with such
skill that it was not long before the shekels started to pour into Farrowsham's coffers. A few years later he bought a vast indigo plantation in
North Bengal. With good management, modern English machinery and
healthy labour practices, he soon converted that too into a gold mine.
Indeed, by the time Caleb Birkhurst retired to Suffolk to devote himself to
the management of his equally prosperous English holdings and to his
duties in the House of Lords, it was said that the Agency minted its own
currency.

Half a century later, however, the Farrowsham ledgers related a different tale. "Rather a sorry picture, isn't it?" Alistair made a face as he
snapped shut the final ledger. "I can't see much hope in all this, can you?"

Willie shrugged. "That's what I've been tryin' to tell you, laddie. Farrowsham's had its day, more's the pity." He had been explaining the
books to young Alistair for days, becoming increasingly depressed in the
process, relapsing often into nostalgia. Now again a faraway look came
into his faded eyes. "T'was na like this once," he said wistfully. "Nae man
alive could juggle borrowin' and lendin' rates like your grandpa, lad.
Company blokes were forbidden direct business activity. Old Caleb persuaded them to hand o'er their savin's to the Agency for investment. I was

a wee lad then, still wet behind the ears, but, God's truth, t'was bloody guid to see him rake in the stuff, e'en through the financial disasters of the thirties." His narrow chest expanded with pride. "Farrowsham made it faster than anyone, 'cept perhaps Trident."

Enthralled by Donaldson's endless fund of stories about his grandfather, Alistair listened eagerly. At the mention of Trident, however, his expression soured. "We made our profits legally, Mr. Donaldson," he remarked with disdain, "not through intimidation and piracy. I find the comparison odious. Besides, I have no wish to talk about Trident."

Donaldson sighed. "Very well, lad. Then let us talk about Mooljee's offer for the Agency and the manse. 'Tis by far the best so far."

"But he's only a moneylender."

"Na any more," Donaldson amended. "Noo he calls himself a merchant prince, hah!"

"And you are sure he can afford to meet the price we have quoted?"

Donaldson sucked in his cheeks. "Well, he trades in silver and gold coin, has a hoard of bullion, owns a bank or two, a stable of racin' horses and shops and property all o'er toon. And he gives seven to twelve percent interest, sometimes more. I'd say he's aboot as solvent as the British Treasury. Aye," he concluded drily with a vigorous nod, "I reck'n he can afford it."

"Oh. Well, does he plan to live in the mansion should we be willing to sell it to him?"

"Withoot a doot, laddie, withoot a doot—that bein' the whole bloody idea." Donaldson made no secret of his disgust. "It'd be a damn sight better to sell to the American although, God knows, that's bad enough!"

The remark brought a smile to Alistair's mouth. "All right then, what about the offer from Behram Dhunjibhai? I should imagine a Parsi millionaire who's lived and traded in Shanghai for four decades is more likely to keep up the house in the manner to which it was once accustomed. As far as Mooljee is concerned, I'm inclined to let him have the Agency. He might not be able to tell French tapestry from a sampler, but as a businessman I've heard he has a nose for profit as keen as that of a foxhound. If anyone can revive Farrowsham, he can." He flicked open another ledger and ran a finger down the column. "Now, these rented shops and houses in. . . ."

For a while they discussed various offers for all the many properties the Birkhurst family owned in the city, rejecting some, tentatively accepting others. Then, when that matter too had lapsed, Donaldson ventured to stir the subject troubling him the most. "That leaves the plantation. What do you suggest we do with that?"

Alistair shrugged and stretched his legs under the table. He fanned himself absently with a large sheet of paper. "You truly believe it cannot be revived?"

"Aye. We'd be bloody fools to try."

"Why? They say no plant in the world can rival Indian indigo in quality."

Donaldson worked his mouth around his shag and spat in the brass spittoon resting at his feet. "True. There was a time when nat'ral Indian indigo had the sharpest blue that e'er was. But that was a long time ago. Noo nae one wants nat'ral indigo. 'Tis a matter of a few years 'ere chemical dyes take o'er the market."

"Surely not the world market?"

"Na yet, but soon. Indigo cultivation's na been remunerative to the peasantry for more than ten years noo. The 'fifty-nine Act to protect peasant-tenants opened the pot of maggots that started the bleedin' rot." He rummaged within a pile of papers on his desk, produced a bound booklet and placed it on the table before Alistair. "Read that, laddie, it's worth a look if you want to learn aboot the indigo belt."

"Yes, yes, I know all about the Famine Commission Report." Alistair threw a disinterested glance at the booklet. "I accept that the Bengal planters themselves are to blame for the messes in indigo cultivation. But what I want to know is, how does indigo in Bihar still prosper despite all these same factors? The peasants there seem happy enough to accept the higher prices planters are offering, and I've heard that cultivation continues to flourish. Why can't we make similar concessions and rejuvenate production on our plantation?"

"It's na only a question of concessions, laddie," Donaldson explained patiently. "The rot goes deeper than that—labour problems, liquidity problems, staff problems. Nae manager wants to live in that hellhole with its bad roads, its squatters and dacoit gangs and chronic bickerin's with local zamindars. If that's na enough, the indigo belt crawls with bleedin' missionaries who go aboot preachin' and convertin' and turnin' native lives upside doon with ideas the peasants and tribals have n'er e'en heard of."

"Well, just as a matter of interest, how much *would* it cost to get the plantation going again?"

Donaldson snorted. "A fortune, laddie, a fortune! An' once you started, t'would be a bottomless pit. 'Tis simply na worth it—if that's what you're thinkin'."

"How much is a 'fortune'?"

Donaldson crinkled his eyes in thought and shifted his wad of tobacco from one cheek to the other. "Thirty, forty thoosand—somethin' like that."

Alistair whistled under his breath. "As much as that?"

"Aye. Maybe more." Donaldson crossed his arms on the desk. "Crichton's sealed off three of the six boilers because of leakages. All the vats need new linin's, the canal's breached with na funds to repair it with, and the pumps ain't workin'. And I'm sick and tired of payin' oot huge sums to the local moneylender to clear Crichton's debts, some fishy as all hell." He added with a look of stern warning, "If 'tis revival you're thinkin' of, I have to tell you that Farrowsham canna spare the cash with profits doon as they are. The money would *have* to come from England, and you know your grandma's views on that. Nae more investment in this damn country, and that's that!"

"All right, even if we can't sell it as a plantation, surely four thousand acres in a block should carry their own value, Mr. Donaldson? And prosperous Indian businessmen like Mooljee, for instance, are surely as hungry for land here as people are anywhere else? That mansion my grandfather built on the estate alone must be worth a tidy sum."

"Aye, lad, but a hoose with nae one to live in it is a liability noo—na like it once was. Your grandpa and grandma used to have o'ernight parties for hundreds, with dance floors laid and canopies under which to. . . ." He delved once more deep into his memories, each one alive and vibrant in the retelling.

When the narration was over, Alistair sighed. "Yes, but the land is still there," he pointed out. "I would have imagined offers would come pouring in for it."

Donaldson shook his head. "Nae for our land, miles from any centre of government, or from any toon, for that matter. T'was a time that was a virtue, but na noo, no any more. Today, you canna get guid English managers to live so far oot. Even Mooljee says he would na touch it with a tent pole."

Having exhausted all his arguments, Alistair relapsed into brooding silence.

Donaldson sat back, regarded the obstinate face of his young master and tapped the desk top with a pencil. "Well, as it happens, there is *one* rather curious offer for the plantation you might be willin' to consider. . . ."

Alistair groaned. "Not Amos Raventhorne's again!"

"Na. This offer is for the plantation only. The cotton mill is na part of it."

"Oh?" Alistair showed his surprise. "Then who from?"

"Kyle Hawkesworth."

"Hawkesworth? You mean, the editor of that weekly paper?"

"Aye."

Alistair looked blank. "What the devil would he want with a derelict indigo plantation?"

"I have nae idea, but that's who the offer's from. He came to see me yesterday, at the hoose."

"Is it a serious offer? I mean, can he pay such a large sum? I thought he ran his paper on a shoestring!"

"He does. But for the land he offers to pay full price."

Alistair slowly sat up, his face brightening. "Well, in that case, why are we delaying? Tell him we'll. . . ." He broke off and his expression changed. "Wait a minute—Hawkesworth is Eurasian, isn't he?"

"Aye. Very much so."

"And a friend of Amos Raventhorne?"

Donaldson grimaced and shrugged.

Alistair's jaw set into a hard line. "Does he think I'm a fool?" he asked coldly. "Hawkesworth wants to buy on behalf of Raventhorne."

"But he's na bid for the cotton mill," Donaldson pointed out, "only the plantation. It's the *mill* that Amos wants, not that danged plantation, and he's na made a secret of that."

"Be that as it may, I am *not* prepared to consider Hawkesworth's offer," Alistair snapped. "There's a trick in it somewhere. I can smell it!"

Donaldson shook his head wearily. "That plantation is a white elephant, laddie—sell while you can. There ain't no more offers comin'. And you're *n'er* goin' to run that goddamned mill!" He raised two clawlike hands to scratch his sparse head of hair in a gesture of desperation. "What the devil are we goin' to do with the blasted thing?"

Alistair gave him a lofty smile. "Last night a chap at the Club said that an American called Landon started and ran a successful cotton mill in Broach, in western India, some years ago. It might not be such a bad idea to follow suit."

Donaldson noticed the glint in the amber eyes and his heart sank. He swore generously under his breath. "By Christ, you take me back to the days of your mother!" His voice was hushed with awe. "I swear I see noo where you get it!"

"Oh?" Alistair picked up the copy of the Famine Commission Report lying on the desk and started to flick through its pages, allowing the silence to expand without making any comment. Finally he asked, very casually, "Well, what was she like when she was with Farrowsham?"

"Your mother?" Donaldson gave him a sidelong glance, not missing the rather overdone nonchalance. For a moment he feigned thought. "Well, if you want the truth, she was like a goddamned mule, that's what!"

"A mule?"

"Och aye. Stubborn." He nodded with great satisfaction. "And as cussed as the hounds of hell. She was wilful, devil may care, blunt as a whetstone and an infernal nuisance all roond." He sat back and glared across the desk at Alistair's startled face. Then he started to chuckle and his watery eyes melted. "But she was 'un of a kind, laddie, 'un of a kind," he said softly, taking a long soughing breath. "There's n'er been a lassie to match her in wits, and that's the goddamn truth." He chortled to himself. " 'Cept for my darlin' Cornelia, I've na known any woman with more gall, with the nerve of bloody Lucifer himself!" He leaned forward, his eyes shining with remembrance. "Know what she did once when a danged creditor refused to settle a bill? She rode down to Vansittart Row 'un weekday afternoon with a terrified bailiff in tow and then, blow me doon if she dinna. . . ."

He related the incident of long ago with such gusto that one anecdote led inevitably to another and then yet another. Alistair asked no more questions but neither did he interrupt. It was obvious that he listened with great concentration, the Famine Commission Report lying forgotten in his lap.

"She was the only 'un who could give that rascal *Kala Kanta* a run for his money," Donaldson concluded with a satisfied cackle.

"*Kala* what?"

"*Kala Kanta,* a black thorn. That's what Jai Raventhorne was known as in the English business community." He slapped his thigh and roared with laughter. "And by Jove, you've n'er kenned a thorn that could prick the sides of the white man harder than *that* 'un!"

Alistair's face was stiff with distaste. "I don't think I want to. . . ."

"Och, shure you do!" Donaldson said with a brisk wave of his hand. "Listenin' does na harm, noo does it?"

Alistair glared at his boots. "Well, what was he like then?" he growled.

"Like her," Donaldson said. "Without a match."

"Odd!" Alistair snorted. "I've heard he was a ripe bastard!"

"Aye, that too in many ways." Donaldson agreed willingly enough. "Satan's pup, if there e'er was one. But by Christ he na lacked for guts either! Given the chance, he'd na stop at challengin' the gods themselves. Noo, as for Master Amos." He peered upwards at the ceiling and stopped.

Alistair let the silence enlarge, then swallowed hard. "Amos?" He did not look at Donaldson.

"Master Amos is a very diff'rent kettle o' fish from his father. A clean, hardworking lad, soft-spoken and a gentleman." He tapped a fingernail on the tabletop and his lips thinned in a pointed smile. "'Least until noo."

"Hah!"

Donaldson ignored the snort of contempt and dug his plough deeper into the furrow he had been preparing. "He's set his heart on that mill, you know."

Alistair shrugged and again picked up the report. "That's his hard luck, not mine. And I would be grateful if you would now accept that the subject is closed."

Donaldson's expression cooled. "Your grandma's given me very spec'fic instructions aboot what's to be done, your lordship," he said, chilling further and reverting to the proper formalities as a mark of his displeasure. "You are to sell the plantation, the manse, the Agency and all other assets, and then return to England. Her ladyship is absolutely clear on that."

"Why?" Alistair countered with a continuing touch of defiance. "If I wish to stay longer, I damn well will, Mr. Donaldson. Together we could perhaps. . . ."

"I would na coont on that, your lordship," Donaldson interrupted icily. "I happen to have other plans for the future."

Despite his best efforts, Alistair's face fell. "You are quite serious then about retiring, Mr. Donaldson?"

"Och aye. And I wrote and told her ladyship so."

"We are both hoping that you will change your mind if. . . ."

"Na, laddie. I canna. Na noo." His irritation vanished in a surge of sentimentality. "I've had a grand life with the Birkhursts, a *grand* life," he muttered, steeped in melancholy. "But since Cornelia went, I find myself thinkin' of Pitlochry and the Isles and oftimes in my dreams I see myself back at Clyde side with the braw fisher lads of the village."

"You're not *frightened* of a fresh challenge, are you, Mr. Donaldson?" Alistair goaded in the hope of provoking him into a change of mind.

Willie Donaldson closed his eyes and laid his head back against his chair. He smiled sadly to himself. No, he was not a coward. In his five decades as an India hand, he had fought many battles in the commercial jungles of Calcutta, some lost, many won. He opened his eyes and looked hard at his young protégé. "Na, laddie, I'm na frightened, simply tired and old and played oot. There was a time when I would na have turned away from a fight such as you're lookin' for with Amos. But noo, with neither the mind nor the body for it, I'm nae langer fit for the cut and thrust of pers'nal rivalries. 'Sides, I'm far too old a dog to learn new tricks, laddie."

Alistair struggled manfully with his disappointment but looked openly crestfallen. "Well, if that is your wish, then I suppose you must retire and return home, Mr. Donaldson. I will, of course, arrange a handsome pension so that you do not lack for any comfort."

"Home!" Donaldson sat mulling over that for a moment, playing absently with his wispy whiskers, then he laughed bitterly. "Scotland for me is a fool's paradise, laddie. I dream of it, but if I went there I'd die a lonely, bleedin' stranger in my own land. I've been in this accursed country since I was a snot-nosed lad. India is the only home I've e'er known. For 'un," he attempted to raise a pale smile, "I've n'er learned e'en to clean my own pipe—I'd be bloody *lost* without my old *khidmutgar!*" He gave a shaky laugh and wiped his eyes with the back of his hand. "There's a patch here in the cemetery that's marked oot for me next to my Cornelia. And I reck'n *that's* where my final retirement'll be."

Seeing the feisty old Scotsman so unusually dispirited, Alistair too felt the onset of depression. He knew that, despite his failing health and advancing years, Willie Donaldson was more than capable of negotiating the sales of the Indian properties on his own. Why then in heaven's name had *he* bothered to come to this damnably alien country that had so little to commend it?

But Alistair knew only too well why he had come. And that depressed him even further.

When Kyle arrived at the lake, well beyond Champatollah to the north of the city, Sir Jasper was waiting for him.

It was soon after the hour of dawn. In the pale light, the world looked somnolent and deserted. The waters of the lake, covered with lime green and splashes of lavender hyacinth, lay still. The air was faintly moist, tasting of mist and humus. On the other side of the waters, rolling softly out of the early morning vapours, was the white cone of a village temple surrounded by an untidy sprawl of thatched roofs and banyan trees. A bank of dark, overweight clouds lowered in a corner of the ash grey sky, ready to strike.

The monsoons were about to arrive.

Kyle had no need to inquire why Sir Jasper had chosen such a strange hour and place for their meeting, nor did Sir Jasper volunteer the information. The reason was subsumed in their tacit mutual understanding. The note summoning Kyle had been written personally by Sir Jasper and delivered by his bearer, and it had brought a smile to Kyle's lips; this was one appointment, he knew, Sir Jasper would not have entrusted Leonard

Whitney to make. In any case, Whitney had been asked to return to his duties in the Lieutenant-Governor's office, already replaced by a young English accountant. Kyle had no doubt that Whitney's return had a direct bearing on his own friendship with him.

Sir Jasper was seated on a small mound concealed from the lake behind a cluster of bushes. As always, his back was ramrod straight, his expression alert and his brow clear of anxiety or even unease. He wore a dark brown corduroy riding habit and gleaming high leather boots, their spurs shining like mirrors. Despite the early hour he looked patrician, confident, in customary control of himself and his environment. Across his lap rested a twelve-bore rifle. Behind him, a gun bearer stood at attention guarding the spare rifles, the boxes of ammunition, a cane picnic basket and all the accoutrements of a gentlemanly excursion. A second attendant sat on his haunches by a kerosene stove, brewing tea. Judging by the size of the morning's haul lying beside the gunny sack under the tree, it was obvious that Sir Jasper had been gainfully occupied for some time. But then, Kyle knew, he was a gifted huntsman, able to sense prey with unerring accuracy merely through sound and scent even when none was visible to the naked sight.

As Kyle rode up and dismounted, one of the bearers took the reins of his horse, a magnificent midnight. The two men stared at each other. It was Sir Jasper who spoke first. When he did, it was with that flattering warmth that had charmed so many, an irresistibly appealing balance between effusiveness and formality.

"Who would have thought that we would meet again after all these years!" The large hand that engulfed Kyle's was energetic and enthusiastic, the smile wide and the expression untroubled. Sir Jasper spoke in Urdu and it was almost as fluent and colloquial as it had been fifteen years ago.

"Yes, who indeed," Kyle murmured in response.

The calm, smiling eyes of the older man made a cursory appraisal. "I would not have recognised you now, Lal," he said using the old nickname. "I certainly did not that first evening when we disembarked at the Ghat."

Kyle shared in the smile. "I would have recognised you anywhere, Sir Jasper."

There was only the slightest flicker in Sir Jasper's eyes as he received what might have been a compliment. A handsome, generously built man, loose-limbed and lithe, he carried his tall frame with more grace than one would have imagined. Not yet fifty and still in his prime, he prided himself on his fitness of both mind and body. His mutton chop whiskers were immaculately trimmed; the cornflower blue eyes sharp and perceptive, the mind behind them even more so. Had it not been for his considerable charm, disarming and often deceptively artless, his skill as a ruthless manipulator might not have been so well concealed. It was said in Whitehall by those who had been closely associated with Sir Jasper over the years that the man had no nerves, or, if he had, they were drawn out of steel.

"The undergrowth here is excellent for hare and partridge when the water level is low, just before the rains," he explained to Kyle. "This used to be one of my most favoured hunting grounds many years ago during my furloughs in Calcutta. I have always been partial to partridge meat."

"Yes, I remember."

They spoke in low voices. Sir Jasper's eyes were half closed, darting about the undergrowth with the keenness of a beagle. He conversed with ease, as if merely continuing a recent encounter, as if they met frequently, as if the intervening years had never been and they were still familiar participants in each other's lives.

There was a rustle in the undergrowth some twenty feet to their right. Both men fell silent. Sir Jasper peered through the rising light for a second, raised his rifle and fired. The bushes fluttered wildly as the leaves danced and a small puff of dust rose like a cloud in the morning air. Then all was again still and silent. Sir Jasper made a signal to the bearer; the man dived into the bushes and re-emerged triumphantly holding a large brown hare by the ears.

"Would you care to have a shot?" Sir Jasper asked.

Kyle shook his head. "It would be wasted on me. Despite your many hours of tutelage, I remain an indifferent marksman." He added after a small pause, "You took me deer hunting once in Lucknow in the forest around Wajid Ali Shah's palace."

"I did?"

"Yes. I volunteered to be your gun-carrier. That was the occasion for my first lesson in gunmanship. You were indulgent enough to allow me a shot then."

"Oh yes, so I did. You brought down a sambhar, if I recall correctly."

"A spotted doe, a nursing mother. She died as she looked at me. There were tears in her eyes. I searched for her sucklings for days, but they too had probably perished. Since then, I have never been able to kill a living creature for sport."

Sir Jasper looked vaguely surprised. "Really? How very curious. Anyway, I taught you how to shoot and you taught me how to fill a chillum. You could call that a fair exchange. I have to admit there is still no one who can arrange a hookah quite as well as you used to." Sir Jasper raised his rifle and peered through the sight at some invisible target. "As a matter of fact, it was my hookah-burdar who brought your memory back to mind," he added lightly.

Kyle acknowledged the remark in silence.

The lines of Sir Jasper's face appeared to soften as his thoughts raced back to another age. "On the whole they were good times, Lal."

"Better for some than for others."

Sir Jasper shrugged. "Yes, but that's the way it always is, isn't it? I often remember those days with great fondness. There was that shop at the corner of that bazaar."

"Hazrat Ganj."

"The one with the Bihari owner that sold those milk sweets shaped in cones and stuffed with nuts and raisins—what are they called?"

"Malai paan."

"Yes. That's it. I used to have a bearer who. . . ." Again he faltered.

"Wali Khan?"

Sir Jasper gave him an amused look. "You always did have an astonishingly sharp memory for detail, didn't you?"

"It is not difficult to remember details of a part of one's life that subsequently influenced the rest of it."

If there was sudden watchfulness behind Sir Jasper's expansive charm, only those who knew him intimately would have been aware of it, as Kyle was. But then the smile again widened and became untroubled. "Well, Wali Khan used to get me a dozen of these sweets for a few pice and I used to sit and enjoy them all by myself. Sometimes I shared them with you, do you remember?"

"Twice."

"Eh?"

"You shared them with me twice. The third time I asked for one, you boxed my head and my nose bled."

Sir Jasper gave an indulgent laugh. "Well, if I did, I have no doubt you deserved it." A bush in front of them near the water's edge rustled and he was again alert, but it was only a large mole blindly groping around for his breakfast. "For all his incompetence as King of Oudh, Wajid Ali Shah truly knew how to enjoy the pleasures of life. He made Lucknow one of the finest capital cities in the north." He nodded in appreciation. "It was from him that I learned to savour every sense individually, to consider each day a gift and to absorb fully whatever it brought." He seemed on the verge of saying something else but then changed his mind.

"And each day did bring you a great deal, Sir Jasper."

He again turned to give Kyle a deep look of appraisal, this time rather more thorough. "Yes, I must say you have come a long way from polishing shoes, running errands and filling chillums!" Nevertheless, he said it pleasantly, taking Kyle's remark in his stride without any sign of offence. "But what you say is quite true, and I have never denied it. It was in Lucknow that the foundations of my career were reinforced. Despite the general slackness of British officialdom before and during the Mutiny—or, perhaps, because of it—even mediocrity stood out like a beacon."

Kyle smiled at the modesty. "But you were never mediocre, Sir Jasper, far from it."

That too he accepted coolly with an imperious tilt of the head, an accolade taken for granted. "I was fortunate enough to serve under first-class men like Henry Lawrence. The apprenticeship has stood me in particularly good stead." He dismissed the subject with a wave. "But all that apart, what truly enchanted me about Lucknow was its ambience of elegance, Lal, its *tehzeeb*—that exquisite tradition of courtesy that sets Lucknow's mannered society apart from all others—and its . . ." He broke off in mid-thought. "You are not known as Lal any more, are you?"

"No."

"Odd that I should never have known your other name. I always called you Lal."

"Or 'boy.' Perhaps you never inquired."

"No, I didn't. I should have." He made the admission freely, with an air of genuine remorse. "Hawkesworth." He rolled the name around his tongue as if assessing a vintage wine. "I suppose you selected that because of your interest in hawking?"

A faint colour touched Kyle's cheeks. "Does it matter?"

"I wouldn't think so." He smiled. "But there was a time, I remember, when you were obsessed with knowing the identity of your father—forgive me if I step beyond my limits."

"It makes no difference now," Kyle replied lightly. "It's just a name, as good as any other."

The morning still was shattered with the strident cry of a bird. It came from a lone peacock perched on a low branch not far from where they sat. All at once, with a graceful spread of wings the bird rose and sailed off the branch, its exquisite plumage sparkling like blue opals in the morning light, its crested head held high with customary hauteur. Even though his thoughts were elsewhere, with a well-trained reflex action Sir Jasper raised his rifle and fired. The huge bird stalled in mid-air. With a final cry of anguished surprise, it somersaulted to the ground, flapped its huge, luminescent wings a few times and then lay still. At a nod from his master, the bearer ran forward and proudly collected the prize of the morning's bag.

"Have you ever tasted peacock meat?" Sir Jasper asked, enormously pleased with himself. "It's the finest game there is."

"No. Many in India consider the peacock to be sacred."

Sir Jasper snorted. "In India, everything is considered sacred, from cow dung to cockroaches!" He bent down to examine with satisfaction the large male bird the bearer presented for his inspection.

"Nevertheless, there was a time when you would not have done that."

"*Autres temps, autres moeurs, mon ami.* If the dinosaurs had realised that, perhaps they might never have had to face extinction." He reseated himself on the rock and laid his rifle down to rest across his knees, finally content with the substantial haul. "To thrive, to fulfil one's potential, one must learn how to grow, how to adapt and adjust, to recognise priorities, to appreciate the inevitability of compromise."

"And of expediency?"

Sir Jasper threw him a quick look. "Yes. That too." He unstrung a small silver flask from a chain attached to his belt and cupped it between his palms. "I learned much during the Mutiny, Lal, every Englishman did—or should have done." He continued to use the old name without being aware of it. "One of the most salutary lessons I learned was that expediency is as much a part of the process of survival as compromise, especially for an Englishman trapped in a colonial maelstrom."

"There was also a time when you might have hesitated to make a confession that branded you a dedicated colonial."

Sir Jasper weighed the remark carefully; he did not smile. All this time he had continued to speak in effortless Urdu. Now, perhaps to drive home his point, he reverted to English. "I have often been told by some allegedly patriotic officials," he said, his manner cooling, "that it is the duty of the

Indian government to think first of the natives, even at the cost of British interests. I no longer accept this thesis. Indeed, I find it offensive, even dangerous. The fact that I am able to participate in your culture, and have passed many pleasing years in this country, no longer conflicts with my essential identity as an Englishman."

"You consider that it once did?"

"Oh yes! When you examine all the factors, Lal, you see that the Englishman's only function in India is to rule. He has no other. There was a period of time when I had lost sight of that." He bent down to tighten a loose shoelace. "As Christian appears to have," he murmured softly. "One can either be fish or fowl or both—but not at the same time."

"You believe that Christian is in danger of losing sight of his identity?"

"Don't you? When missionary zeal supersedes ambition, what is there left?"

Knowing full well to what Sir Jasper referred, Kyle neatly sidestepped the invitation to that particular debate. "But then, is there no more to a man than mere ambition?"

Sir Jasper stared at him hard, his eyes intense. "It is the driving force of a man, Lal, more powerful than any other, and why not? There is no shame in honest ambition."

"No. Only in what one is prepared to do to realise it."

"Sometimes, not even in that, Lal, not even in that."

For an instant, their glances clashed and locked; in Sir Jasper's there was a sort of disarming challenge. But then it was Kyle who looked away. That they could speak after all these years with such brutal frankness came as no surprise to Kyle. Despite their disparities, there was between them a lethal shared knowledge, dormant and as yet deliberately unspoken, but a knowledge of such significance that it made the use of pretence offensive. It was only this knowledge that forged a relationship between them; they had no other common ground to tread. Both had come to this meeting place with an aim in mind. Kyle had no desire for his aim to be diffused by irrelevant dialectics. And he certainly had no desire to launch into a discussion about Christian. He abandoned the argument.

"Why did you want to see me?"

Sir Jasper's shoulders lifted in a slight shrug. "I was curious to know how you had come to acquire the intellectual stature that you obviously have."

"Through a process of very slow, painful evolution, Sir Jasper. And by always remembering that, given a goal—an ambition, if you like—even an unlettered chillum boy might some day find his place in the sun."

"I see. And have you found your place in the sun, Lal?" Sir Jasper asked softly.

"Not yet. But perhaps some day soon."

"Oh?" Sir Jasper frowned, as if uncertain how to proceed further in this very strange and unexpected encounter he would have gladly done without had it not been so vital. There was a minimal silence, heavy and significant; it was no longer possible to postpone reference to the subject uppermost in both minds.

"I was sorry to hear about the death of your mother."

Kyle made no response.

"She was a fine lady, a true artiste. She taught me how to appreciate the nuances of your classical arts. For that I will always be grateful." He got up and, locking his hands behind his back, started to stride up and down. "Had she been alive, she would have been pleased to see you as you are today. I'm glad you have put your opportunities to good use."

"As we both have."

The cornflower blue eyes flickered again. "Yes." He gave a curt nod. "I have already conceded that. Since Lucknow, I have not looked back, nor do I intend to. Anyway, enough of the past." He made a signal to the bearers. "Perhaps you will join me in some *chota hazri?*" As the attendants leapt into action and spread out the maroon dhurrie on the green verge of the lake and arranged two folding stools on it, he patted the silver flask he held in his hands. "A consignment of Cognac has just arrived from France. I can vouch for its excellence."

"Cognac for breakfast?" Kyle raised an eyebrow and shook his head. "I don't drink alcohol during the course of the day. From what I remember, neither did you. In fact, that was one rule you always considered inviolate."

"Well, I don't mind confessing that relaxing that rule has been one of my more pleasurable compromises." His laugh was almost shy, engagingly boyish. "Success is a knife of many edges, my boy. Sooner or later, they start to chafe. The nerves tauten, the muscles creak, and the need for lubrication increases. I find that with the pressures under which I work, a tot or two at any time of the day goes a long way to lessen the inevitable stresses that responsibility brings. Anyhow you will, at least, join me in a smoke while the food is being unpacked—or is that too against all these principles you appear to have suddenly developed?" Lowering himself on to a stool, he invited Kyle to take the other, flicked open a gold cigar case and extended it in his direction.

"By no means." Kyle extracted a cigar, held it up to his nose and nodded. "Fortunately, I have not yet developed the willpower to be able to refuse a genuine Havana."

"A cousin has decided to abandon the civilised world to live in America. It is he who keeps me very generously supplied." There was a moment's silence as they both lit their cigars and, with well-trained carefulness, the bearer placed a cup of tea before Kyle. Sir Jasper unscrewed the cap of his flask, poured himself a drink and sipped. "Did you leave Lucknow soon after your mother passed away?" he inquired casually.

"Shortly thereafter." Kyle exhaled upwards, then stared through the pale blue haze at the opposite bank of the lake where the village was beginning to come alive for the day. "I looked for you everywhere that Friday. I could not find you. They said you had left for Calcutta."

Sir Jasper showed no sign of surprise, nor did he hesitate to identify the day to which Kyle referred. It was a question he had anticipated. "As indeed I had. I was transferred to more urgent duties at an hour's notice. Amid the general chaos of the Mutiny, there was no time for farewells."

He bent down, gathered a handful of wispy leaves that had blown onto the dhurrie and tossed them aside. "Perhaps I should have written to explain, but . . . you know how it was at the time."

Kyle deftly caught a tube of ash from the end of his cigar just as it was about to fall and said nothing.

There was a slight heightening of colour on Sir Jasper's cheeks. He opened his mouth to say something more, but as one of the bearers approached carrying food, he left the thought unsaid. There was a sudden tension in the air between them, soft and humming. With great reverence, the bearer placed a folding table bearing plates of Scotch eggs, cold cuts and neatly deboned roast fowl carved into dainty pieces, before them, then started to butter thick slices of brown currant bread.

Sir Jasper indicated that Kyle should feel free to help himself and lifted a piece of duck onto his own plate. For a while he sat and chewed in silence, his thoughts elsewhere. Then he looked at Kyle and smiled. "There is another reason why I felt I should see you."

Selecting a Scotch egg rather than a portion of the roast fowl, Kyle sliced it into two symmetrical halves. "Yes?"

"I'm not surprised that you chose the career that you have." He discarded the duck and speared a slice of cold meat. "I cannot subscribe to all your views, of course, but I have to confess that you express them well."

"I am flattered by your commendation."

"It cannot be easy to publish a weekly periodical with—if I presume correctly—limited funds." He sliced the meat into small pieces but then merely toyed with them. "I wanted you to know that if I can be of assistance. . . ." He left the rest to be tacitly understood.

Kyle raised an eyebrow. "You offer assistance to a periodical whose views you detest?" he asked, even though he knew why.

"Despite my disapproval of your efforts at rabble-rousing," Sir Jasper clarified with a guileless smile, "I believe there is something to be said for freedom of expression."

Kyle laughed, amused. "You had other views when you threatened to whip that editor in Lucknow—the one whose press was mysteriously destroyed one night."

"As I said, Lal," his expression was undisturbed, "*autres temps, autres moeurs*. Besides, that was a long time ago."

Kyle stared into the green waters of the lake. "I appreciate the thought, but I do not accept donations. They have a way of suddenly sprouting strings."

A trace of annoyance appeared in Sir Jasper's face. "All I meant was that if there is anything that I can do for you. . . ."

"Well, as a matter of fact, there is." Kyle put down his plate and turned towards him. "I have a business proposition that might be of interest to you."

Sir Jasper was somewhat taken aback by the alacrity with which his offer was accepted. "A *business* proposition?"

"Yes."

"I presume you are not unaware that civil servants are prohibited from indulging in business practices while they serve the government?"

"I am aware of that. The proposition I have in mind would not be incompatible with your obligations as a civil servant. On the contrary."

"What kind of a proposition?"

"One that will appeal as much to your community as to mine."

"Oh?"

"Did you, by any chance, happen to read the editorial in my paper this week?"

Sir Jasper shook his head as his lips thinned. "How the devil you manage to stay clear of the Lieutenant-Governor and out of gaol, Lal, I will never know! Yes, I did read it. As usual, it was abrasive and highly exaggerated."

"Abrasive yes, exaggerated no. You cannot deny that the hordes of Eurasian children swarming the alleys and gullies of the city are a source of concern to the English—not out of compassion or conscience, but in the cause of sheer self-preservation."

"No, I don't deny that." The tone was level but there was a tightness around his mouth that made his lips look grey. "Well?"

"The scheme that I have in mind would remove many of these Eurasians from the environs of this city."

"Remove? Good heavens, that does sound draconian!"

"There are means of removal other than extermination," Kyle said drily, throwing him a sidelong glance. "Do you not consider that such a plan would meet with the approval of a great many of your compatriots?"

Sir Jasper shrugged. "I haven't the faintest idea. I don't mean to discourage you, Lal, but to me it sounds like wishful thinking. But then you always were a bit of a dreamer, forever weaving fantasies." He put a small piece of meat in his mouth and washed it down with a sip of Cognac. "Just as a matter of curiosity, where would you remove them to?"

"To a township sufficiently remote from the city to minimise the risk of exposure."

"A township?" He chuckled. "Come now, Lal—we both know that such a township does not exist."

"Not at present. But it could in the future."

"My dear fellow, townships do not materialise out of nothing. They need more than just paper plans and an over-active imagination!"

"The land is already available, almost four thousand acres of it, in North Bengal."

"So?" Some slight signs of impatience were starting to show on Sir Jasper's face. "How does all this concern me?"

"I suggest that the Treasury buys this land."

Sir Jasper first stared, then threw back his head and roared. "Good grief, Lal, if I didn't know otherwise, I would strongly suspect that you've suddenly gone mad!"

"The price would be up to ten pounds per acre for unirrigated land,"

Kyle continued, unperturbed, "and thirty-six pounds for irrigated land. Since the canal on this estate is breached, I presume it would be categorised as unirrigated. That makes the cost just about five lakh of rupees, fifty thousand pounds."

"You *are* mad!" Sir Jasper exclaimed, now more surprised than amused. "And having bought the land, what would the government do with it—build you this ethereal township?"

"No. The government would merely hand over the land as a gift to the Derozio Society. The construction and running of the township would be their responsibility."

"The Derozio Society? What the devil is that?"

"It is an organisation that endeavours to prepare penurious Eurasians for a better life."

Sir Jasper cocked an eyebrow. "You consider the British Government to be a charitable institution devised for the indiscriminate distribution of largesse?"

"Not indiscriminate, no. The fact is that the government does subsidise nineteen thousand patients a day at public dispensaries. It spends almost a million pounds annually on supporting nearly seventy thousand educational institutions in full or part. The budget makes provision for emergency funds in times of national calamities. There is no dearth of headings under which these funds could be made available for the purchase."

Sir Jasper's smile faded. "By Christ, you *are* serious!"

"Absolutely. Given support by the government, the project is not only viable but also advisable—for more than one reason."

Sir Jasper dabbed the corners of his mouth with a napkin and handed his plate to the waiting bearer, even though he had scarcely tasted the food piled onto it. He took a toothpick from a silver container the bearer produced, then sat back, his thoughts racing. He was not a fool; neither, by any means, was Kyle Hawkesworth. The proposition Hawkesworth had made with such impertinence was preposterous, and Hawkesworth must surely know it to be so. It had not the remotest chance of being accepted, either by him or by his government.

The question was, why then had he made it?

As a matter of long-standing principle, Sir Jasper did not believe in precipitate action. No matter how outrageous the obvious, it was his incontrovertible rule never to arrive at a decision on the bases of first impressions. There was certainly some very distinct purpose behind this particularly outrageous suggestion; he would not act until he had discovered what it was.

"Very well, Lal," he finally said, his face expressionless, his thoughts again composed. "So long as you are prepared for disappointment, all I can say is that I am willing to give your proposal my earnest consideration. Could you put it in writing and have it sent to my office?"

"It is already in writing. I thought it might save time if I delivered it to you personally this morning." Kyle walked back to where his horse was tethered and took out a folder from a saddle bag.

Sir Jasper accepted the folder with a brisk nod and handed it to his bearer with instructions for safe keeping. From his waistcoat pocket, he withdrew a watch to ascertain the time. "I regret that I have an appointment at eight. The Lieutenant-Governor has requested me to inspect this new road they are planning." His voice was perfectly normal, his tone pleasantly conversational. It was as if they merely continued a dialogue they had been having earlier.

"The one linking up Dharamtala and Baghbazaar?"

"Yes. As you probably know already, it's been in the planning stage for almost twenty years."

The second bearer hurried up with a carafe of water. He started to pour and, very meticulously, Sir Jasper washed each of his fingers in turn, patting them dry on a small white napkin the bearer presented. The bearer then repeated the ceremony for Kyle's benefit. As Sir Jasper stood up, the bearer ran back to the picnic basket and returned with a long-handled clothes brush with which, very carefully, he brushed down his master's coat and britches. While one bearer attended to the matter of grooming, the other started to clear the dishes and make preparations to depart.

Kyle too rose to his feet. The bearer hurried towards him with the brush, but waving him away, Kyle used the back of his hand for a cursory dusting of his own coat and britches. "The general belief is that the scheme is now moribund and has been postponed indefinitely."

"Well, only because they've run out of money. The Lieutenant-Governor is hoping to negotiate a loan from the Treasury. The original estimate was for eleven lakh rupees. With what was available, they could complete only a third of a mile of the proposed distance. Road building is not my province, of course, but I've been asked to look into the matter."

"Will you sanction the loan?"

"McNaughton appears to believe so." He gave a grim smile. "But then, Bruce has a vested interest in the scheme—as, indeed," he added drily, "he has in every scheme off which money can be skimmed. I'm sure you know that already."

Kyle nodded, his smile minimal. "But you can't deny that the road would relieve some of the traffic congestion along Dharamtala."

Sir Jasper shrugged. "Roads are the responsibility of the local government," he said irritably. "I don't see why we should bail them out of a mess of their own making."

He strode purposefully to the spot where their horses were tethered, and with an athletic jump worthy of a man half his age, vaulted into the saddle. He waited for Kyle to mount his midnight, then extended a hand. "Well, I've enjoyed meeting you again, Lal. You bring back many fond memories of your mother. As I have already said, I hold out no false hopes, but I will certainly look into your proposal as objectively as I can."

Kyle took the profferred hand. "I am most obliged to you for your indulgence, Sir Jasper. I too have enjoyed our little interlude this morning. I hope it will prove beneficial for both of us. It is, after all, a business proposition. I bid you good day." He touched the reins and the midnight galloped away in the direction of the native town.

Arrogant young whippersnapper!

Sir Jasper stared hard at Kyle Hawkesworth's departing back, his bland expression slowly turning into one of acute distaste. He had never liked or trusted Nafisa's son. Even as a boy, he was precocious, shrewd beyond his years, hiding in corners and behind doors listening to that which did not concern him, always exceeding his place. It galled Sir Jasper that circumstances compelled him to meet Hawkesworth, the half-caste bastard of a half-caste dancing girl, as an equal. The encounter had revived all his old impressions of the boy's character. In spite of the fine trappings, his essential deviousness had remained unchanged. He had never been entirely comfortable in the boy's presence; he still wasn't.

He saw now that Hawkesworth's association with his son was not just undesirable, it was dangerous. It was fortunate that the friendship was temporary, that Christian would be away before long. Even so, Sir Jasper's intuition told him that during the course of his encounter this morning with an almost forgotten past, the seed of something noxious had been planted between him and Kyle Hawkesworth. Much had been said; he sensed, however, that what was of far greater significance was what had *not* been said. And it was the same unerring instinct that warned Sir Jasper that that noxious seed had something to do with Nafisa.

The morning had turned warm and sunny, but Sir Jasper shivered. He felt as if someone had suddenly walked over his grave.

Sometime during the night the monsoons broke over Bengal.

For days anxious farmers had been watching the skies, testing the winds against wet, trembling fingers, and chanting mantras to propitiate the whimsical gods of the weather. There had been massive cloud formations but no rain since the nor'westers had ceased; the earth, parched and rock hard, lay gasping in the turgid heat of summer. Unlike the transient nor'westers of April that brought only momentary relief, the monsoons were the life source of India. For three months they nursed the fields, nurtured the newly planted crops, and revived and refurbished into sparkling greenness the gaunt, arid landscapes left by the hot weather. A mean, miserly monsoon meant empty granaries, hungering bellies and desperate hardship; a season of good rain was the harbinger of joy, of guaranteed plenty for the rest of the year.

A light sleeper at the best of times, Maya had woken unusually early. She had not slept well. Indeed, she had not been sleeping well ever since her last encounter with Kyle. The furtive little creatures that scurried about in the hidden darkness of her mind made night time intolerable. Sipping a glass of fresh green coconut water, she sat staring into the wetness outside, remembering something else, something even more fearsome than Kyle's shattering revelations. At the time the few words Joycie had mumbled had made no sense to her, but now, in the light of what she had seen and heard in Kyle's house, they took on a sinister clarity.

He wanna kill dem, you know dat . . . ?

Who had wanted to kill Kyle's mother and that "devil critter chile"—Christian's father? Why, the very idea was absurd, as bizarre as it was malicious, and Maya simply refused to believe it. Nevertheless, she knew that something unforeseen and repulsive had been brought into her life by Kyle Hawkesworth, and she resented that bitterly. Driven by sheer spite, he had tried to defile her future with Christian, to fill their relationship with venom, to create irreparable schisms between them. Maya's every nerve end throbbed with premonition. Try as she might, she could not rid herself of the thought that something terrible was about to happen.

Oh dear God—what if Christian *did* come to know the truth about his father?

The skies opened up again. Whipping gales raced across treetops, making them dance like dervishes. Streaking cracks of white light divided the skies, the thunder became deafening and the rain pelted down on the earth as if determined to flatten it. In between the clamour, Maya could hear faint, distant sounds of horses neighing, obviously frightened out of their slumber. Knowing that Abdul Mian and his son were there to calm the animals down, she turned to the dogs leashed to the balustrades, barking furiously in the expectation of imminent release. She undid their chains. Delighted, they leapt and pranced around her for a moment before bounding out onto the lawn with a fine disregard of the weather, to attend to more immediate priorities.

Just as rapidly as it had risen, the first assault of the storm subsided. Chased off by the winds, the clouds dispersed and the skies started to clear. On the far horizon, entangled in the fronds of an untidy row of palms, the half moon reappeared, balanced precariously on a branch before it slipped away beneath the rim into other realms.

All at once, out of a corner of her eye, Maya caught a movement on the lawn outside the verandah. It was still dark, still drizzling a little. An intruder, at this time of the morning? A hooded figure came scurrying out of the gloom and landed with a heavy splash on the verandah floor. Maya's stomach lurched and she half rose from her chair. But before she had time to feel any real sense of alarm, he threw the hood off his head and she recognised who it was.

"Samir!" She sank back into the chair with a mixture of relief and astonishment. "You scared me out of my wits! What on earth are you doing here so early in the morning anyway?"

He picked himself up from the floor, shook the water from his hair and gave her an aggrieved look. "It is again Sunday. Don't you remember?"

Sunday? She frowned, then started in guilty remembrance. She had forgotten all about her promise to go soon to the mango orchard!

Murmuring a few inaudible regrets, she was filled with both remorse and irritation. The last thing she needed at the moment was the added burden of Samir's perpetually mournful company. Taking note of his altogether sorry state, however, she made a sound of exasperation. "My goodness, just *look* at you—you're sopping wet and quite a sight!"

Grumbling to herself, she hurried inside and fetched him a towel.

Obediently, as she commanded, he proceeded to rub himself dry, then sat down on a chair beside her and sipped at the hot cocoa she ordered him to drink. "So many Sundays have passed and you did not come." He still looked as forlorn as a water-logged cat and his voice quivered with disappointment. "All these Sundays I waited for you. Everyone did."

"Well, so much has been happening, Samir," she said, very much on the defensive as she sought to justify her forgetfulness. "Joycie and Alistair and . . . everything else." She spread her hands with an impatient shake of her head.

He remained sullen, refusing to accept her explanations. "Christian has been away for days. You could have spared some time to keep your promise!"

She was about to make a sharp retort when, in a flash of intuition, she sensed the depth of his emotion and it surprised her. Impulsively, she leaned towards him and touched his hand. "I'm sorry, Samir dear, truly I am."

She spoke with gentleness, realising just how much she had wounded him. The small gesture brought a flush of pleasure to his cheeks. To cover his embarrassment, he started to comb his damp, spiky hair with clumsy fingers. "Then you will come with me now?"

"Now?" Despite her feelings of guilt, she could not quite conceal her dismay. "But it's not even six o'clock!"

"I started from the *bagan bari* at four! Had I been caught in that first downpour, it would have taken me hours to reach. And if we don't make an early start back, the dirt roads will be impassable. Today I have brought a carriage to fetch you. Ma insisted that I should."

"But I can't go today, Samir!" Maya exclaimed, as her irritation returned. "There are millions of matters that I have to attend to in the house and stables."

He removed his spectacles and started to wipe the mist off the glass. "Once Christian returns, you will not want to come at all. And, in any case, the mango season will be over."

His disappointment was so palpable that she could almost touch it, and again she felt ashamed. He had always asked so little of her—a smile, a touch of the hand, a soft word or two—trivial gestures made with ease, yet received with such disproportionate gratitude. Ever since she had known him, he had been the giver, expecting nothing in return. Perhaps because she was already so low in spirits, she felt a sudden rush of feeling at his essential decency.

"Well, since you have come all this way to fetch me," she said before the impulse faded, "I suppose I can't really let you return on your own."

He burst into smiles, his eyes lighting up as if illuminated from within. Joining in his smile, Maya hurried up to change, to leave a note for her mother and to scribble out some instructions for Abdul Mian.

It was still only just after seven o'clock when they started. The orchard was more than two hours' journey to the north, beyond Dum Dum on the road to Jessore, and another downpour appeared imminent. After a cer-

388

tain point, the streets were mere dirt tracks and would almost certainly be turning slushy. As they drove through the crowded native town, however, the thoroughfares were filled with people out in force to rejoice at the arrival of the rains. Droves of children, some in skimpy loincloths, others with not even that, stomped and splashed in the rapidly deepening puddles regardless of their high content of mud, some of which stuck eagerly to their bodies. Even in the heart of town, the scents released by the earth as it quenched its thirst were warm and wonderfully reviving. There was an air of festivity everywhere, a feeling of joy, as if at the return of a prodigal not heard from for a long time. Even jolting along in the carriage well protected from the rain, it was difficult not to share in the spontaneous sense of celebration. Gradually, as the journey progressed, Maya's spirits revived and her mood brightened.

At her first sight of the large slatted gates to the orchard, a tight knot of excitement formed in her throat. She had not been to the orchard since she had left school. Yet, as the lovely, pastoral scene unfolded before her eyes, every detail of it seemed as vivid in her mind as if she had been here yesterday. Nothing appeared to have changed; every leaf was still in its place, every tree and shrub and flower in its given position, producing in her a strange sense of continuity. To their left was the well around which they were forbidden to play even though it was covered, and instinctively, her eyes went up to search the top branches of a large peepul. Yes, the hornets' hive at which Samir had once aimed a wooden ball—with very painful consequences—was still there. She laughed out loud at the memory and, guessing the reason for her amusement, Samir grinned. Despite their fierce tempers when disturbed, the hornets produced the most delicious honey one could imagine—sharp-tasting in winter when the mustard flowers spread thick and golden over the fields, and delicately sweet in early spring when there were luscious lychees to suckle. The rain had again stopped. As they drove towards the main house, the clouds parted and brilliant swathes of sunshine cut across the wet, carpeted grass, making it sparkle with freshness.

"Where have you *been* all these years!" She was greeted with ecstatic hugs and kisses by Samir's two sisters on the flight of marble steps at the entrance where the carriage deposited them. "We thought you had abandoned us forever!" They scolded her very soundly, but only out of affection, far too happy to be truly angry, not really expecting either apologies or excuses.

The splendid country house that was the holiday retreat of the Goswami family teemed with people and activity. It was large and rambling and more than a hundred years old, set in a clearing in the middle of the orchard. To one side was a rolling lawn, beautifully trimmed, where a croquet game was in progress amid much heated debate among a group of young people Maya recognised as some of Samir's many cousins. They waved to her, then continued with their argument. The cousins, all members of the vast, extended family Kali Charan Goswami maintained and sustained, had gathered according to custom to celebrate *sawan*, the season of rains. On several sturdy branches of the trees ropes had been tied and swings devised with little wooden seats and cushions attached to them. Some young girls sat on the swings, flying alarmingly high into the trees, their glossy black plaits arcing back and forth behind them like animated tails. Others scrambled for ripe mangoes in the undergrowth, each discovery announced with shrieks of triumph. The atmosphere was very much like that of a country fair, gay and colourful and marvellously light-hearted.

Beyond the lawn, on the other side of the stream that ran through the estate, lay spreading paddy fields dotted with villages and banana groves; behind the main house were the myriad barns, lofts, stables, servants' quarters, kitchens and other outhouses that comprised the Goswami ancestral estate. The stream, Maya recalled, teemed with carp, and as children they had fished over many happy hours in the clear, flowing waters, as delighted with a catch of tadpoles and minnows as they would have been with a prize carp of more respectable dimensions. Across the stream stretched a rope bridge, but the shallow waters could also be crossed over a pathway of high, flat stepping stones. And, of course, all around was the pleasing lushness of the mango trees, dense with bottle green leaves and plump fruit, green-yellow on the outside, with bright yellow flesh, crying out to be plucked and eaten.

"Well, what are we waiting for?" Minali shouted, making a run for the orchard. "I know a tree where the fruit hangs low enough for. . . ."

They hurried behind her into the orchard in a group, scrambling for positions, jumping up to reach the lower branches, bringing down fruit by the dozen. A little shy, Maya held back. But then, remembering that in a mango orchard at the height of the season fortune does not favour the meek, she joined in with enthusiasm. Soon there were mountains of mangoes stacked underneath the trees, but attacked with much mirth and good-humoured bickering, they vanished with astonishing rapidity. Knives and plates were available for those who wanted the use of them, but nobody did. Instead, they bit the scabs off the fruit with their teeth, plunged them into the giant tubs of water for a perfunctory wash, peeled the thin, luminescent skin off with their fingers, and then ate in huge, succulent mouthfuls with the incredibly sweet juice running down their chins into the grass. No matter how many they ate, there always seemed to be room for just that one more. Working almost as hard as the feasters, an army of servants swept up the mountainous debris in enormous baskets and carried it off to the cowshed for the enjoyment of the cattle. The younger servant lads scraped down the mango seeds with astonishing skill and fashioned them into the traditional whistles known as the *papiha*, blowing hard into the slits to produce sad, mournful notes, like the call of some lovelorn bird.

"The English believe that mangoes should be eaten only in the privacy of one's bathroom," Kali Charan remarked with good-natured indulgence as he strolled through the orchard for an inspection, followed by his retinue of attendants. "I see now that their point is indeed well taken!"

When they could eat no more, they washed their hands and feet and faces and lay in the sun uncaring of the dampness in the grass. Aunt Sarala came and sat near Maya, trying to coax her into eating one last mango. Maya flung up her arms in defeat. "Not even one last bite," she gasped. "I simply *couldn't*—at least, not until after lunch." Everyone burst out laughing and Maya giggled.

"You have not been to see us for a very long time," Aunt Sarala observed with some severity. "Why?"

Maya coloured and lowered her eyes. Much as she disapproved of the absurdly masochistic rituals the determined widow followed, she had always had a fondness for Aunt Sarala, Kali Charan's eldest sister. "I . . . don't know. I cannot explain it. I'm sorry."

The old lady, dressed in white as befitted her widowhood, stopped her with a gesture. "Never mind. Don't make apologies. I get news of your dear mother from my nephew and his mother. I always remember her in my prayers because I know how much sorrow she still bears."

They talked for a while about Olivia and Amos and family matters, and Maya was surprised at the ease with which she found herself conversing in Bengali. One of Aunt Sarala's maidservants arrived, bearing something wrapped in a banana leaf. "Here, this is for you," Aunt Sarala said, laying the leaf in the grass before Maya. She opened it to display a freshly cooked sweet. "I made it because I remembered that these were your favourites."

Maya sat up, touched. Aunt Sarala's passion in life, she knew, was her kitchen; her mission in life, the feeding of friends and family. It was a mission fully endorsed, for she was indeed a superb cook. Recognising the Bengali delicacy, Maya thrust the long, slender pancake roll stuffed with coconut, raisins and sugar syrup into her mouth and closed her eyes. "Hmmmm!" she breathed, entranced. "It's even better than I remember!" Before she knew it, she had eaten two more.

Aunt Sarala nodded. "You know what was my favourite sweet when I was a child? Something made with a strange foreign nut and cream. They were called mon . . . mon . . ." She stopped, searching her memory.

"Mont Blanc aux marrons? They're made with chestnuts cooked in sweetened, vanilla-flavoured milk, sugar and cream."

The widow brightened. "Yes, those. A cousin of mine had a French governess who used to make them. They were delicious."

Maya looked surprised. It seemed odd to think that Aunt Sarala, austere and ascetic, had ever had anything as frivolous as a childhood, much less a craving for French sweets. "Well, the chestnut paste we get here is tinned, of course."

"Yes, I know, I know. She used to put a lot of cream in it and we used to devour it by the spoonful." She gave a self-conscious laugh. "It's peculiar how some childhood memories linger more than others." She stopped and toyed a moment with the bunch of keys tied to one corner of her sari, tossed over a shoulder. "Samir will be leaving soon for England."

"So he tells me."

The old lady looked distressed. "I do not like the idea. Brahmins lose caste when they travel across the seas. My nephew would bring disgrace to the community."

"Times have changed, Aunt Sarala," Maya said gently. "Nobody believes in these superstitions any more."

"There are some things that can never change!" Aunt Sarala retorted severely, waggling a finger in her face. "These are the foundations on which our traditions have been built. If they crumble, we crumble." She dabbed her eyes with a corner of her sari. "But then, I am just a silly old widow. Who listens any more to what I have to say?" Which was, of course, a gross distortion of the truth. As the matriarch of Kali Charan Goswami's joint family, this frail old lady less than five feet tall exerted great influence over the household. Well aware of this, Maya smiled within herself but did not dare to offer a contradiction. Summoned by a frantic maidservant to take charge of some culinary crisis or other, Aunt Sarala got up quickly and hurried off in the direction of her kitchen house.

"Come, let us grab a swing quickly or we'll have to wait for *hours.*" Minali leapt up, again ready to dive into the heart of the orchard.

Maya looked down at her dress, heavily stained with mango juice. "I think I should change but, foolishly, I did not bring another set of clothing."

The girls were both shorter than she, but Barnali's long skirt, a blouse and a veil proved more than adequate in such informal surroundings. Maya put them on amid hoots of laughter and teasing because the skirt did not quite reach down to her ankles and the veil kept slipping off her shoulder. While her ayah took her stained clothes down to the dhobi house, Barnali showed Maya her collection of cloth dolls, one of which Maya had made for her years ago as a birthday gift when they were at the Academy. She remembered the time and effort she had spent in making the rather elaborate doll, dressed as a bride, and in collecting all the shiny bits and pieces that went into its embellishment. It touched her that Barnali should have looked after it so well over the years.

In the orchard, good use was being made of the swings by a host of girls and boys who flew through the air to reach incredible heights, shrieking and squealing with delight. Some stood daringly on the seats, urging the swing higher and ever higher with bended knees and propelling jerks of their young, energetic bodies. Others sat in rather more sedate fashion, content to be pushed to and fro by younger children obediently observing the strict rules of seniority that applied in a joint family. And everywhere, everywhere, all around, right up to the edge of the river, was the rich, sweet, intoxicating perfume of the Bengali *langra* mango, the finest species of the fruit in the world.

"Here, quick!"

One of the cousins almost shoved Maya into the seat of a swing that had fallen vacant. Maya pushed the ground cautiously with the tips of her toes, then, as confidence returned, harder and harder. Before long she too was standing on the seat, remembering all the expert ways in which swings could be made to reach impossible heights without one's falling off. A girl started to sing and everyone else joined in. They sang folk songs in Bengali, songs of the season about rain and cloudy skies and the rich, wet earth and the sad laments of the *papiha*. Without thinking, Maya too joined in, hesitantly at first, then more confidently, astonished that she should still remember tunes and words she had not thought of in years.

Time unwound; the intervening years melted away one by one. She was ten years old again, climbing trees, romping through the orchard, singing at the top of her voice, scraping knees and elbows with uncaring abandon, then sobbing against Samir's shoulder because the bruises hurt. In her memory his voice was soft and soothing as he wiped away her tears, painted tincture of iodine on her insignificant wounds as if creating a work of art, stricken with remorse when it stung and she screamed with brattish temper. The pendulum that was Maya's swing reached its apogee and she looked down. Samir stood below in the clearing, his eyes fixed upon her, anxious and unsmiling, in case she should fall. Meeting his dark, sparkling eyes, Maya felt something strange stir within her, a gentle upheaval, an alien emotion that she had not felt before. She bit her lip and looked away, uncomfortable and angry with herself.

Then it was time for luncheon, served on long trestle tables on the covered verandah in case it rained again. They formed a large, untidy group and there were some faces Maya had either not seen before or did not remember, but everyone seemed to know her. Suddenly there was so much to talk about, so much catching up to do, it was as if she could not get the words out fast enough. Everyone made a fuss of her as little servant girls ran in and out of Aunt Sarala's personal kitchen next to a banana grove by the side of the house, bringing forth an endless succession of courses.

They ate with their fingers off banana leaves and from disposable clay bowls, as was the custom—huge juicy fish heads cooked in lentils, fried vegetables, snowy white rice, prawns baked in coconut shells, sweet curds and, of course, *ilish maach*—the hilsa fish—smothered in a pungent gravy of homegrown mustard seed and chillies. The hilsa was surely the most delicious fish in the world, but also the most difficult to eat because of its bewildering assortment of bones. Samir's father presided over the long wooden trestle table, making constant demands for this, that or the other, and his mother sat at the other end. Aunt Sarala did not eat with them. As was mandatory for Hindu widows, she was a strict vegetarian and refused even to sit close to a table upon which fish, fowl or mutton was being served. However, many of the delectable vegetable and lentil dishes they now ate had been cooked by her in her private kitchen and, as was her custom, she supervised the family meal with hawk-eyed persistence.

Standing at a safe distance from the luncheon table, taking care not to let even a corner of her sari brush against it in case it defiled her person, she nodded her approval at the heap of bones stacked before Maya. "Ah, I see that you have not forgotten how to eat *ilish maach*. I remember you were always very good with the bones."

Maya said nothing. Hilsa was a great favourite with Amos and her mother; it was she who rejected it at home because it had to be eaten with the fingers, a custom she privately considered primitive.

"Why shouldn't she be?" Minali demanded. "She's as Bengali as we are!"

Sitting to one side of her, Barnali whispered with a mischievous giggle, "We liked your Christian Pendlebury, you know—but we hope he wasn't too taken by that beautiful nautch girl."

Maya blushed, accepting the banter in the proper spirit. "Well, if he was," she whispered back coolly, "it's because he has *very* good taste when it comes to the ladies!" Which produced a positive storm of laughter.

When the meal was more or less over, Samir's mother got up from her seat and came to sit opposite Maya, her enormous bunch of household keys tinkling with each step. "I am very worried about your poor mother," she said. "How long is she going to brood like this about Alistair?"

"Until he comes to see her—or leaves—I suppose." Maya took one last spoonful of sweet curds, upturned the empty clay bowls and folded her banana leaf neatly as an indication that she had finished eating. "At the moment he shows no sign of wanting to meet her again."

"Yes. It must surely break her heart, poor dear!"

Mays's eyes lit up. "Have you seen him at all?"

"Once. We passed him walking down Old Court House Street and my husband pointed him out to me."

"He looks very much like Mother, doesn't he?"

"Well, he has her eyes. And his hair is that rich chestnut colour, like hers."

"And mine!"

Abala smiled. "Yes, of course. Has he made any effort to see you?"

"No." She picked up a sliver of lemon and with it carefully wiped the grease off her fingers. "If he won't come to see Mother, I doubt if he would deign to meet me." She squeezed the last drop out of the lemon and pushed it inside the folded banana leaf. "But I would like to know him better. If it weren't for Amos, who's being so dreadfully pig-headed about that wretched cotton mill, I probably would have."

At the end of the verandah, a servant stood with a jug of warm water, soap and towels. As she washed her hands, Maya saw Samir's father pacing the brick patio that adjoined the verandah. Having just left him still sitting at the luncheon table, she was vaguely surprised, but then realised, with a small shock, that it was not Kali Charan Babu at all but Samir. He was walking up and down with his hands clasped behind his back, very much in the manner of his father, talking to a group of people who stood in a silent line at the edge of the patio. From the snatches of conversation that wafted across to her, she gathered that he was conducting business connected with the estate. He was dressed, as usual, in a white cotton dhoti, crisply starched and crimped, and his feet were encased in his customary thonged leather sandals. Yet, somehow, he looked different.

He appeared taller, straighter of back, more confident and in perfect control, with no sign now of those gauche, nervous mannerisms that had always irritated her so much. The voice in which he spoke to his father's tenant farmers was strong and decisive. Whatever he said was said with quiet authority, in measured tones, and everyone listened.

This was an aspect of Samir that Maya had never had occasion to see before. Indeed, it was so much at variance with the way he normally was that, taken by surprise, she seated herself on a chair, watching and listening in silent fascination. Here, in his own milieu, Samir had acquired a presence, a clearly defined identity. Within the parameters of his own world, with no compulsion to prove himself, he was an aristocrat, acknowledged and respected as such. He was no longer a clumsy boy in the alien English environment, constantly defeated by the conjugations and nuances of a language not his own. He spoke now in Bengali, with the fluency of thought and expression that sprang from his roots, entirely in command of what he said. As she sat observing him in this unfamiliar incarnation, Maya felt suddenly pained that out of his own environment he should be reduced to a figure of fun, and that it should have been she who often derived pleasure from ridiculing him.

The same strange and disturbing feelings stirred within her again. She felt a curious empathy with Samir, a feeling of compassion. And she suddenly saw that it was because she truly understood him. They had grown up together; she was an accepted component of his home, his extended family, familiar with so many crevices of his life. In a cruel twist of her mind, she also thought of Christian. How little she knew about *his* life! What did his sister look like, was he good at algebra in school, did he detest brinjals as much as she knew Samir did?

She had a moment of frightening disorientation, not knowing where she was or *who* she was. Was it possible that it was here that she belonged, after all?

But then the moment passed and she was furious with herself for deliberately clouding her priorities. In that instant, Samir turned and saw her. He broke into an involuntary smile and with a gesture dismissed the entourage around him.

"Come with me," he said as he joined her on the verandah. "I have something to show you."

"W-what?" she stammered, still flustered and disoriented.

He would not say more, but led the way to the back of the house. Since she had last seen them, the stables had been renovated and expanded to accommodate the family's horses and carriages. They circled round them to a small paddock at the back. Behind a wooden fence, a foal gambolled around his mother. He was a lively little fellow no more than a month old, with large, shiny eyes and a matching coat of deep brown.

"Well? How do you like him?"

Maya gave a gasp of pleasure. "Oh, he's absolutely beautiful!" Opening the gate of the paddock, she ran in after the foal.

"Can you recognise his breed?" Samir asked, following her into the paddock.

Maya examined the foal with expert eyes and hands, then frowned. "A Marwari?"

"Yes." He looked pleased, proud of her expertise. "It is for you. I will have him delivered as soon as he is weaned."

"For me?" She regarded him in consternation. "You know that I cannot accept this, Samir." She spoke with unintended severity, suddenly not at all at ease in his presence.

"Why not? I know you've always wanted to add a Marwari to your stables."

"Yes, but this is too valuable a gift."

"It gives me pleasure to give you what gives *you* pleasure," he said, his voice very gentle. "You already know that."

She shook her head. "I simply cannot."

"You can and you will." He still spoke gently, but in a tone of authority. Without waiting for her to react, he led the foal into the orchard, encouraging him to run and frisk about to his heart's content. Maya had no option but to follow.

For the remainder of the slow, slumbrous afternoon, Maya sat in subdued silence, watching the boisterous games of *hu-tu-tu* and croquet that were being played on the lawn, content to be an onlooker. She sat on the verge with her knees pulled up tight against her chin, lost in self-examination and not much liking what she saw.

She had forgotten so much. She would not, she vowed passionately, allow herself to do so again.

But that evening when she returned home, Maya's memory was once again to be wiped clean of everything save the present. Waiting on the marble-topped table in the hallway was an ivory white rectangular envelope of the finest quality imaginable. It was addressed personally to her in exquisitely executed calligraphy and, Sheba informed her, had been delivered during the course of the morning by a liveried courier. Wonderingly—and with great care—Maya coaxed open the envelope.

Inside was an invitation to the Pendleburys' *burra khana*.

17

A STARTLED CALCUTTA woke up the next morning to an astonishing advertisement on the front page of the weekly periodical *Equality*. Promising total confidentiality to those who came forward, it requested information about the identities of the arsonists responsible for the fire at the Jai Raventhorne Seva Sangh in Chitpore. What caused the astonishment, however, was the spectacular reward promised for the information, should this lead to the arrest of those responsible: a gemstone called the Roshanara.

Informants were advised to report directly to the Inspector-General at police headquarters.

The advertisement created a mild furore over several breakfast tables in the city.

"The Roshanara? That's that ruby stolen some years ago from the nawab chap, isn't it?" Leaving his kipper half eaten, Lucas Anderson stared at the paper in surprise. "How the devil did Hawkesworth get ahold of it, anyway?"

"Well, I should think that's obvious." Never having heard of the Roshanara, his younger daughter nevertheless gave a disdainful toss of her head. "Thick-skinned as he is, he's probably the one who stole it in the first place."

"Oh, don't be so silly!" Her older sister withered her with a look. "If he had stolen it, why should he advertise the fact on the front page of his paper?"

"Because he is so thick-skinned! There's nothing he enjoys better than to cock a snook at the authorities."

"Well, I think what he has is a fake," Charlotte Anderson suggested after serious deliberation. "Being the reprobate that he is, naturally he has no compunction about passing it off as the genuine article."

"He'd be a fool to try it," Lucas Anderson pointed out, setting the paper aside and returning to the enjoyment of his kipper, "and he's certainly not that."

With a cluck of impatience, his wife put an end to the debate and returned to a subject far more pertinent. "Now, about the Pendleburys' *burra khana.* Sadruddin durzee is waiting on the verandah. Do you want the tussur print, Melody, or the mull?"

Across town at the Bow Bazaar chummery, having just returned from his morning game of fives at the Club, Patrick read the advertisement with great interest. "Come to think of it, old chap, why don't *you* confess to the crime and claim the reward, eh?" he suggested to Lytton, not entirely in jest. "Think of all the debts we could wipe out with that little bauble!"

"Come to think of it, why don't *you?*" Lytton retorted, busy completing his book of odds for a cock fight he was arranging.

"I can't," Patrick replied piously. "I'm a bespoke man, remember? And everyone knows it's stolen property."

"Well, I'm not, and I'd still rather be in debt than in the pokey."

"Why should they send anyone to the pokey? That old mulatto biddy who died had one foot in the grave anyway."

Sir Jasper's eye caught the boxed-in front-page advertisement in bold print just as he was about to leave for the office after breakfast. He halted a moment, picked up the paper and read the announcement with great care. He knew all about the Roshanara ruby, of course; he had been in Lucknow when the Saifabad family had reported it missing. He frowned a moment, then suddenly started to chuckle.

"It's an old trick, that. Trust him not to miss it!"

"What, dear?" Lady Constance had only half a mind on what her husband said, the other half being occupied in making ticks and crosses on a copious invitation list. Without waiting for his reply to her question, she asked, "Have you received word yet from the Viceroy's Secretariat?"

Sir Jasper put down the paper. "Yes. One of the aides delivered a letter to my office yesterday afternoon. I'm sorry, I did mean to bring it home but it slipped my mind."

"A letter arrives from the Viceroy and it slips your mind? Really, Jasper!" She looked very cross indeed. "You know that I've been *waiting* for that letter. All the arrangements depend on whether or not His Excellency and his entourage are to be present. Anyway, what did the letter say? You did, I hope, take the trouble to read it?"

"Lord and Lady Mayo are in Simla, Constance," he said irritably. "How the devil do you expect them to be present at your damned dinner party?"

Lady Pendlebury heaved a tired sigh. "It was *you* who asked for an invitation and letter to be sent to them in Simla, Jasper," she explained with rapidly eroding patience. "You said they planned to make a brief return to Calcutta this month, don't you remember?" He obviously didn't. "Well, is it true or not?"

"No. It is not. As far as I can remember, the letter came in the diplomatic pouch from Peterhof, the viceregal residence in Simla. It made no mention of an imminent return. Neither does the Viceroy's staff here know of any such plan."

"As far as you can remember?" Lady Constance sat back, noticed her husband's plate of uneaten grilled bacon and kidneys, and eyed him with some concern. It was quite unlike him to forget important letters and messages. Besides, he had not been sleeping well at all lately. This morning he hadn't touched his breakfast any more than he had his dinner last night. She put aside the list and balanced her elbows on the table.

"There's something on your mind, Jasper."

"No more than usual," he said shortly. "Now, where has that blasted fellow put my briefcase?"

"You're worried about Christian, aren't you?"

"Stop being fanciful, Constance. No, I'm not worried about Christian."

"Well, I certainly am!" She shuffled her voluminous guest list and stood up. "I'm so glad he comes home tomorrow. Once he's here, Charlotte Anderson believes, we can at least. . . ." But what Charlotte Anderson believed was destined to remain unrevealed; her husband was no longer in the room.

At the Raventhornes' breakfast table, Amos read the piece and was much put out. "Kyle said nothing, absolutely nothing, to me about this reward when we last met," he remarked, annoyed. "And from where has he suddenly acquired the Roshanara, anyway?"

Olivia threw a covert look at Maya, but paying scant heed to the conversation, her daughter did not respond. "I have no idea, dear, but it really is most odd. Do you think he's likely to get into trouble over this?"

"Well, he certainly will with me!" Amos said grimly. "He could have at least discussed it before deciding to announce the reward."

Olivia picked up the paper and again perused the advertisement. "But if a reward is to be offered—and I do think that it should," she remarked thoughtfully, "then surely the offer should have come from us? I do feel ashamed not to have thought of it before. Oh dear!" She gave a worried shake to her head. "I do hope Kyle hasn't landed in a situation from which he cannot extricate himself."

Maya continued to sit in abstracted silence, neither contributing to the discussion nor listening to it. She was deeply engrossed in her own thoughts, uncaring not only of Kyle's advertisement but of the world in general. Ever since she had received the Pendleburys' invitation, she had not been able to think of anything else. Taken entirely by surprise at the sight of the gilt-edged card addressed to her personally, for a moment she had thought she would faint. There was about its frigid elegance something truly awesome, and the refined language in which the contents were couched had quite overwhelmed her. To reassure herself that it was not merely part of a dream, she refused to have it leave her possession even for an instant. She had carried the envelope up to her room and sat up half the night staring at it in silent wonder. When she finally dropped off to sleep, it had remained safely ensconced underneath her pillow.

But then, inevitably, with the morning came a return to reality and the initial flutterings of panic. Casting off her distracted look, she interrupted the breakfast-table discussion with the first thought that comes to the mind of every female ever invited to a party. "I have nothing to wear," she announced flatly. "I shall have to have something new made, Mother. Do you think there is enough time for that?"

Olivia mumbled a reply as, within her, her heart sank. Knowing that the reaction of her son and daughter to the Pendleburys' invitation would be diametrically opposed, she had deliberately not stirred the subject yet with Amos. His manner with her was still deeply resentful and withdrawn. The invitation, Olivia recognised, would do little to improve his temper. Nevertheless, the matter would have to be discussed sooner or later. Resigning herself to the argument that was bound to follow, she decided to get it over and done with as soon as possible.

"Have you had time to read the invitation from the Pendleburys, dear?" she asked Amos.

"Yes."

"Well?"

"Well what, Mother?"

"Do we accept or not?"

He laid down his knife and fork with a clatter. "Accept? Mother, you can't be serious! You would actually consider going to a circus like that?"

Listening in tense silence, Maya bristled. "It's *not* a circus. It will probably be the most fashionable ball of the year!"

"So? That impresses you, does it? Well, it doesn't me."

"What has that got to do with it?" Maya retorted, incensed. "They have made an offer of hospitality. Shouldn't we accept it with some show of grace? How can you be so churlish when they've been kind enough to request our company?"

"Have you stopped to wonder *why* this alleged kindness is suddenly being offered?"

Maya toyed nervously with the piece of toast on her plate "Well, maybe they just want to be nice, considering. . . ." She coloured and lowered her eyes.

"Nice?" Amos echoed. "You think they've asked us because they want to be nice?"

"Well, why else?" Maya's colour heightened, as did her anger. "I . . . I told you Christian has asked me to. . . ." Her voice tailed away as she chewed on her lip.

"And you really believe *that* is the reason for this invitation?" Amos demanded, astonished.

"Well, what else?"

He threw down his napkin in a show of disgust. "If you can't work that out for yourself by now, you're either blind or simply determined not to see."

"But, Amos dear," Olivia intervened hastily, "don't you think that we should at least discuss this?"

"What is there to discuss? Just say we have a previous engagement and that will be the end of it."

"But we don't have a previous engagement," Maya cried, close to tears, "and I want to go!"

"If you want to, by all means do, but don't expect *me* to be part of the humiliating *tamasha.*"

Maya's lip quivered. "I've never been to a ball like this before, Amos. If you don't go, you know that I won't be able to, either."

Amos refused to be cajoled. "Why don't you ask your *other* brother to escort you?" he asked with lacerating scorn. "I daresay you'll cut far more of a dash on the arm of an Englishman."

Maya burst into tears and ran out of the room.

Olivia half rose in a bid to stop her, but then threw up her hands in despair. "Was that really necessary, Amos? Is it not possible to talk about the matter without being so hurtful?"

"What is there to talk about, Mother?"

Olivia sighed wearily. "To tell you the truth, Amos, I'm as confused as Maya is—why have they asked us, anyway?"

"For the same reason that everyone else does." His pale eyes flashed with arrogance. "Because they have no choice! If other members of the Chamber of Commerce are invited, they cannot afford to leave out the Raventhornes, however much they might want to."

"Then you think it has nothing to do with Christian's interest in Maya?"

"Of course it hasn't! At least, not directly. The Pendleburys are simply making a virtue out of a necessity. If they leave us out, tongues already wagging like damned puppy dogs' tails will only wag faster. Any ass can see that!"

"Well, I wish they hadn't asked us at all! But Maya is right—unless you accept, we cannot. And, in all fairness, Amos, you simply cannot let your sister down at a moment like this, no matter what your personal feelings."

He gave her a dark look. "You have no qualms about accepting the Pendleburys' invitation under all these embarrassing circumstances?"

"You know very well that, like you, I would much rather not go," Olivia said, tired out by the argument. "Apart from anything else, it's years since I went to a *burra khana.* I'm not sure that I'm now up to the conversational hypocrisies, the sniggers, the snide remarks behind one's back just loud enough to be heard, the imperious stares. I have forgotten how to pretend that I see nothing, hear nothing, *feel* nothing. . . ."

She covered her face with her palms, trying not to think of past humiliations, fighting off futile emotions. But when she uncovered her face again, Amos had gone.

Upstairs, she found Maya in her room lying on her bed in unhappy silence, her eyes red-rimmed and puffy.

"Did you know that ruby was the Roshanara?" Olivia asked, still worried for Kyle.

"What? Yes. No. I don't remember."

"Kyle said nothing to you about offering a reward?"

"No." Maya turned her face away, crippled with disappointment, and stared at the opposite wall. Olivia sat down next to her on the bed and put a gentle hand on her shoulder. "What Amos was trying to point out, darling, was that. . . ."

"It doesn't matter. I'm not going anyway."

Olivia bent down to kiss her on the forehead. "Yes, you are. We all are."

Maya turned, a spark of painful hope in her eyes. "Amos?"

"Yes, Amos too. When he realises how much this evening means to you, I'm sure he'll decide to be more accommodating."

A tearful smile struggled on her lips. "I've never been to any of these grand occasions, Mother."

"Yes, I know, darling."

She again looked panic-stricken. "But what on earth will I wear? I haven't the *faintest* idea of what might be considered high fashion!"

"As it happens, neither have I," Olivia said with a light laugh. "We're both terribly *démodée*, I'm afraid, but we'll put our heads together and do the best that we can."

Maya did not smile. "Do you think they've asked us because of . . . Christian?"

"I don't know, dear. Perhaps, perhaps not." She took Maya's hand in hers; it was ice-cold. "I want you to promise me something, darling. Whatever their reasons, don't read more into this invitation than there is. Accept it at face value."

Maya squeezed her eyes shut and her mouth quivered. "Oh, I'm so frightened, Mother!"

"Frightened?" Olivia smoothed down her hair. "There's nothing to be frightened of, dear."

Opening her eyes, Maya focused them on the ceiling. "What if I make a fool of myself in front of his parents? What if they don't *like* me?"

"Have you lost your senses, Kyle?" Amos asked without preamble when Kyle arrived at his office later that morning. "The Roshanara ruby is stolen property. How the devil do you expect to get away with this? And how do you happen to have it in your possession anyway?"

Kyle showed no sign of perturbation. "The jewel does not belong to me. It was not my idea to offer it as a reward for information."

"Well, whose then?"

"Someone who wishes to remain anonymous." He dismissed the question with an impatient wave. "Forget about the Roshanara. What I have to tell you is of far greater value."

There was an urgency in his tone that stopped Amos's further comments. "Well?"

"I have received that long-awaited communication."

"What communication?"

"From Thomas Hungerford."

"Hungerford!" Amos sat down slowly, thoroughly shaken. "After all these months of silence, he suddenly decides to acknowledge our letters?"

"With good reason, he indicates. Not only that, he's decided to go one better by coming out here personally."

"He's *here?* In India?"

"So I gather. Ill health compelled him to disembark in Madras some days ago to seek medical attention there. He sent me a letter courtesy of the ship's captain, I received it early this morning. He appears anxious to come to Calcutta as soon as he is physically able."

Amos swallowed. The news was so unexpected that he could not quite assimilate it. "What else does he say in his letter?"

"He insists that he must meet your mother."

"No, not yet! Not until we are satisfied that he has something new to say, not until she can be prepared. After all. . . ." His voice trailed away. Struck by the full impact of what Kyle had said, he felt cold, filled with a strange sort of fear. "Thomas Hungerford," he breathed. "At last, after all these years!"

Kyle watched him for a while, then asked, "You are again doubtful about the advisability of resurrecting him?"

"I don't know." Amos sat fingering his chin, slumped in thought. "Sometimes I wonder if we did the right thing in inducing him here at all, if it might not have been wiser to let sleeping dogs lie. It would be intolerably cruel to make her face him in case"—he shrugged and stopped, unable to complete the thought uppermost in both their minds. But then, with a shake of his head, he again straightened and his jaw set. "When does Hungerford think he will be well enough to travel?"

"He doesn't say. It could be a week, two weeks. Who knows?"

"He writes nothing else?"

"No, except that he has much to reveal."

Amos gave a hard laugh. "Then why has the bloody fellow not revealed it before?" he asked, angered.

"He had his compulsions, he says."

"And we both know what they were!"

Kyle got up and laid a sympathetic hand on his arm. "It is still not too late."

"No!" Amos reacted sharply. "Now, there can be no going back, Kyle. We made a calculated decision when Findlater died. We discussed the risks involved, and we decided that whatever the consequences, we would pursue the truth."

"It would be foolish to raise expectations, pleasant or otherwise, until you've heard what the man has to say," Kyle warned. He might be an utter waste of time, simply out to make a quick quid. That he is greedy and also a congenital liar, we already suspect. And if he has lied before, he could easily lie again."

Amos took a deep breath. "Yes, I am aware of all that. However, to his credit is the fact that he did respond to our communication and has made the voyage out at his own expense." With his fingertips he drummed an impatient tattoo on the desk top. "He gave you his address in Madras?"

"Yes."

"Then, rather than let him languish there doing nothing, let him prepare a written statement about what he wants to say and send it to us in advance of his arrival. It will establish his credentials and save time."

Kyle nodded in quick agreement. "Yes. A good idea." He made to leave. "Whitney's brother-in-law sails for Madras on the evening tide. I can request him to deliver my letter to Hungerford personally. By the way," he halted with his hand on the door knob, "I have to be out of station for a few days."

"Where are you going?"

"To North Bengal. I want to have a look at this plantation and assess its suitability. I should be back within the week, well before Hungerford can be expected."

Amos gave him a curious look. "You're hopeful of being able to acquire it even though Birkhurst refuses to sell?"

Kyle smiled a little. "Yes. Very hopeful."

"Don't let us get in too deep until we are certain of our own strength, Kyle. Did you see Sir Jasper?"

"Yes."

"And?"

Kyle hesitated. He shut the half-open door and, for a moment or two, walked aimlessly about the room, his mood restless. "My friend, I regret that there is a great deal that I have not revealed to you yet." His face was uncommonly grave, even worried. "I promise that you will know everything very shortly, as soon as I return. But for the time being, I beg of you to bear with me."

"Why did he want to see you, anyway?" Amos asked bluntly.

"He was looking for . . . reassurances. More than that I cannot say at this juncture. I told you I was going on a fishing expedition, didn't I?" He appeared greatly amused. "Well, as it happened, we both were!"

Amos had seen Kyle in many difficult situations, admired the panache with which he attacked them, more often than not with satisfactory success. But this time, he could see, Kyle was tense; that supreme confidence with which he tackled everything appeared to be somewhat lacking. Amos felt more than a pinprick of apprehension.

"Don't cross swords with him, Kyle," he cautioned, full of misgivings. "Whatever your business with Pendlebury, the man is shrewd and enormously cunning—quite unlike that blithering ass McNaughton. Be careful, dammit!"

"You don't believe that I'm not also shrewd and enormously cunning?" Kyle laughed. "Don't worry, in this game the stakes are too high. I cannot afford to be anything but careful."

The blithe reassurance provided scant comfort for Amos. For the moment, however, the Roshanara ruby was forgotten.

Christian returned the next morning, bone-weary and terribly dispirited. Neither Patrick nor Lytton was at the chummery, both out at some cock-fighting event, he was informed by Karamat. Relieved, Christian treated himself to the luxury of a long, leisurely hot soak in the bath tub after Karamat had massaged his aching legs and back with oil and seasoned expertise.

Lying back in the tub and filled with despondency, Christian brooded. The district to which he was being posted was lacklustre, with few redeeming features. The countryside was sparse and unkempt, the indigo plantations in chaotic disarray, with petty zamindars, muscled hooligans and avaricious moneylenders ruling the roost with scandalous impunity. He had heard that a recent District Officer and his family had been besieged without food and water for three days by rebellious villagers and had escaped with their lives only after fleeing the district under cover of night. Christian had met one or two British planters, arrogant and callous, and was appalled by their open defiance of the rule of law. The bungalow allocated to him was a mean-looking single-storey structure of bricks and white lime plaster, of limited cheer within and without. But, as it happened, that constituted the least of his worries.

He had had dinner with Cyril Cleaver, the Assistant District Officer whom he would be replacing and whose bungalow he would be occupying. Cleaver was a pleasant enough fellow, well read and obviously competent in his work, and had welcomed him like a long-lost brother. The reason for the overwhelming warmth of his reception was soon apparent. Cleaver confessed that he seldom had occasion to entertain guests with whom he could hold a decent, civilised conversation. Christian's was the first new face he had seen in the remote region in over three months. The planters preferred each other's company to that of the officials, and it was unthinkable for civil servants to hobnob socially with the local people. So great was Cleaver's relief at finally being able to leave his present post that—rather tactlessly and to Christian's great annoyance—he mentioned it several times during the course of the evening. The worst, however, was yet to come.

Soaking in the lukewarm water, washing off the dust and fatigue of his travels, Christian's brooding thoughts now turned to what was, in his opinion, the most sinister aspect of his new situation.

He calculated that, even as a junior officer, he would be responsible for the well-being of a population as numerous as that of England under Queen Elizabeth. Yet his superior officer in this complex, populous region, the District Officer, was one of the most diabolically unpleasant specimens of a civil servant he had ever had the misfortune to meet! The man's name was Humphrey Doyle, and he too had asked Christian to dinner. However, the invitation had been proffered not only grudgingly but, Doyle made it sufficiently clear, more out of deference to Christian's father's position than to any inclination on his part to welcome his deputy-to-be. If the planters were often men without either compassion or conscience, Doyle had even less to commend him. He was openly corrupt, and after the first few drinks of the evening, strutted around the compound of his house freely boasting about the many financial coups he had pulled off in his own interest. Without resorting to any great subtlety, he had made it plain to Christian that the district was his domain. No interference with the way he chose to run it would be tolerated from him, and the sooner Christian understood this the better.

Christian was disgusted. After a veritable ocean of alcohol and a stone-cold, indifferently prepared dinner served almost at midnight, he had finally departed without being able to bid his host goodnight. Soon after dinner, Doyle had collapsed on his bed in a drunken stupour. Christian had left in a hurry as two of Doyle's long-suffering bearers struggled to get their master's heavy, obese hulk into a pair of pyjamas.

Christian had learned later that since Doyle was the favourite son of a Very Important Personage in Westminster, there was little likelihood of his ever being given the boot until retirement—if not his, then certainly his father's.

All the rest of the inadequacies of his posting, Christian felt he could have tolerated. Through sheer force of will, he would have persuaded himself to think of them as challenges worthy of labour and effort such as an intrepid covenanted civil servant is expected to face without complaint several times in the course of his career. But the very prospect of working with and serving under such an ill-mouthed, intemperate, incompetent, conscienceless boor as Humphrey Doyle nauseated him. With so many fine, fine Englishmen serving Queen and both countries with devotion, integrity and honest endeavour, why should fate have made it his lot to have drawn the shortest damned straw?

Later that morning, still heavy of heart and bitterly cursing his luck, Christian hurried to the Raventhorne house. He could not wait to recount his explorations and experiences to Maya. He looked forward immensely to pouring out his heart to her, to receiving soft, feminine—and well deserved—sympathy, however platitudinous. How she would consider the prospect of living in such a God-forsaken wilderness, he did not even think about. Faced with the horror of Humphrey Doyle, all other aspects paled into insignificance; for the time being, domestic trivialities were relegated to second place.

Maya was at the desk in her office in the stable house, idly flicking through a pile of magazines, one cheek cupped in a palm. Even though he had had little time to mope during his travels, Christian realised suddenly just how much he had missed her. For a moment or two he simply stood and watched her, marvelling at her beauty, savouring her perfumed presence, allowing them to soften all the recent ugliness that had so ruthlessly crushed his professional hopes and dreams. She glanced up, saw him and, with a cry of delight, came flying into his arms.

"Oh Christian! I've been counting the *minutes* to your return. I'm so happy you're back!" Giving him a bear hug, she pouted. "I was so worried for you—you only wrote *once*."

Merely hearing her voice, full of concern and loving welcome, made him feel immediately better. "There was never any time to write," he said, husky with feeling. "I seemed to be always on the move. I'm so sorry."

For a moment he held her close as he kissed her mouth and then every corner of her face, murmuring endearments, avowing repeatedly his love for her. Then, as his more immediate worries again took over, he released her and flung himself onto the chintz-covered settee, bursting with the need to voice his woes and share them with her. He plunged into his impassioned saga, brow furrowed in concentration so as not to leave out a single pertinent detail, anxious that she should understand the extent of his frustration. She sat close to him, her head against his shoulder, and listened with unspeaking attention.

When he had explained to his satisfaction all his many grievances, he paused to ask her a question. She made no response. He had to repeat his question twice before she came awake with a guilty start.

"What?"

He stared at her in shocked disbelief as he realized that that she had not heard one word that he had said. Indeed, she appeared to be far, far away in some other world, lost in thoughts that had nothing to do with his own predicament.

He felt a stab of sudden alarm. "What's happened, is something the matter?"

She shook her head quickly, but he saw that she appeared to be in a high state of excitement. Her face was flushed, the eyes over-bright, as if with fever; gripped by some curious restlessness, she could barely sit still. Unable to hold back any longer, she exploded into a breathless torrent of words.

"Oh, Christian, they've asked us, all *three* of us—can you believe it? *I* can't. It's so much like a *dream!*"

He looked blank. "Who has asked whom and to *what?*"

"Your parents, silly! They've invited *all* of us to their *burra khana* next Saturday, including me! Isn't that *incredible?*"

"Oh?"

"Yes! I've been *waiting* for you to come back to show you these." She jumped up to fetch the stack of magazines from the desk. "I simply cannot make up my mind between this"—she rapidly flicked over the pages, her fingers trembling—"and this. What do you think? I think this one here would look *divine* in taffeta, blue taffeta. Mother favours the other one, in white tulle, with layers and layers of stiff under-petticoats. Aunt Edna, on the other hand, who should know, insists that. . . ."

He sat in silence, gaping at the dress patterns she presented to him in a flurry of confusion, letting the deluge of words flow unimpeded.

"Well?" She suddenly took note of his silence and stopped. "Aren't you going to say anything at all?"

"What do you expect me to say?" he asked, his tone curt. "It's only a damned *burra khana.*"

She was dismayed. "But don't you see the significance of the fact that we have been invited?"

"You haven't heard a word I've been saying to you," he said sullenly. "Don't you care about my future, *our* future?"

"Of course I have, and of *course* I do! I've heard every single word that you said—and I'm sorry that it has been such a miserable time for you. But . . . does it really matter? I don't care what sort of place we live in, Christian, *truly* I don't. As long as I am with you, I would be happy *anywhere!*"

She considered that all his worries were about her comfort? He could hardly believe that she had misunderstood the situation so totally! But he also realised that while she was in her present mood, there was no point in pursuing the subject of his posting. They would only end up with an argument, and that, in his present mood, was the last thing he wanted. Reluctantly, he resigned himself to a morning of silly trivia.

"My parents are having a *burra khana?*"

"Yes!" She was relieved that she finally had his attention.

"And there were separate invitation cards for each member of your family?"

"Yes."

It suddenly dawned on him that the matter that consumed her was, perhaps, not quite as trivial as he had somewhat hastily presumed. Quite the reverse!

"You have accepted the invitations?"

"Good heavens, yes!" Did he really think that they would not? "We have been *delighted* to accept. Now, tell me, darling," she hurried on, breathless with anticipation, "who else is likely to be there? Is it a small gathering or a very large, formal affair with dancing and an orchestra and buffet tables?"

"I'm afraid I don't know. I haven't been to see my mother yet." His own enthusiasm started to soar. He felt guilty that his initial reaction should have been so perverse. "But I suppose I could find out."

"Well, I just wondered if it is to be truly a grand affair or something modest and more intimate."

"Knowing Mother, I presume it will be the usual bun fight."

"Bun fight?"

"A crush, with hundreds of guests." He made a face. "Mama doesn't like half-measures, that much I do know. The invitation is addressed to you personally?"

"Yes." Her eyes shone. "I was as astounded as you are!" She searched his face with a trace of anxiety. "You *are* pleased, aren't you, Christian?"

His eyes softened. There was something so appealingly childlike about her excitement. "Of course I am—how can you ever think otherwise? I knew Papa would not let me down. He never has, you know." He felt overwhelmed with gratitude.

"In that case," she busied herself in restacking the magazines neatly, not looking at him, "surely he would not object to speaking to Mr. Ludlow about . . . ?"

"No!" He would not hear of that. "I've already told you, I don't want to ask Papa for any favours. He would be disappointed if I tried to sneak in to a better posting through the back door. These are precisely the sort of underhand methods that he deplores."

"But if the place is so utterly reprehensible?"

"I'm not a child any more," he reminded her sharply. "I can't go mewling to my father every time something in my life goes wrong. A civil servant is expected to take the foul with the fair, and that," he ended flatly, "is all there is to it."

For a brief instant—encouraged by her concern—he was strongly tempted to repeat to her everything he had already said, but then it was too late.

"And you'll never guess what *else* has happened!" Maya said with renewed excitement. "Alistair is here!"

"Alistair? Alistair Birkhurst?"

"Yes!"

Christian had heard about Alistair Birkhurst, of course. There was hardly anyone in Calcutta who did not know of Olivia Raventhorne's earlier marriage. "I was not aware that he was expected."

"Neither were we! He arrived one day quite suddenly. He is here to resolve the Agency's financial problems."

A thought struck Christian. "How has Amos taken Birkhurst's arrival?"

"In his stride." She grimaced. "Well, more or less. We haven't really seen much of Alistair since he arrived." For the moment she withheld mention of the cotton mill. "Is Alistair likely to be at the *burra khana?*"

Christian sighed. "If I know Mama, *everyone* will be at the *burra khana.* Has Amos accepted the invitation?"

"Oh yes." Her chin rose, as if she was challenging him to contradict her. "He looks forward to it as much as we do."

"Good."

Christian got up to leave, still somewhat depressed, still frustrated, but trying bravely not to show it. He was pleased, of course, about his parents' gesture, but he wished he could share in her elation more fully. Putting her arms about him, Maya gave him a lingering kiss on a cheek. "Since you refuse to involve your father, think about speaking to Mr. Ludlow yourself," she implored. "He might consider. . . ."

He shook his head. "No. We will just have to make the best of what there is."

"Well, I meant what I said, Christian," she said quietly. "As long as we are together, I could live anywhere."

This time he felt no irritation. There was about her a simplicity of thought that was touching; she trusted him implicitly. He felt an involuntary lump rise to his throat. For a moment he held her very close. "Yes," he whispered, rubbing his cheek against hers, "so could I."

"Stay for a while, Christian," she begged, reluctant to let him go.

"I can't. Not today. I have to see my parents, or they will be very cross with me. And before that, I intend to visit Kyle. He'll probably be at the press."

"Kyle?" Her heart skipped a beat.

"Yes. My father said he would like to meet him again. I want to find out if he ever did."

Maya froze. Even the *burra khana* was forgotten.

Ever since the first invitation cards had been received by those fortunate enough to be on the Pendleburys' guest list, the forthcoming ball was the talk of the town. Socially speaking, the monsoons brought little cheer. Therefore, any event that promised to lessen the ennui of these soggy months was considered a blessing. As it was, there was considerable curiosity in town about the new Finance member and his socially prominent wife. Reminders of Sir Jasper's clout as an important component of the government were hardly necessary and Lady Pendlebury's social reputation as a hostess had long preceded her arrival from London. That Lord and Lady Ingersoll's presence in town should further whet social appetites was only to be expected. No doubt, the influential, widely admired confidante of the Queen, and her husband, would also grace the occasion, and the prospect of rubbing shoulders—metaphorically speaking—with shoulders that had rubbed shoulders with royalty created a positive frenzy of excitement in town.

Even more exciting, and of infinitely greater practical value, was the expected presence at the ball of the contingent of eminently eligible young competition-wallahs belonging to Christian Pendlebury's batch. Calcutta's frenetic marriage market, in which stakes were often higher and competition stiffer than even at the horse races, thrived best in festive drawing rooms. Indeed, what better place to initiate alliances than these comfortable arenas where prospects and prospectors could be brought together under the same roof in the most flattering and favourable circumstances possible? The misfortune that had befallen young Christian Pendlebury was, of course, universally mourned, and with as much grief as a premature demise. How frightfully tragic that this innocent young man should have met so undeserving a fate even before his flowering as a full-fledged civil servant! But if one had managed to slip through the net and made good his escape, God was still in His heaven diligently looking after His own. The sudden and unheralded arrival of Baron Birkhurst of Farrowsham was received as generous enough divine compensation. Also young, good-looking and wealthy, Alistair Birkhurst was the most succulent plum to have landed in the laps of Calcutta's matronly predators in recent years. It was unfortunate, of course, that his mother was American and of such dubious repute, but then that was hardly the poor boy's fault. Gritting their teeth and priming their weaponry, mothers of spinster daughters set about planning various offensives with all means at their disposal, fair as well as foul.

"Be sure to dance with him at least *twice*," Charlotte Anderson instructed her older, unmarried daughter, Melanie, about whose future she was greatly worried. Tim Harrison of the 2nd Native, of whom she had had such high hopes, had vanished without trace somewhere in the North-West Frontier and had not been heard from since. And Melanie was not getting any younger. "Given half a chance, Verity Twining will slither in through the back door quite brazenly to push that pimply, overweight niece of hers into his lordship's face."

"I can hardly *force him* to write in my carnet unless he asks me to dance," Melanie pointed out, as she sat twirling hot tongs and paper slips in her hair, fashioning ringlets.

"There are other ways of achieving the same objective." Mrs. Anderson pursed her lips and suggested one. "Drop your carnet where he cannot miss it. When he retrieves it, ask him if he prefers the waltz to the polka. No gentleman will need further prodding to do the needful." She eyed her plain, toothsome, older daughter without enthusiasm. "And for goodness' sake, don't open your mouth any more than you need to."

"I have to make conversation, don't I?" Melanie grumbled.

"Learn to make it with your mouth shut," her mother snapped.

Smug in her recent engagement to Patrick Illingworth, Melody giggled, earning a poisonous glare from her older sister.

At the Twining luncheon table, Verity Twining's disapproving glances alternated between her niece's heaped plate of oily mutton pilaf and her pendulous double chins. Isolated in the Mofussil, Clarence's sister had despatched her daughter to Calcutta in order to seek a suitable match. Despite every conceivable effort, Verity Twining was not finding the task easy, and she was beginning to lose both heart and patience.

"No one will ever notice what a lovely smile you have, my dear," she said as she firmly swept half the pilaf onto her own plate, "unless you shed some of that excess avoirdupois. Certainly not anyone as personable as Alistair Birkhurst!"

"I don't want to be married," Deirdre wailed, as weary of the marry go round as her aunt. "I want to be a musician."

Privately, Verity Twining was beginning to doubt that she would ever be either, but she did not say so. "You can get married and still be a musician!"

"Well, he's younger than I am."

Mrs. Twining gave her a hard stare. "You are twenty-one—and don't you forget it, miss!"

"No, I'm not, you *know* I'm twenty-four! I think it's wrong to tell all these silly lies."

Her aunt gave her a look that quite appreciably lowered the temperature in the room. "There are lies," she said icily, "and there are *lies*. Under certain drastic circumstances, one is allowed permissible liberties with the truth."

Quite apart from the domestic friction the eagerly awaited event instigated, it unleashed frantic activity in several other directions. For one, there was not a single decent tailor to be had anywhere in town for love or money. Even the second range of seamsters had been snapped up as eagerly as gold nuggets from a sifting pan. Behind thick, temporary screens erected to ensure privacy, verandahs hummed with the whirr of sewing machines and nimble black fingers flew back and forth cutting and shaping, stitching and smocking, gathering and gophering, into all hours of the night. Those fortunate enough—and fast enough—to have bagged the best tailors in town secreted them in servants' quarters or distant out-houses. Knowing how fickle could be the loyalty of a master tailor before an important social occasion, no one wanted to risk having their own lured away with promises of additional lucre by unscrupulous competitors.

Those whose pockets were simply not elastic enough to stretch to elab-orate new gowns used other methods of outwitting rivals. What they lacked in resources they made up in resourcefulness. Determined not to be left lagging, they set about adding and altering, ripping and remodel-ling, cleverly transforming old favourites into modern confections, fer-vently hoping that no one would recognise last year's Derby Day wear in its new incarnation. Indeed, no mission of the British Foreign Service in Afghanistan could have been conducted with greater conspiratorial finesse and furtiveness than the sartorial preparations for the Pendleburys' inau-gural ball. Whatever else they did or did not prove, they certainly made a mockery of the myth that women cannot keep secrets.

But if domestic premises resembled battle zones as far as the women went, they were no less so for their husbands. Dr. Humphries cursed at great length as he tripped on a strange figure huddled over a complicated apparatus on the floor of his study when he came home for tiffin one after-noon.

"*Do* be careful, Charles," his wife warned, "or you'll ruin the durzee's entire morning's work!"

"Durzee? What is the blasted durzee doing in my study?"

"He's making an evening gown for Emily, what else?"

"In my *study?*" He was livid. "You couldn't find anywhere else in the house to put him?"

"Certainly not!" Dora said coldly. "Apart from the fact that I have to keep an eye on every *stitch* he makes, I'm not having him work on the verandah where everyone can see him."

"Why, he's not in damned purdah, is he?"

"Oh, don't be so *tiresome*, Charles. Do you want *everyone* to know what your daughter will be wearing?"

"What the devil does it matter, as long as it's decent—or is that too much to expect these days?"

Dora fixed him with an acid, accusing stare. "Obviously it is not of the slightest consequence to you whether or not your daughter finds a suit-able match!"

"Suitable match? Good grief, woman, she's only fifteen!"

"Well, unless I start early, how do you expect me to keep the eligible ones from getting away?"

"Lasso them and nail them to the front door, for all I care. But if this fel-low and his trappings aren't out of my study in *five* minutes . . . !"

Terrified for his life, the tailor fled.

Also making hay while the sun shone were the town's leading commercial establishments, haberdasheries, and lesser entrepreneurial talents. Ecstatic pedlars laboriously trundled from house to house, their donkey carts laden with freshly imported bolts of the most expensive materials, made even more expensive by the unseasonal rise in demand. Exploiting female vanity with outrageous flattery, they talked their smooth way into unbelievable windfalls. Whiteaway Laidlaw had not been so busy during the rainy season for years. Through the day came a steady flow of well-heeled memsahibs—or their representative ayahs and bearers and general factotums—to match ribbons and lace and swatches in the race for chic and elegance. Finally, even Whiteaway Laidlaw had to announce, with regret, that the Brussels lace was running out, that there were no more pink and blue ribbons left, and that long stockings in all shades were completely out of stock. Coiffeurs claimed equivalent attention as hairstyling establishments overflowed with customers. By the time the day of the *burra khana* dawned, most of them had run out of hairpins, nets and ornamental tortoise-shell combs, and supplies of hair lacquer were nonexistent.

In contrast to the charged atmosphere of the White Town, the Pendlebury household appeared remarkably subdued. An experienced hostess used to entertaining and being entertained on a lavish scale, Lady Pendlebury was accustomed to moving in elite and exclusive circles. Secretly, therefore, she viewed Calcutta's social scene with dismay. Colonial snobberies, she had noticed, tended to be of colour rather than of class, and quite rightly so. Being in the minority in India, the ruling population had a primary duty to hold together, regardless of the considerations of pedigree that prevailed with such unassailable rigidity back home. On the other hand, this diffusion of social hierarchies in the interests of a united front forced one to mingle with many whose antecedents would have automatically forbidden them entry into any respectable social arena in England. There were some on Lady Pendlebury's list of Calcutta guests, for instance (quite apart from the brazenly pushy Raventhornes), whose accents would not have got them past her gatekeeper's lodge in Buckinghamshire, much less her front door—not that they would ever have had the gumption to even try such an intrusion. Unlike these clod-hopping colonials, people in civilised societies knew how to keep their place and, what's more, did so. If Lady Pendlebury derived any consolation at all from her guest list, it was that the Ingersolls were also on it to provide a touch of exclusivity, and that, she concluded morosely, was better than nothing.

Nevertheless, behind the Pendlebury household's placid exterior, copious preparations were indeed in progress. Despite her many reservations, Constance Pendlebury was a naturally house-proud hostess with an infallible eye for detail, and as such, it was second nature to her to take infinite pains over planning every aspect of a social evening under her roof. She dispensed orders and delegated duties with consummate calm and confidence. She knew exactly what was needed and precisely how it was to be achieved. M'amselle Corinne, her new housekeeper, was a true treasure, her supreme virtue being that she got on well with Pierre. For this tender mercy, Lady Pendlebury was profoundly grateful; the temperamental chef had not had a migraine in days. In fact, he had further surprised her by taking the extensive buffet menu she had devised entirely in his stride with not even a peep of protest. Indeed, there were moments when Lady Pendlebury wondered if the two were not getting on rather *too* well for comfort, but that, she decided, she would worry about later, after her first dinner party and musical soirée were safely behind her.

Even though it was he who had proposed it, the *burra khana* and its preparations constituted a source of irritation to Sir Jasper. He lost no time in taking appropriate defensive action. With workmen in every available room falling out of the woodwork like termites, he spent even longer hours at work, dining out of a tiffin-carrier brought by Tremaine to his office from the house. As soon as he returned home, he hurriedly ordered a hookah and withdrew into his study, sheltering against invasion amid clouds of aromatic smoke. As it happened, there was much that he had to think about in privacy; Harriet Ingersoll's connections with royalty, for instance. He also needed to cogitate in greater detail about his strange encounter with Kyle Hawkesworth, an encounter that disturbed him more than he cared to admit.

Knowing from past experience how futile it was to expect her husband to make intelligent domestic suggestions or decisions, Lady Pendlebury allowed him his solitary pleasures without hindrance. However, two days before the event, she bravely risked suffocation and, clamping a handkerchief over her nose, ventured into her husband's inner sanctum.

Coughing, waving her arms about her face, she sat herself down as far away from Sir Jasper as she could and still remain within earshot. "I thought you might want to know that all the native merchants have accepted, but only one will bring his wife."

"Kali Charan Goswami? Yes, I thought so. I believe she has no objection to mingling with foreigners."

"I should hope not," his wife snapped, then went on to enumerate the names of a few more who had accepted, pointing out the remarkably few refusals. "Anyway, I've avoided both beef and pork in the Indian menu."

"Excellent."

"We are arranging separate tables for those who might have other dietary restrictions. There will be plenty of fish, fowl and vegetable curries made by the Bengali cooks."

"Very thoughtful, m'dear, very thoughtful."

"The champagne we have in stock should be enough, but if you don't wish to serve the Havanas Dudley sent from America, you will need to order more cigars."

"Is young Birkhurst coming?"

"Yes. Mr. Donaldson has written on his behalf."

He fixed her with a hard stare. "And the Raventhornes? Have they accepted?"

Her manner cooled. "Did you expect them not to?"

"Yes. They are known to keep themselves to themselves."

"I daresay, they have good reason to! Jasper, I. . . ."

He held up a hand before she could proceed further. "The subject bears no more discussion, Constance. I have already explained that it is for reasons of expediency that they have been asked. Whatever your personal feelings, I must insist that once they cross our threshold, they be given the same attention and deference as the other guests. There can be no two ways about that."

Lady Pendlebury clenched her fists. "If Christian makes a fool of himself in public, fussing and fawning over that hussy, I will not be able to tolerate it!"

"Why not? He will simply be doing his duty as a host. Surely you would not have it otherwise?"

She glared at him in disgust. "How can you take it all so . . . so *lightly*, Jasper? Don't you find it horribly demeaning?"

"No. I've already assured you that Christian will not marry Raventhorne's daughter."

"So you say, Jasper—but how precisely do you plan to *stop* him, pray?"

"Stop him?" Sir Jasper looked mildly surprised. "Oh, I won't *stop* him. I won't need to. It will be Christian's own decision not to marry the girl."

If Amos's childishly intractable attitude to the *burra khana* was impossible, Olivia found her daughter's extravagant reactions even more nerve-wracking. Ever since that gold-crested, exquisitely penned invitation had arrived, Maya seemed to have lost every semblance of good sense. Her behaviour was irrational, her temper ready to ignite at the slightest provocation. She barely ate at table, but in between meals, she foraged in the larder and devoured whatever she could find. Instead of sleeping at night, she took to sitting up in the verandah, thinking or making copious notes, and in the privacy of her room, Olivia knew, she was driving herself to distraction over those wretched pattern books she carried around like a totem.

The all-important matter of the dress still remained unresolved. Nothing that any pedlar brought was considered good enough for the occasion, even the finest of materials rejected. Eventually. Olivia laid her own wardrobe at Maya's disposal. She unpacked one of her very expensive, unused evening gowns, and suggested that it might be successfully altered. Maya dismissed it with contempt as archaic and unusable, then once again teetered on the verge of a tantrum.

"Just look at the *hem*, Mother! Can't you see how uneven it is?"

"With two hundred people at the party, who on earth is going to notice one solitary hem, for heaven's sake?"

"I'm going to notice it, and *she* is!" Maya cried, the tears starting to well. "She's going to notice every *single* thing about me, including that damned hem—can't you see that?"

Exhausted, Olivia gave up the fight. Just at that opportune moment, Edna Chalcott walked in. Gratefully, Olivia surrendered her daughter into her friend's knowing care.

With unerring instinct and a practised eye, Edna took in the situation at a glance. Marching Maya off to her room, she seated her down on an easy chair. Then, without saying a word, she took the pile of fashion magazines stacked by her bedside and pitched the entire lot into her wastepaper basket. Stern-faced, she positioned herself opposite Maya on a corner of the bed.

"Now, you listen to me, my girl," she said. "Temper and tizzies are not going to get you anywhere—except to a sickbed. During these past days that I have been rehearsing for that musical soirée, I have been observing Constance Pendlebury very closely. She is a highly sophisticated lady. Everything that she wears, even her undergarments, I daresay, is noteworthy, chosen with an eye for exclusivity."

"What are you trying to do?" Maya asked with a sarcastic laugh that sounded suspiciously like a sob. "Make me feel even worse than I already do?"

Edna ignored the question. "Now if you want to make a favourable impression on Christian's mother—and that, I presume, is the object of this entire exercise—then you have to match her on her own ground. What you too have to be is sophisticated."

"*How?*"

"Not with these hoary chestnuts, I promise!" Edna directed a look of contempt at the wastepaper basket. "Since their limited imaginations are incapable of carrying them further, this is where every woman in town will scrounge for inspiration. What you need, my dear, is something that makes you look *different.*"

"Oh, you mean we just wave a wand, do we?"

To that, too, Edna paid no heed. "First of all, we will forget about frills and flounces and miles of lacy frou-frou—that is *precisely* what Constance Pendlebury detests. Most colonial women carry their taste in their mouth, and nowhere else. Decked up like tinselled Christmas trees for the ball, they will be blissfully unaware that they look common and cheap and grotesquely overblown. You, my dear, must not."

"Well then, what do I wear?" Maya asked tearfully. "I've got nothing else, and neither has Mother."

Edna got up and patted her hand. "Leave it to me, my dear. I may not be a great couturiere, but I do have a modicum of good common sense and I know what I'm talking about. As it happens, I have *just* the thing for you in my treasure chest. Now, wash your face and blow your nose. We're going to see the twins at the Home."

A thousand questions milled about in Maya's head, all of which Edna answered with patience and eminent practical wisdom as they made their way to Chitpore. Should she wear gloves? Well, she didn't have any. Was it customary to curtsey when introduced? Should she wear her hair long and flowing, up and lacquered, curled or straight? What cosmetics were commonly used beside lip salve, rouge and eye kohl? And certainly she would need new dancing slippers (flat or small-heeled?) and a poche to match. There was so little time, so much to do and learn and absorb. Whatever else, she must not disappoint Christian, must not do anything wrong!

Oh, merciful heavens—where did one start?

"Start? Well, if you still have your illustrated manual from the Academy," Edna suggested, when they returned after concluding their business with the twins, "I recommend that we start with some dancing practice. I daresay both of us could do with a lesson or two."

Greatly relieved to have her overwrought daughter off her hands for the time being, Olivia again turned her thoughts towards Amos. He was still going to great lengths to avoid her, still sullen and closed within himself. As a concession to his sister's impassioned pleadings, he had finally agreed to escort them to the Pendleburys' dinner party, but with very bad grace. However, although that particular battle had been won, Olivia knew that another still remained to be fought. On the eve of the event, she tackled Amos in his room.

"There's something else that I have to say about this *burra khana*, Amos."

"Oh, for heaven's sake, Mother," he exclaimed irritably, "I've *said* I will go—what more do you want?"

"The reason why you were so against going—still are—is that Alistair will be there, isn't that it?"

He gave her a cold look. "Whether or not he is there is not of the least consequence to me. I do have other matters to worry about."

"What matters?"

"Matters more serious than a damned pukka ball!"

He almost blurted out the information about Thomas Hungerford, but then stopped himself just in time. Instead, he turned away, angry that she should have voiced what was, of course, true. He loathed the prospect of having to come face to face with Alistair Birkhurst.

"There is no law that says that you have to like Alistair, Amos," Olivia said firmly. "I accept that. I also accept that if you don't wish to meet him, you are free not to. Naturally, I am pained, but as a grown man you have the right to make your own choices. There is *one* thing, however, upon which I must absolutely insist." She walked round to where he stood and forced him to look at her. "I insist that if you do happen to come face to face with Alistair in public, as you are likely to on Saturday, you will at least be civil."

"If by that you mean that I should not punch him in the eye in public, I agree." He gave a nasty laugh. "Unless, of course, he asks for it!"

The sharp hurt that she felt showed in her eyes. "I would be perfectly content if you would do just this one thing for me, Amos," she begged, "just this one thing. Promise me you will, darling, promise me!"

He scowled, seething with resentment. "You don't have much faith in me any more, do you?"

"Oh darling, it's *not* that, it's. . . ."

"Don't bother to explain. I understand perfectly."

She grabbed his hand and held it. "Give me your word, Amos!"

He wrenched his hand free. "Yes, yes, *yes*. Now don't bother to mention his name to me again!"

He whisked his neatly folded pyjamas off the bed, stomped away in the direction of his dressing room and slammed the door hard behind him. Nonetheless, Olivia breathed a heavy sigh of relief. Having given her his word, she knew that he would not break it. As Olivia tripped lightly down the stairs on her way to her rose garden at the back, she smiled a secret little smile within herself. She had told Amos that she did not want to go to the Pendleburys'. She had lied. There was nothing in her life that she wanted more than to be at that *burra khana* tomorrow night.

She knew that Alistair would be there. And that she would see him again.

"Sit down, Mr. Pendlebury." Herbert Ludlow waved his hand at a chair as soon as Christian walked in. "I am glad that you could make the time to see me this morning."

Christian did as ordered and smiled to himself. The Chief Commissioner's summons were an order; there was no question of "making the time." He had not been surprised to find the message waiting for him at the chummery after he returned from seeing Maya, asking him to make it convenient to call this morning. No doubt, he decided sourly, it would give Herbert Ludlow considerable sadistic pleasure to interrogate him at length about his trip to Champaran. During the few moments of mandatory casual talk, however, the Chief Commissioner made only routine inquiries about Christian's language and other studies. A squat, portly figure of a man, with little hair and much flesh, Herbert Ludlow had been at Haileybury at the same time as Sir Jasper and Bruce McNaughton, and had also started his working life as a writer with John Company. He was a confirmed and rather pedantic bachelor, and as such, tended to view his married colleagues with genuine pity. Like many bureaucrats, he was inclined to be somewhat more fond of the sound of his voice than modesty decreed—or his listeners might have wished. If Herbert Ludlow had a religion at all, it was said to be the Covenanted Civil Service, and his place of worship, whichever desk he happened to occupy at the moment.

Having dispensed with the preliminaries, he proceeded to the same tedious opening to which he reverted in all his interviews with the raw young recruits brought to him each year by the Civil Service competition, no matter how often he had met them.

"The Covenanted Civil Service, Mr. Pendlebury, comprises the most important class of officials in the country—as, no doubt, has already been impressed upon you at the College."

"Yes, sir."

"It signifies to the natives the very essence of British rule in India. Every officer of the Service stands as a symbol before the people of this country, a material symbol of the intangible mind and motive of Her Majesty's Government. As far as governmental action affects the daily life, the domestic well-being and the mundane, everyday concerns of the people, it is in the conduct of arbitrament for their weal and woe that the Covenanted Civil Service is of the utmost importance. Do you agree?"

"Most definitely, sir."

Pompous ass! Inwardly, Christian suppressed a groan, knowing that he was going to be kept here for hours, forced to listen to flannel he had heard a hundred times before. The expression on his face, however, remained one of deep reverence.

"By the conduct of these few and select officers," Ludlow droned on sonorously, "is measured the very character and calibre of Britannia herself, Mr. Pendlebury. By his disposition, the temper of his conversation, his ability and demeanour, his conduct with the native people of this land, the covenanted civil servant performs a mission such as has not ever. . . ."

Christian stopped listening. Every student who has ever passed through University develops a certain facility which he refines into an art form, and Christian was no different. He heard not another word, but his expression of rapt attention did not change a whit. Borne aloft on the wings of his own oratory, the Chief Commissioner carried on regardless.

Behind his mesmerised eyes, however, Christian's mind was by no means in a trance. He was thinking furiously. When interrogated about Champaran, he wondered, just how forthcoming was it advisable to be? Should he risk mention of Humphrey Doyle and his reprehensible antics (obliquely, of course), or should he avoid that topic altogether? And what if he were to suggest, merely *suggest,* that with a few more creature comforts he might be better equipped to help Britannia's measure?

He saw that Ludlow was in a benign enough mood this morning, as he usually was when sermonising to a captive recruit about his favourite subject. Christian recalled Maya's suggestion and cogitated over it. Well, what if he *were* to take the bull firmly by the horns and make a bold request for a change of posting? Ludlow would be highly displeased, of course, but what was the worst the old windbag could do apart from fulminate and dismiss the request as impertinent? The more Christian considered this option, the more animated he became in his mind. And, while the going was good, he decided, might he not also throw in. . . .

His introspections snapped in mid-thought. He noticed that there was silence in the room; Ludlow had stopped talking. Christian recollected himself with a start, realising with a sinking heart that the Chief Commissioner had asked a question and was now awaiting an answer. Not having heard the question, he was hardly in a position to provide one.

"I, er, beg your pardon, sir?" he stammered, flushing.

"Pay *attention,* Mr. Pendlebury," Ludlow said with marked irritation. "I am not in the habit of wasting my time for the benefit of the walls."

"Er no, sir," Christian said hastily. "Certainly not, sir."

"Well, would you or would you not?"

Feeling an absolute idiot, Christian had no option but to ask, "Would I, er, what, sir?"

Now distinctly annoyed, Ludlow tapped his fingernail ominously with a pencil. "I asked," he said slowly and with more than a touch of sarcasm, "if you are familiar with the name of Lumsdale?"

"Lumsdale?" Christian's mind leapt to attention, every nerve end alert. "Lumsdale, sir? Mr. *Gordon* Lumsdale?"

"If there is another Lumsdale in the Service who is a District Commissioner," Ludlow said coldly, "I would be gratified to be enlightened."

Christian fumbled his way through a hasty apology, his eyes wide with shock. "But Mr. Lumsdale is in the Punjab, sir, if I am not mistaken."

"Of course he's in the Punjab—that is precisely what I have just said, Mr. Pendlebury!" Ludlow thumped the tabletop in exasperation. "What is the matter with you today, sir? Are you not well?"

Grasping the excuse, Christian quickly nodded, pulled out his handkerchief and sniffled into it very convincingly and at some length.

The Chief Commissioner waited with ill-concealed impatience until Christian had finished blowing his nose, the pencil still tapping. "Since you appear not to have heard a word of what I have been explaining to you in considerable detail and with monumental patience, Mr. Pendlebury, I suppose I shall have to repeat it. However, I would like to point out that I take an *extremely* dim view of lack of concentration in any civil servant ordained by Her Majesty's Government to. . . ." He stopped and frowned. "What was I about to say?"

"You were about to say something about Mr. Lumsdale, sir." It was all Christian could do in his eagerness to keep himself still in his chair.

"Ah yes. Well, Mr. Lumsdale, who is at present in the Punjab, has had an unfortunate experience with one of his assistants. In fact, the young man has decided to hang himself."

He spoke with marked disapproval, making it plain that he viewed such an act to be the height of inconsideration, especially since it was committed during the hours of duty.

Christian quickly mumbled his own agreement, callously directing his own sympathies towards Mr. Ludlow and his predicament.

"As you may conclude from this," the Chief Commissioner continued, "the man's lack of responsibility has been the cause of great inconvenience to Mr. Lumsdale and, naturally, to the local administration."

"Naturally." Again Christian agreed. Not having known the unfortunate young assistant, he felt no compunction in endorsing the man's lack of fibre. He waited in an agony of suspense for Ludlow to come to the point, hardly daring to breathe in case he again missed something.

"For all his emotional instability, however, the young man, also a competition-wallah not long out of Fort William College, was a highly competent officer. Lumsdale, a hard taskmaster who spares neither himself nor his deputies, is the first to concede that. Nonetheless, the fact is that he has been left high and dry in the middle of a most vital rural project."

"Yes sir, I can appreciate that." With the violent pounding of his heart within his ribcage, Christian could barely hear his own words and raised his voice. "I have read a great deal about Mr. Lumsdale. Indeed, as a perfect civil servant, he has long been my ideal."

"You don't need to shout, Mr. Pendlebury," Ludlow said irritably. "I am not deaf!" But Christian's comment pleased him. He leaned back in his chair and beamed. "A very worthy model, I might say, Mr. Pendlebury. Very worthy indeed."

"My other ideal is, of course, Sir Henry Lawrence," Christian added, lowering his voice. What he said was true, but he now intoned it, quite shamelessly, with rather overdone reverence. If ingratiation was what the Chief Commissioner wanted at this electrifying moment, then ingratiation was what he would give him. "I consider no civil servant's services to this country greater than those of Sir Henry."

"Ah!" The Chief Commissioner was delighted. "Rather fortuitous that you should choose to admire two men who have, more than any others, made their name in the Punjab, what?"

"Yes, sir." Christian assumed an expression of modesty and a slightly obsequious smile, both of which he knew would go down well with Ludlow. "I have always considered the Punjab to be the most challenging province in the country."

"Have you? Well, that *is* rather a happy coincidence!" Ludlow nodded several times to show his approval. "Lumsdale made a request to me about a month ago, just after this tiresome incident, to select for him a replacement of a similarly high calibre. All said and done, Forrester—the man who died—was an admirable choice. He was a natural linguist. Within eight weeks of joining his duties, he was speaking Punjabi almost as well as a native and so gained great local popularity. Being of farming stock himself, he loved the land and soon established excellent rapport with the indigenous peasantry. He was modest, not at all arrogant, sincerely admired this country and its people, and had a humility of demeanour that increased rather than diminished his competence."

To all this Christian listened closely, ready to burst with expectation. Would the man never get to the bloody point? Knowing, however, that a premature comment would not go in his favour, he forced himself to maintain an anguished silence.

"On my instructions," the Chief Commissioner resumed, suddenly brisk, "the tutors at the College have been asked to recommend a young man of your batch who gives evidence of the same potential and qualities as the ill-fated Forrester." He made a significant pause. "I am pleased to announce that they have recommended you, Mr. Pendlebury. Now, what do you have to say to that?"

Christian had nothing to say. Although he had half expected what Ludlow had just announced, he was still dumbfounded, paralysed with disbelief. Rather stupidly he noticed that a wasp had flown in through the window and was about to settle on the Chief Commissioner's ear. In his befuddlement he might have blurted out a warning and made an ass of himself but, fortunately, he had simply lost all power of speech.

"You have a genuine interest in this country," Ludlow carried on, possibly to give him time to retrieve his voice. "You come here, Mr. Trevors has informed me, with a noble desire to serve the country and its people, and in all humility. Your attitude, your other tutors have said, is precisely what a man like Lumsdale would want. You have, I am pleased to note, not complained once about being posted to a district such as Champaran." He stopped and, overwhelmed by that last remark and the extravagant praise, Christian blushed. "Well, Mr. Pendlebury, what do you say, do you accept my offer?"

Christian gulped and cleared his throat. The wasp, he noticed with relief, had flown back out of the window. "Yes, sir. Most *definitely*, sir."

Ludlow gave a good-natured laugh. "Are you not interested in even knowing where the posting is?"

"No, sir. For an opportunity to serve under Mr. Lumsdale, I would go anywhere in the world, anywhere at all! But, as it happens, I do know the precise location. At present, Mr. Lumsdale is in a village called Gujrat some seventy miles from Lahore on the road to Peshawar. His main project is to build a small but very necessary dam across a minor tributary of the River Jhelum."

"Well done, sir! I see that we have made the right choice for the job, and I am certain Gordon Lumsdale will endorse that. Now, would you be ready to leave in, say, three weeks' time?"

"I would be ready to leave tomorrow," Christian said simply.

"The right spirit, Mr. Pendlebury, but a presumptuous answer," Ludlow reproved sternly. "You would not be ready to leave tomorrow for the very good reason that you speak no Punjabi. Lumsdale insists that his assistants have at least some familiarity with the colloquial language when they arrive."

Christian nodded, his throat choked, his eyes shining.

"Well then, off you go, Mr. Pendlebury. You start your lessons at the College this afternoon with a Mr. Harbinder Singh, a retired havildar-major of the Third Light Cavalry." He chuckled. "From what I hear of his methods, he will have you chattering like one of his own within the week. Now, any questions?"

In the process of floating through the doorway, his feet scarcely touching the ground, Christian halted. "One, sir."

"Yes?"

His colour heightened. "About the, ah, accommodation, sir."

"You will be under canvas, of course. Everyone is, including the District Chief Secretary. Suitable housing will be constructed in due course, naturally, but it is hardly a priority. The dam is. Why do you ask?"

Red-faced, Christian twisted his handkerchief between his fingers. "I ask because . . . because." He stopped. Sheer embarrassment prevented his tongue from formulating the words.

A small gleam of understanding dawned in Herbert Ludlow's eyes. He took his time to reply. First he sat for a moment in thoughtful silence, then he rose and walked to his bookcase.

"It is my duty to warn you, Mr. Pendlebury, that what you face on this posting is a harsh and relentless life." Ludlow spoke conversationally, his back towards Christian as he searched for some book, but his tone was edged with steel. "The winters in the Punjab are bitterly cold, the summers blisteringly hot. The food will be indifferent, the meals irregular, hurriedly snatched whenever there is time to eat. Even if the camp beds prove comfortable, the nights will not. There will be constant hazards from dangerous insects, reptiles and animals—mosquitoes, scorpions, snakes, lizards, spiders and prowling predators—to say nothing of the ever present threat of violence from local dacoits. The working hours will be endless. You will have to consider yourself on duty through twenty-four hours of the day, seven days of the week. Now"—book in hand, he turned to face Christian—"do you wish to change your decision?"

Christian looked horrified. "Oh, *no,* sir, absolutely not, sir! I only inquired about the residential facilities in case . . . in case I. . . ." He coughed and dropped his eyes.

Herbert Ludlow resumed his seat and indicated that Christian should do the same. He placed the book on the desk. It was a volume of memoirs of a civil servant early in the century, often held up as a model to current young competition-wallahs.

"There is one factor involved in this posting that I have not yet mentioned. I had thought that I would bring it up later, at a more detailed briefing, but in all fairness to you, I see that it would be expedient to do so now." He looked at Christian gravely over the pyramid of his fingers against his chest. "The reason young Forrester took such an extreme step as to terminate his life arose out of his rather tragic domestic circumstances. He and his young wife lost two children in the Punjab in quick succession. One was stillborn, and the other, a two-year-old daughter, died ten days later due to the local unavailability of adequate medical facilities. Devastated by the loss of both her children, plagued by ill health herself and unable to endure the unspeakable vicissitudes of life in the open, Mrs. Forrester decided to leave for England, vowing that she would never return to this country." He paused. "In a single month, Forrester lost his entire family. Unable to bear the terrible burden of such a total loss, his mind snapped."

Christian sat in absolute silence. A feeling of profound unease crept up his chest.

"In the Covenanted Civil Service, Mr. Pendlebury," the Chief Secretary continued in the same hard tone, "very often one finds that one cannot serve two masters at once. There comes a time when, inevitably, one has to make a choice. Am I making myself clear?"

Christian shook his head but remained silent.

"Then I must clarify further. Mr. Lumsdale has specified in strong, unequivocal language that he will not, I repeat, will *not,* under any circumstances, consider accepting another married assistant at this location." He picked up his pen to indicate that the interview was at an end. "That will be all, Mr. Pendlebury."

Christian's euphoria evaporated; everything within him went numb. He closed his eyes and remained seated.

Ludlow looked up. "Well? Any more questions?"

Christian opened his eyes and tried to focus his bleary vision on the Chief Commissioner's face. "No, sir. No questions. But I have to tell you that, under these conditions, I regret that I cannot accept the position."

Herbert Ludlow laid down his pen. He could not have looked more shocked had Christian decided to shed all his clothes and perform a jig on the desk. "Cannot? Why the *devil* not?"

"Because I am not in a position to give an undertaking to remain a bachelor for the duration of the posting."

Ludlow slowly eased his great hulk back into his chair. In silence, he studied the colourless, desperately unhappy face of the young man who sat opposite.

"I see." His voice was arctic.

But the truth was that Herbert Ludlow did not see. Christian's association with the Raventhorne girl was no more a secret to him than it was to anybody else. However, dalliance was one thing, normal and expected, but marriage? As a dedicated bachelor himself, he simply could not understand how any intelligent young man could voluntarily consign himself to a state as unholy as matrimony. He was baffled and outraged by Christian's extraordinary response. He waited for further explanations. When none appeared to be forthcoming, he took a deep breath and crossed his arms against his chest.

"Very well, Mr. Pendlebury. In that case, permit me to do you the favour of preventing you from becoming your own worst enemy. Because I believe that you *are* so eminently suited to fill this position, I am going to suggest that you allow yourself time to examine all aspects of the matter. I will give you one week in which to change your mind. After that, I regret, I will be compelled to select another candidate."

He would not change his mind! On the verge of saying so, Christian stopped. He had already blotted his copybook enough for one day. It would be foolish to destroy it completely. He rose and gave a stiff bow. "Thank you, sir. I will inform you of my final decision as soon as the week is over."

"Give it to me in writing, will you?"

"Yes, sir. Thank you, sir." He turned and walked out of the room.

Christian stumbled through the compound of the Commissioner's office, hardly aware of where he was going. In his head swirled a snow-storm of confusion; he felt unsteady on his feet. The only clear thought his brain could manage at the moment was that this had been absolutely the worst morning of his entire life.

CHAPTER

18

A S A MATTER OF UNIVERSAL RELIEF, the day of the Pendlebury
ball dawned clear, with washed blue skies and pale but persistent
sunshine. Nonetheless, refusing to risk being caught unawares,
guests started to arrive early. Despite the city's temporarily depleted European component, at sunset the streets around the Pendlebury's Garden
Reach mansion and the driveway that led to it were choked with an astonishing number of carriages. Their bedecked occupants, eager to reach the
safety of the porch before a perverse shower could flatten ringlets,
starched skirts and, indeed, soaring spirits, pushed and shoved their way
to the front entrance without a shred of embarrassment.

Among the earliest to arrive were Willie Donaldson and Alistair
Birkhurst.

Given a slight difference in terminology, Olivia's conversation with
Amos the previous evening was not entirely dissimilar in intent to that
which Willie Donaldson had had with Alistair Birkhurst in the Agency
office that morning.

"I'll come to fetch you at six, laddie," Donaldson said. "I would be
obliged na to be kept waitin'."

Alistair yawned and looked bored. "I think I have already made it clear,
Mr. Donaldson, that I will not, repeat *not*, be going to the Pendleburys'
party this evening."

"And while you are there," Donaldson continued as if he had not spoken, "you will comport yourself like a true son of Farrowsham. Your
grandmama would na react kindly should the fair name of Birkhurst be
disgraced in public."

"I'm not *going!*" Alistair repeated crossly and loudly. "Didn't you hear
what I just said?"

"Furthermore," Donaldson's monotone droned on, "you will make it a point to approach Amos Raventhorne like a gentleman. You will greet your mama with a kiss, nice and proper, likewise your sister. And you will dance at least once with each of the ladies."

Alistair was outraged. "I'll be damned if I do, sir! Do you think I would lower myself by so much as even *acknowledging* them? In any case," he sat back with a smirk, "they're hardly likely to be invited, are they!"

"They are invited."

Alistair looked nonplussed, but then his chin again firmed. "In that case, I definitely refuse to go!"

"T'would be a guid chance to mend fences."

"I don't *want* blasted fences mended!"

"I've already accepted on your behalf."

"Well then, you can jolly well unaccept! Just say I've been taken ill."

Donaldson looked shocked. "You canna ask me to tell a lie!"

"Then I will, and you can simply deliver the letter."

"It would na be courteous to decline at the last minute."

"I don't care a fig if it isn't! I'm *not* going to lower myself consorting with those half-castes!"

"Better a half-caste than a halfwit," Donaldson said coldly. "Besides, there are guid reasons for you to go."

"Like hell there are!" Alistair gave him an enraged glare. "Give me one!"

For a moment Donaldson reflected upon the flushed face of his youthful charge. "Unless your lordship accepts my most humble suggestion," he said, "your lordship may consider my services to the Birkhurst family term'nated as of this mornin'. Noo, would your lordship consider *that* guid 'nuff reason?"

"What?" Alistair sat up, startled.

Donaldson elucidated further. "To tell the truth, I'm gettin' fed up, bloody fed up of your lordship's 'nfantile shenaneckings. I'm *disgusted* that a young man with as much breedin' should have so few manners and so little 'preciation of God's manifold blessin's, and I 'ntend to put that doon in writin' for your dear grandma's 'nformation. For nigh on sixty years, I've served your lordship's family with love and sweat and bleedin' tears. But I regret that I canna do so any longer. Your lordship can manage the sales withoot my help, I daresay. If na, the Agency can rot and go to the goddam devil!" He rose and pulled himself up to his full height. "Noo, have I made myself clear on all coonts?"

Alistair was speechless.

"Very well, then, I'll see your lordship at the manse at six o'clock this evenin'. *Sharp.*"

Whistling under his breath, he shuffled out of the room leaving his young protégé furious and spluttering.

When Willie Donaldson arrived at the manse at six o'clock precisely, he did so in some trepidation. However, he was pleasantly surprised to be greeted on the front steps by the ninth Baron of Farrowsham, glowering ferociously, true, but nonetheless ready and waiting. Alistair's mood was foul, his manner chilly. The journey to Garden Reach was negotiated without the benefit of a word or a look between them, except for a brief sotto voce exchange as they alighted.

"Dinna forget, your lordship."

"Oh, go to blazes!"

But all in all, Willie Donaldson was well satisfied with his morning's work.

"Why people insist on arriving earlier than invited, I shall never know," Lady Pendlebury grumbled to herself as she pressed a diamond ear bob into a lobe. She stood up from her dressing table, smoothed down the front of the very chic aquamarine lace over taffeta that she had last worn to a Hunt Ball in Shropshire, and prepared to hurry downstairs. "Well, it doesn't surprise me that these colonials should have not even the meanest of social graces!"

Her ayah nodded in vigorous agreement without having understood a word.

At the entrance to the main reception room, however, as she joined her waiting husband and son, Lady Pendlebury's face brightened. For once, since the day of their disembarkation, Christian was correctly clad. His well-starched cream shirt matched his professionally pleated cummerbund. The dark brown velvet lapels and cuffs of his formal coat were brushed into a smooth shine, and his hair was oiled well back with none of those Bohemian tousles that gave him the appearance of a vagrant intellectual. She stretched out a gloved finger to remove a suspected speck from his coat front, but he jerked back.

"Don't fuss, Mama! It's only a bit of fluff."

Despite the meticulousness of his grooming, his face looked pinched, as if he had not slept well, and he was fidgety. His mother's eyes narrowed; putting his apparent nervousness down to the imminent arrival of his lady love, she silently mouthed an oath that she would never dream of voicing aloud. But then, as the indefatigable M'amselle Corinne hurried up with a whispered question and the wheels of another carriage crunched to a stop outside on the gravelled driveway, Lady Pendlebury smoothed her frowning brow and concentrated on her immediate priorities.

The thin trickle of arrivals soon thickened into a deluge. Guests in their best bibs and tuckers spilled in through the wide-open front doors in rapid succession, all ogling eyes and bated breath as they dispensed kisses and curtseys and handshakes. Apart from the Viceroy's palace during the Imperial Levees and First Drawing Room receptions, such lavish surroundings and hospitality were seldom seen in station. Even in the more affluent of Calcutta's households, entertainment was on a far more modest scale.

"Oh my!" Deirdre Twining whispered to her aunt as she cast awed eyes around the glittering reception rooms ablaze with light from the multi-tiered chandeliers and candelabra. "Fancy waking up to this every morning!"

"Well, they don't," Verity Twining snapped, simmering with envy at the splendour they themselves could ill afford on an Inspector-General's salary. "I daresay they have bedrooms to sleep in just like us lesser mortals."

There was indeed no doubt that Lady Pendlebury had achieved miracles with the Garden Reach residence, as much with money as with imagination and faultless good taste. The marble floors, where not overlaid with exotic Persian carpets, shone like mirrors; the antique brass, silver and crystal sparkled with life. Long, sweeping curtains in subdued pastel designs covered the tall, open windows, their silken tassels as gossamer fine as freshly spun candy floss. No corner of the reception rooms appeared to have been neglected. Even the most out-of-the-way niche had been livened with some embellishment or the other: a framed tapestry, a priceless Russian icon, an arrangement of medieval Chinese pottery or Wedgwood plate, and, of course, there were banks of freshly cut flowers everywhere. Through the folding glass doors, past graceful verandah arches, lay the gardens, at the back bordering the river. There was still enough light to see how very effectively the sprawling lawns had been cossetted back into vibrance and the neat, geometrical flower beds pampered into visions of colour. At the end of the garden, in the far right corner, the glass panes of a summerhouse glowed orange and red as they caught the last rays of the setting sun.

Arthur Robinson, wealthy owner of a prosperous shopping establishment who hailed from Clapham, dropped aitches and bricks with equal abandon, but nobody really minded. When it came to supporting the cause of fallen women or impoverished East India merchants, he was the first to dig his hands into his pocket. He now stared around in frankly boggle-eyed fascination. "You done a spiffin' job, yer lidyship, a *spiffin'* job!" He pumped her hand hard between his fat, beringed fingers. "Must 've cost yer a bob or two, Oi bet, all these fancy doodahs and everyfin'." He nudged his wife in the ribs with an elbow. "Ain't it grand, lovie, jes grand?"

Since Mrs. Robinson's life's ambition was to be invited to perform as the solo soprano at one of Lady Pendlebury's soirées, she nodded in eager agreement.

"Too kind," Lady Pendlebury murmured, retrieving her hand with some difficulty and trying not to shudder. "Simply too kind!"

The Indian merchants, suited and booted and punctual to the dot, came in a group, spruce but self-conscious in the unaccustomed Western garb. Even Kali Charan Goswami, in a rare concession to the occasion, sported a three-piece English suit of natty pin-striped grey, and a scarlet bow tie. His wife on the other hand, very elegant in a crimson sari with bright peacock blue and gold border, looked entirely at home though she was the only Indian lady present.

As initial stiffness melted, the reception rooms started to come alive with the low hum of speech and sporadic bursts of laughter. The gentlemen, flashing their medals and moustaches, presented as colourful an aspect as the ladies, from the scarlet, blues and greys of the uniforms to the jaunty yellows and greens of the younger blades and the sober black of the business community. The close to two hundred guests included merchants, bankers, civil servants, government officials, naval and army officers, Port Trust officials, chandlers, stevedores, prelates garbed in the cloth, medical men and missionaries. Presently, they separated into smaller groups according to age, occupation, old friendships, new acquaintanceships, or simply personal preference.

What made Calcutta's limited social scene different and comparatively undemanding was the effective idiom used to simplify personal information. Regardless of dress, manners, virtue or pedigree, descriptions usually consisted of a professional designation together with a pithy use of parentheses. Thus, so-and-so was the Assistant Commissioner of Income Tax (whose eldest daughter eloped with a piano tuner last year and was then abandoned, pregnant and penniless), or the Inspector of Smoke Nuisances (who had two children in a frightfully expensive Edinburgh boarding school—as corrupt as they come, my dear, except that he thinks *everyone* thinks he's as white as a Brahmin's summer dhoti!), or the newly appointed Sudder Judge (who was trying to get his effeminate son married off to the General's daughter and the poor girl had absolutely no idea that the boy was, you know, *one of those!*).

At a signal from the hostess, a succession of white-uniformed bearers with the Pendleburys' initials embroidered in red and blue on their left breasts floated in, bearing trays of anchovy allumettes, Lucille toast and barquettes. To one side of the second reception room, not far from Sir Jasper's study, Lady Pendlebury had arranged a long counter which served as a bar, behind which waiters in white and scarlet turbans from the Bengal Club served drinks that would loosen inhibitions and heighten cordiality: iced champagne, French wines, malt whiskies of the finest brands, brandies, beer, port, sherries and liqueurs. An additional barman, an American, hired for the evening from a visiting steam clipper out of Philadelphia, dispensed the more unusual varieties for the benefit of guests from the New World. Hal Lubbock, prominent member of this community, was not present. Much to Lady Pendlebury's relief, the brash, rough-hewn Southerner, and his swarthy wife and daughter with the chi-chi accents, were still away in the hills.

"I say," the shellac importer from Boston asked, eyeing the bar counter with a salacious look. "You think I could find some bourbon here?"

Kali Charan Babu smiled. "Seeing the arrangements at the bar, I should say you could even ask for your favourite brand."

As at every social confluence, subjects of male debate remained fairly impersonal—commercial constraints and shop talk, sporting events, Britain's disastrous foreign policy vis-à-vis the Afghan problem, and the utter failure of the government to fulfil this or that urgent need. A feisty old India hand collared Bruce McNaughton, the Lieutenant-Governor, in the billiards room just as he was about to start a game with Douglas Hooper, a civil engineer from the Department of Public Works.

"Well, what are you doing about it?"

"About what, Algy?"

"Moving the capital, Bruce, what else? As I said the other night,

Calcutta simply isn't good enough! Twelve hundred miles from Bombay, a hundred and twenty miles from the sea, half a continent away from Simla, the summer capital. I ask you, does this plagued hole-in-the-corner city *deserve* the honour?"

"Well, where would you suggest then?"

"What's wrong with Jubbulpore?"

"Jubbulpore? My dear fellow, you can't be serious. Nobody's ever heard of the place!"

The old India hand bristled. "I have—my daughter lives there!"

Wondering how to disengage himself without seeming rude, Sir Jasper listened with seeming intentness to the dissertation embarked upon by the Bishop of Calcutta. His Grace was in the habit of passing a metaphorical collection plate round at dinner parties, a practice viewed with equal disfavour by the pious and the impious. His host was on the verge of promising a substantial donation for the repair of the church spire when help arrived with only seconds to spare. Lord and Lady Ingersoll were announced by Tremaine, necessitating Sir Jasper's fortuitous presence elsewhere.

One way or another, between them the Ingersolls commanded a formidable sphere of influence in the Eastern Empire. An erstwhile Lady of the Bedchamber, Harriet Ingersoll enjoyed the trust and friendship of Her Majesty the Queen. It was known in Court circles that she had often helped to further this or that worthy cause with a word in the royal ear. It was also known that, at the Queen's request, she corresponded with Her Majesty on a personal level. The correspondence had been initiated when Benjamin Ingersoll came to India on his first assignment as Chief Commissioner of the Central Provinces, and had flourished during each of his subsequent postings in the country. Lady Ingersoll's letters, it was said, provided the Queen with a great deal of informal and lively information about the Eastern dominions lacking in dispassionate official despatches, and she valued them highly.

Rather less striking in outward appearance and personality than his wife, Viscount Ingersoll was a mousy-looking man, small and, at first glance, nondescript. The initial impression was deceptive. As Foreign Secretary in the imperial government, he held a position of immense importance and prestige. He was a canny, gifted diplomat with a natural flair for figures, which made him doubly valuable to the government. Since they were such a renowned couple, as charming as they were distinguished, eyes stared and necks craned with considerable curiosity.

Once the formalities were over, the introductions and presentations dispensed with, and it was ascertained to everyone's satisfaction that the Hands That Had Touched Royalty felt just like everybody else's, everyone settled down to enjoying the evening and all the many pleasures it afforded. True enjoyment, however, in every sense of the word, rested with the ladies. Not caring a jot about where the summer or winter capitals should be located, those recently returned from Simla wore their blooming rose complexions and unashamed complacency like medals earned in a hard-fought war. Impatient to disseminate to their less well-travelled compatriots summer scandals picked up along the Mall and at the fêtes, fiestas and gymkhana races in Annandale, they did so with infuriating patronisation. The unfortunate recipients simmered, commiserating silently with one another, but able to retaliate only by suffocating their chagrin under extravagant smiles and nonchalant shrugs of disdain.

However, petty personal rivalries were soon forgotten as feminine attention finally reverted to matters that *really* mattered—the enviably sophisticated style of living of the Pendleburys, the potential and calibre of the unattached male contingent, what everybody was doing and with whom and behind whose back, and, of course, what everyone else was wearing. Critical eyes swept across the sea of silks, satins, sarsenet, voiles and linens, and yards of frills and furbelows over bell-hoops and crinolines, leaving not an inch of the female territory unexplored. In between, reputations were demolished and defended with vim and vehemence, depending on where one's personal loyalties and interests lay.

"It's class, sheer class. Anyone can see that," was Mrs. Hooper's considered opinion.

"Oh, nonsense, Mabel!" Clementine McNaughton sniffed. "They've got the money, that's all."

"True, but it's simply not enough, is it? After all, one *does* have to be seasoned, like old furniture or scuffed leather."

"Not here one doesn't," Clementine McNaughton countered with a tart smile. "But then, what possible finesse can one expect in a country where ducks are called 'buttocks'?"

Everyone hooted.

"Well, I agree with Mama." Arabella McNaughton contributed her mite as the merriment subsided, vigorously waving her left hand in case anyone had missed her diamond-and-emerald engagement ring. "I think it looks like an auction hall, dreadfully *de trop.*"

"Well, what's the point of having it if no one *knows* you've got it, that's what I say?"

Poor Dora Humphries's refurbished grosgrain failed to pass muster, despite all her valiant hopes and efforts. "She wore it to the Town Hall Ball year before last," one of the station's pair of elderly Spins whispered in Dora's hearing to her undying mortification. "I'd know that awful bric-à-brac anywhere!"

Seeing him in such splendid dress for the first time, Melody made no secret of her admiration for Christian, letting her hand linger in his just a whit longer than necessary as he received guests with his parents at the front door.

"He really *is* frightfully good-looking, isn't he?" she remarked a moment later to Patrick, with remarkable lack of tact.

"Don't waste your drool, precious," Patrick drawled, cut to the quick and very jealous. "He's got other axes to grind, remember?"

"Oh!"

With a furious toss of her head, Melody stalked off in the opposite direction and, very pointedly, took up conversation with a young Irishman with dimples who was an apprentice stevedore. Ever since Genghis Khan had come in third from the wrong end at the charity race meeting (despite Melody's dream), and Patrick had lost a fortune, relations between them had not been totally congenial. Quite unreasonably, Melody had blamed him for the loss, and he simply could not see why. They had had many words—some earlier this evening—and the air between them had turned distinctly frosty.

At the other end of the room where she stood next to her mother, Melanie received a sharp jab in her side. Her mother directed a significant gaze towards a far corner where, trying to look inconspicuous, Alistair Birkhurst stood scowling at a potted aspidistra. On the other side of the plant, rather like a constable on his beat, Willie Donaldson paced up and down with somewhat overdone nonchalance.

"Good evening, your lordship." From behind the safety of the carved ivory fan that concealed her teeth, Melanie smiled and dropped a pretty curtsey. Alistair looked blank. "Don't you remember?" she simpered. "We met at the Smithers' the other night?"

"Oh yes." He gave her a wan smile. "How are you, Miss er . . ."

"Anderson. Melanie Anderson."

"Of course." He could hardly ignore the hand she thrust in his face. Not knowing what else to do with it, he took it in his and, feeling extraordinarily foolish, brushed it with his lips.

"They say it's going to rain again," she ventured, fluttering her eyelashes above the rim of the fan.

"It usually does during the monsoons."

"No, I mean, this *evening.*"

"Oh."

"But it might not tomorrow, because it usually doesn't two days running unless, of course, there are more clouds."

Alistair examined this astonishing piece of information and remained silent, wishing she would go away and leave him to brood in peace.

Realising that she had failed to draw him out, Melanie ruminated a while, then, looking up at the ceiling, she let her booklet slip out of her fingers. It fell at his feet.

"Oh dear, I *am* sorry!" She fluttered her eyelashes again and gave him a beseeching look, but Alistair's gaze was riveted to the main door of the reception room. He failed to notice the booklet lying at the tip of his shoe. Willie Donaldson, however, did not. He hobbled forward, bent down to grope for it, and with a courteous bow, handed it back to Melanie.

Confused at this unexpected change in the projected scene, Melanie blurted out the first thing that came into her head. "Do you prefer the waltz to the polka?"

He shook his head. "Canna tell 'un bleedin' tune from t'other," he announced cheerfully. "They all soond the same to me."

Something very sudden and subtle rippled across the room, a frisson of surprise. In unison, all eyes turned towards the door where the host and hostess were in the midst of receiving the latest arrivals. Slowly, the ripple petered out and settled into a deathly hush. Soon the silence was so deep, the atmosphere so still, that even the most minimal gasp could be plainly heard. It came from Charlotte Anderson, weak with horror.

"The Lord have mercy—what *could* Constance be thinking of?"

"Don't faint now, Mama!" Melody hissed a cross warning. "You *know* how tussur crushes."

Edna Chalcott, who came with the newly arrived group, performed the introductions. Lady Pendlebury took Olivia's hand and her smile was dazzling. "I'm *so* pleased you could come, Mrs. Raventhorne. I have *so* been looking forward to making your acquaintance." Olivia smiled and murmured a matching response.

Further introductions were made, bows, smiles and a few words exchanged all round, and Maya executed a low, graceful and sweeping curtsey. Sir Jasper shook Amos's hand with considerable warmth. "I think you've already met my son, Christian."

"Yes, indeed, sir." They too shook hands and nodded amiably at each other.

Sir Jasper gave Amos a paternal pat on the back, made some light remark and a fragment of laughter floated outward from the group. Christian said something to Maya, his eyes shining with very visible admiration, and her lips curved shyly.

Lady Pendlebury returned her attention to Maya. "What a very attractive dress, Miss Raventhorne," she said with a smile that was tranquil, and in tones that were loud and distinct. "Why, you do look perfectly charming!"

Sir Jasper nodded in agreement, rubbed his hands together, and turned even more expansive. "Well, I think you already know many of those present, Mrs. Raventhorne, but I would like to have the pleasure of introducing you and your delightful family to our very special guests."

It was all admirably smooth and beguilingly effortless—but what effort went into making it so was, of course, quite another story. Before leaving the house, Edna Chalcott had insisted that Maya down a sizeable tot of brandy to steady the quivering of her hands and the weakness in her legs. An extra dab of rouge had been deemed vital to further camouflage the whiteness of her face. As far as Constance Pendlebury was concerned, there was no ambiguity in her thinking; violent differences of opinion within the privacy of the family circle were one thing, a public show of pique quite another. She would rather have laid down her life than let either the side or her smile down in front of the multitude.

If the very presence of the Raventhornes was a sensation, the appearance that each presented was no less. No one had ever denied that they were a strikingly good-looking family. This evening, formally dressed, they looked positively stunning. Amos Raventhorne occasionally attended social functions arranged by the Chamber of Commerce, but neither his mother nor sister had ever been seen at a private *burra khana* in an English home (quite understandably so). That their initial appearance should be here, at the Pendleburys'. . . .

In the dining salon, where she had gone ostensibly to make a final inspection of the buffet tables, Lady Pendlebury stood half concealed by a curtain. Neither her mind nor her eyes were on the gourmet display ranged behind her; both were riveted on the face and figure of Maya Raventhorne, deeply engrossed in conversation with Christian in the adjoining room.

Lady Pendlebury had heard, of course, that the girl was attractive, but she had not expected what was being revealed to her now. Her cold, practised eye dissected Maya slowly and with meticulous precision, from head to toe. The girl's grooming was perfect, the gown she wore hardly what one would expect to see in a clod-hopping colonial town beset with sartorial absurdities. Of thick, ivory Chinese silk, it was fashioned like a sheath and clung to her tall, willowy form with just the right tenacity, tantalising and yet the epitome of decorum. It had a boat-shaped neckline, not quite off the shoulders, and the sleeves were capped. Falling straight down in front, moulded gently at the waist, the dress had an enormous bustle at the back where the skirt opened out like a pleated fan to facilitate movement and dancing. If Constance Pendlebury had not known better, she would have sworn that the gown was of French design, cut and tailored on the Champs-Elysées. Its very simplicity gave it class and style, and to add to the effect, the girl wore it with that air of casual elegance that was the universal hall-mark of sophistication. Filigreed white lace gloves reached up to her elbows. At the base of her long neck rested a diamond-and-sapphire neck-lace, with earrings to match. Most noticeable of all, the girl had dignity and poise. She moved with grace. Her manners, it was obvious, were faultless.

Yes, the girl was ravishing—and Constance Pendlebury was furious!

However, before the first shock of the Raventhornes' presence had had time to fully wear off, there came another. Somewhere in the midst of the gaping throng, his mouth dry, his skin cold with sweat, stood Alistair Birkhurst. For one stricken moment he looked pleadingly at Donaldson standing right behind him, but not a trace of mercy showed in the Scots-man's face as he champed grimly on his tobacco. Seeing that there was no escape without public indignity, the hapless Alistair put a reluctant foot forward and did what he had been blackmailed into with such callous dis-regard for his own feelings.

Walking up to his mother, he gave her a peck of a kiss on the cheek, then repeated the gesture with Maya. Turning to Amos, he bowed and extended his hand. His face was bloodless and without any expression at all, as, indeed, was that of Amos. If Alistair's hand was ice-cold, Amos hardly noticed; his was equally so. Neither spoke a word or exchanged a smile. The ceremony was conducted in total silence.

Once again there was a startled hush. Sentences remained suspended and glasses hung in mid-air; widened eyes stared in disbelief. It was pub-lic knowledge that, since Birkhurst had stolen a march over Raventhorne in the matter of that cotton mill, there was little love lost between them. Indeed, for that (and other reasons!), they absolutely hated each other. Why and how then this strange show of cordiality?

For a while questions, comments and conjecture ran utterly rampant.

The men stood around looking red and embarrassed, pretending they had seen nothing, and the women gathered in tight little knots for appropriate sotto voce discussion. Charlotte Anderson was livid that Constance Pendlebury should have invited the Raventhornes behind her back without saying a word—after *all* that she had done for her! It was a social betrayal of monumental proportions. Calcutta's second Spin, a missionary lady with whom, it was generally accepted, God agreed about everything, hinted darkly at black magic practices by the immoral Raventhorne girl to lure innocent young Englishmen and throw dust in their parents' eyes. The room positively hummed with gossip and glee, each new conjecture wilder than the one before.

But when all was said and done, apart from suspense and mystery, there was also conviviality in the air. The drinks were excellent and plentiful, the food promised to be divine and there was a great deal else to chatter about. Gradually, everyone relaxed, breathed normally, and returned to former preoccupations. The tacit consensus was that it was all quite scandalous, considering what was happening between you-know-who and who, but if the Pendleburys wished to consign their only son to perdition, then who was anyone else to care? That decided, the matter was set aside for the moment and the jollifications resumed.

"Socially, the Raventhornes hardly count, my dear." A large lady in polka-dotted blue organdie comforted a highly aggrieved Charlotte Anderson. "It's *who* you know that matters—and, who do they know, I mean *really* know?"

"Well, they know me," Edna Chalcott pointed out cheerfully, overhearing the conversation as she passed. "*Really* they do."

A great believer in the soothing effect of music on any gathering, Lady Pendlebury sent instructions to the Navy Band to strike up an overture as a prelude to the dancing.

"Oh, damn!" A portly gent, manager of Grindlays Bank, was much put out. "The damage to human spirit and tissue during a gallopade is frightful, truly frightful!" he grumbled to Charles Humphries.

The physician laughed. "I agree. We should do what the natives do—allow the ladies to do our dancing for us while we sit in comfort under punkas and watch."

First on the floor was Christian. Uncaring of stares, he swept Maya away with a laugh and a flourish. They were followed by others, and soon the floor was crowded with swaying couples. "Your hands are cold," Maya whispered with an anxious smile, her nervousness starting to melt in the rhythm of the music and the sheer splendour of the evening. "Are you feeling all right?"

"Of course I'm all right!" A small frown appeared on Christian's forehead as if the question irritated him. "Why do you ask?"

"I just thought you looked a little. . . ." She broke off with a smile and left it at that, not wishing to jar him. It was the first time they had ever danced together. She was enchanted that he waltzed so divinely—and with everyone watching!

435

Standing by the side of the dance floor with a group of girls, Deirdre Twining inspected Amos with a thoughtful eye.

"He doesn't look a bit Eurasian, does he? He looks just like *us!*"

"Well, he isn't," Sarah Smithers assured her.

"Isn't Eurasian?"

"No, silly—isn't just like us. Eurasians smell quite different, Mama says."

Deirdre looked at him wistfully. "Do you think he'll want to dance? Emily says he's very shy of women."

Sarah hooted with laughter. "Shy? Why, everyone knows his father was a *raging* profligate!"

"Then maybe he doesn't know how to dance."

"Well, *she* certainly does, doesn't she?" They both turned again to look at Maya in the arms of Christian Pendlebury, and then at the cluster of young men lounging on the sidelines impatiently awaiting their turns, their eyes riveted on Maya. Even the very supercilious Lytton Prescott had stopped to stare in grudging admiration.

"*Et tu, Brute?*" asked one of his batchmates with a grin, following his gaze.

"Not in the least!" Lytton said with a shudder. "Dalliance under a tatty within reach of a tub of ice is one thing. Brandishing Cupid's torch in the Tropic of Cancer when it's a hundred in the bloody shade is *quite* another." Dragging his eyes away, he sauntered off in pursuit of another brandy pani and one Marigold Ponsonby, recently arrived stepdaughter of the Superintendent of Prisons.

Unaware of his good looks, Amos had no idea how dashing he appeared in his formal maroon dinner jacket and trousers, and he simply couldn't understand why all these women kept following him whichever way he went. Having eventually done his duty on the dance floor by his hostess, his mother and Lady Ingersoll, at the first opportune moment (and much to Deirdre Twining's dismay) he escaped to the bar counter. He was not a habitual drinker, but feeling most comfortable in this strictly male preserve, he ordered himself a glass of champagne. As he sipped, he tried not to think of the gossip still buzzing around the room. Being Jai Raventhorne's son, he was a seasoned target for unkind talk. Like his mother and sister, over the years he had learned to ignore it. But tonight, somehow, it truly nettled him. With an effort he concentrated on the conversation at his elbow, which was about someone called Witherspoon, obviously not one of present company.

"The man, sir, is a drunken sot who simply can't hold his liquor!" A tall, thin, monocled actuary with an insurance firm snorted into a frothing tankard of beer. "He made a revolting mess when he brought up the wine all over the Smythes' lace antimacassar the other night, remember? If he misbehaved here, Constance would throw a fit."

His companion, an importer of European wines, disagreed. "Oh, I think Constance would be pleased to forgive him," he countered pleasantly, "as long as he brought up the white wine with the fish." He turned to Amos and winked, then guffawed at his own joke. It seemed to sum up Lady

Pendlebury's social proprieties rather neatly, and Amos had to smile.

"I say, Raventhorne," Amos found Clive Smithers by his side. "I hear you've completed construction of that godown with modern insulation?"

"Yes, almost. It should be ready in a week or so." Smithers traded in furs and was anxious to rent space for his stocks in Trident's new warehouse.

"Well, I have a consignment coming in from Shanghai early next month. Do you think you could see your way to . . . ?"

They relapsed into business talk.

Few of the Pendleburys' guests were unacquainted with Olivia Raventhorne, if not in person then certainly by name. There were several she recalled well from the old days, some of whom she had met through Estelle. Polly Drummond, once a close friend of her cousin, was frankly delighted to see her again, as were Susan Bradshaw, David Crichton and Lily Horniman, who still spoke through her adenoids. Of course, the years had wrought many changes. The girls were all married, with children and successful husbands. David Crichton, then a shippie, was now a naval commander stationed in Malta, with a wife and four children. They all inquired after Estelle.

"Thy sed she'd perished in that 'orrible Cawnpore haffair," Polly—now the wife of an Inspector of Opium Godowns and Salt, no less—said in her unashamed Cockney, "but no one hever confirmed it, me 'arold sez. Is it true, then?"

Olivia hesitated an instant before replying. Her correspondence with Estelle had flourished over these past weeks. Indeed, she had received an effusive letter from her cousin not three days earlier, thanking her for the exquisite emerald ear drops she had sent the new bride. However, the fact that her cousin was alive and well, albeit in bizarre circumstances, was something Olivia decided she simply could not share with anyone just yet. Estelle would never forgive her for a disclosure she was still not prepared for. In response to Polly's question, therefore, she simply nodded and then changed the subject.

Tonight, not even talk of Estelle could have dampened Olivia's buoyant spirits. What Alistair had done had moved her deeply. She had no idea what his motivation might have been, nor whether the effort was prompted by genuine emotion. She simply didn't care. The fact was that he had kissed her, kissed Maya, shaken hands with Amos, and then danced with her, all in full view of everyone! He had swallowed his pride to make a contribution to a better relationship, and she was overwhelmed with gratitude.

Having met Alistair properly for the first time, Maya too was thrilled by his show of cordiality. She observed, however, that he had not approached them again, that he maintained his distance. Curious to know him better, to cajole him into friendship as a brother, she decided that one considerate gesture surely deserved another. If he had shown such magnanimity in public, well, so would she, as soon as she could get away from Colonel Fitzpatrick-Browne.

The Colonel was relating to her, at considerable length, the rather tedious details of a very enjoyable and very long sojourn in the Simla Hills, away from what he called "this cruel graveyard of the expatriate." Maya listened with rapt attention—but did not hear a word. She had often seen Colonel Fitzpatrick-Browne walking his basset hound along the Strand in the evenings. According to Grace Lubbock's mali (who also worked for the Colonel), Mrs. Fitzpatrick-Browne, his rather faded wife with the pinched face and vacant smile, was a secret tippler. The Colonel himself, so Grace had told her, often sought his pleasures elsewhere, mostly at the Golden Behind. It seemed unbelievably exciting to Maya that she could be here, chatting so confidently with a man known to be a doyen of British society in station, standing no more than a foot away from him, close enough to pluck a whisker out of his beard.

Forgetting about Alistair for the moment as another young man claimed her for the next dance, Maya continued to float on air. Her feet hardly touched the ground—or so it appeared to her—as she whirled round and round the marble floor in the arms of this gentleman or the other. She danced every dance, scarcely allowed to sit for a moment. Whether the waltz, the quadrille, or the polka, the minuet or the gallopade, her expertise with each was astonishing. She danced with soaring confidence, without the embarrassment of a single stumble or misstep. There was no doubt that that timely tot of brandy had indeed stood her in excellent stead, and she blessed Edna for having thought of it. Christian had remained a wonderfully attentive host. He had introduced all his friends to her, seen to her every need, enjoying her enjoyment as much as he did her success. If, occasionally, he appeared abstracted and his smile dropped, Maya attributed his tensions either to the exigencies of the situation or simply to the heat. It was a petty matter; she dismissed it from her mind. Why, even Constance Pendlebury had smiled at her, shown approval of her dress, pronounced her charming. What more could she want?

Even as she conversed with Harriet Ingersoll, Lady Pendlebury could not stop her thoughts from wandering. Her mouth moved mechanically, dispensing small talk and smiles with equal facility, but it was still Maya Raventhorne who claimed all her attention. The girl was again on the dance floor (indeed, had hardly been off it!), now held in the arms of a young army lieutenant. Her eyes, large and lustrous, were fixed on her partner's face; coral lips, slightly parted, glistened in a half smile, and her petal smooth skin was polished and aglow. Her hair was brushed up in a high chignon, making her even taller and more slender, a few tiny curls scattered across her forehead. The young man made some amusing remark. The girl threw back her head and laughed, not with vulgar excess but with delicacy and refinement. As her face turned upwards, her extraordinary violet eyes caught the lights of the crystal chandelier. They burst into a thousand sparkles and quite dazzled the young lieutenant.

Constance Pendlebury's smile never wavered, but within she twisted with anguish—what chance did her innocent son stand in the face of such overwhelming temptation? Christian was weak, easy to impress, a gullible idealist. This girl, on the other hand, was a siren, a tenacious huntress, well versed in the art of seduction and equipped with all its accoutrements. If half the men in the room looked smitten, what possible defences could she expect from her poor besotted darling boy against such a determined onslaught? Starting to tremble, she finally escaped into a deserted passageway. Closing her eyes, she leant against the wall and devoured long, deep breaths to compose herself. When she returned to the drawing room and looked around, she found herself gazing straight into the amber eyes of Olivia Raventhorne. Lady Pendlebury coloured and, with a quick smile, turned away. But in that intercepted look, Olivia had seen much. If Maya's appearance and success this evening brought Constance Pendlebury little joy, they brought Olivia even less. There was no doubt that Edna's brainwave in re-fashioning her own wedding dress into an evening gown for Maya, according to French cut and style, had been little short of inspired, and the deft fingers of the twins had indeed wrought a miraculous transformation. Even so, Olivia's heart filled with pity for her misguided daughter. How little Maya knew of the ways of the world—and at what high cost she was destined to learn!

Egged on by her mother, Melanie again set off in search of Alistair. He was at a far end of the verandah, engaged in a somewhat animated conversation with Lytton, Patrick and one or two others. Alistair broke away from the group and started to walk off on his own. At that precise moment Melanie arrived and, as it happened, also Maya Raventhorne. The girls stopped, sized each other up warily, then exchanged swift, cold smiles. Quick as a blink, Melanie stepped forward and triumphantly dropped her booklet at Alistair's feet.

Maya took only a second to assess the situation. Before Alistair could react, she bent and retrieved the object. "I think this is yours?" she said sweetly, returning the booklet to a livid Melanie. Then, while Alistair looked baffled and Melanie looked daggers, she pierced him with a gimlet eye. "You said you would like to dance a waltz with me? Well, they've just started playing one."

Alistair's hunted gaze alternated between the dreadful girl with all those teeth and the knot of giggling daughters and determined mothers within striking distance, poised to swoop. It took him only a split second to decide upon his remaining option. All inhibitions forgotten, he flew into Maya's arms like a homing pigeon.

"My God," he said feelingly as she whisked him away from the danger zone, "for a moment I thought she had me! I didn't have the nerve to pretend not to see her wretched programme twice running." His mouth opened wide in a smile of unmistakable relief. "Thank you."

"My pleasure," Maya murmured shyly, studying his face with interest as they started to dance. How very much like Mother he looked when he smiled!

The significance of having her as a dancing partner suddenly dawned on Alistair, and he flushed. For a moment neither knew what to say, equally awkward. In his confusion, he only hoped Donaldson was watching and that it would not be a wasted exercise. But Donaldson was nowhere to be seen. Deciding that he had done his bit for the honour of the Birkhursts, he had repaired to the bar counter to slake a long-pending and impatient thirst.

"You made Mother very happy, Alistair," Maya finally said. "You cannot possibly assess what your gesture meant to her."

He nodded stiffly but showed no other reaction.

"Will you . . . come and see us again?" she asked, careful not to sound as if she nagged.

"I don't think so. I *am* rather busy."

"Oh."

He amended his brusqueness with a rather superior smile. "Perhaps we will bump into each other again at one of these confounded dinner parties," he said with a shrug.

"We don't go to dinner parties."

"You don't?" he exclaimed without thinking. "I thought that's all anyone did in this gruesome place with such little imagination!"

"Yes, but we don't. We're not invited to those parties to which you might be. This is rather an exception." It was strange how easy she found it to talk to him. Her bluntness was rather discomfitting, of course, but in some odd way it was also rather charming. She had spoken without anger or sarcasm, just very simply. He searched for something else to say, but could think of nothing. Then he remembered that the girl kept horses.

"Do you go yourself to the Byculla auctions?" he asked.

"You know about those?" She was surprised.

"Oh yes. My grandmother has an agent in Bombay. She often buys Arabs through him for our own stables."

Maya's eyes lit up; now she was on secure ground. In her answer to his question, he found cause to ask several others, and the conversation became easier. He told her about the Farrowsham farm and their problems last year with the Jersey herd. One dance led to another without either noticing. Alistair was surprised at how well she knew her subject, even more surprised that he found her not unpleasant company. She was very pretty, of course—in a Eurasian sort of way—but that was not where her appeal lay. She was also naïve, devoid of artifice and straightforward of speech. By the time the second dance ended, to his own astonishment, he heard himself promise to visit her stables, although of course he had no intention of actually doing so.

On the whole, however, he was relieved that the music had stopped. There was a limit to how much one could say about horses and cattle and wheat farming.

But whatever Alistair's reservations, Maya had none. Her cup was full; she could have asked for nothing more.

Amos was bored.

The social demands of the evening were proving beyond his capacities, stretching his tolerance to its very limit. For other, more obvious reasons, he found the occasion acutely embarrassing. His sister's blatant enjoyment of the rousting and revelry—particularly, of the very substantial male attention she received with such unalloyed delight—incensed him. Considering the circumstances of their presence, and the hypocrisy that had provoked it, he found her gaiety offensive and impossible to swallow.

Apart from all that, Amos also found it a confounded penance to make small talk. As head of Trident, he was known to almost all the men present, well used to being sought after in matters of business. He was perfectly at ease discussing freight rates and tea tariffs and the lease of warehouses with men of any colour, community and nationality, but when it came to the women, he was entirely at a loss. With the exception of Lady Ingersoll—whom he had discovered to be refreshingly erudite—he considered the female contingent abysmally dull. He did not have the faintest idea what to talk to them about.

"Talk about *them*," Edna Chalcott had advised. "Better still, let them talk about themselves." He had rejected both suggestions. He could not think of a more dreary way to waste an evening.

His jaws now ached with the vacant smiles that courtesy forced him to dispense. The weight of his maroon jacket had made him perspire and he was soaked to the skin through his starched white shirt beneath. The tightly wound cummerbund was beginning to feel like a straitjacket, and his blasted shoes pinched.

Worst of all was the fact that, whichever way he turned, he seemed to bump into Alistair, although he made every effort to avoid him. He sensed a trick in the man's show of cordiality; it was fulsome and palpably false, designed only to make *him* feel small in the eyes of the spectators. Several times he had caught the blighter staring straight at him, and this show of insolence constituted an extra irritant. Had it not been for that promise his mother had extracted from him against his better judgement, he would have walked right up to the impertinent wretch and read him his fortune.

As if all this was not enough, he had happened to overhear the Smithers girl's remark about his father and it had decimated him. Amos had, of course, heard many stories about his father's frequent indiscretions. Had he heard them about anyone else, he would have laughed as loud as the next man, for he certainly was no prude. But that such remarks should be passed about his own father was to Amos a matter of embarrassment. There was no doubt that some of the stories were unforgettably shameful. For instance, that much-tossed-around incident about his father's involvement with the Slocum girl, sister of Barnabus Slocum, then the police chief. He had come to know of it at school through a friend and he had been devastated for days. That his father's peccadilloes dated from before his marriage to his mother brought little comfort to Amos. The very fact that their existence was still a basis for loose talk remained for him an intolerable humiliation.

As the tempo of the music accelerated, the dancing became increasingly aggressive and, with it, the demands of social chivalry. Amos decided that this then was the absolute outer limit of his indulgence. It was not that he was insufficiently acquainted with the mysteries of the gavotte or the eightsome. As it happened, to the chagrin of most of the boys at the Academy, dancing had been a compulsory social discipline, given great importance by the school authorities. But, Amos vowed, he was damned if he was going to spend the evening prancing about an alien floor with his arms about some dung-headed ninny he neither knew nor cared to. Artfully, but with grim determination, he dodged his mother's ever watchful eye on the other side of the room, grabbed another glass of champagne and slipped out through a side door into the back garden.

People had trickled out onto the front lawn bordering the river, but the back garden, Amos saw with relief, was mercifully deserted. Even though the sky was mildly overcast, there was as yet no rain. Noticing the summerhouse at the far end of the lawn, well concealed by a cluster of pretty gulmohars, he bounded across the grass towards it. There was no one inside. Amos walked in, sank down on a stone bench, and with a loud groan of relief to be on his own at last, slipped out of his shoes to give his inflamed heels a rest.

Taking small sips of the champagne, iced to perfection, he leaned his head back against a glass pane, enjoying the moist night air, the perfume of damp earth and the wafting fragrance of night bloomers. From a waistcoat pocket he pulled out a matchbox and lit a cheroot, exhaling up into the air with his eyes closed, imbibing with momentary contentment the familiar sounds of a monsoon night. From the glass roof came the musical patter of a fine drizzle; outside, in the bushes, frogs made foghorn calls to their mates and cicadas chirruped in mournful unison. Lazily, Amos's tensions unwound; his mind started to amble. With a strangely intense longing, he again thought of Rose Pickford. For a while he luxuriated in his charming memories of her, devastated that he might never have a chance to reveal to her his feelings. Then, rather more worriedly, he recalled his last meeting with Kyle.

Thomas Hungerford . . . would he be worth all the effort?

About a half hour elapsed and Amos was just starting to wonder if he should risk another thirty minutes of blessed solitude, when he heard voices outside. Dismayed at the prospect of unwanted company (God forbid, that Twining girl!), he shuddered. But then he recognised the voices as male and loosened somewhat. There were three, possibly four, men outside. One, Amos could tell immediately from his voice, was Christian Pendlebury. Of the other voices, two probably belonged to that insufferable duo who were his chummery mates, Illingworth and Prescott, and the third, with a strong Irish accent, that of the rather pleasant young assistant in the stevedoring firm with which Trident did much of its business.

Contemplating his next move, Amos was quietly putting on his shoes when he realised that out there, some sort of quite heated argument was in progress. The drizzle had stopped but a gusty wind had risen. Only a few intermittent snatches of words and phrases that happened to blow in his direction were intelligible.

"She doesn't give a bloody whore's *fart* for you." The language was crude and the words slurred. This one, at least, was drunk.

"Now, *look* here . . . mumble, mumble . . . your damned *business!*"

". . . lick her arse . . . ?"

"I said, *drop* it, Lytton, or else." This, very clearly, in Christian's raised voice.

By the sound of it, the dispute was turning ugly. Amos stood up, trying to work out a strategy of discreet escape, but it was impossible to leave the summerhouse without being seen, and this he wished to avoid. Outside there were sounds of a scuffle, of oaths and curses, and inevitably, distinct and unmistakable, the crack of a fist connecting with hard bone. Then, in quick succession, came a flurry of shuffling feet, much crunching and grunting, more knuckles colliding with more flesh and shoes skidding about in the soggy earth.

Under his breath, Amos muttered a few hearty curses of his own. He had absolutely no wish to be involved in somebody else's brawl. The problem was, how the devil was he to get away from here without being seen? A cautious peep through the summerhouse opening, however, was sufficient to make a lightning decision. It seemed unlikely that anyone in that confused jumble of legs and arms would have the time or the inclination to spare him a glance. Putting a firm foot forward, he prepared to make a dash for the house.

Just then, a guffaw of derisive laughter blew his way and with it, very clearly, Amos heard the name "Raventhorne." He froze, his leg halfway through the opening.

"You say that *once* more, you filthy, foul-mouthed son of a . . . !"

"All right, I will. She's been a slut all her. . . ."

The rest was cut off by the thump of a fist in obvious collision with a face.

Oh, sweet Lord—the brawl was about his sister!

When Amos emerged from his shock, his immediate inclination was to leave it well alone. As far as he was concerned, they could kill each other, and that too with his blessings. Pendlebury had made his bed; let him now bloody well lie on it! But then, as second thoughts arose, Amos felt ashamed. It was obvious that Christian Pendlebury was fighting for the honour of his sister. Could he, in all conscience, walk away and leave the man aiming to be his brother-in-law to do battle on his own?

Cursing his luck at this unexpected disaster, Amos pulled in a long, deep breath and stepped out into the open.

He couldn't see too clearly, but he discerned enough to know that two of the combatants were ranged against one, Christian. The fourth man, the Irish stevedore, appeared to have opted for discretion over valour and fled. Flailed from two directions, Christian defended himself as best he could, but the odds were against him.

"Leave him alone!"

Amos's warning, unfortunately, came a split second too late to prevent a final blow from one of the fists. It connected particularly well. There was a sickening crunch and, with a cry of pain, Christian crumpled to the ground. The two aggressors stood staring at Amos in astonished silence.

Then Patrick Illingworth, deep under the influence, swayed from side to side and his expression of surprise turned into a sneer. Very deliberately, he prodded the supine figure with his shoe and kicked it. He waggled a wavering finger at Amos.

"*You* stay out of this, you bloody, black-arsed nigg. . . ."

Before he could complete the sentence or, indeed, before Amos's brain could register what his fist was doing, it had shot out and smashed the remaining words back into the offending mouth, filling it with blood and broken teeth. As Patrick fell back into the shrubbery, his friend Lytton threw himself at Amos with a roar of rage and a shower of obscene language. But, like Patrick, he had had too much to drink. He was no match for Amos—taller, heavier, cold sober and strong as an ox. A few half-hearted feints and some colourful oaths later, Prescott turned tail and loped off into the shadows. When Amos looked again at the bushes, Illingworth too had vanished. Only Christian still lay on the ground, groaning and obviously grievously hurt.

Amos gave several sharp shakes to his head to clear it, breathed in large lungfuls of air, and recomposed himself. He bent over Christian's moaning form. "All right, you can get up now, they've gone. Come on, I'll help you into the house."

Christian shook his head and clutched his arm. "I can't," he gasped. "I think it's broken. . . ."

Amos offered him a hand. "Take this with your good arm, then hoist yourself up slowly. I'll support your back."

Christian nodded; with a wince, he reached up and did as told. In the process, he turned towards him and Amos remained rooted. This man was not Christian Pendlebury at all. It was Alistair!

Amos gazed down in bewilderment and horror. How could he have made such a stupid mistake? And Alistair Birkhurst had been fighting for the honour of the *Raventhornes?* Why, it was impossible! In a lightning reflex, his body straightened and his hand jerked back.

"If I had known it was you," he snarled, "by God, I would have let them paste you to pulp!"

"I didn't ask for your help! Why did you have to butt in, anyway?"

"I thought you were . . . never mind." Amos bit his lip and scowled. "We don't need *you* to fight our battles for us! Just keep your damned nose out of our affairs, understand?"

"Oh, leave me alone!"

"As you wish." Amos glared at him a moment then, spun on his heel and walked away.

Halfway across the lawn, he stopped and looked down at his clothes. His shirt was torn. The left sleeve of his jacket was ripped at the top seam and his boots were covered in wet mud. One of his knuckles was still bleeding and he had no doubt that his face was a mess. There was simply no way he could return to the party in his present condition. For a few seconds he contemplated his sorry situation—and also, in retrospect, the extraordinary reason for that blasted brawl.

"Oh, what the hell!" He shook his head, sighed, and retraced his steps back to the summerhouse.

Alistair lay in exactly the same position, obviously unable to move. Amos clenched his teeth and roughly thrust out his hand. "All right, take it."

Alistair stirred. "I don't need your goddamned help!" His voice was faint, the speech blurred with pain. "I can get up on my own. . . ."

"In that case, please yourself." He moved back, put his hands on his hips, and waited.

Alistair turned over, tried to get up, but then again doubled over. Amos made no move towards him. Again, slowly and with great difficulty, Alistair levered himself up, inch by inch, until he was on his knees. Then, with a final mighty heave, he pushed himself upwards and was on his feet. Vertical for barely a second, he lurched to one side as if about to slump again. Instinctively, Amos's hand reached out, but angrily Alistair shook it off and somehow steadied himself.

"Take your confounded hands off me, Amos Raventhorne! I'd rather *die* here than let you. . . ."

And with that, he fainted. Had Amos not leapt forward to catch him, he would have crashed to the ground. One arm hung down limp and lifeless, and at a curious angle. He was still bleeding. The front of his shirt was soaked with red.

"Oh Lord!" Amos groaned. "That makes the evening perfect, bloody perfect!"

The drizzle, this time more persistent, had returned and threatened to expand into a full-blown shower. With Alistair's dead weight on his shoulder, Amos looked around for help. Although the sounds of revelry coming from the house were loud and resonant, there was not a soul about in the garden.

Bitterly resentful, Amos staggered into the summerhouse with the limp form slung over his shoulder. Not quite sure what to do next, he laid Alistair on the stone floor and sat down to think. For a fleeting second he felt an overpowering temptation to leave the man where he was, send a message in to Willie Donaldson and then simply take himself home. But, grudgingly, he was forced to reconsider.

When last seen, Donaldson was at the bar, already propping it up with difficulty. By now—as was his well-known custom at any *burra khana* he graced—he would have secreted himself in some forgotten corner to snore away the night, and that corner could be anywhere in the house! The ideal solution, of course, was to abstract Dr. Humphries discreetly from the party and let him take charge. However, Dora Humphries—notorious for her sharp ears, active tongue and utter ignorance of the word "discretion"—was bound to pick up even the faintest whisper and then sound a general alert. The entire female battalion present would respond to the clarion call with enthusiasm. There would be a barrage of questions, counter-questions, instant conjecture and conclusions, and there would also be ruination of whatever remained of Lady Pendlebury's dinner party, for which, undoubtedly, he would be blamed. Swearing under his breath, Amos took the only remaining option. He set out down the drive to try and find the Birkhurst carriage and attendants. The sides of the streets were thickly lined with dozens upon dozens of carriages, and Amos had no way of identifying which one belonged to Alistair Birkhurst. Getting more ill-tempered by the minute, he finally located his own brougham and shook awake his coachman lying fast asleep inside. With the carriage positioned halfway up the long drive, Amos prayed that nothing would transpire to create a commotion before they could safely get away. Helped by his coachman, he carried Alistair to the brougham and, together, they propped him up on the seat. Still unconscious and bleeding, Alistair slumped sideways, his broken arm sprawled across his stomach at a grotesque angle. Positioning his own body so that Alistair could rest against it, Amos ordered the coachman to drive like hell to the nearby house of Dayananda Babu, the modest but competent herbalist known as an expert bone-setter and used on occasion by many of the Trident staff.

As the carriage came to a halt outside the herbalist's house, Alistair came awake with a drowsy start. "Where?"

"At the doctor's," Amos said shortly.

Alistair shook himself free of Amos's supporting arm. "I don't want any bloody native butcher to. . . ."

"Shut up and do as you're told!"

Alistair opened his mouth to issue an indignant retort, but before he could produce a sound, he again slipped into unconsciousness.

The bone-setter's premises were in darkness, the household asleep. However, once awakened, the wizened old healer reputed to have magic in his fingers worked swiftly and in silence. Within the hour the bleeding was stemmed, the wounds and bruises cleaned and swabbed, and the broken bone set, splintered and securely bandaged.

"The wounds are not deep, but the bones will need time to join," Dayananda Babu said, dispensing herbal tablets, poultices and instructions. "You can take him home now, but make certain that he remains in bed for a few days and keeps his arm in a sling. Would you like me to visit him in a day or two to continue the treatment?"

"What he does now is up to him," Amos said coldly. "I have nothing more to do with the matter."

"But he will need care, looking after. . . ."

"Well, I'm not his damned nursemaid!" Amos said irritably. "Whoever does the looking after, it isn't going to be me!"

"Who then?" the old man asked.

"How do I know? His bearer, I presume."

Dayananda Babu frowned and peered into Amos's face. "He is not a friend of yours?"

"No," he said tightly. "An . . . acquaintance."

"Someone will need to accompany him to his house. Where does he live?"

"On the Esplanade."

"Ah!" Realisation dawned in the old man's eyes as he guessed the injured man's identity. He knew Amos well, of course. The hostility that existed between him and his recently arrived half-brother was all over the Trident establishment and certainly no secret in town. Judging from the appearance of both, he assumed that the hostility had finally erupted in a bout of fisticuffs, but he felt it was not his place to ask questions. Instead, he pointed to Amos's forehead and knuckles. "I think *those* need some. . . ."

"No, I'm all right." Amos brushed the suggestion aside. "We've got to get him home somehow."

"Well, if you so desire, I will ask my son to escort the sahib to the Esplanade," the herbalist ventured. "My son will ensure that he is entrusted to his bearer's good care."

Amos was relieved and showed it. "I would be obliged to you and to your son if that could be done, Dayananda Babu. Thank you for your trouble."

"How will my son go? I do not own a carriage."

Amos struggled for a moment. "Well . . . my carriage is at your son's disposal," he said with little show of grace.

"But then, how will you reach your own home?" the herbalist wondered.

"Do you have a horse to lend me? Even a hack?"

The old man shook his head sadly. "No. Only a mule."

Once again Amos struggled silently with himself, then cursed under his breath and clenched his teeth. "In that case, I suppose I shall have to damn well walk, won't I?"

It was almost three in the morning by the time Amos arrived home— exhausted, footsore, drenched, bedraggled and in a vicious temper. His mother, sister and Mrs. Chalcott were not yet back from the *burra khana*, and this enraged him even more. He stripped off his bloodstained clothes and tossed them into the laundry bin, sloshed cold water all over his body to refresh it and dabbed tincture of iodine on his sorely bruised knuckles. Then he poured himself a double tot of brandy, tossed it down in a gulp and fell into bed.

His last thought, before his head hit the pillow and he slumped into aching sleep, was that he should have *strangled* the blighter when he had the chance.

"She's an enchanting young thing, isn't she?"

Engaged in conversation with Lucas Anderson, Sir Jasper turned to see who had made the remark and about whom. Behind him stood Lady Ingersoll, staring very intently at Maya.

The buffet dinner had been announced shortly after eleven and guests were crowded around the long tables in both reception rooms, gourmandising as much with the eyes as with the stomach. The display on the endless line of trestle tables was sumptuous, the embellishments a veritable feast of trompe d'oeil. Jane Watkins was devastated to learn that, mistaking it for a sculptured tomato, she had eaten part of a flower arrangement. But there was no doubt that Monsieur Pierre had indeed excelled himself. Menus, written in French, were fitted into silver frames and ranged at regular intervals along the tables. ("Is one allowed to eat without being able to pronounce all that?" Edna Chalcott whispered worriedly to Nigel Crockett, and was greatly relieved when he nodded.) White napery crackled with starch; silver cutlery, carved and monogrammed, lay beside goblets of heavy Czechoslovakian crystal. Wines, both red and white, were served at suitable temperatures by a rigidly correct Tremaine and his tribe of underlings. Nothing was casual, not even the cruet stands: the salt in the silver containers flowed fine and fluent in utter defiance of the monsoon's humidity.

Excusing himself from Douglas Hooper, Sir Jasper hurried to Lady Ingersoll's side to endorse her remark. "Indeed, quite the belle of the ball, I entirely agree."

"And her brother has such impeccable manners," Lady Ingersoll went on. "He appears to have inherited a great deal of his mother's reputed intelligence." She studied her host's empty plate and raised a questioning eyebrow. "You do not partake of this positively *Lucullan* banquet your wife has so cleverly devised for our pleasure?" She helped herself to another minuscule smoked breast of quail and popped it into her mouth.

"Oh, I dó, indeed I do." Rather absently, Sir Jasper piled food onto his plate. Regardless of its Gallic ancestry, he sprinkled it with chilly powder, reducing poor Monsieur Pierre to tears as he watched from behind a door. "Your ladyship does not intend a holiday in the hills this summer?" he asked, anxious not to let the conversation lapse.

"Simla? Well, Benjamin is off tomorrow to say his salaams to the Viceroy, but I have to find suitable personal staff and get the household into some sort of decent order by the time he returns. Besides," she jabbed her fork into a truffle and made a face. "I loathe the place. Can't tolerate the social hysteria and the bureaucratic cliquism—to say nothing of the extraordinary colonial talent for devouring and regurgitating scandal."

"I have to agree," Sir Jasper smiled. "Simla isn't my favourite watering hole either. What troubles me greatly is the lack of efficient communication with the outside world. Simla is completely cut off despite the telegraph."

"Communication?" Lady Ingersoll raised a caustic eyebrow. "On the contrary, that is the one thing the government *doesn't* need to worry about in Simla. The reach and speed of the human tongue, I assure you, are far greater than those to which any electric telegraph could aspire!"

Sir Jasper laughed with genuine amusement, then noticed that Lady Ingersoll's gaze had again wandered to the spot where Maya Raventhorne stood surrounded by a coterie of male admirers.

"Yes, an altogether attractive family," she remarked, returning to her original subject. "I am so pleased that you and Lady Pendlebury elected to invite them. It could not have been an easy decision to make."

Harriet Ingersoll was a somewhat masculine woman with greying hair, large-boned limbs and scant interest in what she wore. She had, on the other hand, considerable personal charm, a soft smile and a sharp mind capable of very acute perceptions. Her final comment caught Sir Jasper unawares. She was known to be uncommonly forthright, but he was surprised as much by the extent of her candour as by her choice of subject.

"The Mutiny is dead history, your ladyship. Many consider that it is time to bury it." He chose his words with caution, anxious not to make the wrong responses. "Naturally, it can never be *wholly* forgotten. Nor, perhaps, should it."

"Oh, I couldn't agree more! But I find it so *tiresome* when people persist in old enmities and use them as an excuse to perpetuate prejudice." She paused to eat a vol-au-vent and sip at her wine. "It is because of this that I took the liberty of commending your own obviously liberal views."

It suddenly occurred to Sir Jasper that her oblique references might well concern the gossip rampant about Maya Raventhorne and his son. He was not obliged to make clarifications, of course, but he chose to. "There is no better way to counter rumour, your ladyship," he said with an offhand shrug, "than to meet it head on. It takes the wind out of the gossipmonger's sails."

But Lady Ingersoll appeared to be unconcerned with the gossip. "If one were to let rumour run one's life," she said impatiently, brushing his explanation aside, "where would be the time for productive endeavour? But do forgive me if I intrude in matters that are private, Sir Jasper—that is not my intention." She made a wry face and laughed. "My husband is convinced that I have made a special study to say things that I ought not to."

In that case, her host wondered briefly, just what *was* her intention in making the oblique observations? But before he could find the words to frame a polite inquiry, she spoke again. "All said and done, the Raventhornes have been luckier than most, wouldn't you say?"

"I beg your pardon?" He was vaguely discomfitted by the subject but, at the same time, curious to see why she persisted in it.

Lady Ingersoll reached for a seasoned breadstick, dipped it in a small mound of pâté de foie gras, and bit off the top with every sign of enjoyment. "I was referring, Sir Jasper, to the general state of the community to which they belong. Not many Eurasians have enjoyed the privileges that the Raventhornes have, although, of course, Jai Raventhorne worked long and hard to acquire them. Given the unwelcoming environment, it could not have been easy."

The conversation had taken a quite unexpected turn and, greatly intrigued, Sir Jasper was anxious to pursue it—but not in the middle of a crowd where one was forced to raise one's voice simply to be heard. Using the cloying heat of the room as an excuse, he urged Lady Ingersoll out onto the back verandah, where it was not only cooler but more private. Having settled his guest comfortably on a marble bench facing the lawns and the river, Sir Jasper took his position opposite her on a stool.

"You were saying?"

"I was commenting on the difficulties faced by the unfortunate

Eurasians in India. The odds against which most struggle must be quite soul-destroying."

Sir Jasper fell silent to give himself a moment or two of thought. The Eurasian problem was the very last subject he had expected to discuss with Lady Ingersoll. Evidently, the opinions she held were strong, and that astonished him even more. "You believe that we have not been just to the Eurasians?"

"Well, search your heart, Sir Jasper—*have* we? Even in our modern, democratic age, they are constantly being denied self-fulfilment. I am referring not only to the abhorrent prejudices that prevail, but to simple social justice. I find it shocking that a nation as fair-minded as ours should have done so little to enhance the well-being of those who exist *only* because of us. I don't mind telling you, Sir Jasper, that this deplorable lacuna in our governance is a source of grave concern to some in certain very high circles back home in England."

Sir Jasper sat still; only his hand holding a fork moved to toy with a plover's egg set in aspic that was fast melting on his plate. He had no doubt as to the identity of those "certain very high circles" to which Lady Ingersoll referred. He came to a lightning decision.

"It seems rather an odd coincidence that your ladyship should broach the subject at this particular juncture," he said very smoothly. "As it happens, the Treasury, at this very moment, is in the process of devising a scheme to fill precisely the lacuna that you mention."

"Oh really?" She leaned forward, deeply interested.

"The project is still very much in its infancy, on the anvil, so to speak." He gave her a sombre, direct look. "I mention this in the greatest of confidence, your ladyship. Not even members of the Cabinet are aware of the scheme yet."

Lady Ingersoll nodded. "A scheme devised by yourself?"

He met her gaze with confidence. "Yes."

She laid a hand on his arm. "Well, I will not breathe a word, not even to Benjamin, I promise. But I *do* applaud your initiative. And I look forward to hearing more about this project of yours when you are ready to announce it. Now," she rose, "shall we go in and join the others? I simply must ask Lady Pendlebury's advice on how to acquire a trustworthy cook—if such a creature exists outside mythology. Benjamin *swears* the one we have is being paid by the Czarists to poison him, one way or another."

Sir Jasper was frankly delighted with this conversation. Unbidden and quite unexpectedly, Harriet Ingersoll had provided him with a tool so perfect for his purpose that he could scarcely believe his good fortune. In a state of high elation, he returned to the reception room and looked around for Amos Raventhorne. Unable to locate him, his eyes settled on Maya, being escorted out of the room by Herbert Ludlow. Spying Douglas Hooper, he joined him again and, taking his elbow, guided him into a corner.

"How does it go in Molunga, Douglas? Still having trouble?"

Hooper paled and threw a furtive glance over his shoulder. "For God's sake, Jasper, not *here*." It was known among his close friends that he kept a native woman in the Molunga bazaar, by whom he had had two children.

"Well, just answer one question. How would you like it if they were sent away, so far away that you never needed to see them again?"

Hooper's eyes glinted. "Are you serious?"

"Perfectly."

"Well, how?"

"Then you *are* interested?"

"What do you think—of course I'm interested! The wretched woman's demands never stop, and if Mabel comes to know, I'm a dead duck."

"Very well, come to the Treasury tomorrow at ten. We'll talk about it then."

It was as the desserts were being served that Olivia sought out Abala Goswami, engrossed in animated debate with a rather bemused army colonel, who looked distinctly hunted, about the myth that the sun was harmful to the English complexion. "Have you seen Amos anywhere?" Olivia asked, interrupting the debate with an apologetic smile and pulling Abala aside.

"Amos?" Abala looked around, but it was impossible to identify anyone in the crush. "Come to think of it, I haven't seen Alistair either for quite some time."

Suddenly uneasy, Olivia hurried off to make inquiries in another direction. It was very probable that, unable to tolerate each other's presence under the same roof even for a few hours, they had simply taken off for their respective homes, and the thought of such gross discourtesy angered her. On the other hand, there was the rather wishful prospect that they might be together somewhere, conversing, agreeing mutually to bury hatchets. The two letters she had already written to Lady Birkhurst had been truthful and cheerless. How wonderful if a third could convey more joyous tidings!

But then Edna came up to relate a rumour that was circulating in the room.

"A fight in the garden?" Olivia's stomach lurched. "Who?"

Edna shrugged. "No one seems to know. Apparently, someone got drunk and took a slug at someone else over something, it's all rather vague." Noting Olivia's expression, she quickly gave her hand a squeeze. "I'm sure neither Amos nor Alistair had anything to do with it, my dear. Don't worry before you have to." It was sane advice and Olivia accepted it as such, but her vague sense of unease persisted.

"I have been waiting for an opportunity to speak to you alone, Miss Raventhorne, for a very special reason." Herbert Ludlow finally came to the point as he chatted with Maya in an alcove.

She had been apprehensive when he ushered her out of the room, and still was. Knowing how vital the Chief Commissioner was to Christian's future, Maya's heart missed a beat. "You have?"

"Yes. Let us sit down a moment, shall we? I wanted to talk to you about Morning Mist."

"Oh." She made no secret of her relief.

"I saw him race that recent afternoon and, I must say, I have seldom seen a finer specimen of an Arab grey. I had a word with Shooter in the weighing room and he confirms my assessment."

Maya was enormously pleased. "Yes, he has excellent potential as a racer. I was very lucky to have got him at the auctions."

"Do you plan to sell him?"

"Well, yes." She thought an instant, careful not to allow her awe of the man to cloud her sense of business. "But only when I can get the right price for him—and the right home," she informed him firmly.

"Shooter tells me you have had several offers already?"

"A few."

"One, I believe—a very insistent one—was from that reprobate, Aaron Nicholas?"

"Well, yes, but I have decided not to sell to him."

"Then, I take it, you have not yet made a commitment?"

"No. Not yet."

"In that case," it was Ludlow's turned to look pleased, "I would be obliged if you could let me have first refusal. When would it be convenient for me to call at your stables?"

As soon as the appointment was made and the Chief Commissioner had disappeared round the corner, Christian approached her. He looked tense and worried. "What did Ludlow have to say?"

"We talked about horses," Maya said, still a little dazed. "He wants to buy Morning Mist. He saw him win at the charity races."

"He said nothing else?"

"No." She laughed and her eyes shone with a wicked sparkle. "Maybe I can persuade Mr. Ludlow to exchange Morning Mist for a more attractive posting for you, Christian—how does that appeal to your sense of humour?"

It didn't. Indeed, he was suffused with anger. "You've had too much to drink," he snapped, and walked away in a huff. Far too happy to take offence, Maya only laughed.

And then, quite out of the blue, Sir Jasper approached her for a dance.

As she was making her way towards her next partner, who was waiting patiently for her by the door, her host of the evening suddenly appeared in her path, bowed with great courtesy and requested the pleasure of the waltz. He did not wait for her response, taking her acceptance for granted. Which was, perhaps, just as well. Maya would not have been able to say a single word anyway.

I wonder what he thinks of me? Maya asked herself in a daze, overwhelmed by the honour, her stomach full of fluttering butterflies, as Sir Jasper whirled her round and round the floor with far more energy than expertise.

Had she been able to read Sir Jasper's thoughts, however, Maya would have been very discomfited. Uppermost in his mind, and occupying most of it, was the question—how soon would it be possible for him to meet Kyle Hawkesworth again?

452

CHAPTER

19

I T SEEMED TO OLIVIA that she had slept no more than a few minutes
when she was shaken awake the next morning by an agitated Sheba.
Salim, Alistair's bearer, was downstairs waiting with alarming news:
last night the laat sahib had had a terrible accident and was badly
wounded. She must come with him immediately or his poor sahib would
surely die! Bursting into tears, he started to wail and beat his chest.

All the drowse vanished from Olivia's sleepless eyes as the rumoured
fracas of last night in the Pendleburys' garden sprang to mind. In spite of
being dreadfully frightened, she wasted no more precious time in questions but turned and ran back up the stairs in order to change. Halfway
up on the first landing, Sheba barred her way. In her arms she cradled her
favourite toy, the laundry basket. "I have something to show you."

"Not now, Sheba!" Impatiently, Olivia waved her away. "I *must* get to
Alistair."

"I think you should see these first." Resolutely blocking her path with
the laundry basket, the housekeeper held up a garment. It was the boiled
white shirt Amos had worn to the ball last night. The frontage was
encrusted with red.

Whatever Olivia was about to say died in her throat. She snatched the
shirt out of Sheba's hands and fingered it; there was no doubt that the
encrustations were of dried blood. Her own ran cold. "Oh my God! Where
did you find this?"

"In Master Amos's laundry bin. His coat is torn, and both his coat and
trousers are soaking wet. There is thick mud on his new black shoes."

"Where is Amos?"

"He is still asleep. His pillow is also stained with blood." Her eyes were
wide with fright.

Olivia ran into Amos's room, as concerned for him as she was for Alistair. He lay deep in sleep, his right arm flung over the side of the bed. She examined the knuckles without touching them; beneath the iodine stain, there were bruises and abrasions. Above one eyebrow, the blood had coagulated over a nasty cut which had obviously bled onto the pillow during the night. He slept soundly, his breathing regular and normal. Olivia laid a light palm on his forehead; it was damp but cool, and there was no fever. With a sigh, both of relief and of despair, she sat down for an instant to recover her dissipating senses.

Her worst nightmare had come true!

Hardly aware of what clothes she threw on, somehow Olivia dressed herself. Amos's injuries were minor; from what she had heard, it was Alistair who had come off the worse of the two. Within her boiled a rage more insane than she had ever felt before. How *could* Amos have broken his promise to her to do something as unforgivable as this? How *could* he?

Downstairs, in the lobby where Salim waited, Olivia almost fell over Christian, who stood quietly by the hat stand.

"Good morning, Mrs. Raventhorne. I . . ."

"I can't stop now, Christian dear," she gasped, scarcely giving him a look. "I have to hurry!" With a few mumbled words of apology, she flew out of the front door and into her carriage.

Christian looked puzzled. "Has anything . . . happened?" he inquired in vague alarm of the housekeeper.

"No, nothing at all, sir." As loyal and dependable as ever, Sheba blurted out the first excuse that came into her head. "Madam merely goes for a . . . drive."

A drive—so early in the morning? Christian was even more baffled, but with a shrug he put the matter aside. Not having slept at all himself, he was leaden-headed and irritable, with other worries to contend with. First of all, it was imperative that he talk to Maya. The weight of his interview with Herbert Ludlow lay heavy upon his conscience. He simply had to share it with her or he would surely explode.

When he learned that Maya was asleep, quite irrationally, his temper stirred. He refused Sheba's offer to rouse her, announcing coldly that he would wait on the verandah until she chose to rouse herself. He was angry that last night, too engrossed in her silly flirtations, basking in the admiration and adulation of other young men, she had not asked him once about what had transpired between him and the Chief Commissioner—if she even remembered that an interview was due.

Smarting under her thoughtlessness, worn out with tension and lack of sleep, he threw himself into a chair on the verandah in front of the tray of tea Sheba presented, and waited with growing impatience for Maya to make an appearance. She did not. When Sheba returned from the dhobi house an hour later, she found the tea untouched, still no sign of Maya, and Christian fast asleep on the chaise-longue. Taking pity on the distraught young man who would soon be her darling girl's husband, she hurried upstairs and shook a reluctant Maya firmly awake.

"We got home at four, Christian. I've hardly slept at all," Maya began petulantly, as she came down into the verandah, as exhausted and irritable as he. "Whatever it is, couldn't it have waited?"

"No. I have to talk to you now," he said tersely. "It's important."

She forced her eyes open, unnerved by his odd behaviour. "I did something wrong at the *burra khana?*"

"It's nothing to do with the damn *burra khana!* I wanted to tell you that Ludlow has offered me another posting."

"Oh." She made an effort not to let her interest wane. "Well, that's wonderful, Christian." She sat back and yawned, still not fully awake. "It was a *wonderful* evening, wasn't it? I've never enjoyed anything so much in all my life!"

He did not hear what she said. "I've been waiting for a chance to talk to you about it in detail. I couldn't earlier."

She throttled another yawn and nodded.

At meticulous length he related to her what had transpired between him and Herbert Ludlow. "I was really taken aback, Maya," he ended, animated again, "and, of course, enormously flattered."

Maya made no response. With the back of her head leaning against the wall, she was once again asleep. Before he could react, however, the sudden silence wakened her and she got up with a start.

"Where did you say the posting was?"

He gave her an impatient look. "In the *Punjab.* With Gordon Lumsdale."

"Lumsdale," she repeated with a frown, struggling with both her memory and the persistent yawn. "The name sounds familiar—should I know it?"

"You should, but it doesn't matter. Well, he's in the Punjab. Remember I told you about him once?"

She didn't, but she nodded anyway. And yawned again.

"Aren't you interested in what I have to say?" Christian was very cross. "Dammit, I haven't slept a wink either in order to see you this morning!"

"Of *course* I'm interested!" She sat up with an effort and rubbed her eyes into wakefulness. "I'm sorry, but I'm just so tired. Anyway, please tell me again, what did Mr. Lumsdale have to say?"

"Not Lumsdale, Ludlow! Gordon Lumsdale is in the Punjab, I just told you! He happens to be one of the finest officers the Civil Service has ever known, one of the men I admire most. I've read every word ever written about him, his work and his achievements. He has an amazing understanding of the Indian mind, and his passionate dedication to. . . ." Noticing that her eyelids had started to droop once more, he broke off with a muttered oath. "Anyway, let me cut it short so as not to bore you to death. Ludlow has offered me a chance to work with Lumsdale in the Punjab. It's what I have always wanted—*if* you still remember."

"Of course I remember!" What Christian had said finally registered in her befuddled brain. "Oh, Christian, that's absolutely *splendid!* Why, I'm delighted for you!" Her belated enthusiasm was so genuine that he was marginally pacified. His smile, however, was bitter. "Well, don't be." His shoulders sagged. "The posting is for a bachelor."

"A bachelor?" Maya's eyes flew wide open. For the first time he had her total attention. "And what did you say?" she asked in a nervous whisper.

He closed his eyes. "I refused it, of course. What else did you expect that I would say?"

"Oh." She breathed again, overwhelmed with a relief she dared not show him. "In that case, it is still Champaran, is it?"

"Yes. I can't see him offering me another option."

Maya's eyes softened. She took his hand in hers and laid a kiss on his palm. "It doesn't matter, my dearest. We'll manage somehow, I promise."

Christian remained silent, desolate that she should have so little understanding of his needs, his ambitions, his true feelings. But then she smiled with such tenderness that the sense of disappointment evaporated. They were on their own in the verandah and no one was watching. He bent over and kissed her on the lips.

Her eyes again sparkled. The matter settled to her satisfaction, she returned to the subject closest to her heart. "Did I behave well last night, Christian? I didn't disappoint you in any way, did I?"

Despite his anxieties, he was touched by the question. "No." With great tenderness, he stroked her cheek. "You were magnificent. Everyone said so."

"Your parents too?"

"I haven't seen them yet, but I cannot believe that they were unimpressed. Father actually danced with you—and I know how much he hates to be on the floor."

"I was petrified in case I stumbled, but I didn't. I didn't miss a single step!" Her face was triumphant. "Don't you think it was handsome of Alistair to do what he did? It meant so much to us all, especially to Mother. Even Amos was nonplussed." She suddenly giggled. "Did you see what Melanie was wearing? That dreadful thing in pink and purple with sleeves like bat wings? And that *look* on her face when. . . ."

Christian resigned himself to his fate and listened in silence. However, he displayed such an air of boredom and his manner was so abstracted that Maya was frankly relieved when he eventually left. Also, she longed to return to her bed to sleep—and again to dream! Later in the day, when she was on her own with her beloved Sheba, she would recount every precious, unforgotten detail of the evening. Sheba would listen with unwavering attention, want to know about every pleat and frill and furbelow worn, every morsel of food served, every dance danced and every compliment that she had received and from whom.

Elated again, Maya floated across the breakfast room on her way upstairs and then halted with a jolt. Amos was at the table nursing a cup of coffee. He looked frightful! The hand holding the cup was bandaged, and there was a bad cut above his right eye over which he had applied some dark ointment so that it looked even more sinister.

"What on earth have you been doing, Amos?" She was concerned but not truly alarmed. With his sporting interest in pugilistics, he often came home looking far worse.

"I had an accident," he said shortly.

"A fall?"

He took the easy way out. "Yes."

"Cavalcade threw you?"

"Yes."

"You haven't broken anything, have you?"

"No!" The questions made his temper as unpleasant as his appearance. "Now leave me alone, will you?"

"My goodness, just because Mother forced you to escort us to the *burra khana*, you don't have to bite my head off!"

"Well, then, shut up and mind your own confounded business!" He slammed his cup down so hard that it cracked and the coffee leaked all over the white tablecloth, which did little to improve his temper. He shouted for Francis, vented his anger on him for a while, then without completing his breakfast stalked out of the room.

Maya stared after him with her hands on her hips. "Now, why is he like a bear with a sore head this morning, I wonder?"

She did not have to wonder long. Herself in quite a state, Sheba was only too eager to enlighten her.

It did not take long for news of Christian's meeting with Herbert Ludlow, and most of its contents, to arrive at the chummery by means of that most efficient and swift information circuit yet devised by the colonial world—the Indian domestic servant.

Not a little put out by Christian Pendlebury's extraordinary response to the offer of a plum posting, Herbert Ludlow happened to make mention of the matter with some annoyance to a luncheon guest that very afternoon. As the Chief Commissioner bemoaned the incomprehensible demands of the younger generation these days, he was unaware that his bearer listened with as much interest as did his tiffin table companion. Ludlow's bearer, who understood far more English than Ludlow suspected, happened to be married to a first cousin of Christian's father's *khidmutgar*, whose sister bought her groceries from the same bania patronised by the aunt of a kinsman of Christian's personal servant, Karamat. Consequently, as soon as luncheon was over, Ludlow's bearer lost no time in conveying the news to Sir Jasper's *khidmutgar* who, as his bounden duty, consigned it to the next person, who did the same to the next, until it finally reached Karamat's ears with remarkable despatch. Being a business partner of Illingworth's bearer in the matter of the morning's bazaar purchases, naturally Karamat mentioned it at once to his colleague and his colleague offered the snippet to his master in lieu of a handsome baksheesh. As was to be expected, Illingworth passed the juicy tidbit on to Lytton Prescott.

Therefore, by the time Christian returned to the chummery after seeing Maya, details of his meeting with Herbert Ludlow were known not only to his chummery mates but, in all probability, to at least half the White Town.

"You'd be a damned *fool* to turn down that posting with Lumsdale," was Lytton's opening remark the instant Christian came through the door. "It's the chance of a lifetime, you ass."

Already in a beastly mood, Christian slammed the door hard behind him. "I wonder why they bother with the expense of an electric telegraph," he sneered, furious, "when a pair of tom-toms would do equally well. In any case, whether I. . . ."

He broke off, suddenly taking note of the rather less than healthy appearance of both his co-inhabitants. Patrick sat with his feet in a basin of water, a large piece of meat pasted over one eye. His lips were swollen to double their normal size, and when he opened his mouth to wince, Christian saw that one of his teeth was missing. Lytton, on the other hand, merely lay on the divan groaning under his breath, one bandaged hand clutched to his brow, the other clamped to a hip.

Christian was considerably cheered. Not having heard rumours of last night's battle, and too preoccupied to remember even if he had, he looked from one to the other, grinning widely. "Good heavens! Don't tell me another Afghan War has started and I know nothing about it?"

Patrick gave him a venomous glare. "Aw, shut up!"

Understandably, Patrick's own mood was far from congenial this morning. He had taken a licking from a half-caste guttersnipe, his mouth ached like billy-ho and he could only see out of one eye. Furthermore, he was still smarting under Melody's entirely uncalled-for remark about Christian Pendlebury's good looks. Unable to return to the dinner party following the pasting and the ruination of his best suit—to say nothing of his injuries—he had not been forgiven for a disappearing act for which he could offer no explanation. This morning, Melody had returned his engagement ring, and the future of the relationship hung precariously in the balance. To top it all, he was broke.

As a means of ridding himself of his own simmering frustrations, Patrick gave an ugly little laugh and geared up for further argument. "Well, if you want to throw away the chance of a lifetime over some silly popsie, it's your bloody funeral."

The smile whipped off Christian's face and it darkened. "I've warned you not to use that word again!" His hands clenched by his sides.

"What, 'popsie'?" Had it not been so painful to do so, Patrick would have laughed. Instead, he merely smirked. "Why not, if that's what she is? My dear chap, wine-tasters are not required to swallow, only to *sip*." With his one open eye he winked. "Get my meaning?"

"No, I *don't* get your meaning. And, what's more, I find your filthy innuendos disgusting!"

Moaning with the effort, Lytton turned on one side. "Come on, old boy, listen to reason—all we're trying to do is point out something that everyone already knows. With the Raventhorne women, being a mistress is something of a tradition. Your little dolly's mother lived with the man for two years before they were married. It's common knowledge. If you're lucky, like mother, like. . . ."

In a lightning leap, Christian was at his side and had him by the shoulder. "One word more," he hissed, "and I'll push your face in so far back you'll never be able to get it right again!"

"You'd hit a man when he was down?" Lytton asked with a gasp of pain.

Christian let go his shoulder and stood back. "Well, then, don't talk rubbish," he muttered, angry but ashamed.

"It's *not* rubbish, Christian, it's the truth." Feigning patience, Patrick baited him further. "You could have both, you silly twit—the girl and the posting. If you'd drop your blinkers for a moment, you'd see it for yourself. We do, don't we, Lytton?"

"That's it, then!" Enraged, Christian slammed a fist hard into the door. "I . . . demand satisfaction! Tomorrow morning, at six, on the Maidan."

"Oh, don't be so daft!" Lytton sighed, turning his face again to the wall, as Patrick hooted. "I couldn't *crawl* to the Maidan, much less ride—and nobody goes duelling these days anyway. It's terribly *déclassé*. It's also against the law."

Feeling inordinately foolish, Christian let loose a string of invective and flung himself out of the door.

"A chipped front tooth, a gash on the chin—which is what bled so profusely—a bump on the head, probably from a fall, a torn fingernail, plenty of abrasions and bruises and, of course, a forearm fracture." Cheerfully, Dr. Humphries gave Olivia an inventory of Alistair's injuries. "He might look as if he's been fired from a cannon, but he'll be as right as rain in a week. As far as I can tell, it's a fairly clean fracture. It should heal well in due course. He's lost some blood, of course, but nothing he won't recover with proper nourishment."

Olivia's shoulders sagged in relief.

"I must say, he was lucky to get medical attention as fast as he obviously did. Do you know to which doctor he went?"

"No," Olivia replied. "All Salim can say is that he was brought home well after midnight by some Indian well-wisher."

"Well, I suppose it doesn't really matter. Whoever the doctor was, obviously a herbalist, he did a neat job of it." He started to scribble a prescription. "Two tablespoonfuls thrice a day. This will dull the pain and keep him sedated until the broken bone starts to set." He jabbed his pen in the inkpot on the desk and then wrote again. "Do you know how he hurt himself? He seemed perfectly well at the *burra khana*."

Olivia matched his look of puzzlement. "No. I'm sorry, I don't. He probably had a fall."

"A fall?" the doctor chuckled. "A high-spirited set-to, more likely. Well, I'm not surprised. Some of those lads were certainly knocking the stuff back fast enough last night. Anyway," he tore off the prescription and handed it to her, "my compounder will make this up for you while I'm on my rounds. Does he live alone? Young Alistair, I mean?"

"Yes."

He stared down at his sorry-looking patient. "Then who will be looking after him, you?"

"Of course. I intend to stay here as long as it is required."

"Good. For an instant it had slipped my mind that . . . anyway, he's lucky to have you here. I hope the patient appreciates the nurse as much as the nurse evidently does the patient!"

Olivia laughed. "Well, both nurse and patient are greatly appreciative of the speed with which you arrived, Dr. Humphries. I don't know about Alistair, but I certainly feel so much better already."

He placed a comforting hand on her shoulder. "Don't worry, Mrs. Raventhorne. He's young, he's healthy, and last night he was obviously fortunate enough to find a friend to help him when he needed help most." He rose and started to pack his black medical bag. "The pain will persist for a while, of course, but it should subside in a day or two. By the end of the fortnight, he will have little to show for the, ah, accident—except a sling."

Willie Donaldson huffed and puffed his way up the stairs and into Alistair's bedroom suite as soon as Dr. Humphries had departed.

"I was na well myself this mornin'," he explained, not meeting Olivia's eyes. "I awoke with this cripplin' headache." He touched his temple and winced. Olivia suppressed a smile and made sympathetic noises. Donaldson took a closer look at the unconscious figure on the bed and gasped. "Jumpin' Jupiter! What did *he* run into—the side of a bleedin' barn?"

"No. Amos." With the relief also came the return of Olivia's anger. There was, of course, no question of keeping secrets from Willie Donaldson. "Apparently, they had a fight last night sometime during the course of the *burra khana.*"

He was incredulous. "He fought with Amos? Last night?"

"Well, who fought with whom I don't know, but being the older brother, Amos should certainly have known better!"

"But that's na possible, lass!" Donaldson exclaimed, shocked to the core. "Amos would na do such a thing, *ne'er!*"

"Well, he did." She could no longer hold back her bitterness. "There's blood all over Amos's clothes, too. His hand and face are covered with bruises."

"Did anyun' see the fight?"

"No. There were some whispers wafting about but nothing specific."

"Have you asked Amos about it?"

"Not yet. He was still asleep when I left the house."

Donaldson was reduced to silence. That it should have come to this despite all his efforts, despite his threat to Alistair! He could not conceal his own bitter disappointment.

"You want for anythin', lass?"

"No, nothing. Thank you. The house seems to be well stocked with all the essentials."

"I reck'n you'll be needin' help, perhaps a nurse?"

"No, Willie, dear. There are plenty of servants here with little enough to do. They will be perfectly adequate."

Satisfied that his charge was in the best hands possible, Donaldson left, promising to return in the evening.

Maya's reaction, when she arrived a few moments later, was also one of indignation and disbelief. "Oh, don't be ridiculous, Mother! You can't possibly believe Amos to be guilty of this! Why, Amos wouldn't hurt a fly if he could help it. There *must* be some other explanation."

"I hope so," Olivia replied grimly, "but don't underestimate your brother's temper under provocation—it can be as savage and uncontrolled as his father's."

"Well, I don't believe it." Maya remained staunchly defensive of her brother. "They shook hands in full public view, Mother, and it was Alistair who took the initiative. Amos would never rebuff such a worthy effort, no matter what the provocation!"

"I don't know what or whom to believe any more," Olivia said wearily. "But if Amos *is* to blame, I will never forgive him, never—he gave me his *word*."

"Would you like me to stay here with you?" Maya asked, looking around the room. "There seems to be an awful lot to be done through the day."

"No, darling." Olivia shook her head, reluctant to let anyone share her precious hours alone with Alistair, even her daughter. As a mother, it was as much her right to nurse him as it was his as a son to expect it of her. "I can manage quite well with Salim's help." Seeing that Maya was about to argue, she quickly spoke of something else. "What was Christian doing at the house so dreadfully early this morning? Nothing is amiss, is it?"

"No. He merely wanted to talk about the . . . *burra khana*."

"Oh. Anyway, you go back and rest, dear. You didn't sleep much last night either."

Maya smiled and lazily stretched her arms above her head. "Oh, I'm wide awake now, much too excited to rest! I need to do something with my hands. I think I'll have the carriage house and stables cleaned out today. Mr. Ludlow wants to come and see Morning Mist later in the week. Tomorrow, I'll have to spend the day in the kitchen."

"In the kitchen?" Olivia was amused. Cooking was not one of Maya's favourite occupations. "What are you going to cook?"

"Well, I thought I'd try my hand at Mont Blanc aux marrons. I managed to extract a recipe from M'amselle Corinne last night when no one was watching. I'll send for the ingredients this evening." She opened her eyes wide and yawned. "It was a *marvellous* evening, wasn't it, Mother?" she said dreamily, then added in rueful haste, "I don't mean what happened to poor Alistair, of course—that was quite awful. I mean otherwise."

Noticing the pain in her mother's eyes, Maya put her arms around her shoulders. "Why don't you find out the truth from Amos?" She suggested gently. "He deserves to be given a chance to explain."

"Oh, I intend to." Olivia assured her. "I *intend* to—just as soon as I see that Alistair is on the mend. In the meantime, I'd rather you didn't say anything to him about it."

The moment she was again on her own, Olivia busied herself about the house. There was much that wanted doing, but first of all Alistair's needs had to be attended to. He was still in the clothes he had worn last night. Only the jacket had been cut open and removed, obviously by the Indian doctor, to facilitate treatment of the damaged arm. Salim confessed that he had been too frightened to interfere with the laat sahib's clothing in case he unintentionally caused further injury. Now, guided by Olivia, he unclad his master with great care. Watching from a distance, Olivia's thoughts flew back to the days when the loyal old bearer used to perform the same duty for Freddie each time he was brought home drunk and incapacitated. Under her instructions, Salim carefully sponged Alistair's body with soap and warm water, then draped him in a loose nightgown slit down the back. Alistair remained oblivious of the ministrations, restless and muttering incoherently from time to time, still without full consciousness.

Through the rest of the day Olivia remained by his side, keeping vigil. She positioned her chair not a foot away from the bed, her eyes fixed to her beloved son's face, her hand never far from his forehead. Within herself, quietly, she cried; she could not bear to watch his suffering. Physically, she could not share his agony, but in her mind, each time he moaned she felt a shaft of pain, as if the broken bone was lodged not in his body but in her own. Yet, paradoxically, there was something about Alistair's state of helplessness that brought her immense satisfaction. For the first time in both their lives, he was dependent on her, once again the infant she had been denied. He lay sleeping, unaware and unconcerned, his closed eyelids concealing from her the anger that simmered within him. She devoured him greedily, looking her fill, memorising every little feature, every mole and freckle, storing it away in her treasury of precious memories. The ripple on the lobe of his left ear; the half moon that was absent from a thumbnail; the long, brown lashes that curled upwards; the whirlpool on top of his head amidst the thick chestnut curls so much like Maya's and her own. How extraordinary! Each little exploration ended in some minor discovery that filled her with ridiculous joy.

Presently, unable to sit still, she placed Salim by the bedside and set about performing necessary chores about the house, exactly as if she had never left it. She assigned duties to the substantial staff that Willie Donaldson still retained for the maintenance of the house. The bathrooms needed a thorough scrubbing, the curtains had to be taken down and washed, the front lawn, neglected and overgrown, cried out to be trimmed.

Sending for a kerosene stove, she had it installed in the verandah that was part of the suite. On it she boiled nourishing milk with cocoa, chicken broth with barley and vegetables fetched fresh from the market, and some kedgeree. She gave Alistair his medicine at regular intervals, and every hour she coaxed him into eating a little until, like a sleeping child responding to a known touch, he obediently opened his mouth each time the spoon made contact with his lips.

In between, she set about tidying his bedroom suite, arranging his scattered books neatly on the shelves and sorting out his clothes in the capacious almirah that had once belonged to Freddie. As she listed his apparel, she again bemoaned the absurdly inapt clothing he had brought with him, with not one sensible superfine calico shirt or cotton half hose or short-wove cotton drawers, so essential in this murderously humid heat. Refusing to be helped, she wanted to do it all herself, revelling in her unexpected responsibilities. She separated Alistair's clothes into neat little piles: some went to the dhobi house for a boil wash, others to be pressed or brushed. One pile she kept aside for mending when she had a moment.

The day slowly melted into evening. She sent one of the servants to fetch a change of clothes and some toilet articles for her from the house. She knew that Amos would not come to visit, but she still hoped that he might relent and surprise her. He did not. As he had promised, however, Willie Donaldson arrived at sundown, still deeply distressed.

"I canna believe what you tell me aboot Amos, lass. It breaks my old heart, by God it does!"

If only he knew how thoroughly it had broken hers!

After Willie had gone, Olivia prepared supper. Although still heavily sedated, Alistair downed each spoonful hungrily. Later, at Salim's insistence, she nibbled at some toast and an omelette, and settled herself on the couch. The bearer, as concerned about her as he was about his young master, spread his own mat outside the door on the landing in case she required his services during the night. Restless for most of the night, Alistair whimpered often, changing sides frequently, murmuring gibberish as if in a state of delirium. Lying on the couch in the half dark, watching the flickering night light on the table, Olivia remained wide awake and alert. Each time he moved or made a sound, she hurried to his side to cradle him in her arms, murmuring comfort, kissing his moist face, loving him as she had never before had the chance to. But finally, towards the small hours of the morning, Alistair stilled. Tired out by his physical exertions, he slipped into a tranquil, healing sleep.

Her own body exhausted and drained of energy, Olivia too slept. When she opened her eyes again with a start, the sun was already high in the heavens. It was almost noon. Her eyes flew towards the bed, but Alistair still slept. She felt his forehead; it was damp, but there was no fever. His breathing was shallow and regular. Ordering Salim to light the stove and heat some milk, she went into the bathroom to wash and change. When she returned to the room, Alistair's eyes were open.

Drowsy and bleary-eyed, he stared up at her. "Who are you?"

She walked over to the bed and wiped dry his forehead. "A friend. Go back to sleep."

"What is wrong with me?"

"You have been . . . unwell."

He tried to struggle up, but then fell back with a groan. "Have I got cholera? Will I die?"

She laughed. "No, you have not got cholera and you will not die." Her eyes softened. "Is the pain any better?"

"My head aches." He closed his eyes, not hearing her question. "I feel so tired, so *tired.*"

She fed him a dose of medicine and some oatmeal porridge, then sat and massaged his forehead. He gave a sigh of pleasure and lay in a shallow sleep, dozing. Remembering the mending that needed doing, she instructed Salim to fetch her needle, thread and scissors, and sat down to sew some missing buttons on a shirt. As she worked, she hummed, once again happy. She was in the middle of darning one of a pair of Argyle socks when Alistair suddenly spoke.

"Why are you doing all this?"

She gave a start and looked up. He was wide awake and in his eyes there was recognition. "What?" she asked, flustered.

"I asked, why are you doing all this for me? You are not obliged to."

"No. I do it because I want to."

"But why?" he persisted. "It is so unnecessary."

"I do it because for me it *is* necessary, because you are my son." She was surprised at the ease with which she said it. "Anyway, how do you feel now?"

He muttered something that sounded like "Better."

"Is the pain improving?"

He felt his arm, winced and then nodded. "A little."

"Dr. Humphries says the doctor who splintered your arm did a very good job. Who was he?"

Alistair frowned, trying to remember. "It was all so confused. . . ."

"Well, never mind now. Do you think you could manage some chicken stew for tea?"

He didn't reply. Noticing that his clothes had been changed, he blushed a rich pink. "Who?"

"Salim. I wasn't even in the room." She rose and set about preparing his meal.

Alistair ate without protest but in awkward silence, propped up against a bank of pillows, keeping his gaze fixed on the bowl. Respecting his need to be quiet, Olivia fed him by the spoonful, delighted to see that his appetite had returned. After the bowl had been wiped clean, he lay back and closed his eyes, tired out by the effort. But he had eaten well and there was again colour in his cheeks.

Olivia summoned Salim to light the lamps, then, very quietly, asked, "What happened that night, Alistair? How did you get hurt?"

He face became blank. "I . . . don't remember."

She swallowed hard. "Did . . . Amos have anything to do with . . . whatever happened?"

He closed his eyes and said nothing.

"I want to know the truth, Alistair, was Amos there?"

"Yes."

She started to tremble. "Was it he who . . . broke your arm?"

"Amos . . . ?" He struggled to speak but didn't.

"*Was* it, Alistair?" He still said nothing.

"You are hiding something from me," she implored, grasping his hand. "What is it, tell me!"

Alistair squeezed his eyes shut, his mind in a turmoil. He snatched his hand out of hers and turned his back to her. "I can't remember," he whispered. "I don't remember *anything,* can't you understand that?"

"You *can* remember," she cried, "and you do! You're only trying to protect Amos, isn't that it?"

Lying with his face to the wall, Alistair tried to tell her the truth, tried to refute what she said, but he couldn't. The words seemed to stick in his gullet and he simply could not get them out.

Furious and frustrated Christian ran all the way to the embankment after leaving the chummery, rested a few moments, then ran another mile without stopping. Having released some of the steam waiting to explode from within, he sat down, recovered his breath and regrouped his skittered senses. He remained by the river on a far stretch of the embankment whiling away the hours, unheeding of the passage of time as he strolled up and down with his hands in his pockets. Then, as the sun started its descent over the western horizon, his thoughts turned in an unfailingly comforting direction. He got to his feet and started to walk towards Garden Reach. He had a desperate need to talk to his father.

It was the evening after the *burra khana.* Not particularly anxious to encounter his mother today, Christian approached his father's study through the back garden. The windows looked dark and his heart sank; what if his father was out on a social visit, or still at the office with that dignitary from the Arabian sheikhdom? But then he saw that the room appeared dark only because the curtains had been drawn fully, and his spirits revived. With a spring in his step, he almost ran through the door, enormously relieved to see his father sitting in his favourite seat puffing at his hookah.

"Ah! Just the man I was thinking of," came the cheerful greeting. "Your mother's worn out after last night's capers and has threatened to retire early without supper. It seems to me a perfect situation for an extended chess session."

"Rather!" In his relief Christian laughed and immediately felt lighter.

"Your mother isn't expecting you, is she?"

"I hope not."

"Well, in that case, you can join me in a spot of supper. If the *baburchi's* biryani is as good as I hear it is, I may even allow you to win a game or two."

"Allow me to win? Hah, hah!"

"We shall see, we shall see. Now, care for some chilled champagne? I think there's still some left from last night, and of course, there's plenty of beer."

Christian settled for the beer, all his tensions melting away, as they always did when he was with his father. He flung himself into a corner of the deep, spongy sofa opposite his father's winged chair and, feeling completely at ease, stretched out his legs over a footstool.

They chatted for a while, relaxed and unhurried, laughing over this or that happening at the *burra khana*. Then Christian asked a little shyly, with a heightening of colour, "What did you think of Maya?"

"What everyone else did. She's an enchanting young lady, intelligent and, of course, very beautiful. Lady Ingersoll was very taken with her, indeed, with all the Raventhornes." He slapped a thigh and laughed. "By Jove, if only to see the shocked looks on all those faces, it was worth asking them, wasn't it? No offence, old boy!"

Christian smiled. "None taken, Papa. And . . . Mama? Did she express any opinion?"

"No." Sir Jasper sobered and regarded him solemnly. "You know what your mother's opinion is. That, I regret to say, has not changed."

"No. I suppose not." Christian shrugged, not particularly concerned. As long he had his father's understanding and support, there was no need for him to worry. "Herbert Ludlow summoned me earlier in the week."

"Oh? About your visit to Champaran?"

"No. He made no mention of that. He offered me another posting."

Sir Jasper raised a surprised eyebrow. "Really? Where?"

Christian took a sip of his beer, holding his father in suspense and enjoying it. "In the Punjab. With Gordon Lumsdale."

"Did he now!" his father exclaimed, satisfactorily surprised. "Well, that certainly must have warmed every cockle of your heart."

Christian's smile faded and he put down his tankard. "Yes."

At the distinctly tepid response, Sir Jasper paused to peer closely into his son's face. But seeing that Christian appeared reluctant to expand on the cryptic monosyllable, he held his questions in abeyance. Instead, he rubbed his hands together in anticipation.

"Well then, shall battle commence?"

Dutifully, Christian got up to fetch the beautifully carved ivory chess pieces and board and arranged them on a table between them. They tossed, Christian drew white and he moved a pawn. Before the next five moves were over, he had lost his queen and then, with remarkable despatch, the game. In the return match he fell easy prey to an obvious knight fork and was forced to sacrifice a rook and, in swift succession, his own knight and a bishop. He was two moves away from the second checkmate of the evening when his father sat back with a sigh.

"Much as I enjoy slaughtering your scandalously incompetent troops, Christian, there's not much pleasure in a Pyrrhic victory. Why don't we have supper and you can tell me what it is that keeps you from concentrating."

Christian nodded and sighed. "Yes."

Over the excellent biryani, succulent with chicken legs and aromatic with saffron, golden fried onions and roasted almonds, they conversed sparingly, the attention of each focused on the task at hand. Occasionally they again shared a laugh or a comment about some amusing incident from last night's revelries, but on the whole they ate in companionable silence.

After dinner, when Tremaine had cleared away the trays and the dishes and they sat sipping at their snifters of brandy, Christian related to his father the pertinent details of his meeting with Ludlow. And, very feelingly, the grossly unfair condition attached to the posting.

Having listened in silence, Sir Jasper now asked a first question. "Well, what is to be your response, then?"

"I will refuse it, of course. What else can I do?"

"Good. That is what any gentleman would do."

"You approve?" Christian asked, taken aback.

"Certainly I approve—but my approval is not important. The decision is yours to make, that is all that counts." He scanned Christian's uncertain expression. "You have reservations?"

"No, of course not! But . . . I have to confess that I feel rotten about it." He made a sour face. "As you know, it has always been my ambition to work with Lumsdale."

His father nodded, very serious. "Yes. I know."

"The problem is," Christian combed his hair with agitated fingers, "I want to have my cake and eat it! Isn't that illogical and absurd?"

"Yes, regrettably. You know where your commitments and obligations lie, Christian. It is for you now to honour them."

"Naturally, I intend to!" He inched forward on the sofa. "But tell me, Papa, is that what you would do in my place. Refuse the posting?"

"Without a shred of doubt! I wouldn't hesitate to do so for a moment. However," Sir Jasper raised a warning finger, "you must not allow yourself to be influenced by my way of thinking. You will have to make up your own mind."

"I have made up my mind!" Christian cradled his head in his hands and shook it. "I have to give Ludlow my reply by the end of the week, and I am still confused. I can't help feeling, well, disappointed. . . ." He broke off, guilty about the thought, ashamed to have voiced it.

There was a long silence. The hookah-burdar returned to refresh the chillum and fan it into life. An annoyingly vocal housefly buzzed around the spot where they sat. Picking up the swatter, Sir Jasper demolished it with a sharp flick as it settled within reach, then watched with undue concentration as the hookah boy cleared up the messy remains.

"You take me back, you know." Sir Jasper heaved a small sigh as his attention wandered.

Christian usually enjoyed his father's reminiscences about the "good old days." He had a marked talent for relating amusing anecdotes from the past. But tonight Christian did not feel in the mood for lightweight diversion. He nodded absently.

"I am reminded of someone I once knew many years ago when I was stationed in Peshawar."

"Who?" Christian asked without much interest.

"A man called Nesbitt. Warren Nesbitt."

He said nothing more, forcing Christian into another inquiry. "Well, who is Warren Nesbitt?"

"Was. The poor man died some years ago. Fell down a ravine in the Karakorams. They never found his body, haven't to this day. He left a widow and three children."

Somewhat at a loss, Christian nodded again.

Sir Jasper roused himself out of his musing. "Well, I won't bore you with all the gory details of the man's misfortunes. It's just that poor Nesbitt also happened to find himself in a predicament not unlike yours." He pointed to the chessboard. "Now, one last chance to recover some of your lost self-respect, what?"

A spark of interest flickered in Christian's eyes. He waved aside the offer. "How was his predicament like mine?"

"It was just an idle thought, Christian, nothing substantial or of any great significance. The story of Warren Nesbitt merely came to mind because of what you said."

"In that case, I would like to hear it."

Sir Jasper shrugged. "Very well. Nesbitt was an army major with the Guides in the late fifties. He too was deeply devoted to his fiancée, a very comely young lady, I heard, but having been posted to a non-family military station in the northwest frontier, he was forced to make a rather painful decision."

"He refused the posting?"

Sir Jasper exhaled a spiral of smoke. "No. Not quite. They devised satisfactory means to be together during his posting."

"Oh? What means?"

"He hired a house for her in Peshawar which was about twenty miles from his encampment, and spent time with her on each of his furloughs. He told me it did much to relieve the heartbreak of a long wait."

"Ah." Christian sat back, disappointed. "That's not quite the same, Papa. You see, I am forbidden to marry at all for the duration of the posting."

"So was Warren."

"Then how?" Christian straightened, frowning. "You mean, during all this they remained . . . unmarried?"

"They were obliged to, yes."

"I see." His expression closed. "She stayed in Peshawar as his mistress."

Sir Jasper shrugged. "As his affianced, I would say." His expression turned severe. "Mind you, I personally considered the arrangement rather, well, Bohemian, but as long as it suited them, it was none of my business. As far as I could see, both remained perfectly satisfied with—as you yourself put it—having their cake and eating it."

Christian was incensed. "Well, I think it was a despicable ruse with which to resolve the matter, and cowardly to boot!"

"Oh, absolutely. I was merely giving you an example of the tricks sometimes used by those men posted to non-family stations."

"And the lady's family allowed such a scandalous situation to prevail? I find that astonishing!"

"Yes, I did too. But it seems that they raised no objections, indeed, approved heartily of the arrangement." He pressed the tobacco down firmly in the chillum with a small, flat silver hammer designed for the purpose. "They were Eurasian, you see," he added casually. "I suppose that explained it. In their ignorance, many Eurasians believe that by taking Englishmen as lovers, their girls will gain status in the eyes of their peers."

Christian flushed. "Well, I consider that point of view quite reprehensible, sir," he said stiffly.

"As every true gentleman would. I simply point out that there are communities that do not consider these matters in the same light as we British do."

"Well, the Raventhornes are different," he muttered, not looking at his father.

"Who can deny that? I only related the incident to you because you insisted. Olivia Raventhorne is an admirable example of proud, courageous womanhood. That the poor lady was driven to co-habit with Raventhorne outside of marriage reflects not on her, but on the perverse configuration of her stars and circumstances. However unkind the gossip, I have nothing but respect for Mrs. Raventhorne." He brushed aside the subject. "Now, enough of Warren Nesbitt and his ilk. There are other vital matters awaiting our pleasure. What do you say to a concluding game? That is, if you're intrepid enough to risk a third rout!"

When Christian left later that night (after having added a final checkmate to his sorry score of the evening), he was faced with the prospect of a long walk back to the chummery. He had not brought his own horse and had refused his father's offer of one, but that did not worry him. He had plenty to mull over, and the fresh air and exercise would help him to think. It occurred to him that this was the first time he had ever left his father's presence in a state of mental dislocation. The realisation brought with it a small sense of disappointment, and he found this strangely painful. He felt a sudden longing to talk to Kyle. But, as he had learned when he had gone to the press after seeing Maya, Kyle was out of station for a few days, and his sense of disappointment compounded.

He suddenly remembered that, in his preoccupation this evening, he had quite forgotten to ask his father if he had ever got round to meeting Kyle again. In the quiet of the intense dark, an involuntary smile came to his lips. Acerbic or not, Christian had no doubt that the encounter would have been mutually stimulating. He felt a stab of regret at having missed it.

20

THIS TIME MAYA took no chances. She dispatched Sheba to Mr. Barton's store not only for the tinned chestnuts but also for castor sugar, cream and all the other ingredients. She followed very carefully the recipe she had obtained from M'amselle Corinne and, as a consequence, the Mont Blanc aux marrons turned out perfectly.

Since it was not often that Maya could boast of an unqualified culinary success, she was thrilled. Proudly, she set aside a small mould of the marrons for her mother and brother. The larger mould she packed neatly in an empty biscuit tin, then wrapped the tin in a sheet of red paper and adorned it with a bright blue ribbon. She smiled to herself as she worked; what a surprise the delicacy would be for Aunt Sarala! Still in a state of euphoria, she felt wonderfully lighthearted. Sheba's enthusiastic responses to her accounts of the *burra khana* had been everything she could have wished for, but there was still a need to share her glowing memories with girls of her own age—Minali and Barnali, for instance. Both their parents had been at the Pendleburys' that night; part of their curiosity must have surely been assuaged, but, hungry for detail, there would still be many questions they would want to ask her, many gaps they would want filled. And in the prospect of reliving the night yet again in all its glory, Maya trembled with elation, praying that she would find both at the *bagan bari* and that they would be able to chatter to their heart's content.

She slept soundly that night, her slumber filled with lingering strains of music and laughter. The following day she rose late, refreshed and relaxed. By early afternoon, after a light luncheon, she was on her way to the Goswami family's farm house in her neat little carriage. The coachman and her ayah were perched on the high seat with the precious box resting between them.

The mango season was over and the orchard was deserted. Only two workers moved about under the low, leafy branches, sweeping up wet leaves and rotting fruit and carrying them in baskets on their heads to the compost heap near the well. The sky curdled with dark grey clouds and in the sharp winds there was promise of another downpour. On the wet, windy afternoon everyone appeared to have sought refuge indoors, unaware of her arrival. But that didn't bother Maya—she knew that this was one home where she would be welcome no matter when she chose to visit. She had the carriage stopped short of the front steps and, knowing her way about, made straight for Aunt Sarala's kitchen.

There was no sign of the old lady, but one of her white-clad, widowed maidservants sat stirring a pot that simmered on the earthen stove above a wood fire. The maidservant stared in surprise at Maya's approach and informed her, much to Maya's disappointment, that both the girls were away for the day. Their aunt Sarala, however, was down by the riverside performing part of her daily religious rituals. Maya had never been inside Aunt Sarala's kitchen before. When they were children, she remembered, they were warned not to play near her sanctum. Eyes dancing, Maya now quickly removed her shoes, washed her hands underneath the tap beside the door, and stepped into the kitchen. With a little giggle, she put her gift on a shelf near the door where the utensils were ranged.

Placing a warning finger across her lips, she said with an impish smile, "Don't say anything when she returns from the river. Let her find it for herself. I want it to be a surprise."

The Brahmin widow said something, her eyes wide and frightened, but in her excitement, Maya paid no attention. She stepped out of the kitchen, slipped on her shoes, and with a satisfied laugh, ran into the orchard to stand behind a tree and wait for her gift to be discovered.

A few moments later, the old widow walked up from the river bank. As usual, she was dressed in a borderless white sari. Her string of prayer-beads was looped over the fingers of one hand, a shining brass water vessel held in the other. As she walked, the large bunch of household keys tied to her sari over one shoulder made a tinkling sound. Her lips moved silently, reciting mantras; her expression was one of great serenity and devotion. She stopped outside her kitchen doorway, removed her wooden clogs, rinsed her hands under the tap and dabbed them dry on her sari. Still mouthing incantations, she stepped inside her kitchen.

For a moment there was silence. Then came the murmur of voices in conversation, followed by a hush. Greatly excited, Maya was about to step out of her place of concealment when, it appeared to her, all hell broke loose. It started with an ear-piercing scream followed by a deafening crash, then another and then yet another. In a matter of seconds, it seemed as if Aunt Sarala's entire kitchen house was being demolished by an army of violently destructive demons.

Maya's first instinct was to run in and render such assistance as might be necessary in what was evidently a major crisis. But then, before she could make a move, a missile came hurtling out of the kitchen doorway.

Maya had no difficulty in recognising the package decked in red paper and tied with a bright blue ribbon. As it hit the ground, the box flew open with the force of the impact, the paper ripped, and the lovingly prepared marrons mingled with the wet earth, beyond redemption. Bewildered, Maya remained rooted. In swift succession now came saucepans, trays, metal tumblers, plates, spoons, ladles, basins and bowls, of every size and description imaginable. It seemed that the kitchen was being relieved of every single item it had hitherto housed.

Then, followed by a sobbing maidservant who clung to her mistress's sari in supplication, Aunt Sarala marched out of the kitchen door. In her hands she held a traditional domestic broom made of thick, hard twigs bound together with string. Raising the broom high above her head, she started to rain blows on the maidservant's shaven head, calling her names, cursing her with merciless abandon. The wretched woman fell to her knees and crossed her hands over her head. Howling with pain, she pleaded for mercy and forgiveness, again and again clutching at her mistress's feet.

Shocking as this sight was in all its ugliness, the true horror of the moment lay in the expression on Aunt Sarala's contorted face. Gone were the serenity, the piety and the devotion; in their place were malice and cruelty and a terrible hunger for revenge. The lips, moulded around honeyed mantras only a moment ago, were twisted with wrath as they spewed vile curses. It was a scene so unexpected and so abhorrent that Maya could barely assimilate it.

"How could you allow her to step foot inside my kitchen, you black-faced, dung-headed witch!" the old lady screamed. "Are you a Brahmin—or the daughter of a night-soil sweeper? Don't you know why she brings me these gifts, what she is after, that *impure* one?"

People came running into the orchard from all sides, alarmed by the commotion. One of the first on the scene was Samir. The widow contained her hysteria and turned upon him in fury.

"It's all because of you!" she said, so angry that she could hardly raise her voice above a quivering croak. She spoke in Bengali, of course, but the rush of words was rapid and only intermittently comprehensible to Maya. She ranted for a while, not allowing Samir to speak, refusing to be pacified. "This would never have happened if you hadn't encouraged her to step beyond her limits!"

"But, Aunt Sarala, she only. . . ."

His protest was sliced off with an infuriated gesture. "Don't try to make excuses, you besotted fool! Do you think I don't know what's been going on behind my back? Listen to me, Samir, and listen well." Suddenly her rage evaporated, replaced by a hard, icy calmness. "I'd rather you went across the seas and shamed your caste, I'd rather you *died* than defiled the purity of your lineage in the manner that she wants you to!"

Samir turned. His eyes met Maya's, only half concealed by the tree, and he looked crushed. The old lady said something more, but Maya did not hear it. In her state of stupefaction, only one word remained trapped

472

within her consciousness, reverberating inside the confines of her skull.

Impure!

The commotion died down; everyone started to disperse. Someone touched her on the arm. It was Samir. "Come away, Maya. Come with me."

In a trance, she allowed herself to be led away from the orchard towards the stream and beyond, her feet moving forward of their own volition. She turned and, over her shoulder, stared once more at Aunt Sarala's face, unable to drag her eyes away. The old widow stared back at her, hostile and unforgiving, as if what she gazed upon was an abomination.

Maya sat by Samir's side on the wall that bordered the stream, far beyond the house and the orchard. They did not look at each other.

"It was my mistake," Maya said dully. "I should not have gone into her kitchen."

"I did not know that you were listening," he mumbled, his face full of misery.

"What else did she say?"

He shook his head. "Nothing. You know how she is."

"What else, Samir?" she insisted. "Please tell me."

He tossed up his hands. "It is not important, Maya."

"It is to me. *Tell* me!"

He shook his head again, this time angrily. "She is an ignorant, senile old. . . ."

"You will have to tell me, Samir." She caught his hand and held it, her voice hushed in its urgency. "I have a right to know!"

"Let it go, Maya, you cannot understand!"

"I will not let it go—she said I was impure. *Impure!*"

He looked at her frozen white face, her stricken eyes, and his fury soared. "She knows nothing of life, of the world, people, anything! She is simply an illiterate woman who lives in a hole in the ground surrounded by mildew and maggots and the decomposed remains of a bygone age!"

"She considers me impure because I am Eurasian."

"She is frightened of you, Maya, she feels *threatened* by you. Can you not understand that?"

Maya sat very still. Then she shivered, pulled up her legs, and tucked her knees under her chin. "Yes."

The promised rain started to descend in a shower of steady droplets, making amusing patterns on the surface of the water. A carp put its rounded lips above for a second, as if preparing for a kiss from an invisible lover, then, thinking better of it, ducked under again. Samir sat tossing stones into the water, his dark eyes glazed with despair.

From a distance Maya watched the crescent of people gathered around the kitchen door. On the ground to one side, Aunt Sarala squatted, sobbing quietly into her sari, surrounded now by more family members. Trying to console her with nervous, helpless gestures was a highly agitated Kali Charan. "How was she to know?" he kept asking, quite distraught. "After all, she is not one of *us*." A little away, Abala stood comforting the erring maidservant.

473

By her side Maya heard a sharp intake of breath. Samir curled one hand into a fist. "They are hypocrites," he breathed with a contemptuous jerk of his head in their direction, "arrogant, bigoted *hypocrites*. They fight noble public battles, yet they tolerate the cesspools that lie under their noses." He turned and spat into the stream. "They disgust me."

Not one of us. . . .

Maya barely listened, uncaring of the drizzle. "I thought she was fond of me."

"Fond? Yes, she is fond of you—as long as you remain at a distance."

"She made special sweets for me to eat."

"Forget her. Forget them all!" He spoke with lacerating scorn, his mouth filled with bile. "They no longer matter."

"Then what does matter?" she asked, her mind in a daze.

"You and me—nothing else." He slipped off the wall and started to walk back and forth.

"You and me?" she echoed, startled. "In spite of everything that she said?" He winced and hung down his head. Maya's eyes hardened. "I constitute no danger to you and your family, Samir. In any case, you are leaving for England soon."

"I will not go to England. I cannot."

"Because you might lose your precious caste?" she taunted.

"No. Because I cannot leave you, because you might need me some day."

She was ashamed that she should alleviate her own injuries by wounding him. "I will not need you, Samir. I . . ."

"Marry me!" He suddenly blurted out, unable to contain himself. "If you agree to come as my wife, I will go to England."

She was flabbergasted. "You want to marry me?" she asked foolishly. "In spite of everything? *Why?"*

"Because I love you. Because you are the axis around which I revolve. Because without you I will simply wither away and die. And because you will make my life complete."

Beneath the even cadences in which he spoke lay intense passion, like a deadly undertow pulling at a calm sea. Maya was taken aback by the depth of his feeling. To cover her own confusion, she laughed. "I will complete your life even as I defile your lineage?"

"We will live separately," he vowed, elated as he gathered confidence. "And in England you will have your own house, your own kitchen! There will be no compulsions, no obligations. I can heal what she has done to you, Maya, I can look after you, protect you, make you happy."

She searched his glowing face in wordless surprise, silenced by the enormity of the sacrifice he was willing to make, foraging for words, finding none that were adequate.

"Why do you look so surprised?" he cried with sudden asperity, not understanding her silence. "Isn't that what you have always wanted? To go to England?"

She almost told him about her imminent marriage to Christian, but she couldn't bring herself to voice words that would wound him even more. "I love you as a . . . friend," she said, sounding forlorn, cringing at the meaninglessness of the platitude she offered but knowing that she could offer nothing more. "Between us there can never be anything other than friendship."

"Why not?" His throat was thick with emotion.

"I do not love you."

"You do not love Christian!"

He had not mentioned Christian before. Now that he did, she was angry but she did not react visibly, moved by his deeply unhappy face, his lustrous eyes shining with sincerity. And once again she felt that strange current move within her, that half emotion that defied identification. Wanting to blot out his torment, she closed her eyes. She was astonished at the extraordinary hallucination that rose unbidden behind the shuttered lids. It was so clear, so graphic in its every detail, that she kept her eyes shut, holding on to the captive vision, allowing it to unfold in the privacy of her mind.

Clad in his crisp, starched dhoti, an embroidered shawl thrown across one shoulder, she saw Samir sitting on that same brick platform where he had sat on that Sunday afternoon. Next to him, someone had placed another chair, and in that reclined a beautiful young woman with long, plaited hair, a red mark on her forehead. In the parting of her hair was a line of red powder, the sign of a married woman. She was dressed, Bengali style, in a sari of pure white silk with a red and gold border. To a corner of her sari, in the traditional manner, was knotted an enormous bunch of keys, the keys of their household. She wore bangles up to her elbows and exquisite gold jewellery. Samir turned to her to ask her a question; she replied with a smile, the shy, tremulous smile of a bride. He clapped his hands and, lo and behold, a row of women emerged from the house bearing fruit and sweets and gifts on round silver thalis. As she turned to receive them, she raised her face and Maya saw that the woman was herself. . . .

And she was one of them!

She gave a small cry and her eyes flew open. The vision vanished, replaced by the reality of Samir's anxious face hovering above hers in bewilderment.

"What is it? You look . . . odd!"

She flushed and returned to her senses, filled with anger. "No!" she said harshly. "Of course I cannot marry you—the very idea is ludicrous!"

Hot tears singed her eyes as she grappled with his heartbreak, with her own inexplicable sense of loss. Ironically enough, in the same moment that she crushed his hopes, she came closer to hearing the sound of his heartbeat than she had ever done before, closer to feeling for him what she believed she never could. Quickly, she slipped off the wall, lifted her skirt to her ankles and waded back through the stream. He followed in desperation.

"You will never lack anything that you desire, Maya," he pleaded, clinging on to the tail of his vanishing dream, unable to let it go. "I can give you everything that you need, *everything!*"

She turned to look back at him sadly. "You can give me everything *except* what I need."

Samir's mother came into view, hurrying towards them. Without saying a word, she folded Maya in an embrace and kissed her forehead. She was crying. "Oh my dearest child, I am so sorry, so very sorry."

Maya said nothing. She did not return the embrace.

"You must forgive her, you must understand that she is old, set in her ways."

Maya smiled. "Yes, I understand."

"She cannot see that society must change, that there must be new thinking, new ideas. You must not take it to heart, my dear, you simply must not."

"I won't. It was my fault. I should not have entered her kitchen."

Abala kissed her again and again, loath to let her go, mortified by what had happened, trying hard to make amends.

Gently, Maya released herself. "I think I must go."

"But your clothes are all wet—you cannot leave in this condition!"

"I will change as soon as I reach home."

"You will not stay for supper?" Abala cried. "The girls will be back from town any moment, they will be heartbroken to have missed you."

Maya shook her head. "Mother is with Alistair and Amos is on his own. He will be waiting for me."

"You will come another time?" Abala asked anxiously.

"Yes. I will come another time."

But Maya knew that she would not. She knew that she would never again return to the *bagan bari.*

Sitting beside her in the carriage, Samir saw her off to the gate of the orchard. They rode in silence. At the gate, the carriage stopped and he prepared to get off. Maya saw that his long, black lashes were wet with tears. He raised a hand and, very tenderly, stroked her cheek with it. For a bare instant she clung to his hand, then let it drop. They both knew that they would not see each other again.

A sliver of bright orange sun still showed above the horizon. Then, in the blink of an eyelid, it was gone. With it went something of Maya's own world. The sun would rise again. What she had lost today would never return.

Kyle returned from North Bengal to find two urgent messages waiting for him, one from Clarence Twining, the Inspector-General of Police, and the other from Sir Jasper. Both needed to see him urgently. Neither of the messages came as a surprise to Kyle. He had been expecting both.

Also awaiting his return, together with the usual letters, bills and circulars, was a rather more bulky envelope. This he set aside for perusal later.

He calculated that Clarence Twining's anxiety to meet him must be truly acute by now, and the thought brought a smile to his lips. Nevertheless, he decided to let Twining wait a while longer. The longer the wait, the more satisfying the encounter.

The summons Kyle had no wish to defer was the one that came from Jasper Pendlebury. There was much that they had to discuss; it would be in his own interests to do so as soon as possible. He replied to Sir Jasper's message with a suggestion that they meet at the Treasury on Sunday afternoon when the offices would be suitably deserted. There was no need to specify a reason—Sir Jasper would soon understand the need for secrecy. Having despatched the letter, Kyle finally turned his attention to the bulky envelope that had also arrived in his absence. It contained several loose sheets of paper, each closely handwritten. He would have to read them all tonight. Tomorrow they would have to be delivered to Amos.

He spread out the sheets and commenced his perusal of the statement of Thomas Hungerford.

"It sounds like gibberish to me!"

Amos tossed the papers down on his desk, his expression struggling to remain sceptical. Nevertheless, a nerve palpitated visibly in one of his temples. It was very evident that he was shaken and trying not to show it.

Kyle held his tongue and waited.

Restless, Amos stood up and went to stand by the window of his office room, peering out of the slatted bamboo curtain at nothing in particular. By his sides, his hands clutched and unclutched, unable to stay still. Across his bloodless face emotions chased each other in quick succession: disbelief, anger, bewilderment, shock. But most of all anger.

The closely scribbled several pages were badly written, ungrammatical, in some places illegible and in others utterly incomprehensible. But none of these literary lapses were of any consequence in the larger scheme of things. What Hungerford hinted at—without actually specifying details—held promise of a narrative beyond Amos's wildest imagination.

He did not believe a word of it!

"I concede that it's a clever bait. Hungerford has fabricated it well. But that's all. It has no credibility."

"You have concluded that to your satisfaction?"

"Undoubtedly." He returned to his desk and swung his feet on top of it. "The man admits he is a perjurer and a cheat. He and Findlater deposed falsely before General Havelock."

"The fact that he wishes to confess now—does that not say something in Hungerford's favour?'

"He confesses after causing untold misery over *thirteen years*—and for that he deserves a medal?" Amos gave a hoot of derision, then his face again darkened. "Mother cannot be exposed to this . . . this burlesque now, Kyle. It is unthinkable!"

"And if what he intends to reveal is the truth?"

"It cannot be."

"But let us say for the sake of argument that it is. What then? You still feel that you have the right to keep it from your mother?"

"She has finally reconciled herself to the Viceroy's dictum. She has accepted that the files are closed, that they will not be reopened. I am not convinced that it is judicious to disturb the status quo for the sake of this claptrap." He jabbed the sheaf of papers with a contemptuous finger.

"The status quo—refuge of cowards!" Kyle said, suddenly also angry. "You know as well as I do that she *will* want to meet Hungerford—whatever you may think of his testimony. True or false, she has a right to know it. She has searched for the man through all these years, prepared to face him, to listen to him, regardless of the hideous role he has played in her life. Do you consider it just that she be denied this now?"

Amos groaned and cradled his head in his hands. "It will open old wounds, Kyle, make them bleed again—and she has bled enough. We all have, damn it!" He gulped. "Besides. . . ." He did not continue.

"Besides, you are afraid." Kyle completed the sentence softly. "You are afraid that Hungerford might, just *might*, confirm what everyone believes about your father. Isn't that what is your true concern?"

Amos nodded, feeling wretched, knowing that he could pretend with anyone else but not with Kyle. "Yes."

"It is a very valid concern, Amos, let us not make any mistake about that. There is much that Hungerford has left out, as he himself writes. Neither of us can predict what is yet to come."

Amos closed his eyes in despair. "Not even you will deny that my father was a vengeful man, eaten away by his hatred of the English. He could have, in the heat of the moment. . . ." He faltered, disgusted by his thoughts and unable to voice them. "Don't you see, Kyle, that as long as there is doubt, we can bear it. Our salvation lies not in knowing but in *not* knowing!"

"We knew the risks involved in locating Thomas Hungerford after we saw Findlater's obituary, Amos. We discussed the matter at length. We both agreed to pursue our search for the man and somehow induce him to make himself available for interrogation. As it happened, he needed no inducement. He decided to make the journey to India of his own free will, at his own expense."

"Yes, I know, I know," Amos conceded, spreading his hands, "but then it was all so far in the future, so tenuous! But now that he is actually here, on our doorstep. . . ."

Kyle looked into the unhappy eyes of his friend and his expression mellowed. "It will have to be faced sometime, Amos," he said, quietly. "Whatever the outcome, you cannot leave it unresolved. You cannot continue to live under a stigma that is undeserved."

Amos gave a hard laugh. "You are certain that it *is* undeserved?"

"Yes. I believe your father was innocent."

Amos said nothing. He only wished that he could believe it too.

Kyle surrendered the debate. He knew that Amos was not himself these days. He had not been himself ever since Alistair Birkhurst had arrived and appropriated that mill Amos had begun to think of as his own. Lately, there had been whispers of a fight; the injuries Amos bore gave testimony of that. But now, Kyle let the matter lapse. He asked no more questions. Hungerford's statement had stirred up that nest of demons that had haunted the Raventhornes since the Mutiny. Amos needed time to regain his equilibrium, to mull over the offer and prepare himself for all its possible implications. For the moment, it was pointless to argue.

"Hungerford will be here within the week, he writes." Kyle got up to go. "There is still time to consider—and to condition your mother for the ordeal—should you decide to let Hungerford meet her."

Under Olivia's loving, conscientious care, Alistair regained his strength rapidly. After three days Dr. Humphries pronounced him well enough to get out of bed. Two days later, he was walking about quite normally with his arm in a sling, no longer in need of special nursing. Delighted as she was by the speed with which he had bounced back to near normalcy, Olivia was despondent at the thought of returning home, still not certain that he would want to see her again.

Despite his physical recovery, she could see that Alistair's spirits were low and she was at a loss as to the cause of his depression. Willie Donaldson had made it a habit to join them at the evening meal each day and Olivia was grateful for his company. With him Alistair appeared fairly comfortable, but with her his manner remained formal, that of a distant stranger. He conversed with her courteously enough, but without either ease or effusiveness, and he always kept his eyes lowered. If their glances did happen to clash, he blushed and hastily turned away. The questions he asked her now were superficial and impersonal, and he evinced no great interest in the answers she gave.

About the fight, he refused to say anything at all. Indeed, each time Olivia stirred the subject, he became so agitated that she was forced to abandon it. He spoke freely and with some semblance of animation only about his home in Farrowsham and his grandmother, saying he missed both. It hurt Olivia that despite all her efforts and her many displays of love, he should remain wary of her, unable to give her his trust. It hurt her even more that, when the time came for her to return home, Alistair made no secret of his relief.

Profoundly disappointed in one son, Olivia returned home dreading the prospect of confronting the other and facing further disappointment. She yearned to give Amos the benefit of her doubts, longed for him to say just a word or two to assure her of his innocence. She decided to present him with the opportunity to exonerate himself on the very day of her return.

When Amos reached home after work that evening, he found his mother having tea on the verandah and waiting for him. He had not seen her since the evening of the Pendleburys' dinner party, but the spectre of the unwanted prodigal had been present as a barrier between them ever since he had arrived. The fact that she had been away nursing and cosseting Alistair had only helped to aggravate him further. In Amos's considered opinion, the arrogant brat was pampered enough as it was.

Now, on the verandah, Amos bent down and gave his mother a perfunctory kiss on the cheek, made a few mumbling noises and then prepared to go up to his room. He did not inquire after Alistair.

"Sit down, dear," Olivia said. "Would you like a cup of tea?"

He shook his head. "Not yet, thank you. I want to have a bath first. It's beastly hot outside."

"Yes, I know. I only just got back myself. Anyway, sit down for a moment. There's something I want to talk to you about."

Given no choice, he shrugged and pulled up a chair. "Well?"

"I think that there are some explanations due to me, Amos," she began in a conciliatory tone of voice.

"Explanations? What about?" He met her eyes without blinking.

"About what happened at the Pendleburys' that night."

"Many things happened at the Pendleburys'! To which particular incident are you referring?"

She kept her temper well leashed. "You know very well the incident to which I am referring—you and Alistair had a fight!"

A flash of surprise showed in his eyes. "Oh? And how precisely do you surmise that?"

"Don't bandy words with me, Amos," she said sharply. "You fought with each other in the garden. What I want to know is, why, and did he start the fight or you?"

Amos's lips tightened. He said nothing.

"Tell me what happened, Amos. I'm merely trying to arrive at the truth."

"Didn't your precious Alistair tell you what happened?" he sneered. "I should imagine you would have had plenty to say to each other over all these days!"

She ignored the taunt with an effort. "Whatever the reason for the fight, you are the older brother, Amos. It was for *you* to keep yourself under better control."

He leapt to his feet. "I had no fight with him. I have no idea what you are talking about."

"Don't lie to me, Amos!" Olivia's patience snapped. "Your bloodstained clothes were in the laundry bin, soaking wet and absolutely ruined." She reached out and grabbed his right hand where his knuckles still showed bruises. "And what about your hand? If you didn't have a fight, how did you get all these?"

He shook his hand free with a jerk. "Is that what Alistair told you?" he inquired quietly.

"No. But he didn't deny it either. He tried his best to shield you, Amos."

"Did he now?" he said, furious. "Well, that was generous of him, I'll give him that!"

"You *promised* you would be civil with him, Amos, you gave me your *word!*"

Amos drew back his lips at the corners in a travesty of a smile. "I appreciate your faith in me," he said with biting sarcasm. "I am touched by it, Mother, *truly* touched!"

"Don't be insolent with me!" Olivia cried, her temper flaring. "All I'm trying to do is to find out what happened. I simply don't know what to believe!"

He gave her a very strange look. "Believe whatever you wish," he said coldly. "I don't particularly care one way or the other. But I do regret one oversight—I should have broken both his arms while I was about it!"

With no wish to discuss the matter further, he vanished inside the house.

With a cry of frustration, Olivia buried her face in her palms and burst into tears.

Dinner that night, shared between Olivia and Edna Chalcott, was a dismal affair. Not even Edna's cheerful presence and her attempts at light-hearted chatter could relieve the gloom that prevailed at table. Knowing Olivia's enthusiastic plans for the annexe recently acquired by the Home, Edna made valiant efforts to distract her with questions about the various expansions they had been discussing avidly for weeks, but it was futile. Taking refuge in monosyllabic responses, Olivia continued to brood, too dejected to talk. Amos himself had disappeared from the house, leaving word with Francis that he would not return for dinner. And there was no sign of Maya. According to Sheba, she was in her room nursing a migraine. When she finally chose to appear, the main meal was over and the pudding was being served. She slipped into her seat with a mumbled apology, spooned some caramel custard onto her plate and proceeded to eat it in silence. Annoyed, Olivia was about to offer a rebuke when she suddenly noticed her daughter's appearance and the words froze in her mouth. The girl looked absolutely dreadful!

Olivia had not seen Maya since the morning she had called at the Birkhurst mansion to visit Alistair. Indeed, she was surprised and a little hurt that Maya had not bothered to call again to inquire after Alistair's condition. But looking at Maya now, Olivia forgot all her complaints. Her daughter's skin looked pasty, devoid of colour; there were grey rings around her tired eyes, as if she had not slept in a long while. Even her hair, usually glossy and dense, hung limply about her pinched face, unbrushed and neglected. The contrast between her appearance now and as it was on the evening of the dinner party was so marked that Olivia could only stare in astonishment. Even Edna, chattering away nineteen to the dozen, stopped in mid-sentence, shocked by the unprepossessing picture Maya presented.

"You have another migraine, I hear," Olivia said, softening. "Is it unbearable?"

"No. I'm all right."

"But you're not!" Olivia exclaimed. "I can *see* that you're not. Perhaps we should send for Dr. Humphries before it gets any worse?"

"There's nothing wrong with me, Mother." Even her voice was listless, its usual edge dulled. "It's just . . . that time of the month, that's all." Gulping down a final spoonful of the pudding, she excused herself and ran back upstairs to her room.

"Well!" Edna dabbed the corners of her mouth with her napkin and sat back. "She didn't even mention the ball! I was sure she would want to talk about nothing else all evening. Now, that *really* has me worried!" She made the remark brightly in an effort to lighten the gloom, but Olivia did not participate in her smile.

Later that evening they strolled arm in arm by the river, enjoying the brief respite from the cloying humidity of the day, taking advantage of the breeze-filled interlude between showers. The stars were out in full force, twinkling defiantly, playing hide-and-seek with the swiftly moving monsoon clouds.

"What is wrong with all three of my children, Edna?" Olivia suddenly asked, halting dead in her tracks. "I simply do not have the energy to understand any of them any more. I now wonder if I ever did!"

"Can anyone ever understand their children?" Edna asked in return. "One may think one does, but they all seem to have the inborn capacity to take one by surprise, no matter how prepared one believes oneself to be." She squeezed Olivia's arm in a gesture of sympathy. "Anyway, sibling rivalry is only to be expected between brothers a year apart in age, my dear, especially when their upbringing has been so divided and divergent."

"Alistair still refuses to make concessions, and Amos—my soft, gentle Amos!—says he's sorry he did not break both of his brother's arms."

"He didn't mean it, Olivia."

"The terrible thing is that he *did* mean it! I could see it in his eyes." They arrived at the steps and, with a sigh, Olivia sank down on to her favourite seat. She picked up a twig and started to make patterns in the water lapping at her feet. "This has always been my recurring nightmare, Edna. Deep down inside me I have always known that some day Alistair would return, that Amos and he would be at each other's throats, driven insane by mutual hate and jealousy."

"It's that wretched cotton mill, of course."

"No. The mill is only an excuse. Had it not been that, it would have been something else. As for Maya. . . ." She broke off with a gesture of utter helplessness.

Edna frowned. "Yes. I must say, Maya *does* surprise me. I would have thought she'd be on top of the world, full of her sparkling success at the Pendleburys'. She told me that Herbert Ludlow wanted to buy one of her horses. She was thrilled to pieces about that, too." Dusting the surface of the step with her handkerchief, she sat down next to Olivia. "Do you think something could be amiss between her and Christian?"

"Oh, sweet Lord—I wish I knew!" The twig slipped from Olivia's fingers; she followed it with her eyes until it was swallowed up by the night. "But he did call the morning after the party. Sheba says they spent an hour together and seemed perfectly content in each other's company. Later in the day, Sheba says, Maya was still full of the dinner party. Apparently, she could hardly bear to talk of anything else."

"And when she went to see Alistair?"

"Well, she seemed happy enough then too, preparing to go to the Goswamis' *bagan bari* with something she had made for Samir's aunt." Her forehead creased. "According to what Sheba tells me, she's been behaving very oddly ever since she returned from that orchard."

"You think she's upset about something that happened there?"

"Oh no, that's highly unlikely." Olivia shook her head. "They're all extremely fond of Maya, especially Samir. In fact, I think he has quite a case on her, always has had."

"Constance is having a musical soirée next week," Edna said, digressing. "You haven't been asked by any chance, have you?"

"No, but then I don't expect to be. What I do expect, however, is some indication—either from them or from Christian—as to what they have in mind for the future."

"Christian is being posted to that ghastly place, Champaran, I hear."

"Yes. He is due to leave shortly."

"And there has been no more talk of the marriage?"

"Not a word! I just don't know what to make of the situation, Edna. I have absolutely no idea how to proceed—if at all."

"Well, judging from the attention they lavished on all of you that evening. . . ."

"For what *that* was worth!" Olivia made a grim face. "I can't help feeling that they merely mounted a charade, played a game with us. In fact, I sometimes feel that *everyone* is playing some game or other, Edna, even my children. They seem to be keeping things from me. It's just a suspicion I have, an instinct, I can't define it." She threw up her hands in a burst of exasperation. "Tell me, Edna. Am I going mad or are they?"

That night, before going to bed, Olivia went into Maya's room. She found her lying on her bed, fully dressed, staring up at the ceiling. Olivia pulled up a chair by the bedside and, with great tenderness, took hold of her hand.

"What is wrong, darling? Tell me, are you truly unwell?"

Maya closed her eyes and remained silent.

"Well then, have you had a row with Christian?"

"No."

"Then what is the matter? Something obviously is." Maya shook her head and tried to turn away, but Olivia wouldn't let her. "Talk to me, darling! Can't you see that I want to help, that I hate to see you like this? Are you upset about something that happened at the *bagan bari*?"

Maya looked at her with vacant eyes, and for a moment, Olivia wondered if her daughter had heard her at all. But then, after a long silence, she finally spoke.

"I've found out something that I didn't know before."

"What?"

"I've found out why I frighten people."

"*Frighten* people?" Olivia peered at her closely. "Who is frightened of you?"

"Oh, just . . . people." Maya's shoulders moved in a minimal shrug. "Anyway, it's not that important."

"If it weren't, you wouldn't be in the state that you're in. Tell me, why are people frightened of you?"

But once again curled up within her shell, Maya had retracted beyond her mother's reach.

Sir Jasper thought a great deal about his unsolicited conversation with Harriet Ingersoll. He had made a commitment to her on the spur of the moment. As a responsible government servant and a normally cautious man, he was not in the habit of acting on impulse, and he was astonished that he should have done so. However, since then he had had time to give the matter serious and prolonged consideration. He now saw that having made the commitment there was no reason to retract or, indeed, regret it.

As an inseparable corollary to these reflections, Sir Jasper also thought of Kyle Hawkesworth. When the fellow had first put his proposition to him, he had considered it proposterous. In fact, he had been outraged by it. But now, since the night of the *burra khana*, he had started to see it in quite a different light. The project, he realised, had immense potential vis-à-vis his own requirements. It was ambitious and imaginative. If implemented, it could achieve several worthwhile ends at the same time. His initial bias against it was because he had allowed his personal dislike of Hawkesworth to interfere with his capacity for rational assessment, and that had been a mistake. A plum—rich and juicy and ripe for the eating—had fallen unbidden into his lap. He would be a fool to waste it.

It was not often that Sir Jasper allowed himself the luxury of emotions he considered vulgar. But, as he sat waiting for Kyle to arrive at the deserted Treasury on Sunday afternoon, he could not deny feeling a frisson of excitement.

There were, however, two flies in the ointment that needed to be removed. One, Leonard Whitney, he had already dealt with. Sir Jasper regretted losing such an undeniably competent aide, but Whitney's close association with Hawkesworth (an association he had tried to conceal) made it dangerous to retain him at the Treasury any longer. There had been, therefore, no option but to return the man to McNaughton's office before he could conspire with Hawkesworth to do whatever damage was intended.

The other fly in the ointment was, of course, Hawkesworth himself.

Sir Jasper's mouth tightened; no, there was no way now that he could risk leaving station for Simla even for the Council meeting. He had already missed one meeting and he knew that he courted serious viceregal displeasure. But he was confident that the project he had in mind would go a long way to mitigate that displeasure, considering the moral benefits to the imperial government—especially now that he could expect the active support of Lady Ingersoll.

"Well, Lal, as I promised, I have been deliberating at some length on your proposition." Following a few meagre preliminaries, Sir Jasper plunged directly into the heart of the matter as soon as Kyle arrived. His mood was still cordial, his smile still open and untroubled, but his manner was briskly formal. "On deeper reflection I find that the project is not so far out of the realms of possibility as I had initially imagined. In fact"—he opened the folder Kyle had given him—"it might even be feasible. Before we proceed, however, I have to confess that I have certain reservations. And, of course, several questions."

"Yes, naturally."

"Well then, first the questions. There is one point on which I am rather curious. It's not important, but nonetheless I would like it resolved. With the rich and influential Raventhorne family as patrons, why did you need to come to me with this project?"

"The Raventhornes are already the main financiers of an ambitious marine school project for which they have donated a clipper. It is unfair that they should be expected to bear another heavy financial burden."

"And is that the only reason?"

Kyle hesitated briefly. "No. The land that we have found to be most suitable for our purposes is, for personal reasons, not available for purchase by the Raventhornes."

"And you do not have other sources from which to raise the requisite funds, is that it?"

"Yes."

"You say the land is already available. Where?"

"That I would rather not say at this juncture."

Sir Jasper waved a hand indicating that it didn't matter. He knew already that the plot in question was the Birkhurst indigo plantation. "About four thousand acres, I think you told me the last time? Agricultural or with habitation?"

"Mostly agricultural," Kyle replied, having no doubt that Sir Jasper would have already discovered the location, "although there is a scattering of villages."

From the file Sir Jasper withdrew a large map, unfolded it and spread it across the table. He examined it for a moment and then regarded Kyle over the tips of steepled fingers. "Your architect's plan for the proposed township is satisfactorily detailed, but also extremely optimistic. I presume you are fully aware of the immense problems involved in establishing and sustaining a self-sufficient township such as this envisages?"

"It would be naïve not to be. However, whatever the problems, I believe if people have sufficient enthusiasm—as I hope they will have—at the end of the decade we should have at least a partially functioning settlement."

"If the government were to accept the proposal that I intend to present to the Cabinet," Sir Jasper said carefully, "it would naturally wish to participate very fully in the project."

"Participate? How?"

"Well, purchase of the land would be only the first step. After that I expect we would need to subsidise construction and other expenses."

Kyle leaned forward, his eyes intent. "In return for . . . ?"

"Ah!" Sir Jasper raised a finger as if in warning. "Here we come to my major reservation. Should the government acquire this land and make further large investments, what it would want in return are two things. The first is recognition."

Kyle smiled. "Recognition! Yes, of course—I can see that applause from the populace would certainly be one of the conditions. Well, that is acceptable." He shrugged. "Who gets the credit is not of any great consequence to me. And your second condition?"

"The government would be responsible for the administration of the township."

"No." Kyle shook his head. "I'm afraid that condition will *not* be acceptable."

Sir Jasper arched an eyebrow. "But surely, you don't expect these vast amounts of government funds to be placed in the hands of private individuals?"

"They would not be in the hands of private individuals. The Derozio Society has been registered as a charitable organisation. Its office bearers are known professional people of irreproachable integrity. The funds would be regulated for the Society by a reputable firm of accountants."

Sir Jasper sat back, stroked his chin and looked dubious. "Nevertheless, such an arrangement would not find favour with the government, Lal. I can promise you that."

"The Society would have no objection to a member of government, maybe two, being nominated to its board of directors."

"It would not be enough." Sir Jasper's tone developed a fine edge of steel. "What difference would it make *who* administers the township? As long as it is built and functions efficiently, surely that is the priority?"

"The difference is a very vital one!" Kyle's attitude also hardened. "In the final analysis, the reason for the government's alleged interest is to make political capital in Westminster, to win votes in England, to ingratiate itself with the people by projecting an image of compassion and fair play."

"Oh, come now, sir." Sir Jasper's smile was disarming. "Aren't you being unnecessarily touchy?"

"No, I don't think so." Kyle leaned forward again, his voice intense. "Perhaps there are some politicians who have genuinely wanted to evolve means to benefit Eurasians. This project, however, is the first that presents government with a *concrete* opportunity to establish its bona fides. The reason why my project appeals is that it promises to kill two noisome birds with the same stone. It will remove unwanted progeny from immediate sight, and it will do so painlessly and profitably, in the name of altruism."

"A township such as this cannot be administered competently without governmental control," Sir Jasper said sharply.

"*If* the township is built at all!" Kyle countered with a dry laugh. "We both know what is on the cards, Sir Jasper. Once the land is acquired, the clarions sounded, the newspaper articles written, credit harvested, publicity gleaned, applause given a chance to die down and," he paused a minim, "promotions granted, the project will stagnate. A committee will be appointed to give recommendations. Its report will take years to materialise. As soon as public interest in your good deed fades—as it will shortly—funds will be quietly siphoned off to other projects considered more urgent, and the project will lapse with all involved having got what they wanted."

Sir Jasper felt a stab of annoyance. "And you consider that the Opposition will sit quietly through all this without raising a furore?"

Kyle shrugged. "Only a handful of members in Westminster give more than a fig for what happens in India. If someone does make a fuss, there's always room for one more committee to be sent out here to look into the matter."

It was quite true that from time to time, some pious member would stand up in Parliament and, to a few "hear, hears" and many snores, pay lip service to the need to improve the lot of Eurasians. Impassioned speeches would be made, questions asked and answered, vague and sanctimonious resolutions passed, and then yet another committee would be appointed to look into the matter, after which the entire exercise would be forgotten. What incensed Sir Jasper was that Kyle should have pinpointed this with such accuracy. However, he concealed his anger well behind an indulgent smile and a wry shake of the head.

"Do you truly consider that such cynicism will help to serve your cause better, Lal?"

"Not cynicism, Sir Jasper, realism! The reality is, nobody really cares a damn about the Eurasian except the Eurasian. Therefore it is only reasonable and just that it should be the Eurasian who runs his township."

"You mean your Society?"

"Yes. It is composed of people who feel strongly and genuinely for the community. We know what is needed, we can recognise the people who need to be helped. To us it would be a human problem, not a mere publicity trick." Having made his point, Kyle again sat back, once more calm. "I regret that your second condition is not acceptable, Sir Jasper. If the government is to acquire the land at all, it is to be donated to the Derozio Society." His smile was hard and knowing. "As for the kudos, you would be welcome to them, Sir Jasper."

Sir Jasper's colour heightened, but imperceptibly. "That, I regret, will not be acceptable to me—any more than it will be to the government. In any case," he leant back in his chair and pointed out quite amiably, "there is one aspect you seem to have overlooked, Lal. Should the government wish to proceed, it can do so on its own. There would be no need for participation from you, or from anybody else."

"I disagree," Kyle said softly. "There would be every need."

"How so? You certainly can't prevent us from purchasing the land and initiating the project on our own if we so wish."

"Oh, but you see, I can."

Sir Jasper looked at Kyle's face, saw something in it that he had not seen earlier, and his eyes narrowed for an instant. Much had been left unsaid during that first encounter at Champatollah. He saw now that the voids were about to be filled. "Is there something that you are trying to tell me?" he asked, as cool and collected as ever.

"Yes." Kyle pulled out his Meerschaum from his belt and held it up with a silent question. Sir Jasper nodded, then waited with impatience while the pipe was lit. "The other morning, if you recall, I mentioned that this was a business proposition."

"Yes, you did. So?"

"How would you define 'business,' Sir Jasper?"

"Is that a serious question, Lal, or are you just wasting time?"

Kyle paid no heed to the protest. "Very well then, I will tell you. Business is a matter of supply and demand, of buying and selling products, entertainment, services." He paused. "And silence."

"Silence?"

Kyle stared him directly in the eye, without blinking. "The other day you mentioned two reasons why you wanted to see me. You did not include a third, but that, in fact, was the *only* reason." His tone changed. "You wanted to find out if it is generally known that, at one time, my mother was your mistress."

There was a moment's silence, then, with no change of expression, Sir Jasper chuckled a little. "My dear fellow, you can't seriously believe that! Of what interest would that be to anyone now? It's all past history." He got up as if to stretch his legs and strolled to the far end of the room. "But since you bring up the subject—is it?"

"Generally known? If it were, would it embarrass you?"

"No." Sir Jasper turned. His unswerving gaze matched Kyle's. "Why should it? Men of the world accept that those away from home for long periods of time need to expend certain energies in order to conserve others. It is hardly unknown for Englishmen to have Indian mistresses. It may not be the subject of overt conversation, but it is certainly a matter of tacit understanding."

"In that case, you have no cause for concern at all."

"Concern? Merely because I happen to have had a native mistress?" He laughed with some amusement. "In any case, the native mistress I had, and was extremely fond of—make no mistake about that—is dead. Who would possibly care about it now?"

Kyle swung around in his chair so that he faced Sir Jasper. "You were transferred out of Lucknow because Sir Henry Lawrence, a straitlaced man of strong moral convictions, disapproved of your relationship with my mother. He could have ruined your career with an adverse comment in one of his despatches."

"That is simply wild conjecture!"

"You are a man of extraordinary ambition, Sir Jasper," Kyle continued, ignoring the interruption. "Contrary to what you would have others believe, your reputation, hitherto unsullied, is of the utmost importance to you—*especially* now that you are so close to the highest echelons of power. You badly want that peerage the Prime Minister is rumoured to have promised you. And one day you fervently hope to be a candidate for the Viceroyalty of India—your ultimate goal. A scandal at this stage would be professionally disastrous. If that doesn't quash your hopes of untold power, then certainly Lady Ingersoll's royal connections will."

Sir Jasper threw back his head and roared. "Oh dear me! If moral propriety were the sole criterion for selecting high officials, by gad, few of us would be here!" Still laughing, he walked back to his desk, sat down and leaned his elbows on it. There was not a shadow of anxiety in his clear, blue eyes, not a whisper of fear. "What counts in those 'echelons of power,' as you call them, my dear fellow, is simply this." He rubbed his finger and thumb together to denote money. "As long as I can increase the inflow of shekels into the government's coffers, very little else would be taken into account, believe me."

"Regardless of that, your Queen's views on moral turpidity are well known, Sir Jasper. If she learns about all your good deeds from Lady Ingersoll, she might also learn about your lapses."

"So! As far as I can see from this rather entertaining conversation, Lal, your plan is to weave a belated scandal around my name and expose me to royal censure, is that it?"

"No." Kyle sat back comfortably and stretched his legs. "That is not my plan. The destruction of your career brings me nothing from which I would benefit. All I want is for the Treasury to purchase that land, give it to the Derozio Society—harvesting whatever crops it can by way of political gain—and then withdraw from the scene. However, subsequent help in acquiring bureaucratic permissions and resolving various legalities would be greatly appreciated."

"Good God, you don't want much, do you?" Sir Jasper asked, still with no sign of agitation. "And what if I refuse?"

"You will not refuse."

"Oh?" He stilled. "There is something else to come, isn't there?"

"Yes. There is something else." Kyle drew deeply at his pipe, then exhaled a perfect smoke ring. It was instantly demolished by a gust of air from the punka swinging overhead. "The midwife lied, Sir Jasper. My mother is still alive."

"Ah!"

The exclamation sounded like a sigh, subtle and muted. But not by a flicker of an eyelash did he offer any other reaction. He merely nodded, as if not entirely surprised. "Well, for your sake, Lal, I am certainly happy that she still lives. But that changes nothing."

The man's control was remarkable. "I beg to differ. That changes everything! Your society might condone youthful dalliance away from home, but I doubt if it would condone attempted murder."

"Murder?" Sir Jasper cocked an eyebrow. "That's a strong word, Lal.

Aren't you allowing your imagination to run away with you a little?"

Kyle toyed idly with the tip of a pencil. "When my mother told you she was with child, you were furious."

"I was upset, naturally. I had no great wish to father a string of bastards! What man in my position would?"

"You saw your career in shambles," Kyle continued, "even before it had had a chance to get under way. If Sir Henry disapproved of native mistresses, he would not hesitate to cashier a man who had fathered an illegitimate child."

Barely a muscle twitched in Sir Jasper's face. His only concession to the allegation was that he did not speak. He waited for Kyle to continue.

"You made two miscalculations, Sir Jasper. The midwife was not as strong as you had thought, my mother not as weak. When she realised the midwife's intention, she fought hard for her life. Wounded and bleeding severely, she finally escaped into the forest."

With great deliberation, Sir Jasper opened his cigar box, chose a Havana and took his time lighting it. He did not offer Kyle one. "Pray continue."

"Eventually, it was I who found her in the forest the next morning, barely alive. A woodcutter helped to carry her to a herbalist in a nearby village. He saved her life. What he could not save was her right leg. Since then, she has had to live with a limp."

For the first time something flashed across Sir Jasper's eyes, perhaps a shadow of regret, as he saw the vision of a once young and beautiful dancer no longer able to dance. Then it was gone. "The child?"

"The midwife could not abort it."

"It too lives?" he asked, but with such casualness they might have been discussing a duck shoot.

"Yes, a boy. He is now fifteen years old."

Sir Jasper nodded. "He would be about that."

He continued to pull at his cigar, enjoying it, his posture relaxed and comfortable. There was no shock, no outburst of temper, no expression of remorse, not even a denial, simply cold and nerveless acceptance. The nonchalance of the man was chilling.

"Whether it was due to the ministrations of the midwife or an act of God, the boy was born physically deformed. Mentally, there is some intelligence, but no speech. My mother has chosen to name him Montague."

For a long time Sir Jasper sat still. When finally he stirred, it was with a small shrug. "I never had anything to do with that midwife."

"No, that at least is true. It was Wali Khan, your bearer, who arranged everything. Incidentally, he still lives, old and ailing but very much alive. Out of loyalty to you, he refuses to put his thumbprint upon a written statement."

Sir Jasper raised an eyebrow in admiration. "By George, you *have* been thorough in your investigations! But tell me truthfully, do you believe you can prove any of these bizarre charges?"

"No."

"That midwife is long dead. Wali Khan will not speak, and I hardly

490

think the word of your mother, a sometime dancing girl of dubious Eurasian antecedents who cannot tell who it was that fathered her older son, would be of much consequence. There are a hundred other courtesans who have tried to make capital out of their liaisons with English officers."

"Perhaps."

"As for your own reputation." Sir Jasper shrugged. "Your vitriolic pen enjoys little credibility with the authorities, Lal. Who would ever believe you?"

"Not many, I agree."

"You could not damage my reputation even if you approached Lord Mayo himself!"

"I was not thinking of Lord Mayo."

"Oh? Who then?" Sir Jasper mocked. "Her Majesty the Queen?"

"No. I was thinking of Christian."

For an entire minute, total silence fell between them. At last, Jasper gave evidence of a reaction. His eyes went as frigid as marbles; his skin turned grey. Within him, all at once, rose a terrible rage—a cold, murderous rage—but, with monumental effort, he kept his voice under control.

"Yes," he said, his tone flat, "yes. I have to confess that, for a moment, I had quite forgotten about Christian."

"My credibility with Christian, as you well know, is extremely high," Kyle pointed out with a faint smile.

Sir Jasper again rose and started to pace. "So *that* was your motive in befriending him! I have often wondered. And you really think he would believe your word against mine?"

"Yes. If he met my mother and saw his . . . half-brother."

The term brought a fleeting grimace of distaste to Sir Jasper's handsome face. "You . . . plan such a meeting?"

"No. Not unless you make it necessary. I bear Christian no ill-will, no grudge. He is an innocent participant. I would not like to see him destroyed for no fault of his own."

"Well, that is noble of you!" Sir Jasper murmured with a low, caustic laugh. Then he asked lightly, "I suppose you do know that blackmail is a criminal offence, Lal?"

"So is attempted murder."

"The intent was not to kill her, merely to abort that unformed child."

"But had she died in the process, her death would not have been unwelcome."

Sir Jasper made no response to the taunt. He merely said, very calmly, "There are certain times in one's life when a man has to do what he must." His tone changed. "You will not tell Christian any of this, Lal!"

"If you agree to my terms, there will be no need to."

Sir Jasper sat for a moment, motionless and silent. Then he asked unexpectedly, "Do you play poker?"

It was an extraordinary question, on the surface irrelevant and frivolous. But Kyle was instantly on the alert. He knew that Sir Jasper was not in the habit of wasting time either on irrelevancies or on frivolities. He studied him guardedly.

"Occasionally."

"Do you know what is the highest hand that one can hold?"

"A royal flush."

"Yes. A royal flush." Sir Jasper pushed his chair back and stood up. There was an air of finality about the gesture, as if it were a sign of dismissal. "I do not deny that you hold an ace or two, Lal. How can I when your cards lie face upwards on the table?" He laughed under his breath, caressing the tips of his exquisitely groomed whiskers. "But you cannot see *my* hand, Lal, now can you?"

"And you have a royal flush?"

"Yes. I have a royal flush." He whipped the smile off his mouth so fast that it might never have been. "You will tell Christian nothing of this, Lal. *Nothing!*"

For the first time that afternoon, Kyle found his confidence slipping. He felt uncomfortably out of his depth, unable to negotiate the unexpected undertow.

"You can prevent me?" he asked uneasily.

"Yes. I can prevent you."

"How?"

Sir Jasper's smile returned, this time triumphant and full of complacency. "I hold knowledge that happens to be very precious to your Eurasian community."

"Oh?"

"Indeed! You see, Lal," Sir Jasper explained softly, "I am the only man alive who can prove that Jai Raventhorne was innocent of the Bibighar massacre."

21

S TILL FERMENTING OVER Hungerford's claims of extraordinary information, still unwilling to accept his bona fides, Amos reacted to news
of Sir Jasper's astonishing declaration with even sharper scepticism.
"It's sheer *twaddle!* Why should he suddenly pull this rabbit out of his
hat with neither rhyme nor reason?"

Kyle, more serious than Amos had ever seen him before, looked disturbed. "There is a reason."

"What?"

Kyle sighed. "My friend, as I once said, there is a great deal that I have
been keeping from you. There was a time when secrecy was of the essence,
but no longer. In fact, now it is not only fair but mandatory for you to
know everything that has been happening."

It was still early morning. They were again sitting on the deserted river
bank, where the air was cool and quiet and there was little risk of intrusion. Across the cloud-studded pale pink sky, flocks of birds made their
way outwards from their nests in search of sustenance for the day. Further down the shore a fisherman loaded his craft and prepared to take it
mid-stream.

In a quiet voice, Kyle related to Amos the curious details of his long
association with Sir Jasper Pendlebury, right up to their volatile encounter
the previous afternoon at the Treasury. He spoke frankly. He omitted
nothing, including in his narrative even those intimate details that he had
never before shared with another. His tone was even, without passion, but
when he was done he looked emotionally drained and filled with inner
pain. They both sat in hushed silence. Neither said a word, nor looked at
the other.

An itinerant green coconut pedlar stopped where they sat and, putting his basket down, began to extol the virtues of his wares. He continued his earnest patter for several minutes, then, when no responses appeared to be forthcoming, he shrugged, picked up his basket and walked away grumbling.

"It's . . . a strange tale, Kyle," Amos said, staggered.

"That it is!"

"I cannot imagine your poor mother's anguish."

"Yes. The anguish remains, will always remain."

Amos clenched his fists. "My God, had I had even an inkling about this, I would have smashed his face in at that damned *burra khana!* The man deserves to be horsewhipped!"

"True. But that will not get us what we want."

Amos abandoned futile temper and quietened. That Kyle's acquaintanceship with Jasper Pendlebury went back a long way, he had always suspected. But that the involvement had been so intimate, and so tragic, had never entered his thoughts. He was taken greatly by surprise, of course, but he was also alarmed. He had never been comfortable with Kyle's methods—street justice, he called it—nor was he now. Destiny had forced Kyle to cross swords with one of the most powerful men in England's Government of India. How could he possibly escape unscathed?

"So much has been happening that I knew nothing about," Amos murmured, more in wonderment than in pique, setting aside his other apprehensions.

"Yes, for that I apologise most abjectly."

"There is no need to. I understand your compulsions, Kyle. I sympathise with them. The question now is, where do we go from here?"

Kyle's shoulders lifted in a shrug. "We are at an impasse. I was not prepared for the claim he made yesterday. I have to confess, I haven't the faintest inkling what to do next."

"Well, I still think his claim is a bluff, an impromptu trick to silence you for a while."

"Perhaps. However, I know the way Jasper Pendlebury's mind works. He's ruthless, a Machiavellian manipulator, but I doubt if he would resort to bluff."

"Well then, how could it possibly have benefitted him to remain silent for all these years, Kyle?" Amos continued to scoff. "Hungerford might have axes to grind, but Pendlebury has none—or, at least, none that I can think of."

"Who knows? All I can say is, *nothing* Jasper Pendlebury says or does should be taken lightly."

Amos gave him an oblique look. "You threatened to expose him to Christian. You seriously consider doing that?"

"No." Kyle made a sour face. "That, my friend, *was* a bluff. I cannot bring myself to destroy the boy. Unfortunately, Pendlebury suspects my misplaced sense of nobility. Perhaps," his smile was embittered, "he knows me as well as I claim to know him."

Amos had never seen Kyle so dispirited, so much at a loss. He stood up, thrust his hands in his pockets and walked back and forth in a storm of restlessness. "I suppose Pendlebury will now make a bid for the plantation?" he said, sharing in the disappointment.

"Undoubtedly. The tragedy is that it is perfect for our purpose. I rode over every inch of the property. There are problems, of course, many problems, but none that we could not have resolved in time."

"What he said was true. How *can* we prevent him from forging ahead without our participation?"

"We cannot." Overhead, a bank of clouds gurgled. Kyle peered upwards, crinkling his eyes against the glare. "If he can put the project forward as his own invention, which is his aim, he stands to make handsome political capital. That is the only reason for his interest. It takes him one step closer to the peerage."

"Then we might as well forget about the township," Amos said, his tone flat.

"Yes." Kyle left it at that and his manner changed. "I think you should now seriously consider giving Hungerford a hearing, Amos."

Amos shuffled a small heap of pebbles around with the tip of his boot, then kicked one hard into the water. He asked, "Tell me, Kyle—do you honestly give this fellow credence?"

"Yes."

"Oh? Why the sudden vote of confidence?"

"Hungerford no longer has reasons to lie."

"How do you deduce that?"

"The man is dying. He has only a month or two to live."

"He writes that?" Amos asked, startled.

"Yes." The day was starting to warm. Kyle wiped his forehead with the back of his hand. "With his own letter, he has enclosed one from the doctor who treated him in Madras." He stood up and stretched his arms above his head. "In view of Pendlebury's contention, Hungerford's testimony assumes greater importance. It would be unwise to ignore it."

Grudgingly, Amos conceded the point with a nod.

"You must prepare your mother to receive him."

"Yes."

"Ambiguous and confused as it is, do you intend to show your mother Hungerford's statement before she meets him?"

"I feel I must. It would at least serve as a forewarning. When is he expected, does he say?"

"Very shortly."

"I hope you will be with us when he comes?"

"I think not. My presence would be an intrusion."

"Intrusion! How can you say that, Kyle?" Amos protested. "It is because of your efforts that Hungerford is here at all. Had you not seen that obituary and found him through Findlater's widow. . . ."

"No, Amos." Kyle remained adamant. "The meeting with Hungerford will be charged with emotion, with grief. It is a private affair, to be dealt with within the family."

Amos relapsed into silence and stood lost in thought for a few fleeting instants, mentally revisiting the past. The hopes and humiliations and heartaches, the bitter, bitter disappointments, the futile explorations up and down blind alleys that led nowhere . . . he remembered them all.

Would the nightmare now start all over again?

That evening, for the first time in several days, Amos sought out his mother. He found her in the conservatory at the side of the house, engrossed in trimming her treasured roses.

"There is something that I have to tell you, Mother."

She didn't answer immediately. Instead, she took her time to snip off another stem, carefully clean and lay down her secateurs and remove her gloves. "Have you finally decided to confess the truth about your fight with Alistair?" she asked, still distant and unforgiving.

"No."

"Well then, whatever it is, I don't want to hear it!"

"I think you do."

He laid the bulky envelope on the table in front of her and told her about the advent of Thomas Hungerford.

Jasper Pendlebury and Bruce McNaughton were both Haileybury men, both civil servants of long standing. They shared the view that it was the ultimate absurdity for India to be governed directly from London, and that the capital of British India should be moved from Calcutta to a more central location in the north. Apart from that they had little in common. Their viewpoints on just about every other matter were widely divergent, as indeed were their respective greeds. Whereas Jasper Pendlebury's abiding hunger was for political power that would give him authority over his fellow men and ensure him a place in colonial history, the Lieutenant-Governor lusted merely after wealth.

Which was why it was with considerable surprise that Sir Bruce received the Finance member's very cordial note suggesting a game of billiards and perhaps a spot of cold supper at the Lieutenant-Governor's residence. The informality was quite unlike Sir Jasper, and Sir Bruce's considerable surprise was tempered with considerable suspicion. And considerable alarm! Had Sir Jasper heard something that he should not have? Why otherwise should he suddenly seek him out for a social evening when they had met no more than a week ago at the *burra khana?* It could hardly be a matter of business; after all, they met often enough in the course of their duties during the week.

"We don't see enough of each other, Bruce," Sir Jasper said, as they settled down to their whisky-sodas after Lady McNaughton had withdrawn and left them to themselves. The billiards-room bearers were brushing the table, arranging the triangle of balls and chalking the cues.

Sir Bruce thought otherwise but he did not say so.

"You should be leaving for home shortly for Arabella's wedding, if I am not mistaken?"

"Yes. We sail in six weeks."

"Away long?"

"The usual. About half a year."

"Your future son-in-law is a very fine young man, I hear. Someone was saying just the other day that. . . ."

Presently, social chitchat developed into shop talk. Sir Bruce was further surprised, and pleased, at how similar their viewpoints on all subjects appeared to be tonight. Sir Jasper encouraged him to talk about himself and Sir Bruce enjoyed talking about himself. He knew that he was not a well-liked man, that behind his back people called him a bore, and this peeved him. Now, given the freedom of a leisurely platform and the loan of a pair of erudite ears prepared to listen with such flattering attention, he expounded to his heart's content. Whatever he said, Sir Jasper accepted with solemn nods of agreement. If he refuted a contention, it was mildly, with humour and indulgence. Gradually, as the game progressed, Sir Bruce started to loosen.

Indeed, so affable was the prevailing mood of the evening that Sir Bruce would have been astonished to learn just how intensely his amiable guest disliked him. Secretly, Sir Jasper found his corpulent host's conceit intolerable, his complacency worse, and he was irritated beyond endurance by his garrulous pomposity. That Bruce McNaughton was incorrigibly corrupt, Sir Jasper knew; that he was also cold-blooded and unscrupulous, he strongly suspected. He had heard about that little affair in Sind years ago, for instance, and about the deftness with which the matter had been swept under the carpet. And, of course, he had heard the present sinister whisperings about his devious host's covert attempts to secure the lucrative Dharamtala-Baghbazaar road-building job for a local contractor of dubious repute (and an equally lucrative consideration for himself, naturally). Ironically enough, it was precisely this villainy that appealed most to Sir Jasper this evening, for purely selfish reasons. Privately, he applauded the fact that Bruce McNaughton was a man entirely without moral fibre or, indeed, conscience.

As it happened, Sir Bruce was also an appalling billiards player. Therefore, Sir Jasper had to put in considerable effort to seem even less skilful, much to his host's frequently expressed glee. Time and time again the Lieutenant-Governor found himself winning with comfortable ease. Even his lowest scoring breaks appeared to be far beyond Sir Jasper's rather more modest capabilities. By the time they had hung up their cues and the cold supper had been served in the billiards room by a flurry of bearers, Sir Bruce had won three games in a row and was at his most expansive, self-satisfied best.

"I'm afraid you're far too good for me, Bruce," Sir Jasper said with a rueful smile as he pulled out his wallet. "Now, how much are the damages?"

"Five rupees eight annas, old boy. Not having a good run of luck this evening, are you?"

"Rotten!" Sir Jasper hated being called "old boy," but he tolerated it with a smile and cheerfully laid his dues on the table.

"Not a bad chap at all," Sir Bruce thought to himself, well pleased with his substantial winnings. "In fact, not half as high and mighty as they make him out to be."

They talked as they ate. Sir Jasper commended his host on the continuing reforms and reorganizations in the police force. Sir Bruce reciprocated by pronouncing the *burra khana* the most entertaining social event he had attended in the last two seasons.

"Incidentally, how is your scheme to eliminate the scourge of the cobras from residential areas proceeding, Bruce?" Sir Jasper inquired over the chicken breasts in aspic. "I see that lately there's been a great deal about it in the papers."

Sir Bruce's florid face turned redder. "It's a fiasco, Jasper, an absolute bloody disaster!"

"Oh? That surprises me. Just the other day the servants caught and killed an eight-foot hamadryad among our banana trees. They're getting to be quite a hazard, I must agree. I think your scheme is an excellent idea."

"Of course it is! Or would be were it not for the incompetence of those blithering idiots in our districts!" His face darkened as he wiped the dribble of gravy from the corners of his mouth. "That damned fool of a Deputy Commissioner in Sonthal Parganas says he hasn't had any results at all in the past eight months—and do you know why?"

Sir Jasper confessed that he did not.

"Because, he says, he forgot all about it! *Forgot!* Can you believe that any government officer could reach such heights of asininity?"

Sir Jasper admitted that he could not.

"And the excuse of the chaps in Dacca is even more of a laugh—they say they simply mislaid our circular authorising payments! So, naturally, not a single cobra, dead or alive, has been delivered to date by the populace."

"How much is the inducement?" Sir Jasper smothered a yawn and continued to look fascinated.

"Two annas per cobra, dead or alive. Not a pittance by any manner of means."

"Well, can the budget not be stretched to, say, four annas? Surely that much filthy lucre would tempt even the most inert citizen to bestir himself with some modicum of enthusiasm?"

The sarcasm was lost on Sir Bruce. "As a matter of fact," he replied very seriously, "we have written to the Supreme Government to sanction an increase in the amount. But so far, not a word in reply—typical, *typical!* I say, old chap, I wonder if you could look into the matter and get these bloody fellows off their arses? I should imagine the letter is gathering dust with your bunch of slothful babus somewhere in the Treasury."

Sir Jasper promised that he would see what he could do.

That subject exhausted, they repaired to Sir Bruce's study and settled down to their glasses of post-prandial Cognac. Sir Jasper casually lifted up the morning's paper lying on a nearby table. He pointed to an item on the front page in which the Lieutenant-Governor had been soundly chastised for some unpopular measure or other.

"I think this is a grossly unfair stand to take, wouldn't you agree, Bruce? After all, you only did what was your duty."

Expansively, Sir Bruce waved a careless hand. "Oh, they have a right to their opinion, I suppose. Freedom of speech and all that, old boy."

"Nonetheless, an excessively biased opinion, if I might say so. I'm surprised that you are able to take it in such good spirit."

Sir Bruce shrugged. "Sticks and stones, et cetera, et cetera. On the whole, I must say, the Anglo-Indian Press is not as out of control as it sounds. Mind you, occasionally they do step too far out of line and then we rap them over the knuckles, perhaps even deport one or two. But most of what they write is simply hot rhetoric, especially in the vernacular Press. They carp and nitpick like hell, but then that is the rabble-rousers' job, isn't it? One learns to accept it as an indication of educated public opinion. Hah!"

Sir Jasper laid down the paper. "In that case, I must admire the manner in which you discharge your obligations to democratic tenets, Bruce. I am really very impressed."

"Oh, this isn't the view I hold, Jasper, perish the thought!" Sir Bruce hastened to correct the misinterpretation. "This is the view I have been instructed to hold by those nincompoops who play God with the colony."

"Is that so?" Sir Jasper remarked, most interested. "Having arrived fairly recently, I have to confess that I am not entirely familiar with the policies that prevail here with regard to newspapers, but I've noticed that there *are* one or two that persist in offensive writing." He gave a good-natured laugh. "Come to think of it, they are the true cobras that need to be exterminated from our society, what?"

"Eh?"

"Well, that fellow, for instance." Sir Jasper's forehead creased in a frown as he foraged in his memory. "What is his name? The Eurasian. . . ."

There was the sound of a sharply indrawn breath. "Hawkesworth?"

"Yes. That's the one. What a slur on the noble profession of journalism. I am truly astonished at the extent of your forebearance, Bruce."

Sir Bruce's stomach gave a sickening lurch; a gleam of caution leapt into his faded blue eyes. His spies had informed him of that early morning meeting between Pendlebury and Hawkesworth near the Champatollah pond . . . was *that* connected with the purpose behind this evening? Sir Bruce threw his guest a sidelong glance, but Sir Jasper's expression seemed open and innocent, devoid of subterfuge as he puffed contentedly on his cigar.

"That extraordinary announcement about the Roshanara, for instance," Sir Jasper continued. "How does the fellow get away with it, Bruce? I presume you do know that this is stolen property?"

"Well, of course I do." Very cautiously, Sir Bruce started to breathe again. "Twining is investigating the matter. With some luck, he should have the man behind bars in very short order."

Sir Jasper flicked the tube of ash from his cigar very carefully into a Bohemian glass ashtray. "I wonder where he gets the funds to publish all his drivel?"

McNaughton relaxed further. He snorted. "Probably from that Raven-thorne boy. They're as thick as thieves, you know." Seeing that there was no imminent danger of an inconvenient diversion, Sir Bruce allowed his nervousness to turn into righteous anger. "By God, Jasper, you're right—that Eurasian bastard *is* a snake, a poisonous viper! Some day someone is going to take a whip to his miserable hide and tan the bloody trousers off him!"

Sir Jasper showed some amusement. "As bad as that, eh?"

"Worse! The man is absolutely loathed in the city." His face twisted with malice. "For two pins, I. . . ." He stopped and pursed his mouth before he could say too much.

Sir Jasper appeared lost in his own thoughts. "You know," he mused as he stared up at the ceiling, "it brings back to mind an editor of an Urdu daily I met once or twice when I was posted in Lucknow. The fellow was a rather tiresome firebrand, violently opposed to the annexation of Oudh. The pages of his rag were filled with ravings and rantings against the administration. General Outram hated the man, although I must say I found his writings rather entertaining. I never took them seriously, you see." Noticing that his cigar had gone out, he stubbed it against the bottom of the ashtray and wiped his fingers with his silken cream handkerchief. "I was quite sorry that he came to a somewhat sticky end."

"Outram cooked his hash right and proper, did he?" Sir Bruce asked eagerly.

"Oh, dear me, no, nothing like that! But *someone* did. Fortunately for us, the man had no shortage of enemies. We British didn't have to lift a finger. One night intruders smashed every machine he had in his press and then torched the whole lot, including the building."

"And they got away with that?" Sir Bruce marvelled.

"Apparently." Sir Jasper shrugged. "The exercise was neatly carried out and obviously professional. It was never discovered who was responsible. The police could have had their pick of a dozen suspects. It was most mysterious. Eventually it was assumed that the motive was some long-standing personal vendetta and the file was closed."

"No one made a fuss about it, not even the natives?"

"Well, some local people did, naturally. There were many who agreed with his inflammatory writings. But the English community was, frankly, delighted. In fact, if I remember rightly, the Thirty-Second were posted there at the time. They held a Regimental Ball to celebrate the occasion."

"What happened to the editor?"

"Oh, didn't I mention it? He and his family perished in the fire. It was most unfortunate."

Sir Bruce had been listening very intently. Now his eyes glinted. "By Jove, sir, given a chance I'd do the same with this vermin, Hawkesworth. I'd like to break every machine he has in his press and every damned bone in his miserable body!"

Sir Jasper looked faintly shocked. "But my dear Bruce, you must expel that idea instantly from your mind! If we, the civilised nations, do not protect and respect the liberty of the modern Press, then who, pray, will?"

"But of course, of course!" The Lieutenant-Governor hastened to make reparation for his outburst. "Come on, Jasper, I was only speaking in jest. Naturally I would never contemplate compromising the dignity of my high office with such lawless and irresponsible behaviour."

"Good. I am glad to hear you say it." Swallowing a yawn, Sir Jasper got up to go. "I should imagine, some day someone here too will be only too glad to do the needful with your particular *bête noire*, Bruce—with a bit of luck, of course!"

To show that he too spoke in jest, he laughed with full-throated humour.

Sir Bruce did not believe in luck; he believed in swift and positive action. That night he did not sleep well and the next morning he was up inordinately early.

Dawn had barely broken on the eastern horizon when he sent for Aaron Nicholas.

After his talk with Kyle, Amos repaired to his office and sat brooding at his desk, sipping his morning cup of tea in silence. His mood was black, his thoughts turbulent. He could not dispel the feeling that once again they stood on the edge of a precipice, only a step away from disaster. Whatever Hungerford's revelations, however well they were prepared for them, they would ravage his mother, and their lives—and the household—would again be in upheaval. His father's life and death were history. Why reopen sepulchres long closed, sealed and forgotten?

On the one hand there were Hungerford's and now also Pendlebury's extravagant contentions. On the other, were his sister's complex problems and, of course, Alistair Birkhurst. Merely thinking of the little rat and the despicable machinations that had produced bad blood between him and his mother, Amos simmered. The worm, the loathsome, lying, ungrateful . . . !

A knock on the door cut off his train of thought. Hari Babu entered. "There is a sahib who wishes to see you."

"Tell him to talk to Ranjan Babu. I don't want to see anyone today."

"The sahib insists." Hari Babu placed a visiting card on the desk.

Amos stiffened and his face suffused with colour. "I thought I had given *specific* instructions that this . . . gentleman was not to be allowed on the premises—*ever!*"

"I tried every excuse I could think of," Hari Babu pleaded nervously, "but the sahib is very persistent. He refuses to leave until he has seen you."

"Well then, have him thrown out! Get the two watchmen from downstairs. . . ."

"That will not be necessary," a voice interrupted from the doorway. "I do not intend to stay a moment longer than I have to."

Hari Babu spun round, his mouth agape, and Amos froze in his seat.

Very calmly, Alistair Birkhurst walked into the room and positioned himself on the other side of Amos's desk. The two stared at each other for a moment in silence, Amos cold and furious, and Alistair (his arm in a sling) without any discernible expression at all. Then Amos made a sign to dismiss his assistant. Hari Babu scuttled out of the room and closed the door behind him.

"What do you want?" Amos asked rudely. "I'm busy." He did not ask Alistair to sit down.

"I don't want anything. I just wish to say something."

"There is nothing you have to say that I want to hear!"

"Nevertheless, hear it you will!" Alistair fisted his good hand and thumped it on the desk. "I'm not leaving until I've got it all off my chest, so you might as well listen."

"Well, make it quick. I can't spare you more than two minutes."

"Two minutes are all I need. I wouldn't want to stay longer anyway." Lowering his eyes, Alistair went on, "I wanted to thank you for . . . what you did the other night."

The infernal gall of the man! "Oh, did you now? Well, I can do without your hypocritical gratitude. Now get out!"

"I will. As soon as I've said everything that I intend to," Alistair gulped, his face bright red with effort, embarrassment and determination. "You needn't have done all that you did."

"You're damned right I needn't have!" Amos half rose out of his chair. "Now listen, you double-faced, mealy-mouthed, lying pipsqueak! You . . ."

"Oh, shut up and sit down, will you?" Alistair threw up one hand in matching temper. "Damn it, do you know how difficult it was for me to come here today knowing that I would be insulted? For two pins, I'd rather punch you in the nose and give *you* a taste of what I got that night!" Breathing noisily, he raked his hair clumsily in an attempt to still the turmoil in his mind. "That night you saved my life."

"Oh, don't be so bloody melodramatic!" Amos snapped, making a sound of disgust. "I did what I did because I had no choice, that's all there is to it."

"You could have left me there."

"I *should* have—I almost did!"

"But you didn't. I went to that doctor bloke again. He said I could have bled to death. I *am* grateful, Amos."

"Oh, really?" Amos sneered. "And it's because of this overwhelming gratitude of yours that you lied to Mother, I take it?"

Alistair crimsoned further. "I didn't lie to her," he mumbled. "She simply presumed the rest."

"And, of course, during seven days of babying and cossetting, you found no opportunity to correct that presumption!"

"Well, I tried to. . . ." He broke off. His chin thrust forward and his nose rose up in the air. "No. To tell you the truth, I didn't try to!"

"Why the hell not, you little rotter?"

Alistair again dropped his gaze. "You know why not."

"No, I do not. Why don't you enlighten me?"

"I didn't want her to know the truth, *that's* why!" He gave a defiant toss of his head and glared at Amos. "I wanted her to think badly of you, I *wanted* her to be angry with you!"

"Why, in heaven's name, why?"

Alistair looked at him hard and shook his head fiercely from side to side. "I'm *not* going to say it, Amos. It's humiliating enough as it is. And if you can't guess, you're a bigger damned ass than I thought!"

Amos narrowed his eyes. "You're . . . jealous of me, aren't you?"

"And you of me!" Alistair retorted, but then his shoulders sagged and his face crumpled; he looked stricken. "You've had her all your life," he said bitterly. "I didn't even know what my mother looked like until two months ago!"

Reduced to silence, Amos sank back into his chair. He could think of absolutely nothing to say.

In mutual embarrassment, they avoided each other's eyes. Amos gazed steadfastly out of the window. Alistair seemed mesmerized by a long, brown lizard on the wall inching its way towards a somnolent moth left over from the nightly invasion. Then he cleared his throat and dug his hand inside the pocket of his jacket. He threw something onto the desk. It was an envelope.

"I've brought you this."

"What is it?"

"Open it and see. Presumably, you can read!"

Amos slit open the envelope with the paper-cutter on his desk and pulled out some sheets of thick paper.

They were the title deeds for the Sutherland Cotton Spinning and Weaving Mill in Cawnpore.

Amos's breath caught. For a while he could not speak. Then, with supreme effort, he pulled himself together and coughed at some length to clear the obstruction in his throat.

"What is th-this?" he finally spluttered, covering his confusion with a dark, suspicious scowl, "a silly joke?"

"Take it. It's yours," Alistair said dismissively. "I never wanted the damn thing anyway." He shifted his weight from one foot to the other. "You could at least ask me to sit down now," he said plaintively. "My feet are killing me!"

"You won't be here long enough to sit," Amos said, but somewhat absently, quickly reconstituting his face. Behind his carefully constructed impassivity, his mind raced. Taken unawares, he could not decide how to react. Was the blighter serious?

Alistair muttered an oath, pulled out a chair, and with an air of defiance, sat down anyway. Amos folded the document and returned it to the envelope. He held it out to Alistair. "I don't accept charity," he said coldly, "especially yours. You can leave now."

"Who the hell said anything about charity, you idiot? If you want it, you can jolly well pay me full price for it!"

Amos struggled to contain his euphoria. "Well, how much is the full price?"

"What I paid for it."

"Not acceptable. I will pay you what I have already offered—the price you paid *plus* thirty percent over it."

Alistair laughed and shrugged disdainfully. "More fool you! But if that is how you want it, naturally I agree."

Amos nodded, pretending to study the document, not daring to raise his eyes in case he gave away his jubilation. His mind was in a whirl; he simply couldn't believe his luck.

"You can send your Mr. Moitra to see Donaldson to settle the legal details. Donaldson has my power-of-attorney."

Alistair hesitated for a moment, as if waiting for Amos to say something. But when Amos did not speak, he rose to his feet and prepared to leave. He was almost at the door when Amos stopped him with a sudden question.

"The plantation . . . ?"

Alistair retraced his steps and again seated himself. "Are you really interested in that?"

"I offered to buy it with the cotton mill, didn't I?" Amos reminded him, his heart in his mouth.

"I thought that was just to dangle a carrot!"

"Well, it was. But is it still available?"

Alistair frowned. "I have an idea it's already sold."

Amos's heart dropped with an almost audible thud. He somehow managed a sarcastic laugh. "Trying to raise the price with that old chestnut, are you?"

"Oh, don't be daft! It doesn't matter to me if it's never sold, you already know that. But there has been an inquiry for it very recently."

"Who from?"

"Some government department."

Amos's mouth went even drier. "What would any government department want with a defunct indigo plantation?"

"How should I know? He said they needed the land for some new rural construction project or the other. At least, that's what I *think* Donaldson said the man said."

"Which man?"

"Someone from the Treasury. One of Sir Jasper Pendlebury's assistants."

Amos felt very sick indeed. "Has the agreement already been signed?"

"I'm not sure. I'll have to find out from Donaldson. But if you seriously want it. . . ."

Very cautiously, Amos started to breathe again. "Yes. I seriously want it." He spoke as calmly as he could. "How much do you expect for it—considering it's defunct and gone to the dogs anyway?"

"Oh?" Alistair cocked a mocking eyebrow. "Is that why you're ready to give your eyeteeth to get it?" He gave a low chuckle. "Well, make me an offer."

"I'll give you twenty percent above whatever the Treasury offers."

"My, my. For a defunct plantation gone to the dogs, mine certainly seems to have suddenly developed mysterious value!"

Amos glared at him. "Don't waste my time with imbecilic remarks," he snapped. "Either sell or get out!"

"Oh, I'll sell all right," Alistair said easily. "It's no skin off my nose who buys it. I'll tell Donaldson to halt the negotiations with the Treasury. You can complete the sale with him after I've gone."

"Gone?" It was an involuntary reflex, and having blurted it out, Amos coloured. What the devil did it matter to *him* whether he went or stayed?

"Yes. I sail later in the week. One of your clippers, as it happens. They say the grub kills you in a week on P&O, but on yours it takes almost a fortnight."

Amos laughed, then quickly scowled again. "Well, I can't say I'll be sorry to see the back of you."

"Likewise," Alistair retorted, again standing up to leave.

"Tell me, just as a matter of curiosity," Amos again stopped him as he was about to talk towards the door, "what *was* that brawl about, anyway?"

Alistair's expression closed. "I don't consider that to be any of your damned business."

"I consider otherwise. Why should you, of all people, suddenly decide to champion the cause of the Raventhornes?"

"I told you, stay out of this!" Alistair growled, clenching his fist, then quickly hiding it behind his back.

"They made insulting remarks about Mother, didn't they?" Amos suggested softly.

"Hah! Why the hell should I care about that?"

Amos studied him with sudden interest, then shrugged and abandoned the subject.

He rose to his feet. In his hands he still clutched the envelope Alistair had given him. Casually, he put it down on the table. He hesitated an instant, then said two words he had never imagined he would ever in his life find occasion to say to Alistair Birkhurst.

"Thank you."

Alistair stood rooted where he was, equally startled. Amos suddenly thrust a hand out at him across the desk. For a split second Alistair gawked at the hand as if it were some arcane object he had never seen before. Then he grasped it and his mouth split in a wide grin.

"Oh, to hell with you!"

He bounced out of the door and slammed it hard behind him.

Amos picked up the envelope gingerly, in wonderment, then ran a cautious finger all round its edges to assure himself that it existed, not as a hallucination but as a tangible reality. In that envelope reposed a dream he thought had been lost to him forever. He could not bring himself to believe that he had actually regained it.

For the moment even Thomas Hungerford was forgotten.

Striding to the door, Amos flung it open with a flourish. "Ranjan Babu?"

he yelled at the top of his lungs. *"Ranjan Babu!* I want you here this very instant!"

A terrified Ranjan Moitra came hurtling round the corner and into the room a second later, the folds of his plump face all aquiver. Without saying a word, Amos handed him the envelope. Moitra took it with quaking fingers, whisked out the document and read it at a glance. He clutched his brow, staggered towards a chair and collapsed into it. Then he muttered something no one had ever heard him say before:

"Well, I will be *damned!"*

It was time to answer Clarence Twining's summons. Kept waiting any longer, Kyle knew that the Inspector-General was likely to lose both his sense of humour and his temper. Much to his surprise, however, just as Kyle was about to leave the house for the police headquarters, he saw the massive figure of the worthy gentleman himself alight from the rather splendid curricle that was the envy of many, and lumber through his gate. With an imperious gesture, he commanded the two constables who accompanied him on horseback to wait for him outside.

"Not expecting the mountain to come to Mohammed, were you, Hawkesworth?" Twining barked with a grim smile.

"Since you ask, sir, no." Kyle ushered him into his study and despatched his young servant lad to bring refreshments. "Indeed, I am quite overwhelmed by the honour. I was about to make myself available at your office."

"Well, don't flatter yourself, Hawkesworth," Twining said, settling his oversized bulk into an easy chair that creaked ominously under his weight. "I happened to be passing, and knowing that you have been back in station more than two days, I thought I might as well get this matter settled at my convenience rather than yours. Didn't you get my note?"

"Yes, but I have been rather busy."

"Not too busy to sit dawdling by the river with Amos Raventhorne, I learn."

Kyle lowered himself in his usual chair on the other side of the desk. "You've been having me followed?" he asked easily, not in the least perturbed. "Well, I must say, I'm impressed by Her Majesty's espionage network."

"I should damn well hope so! What makes you think you're the only one in town who knows what everyone is doing, eh?"

Kyle laughed. He liked and respected Clarence Twining, as almost everyone did. The police chief was a scrupulous man, difficult to hoodwink, fair and straightforward in his dealings, if sometimes unorthodox in his methods. Straight as a die himself, he tolerated neither indiscipline nor wrongdoing in others, but he also believed in compassion. For these many virtues, he enjoyed the trust and regard of all communities. He was also known to possess a lively sense of humour, unfortunately not much in evidence this evening.

The young servant lad returned bearing a tray with bottles of beer and bowls of roasted pine nuts.

"I don't drink on duty, Hawkesworth," Twining said sharply. "And make no mistake, I *am* here strictly on duty." He waved aside the refreshments. Kyle gave a signal to the lad and, leaving the tray on the table, he went out of the room.

"I suppose you know why I am here?"

"No. I'm afraid I have absolutely no idea, sir."

"Like hell you haven't!" Twining leant forward and pincered him with slitted eyes. "You have some *gall*, Hawkesworth, printing that advertisement without either my knowledge or my permission."

"If I had asked your permission would you have given it?"

"Certainly not!"

"Well, there you are, then. It was printed in a worthy cause, the pursuit of justice. If the means were, well, impertinent, I hope they will be proved justifiable by the ends."

"And if they are not?"

"Then," Kyle assured him blandly, "Her Majesty's Government will be entitled to my unconditional apology on the front page."

Twining snorted. "By God, Hawkesworth, you have an infernal nerve! Had you been in station, I would have clamped you in irons for your confounded effrontery—which, I regret to say, becomes more of a habit with each blasted day."

"The point is, has the advertisement borne any fruit yet?"

"Has it borne *fruit?*" Twining roared, the mottled pink of his face turning aubergine. "It's borne enough fruit to fill the whole bloody Municipal Market, *that's* what it's borne! I have every petty criminal lining up outside my headquarters practically begging to be charged with arson! I have aspiring arsonists falling out of the brickwork, a dozen more each time I turn my back. My men are going mad trying to fend them off—I can barely get into my office without someone clutching at my feet begging to be arrested." He sat back huffing and puffing and patted his handkerchief across his forehead. "You've started a ruddy circus going at my headquarters, man, and I can tell you, the Lieutenant-Governor is livid, bloody livid—not that *I'm* not!"

"Why? Because the promise of a sizeable reward has flushed all the rats out of the sewers?"

"No, my friend, because—as if you didn't know!—you're flaunting possession of stolen goods, that's why!"

"Stolen goods? I'm afraid I don't understand, sir."

Twining heaved a weary sigh. "Don't play silly games with me, Hawkesworth. The Roshanara ruby is stolen property. I can hardly believe that you, who know what I had for breakfast last Tuesday, are not aware of that fact."

"Of course I am. It's common knowledge."

"Well, the Saifabad family have reacted violently to your advertisement. They have demanded an immediate investigation and, consequently, an arrest."

"Rightly so. In their situation, I would do the same."

Twining's beady little eyes glittered from amid rolls of pink flesh. "And still you claim that the Roshanara is in your possession?"

"It is in my possession, yes."

Twining sat back and drummed on the desk with his fingers. "I must tell you, Hawkesworth," he said frigidly, "that whatever skulduggery you are up to, I am not amused. The Saifabad people are furious, the Lucknow authorities are furious, the Lieutenant-Governor is furious and, to be honest, I myself am closer to murder than I have ever been before. Now, if what you claim is true, then I hope you realise that I will have absolutely no option but to arrest you."

"Naturally. The law must take its course under all circumstances."

Twining's chest heaved up and down, as if he breathed with an effort. "All right," he grunted, "let me get this absolutely straight. You confess that the Roshanara *is* in your possession, or that you have access to it. Do I surmise correctly?"

"Yes."

"You actually have it here, on the premises?"

"Yes, of course. Where else?"

"In that case you would have no objection to showing it to me, would you?"

"None whatsoever."

Twining steepled his fingers and played them against each other. "Fetch it."

"As you wish."

Kyle rose and left the room. He returned a few moments later bearing a brown paper packet. This he laid on the desk before the police chief. He reseated himself. Twining fumbled in his breast pocket, took out a gold-rimmed pince-nez, hooked it over his fleshy nose and gave Kyle a look rife with suspicion. From within the paper he extracted a small red jewellery box. He opened it, took out the item reposing within and, draping the chain and pendant over his hand, examined it closely. He stared at the pendant for a whole minute. Slowly, his face changed colour and he looked up.

"Is this some kind of jest, Hawkesworth?"

"Jest, sir? I regret I don't follow your meaning."

Twining held up the pendant. "This isn't a ruby, it's a bloody sapphire!"

Kyle looked faintly puzzled. "But of course it's a sapphire."

It was Twining's turn to look confused. "But the Roshanara is a *ruby*, dammit!"

"Well, my Roshanara isn't," Kyle said smoothly. "My Roshanara has always been a sapphire. It was given many years ago to my mother by her mother who got it from *her* mother. It has been in our family since 1783. My great-great-grandmother was called Roshni Begum. It was named after her."

Twining sat through the explanation stone-faced. "It won't work, Hawkesworth. You advertised the Roshanara *ruby* as a reward!"

Kyle looked aghast. "I think you are mistaken, sir. I certainly did not."

"Like *hell* you didn't! Give me a copy of that confounded paper. . . ."

Kyle abstracted it from a pile on the desk and handed it to him. Twining laid the paper flat on the desk and smoothed it out. He adjusted his pince-nez. "Here it is, by God!" He jabbed the advertisement so hard with one finger that it made a hole in the paper. "Right here, *right* in front of your eyes and mine! If you think you can wriggle out of this one, you. . . ." He stopped abruptly, his gaze riveted. He scrutinized the advertisement twice, very closely, and then once again. Slowly, he removed his pince-nez, slipped it inside its case and returned the case to his breast pocket. He looked up at Kyle, then sank back in his chair without saying a word.

"I trust that satisfies you, sir?" Kyle smiled a little. "I advertised *my* Roshanara as a reward. The word 'ruby' was never mentioned. I haven't the faintest idea where the Saifabad Roshanara is. I can only vouch for my own."

Twining sat deep in contemplation, stroking the topmost of his several chins, by no means deceived. He cocked his head to one side. "And you know nothing of the whereabouts of the Roshanara ruby?"

"No, nothing."

"You've never seen it?"

"No."

"And it is not in your possession?"

Kyle looked shocked. "Certainly not! I could not, in all conscience, even consider harbouring stolen property."

Twining propped his elbows on the table, closed his eyes and cradled his chins on his knuckles. "The rumour is that it was Miss Crum who abstracted it from the nawab's family."

"Well, if she did," Kyle said drily, "I would say the old lecher certainly made her earn it."

"They claim she *stole* it."

"Under the circumstances, that charge might be difficult to investigate— unless Her Majesty's espionage network also has representation over-head."

"Don't be impertinent with me, Hawkesworth!" Twining snapped. "I'm not in the mood for it. You're a cool customer, too damned cool for your own good, but don't for an instant think I'm satisfied with your glib expla-nations, I am not. Anyway," he straightened his back and sat up, "as it happens, your ill-advised announcement has served the cause of justice, after all." His expression as well as his tone mellowed. "After separating the wheat from the chaff, we have struck what my American friend Hal Lubbock might well call pay dirt. If you will forgive a shockingly mixed metaphor."

Kyle raised an astonished eyebrow. "Really?"

He reached for the beer, poured out two glasses and offered one to Twining. The police chief accepted with a nod, without protest. "Are you acquainted with a man called Bansi Dhar?

"No."

"I wouldn't lie any more than I had to, Hawkesworth," Twining said pleasantly, "or you'll find yourself up for perjury faster than you can say ruby! In the meantime, I will pretend to believe that you know nothing of this Bansi Dhar, so humour me by listening, will you?" He took a large mouthful of beer and paused to wipe a line of froth from his upper lip.

"Bansi Babu is a *munshi* in the employ of Nalini Chandra Ganguly and his brother for the purpose of keeping accounts. A few nights ago, the fellow came to my house in stealth, and in a state of high agitation and hysteria related to me some very pertinent information—the names of the men Nalini Chandra hired to torch that Chitpore Home. Not only that, Bansi Babu says he also has proof by way of payments made to the men by the Ganguly brothers, and claims to have overheard much of the plotting."

"You have verified his testimony?"

"As far as we could, yes. Nalini Chandra, of course, denies everything, but when faced with incontrovertible evidence, he will not be able to sustain his claim of innocence. There is already friction among the conspiring brothers, I learn. In very short order, they will start blaming each other and seal their own fates in the process." He scratched his nose. "But having come this far, I regret to say, the investigation has come to a halt."

"Oh?"

"Yes. Bansi Babu has gone into hiding. I am informed by my constables that he will not put even one word to paper, or emerge from his hiding place, until he has been assured of the reward."

"I see. Well, what do you want me to do about it?"

Twining took a handful of pine nuts and tossed them into a cavernous mouth. "Produce the damned reward, what else?"

"Not until the Ganguly brothers are convicted."

"Well, perhaps you would be kind enough to explain that to Bansi Babu when you see him next." Kyle opened his mouth to make a protest, but as Twining gave him a warning look, quickly closed it again. "I know that you are not a fool, Hawkesworth."

"I am relieved that you should think so, sir."

"In fact, you are a disturbingly clever young man."

Kyle remained silent and waited.

"Therefore, I would be obliged if you could do me the return courtesy of not thinking *me* a fool either." Twining struggled out of his chair with some difficulty and stood up. Kyle rose too. "Whatever it is that you have pulled off, Hawkesworth, you've pulled it off well, I grant you that. Frankly, I am delighted that poor Joycie Crum's murder will not go unpunished, whatever the means used to catch the guilty. If the Ganguly men can be brought to justice, I am content. But, a word of advice." Somewhere in the depths of his highly perceptive eyes, a twinkle appeared. "If I were you, I'd get rid of the *item* in question as soon as possible. Should I happen to find it on your premises, you can look forward to hospitality as Her Majesty's guest for at least five years, that much I promise. Thank you for the beer. Goodnight."

He lumbered across to the front door and let himself out. As he did so, he chuckled under his breath.

As soon as the sounds of the departing carriage had died down, Bansi Babu crept out from behind the door of the next room where he had been hiding. "Your Roshanara is a sapphire?" he asked, outraged.

"Yes," Kyle confirmed. "But yours, my friend, will be the *ruby*, as promised. You will have it as soon as you have submitted your signed statement to Mr. Twining, as soon as the trial is over and *after* Nalini Chandra and his brothers are convicted."

"I'm a poor man with. . . ."

"And not a day earlier than that on which you embark for Mauritius!" Kyle gave him a stern look. "The rest of the understanding is clear, I hope?"

"How can I live there?" the *munshi* wailed, wringing his hands. "I do not even know where this place is!"

"Mauritius is an island in the Indian Ocean."

"I have a wife and seven children, an old mother and father, an aunt who. . . ."

"It may be an island, but I assure you it's large enough to accommodate even your prolific family."

"But I do not know anyone there, no relations, no friends!"

"You take enough relations with you to satisfy all familial requirements, and you will make friends. There are plenty of Indian settlers on the island working in the sugar-cane fields."

"And the boat tickets? You expect me to purchase boat tickets out of my *own* money?" he asked, dismayed.

"No. *My* Roshanara will take care of those. Now, if you're having second thoughts. . . ."

Quickly, the *munshi* shook his head. "No, no, *no* second thoughts." His eyes flashed with greed. He smiled and his face lit up. "There are *Bengalis* in Mauritius?"

"More than you can count. But remember—if you ever return to this country with that ruby," Kyle warned, "I will not be responsible for the consequences. Now go to Mr. Twining and do exactly as he tells you."

Later, over supper, Kyle's mother asked, worried, "There will be no trouble for you, my son, will there?"

"No, none."

"And those men will be caught?"

"Twining will see to that. He is a good man."

Her sad, sea green eyes brimmed. "I'm glad that accursed ruby will soon be out of our lives forever, but it has served its purpose well. True, in a way, it was responsible for the loss of my beloved Joycie's life. But in another, it is the instrument that will punish those who deprived her of it."

Somehow, with supreme effort, Maya cast aside her mantle of all-pervasive melancholy and prepared herself for Herbert Ludlow's visit.

Despite her painful distractions, she had not forgotten that most important appointment. In a way, the mere fact of preparing her establishment for the Chief Commissioner's inspection was healing. In the hurry and flurry of cleaning out the stables and the lofts and attending to the thousand and one rituals of grooming Morning Mist, she had scarcely a moment left to think, let alone brood. She drove Abdul Mian and his son, Rafiq, into a tizzy as she fussed about giving last-minute instructions. Now the stables positively sparkled with elbow grease; in his stall the handsome grey, the star performer of the day, stood meticulously groomed, his coat sheened like a pearl. No less resplendent, the two grooms sported new overalls and looked as pleased as punch. Abdul Mian moved about stiffly, as if nervous of subjecting his smart new garment to excessive wear and tear, and his son, rather more nonchalant, strutted around with an air of great self-importance. Neither spared himself in the pursuit of his assigned duties for the day, convinced that their missy memsahib was entertaining one no less than the Viceroy himself.

As she put finishing touches to the flower arrangement in her office—where they were to have tea—Maya wished Christian could have joined them this afternoon. She had not seen him since the morning after the ball, but she realised that he was probably busy winding up his affairs before he departed for Champaran. She wondered when she would see him again once he had left. Soon, he had promised, *soon*; the comforting prospect finally induced a smile to struggle up to her mouth. In her sense of desolation over the past few days, she had not even had the will to dwell on memories of the *burra khana*. She did so now, and the smile widened. She recalled several little forgotten tidbits that she had not narrated to Sheba, Melanie Anderson's silly antics with Alistair, for one. Goodness, what a fool the girl had made of herself! Amused by the memory, Maya laughed. She would have to rectify the omissions as soon as she had concluded her business with Mr. Ludlow, and Sheba her domestic duties.

For tea, Maya had ordered Anthony to prepare buttered crumpets, sardine sandwiches, chocolate éclairs and angel cake. The splendid fare, tastefully arranged in silver dishes, was now being arrayed in her office room on a table overlaid with the finest Brussels lace tablecloth and napkins Sheba could produce from the household's linen storeroom. In a Dresden china dish set out as the centrepiece of the table, Sheba had placed the Mont Blanc aux marrons that Maya had set aside for the later pleasure of the family and subsequently forgotten. Maya stared at the dish with abhorrence. Then she picked it up and handed it back to Sheba.

"You want this kept for after dinner?" the housekeeper asked.

"No. Just throw it into the river."

About the incident at the *bagan bari*, Maya forced herself to think as little as possible. It was in the past. Whatever had been left behind there would remain there. She thought of Samir with a wrench, but then that thought too she discarded. She would always remember him as a friend and love him as such. But other than that, there was no place for him in her life—any more than there was for her in his. Now she was surrounded by new horizons. She had no intention of ever, ever looking back!

By the time the clock struck three, the time for Mr. Ludlow's arrival, she felt immeasurably brighter.

The Chief Commissioner arrived on the dot, as Maya knew he would. Dressed in riding habit, crop in hand and hat under one arm, he strode across the lawn looking very grand indeed. Involuntarily, Maya's gaze flew up to the Andersons' bedroom windows. Were they watching? She received Herbert Ludlow shyly, with a smile and a curtsey, overcome again by the realisation that this was the powerful official who controlled Christian's destiny. And consequently hers!

Not a man given to frivolous chitchat, Ludlow nevertheless paused to comment with admiration on the well-kept lawns, the very elegant mansion and the spaciousness of the paddocks in which the foals gambolled. He stopped a moment more to play with the two dogs that pranced around his boots with excited yelps, then, impatient to get down to business, he asked to be escorted to the stables.

En route, stiffly at attention, stood the grooms. As they almost swept the ground with their hands in a low salaam, Ludlow studied Abdul Mian from head to toe. "I say, he does rather remind me of my old syce up in Baluchistan! Quite a card, mind you, quite a card, but a better horse-wallah I have yet to find. Could *sniff* out a colic even before the gaseous distension started."

"Well, Abdul Mian goes one better than that," Maya informed him proudly. "He can diagnose spavine merely by a touch of his fingertips."

"Can he, by George!" The Chief Commissioner nodded in approval and Abdul Mian beamed. "Now, I've already seen your frisky feller at fairly close quarters. I'm jolly impressed, as you know, but I can hardly be expected to pay the king's ransom you will no doubt demand without personally inspecting every hock and hackle, what?"

He spoke with humour, of course, but Maya hastened to usher him into the stable house without further delay. Before entering the stall, Ludlow crossed his arms on the half gate and subjected Morning Mist to a very thorough visual examination.

"Rug him at night?"

"Yes. But only with a cotton sheet. I find it keeps the gloss in the summer coat."

"Good. Ever had nasal catarrh?"

"No."

"Ringworm, acne, the like?"

"No."

"Hmph!"

He slipped into the stall, stroked the grey's snout very gently until the animal neighed with pleasure, then went down on his knees, feeling the horse's legs and tendons with fingers not much less sensitive than Abdul Mian's. He lifted a hoof and examined it closely.

"Hoof oil?"

Maya nodded. "Every day. Right up to the coronet."

"Strapping?"

"Yes, with a straw wisp."

"Excellent. Good for the neck and quarters' muscles. Clipped in winter?"

"Well, I only got him this spring. But yes, I was intending to clip him this year once the cold weather started."

"Full clip?"

"No. He wouldn't need that. A hunter clip should be adequate."

However loquacious with young civil servants still wet behind the ears, there was no doubt that, outside his office, Herbert Ludlow was a man of remarkably few words. He now grunted and rose to his feet, still firing off staccato questions about the horse's weight, diet, bowel functions, ailments and so on, until Maya almost ran out of breath trying to keep pace with him.

He examined the horse's head, mouth, eyes, back, underbelly and flanks, occasionally peering through an eyeglass at something or other on the immaculate coat, barking comments or further questions, not missing a single aspect of the horse he had set his heart on buying. Maya could not help being amused by Ludlow's fastidiousness, but at the same time she was greatly impressed by his practical knowledge. She had been surprised that he had not brought a veterinarian with him, and now she saw why. Ludlow was more of an expert on horseflesh than any veterinarian in town; he simply did not need one. More than anything else, Maya noticed the gentleness with which he conducted his investigations, talking constantly to the animal, making friends with him. There was no doubt about his great love of horses, and this pleased her. Morning Mist would be in safe hands. He would tend him as lovingly as she had.

Ludlow finally concluded his task and stood back. "Well, no odd bone growths, parasites or fungal infections there. In fact, I must commend you on your maintenance, Miss Raventhorne. He's in very fine fettle, very fine indeed. Every word Shooter said was true and, by gad, *he* should know his onions!"

He stepped out of the stall and Abdul Mian leapt forward with a jug of warm water, a basin and a soap dish, and Rafiq followed with a fresh white towel. Ludlow scrubbed his hands with characteristic thoroughness, then asked permission to take Morning Mist for a trot and a canter. The horse was quickly saddled and, accompanied by Rafiq on Scheherazade, he galloped away down the embankment. He returned a half hour later, huffing and puffing, but quite openly delighted.

"Goes like a ruddy cavalry charger!" Ludlow declared as he dismounted. "By Jove, I'd like to get him to Newmarket for the Two Thousand Guineas. He'd soon give those toffee-nosed thoroughbreds a run for their money!"

"Then you intend to race him, do you, Mr. Ludlow?" Maya asked, hugely chuffed by his very eloquent approval.

"Just as soon as I can get Shooter in the saddle! He'll need to be put through his paces, naturally, but Shooter will have him ready for the winter season."

And then it was time for tea.

As they sipped and nibbled and Ludlow went over her written records about Morning Mist, the conversation remained centred on horses. As punctilious a sportsman as he was a civil servant, Herbert Ludlow's passion for horseflesh was second only to his devotion to the Service. He had a fund of anecdotes about his horse-racing experiences in Bombay, Bangalore and Poona, and he was an amusing raconteur. But as soon as tea was over, briskly he reverted to business.

"Well now, Miss Raventhorne, what is your decision? Are you willing to let me have this splendid specimen or am I to be returned empty-handed?"

Maya smiled at his modesty. "No. You are not to be returned empty-handed, Mr. Ludlow. I would be delighted to have you acquire Morning Mist."

"Even before you have heard my offer?" he asked with a surprised laugh. "You said you wanted a fair price for him. Well, you might not consider my offer fair!"

"Whatever you offer, Mr. Ludlow, it will be acceptable. I want a good home and a caring owner for my horse. I now know that with you he will have both." Herbert Ludlow could not have been more jubilant.

As they walked out of the stable house onto the lawn, he suddenly took particular note of one chestnut foal that was frisking about in the smaller paddock.

"Ah, a Marwari, I see! I thought you only went in for Arabs, Miss Raventhorne?"

Maya's colour heightened. "This is the only Marwari I have in my stables. He . . . came to me through a friend."

"Well, a colleague of mine in the Secretariat has been hunting frantically for a good Marwari foal. He would be most interested to have a look at yours. May I suggest that he gets in touch with you?"

Maya hesitated. This was the foal Samir had reared specially for her. As he had promised, it had been delivered shortly after her earlier visit to the orchard. "Well, I am not sure that I. . . ." She broke off, uncertain what to say.

Ludlow peered into her face. "He *is* for sale, isn't he?"

Maya thought for a long moment. Then she squared her shoulders and gave him a very direct look. "Oh yes," she said. "He is for sale. I would be pleased to show him to your colleague."

"There are many others I know," Herbert Ludlow said as they walked towards the main gate at the top of the drive where his rather splendid blue roan awaited with the syce, "who are looking for good equine bargains in which they don't get cheated. I will make a point of recommending your stables to them, Miss Raventhorne, if you will permit me to do so."

515

Touched by his thoughtfulness, she thanked him.

Buoyant at having achieved his objective, Ludlow was again his normal voluble self. As they stood by the front steps, he continued to talk, but as it happened, Maya could not pay attention to a word that he said.

She had been nervous of meeting Herbert Ludlow. She had been expecting a dry, stern, humourless man who would drive a cold, heartless bargain. Ludlow's affability and charm had come as a surprise. She now felt completely at ease in his company, not in the least intimidated. She could see that he too was greatly taken by her, impressed by her professionalism and the meticulousness with which she maintained her stables and animals.

That Christian had refused the posting with Gordon Lumsdale, Maya already knew; Christian had told her so himself the morning after the *burra khana*. She was relieved, of course, but she also had a corroding sense of guilt. After all, in a way, it was because of *her* that Christian was being denied an opportunity that he cherished. Under normal circumstances, Maya would never have dared to broach the subject with Herbert Ludlow. But the man's manner was so courteous, so informal and friendly, that she wondered—should she risk an indiscretion that might displease him and would certainly infuriate Christian?

She decided that she must.

"Please forgive me for taking such a liberty, Mr. Ludlow," she began firmly as they reached the main gate at the end of the drive, "but there is something that I would like to ask of you."

He stopped where he was. "Yes?"

"It's about . . . about Christian's . . . Mr. Pendlebury's posting."

"Oh yes? What about it?"

"Christian . . . Mr. Pendlebury told me of your great kindness to him in making him an alternative offer."

"Which alternative offer?"

"The posting with Mr. Lumsdale in the Punjab."

"Ah, that." He waited, looking at her questioningly.

"Mr. Pendlebury is a dedicated officer, Mr. Ludlow, devoted to the Service and to his duty. Wherever he is posted, he will acquit himself with honour."

"Oh, absolutely. I have not had reason to doubt it."

"He would never let you or the Service down, Mr. Ludlow." she went on earnestly. "Wherever you send him, he will do you proud—even in Champaran."

Ludlow was beginning to look slightly bewildered. "But of course. Neither Mr. Pendlebury's devotion nor his talents have ever been in question. He is considered by his tutors and by myself to be one of the best of this latest batch of competition-wallahs."

Maya filled her lungs and took the plunge. "But then, Mr. Ludlow, why relegate him to a wilderness, a district considered unworthy of even the least capable among civil servants! Is he not deserving of a better posting?"

"A better posting? Where?"

"Well, he loathes the idea of Champaran!"

"Naturally. They all do. It's a perfectly dreadful place, dreadful, but Champaran is considered useful for new recruits who need to be thrown into the deep end, so to speak." His forehead puckered and he looked puzzled. "But I was not aware that young Pendlebury felt the same about the Punjab. Why, he gave me to understand that he would sacrifice his right arm to work under Gordon Lumsdale."

It was Maya's turn to look baffled. "Yes, of course he would! But you already know the reason why he felt he could not possibly accept the post."

"The post with Gordon Lumsdale?"

"Yes. He was heartbroken at having to refuse it!"

"Refuse it?" Ludlow echoed. "But he has not refused it after all, Miss Raventhorne. I already have his acceptance in writing. Pendlebury undertakes to leave for the Punjab within the week."

22

O LIVIA LAY in her darkened room listening absently to the sounds of the monsoon outside. Against the rumbling growls of thunder that rolled across the lowering clouds from time to time, thoughts of Thomas Hungerford and all that his advent presaged for them seemed even more ominous. She had often tried to imagine what it might be like, this moment when she finally achieved the edge of the great divide between truth and conjecture. But now that the moment was upon her, she found that she was frightened, ill-prepared even after all these years of assiduous self-indoctrination. Hungerford's incoherent, fevered protestations contained in his statement revealed little; but the knowledge that they promised—despite the cautious, convoluted phraseology—was enough to chill her to her stomach. Could it be that he *did* know the truth they had sought for so long, the truth about the final days of Jai Raventhorne?

If so, did she still possess the resources to brave it?

It was just as Olivia had completed reading Hungerford's letter for the tenth time, longing to dull her racing brain with a blessed dose of laudanum, that the housekeeper entered to announce the arrival of Lord Birkhurst.

Olivia's heart somersaulted. Alistair? Here, to see *her?*

She had not seen Alistair since she had returned home from the mansion on the Esplanade. She had made daily inquiries about his progress, but he had not called, or even thought to respond to her inquiries with a written message. Knowing that a visit from her would not be welcome, she had hardened herself against the temptation to call personally, despairing of ever being able to penetrate the indomitable resentment behind which he hid himself from her. Indeed, she was beginning to wonder if she would ever be able even to see him again. Already in a fragile state of mind, Olivia felt her mouth run dry with nervous excitement even as her spirits soared. He had chosen to come here of his own accord. Oh blessed day—perhaps the tide was about to turn after all!

She quickly got out of bed and set about tidying the room to give herself time to leash her emotions. He disliked displays of sentimentality; she must steel herself against even the slightest hint of emotional self-indulgence.

"Ask him to come up," she instructed Sheba, slipping on a bright red Chinese silk kimono. "I simply do not have the energy to dress and go down."

When Alistair was ushered in a few minutes later, he found his mother seated on the couch in her private sitting room overlooking the back lawn, glancing through a periodical. He approached her with uncertain steps and made a bow. Smilingly, she waved him into a chair on the other side of the low glass table so that he sat opposite her. Although it had rained steadily since the early morning, the day was warm and humid. Yet he was dressed with customary formality in dark coat and trousers, striped shirt, cravat and pointed black boots. His left arm was still protected by a sling. It was hardly surprising that he looked flushed and hot. He had arrived by carriage, Sheba had said, but even so there was a spattering of rain droplets on his cheeks and his shirt looked damp. Olivia rose and fetched him a towel. He nodded his thanks and silently dabbed himself dry.

"I am sorry that I did not reply to your messages," he ventured in a low, sombre tone. "I was waiting for an opportunity to come and see you personally." His voice sounded strained, and as was his habit, he addressed her without meeting her eyes.

"Are you well?" Olivia asked, wondering idly about the purpose of his visit, not really caring, overjoyed simply to have him in the same room as her.

"Thank you, yes."

"And the arm? Healing satisfactorily, I hope?"

"It seems to be." He moved it back and forth, flexing and unflexing his fingers for her benefit.

She nodded, relieved that he mended well. "And the cut on your chin, the injury that did the most damage?"

"It pains only if I press down on it. The outward rawness seems to have disappeared."

"Well, I'm pleased to hear that. Given a month or two, not even the scar will remain." He nodded and there was a pause in the conversation. To fill it, Olivia asked, "Have you any recent news of your grandmother? I have written to her twice, but I don't expect a reply much earlier than the end of the month."

In mutual relief, they plunged into safely neutral talk, chatting about the old dowager, about the Farrowsham estate and about Willie Donaldson. She could tell that he was still jittery in her presence, visibly ill at ease. She pretended not to notice, chatting on brightly. He offered various comments about the weather, declaring himself surprised that the monsoons could be so ferocious. Olivia replied that it was a good thing they were. Without the annual rains, farmers would be hard put to make a living and, of course, the shortages in food, especially staples, would be horrendous. The government should think of introducing modern irrigation methods, Alistair suggested; it was foolish to depend so heavily on unpredictable rainfall. Oh yes, she agreed, it should, but then this was such a vast, ancient country and farmers were known universally to be conservative.

As Sheba came in with glasses of iced lemon sherbet, Alistair inquired after Maya ("Miss Raventhorne"). The housekeeper said that she was not at home but had gone with the two grooms to fetch some supplies from the wholesale fodder market. He expressed remorse that he would miss her, since he had looked forward to inspecting her stables. And then, having presumably said all he could think of, he slumped into silence.

It was after Sheba had left the room that he suddenly blurted out, "There is something that I have to tell you."

Olivia's heart skipped a beat. "Yes?"

"I went to see Amos in his office yesterday."

She almost stopped breathing. "Oh?"

"I wished to apologise to him." His face was sheened with perspiration and he kept his gaze firmly focussed on the tip of one boot.

"Apologise? But surely it is *Amos* who . . . ?"

"No." He winced, not letting her finish. "No! It is not Amos who was at fault. It is I." Speaking quickly and with dispassion, he related to her what had happened that night at the Pendleburys' between Amos and himself. He made no effort to spare himself.

"But why didn't you tell me all this before?" she asked when he had finished, quite bewildered. "Why didn't Amos?"

He merely lowered his flushed face.

As the full implication of Alistair's confession dawned on Olivia, she felt a sickness rise in the pit of her stomach. "It seems then that I have done Amos a terrible injustice," she said slowly, keeping from him the depth of her distress, "I had no idea. . . ."

"No, how could you have had?" he asked, stone-faced. "I should have clarified all this earlier. I'm ashamed that I didn't. But you see, I . . . couldn't. I don't know why. I'm sorry if I caused you unnecessary anguish."

She knew why, and filled with sudden compassion, she softened. He looked so miserable, so full of remorse at his transgression, and yet trembling with relief that he had finally had the courage to make the humiliating confession. Seeing how difficult it must have been for him to have said what he had, she waved a dismissive hand and quickly raised a smile. "Well, as long as it's all out in the open now." She halted a fraction and peered at him hard. "You say you went to see Amos at his office?"

"Yes."

"He . . . received you well?" She marvelled that he had received him at all!

"Well enough."

"You shook hands?"

"Yes."

Her throat tightened. "Well then, it's over. We will consider the matter closed." She frowned. "But what was the reason for that fight, Alistair? Had you had too much champagne to drink?"

"No." His cheeks reddened. "The reason was personal," he mumbled and said nothing more.

Olivia took a deep, slow breath. "You've made me very happy, Alistair," she said, trying not to let her voice quiver. "All my life I have prayed that if ever Amos and you met, you would not consider each other mortal enemies." Throwing caution aside, she risked a bold suggestion. "Who knows, perhaps some day you might even consider yourselves . . . friends?"

"That will not be possible. I sail for England tomorrow."

"Tomorrow?" she echoed stupidly, his words falling like lead in her consciousness, deadening it. "You sail tomorrow?"

"Yes. With most of the major problems taken care of, I have no more business in Calcutta."

Having got his shameful confession off his chest, he was visibly more relaxed. As he told her about the imminent sale of the Agency to Mooljee and of the mansion to the Parsi silk merchant from Shanghai, he even smiled, unaware of what he had destroyed within her. He said nothing about the plantation or the cotton mill; neither did she remember to ask. She merely sat struggling to accept the reality of his abandonment, struggling to keep from him the extent of her inner devastation.

She ran the tip of her tongue over stiff, cold lips. "Why must you leave so soon?"

"My grandmother needs me, so does the estate. Here, Donaldson will complete the formalities of the various sales and the procedures of closure, but at Farrowsham I must supervise everything myself."

"You have no plans to return?" she asked, her eyes vacant.

"No!" He took a sip of sherbert and the lines of his mouth hardened. "No," he repeated very firmly. "I will never come back. I have hated it here, *hated* it! I find everything about this country loathsome, an offence to human dignity—the obsequiousness of the natives, the arrogance of the Europeans, the pretensions of both, the abominable climate, even the terrain and the smell of their food. I can't tolerate any of it!"

She was surprised at his outburst. "Apart from all that, surely there is also much that is of value here?"

"Not for me," he said, adamant. "I could never make a good colonialist such as my grandfather was. There is a brutality inherent in colonialism that we delude ourselves into believing is civilisation. What we actually practice is a sort of social cannibalism. We garnish the skin but we gnaw away at the entrails, suck out the marrow from the bones. I cannot understand why we are here at all." He turned on her, impassioned. "I can-not understand why *you* are here, how you could remain here all these years, tolerating what they say about you!" He broke off and savaged his underlip.

"What do they say about me?" she asked, forcing herself to sound light and uncaring. "That I am a loose woman? That I lived with a man out of wedlock? That I loved and married a Eurasian?"

"That and more," he muttered, flinching at the bald enumeration. "I mean, doesn't it make you want to punch them in the noses?"

"It disturbs you?" she asked gently. "What they say about me?"

"No. *Yes!* Yes, of course it disturbs me! It's humiliating for a man to hear people talk about his mother, regardless of . . . of . . . anything else."

"Is that what the fight with those boys was about?"

His face turned a telltale scarlet as he averted it. "I . . . I only asked," he replied stiffly, "because I was curious to know why you chose to stay on here."

"I stay on here because I am compelled to." Her voice tailed away. For a moment she sat in frowning silence, then her frown lifted and she shook her head. "No, that is not true. I stay because there is nowhere else for me to go."

"Nowhere else?" He was astounded. "But you are American, you could return to America! After all, that is your home!"

"Is it? You know, sometimes I wonder."

The rain pelted down even harder outside, crashing against the window pane, dripping in through an inadvertent chink. She got up and went to adjust the slightly open casement, but before she could reach it he was there. He wrestled with it a moment, then shut it securely. He stood beside her as she remained staring out into the garden. In the onslaught of the rain and wind, the grey, metallic surface of the river looked pockmarked, the sky lying almost flat upon the earth.

At the window, Olivia pointed to the left of the lawn. "See that mango tree? I planted it from a seedling the year Maya was seven. And that there, the bush of Chinese chillies? That came from a cutting I brought from Kirtinagar. Amos planted it on his eleventh birthday. Maya buried her first tooth under the double hibiscus and made a wish. She would never tell me what it was." She turned to him, desperate for him to understand. "You see, Alistair, every memory that I cherish, everything that has had meaning in my life, is here."

"But America is your *home!*" he insisted, unable to accept her perverse attachment. "Surely, nothing can have more meaning for one than one's home?"

"Home. . . ." She swilled the word around in her mouth as if tasting a new flavour. "I've often wondered just what home is, you know. Perhaps it is an intangible, an attitude of mind, a feeling. That is all that America is for me now, a feeling, a shadow in time. An illusion, if you like. I return to it occasionally, when I am lost and lonely. I stroll through the paddocks and corrals and across the hills and the low streams, and I breathe in the reviving fragrance of Sally's doughnuts and the newly mown grass and my father's dreadful pipe tobacco." She laughed, a small, forlorn laugh that held pain such as he could never imagine. "But I never stay there long. Even in an illusion, one can become homesick for what has become a

522

habit." She noticed his expression of incomprehension. "You don't understand what I am saying, do you?"

"No."

"Well, maybe some day you will," she said with a return of the forced lightness, "when you are older. As you will recognise that places one loves are really people that one has loved there." She stared at the embankment. "This is where I first met Jai, in this very house, on those steps, there, by the river at the back." Lost in her melancholy world, she shared it with him even though she knew that for him it held no significance. "He spent his last days in this country, Alistair. This is where he remains, although I know not where. Until I can discover every detail of those last days of his life, I cannot abandon India."

Then, because the man was so much on her mind, she told him about Thomas Hungerford. As she continued to talk of a segment of her life in which her second son had played no part, he listened intently but without comment. When she had finished, he struggled for a moment between resentment and curiosity, but then could not refrain from asking a question.

"This man, Hungerford—you believe that he will give you true information?"

"I don't know. I can only hope. And pray. I know that my husband was innocent. I must stay to ensure that his innocence is publicly acknowledged. Anyway," she discarded the subject, "tell me, what are your plans for the future?"

A future without her. . . .

He told her, his enthusiasm gathering as he talked. He planned to expand the Farrowsham dairy, modernise the machinery, reinforce the herd with sturdy Herefords, experiment with fresh breeds, try a new form of crop rotation someone had told him about in Calcutta. In his enthusiasm he forgot his shyness, driven by the volatile energies of youth, fired by ambition. Each word that he said cut deep into Olivia, emphasising his distance from her, an acid reminder of the divergence of their paths, their separate lives. And then he said it was time for him to go. Pain sluiced through Olivia's body, but she did not restrain him.

"Do you think you could write to me?"

"Yes, if you like."

"This evening I will send to your house a letter for your grandmother."

"I would be happy to deliver it."

She felt hot, sharp stings at the back of her eyelids. "I did not know that you would leave so soon. I have thought of nothing to give you."

He played with his hands and stared at them hard. "Well, there is something that I would like to have. . . ."

"Anything!"

He did not reply immediately but walked to the bureau upon which rested a photograph of her in a silver frame. Arvind Singh had taken it in the Maharani's garden in Kirtinagar in the process of showing off his recent acquisition of brand new and very modern camera apparatus.

Alistair held it up shyly. "This?"

She nodded.

He frowned, his face again stern. "For my grandmother," he explained quickly. "She would like to see how you look now."

"I understand." She held on to the pieces of her heart, trying not to let them scatter. "Will we meet again?"

He did not know how to answer that and his frown deepened. "Perhaps. If you should ever happen to come to England. . . ." He stopped.

"If I should come to England, would I be welcome?"

"I don't see why not." He cleared his throat. "I have no doubt that my grandmother would be very happy to receive you."

"And you?"

"It would also be my pleasure," he responded formally.

"It was good of you to come, dear. I'm glad we have had a chance to . . . talk a little."

"Grandma would not have forgiven me if I had not!"

"And is that the only reason?"

"No. I suppose"—he swallowed and shuffled his feet—"I would have come anyway."

She longed to take him in her arms, to kiss his shy young face, to tell him that she loved him, that just as Amos was one limb, he was another. But she didn't; he would never forgive her if she did. She saw that he had thrust a hand out towards her. She took it in both of hers and, wordlessly, pressed it between her palms.

"I regret that I have not seen Miss . . . Maya. Please convey to her my best wishes."

"I will. She will be sorry to have missed you."

"Yes, I was looking forward to inspecting her stables."

"She will be back soon."

But he declined the offer. "Donaldson awaits me at the house. There are still a few loose ends to be tied." Gently, he released his hand. "Well, I suppose I ought to be going."

"Yes."

"The ship sails early tomorrow. On the first tide. One of yours."

Finally, her eyes brimmed. "Go with my blessings, my son. Remember that wherever you are, a part of me will always remain with you."

It was all that she could allow herself to say—or that he would allow her to.

He suddenly leant forward and kissed her on a cheek.

"Goodbye," he said, grabbing the photograph, "Mother."

And with that he was gone.

When Amos returned that evening, he found his mother sitting by the river. The showers had stopped; there was a coolness in the air that was pleasant and refreshing. He perched himself on the low wall that enclosed the stone steps.

"Thomas Hungerford has arrived. I will fetch him here tomorrow morning at ten."

She felt the familiar prickles of fear along her spine and sensed that he felt them too. But then she recovered and quickly said, "Alistair came to see me today."

"Oh."

"He sails tomorrow."

"I know."

"He told me . . . everything."

He looked away, wordless.

She got up, went to him and encircled him with her arms. "Forgive me, my darling, if you can."

Her ear, resting against his shoulder, picked up his indrawn breath, a faint sigh of relief. For a long moment he did not move. Then, slowly, his arms rose to circle her waist and he smiled to himself. He told her about the acquisition of the cotton mill and the plantation.

Olivia was surprised to see how small he was.

Over the thirteen years that he had haunted her imagination, he had grown to assume the dimensions of a giant, monstrous-looking, a perpetrator of evil. But in reality his stature was short, like that of an overgrown child. Even so, he walked with a stoop, the mere weight of his head too much for his shoulders. The ravages of illness were upon him everywhere. His skin hung loose about him, like an ill-fitting garment within which his body had shrunk. The face, puckered and the colour of putty, was dominated by large eyes, lifeless and immensely weary, ringed with dark grey. Blue lips, stretched over unkempt teeth, were adorned by a wisp of a moustache; there was hardly any hair on his head. He looked old and spent, although they knew that he was not yet forty. The man was an unprepossessing specimen, but there was no doubt that he was extremely sick.

Amos made the introductions. "Mother, may I present Lieutenant Thomas Hungerford, formerly of the First Madras Fusiliers."

Hungerford extended a shaky hand. Olivia did not take it. She gave him only a cursory glance, her eyes remote and unrelenting. Maya did not even look at the man. She merely sat in a corner quietly, her face expressionless. Hungerford bowed, unsteady on his feet, his gaze fixed to some spot beyond Olivia. Then he simply turned and sat down in the chair Amos indicated. Amos walked to the other end of the room and stood with an elbow resting on the mantelpiece.

No one spoke. The silence expanded. Where was one to begin?

It was Hungerford himself who broke the silence. "Before we commence, Mrs. Raventhorne, I feel there is something that I must clarify." He spoke in a strange voice, dull and without inflection, as if reciting a prepared piece. "I am aware that by remaining silent for all these years, I have caused you and your family much grief. I make no excuses for my behaviour because I have none. It would be hypocritical of me to express remorse. I feel none. I did what I did because at that time it appeared right, or rather, expedient—and, of course, profitable. Nevertheless, I seek your indulgence. . . ."

"You hanged my husband!" Olivia's voice scythed through the sentence, cutting it in half. "In this house there can be no indulgence for you, Lieutenant Hungerford! Were it not that you profess to have undeclared information about my husband, you would not be allowed to set foot within our portals. Are you not ashamed to make all these barefaced, belated admissions?"

"No, Madam. I am past shame. Indeed, past everything—as Mr. Hawkesworth must have already explained to you."

"Then why have you bothered to come forward at all? To make more profit?"

"I have no more use for profit. The sickness had already gripped my lungs by the time I received Mr. Hawkesworth's communication through Mrs. Margaret Findlater. The Findlaters and I shared a semi-detached house in Tunbridge, you see. Anyway, my decision to respond to Mr. Hawkesworth's call, like everything else in a misspent life, was motivated by self-interest. I wished to die in India. I would have come anyway. Being beyond earthly justice, I now have nothing to lose." His face contorted in a spasm. "The reason I am here, in this house, is also, regrettably, selfish. I lack the courage to face my Maker bearing the burden of knowledge that I should have shed long ago."

It was extraordinary that the man could speak without even a vestige of emotion!

"Well, at least you are honest about your motives, I'll give you that," Amos said with ill-concealed contempt. He looked questioningly at his mother and she nodded. Seating himself opposite Hungerford, he picked up the papers lying on the table beside him as a prelude to commencing the inquisition. "There is much in your statement that is confused or illegible, Lieutenant. Some parts make no sense at all."

Hungerford attempted a wan smile. "Forgive me. My fingers are not as steady as they once were. I have trouble holding a pen and I lack concentration." He nodded and folded his hands in his lap. "I am ready to answer any questions that you might wish to ask."

"Just as well, Lieutenant Hungerford," Amos remarked drily. "There is a great deal here that demands explanation. The claims you make are, frankly, outrageous, beyond the limits of credulity."

"Truth often is, Mr. Raventhorne. Incidentally, since I resigned my commission in 'fifty-seven, I prefer not to use the military designation."

"Very well. We will dispense with that. Mr. Hungerford then." He examined the document. "First of all, the initial fact that I would like to confirm is what you say here, on page one, that the deposition you and Captain Findlater made to General Havelock was not entirely accurate."

"Yes, that is correct."

"In other words, you both lied through your teeth!"

"Yes."

"If you could perpetrate such a fraud on an official deputation," Amos asked, incensed, "then what proof do we have that you will tell us the truth now? You, a man habituated to perjury in the cause of self-advancement!"

"None. Or, at least, none that I am prepared to offer at this juncture. For the time being, you will have to take my word for it." Hungerford coughed, then put a quivering hand up to his forehead. "I asked for your indulgence, Mrs. Raventhorne, because of a fact I did not include in there." He jerked a hand at the papers Amos held. "You see, we did not hang your husband."

There was a chill silence in the room. For a whole minute no one spoke. Even Maya, lost in her own silent world, gasped and snapped back to attention. Amos was the first to find a voice. "I would be obliged if you could repeat what you said, Mr. Hungerford," he said evenly.

"Neither Captain Findlater nor I hanged Jai Raventhorne. I swear that that is the truth."

"You mean, you had no *complicity* in the hanging?"

"Yes. Nor any knowledge of it. In fact, we were not even witnesses to the execution. The body was already on that tree when we arrived at the clearing."

"But then, who . . . ?"

Hungerford waved the question aside. He closed his eyes and pressed his lids down with his fingertips, as if to squeeze out an ache. "There is so much to tell," he said. "So much! Perhaps it would be easier if you would permit me to recount the sequence of events in my own words?"

Amos replaced the papers on the table. He sat back. "By all means, if that is what you prefer. But I promise you, Mr. Hungerford, if I detect one lie, even *one. . . .*"

"There will be no lies," Hungerford said wearily. "I have neither the strength nor, indeed, the ingenuity left to devise more." He tried to clear his throat but then almost choked with the effort. "First, please, some water," he gasped.

It was only after he had drunk thirstily, his throat obviously parched, that he could begin his narration. He spoke dispassionately but quickly, as if he could not to wait to unload the weight of the words bearing down inside his mouth.

"It all started," Thomas Hungerford said in a low monotone, "on the morning of seventeen July 1857. It was a Friday, I remember. As part of the Madras Fusiliers, we marched with General Havelock and his troops towards Cawnpore. In the chaos prevailing, Captain Findlater, myself and a handful of our sepoys became separated from our regiment during the night and wandered about for a while, lost. It was then that, in the very early morning, we chanced upon that clearing and the body hanging from that peepul tree. A crowd of villagers was collected around it, passive and frightened. The body was still fresh, but none of the peasants knew how it had arrived there. A miracle, Findlater called it, manna from heaven!" He gave a thin, humourless smile as he paused, his vision rooted deep in another dimension.

"There was a price on Jai Raventhorne's head," Hungerford resumed his account. "Rumours were rife about his active participation in the Bibighar massacre the previous day. Everyone had a horror tale to tell, true or imagined. No one had the will or the time for investigation. British soldiers ran amok, hanging and shooting anyone who aroused even the faintest suspicion, even many who did not. It was open season on the natives. Impromptu executioners quenched their thirst for revenge with abandon, or simply killed for sport. Hundreds were caught and strung up upon whichever branch could hold their weight, regardless of their affiliations. General Neill's orders to Major Renaud were very clear: villages in the neighbourhood to be ransacked, men to be slaughtered, sepoys without papers to be hanged, no prisoners to be taken. A signal example was to be made, no punishment to be considered too severe as retribution." He shuddered, giving a first indication of emotion. "It was horrible, horrible! There was the stench of blood and madness everywhere. No one who was not there can imagine what it was like, a landscape of hell, men transformed into devils."

It took him a few moments to recompose himself. Then he continued in the same monotone.

"The features of the dead man's face had been mutilated, but we could see that the complexion was unusually fair, the staring eyes pale. He wore only a loose jacket in the pocket of which were some personal possessions—a silver pocket watch, a penknife, some letters, one obviously a call for help from some lady besieged in the Cawnpore entrenchment. Findlater sat down to compose a report."

"Who identified my father's body?" Amos asked in a hushed voice.

"I did. I was brought up in Calcutta. I had seen Mr. Raventhorne on several occasions." He paused to stroke his chest, as if to ease the tension of his lungs. "The reward for Jai Raventhorne's capture, dead or alive, was fifty thousand rupees. As far as we could see, there appeared to be no other claimants for it. Findlater wrote in his report that it was we who had captured and executed Jai Raventhorne as he fled from the scene of the Bibighar massacre. We both signed the report and then submitted it to the military authorities together with . . . with. . . ." He gulped, the words stuck in his gullet like a fishbone.

"Together with my husband's head," Olivia supplied, seemingly nerveless. "Is that what you find difficult to say?"

Hungerford lowered his own head, unwilling to meet her eyes. "Yes. It was needed for identification. Without that we would not have qualified for the reward."

Olivia half rose from her seat, her hands clenched. "Then what you deposed before the committee, that you saw my husband flee from the scene of the Bibighar . . . that too was a falsehood?"

"Yes." He still did not raise his head. "We were never anywhere near the Bibighar."

"Oh my God! How *could* you?"

"Let him finish, Mother." Quickly, Maya came and sat beside her. "He is not yet done." Olivia caught her hand and clung to it, her nails biting into Maya's flesh with the force of her grip.

Amos cleared his throat. "Is there more that you have to tell us?"

"Yes, there is more." Hungerford leant forward to pick up the shoddy little cloth bag resting at his feet. "Forgive me, Mrs. Raventhorne, this will be a painful moment for you. But it is essential that you answer the two questions that I am about to put to you, or I will not be able to continue with my narration." From the bag he extracted a packet and a brown envelope. He unwrapped the package and held an object up to them all. It was a knee-high black leather boot, worn and cracked with age, long beyond redemption.

"Would you say that this belonged to your husband?" he asked Olivia.

Amos voiced an oath, flushing with anger. "What trick is this, man? Can you not see the torment that my mother already suffers? What is the point of this unfeeling display?"

"There is a point. I will not be able to proceed unless the question is answered."

"No. The boot is not that of my husband." Olivia settled the debate quickly, giving it only a fleeting glance.

"Are you sure, Mrs. Raventhorne?" Thomas Hungerford asked.

"Yes. This is at least two sizes too small. My husband had very large feet. I used to tease him about them. Whose boot is this, anyway?"

He did not reply. Instead, with some difficulty he struggled out of the chair and came to stand before her. From within the brown envelope, he now withdrew something else: a tuft of hair about an inch thick. He did not offer it to her but merely laid it in the palm of his hand and displayed it. "Would you say this came from your husband's head?"

Olivia stared at his palm and shook her head. "This is dark brown. My husband's hair was black." She looked at Amos, bewildered. "What is the meaning of this macabre exercise? Where did this man get these . . . these things?"

It was Hungerford who answered. "From the body that we found hanging on that tree."

"But how is that possible?" Olivia cried. "These don't belong to my husband!"

"I know." Hungerford said gently.

"Then why . . . ?" She stared at him, frightened.

Amos strode up to where Hungerford stood and grabbed him by the collar. "I forbid you to torture us any more! What the hell *is* it that you are trying to tell us?"

As he let go, Hungerford staggered back to his chair and collapsed into it. He devoured several rasping lungfuls of air, coughing and spluttering until his breathing again stabilised. He wiped his sweat-drenched forehead and closed his eyes.

"What I am trying to tell you is that the body we found hanging in that clearing was *not* that of Jai Raventhorne."

Once again, silence descended upon the room like a shroud, thick and cloying. Outside, a bird gave a shrill call; it sounded like a scream. Amos started, but Olivia sat frozen. Even her eyes remained unmoving.

"Kindly explain yourself, sir!" Amos commanded, fighting hard to sound normal. "My father's personal possessions were in the pocket of this. . . ."

"Yes. I removed them myself. They were handed over to the authorities. Presumably, they are once more in your family's possession."

Amos's laugh was one of outrage. "Are you actually asking us to believe that Findlater and you passed some unknown man off as my father? That the military authorities *accepted* your claim? Good God, man, do you really expect us to swallow all this rot? What do you take us for, fools?"

"I expect you to believe what I say because it is the truth." Hungerford said composedly. "Although he had never met or even seen Jai Raventhorne, Findlater had good reason to hate him. More than anything else, he wanted to be the one to capture him and grab the reward money. He wanted this so desperately, so obsessively, that I decided to oblige him—and myself, of course—with a calculated lie. Findlater knew that I had been brought up in Calcutta. In his eagerness, he accepted without question my identification of the body. What made the lie more plausible was the fact that the corpse hanging from the tree was indeed Eurasian." He looked directly at Olivia. "But apart from that coincidental common factor, the dead man bore no resemblance to Jai Raventhorne."

"And that one coincidental common factor was all that was needed to deceive General Havelock and the military authorities to whom you presented the head?" Amos demanded sarcastically. "I suppose none of *them* knew my father either!"

"Some did, but only by sight." Hungerford slid forward so that he was on the edge of his seat and straightened his back, possibly to be able to breathe better. He again addressed Olivia directly. "What I am about to relate now is unpleasant, even nauseating. But in a war such as this, fed on a daily diet of death and diabolic suffering, men become brutalised in the pursuit of survival." He was again briefly bitter. "However unsavoury the details, all your questions must be answered, and for this I again crave your indulgence."

He turned to face Amos. "You must remember that the features of the dead man were badly disfigured. Also, in the heat of the overhead sun, the flesh decomposed rapidly. By the time we cut off the head and carried it to Cawnpore to lay before the authorities, it had become carrion and stank to the heavens. No one at General Havelock's headquarters could or would go within a mile of it. We were simply asked to lay our grisly trophy on the ground in the compound. First it was inspected by a group of army personnel, then by Havelock himself, all with cloths held tightly over their mouths and noses. Someone removed the flap from the man's face with a long stick, saw the white skin, the pale staring eyes, and then quickly replaced the cloth. The identification could not have been swifter. Everyone was jubilant and cheered. No one remembered to make any but the most perfunctory of investigations." His mouth puckered with distaste at the memory. "You must understand that men were spent, satiated and footsore, sick with the heat and the gore. There were few energies left for procedures and paperwork, for the proprieties of justice. You see, nobody cared any more."

Amos looked anxiously at his mother. She sat in the same position, hewn out of stone. "Why did you retain the boots and that hair?" he asked.

Hungerford shrugged. "I don't know. Perhaps I foresaw even then that some day I would have a call of conscience."

"The call has come rather late, hasn't it?" Amos remarked sourly. "You could remain silent over all these years, knowing that my father was being wrongly vilified through your fabricated testimony!"

"I had no wish to be sent to prison for perjury. Besides. . . ." He stopped and stared at his feet.

"Besides?"

"Besides, Findlater knew that I had lied for my commission in the Indian Army, that I had lied my way into Sandhurst with forged papers." He paused. "You see, my mother was half Indian. I am Eurasian. I may not appear so, but I am. I was not entitled to be a British military officer."

"Findlater blackmailed you into sustaining the lies?"

Hungerford gave a thin smile. "I could blame it on Henry very conveniently, but that would not be entirely true. In the main, I lied because of greed and sustained the lies because of fear. I wanted to remain free to enjoy that reward money."

"And what if my father had caught you, what if he . . . ?"

"Your father constituted no danger to me."

"Oh? And how precisely did you deduce that?"

"For a very good reason." Hungerford took a few sips of the water at his elbow. "The body we found was that of the Eurasian butcher, one of the five executioners brought in by the Nana Sahib's henchmen to slaughter the women and children at the Bibighar."

"You said you were never *near* the Bibighar!"

"No. But I knew the man from his shop in the Cawnpore bazaar. About his complicity I learned later."

"And who killed him?" Amos persisted.

Gradually through the telling, Hungerford's manner had changed. His eyes had begun to shine as if with fever; his hands twitched and his colour was rich. It was obvious that his recollections were taking their toll, that he was not far from total exhaustion. Somehow he found the strength to continue.

"Your father."

"My *father!*"

"How else could your father's personal possessions have got into the dead man's pocket? Your father killed him to be able to establish his own 'death.' He *wanted* it to be believed that the corpse was that of Jai Raventhorne."

Nobody spoke. For the moment, their questions remained unvoiced in their befuddled eyes.

"The question I asked myself over and over again was the same that you now ask yourselves—*why?* Then finally, and quite by accident, I assure you, I stumbled across the answer." He again drank thirstily, gulping the water down in huge mouthfuls. "Your father needed an alibi. What better alibi than to be dead?"

"But an alibi for *what?*"

So far sitting silent and transfixed, Olivia jolted herself out of her trance. "What does it matter, who or why or what?" she cried. "If it was not my husband who died that day, then where was he . . . *is* he?" She started to tremble. "Oh dear Lord—can it be that he is still *alive? Is that* what you are trying to tell us?"

Hungerford shook his head. "No, Mrs. Raventhorne," he said quietly. "That is not what I am trying to tell you. I deeply regret to confirm that your husband is dead."

"How do you know?" she challenged, now so agitated that she could no longer sit. She leapt to her feet. "How can you *say* that with such confidence?"

"I can say it because. . . ." He broke off with a gasp, again struggling for breath.

"Because what, Mr. Hungerford, because *what?*" Before anyone could stop her, Olivia was upon him and had caught his arms in a viselike grip. "Because of what? *Tell me!*" She started to shake him violently, utterly out of control.

Both Maya and Amos rushed to the man's aid. "Mother, he's ill!" Maya cried. Together they prised loose her fingers and led her away from him. "He can't speak, Mother, give him a moment or two to recover."

Quickly, Amos poured him out another glass of water, but too weak to hold it for long, the ailing man took only a few sips, then lay back panting.

With a cry, Olivia sank back into her seat, appalled at herself and yet driven almost senseless with suspense. As she sat with her face buried between her palms, Maya's arms about her shoulders, Hungerford continued to cough into his handkerchief for another moment or two. When he finally finished and removed the hanky from his mouth, he was utterly spent. The cloth in his hands was soaked with blood.

Still holding the glass, Amos waited a moment, then asked quietly, "Because of what, Mr. Hungerford? How can you be so certain that my father is dead?"

Hungerford did not, perhaps could not, open his eyes. But through sheer force of will, he somehow recovered a faint voice. "Because I was with him when he died," he whispered. "It was I who buried Jai Raventhorne."

He tried to say more, but the words were drowned in another violent paroxysm of coughing. Clutching his chest, Hungerford heaved and convulsed as if he would spew out his heart. It was the most harrowing, pitiable sound imaginable, and when the coughing had subsided, there appeared to be no more breath left in his body.

"We've got to get him to bed, Mother," Amos said urgently. "Send for Dr. Humphries."

"No, no doctor," Hungerford gasped, "No doctor. Medicine. In my bag."

Amos found the bottle and poured a dose of the dark-coloured liquid into Hungerford's mouth. After a while he opened his eyes, but it was obvious that he was now beyond immediate recovery. Several of the menservants were summoned, and between them they carried the frail figure into the spare room next to the study while Sheba scurried about fetching essentials. The medicine was obviously a sedative. Soon Hungerford slipped into a sound sleep. His breathing was ragged but it was regular. There was an oddly placid expression on his face, as if in the shedding of the cross he had borne so defiantly for so long, he had, finally, found some inner peace.

In her room upstairs, Olivia collapsed onto her bed, wrung dry of all feeling. Her hand automatically reached for the bottle of laudanum on her bedside table. Dear God, how she too longed to sink into oblivion, to obliterate her mind and every thought in it! But then, with an angry shake of her head, she retracted her hand. Instead, with superhuman effort, she dragged herself to her desk and sat down to compose a letter to Arvind Singh and Kinjal:

"My dearest friends," she scribbled in a frantic rush:

> *There is news, strange news, disturbing and confusing, about Jai. I am frightened, I can understand nothing, absorb nothing. Amos and Maya are too young, too unprepared, their shoulders not yet strong enough to bear this callous burden. My own brain is stricken with paralysis, it refuses to function. I need your help. I beg of you, come as soon as you can, nay, as soon as you see this. Beloved people, please hurry!*

She entrusted the letter to Rafiq for delivery that same night. Kirtinagar was no more than five hours' ride away; he would reach it easily before dawn.

"Is he comfortable?" she asked Amos as he came into her bedroom.

"As comfortable as can be expected. The medicine he carries seems quite effective. Maya fed him some broth. He took a few mouthfuls, but now he is sleeping."

Her son wandered aimlessly about the room, awkward, not looking at her. Neither had the courage to discuss Hungerford's incredible disclosures yet; it would take time to accept and digest them, to assess their far-reaching implications. "Francis has laid supper in the dining room," he said. "Shall I send a tray up for you, or do you feel inclined to come down?"

Olivia shook her head. "I'm not hungry. Perhaps I'll ask Sheba to fetch me something later." He did not press her. "I think I will now go and sit by Mr. Hungerford."

"But he sleeps, Mother! The sedative is strong. He won't get up for hours."

"It doesn't matter. He might say something in his sleep. If he does, I want to be there to hear it."

He gave in, as drained, as taut with tension, as she. "Very well. As you wish. But please, Mother, try to get some rest yourself. Tomorrow you will need all your strength. It is not yet over."

No, it was not yet over . . . !

She loosened her hair and ran her fingers through it, braiding it into a plait. "You and Maya eat. Talk to her, Amos. The poor child is as shattered as we are." She thought fleetingly of Alistair and was filled with such an intense feeling of bereavement that, fractionally, she even forgot Thomas Hungerford. "He wanted to see her. He wanted to bid her farewell."

"Who?"

"Alistair. He said. . . ." She bit back the rest. What was the point? "Where is Maya?"

"In the stables."

"Oh?" She had lost touch with reality; she had no idea whether it was day or night. "Is it morning already?"

"No, Mother. It's half past nine in the evening."

"Is it? Then what is she doing in the stables at this hour?"

"I don't know. I think I heard Sheba say something about Christian Pendlebury."

Olivia nodded vaguely, not paying attention. Returned to her feverish state of anxiety, she was again entirely selfish, even callous, concerned only with her own need.

Oh dear God, she prayed, *don't let him die before he has told me everything!*

Maya sat by herself in the stables. She tried to dwell seriously upon what Thomas Hungerford had revealed, but her mind played truant, refusing to let her concentrate. She knew that what he had related was shocking, in some way a milestone in all their lives, especially her mother's. But during his recital her attention had wavered constantly; what her ears had carried into her consciousness had been incomprehensible and sketchy.

Even as Hungerford talked, her thoughts kept returning to what she had learnt from Herbert Ludlow. Indeed, over the past two days she had thought of little else.

When the groom came to announce Christian, it took Maya an instant to take in what he said. She quickly went into Morning Mist's stall, lifted his front leg and pretended to occupy herself in feeling for nodules of grime and mud on the inside of the pasterns, although she knew there would be none. She positioned herself so that her back was towards the stall gate. Christian stopped at the gate and leant over it above her head. Immediately, she smelt the alcohol in his breath. She crinkled her nose and turned away, maintaining a frigid silence.

"Well, how did Ludlow's visit go?" Swinging open the gate, he joined her in the stall. "Did you conclude the sale of the horse?"

"Yes." She did not look at him. Instead, she put down the hoof and, reaching behind her, unhitched a harness from a nail on the wall. Positioning herself to catch the light of the suspended lantern, she started to polish the brass pieces.

Christian perched himself on an upturned bucket nearby. "So he agreed to your price, eh?"

"Yes."

"That is surprising! The old codger isn't exactly known as a spreader of largesse. In fact, he's as tightfisted as a newborn babe." He guffawed, either unaware of her glacial mood or deliberately ignoring it. "What else did you talk about?"

"Nothing much."

He watched her silently for a moment, then made a sound of impatience. "When do you plan to finish?" he asked irritably.

"What?"

"Whatever you seem to be doing."

"Why?"

"Well, aren't you going to talk to me at all?" He seemed undaunted by her monosyllabic responses.

"Then there is still something to talk about?"

"Good heavens, what's wrong with you today? I've never known you to be quite such a sourpuss!"

She made no immediate response. Instead, she finished what she was doing, hitched the harness back on the nail and wiped her hands on her apron. Getting to her feet, she gave him a direct look.

"Can you stay a while or are you in a hurry?"

"Of course I can stay—that's why I've come, damn it!" Casting a glance behind his shoulder to make certain the grooms were not present, he tried to take her in his arms, but she evaded him.

"Not here. Let us go into my office."

He followed her in, now a trifle nervous. "Well?"

"You've accepted the position with Lumsdale. Why did you lie to me?"

He did not deny it. "Did Ludlow tell you?"

"Yes."

His face darkened. "You discussed me behind my back!"

"We didn't *discuss* you. The subject just happened to come up."

He wandered around the room, fidgety and on edge. "Well, it's true. I have accepted the position."

"Then why didn't you tell me?"

"I've come to tell you now. In fact, that's the sole purpose of my visit." He voiced a shaky laugh. "And I've come to tell you why I lied."

"I know why you lied," she said coldly. "You didn't have the courage to tell me the truth—or the heart to refuse the posting."

"Yes. That I cannot and will not deny!" He grabbed her hand and held it between both of his, refusing to let it go. "Ever since I was at school, Maya, I've wanted to do something significant in India, follow the example set by my father. Now that I am offered the opportunity, I cannot spurn it. I simply can't, it's not fair to expect me to . . . I might never be given another chance like this." His breath came in rasps; he quavered with passion.

"You've been drinking!" She twisted her hand free and looked at him with disgust.

"Just a beer or two. I felt I must celebrate."

"Celebrate!"

"Yes, celebrate!" He pulled himself together and laughed more heartily. "Celebrate that I have finally, *finally,* resolved the dilemma, my darling. I've calculated how to have my cake and eat it! Now what do you have to say about that?"

Too confounded, she had nothing to say.

He knelt at her feet and again clasped her hands in his. "The reason I lied was that I needed time to work it all out. Now I have. My precious, we need *never* be separated!"

Her eyes opened wide with surprise and in them hesitant hope flickered. "Truly Christian, truly?"

"Yes, truly." He stood up and, on the way, placed a swift kiss on her lips. She did not pull back. "You see, I *do* want you with me, all my life, every moment that I can have you."

"And I can go with you to the Punjab? On this posting?"

"Well, not *with* me, but yes, you can join me later."

"But how, Christian?" she asked in wonder. "How did you manage that? Why did you not tell me earlier?"

"I wanted to tell you when I was ready with all the answers. You see, I had to make inquiries, arrangements. I leave for Lahore at the end of the week. The first thing I plan to do when I arrive is to rent suitable accommodation. I met a chap who's just returned from Lahore. He tells me there are plenty of commodious, well-furnished bungalows to be had, with gardens and stables and outhouses. There's no dearth of hired carriages, either. He says it's a marvellously well laid out city, thanks to Henry Lawrence. When Lawrence was there, he transformed it into a paradise, with tree-lined avenues and parks—one named after him—and fine picnic spots around old tombs, monuments and splendid Moghul gardens. And there are squash and fives' courts, whirligigs, clubs, libraries, a public bandstand. . . ."

"Lahore?" Maya put a hand to her forehead and laughed, left breathless by this deluge of words. "But it is not to Lahore that you have been posted, surely? You said you would be in some God-forsaken place miles from any city!"

"Yes, but you see, there is so much to do in Lahore that you would simply have no time to be bored! You could even set up another stabling establishment, perhaps start a riding school for children. Goodness knows, there's more than enough space to be had. And then there's Simla, right round the corner, and Kashmir! Honoria Lawrence was the first white woman to go to Kashmir, did you know that?"

"But Christian, where will we be married?" Maya asked in wide-eyed bewilderment, but also starting to share in his bubbling excitement. "Not in Lahore, surely!"

"No, of *course* not! We will be married in Calcutta, naturally. Either St.

John's or the church near Kidderpore, whichever you choose. It will be a grand affair, a *grand* affair, Maya, because by then Papa will have his peerage."

"By then? When, Christian?"

"Why, as soon as my posting is over."

"And how long is that likely to be?"

"No more than a year or two. Maybe three."

"Three *years?*" She stared at him, flabbergasted. "But what do we do during those three years, Christian? I can hardly live alone in Lahore, can I?"

He laughed, very merry indeed. "You will not be alone, my precious, you will have a full staff. And then, I will be there with you."

"But what about your work at the site of the posting?"

"Well, there will be holidays and furloughs. I will have time off. Even Lumsdale can hardly expect. . . ."

"You will be with me only on holidays?"

"And then there will be long leaves—Easter, Christmas."

"You intend us to marry after three years?"

"The minute this posting is over, my darling, that very *minute!*"

Nothing in Maya's face moved; she went totally still. Then she released her hand from his and went to stand by the window. A branch of the gulmohar tree outside brushed to and from across the glass panes, making a soft, soughing sound in the vast dark outside.

"You want me to live in Lahore as your mistress."

"No!" He looked genuinely shocked. "As my beloved, my betrothed, my fiancée!"

"But not as your wife."

"You *will* be my wife, damn it, just as soon as the posting is over, I've already explained that."

"But *during* the posting I remain a mistress!"

He was terribly wounded. "I thought you loved me," he cried, aggrieved. "I thought you were prepared to spend the rest of your life with me!"

"I do, Christian, and I am," she repeated. "But. . . ."

"But what?" He started to lose his temper. "What's so different between a wife and a *future* wife, eh? We will at least be together, doesn't that count for anything?"

"It counts for something, but not everything. To be together, I will need to be a wife."

"Mine? Or just any Englishman's?"

Maya went white; she said nothing. In his addled state of mind, Christian was vaguely surprised at what he had said, but having blurted it out, he turned obstinate. "Have you any idea how much time and trouble I've taken to make this arrangement feasible?"

She started to ache. "I will not live as your mistress, Christian," she said quietly.

"Stop using that word, damn you, it offends me!"

"It offends you? And you don't consider that it offends *me?*"

"Why should it offend you?" he shouted, losing control. "After all, in your family. . . ." He stopped short of completing the sentence.

"In my family . . . what?" Her tone was dangerously level. "Don't you have the courage to say what you were about to?"

He turned sullen. "You know what I was about to say," he muttered. "I was simply going to remind you that even your mother. . . ."

Maya's hand lashed out. She slapped him across the face with all the force she could muster. He stepped back with a cry, rubbing his cheek with a palm. Then, with an angry oath, he lunged at her and grabbed her with both arms, twisting one of hers behind her back. "Don't play the sanctimonious virgin with me, Maya," he breathed against her ear. "Everyone knows what rules apply in Eurasian families." Very roughly, his mouth came down on hers and she felt his hand grope for her breasts.

"No!"

Maya wrenched her face away from his, threw off his hand, and pushed with all her strength, her palms flat against his chest. He fell backwards onto the divan and hit his head against the wall. He groaned and then lay still, with his eyes shut, breathing heavily. She could not look at him but turned away, shaking, and hugged herself tight.

Christian heaved himself up, whisked his head from side to side trying to clear away the cobwebs, blinking himself back into sobriety. He lowered his face on to his knees and moaned, his throat choked with dry little sobs.

"Oh, Christ! I shouldn't have said all that. I must be *mad!*" He made a strangled sound and looked at her, his face anguished. "Forgive me, forgive me . . . can you ever forgive me . . . ?"

Maya said nothing. Neither did she acknowledge his implorings with a look in his direction.

He started to plead with her, the words tumbling out in an incoherent spate of affirmation and apology and protestations of undying love. He repeated himself constantly, distraught and beside himself with remorse, as he begged for a smile or a word of forgiveness.

"Say something, my darling, *say* something!"

Maya remained unhearing of his pleas, unseeing of his face. Her inner eyes and ears were engrossed elsewhere. She saw a grave, a mahogany coffin, its inhabitant resplendent in bridal finery destined to be worn only in death. And she heard the sounds of laughter, full of hope and joy and future dreams, as lovers picnicked on the banks of a river. . . .

Something within her died.

Christian had stopped talking, and in the silence, Maya's vision evaporated. He had asked her something but she hadn't heard his question.

"What?"

"Why are you so quiet? What were you thinking?"

She shook her head.

"Tell me," he beseeched, "don't shut me out now, I beg of you. Say you forgive me, *say* it, my dearest!"

"Yes. I forgive you." She thought for an instant, then asked, "You truly want me to be with you in Lahore?"

He gave a gasp of delight. "Can you doubt it? Can you ever doubt that I . . . ?"

"In that case, I need time to think. I cannot make such a vital decision in a hurry."

Desperate to make amends, he agreed instantly. "Of course you must have time to think! I'm an imbecile, an insensitive *lout*, to have sprung it upon you without any warning! But I leave soon and. . . ."

"How soon?"

"Friday morning. The train goes at nine."

"Very well. You will have my answer on Thursday evening. Will that do?"

He was ecstatic. "Yes, a *thousand* times, yes! On Thursday, I shall present myself here."

"No, not here."

"Then where?"

She looked at him, waxen-faced but once again composed. "I will meet you on the Strand at seven, near the wharf."

He clasped her hands fervently and placed reverent little kisses in her palms. "You will not regret it, Maya," he whispered, his voice tight and husky. "You will never regret it."

She smiled. "No. I know I will not."

All night Olivia sat by Hungerford's bed, watching his every move, listening to the agonising breaths being dragged in with such painful effort, praying for his life—not for his sake but for her own. On the couch, unable to remain awake but unwilling to allow his mother to keep her vigil alone, Amos lay sprawled, sleeping soundly. Sheba dozed on the divan in the study next door, equally determined to be on call in case she was required during the night.

Only Maya was absent. She had sent word that Morning Mist had developed a slight cough due to the damp weather. As she sometimes did when one of her horses was ill, she would spend the night in her office.

As she sat watching Thomas Hungerford, Olivia did something she had not been able to bring herself to do for years: she went through Jai's final letters to her. On the table by her side was the small cardboard box that held the paltry possessions the military authorities had returned once the investigations were over. A penknife. A silver pocket watch. Scraps of paper, scribbled notes despatched on the run, whenever an opportunity occurred. Estelle's terrified cry for help from the entrenchment, a cry he had failed to respond to. . . .

His sketchy little messages to Olivia in Hawaii contained little information, perhaps their sole intent being to establish some sort of unspoken bond across all the oceans and landmasses that divided them. Some were dated, others not, yet others contained disjointed phrases and odd jottings. She treasured them all, satisfied with just the sight of his handwriting. *"I live like the stars,"* he wrote in one message, *"in time segments of a night at a time."* In another, one of his last, his gathering bitterness spilled over: *"I am entangled in a battle of bestiality. I fight a war without honour."* The very last note she had received from him was the most poignant, crying out with disenchantment and despair: *"Men turn into monsters and all is dark. The light extinguishes fast. Where does the tunnel end?"*

She heard a rustle of bedclothes and looked up. In the dim light of the single candle burning near the bed, she saw that Hungerford was awake, his feverish gaze fixed upon her face. She went up and put her hand on his forehead. It was still hot but his eyes flickered with something, a mere spark. She fed him a few spoonfuls of barleywater.

"I am truly sorry. . . ."

"How do you feel?" She dismissed his apology.

He nodded, too drowsy to say more.

Olivia glanced at Amos's sleeping figure; he remained dead to the world. "Can you answer one or two questions?" she whispered urgently, touching Hungerford on the shoulder. "I will not tire you, I promise."

He nodded.

"You said that you buried my husband?"

"Yes." He too spoke in a whisper.

"You were with him when he died?"

"Yes."

"The date, do you remember it?"

"Two days after Bibighar."

"After the sixteenth? The eighteenth of July?"

He nodded.

"How did he die?"

He mouthed a word: "Injured."

Her throat tightened. "If you buried him, then you must know where his grave is?"

"Yes."

"Can you take me there?" The questions came pouring out, her chest cleft with emotion.

He smiled and shook his head, then indicated with movements of his hand that he could draw her a map.

"Have you marked the spot?"

"Yes."

She swallowed to relieve the constriction in her throat. "Tell me what he said before he died, every word."

He looked at her sadly, then again shook his head.

She had no idea what he meant and almost cried out with frustration, but it was obvious that, at the moment, he would not be able to say more. The effect of the sedative was still strong on him; his eyelids started to droop. Abandoning the attempt, Olivia returned to her seat. How long would she have to wait before she had all the answers? And how would she ever know that he *was* telling the truth?

540

Perhaps he sensed what passed through her mind. A minute or two later, she heard him call. He held up a hand and pointed to his cloth bag lying in a corner.

"Medicine?" Olivia asked.

He shook his head. She picked up the bag and took it to him. He pulled open the drawstring, fumbled within and took out a rough ball of paper. He held it out to her.

"What is it?"

His nod indicated that she should open it. She did as he said; from inside the ball, she took out an object. With a swift intake of breath, she sat down heavily and stared in disbelief at what lay in the palm of her hand.

It was Jai's missing silver locket!

She took the ice-cold metal to her mouth and pressed it against her lips. "Where?" But it was no use; he was again asleep.

The rectangular pendant and chain, a cherished part of her all too brief life with Jai, had once belonged to his mother. Many years ago, on the very night that Amos was conceived, he had given it to her as a symbol of his love, his commitment. Eight years later when he sailed for India from Honolulu, she had returned it to him, slipping it around his neck with a prayer that it might protect him, keep him safe, bring him good fortune.

Good fortune—what a mockery fate had made of that forlorn hope!

At noon a royal messenger presented himself from Kirtinagar to announce the imminent arrival of His Highness, the Maharaja. A half hour later Arvind Singh arrived in his splendid carriage, escorted by outriders and a small contingent of his state cavalry. Olivia flew out into the porch to receive him and, as she did so, she found herself laughing. Oh, it was good, so *good,* to see the calm, confident, reassuring face of Arvind Singh again.

But she stopped when she saw that he had arrived alone. "Kinjal?" Olivia asked anxiously.

"Alas, she is laid low with a seasonal ailment," Arvind Singh explained as she led him into the house. "Temporarily, I hasten to add."

"Then I will not see her?" Olivia asked, numb with disappointment.

"Oh, indeed you will," he comforted her quickly. "I have been commanded not to return home unless I bring you with me."

Over cooling refreshments in the drawing room, Amos made a few initial explanations and then, over luncheon, he presented a detailed account of what Hungerford had told them the previous day. Arvind Singh listened with unwavering attention, interrupting only to ask pertinent questions. Hungerford himself still slept; it was unlikely that he would awaken before evening.

"It still sounds rather fanciful to me," Amos concluded with a dubious shrug. "He speaks with conviction, but I'm still not sure if we can believe him."

"We can believe him." Olivia roused herself to answer his question. She showed them the locket missing over so many years, the precious locket that she thought she had lost forever.

"He could have stolen it," Amos muttered, still nursing his suspicions.

"Yes, but he didn't. I know instinctively that he didn't."

"Well, for the time being, let us agree to give him the benefit of the doubt," Arvind Singh suggested. "I cannot deny that I am most curious to learn the remainder of this man's testimony." For a while, he made no further comment; he simply sat submerged in thought. Then he said, "I would like to get the dates clear in my mind. July sixteen, did you say?"

"No, July seventeen," Amos replied. "The day *after* the Bibighar massacre."

"And the suicide staged by the Nana Sahib?"

"The suicide?" Amos looked puzzled. "I'm sorry but I don't remember. What does that have to do with my father?"

"It might have everything to do with your father!"

"Oh?" Also at a loss, Olivia nevertheless rose from the luncheon table. "In that case we'd better go into the study where all the files are stocked. They're rather dusty, I'm afraid. We haven't looked at them in months."

In the study, she unlocked the special cabinet containing all the mountainous documentation of the past thirteen years. Amos removed the files, dusted them thoroughly at an open window, then riffled through them until he found what was needed. "The date of that suicide was July the seventeenth. It was a Friday." He gave the Maharaja a questioning look. "Well?"

Arvind Singh's face was still deeply thoughtful, but in his dark eyes there was a strange gleam. "It was towards the end of that month, July, that I first heard the whisper of a rumour brought to me from Bithoor by one of my most capable intelligence agents, a man of unimpeachable integrity. It was a most bizarre rumour, wilder and more outrageous than any spawned by that rebellion. Of course, I discounted it immediately."

Olivia leant across and touched his hand. "And all these years you have kept it from me?"

"Yes." He did not deny it. "It was so preposterous and unlikely that I felt it would be irresponsible to repeat it to anyone, even to you. I gave it absolutely no credence then, but now. . . ."

"Now?"

"Well, now, in the light of this man's testimony, I am wondering if I was not too hasty in my judgement."

"You are having second thoughts about what you heard?"

"Perhaps. As you know, I have always considered the official accounts of Jai's death suspect, not because of what they say, but because of what they do *not* say!" He sat back and nodded, as if in agreement with some inner thought. "I see the glimmerings of an emerging pattern, Olivia. The factors that have never before added up, perhaps will do so now."

His excitement was controlled, still held in abeyance. Even so it communicated itself to Olivia. Her voice shook. "Factors such as . . . ?"

542

He waved a hand. "Well, the general vagueness of the official accounts. I have always wondered why there is no record of where the body of that Eurasian—the man they accepted as Jai—was buried. Also, how it was that nobody at that time questioned in greater detail the highly contrived testimony of this Hungerford and Findlater. No matter how decomposed the man's head, for what reason was the identification so laughably swift and cursory? The reward of fifty thousand rupees was hardly an insignificant sum, yet these men received it within weeks of having made their claim. Why, without a thorough investigation?"

"Hungerford explained that," Amos started to say.

"I do not accept his explanations," Arvind Singh interrupted bluntly. "I am not saying that he lies. I am simply questioning the rather haphazard actions and reactions of the military authorities. Anyhow," he made an abrupt change of topic and his brows came together in a frown, "we went through that region together a year later, Olivia. Amos was only a boy then, but you, I'm sure, must still recall our own investigations very clearly."

"Yes, I do. Every detail of them."

"After going through that clearing and the village near it, we went to Bithoor. How far would you say the clearing was from the section of the river that ran through Bithoor—five miles, maybe six?"

"Yes. Something like that."

He nodded. "Well within the capacity of a man to traverse on foot over a few hours. Do you have a map of the region somewhere in those files?" he asked Amos.

"Yes, a rough one."

"It will do."

He took the paper Amos offered and smoothed it out over the table. He jabbed a point on the map. "Here, on the River Ganges, stands the village of Bithoor. On that night—the night of the much publicised suicide—this is the point that marks the steps from which the Nana Sahib set off in a boat with members of his family. The crowds were gathered here, as they watched the ritual sacrifice of their ruler to the Mother Goddess Ganga." In the recapitulation, his excitement seemed to mount. "The plan was that, as the boat reached mid-stream, all its lights would be extinguished. The Nana Sahib would then plunge into the water and drown."

Amos snorted. "Well, everyone knows now that it was a hoax staged for the benefit of General Havelock, who was waiting to attack Bithoor. The man had absolutely no intention of giving up his life!"

"True, but that was not to be known until two or three days later. In the meantime, confusion and uncertainty prevailed, especially among the British ranks. General Havelock was forced to postpone his advance on Bithoor in case the Nana Sahib's body *was* washed ashore and the death confirmed. By the time Havelock realised that it was, indeed, a hoax, the Nana Sahib had swum ashore and was miles away, regrouping his troops for another battle."

"But why do we dwell on dead history?" Olivia asked uncertainly, impatient with the Nana Sahib and his devious politics, yet well aware that Arvind Singh was not one given to idle talk. "Something that we have missed is passing through your mind, I know, but I fail to see any connection."

Arvind Singh's hand holding the roughly drawn map shook slightly. "Perhaps there isn't one," he conceded. "What passes through my mind is still conjecture, mere speculation. Hungerford may have nothing to contribute to my rather extravagant theory."

"Extravagant or not, does it lead us anywhere?"

"Maybe. We shall have to wait and see. Who knows, it might even lead us to the truth that we have sought for so long, Olivia, the truth about those vital last hours."

Sheba came in bearing the coffee salver. In the charged atmosphere of the room, the musical tinkle of the eggshell-fine porcelain cups brought with it a note of everyday reality. Hungerford, the housekeeper informed them, was now awake and feeling better. He had expressed an eagerness to recommence the interrogation as soon as he had eaten luncheon.

Olivia started to pour the coffee and Arvind Singh reminded her of the Maharani's insistence that she return with him to Kirtinagar after they had finished with Hungerford.

"You have heard much that is traumatic, Olivia," Arvind Singh said gently, "and there is still more to come. It will all have to be assimilated, sifted, discussed, and verified. There will be much to talk about, many questions to be asked and answered. In Kirtinagar, I will have the time to do so with full concentration, and you, I am certain, will be much more at peace in the company of my wife."

"Yes, you must go, Mother," Amos insisted. "It will do you good to be away for a while."

"When do you have to leave?" Olivia asked.

"Unfortunately, tonight. I have to be back in Kirtinagar by the morning. You have waited so many years for this, Olivia. You can afford the expense of another week to mull over it and regain your emotional balances. When you feel up to it, we can decide what is to be done next."

Olivia nodded, too tense and tired to argue.

About to sip his coffee, Amos paused. "Exactly what *was* that rumour that your agent brought to you from Bithoor?" he now asked curiously.

Arvind Singh stared into his cup as he stirred it with great diligence. "He reported strange whisperings within the Bithoor palace. They suggested that the Nana Sahib did *not* survive his swim in the river that night, that he never re-emerged from the water."

They were stunned. "But that is absurd!" Olivia exclaimed. "His survival is a matter of record, of *history*. He fought the British several times after that. It was not until more than a year later that he escaped into Nepal, which is where he eventually died of swamp fever."

But Arvind Singh refused to say more. "I think we must leave the rest to Hungerford—if there is a *rest*. There is every likelihood that in my conclusions I am wrong."

But, as it happened, Arvind Singh was not wrong. At least, not as far as Thomas Hungerford's testimony went.

Refreshed after his long sleep, Hungerford looked alert and considerably revived. There was still little colour in his cheeks, but his expression was bright and he breathed easier. However, because he was still running a low fever, it was decided to question him where he lay so as to save him the exertion of getting out of bed.

"Tell me, Mr. Hungerford," Arvind Singh said after a few brief preliminaries, "when was it that you resigned your commission?"

"In October of 1857."

"Captain Findlater resigned too?"

"Yes."

"May I ask why?"

"With the five thousand pound reward money between us, neither needed to work any longer, nor did we wish to."

"I see. Well, coming now to the matter of July seventeen—you say you went to the banks of the Ganges later in the day?"

"Yes. I was at the riverside in Bithoor that night."

"Why? Where was your regiment, the Madras Fusiliers?"

"We had become separated, as I explained earlier. We had no idea where they were. General Havelock had entered Cawnpore on the seventeenth, but neither Findlater nor I was in the mood to rejoin immediately. Like everyone else, we were fed up with the war, exhausted by the heat, the long marches and the constant threat of cholera. We decided to take another day off before we reported for duty. In any case, we both felt we had an adequate excuse to remain absent."

"And the Eurasian's head? What had you done with that?"

"Buried it until we could take it to where Havelock and his troops were bivouacked outside Cawnpore." He made a sound of disgust. "I tell you, we were both sick to the stomach. Findlater had gone somewhere to celebrate and get drunk. I simply wanted to get to that river and wash out the stench of death from my nostrils. Thousands had already gathered on the Bithoor side of the river to watch the *tamasha*. From where I was, I could see the landing steps quite clearly. They blazed with flaming torches and lamps."

"You bathed in the river?"

"Yes. Not where the crowds were, but about a mile upstream. After that I lay down in the tall grasses and slept for a while. When I wakened, it was to loud chanting from the crowds. I saw the Nana Sahib's boat leave the steps and glide away mid-stream. It had plenty of lights on it, candles, I think. I didn't believe the old coot would drown himself any more than anyone else did, but I was curious to see what would happen."

"You saw the lights extinguish on the boat?"

"Yes. I also heard the splash of his plunge into the water, followed by a muted rippling, as if someone was swimming very cautiously and quietly. The sounds seemed to be approaching the shore where I happened to be.

Nervous of discovery, I moved further down the bank. I was sure he would see me, but then. . . ."

"You saw no one else?"

"Not then, later."

"Who?"

"I'm coming to that."

"All right. Then?"

"Well then, quite suddenly, the rhythm and quality of the swimming strokes changed. They became louder, irregular, with much splashing and thrashing about. It sounded to me as if someone was scuffling in the water. My first thought was that the man was being attacked by a crocodile, but there were no screams for help as one might consider natural. And then I distinguished two human voices, each distinct from the other. No words were said but there were plenty of grunts, groans, curses, even a half scream that was quickly throttled. After that, nothing. Just silence. At least for a while."

Small droplets of sweat had started to collect on Hungerford's forehead. He wiped them off with a corner of the sheet and Olivia signalled for the punka-wallah to redouble his efforts. The speed of the cloth fan immediately accelerated.

"But you *saw* nothing? Heard nothing more?"

Hungerford gulped and nodded. "I did, a few minutes later. A figure heaved itself out of the water not far from me, then dragged up another. This I saw very clearly—they were no more than ten yards away from where I lay hidden. Not having the faintest idea what was happening, I remained very still, hardly breathing, frightened out of my wits in case my horse, grazing somewhere in the forest, suddenly returned and I was exposed." In reliving the fear released by his memories, he had turned even paler. "By now it was obvious that one of the two men was dead, killed by the other, and that it was part of a plan."

"How could you tell that?"

"The man who survived had come prepared. He now uncoiled a long rope from his waist, tying one end around the dead man's neck and wrapping the other tightly round a large rock. His movements were confident, but there was something odd about them. I saw that he was using only one leg, dragging the other behind him as if it were dead weight. I could hear it scraping against the rough grass. It was obvious that he was in pain, for as he laboured he occasionally groaned. The wounds that he had received during that skirmish in the river were evidently severe. Nevertheless, I had the feeling that whatever he did had been previously thought out. Having secured both ends of the rope, he rolled the body to the edge of the water, leaned himself against a tree trunk for support and, with incredible effort, lifted the corpse as far as he could. Then with a last mighty heave, he tossed it into the river, doing the same with the stone.

"In spite of his injuries," Hungerford went on, "he worked remarkably fast. The entire exercise could not have taken more than a few minutes. Then, without looking either left or right, he turned and loped off into the forest. He passed so close by where I lay that I could actually hear his breathing. It was harsh and irregular, as if he took in air with difficulty."

"You saw the man's face as he passed?"

"Yes."

There was a long silence. Olivia's hands clutched at each other and her knuckles gleamed white. Amos got up and went to stand by the window. Only Arvind Singh appeared composed, in control of both the situation and himself.

"Was it the face of Jai Raventhorne?" he asked.

"Yes. The man was Jai Raventhorne."

"*Ah!*"

The sound of the sharply inhaled breath came from Arvind Singh. There was not a whisper from anyone else. Sometime during the recital, the door had opened and, like a shadow, Maya had slipped into the room and positioned herself in a far corner. No one was aware of her presence, or indeed noticed how long she had been there. Having answered the question, Hungerford had laid his head back against the bank of pillows supporting his shoulders. His face again looked ashen.

"Do you want to stop?" Arvind Singh asked kindly. "Perhaps we could continue later?"

Hungerford jerked upright again and shook his head violently. "No!" he gasped. "I have to say it all now, *now* while it is fresh before my eyes."

"Very well. What did you do next?"

"I followed him into the forest. Now I was without fear. I knew that he was badly wounded. Even though his footfalls were very soft, they were unsteady and his gait was awkward, like that of a man with only one leg. We must have gone about half a mile into the trees when the sounds came to a halt. I heard a soft moan and then a crash. I realised that his strength had given way, that he had fallen. I finally found him lying in between the roots of a banyan tree. He was barely conscious. His face, which I touched, was burning hot. His breath came in spurts and irregularly. I could see that. . . ." He broke off and glanced uncertainly at Olivia.

"Go on," she said, dry-eyed and nerveless, every emotion suppressed. "Don't stop. I want to hear everything."

He continued: "I could see that he had not long to live. His left leg had been almost severed from below the knee, obviously from a sword slash. The wound was fairly recent, for it still bled. I had a scarf in my pocket. I tore it and tried to staunch the bleeding as best I could, but it was hopeless."

"Did he say anything?"

"No, he could not. He did not have even the energy left for delirium."

"What did you do?"

"There was not much that I *could* do, so I gave him a tot of rough firewater from a flask that I carried. At first he could barely swallow, but then, as it went down, he revived marginally. He opened his eyes. I could tell because I could see them glisten in the dark. I remembered then that he had strange, pearly eyes, unlike any that I had seen. 'I am not an enemy,' I said. 'And I know who you are. Is there anything that I can do for you?' He understood, because he nodded, fumbled for my hand, and carried it to that locket he wore round his neck. He clasped the pendant, took it to his lips and kissed it. Then, with a long sigh, almost of deliverance, he lay back. It was then, in that instant, that the life passed out of him. He died with one hand in mine. In the other he still clasped the pendant."

For the first time, Hungerford's face showed emotion. "For whatever the opinion of this miserable creature might be worth," he said bitterly, "I consider that Jai Raventhorne died as he lived, with courage, with dignity, and like a *man*." The words clogged his throat; he averted his face to the wall.

"You buried him that night?" Arvind Singh asked after a hushed silence.

"Yes." He heaved a sigh, moved despite his determination not to be. "I buried him that night under that banyan, in a grave deep enough to be safe from predators. I carved the date and his initials on the main trunk of the tree. They were roughly cut because I had to work fast. Perhaps they are still there."

The atmosphere in the room pulsated with feeling. It seemed that every corner of it held evidence of a long-awaited living presence resurrected from the past. Olivia sat unmoving, as if transformed into stone.

It was Amos who broke the dense silence with a question. "You just happened to carry a shovel with you?"

"Oh yes." Hungerford took no cognisance of the sarcasm as his thin lips spread in a humourless smile. "A shovel was part of our standard equipment. You never knew when you would need it."

Hungerford's revocations had been so graphic that, unable to dwell on them yet, Olivia closed her eyes and tried to squeeze out from behind her lids the hideous visions. In her anguish, her thoughts turned to trivialities. With some remote part of her brain she noted that Maya was no longer in the room, that once again she had slipped away without being noticed.

But then, as Arvind Singh posed another question, she forgot about Maya. "Could you identify the other man, the man who was killed?" he asked.

"No. I never saw his face," Hungerford replied. "But I am convinced that it was the Nana Sahib of Bithoor."

Olivia got up and, without a word, fled from the room.

She ran all the way upstairs, locked her bedroom door behind her, and then sat down and wept. Quietly, in the merciful privacy of the anonymous dark, she revived her long-dormant grief; one by one, she allowed each of her inner wounds to reopen and suppurate. She was unconcerned with politics, unaffected by Hungerford's shocking final pronouncement. All she could think of was Jai's last, lonely night in that forest as his breath ebbed. That he had not spoken her name did not matter; she knew that in those last moments he thought of her, saw her face, held her to his heart. She had not been destined to share fully in his turbulent life. It was yet another irony of her perverse fate that she should have been denied a part also in his death. Yet she was grateful that he had not died alone, that there had been someone by his side to hold his hand, to help ease the life gently out of his broken body, and then to consign him to the bosom of that soil that he had loved with such passion. Thomas Hungerford's misdemeanours had been many, his long silence unforgivable and cruel. But for his final mercies, for having shared with her his vision of Jai's last night on earth, she would forever remain in his debt.

Later, when the sharpness of the agony had receded, the cutting edges of pain dulled and the wellsprings of sorrow depleted, Olivia bathed in cold water, changed her clothes and started to prepare for her journey to Kirtinagar. When she was finally ready to go down again, all that remained within her was an aching emptiness. But that she was used to; that she had already lived with for many years.

Arvind Singh awaited on the verandah, ready to leave. She hugged Amos for an instant, overcome by love, by relief that he had been by her side, giving her support. "Take care of Mr. Hungerford. He needs help." Amos nodded. Olivia looked around. "Where is Maya? Still in the stables?"

"No," Amos said. "Apparently she has gone out on an errand. She left word that she will be late for dinner."

"On an errand? Where?"

Amos waved a weary hand. "Who can ever tell with that girl? Anyhow, she's taken Abdul Mian with her. At least she is not unescorted."

It was as she was about to step into the Maharaja's carriage, standing beneath the front porch, that Olivia voiced a thought.

"Nothing that Mr. Hungerford has told us proves Jai innocent of the Bibighar massacre," she said, crippled with bitterness. "He still has no alibi for July the sixteenth."

It was a thought common in all their minds. But no one had had the courage to actually voice it.

The Strand was almost deserted. A fine mist of rain had started to fall and the street shone with puddles left from an earlier downpour. Holding the reins of Scheherazade in one hand, Maya stood beneath a makeshift shelter by the side of the road. It was just a sheet of tin propped up on bricks, with heavy stones placed on the roof to hold it down in the gusty winds. The shelter had probably been left behind by the Public Works Department. Like all roads during the rains, the Strand too was in constant need of repair.

Maya stood well concealed by the structure—not that there was any need for concealment. There was hardly anyone about at seven in the evening and in such inhospitable weather. She was dressed in her riding britches, with a peaked cap on her head and a cape thrown over her shoulders as protection from the rain. She was alone. Abdul Mian had been left behind at a tea shop in the bazaar with instructions to await her return.

The sound of galloping hooves came from a distance. Maya peered into the gloom and, gradually, a moving figure emerged out of it. She stepped into the middle of the road. As the horseman approached, she waved. He reined sharply and the horse reared up on its hind legs and neighed in protest.

"What an abysmal night and venue for a rendezvous," Christian remarked as he dismounted, much put out. He quickly entered the shelter, bending over almost double, and Maya followed him inside. If it was gloomy outside, it was worse inside the shelter. They could barely see each other's faces.

"I'm sorry, I thought it would be more convenient to meet here," Maya said.

"Convenient? Ye gods!" The whites of his eyes glistened as he rolled his eyes heavenwards. "Anyway, I don't have much time to spare. I haven't finished packing my traps yet. And Karamat's accounts are in a damned mess, as always. I still have to sort them all out before I can give him his dues."

"This won't take long." She felt rather than saw his hand fumble for hers in the dark, and stepped out of its path.

"Well?" he asked, still disgruntled but also tight with suspense. "You said you would tell me of your decision tonight?"

"Yes."

"You have arrived at it?"

"Yes. I have decided to accept your offer."

His breath caught, all his bad humour forgotten. He could scarcely believe his ears. "You will join me later in Lahore?"

"Yes."

"And you approve of the . . . the, ah, *arrangement* that I had suggested?"

"Yes.

"No more reservations or doubts?"

"None."

"And you do trust me, don't you? You do believe that I love you with all my heart, that I want to marry you as soon as the posting is over?"

"Yes. I believe you."

He hesitated, suddenly unsure, fumbling to use the right words. "You have . . . spoken to your mother?"

"She has gone away for a few days. I will speak to her when she returns."

"And if she objects?"

"Why should she? After all, she too was a mistress once!"

In the dark he felt the heat climb up his face as he flushed. "I wish you wouldn't. . . ." He stopped, remembering with a pang that this was the last he would see of her for some time. "And Amos?"

"Amos? No, I haven't spoken to Amos, nor intend to. After all, it's my life, not his."

He again searched for her face, embarrassed and disoriented, feeling a fool in this bizarre setting. Not finding it, he shivered. "Did we *have* to meet in this God-forsaken hole? Couldn't we have had this conversation elsewhere? Maybe even at home?"

She refreshed her lungs with a breath. "The reason I chose this place is because it is close to where we must go now."

"We're going somewhere else? Now? Good grief, Maya, you *know* how pressed I am!"

"I know. You will return to the chummery in good time to finish your packing and do your accounts." She touched his hand. "Come."

"Where are we headed, anyway?"

"Just a short way up the river bank."

"Up the river bank? In the pitch dark?"

"I know the place, Christian. Trust me."

He peered up at the sky. "And what about the rain? We'll be drenched!"

"It's only a drizzle. It won't do any harm."

There was something about the manner in which she inflected her words, something about the flat tone in which she spoke, that puzzled him. He tried to discern her mood and could not. She seemed strangely somnolent, drugged and far away, as if she walked and talked from within a deep sleep.

"Are you all right, Maya?" he asked, faintly alarmed. "You sound so . . . unlike yourself!"

"Do I? Yes, I am all right. Come on, we must hurry."

"Very well then." He shrugged and gave a resigned laugh, too satisfied at the moment to want to argue, convinced that she was playing some childish game solely to tease him. "Lead on, Macduff!" he called out gaily.

She vaulted into the saddle and set off at a canter. Christian followed, spurring his horse to keep pace with hers. As he came alongside Scheherazade, he asked, "Now can you tell me where we're supposed to be going?"

"Yes. There is someone that I would like you to meet."

"At this ridiculous hour?"

"Yes."

"Well, all right." He gave an exaggerated groan. "Who is it, anyway? I presume he *does* have a name?"

"Yes. His name is Montague."

CHAPTER

23

S HE ISN'T HERE—her bed has not been slept in!"
Amos regarded Sheba's worried face with irritation. "Who on earth are you talking about, Mother? You know very well that Mother's. . . ."

"No, missy mem, your *sister*. I can't find her anywhere!"

"Maya? Well, she's probably still out riding." He brushed the housekeeper off with a wave. "There's no need to make such a fuss, Sheba. Now run along, there's a good girl. Can't you see I'm busy?" He relaid his head back on the cushion propped up in the chair, closed his eyes and gestured for the ceremonies to commence.

Amos had been waiting all week for the luxury of a professional shave and massage. The barber, an expert in the art of *champi*, scalp massage, had been summoned all the way from Burra Bazaar with instructions not to accept any other customers for the morning. Knowing from experience the size of the reward he was likely to receive from his young and generous customer, the barber—now standing poised for action on the Raventhornes' back verandah—had been only too happy to comply. At Amos's signal, he tucked the white sheet neatly under the waiting chin, sharpened his tools against each other with the flourishing grace of a dancer, and joyously leapt into action. With a sigh of pure rapture, Amos emptied his mind of all other considerations and abandoned himself to the enjoyment of his long-awaited tonsorial pleasure.

The past forty-eight hours had exacted their toll of him as ruthlessly as they had of his mother. Wound up like a tightly coiled spring, he had been unable to sleep last night. Instead, he had sat up for hours composing Hungerford's volatile revelations into a chronological account of presentable lucidity and comprehensiveness. And in the recapitulation, he had lived through his father's nightmare all over again, haunted by images and spectres resuscitated from a fevered childhood imagination. Fearful to close his eyes even for a moment, he had started his day's work at the first flicker of dawn light. Now, with most of his immediate priorities taken care of, he was mentally and physically sucked dry of energy, relieved that his mother, at least, was away for a much needed rest in the good, caring hands of friends.

Summoned at the crack of dawn, Ranjan Moitra had arrived at the Raventhorne house within the hour. Without giving the poor man time to recover from his overwhelming sense of shock at what the statement contained, Amos had sent him off to rouse the Trident lawyer in whose presence Hungerford had signed and certified the veracity of his written testimony. Later, Hari Babu had been despatched to Kirtinagar to deliver the precious document to Arvind Singh. That done, Moitra had taken Hungerford to a hospital run by Jesuits for whatever medical succour they could provide for his immediate relief. Directly from there—in accordance with Hungerford's own wishes—the ailing man would be escorted to Burdwan, where his aged mother still lived. Because Hungerford was now penniless, Amos had provided him with a sizeable sum for his immediate needs and arranged for a subsequent monthly stipend to take care of his medical and other expenses for whatever span of life remained to him. Before he left, Hungerford had requested one further favour: after his death his mother, blind and totally helpless, should continue to receive the monthly stipend until the end of her days. Amos had agreed only too readily.

"I have denied her all these years because she is half Indian," Hungerford had muttered bitterly as he left for the Jesuit hospital. "But, ironically, it is to her bosom that I return to die because I have no one else to turn to."

"Tell me," Amos suddenly asked as he helped Hungerford into the carriage and adjusted a pillow behind his head, "why did Captain Findlater hate my father?"

"Eh?"

"You mentioned in your verbal testimony that Findlater hated my father, that he was obsessed by him. I want to know why."

"Ah." Looking minimally discomfitted, Hungerford shrugged. "Because of the . . . Slocum girl."

Amos flushed and remained silent.

"Years ago—long before you were born, I reckon—your father had a, well, an *involvement* with the sister of Barnabus Slocum, the police chief at the time. They had gone away together for a few days and then, well. . . ."

"What did all that have to do with Findlater?" Amos cut in shortly.

"Henry was engaged to the girl. She had come out from England to marry him. After your father had . . . been with her, she broke off her engagement to Henry. Six months later, rejected by your father, she killed herself." He made a rueful face. "Henry never forgave your father. He swore that one day he would get even with him."

"Findlater told you all this?"

"No, my friend Samuels. He was a drummer with the Sixth Native Infantry, also a Eurasian and a Calcutta man. He died of cholera during the march to Cawnpore."

Reminder of the old scandal had tarnished some of Amos's sense of deliverance at Hungerford's eventual departure, but with a determined set of his chin, he decided to put all that behind him; there were far more urgent matters claiming a right to his attention. First and foremost, he had a moral obligation to see Kyle at the earliest possible opportunity. After all, it was only through Kyle's assiduous efforts that Thomas Hungerford had been found and Jai Raventhorne's last few hours of life made available to his family. Now, as the barber's expert fingers revived Amos's energies, dancing and prancing and pinching and pressing on his scalp, his temples again throbbed with the welcome gush of blood, forcing his tensions to uncoil and his limbs to loosen. As his mood lightened, he directed his thoughts down more pleasant avenues, lingering over other unexpected aspects of his life.

He thought about the cotton mill.

Over these past days, he had not had much time to dwell upon the astonishing windfall. Now, at leisure, he allowed himself the luxury of again savouring the extraordinary turn of events that had precipitated that windfall. Inevitably, he also thought about Alistair Birkhurst, about his curious compulsions and deprivations, and for the first time, he thought about him without anger. He would rename the mill after his father, Amos decided; that was only in the fitness of things, and it would certainly please his mother. Alistair had been as good as his word about the plantation, no less a windfall than the mill. Once the project was formally announced, the community would be jubilant at its acquisition by the Derozio Society at such a reasonable cost. There would be no dearth of willing minds and helping hands to urge the dream of a settlement forward into triumphant reality. His own participation in it, however, would have to wait. There were still far too many familial obligations remaining for him to fulfil before he could involve himself either in active work for the township or, indeed, in the massive endeavour of setting the wheels of the cotton mill spinning again.

First and foremost, he would have to escort his mother and sister to Cawnpore. A search for his father's obscure grave would have to be mounted, and honour done to it according to his mother's wishes. It would be a traumatic pilgrimage for them, one that would take further toll of their depleted emotional resources. But, nevertheless, it had to be undertaken and borne with endurance.

He had no idea yet how Arvind Singh planned to use Thomas Hungerford's testimony, and for what end. No doubt there would be more discussions, more heated debate, more friction, with the Viceroy's Secretariat, with the military authorities, with Whitehall and with bureaucrats. Just thinking about the complexities and legal complications that very possibly lay ahead, Amos's heart started to sink, but, grimly, he refused to let it. Instead, he gritted his teeth and resolutely diverted his attention into other, more pleasurable channels—channels that set his flagging spirits soaring again.

He allowed his thoughts to waft gently in the direction of Rose Pickford. . . .

"Abdul Mian has something to say to you."

Sheba's voice, quivering and shrill, cut into Amos's reverie and jerked him out if it. His eyes flew open.

Standing at the foot of the verandah steps, Abdul Mian salaamed. "I went to buy fodder before going into the stables this morning. When I returned, my son told me Scheherazade was not in her stall. She had not been in all night. Do you know where missy mem might have taken her?"

A frown shadowed Amos's face, replacing the initial look of renewed irritation. "Were you not also with my sister when she went out last night?"

"Yes. But missy mem left me at the tea shop at the corner of Dharamtala and asked me to wait for her to return."

"Well?"

"She did not return."

"And you did, *without* her?"

"I presumed she had forgotten about me and come home on her own. She has sometimes done that before."

"Where did she go after she left you?"

"To the Strand."

"At that time of the evening? *Alone?*"

"No, not alone." The groom lowered his eyes. "I received the impression that the missy mem had made an arrangement to meet someone near the jetty."

Amos's lips set hard; he had no need to ask whom.

"Something's been eating away at my little girl over these past days!" Sheba burst out, on the verge of tears. "You've all been too preoccupied to notice, but I haven't. She's been miserable, *miserable,* ever since she went to that orchard, ever since the Ludlow man came to buy her horse that afternoon. And that night when Master Christian came, well, they talked and argued for a very long while inside the stables, didn't they, Abdul?"

The groom nodded.

Sheba started to cry. "She's not been herself at all," she sobbed. "Your mother knew, but nobody did anything!"

The housekeeper's agitation communicated itself to Amos, and he felt the first prickles of alarm. "She can't have vanished into thin air," he muttered. "She must be somewhere in the house."

With a wistful sigh, he abandoned the rest of the barber's soothing manipulations and paid him off. Then, ordering the servants to fan out in different directions, and with Sheba in tow, he set off for another thorough search of the main premises and the outhouses.

Maya was nowhere to be found.

Amos and the housekeeper returned to the verandah, silent and dismayed, the same unspoken thought in both their minds: The foolish, reckless girl had gone and *eloped* with Christian Pendlebury!

It was not long before they discovered that the reality could not have been more different. Kyle came cantering down the embankment and up the back lawn on his handsome midnight, trailing Scheherazade behind him. He jumped off the saddle, handed the reins over to a surprised Abdul Mian, then vaulted up the steps into the verandah and flopped down heavily in a chair. His hair was spiked with moisture, his face scored with lines of tiredness and sweat.

"Kyle!" Amos was enormously relieved to see him. "I wanted to come to the press earlier, but Hungerford. . . ."

"Hungerford will have to wait." Kyle cut him short, his manner brusque. Indeed, he looked altogether strange. "Something happened last night, something unplanned, something unspeakably tragic. But first, is Maya home?"

"No. But how . . . ?"

"I'll tell you in a minute. Are you certain?"

Amos nodded, now seriously alarmed. "We've searched the house twice." His lips tightened. "Do you consider that she could have . . . run away with Pendlebury?"

The unwitting irony of the question brought an acid smile to Kyle's mouth. "No, my friend. If only it were that simple!"

Without further ado, he told him about Maya's visit to the tunnel the night before with Christian.

"Maya took him there?" Amos asked blankly, utterly bewildered.

"Yes. Christian saw everything, knows everything." Kyle closed his immensely weary, red-streaked eyes. "He saw Montague. . . ."

"*Oh Christ!*" Amos held his head in his hands. "But why did she do it, Kyle? I had no idea that she even knew!"

"She knew because, in my great wisdom, I told her," Kyle said bitterly. "Or, at least, part of it. The rest she obviously deduced for herself—or picked up from something Joycie might have said. Why did she do it? After what I saw last night, it wasn't too difficult to guess. Anyway, that at the moment is not important. The question now is, if she didn't return home last night, where is she? I would have come earlier, but I only noticed her damned horse a half hour ago grazing on the embankment across from the press. My initial reaction was that for some eccentric reason of her own, she had decided to return home on foot."

"Well, she didn't."

They stared at each other in an instant of shared dread.

"Come on." Kyle leapt to his feet. "She's got to be found. You have no idea of the state of mind she was in when she left the tunnel."

Amos laid a restraining hand on his arm. "You don't think there is a chance, however slender, that she might be with Christian after all?" he asked hopefully, still understanding far less than Kyle did.

Kyle spun around, grim-faced. "There's no time to tell you everything now, but let me just tell you this—last night, after she told Christian about Montague, he simply went mad. He tried to kill her. Had my mother and I had not been there to stop him, he would have." His smile was tight as he shook his head vigorously. "No, my friend, I doubt very much if your sister is with Christian Pendlebury—or ever will be again!" He strode back into the garden where the midnight grazed tethered to a tree stump, and paused with one foot in the stirrup. "Where do you suggest I look first?"

Amos gulped, his mind momentarily paralysed, his stomach heaving with panic as he grappled with all the ghastly probabilities. "Along the embankments and in some of the forests to the south. I'll go north, to Shibpore. She often went to the banyan forest." He put a shaking hand to his forehead. "I . . . just can't seem to think. . . ."

"If she it not found by the end of the day, we will have no choice but to inform Clarence Twining."

Amos shivered. "You say Christian tried to *kill* her. Supposing he's gone after her, managed to . . . to . . . ?"

"No," Kyle said with with a hard smile. "Christian has not gone after your sister. In all probability, at this precise moment, he is with his father."

But as it happened, Kyle was wrong. Christian was not with his father.

Just as Kyle left to go in one direction and Cavalcade was being saddled for Amos to go in another, Francis announced an entirely unexpected visitor: Lady Constance Pendlebury.

"Good morning, Mr. Raventhorne." Before Amos could even react to the announcement, Lady Pendlebury swept into the drawing room behind the bearer. "You must forgive me for barging in like this without any intimation, but I wonder if I might have a moment or two with your mother?" She spoke formally, each word tipped with ice. There was not even a hint of a smile on her face.

Amos swallowed his astonishment and quickly rearranged his features into a similarly formal mould. "I regret that my mother is not at home, Lady Pendlebury. She is away from station for a week."

"I see." She brushed off his offer of a seat and remained standing. "And your sister?"

"My sister?" Amos's breath shortened. "My sister is . . . out."

"Yes," she said softly, her cold, crescent smile sly and full of meaning. "I'm sure she is!"

Unable to divine the drift of this unforeseen conversation, Amos cooled his tone further in order to hide his consternation. "My sister rides every morning," he informed her curtly. "Can I be of any assistance?"

"Perhaps." She changed her mind and sat down, draping her arms over the two side rests of the upholstered chair. "I don't know if you are aware of it, Mr. Raventhorne, but Christian was supposed to leave for the Punjab today to resume his posting."

"Punjab? I was under the impression that he had been posted to Champaran."

"Well, he had, but a vacancy occurred with Gordon Lumsdale in the Punjab, which he opted to accept. Anyway, he was due to catch the train this morning, but he never arrived at the railway station. Mr. Ludlow is extremely vexed and I have been beside myself with worry. My son was supposed to spend his last night in Calcutta with us. He never came. Nor is he at the chummery where his bearer awaits with his traps. Mr. Illingworth and Mr. Prescott have not seen him since yesterday evening. They have no idea where he might have gone."

Amos felt his tongue thicken and stick to his palate. "Well, he certainly isn't here, Lady Pendlebury."

"And neither is your sister!"

Amos reddened at the innuendo. "I have no idea what your ladyship might mean. . . ."

"Haven't you, Mr. Raventhorne?" she interposed, her eyes hard and furious. "From my son's bearer I have come to learn that last night your sister had a rendezvous with my son on the Strand. They were due to meet at seven o'clock near the wharf, Karamat says. Christian had told him that he would return half an hour later. Well, he did not. Nor has he been seen since and neither, I strongly suspect, has your sister. I can only presume the obvious, Mr. Raventhorne. Somehow, your sister has prevailed upon my son to abandon his career and agree to an elopement!" In her rage, she could barely enunciate clearly. "I have absolutely no doubt that they have gone away together!"

The unwitting humour of her contention almost made Amos laugh out aloud, but, of course, he did not. "That, if I may say so, is utter rot," he said calmly, feeling an involuntary stab of pity for the woman in her ignorance. "My sister has no need to. . . ."

"My son wanted this posting more than anything else in his life, Mr. Raventhorne," Constance Pendlebury continued, again cutting him short. "He is hardly likely to have thrown it away with such cavalier disregard. Unless the alternative inducement offered was even more irresistible!"

"My sister is out riding," Amos persisted doggedly, starting to feel helpless but refusing to be browbeaten. "With all due respect, Lady Pendlebury, I assure you that your assumptions could not be further from the truth."

"Do you really, Mr. Raventhorne?" She recomposed herself with a visible effort and regarded him coolly. Only her quivering lips gave indication of the depth of her emotion. "My son is weak, Mr. Raventhorne, and your sister is wilful, tenacious and endowed with considerable charms that she has learned to use well. As such, it is an uneven, pernicious battle that my innocent boy has been waging all these months." She rose out of the chair and pulled herself up to her full height. "However, if your family's stance is to ignore the reality, so be it. But I warn you, Mr. Raventhorne—*if* your sister has indeed induced my poor son to flout public opinion and prevailing norms of civilised behaviour with this unspeakable act, then the consequences for her, and for your family, will not be palatable." She turned to leave. "This evening I hold my first soirée of the season. . . ."

"Soirée . . . ?" Amos echoed blankly.

558

She made an impatient gesture. "Yes. With supper for a select few. I can hardly cancel it at this eleventh hour without causing unsavoury speculation. Also, today my husband entertains an important delegation from Turkey, so I have fobbed him off with excuses on my son's behalf. The last thing I want is to instigate a public crisis, but"—her voice broke a little at the hideous prospect of a scandal—"if there is no news of my son or your sister by tomorrow morning, I intend to inform my husband and see that he takes appropriate action, regardless of the consequences. Naturally, Clarence Twining will have to be informed and I will *personally* ensure that, when he catches her, he will put your immoral sister where she rightfully belongs—behind bars!"

Leaving Amos with his mouth agape and his eyes livid, Constance Pendlebury turned on a heel and swept out of the room.

It was an inexplicable instinct that eventually led Kyle to the Lower Circular Road Cemetery. Sparked by some mysterious sixth sense, he suddenly had an overwhelming conviction that, given her strange state of mental dislocation, this was where he would find Maya Raventhorne.

He was not disappointed.

She sat on a grave overlain with a marble slab, her head lowered, her unkempt hair hanging long and loose, like a curtain devised for protection from the painful realities beyond. Her body was still; only her hands moved—her fingers flying back and forth over an array of wild flowers, ferns and leaves as she fashioned what appeared to be a circlet. Totally engrossed in her labours, she did not look up as Kyle approached, unhearing of his footfall, unaware—or uncaring—that she was no longer alone. The grave upon which she sat was that of Joycie Crum.

He perched himself on a nearby tablet, trying not to startle her in her isolation, and watched in silence. Although he sat facing her, she still did not spare him a glance. Her forehead remained puckered with concentration. Her eyes, wide and vacant, were focussed on the frantic fingers, which twined and threaded and made pretty patterns with the foliage, then patted them into shape against her lap. Her clothes—the riding habit she was wearing last night—were soaked through. The jacket clung to her back like a wrinkled wet skin. Her boots were covered with mud, some of it caked hard over the britches stretched taut over her long, slender thighs. Despite the storm clouds overhead it was hot and muggy, but she seemed as indifferent to the weather as she was to his presence. It was obvious that this was where she had remained all night, in the rain, in her search for solitude and silence, gone to earth among the understanding dead.

"For Joycie."

Maya suddenly lifted her head, smiling slowly, secretly, and held up the impromptu circlet. She appeared not at all surprised to see him, almost as if she had been expecting him or, perhaps, had known all along that he was there. She spoke as if she merely continued a conversation they had been having earlier.

"What are you making?" Kyle asked.

"A wreath. She said she would like one. She said it would be . . . appropriate." She spoke in strange, sing-song cadences, but there was no substance to her voice.

"You stayed here all night?"

"Yes."

"Alone? Just sitting by yourself in the dark?"

"Oh no. Joycie was here. We talked to each other."

"Joycie is dead, Maya."

"Oh, I know." She laughed, surprised. "Why else should she be here? In the cemetery?"

He got up and went to her. "Come on," he said gently. "I'll take you home."

She shook her head. "No, not until I've finished this. I have to have it ready for tonight."

"Why tonight?"

She laid the wreath down on her lap and clucked in irritation. "Because Joycie's getting *married*, silly! Why else?"

He took her arm. Her skin burned against his fingertips. "Come on."

She jerked herself free, suddenly animated. "I told you, *not* until I'm finished with this! I promised Joycie I'd let her have it this morning. Besides"—she inched herself away from him—"I want to stay here. What will Joycie think if I leave her now, now, when she *needs* me?" She relapsed into angry mutterings, none of which Kyle could understand.

He asked cautiously, "About last night—do you remember what happened?"

"Last night? Of *course* I remember!" She looked up and smiled again, her blank sleepwalker eyes looking through him as if he were a sheet of glass. "We went on the whirligig in Mr. Lawrence's gardens, and then to the Club. There was a tomb there, a Moghul tomb. Christian said it was built by Jehangir for . . . someone. Anyway, we picnicked there."

"We must go now," Kyle suggested with a little more urgency. "They're very worried about you at home. No one knows where you are."

"Home?"

"Yes. Home to Amos."

She shrank back from him. "I can't go home now! I have to be in Lahore, with Christian. I'm going to start a riding. . . ."

Her face was hot and crimson, sheened with sweat, but her eyes were cold and sightless, like hyacinths frozen in an icy waste. She rambled mindlessly, floating in and out of some secure dreamscape, meandering through an acceptable reality she had fashioned for herself. Kyle sat down again, listening with patience, sensing the destruction of her precarious emotional edifice, understanding why she had no memory of the terrible events of last night. Unable to face them, she had merely excised them from her consciousness and moved far away into another time and dimension.

Last night he had been filled with rage against her; this morning all he felt was a sort of despairing pity. She was not a perpetrator, she was a victim. And there would be more, many more. . . .

"It's going to rain again," he said, defeated and tired. "If we don't go soon, we'll be drenched."

The sky belched in confirmation and a jagged bolt of lightning streaked through a cloud, piercing its entrails, making it groan as if with pain. The wreath finished to her satisfaction, Maya draped it carefully over the pointed head of the tombstone, dusted her hands on the sides of her britches, and stood up ready to leave. Not entirely secure on her feet, she swayed; he steadied her with an arm.

She clung to him in sudden fear. "Why am I here," she whispered, "with all these dead people? Am I dead too?"

"No. You're not dead."

"Then how do I talk to Joycie?"

"You're not dead but you are very sick. You need to be put to bed. You need to rest."

"Where are you taking me, to Lahore?"

"I'm taking you home to your brother."

Her lips trembled. "I want to go to Mother!"

"She will be with you soon, very soon, I promise."

Her legs gave way and she collapsed against his shoulder, mumbling feverishly to herself, only half conscious. He looked around for help. Spying one of the gardeners sitting on his haunches not far away trimming the verges, he summoned him with a shout. As the man came running, Kyle thrust his hand into his pocket, handed him some coins and sent him off to hail a carriage and bring it to the nearest gate. With one arm about Maya's waist, he slowly manouevred her towards the exit, and as the carriage arrived, lifted her into it. He hitched his own horse to the back of the rather decrepit vehicle and climbed in beside her.

Aroused by the jolting of the carriage, Maya came awake and peered into Kyle's face, her expression hostile and mistrustful.

"You're not Christian!" she accused. "Who *are* you?"

Kyle sighed. "I'm a friend. Believe me, I'm a friend."

"But I do not know you!"

He probed deep into the brilliant blue eyes that looked at him but did not see him. "No," he said quietly. "No. You do not know me."

The thunderstorm finally subsided late in the afternoon. Residual high winds teased the surface of the river into little white-capped wavelets, tousled the treetops and carried a cool, moist evening across the city. As dusk crawled over the back lawn of the Raventhorne house, Amos slouched on the river steps, exhausted, trying to revive his depleted mind and body with a double pouring of whisky. Kyle strolled back and forth along the embankment, lost in silent thought.

"I've been wondering if I should send a message to Mother to return," Amos mused, breaking the prolonged silence. "I'm not sure I can cope with a situation as . . . as *volatile* as this!"

"Leave your mother in peace for a while." Kyle ambled back towards the steps. "She needs time to recover from the shocks she has already had." He picked up the glass he had left balanced on a stone parapet and positioned himself on the low wall bordering the steps. "Besides, she can hardly do more than Dr. Humphries already has—and Mrs. Chalcott and Sheba will surely manage the rest quite admirably."

Amos heaved a sigh. "Yes, I suppose so. I was merely thinking aloud." He gave an involuntary shudder, unable to shake off the persisting feeling of sick horror. "The cemetery! What in heaven's name made her go to that damned cemetery?"

Kyle's response to the repeated question remained a determined silence and a dismissive shrug.

Shivering with uncontrollable rigor and in high delirium, the semiconscious Maya had been stripped, sponged and whipped into bed by a frantic Sheba the minute Kyle had brought her back home. The doctor had come and gone, puzzled by her strange symptoms, but not unduly alarmed. She had merely caught a severe chill, he pronounced. What else did the foolish girl expect if she insisted on capering about in the early morning rain? Medicine had been prescribed and a dose already administered. Frequent application of an icebag to the forehead, Dr. Humphries had recommended, would help to bring down the fever.

"Well, what's it all about, then?" Edna Chalcott asked, arriving within an hour of receiving Amos's urgent message. "What's the girl been up to this time?"

There were no secrets in the Raventhorne household from Edna Chalcott. Amos gave her a candid account of the past two days' happenings, including a brief résumé of what Thomas Hungerford had revealed to them. She was shaken to her roots, of course, but being a confirmed pragmatist, she soon put it all in its proper perspective, emerging with priorities commendably unimpaired.

"Let's get the girl back on her feet first," she said firmly, brushing the rest aside for the moment. "We'll worry about all that later."

In very short order—to Amos's enormous relief—she took charge of everything with her usual no-nonsense competence. "I'll have to be away for a while in the evening, darling," she said apologetically. "I've promised to play at Constance's soirée. I can't really let her down at the last minute. She'd never forgive me. I'll return with some clothes and toilet things the *instant* the wretched do is over."

Despite Edna's many reassurances, Amos found it impossible to rid himself of his deep unease as he tried to relax with Kyle in the cool of the evening. "The fever shows no signs of abating," he said, hollow-eyed with anxiety despite his relief that his sister had been found alive and unharmed. "And she's still delirious, still talking gibberish."

"That will pass," Kyle said, taking a careful sip of whisky and staring

562

at the vanishing sliver of the tangerine sun as it slipped over the horizon of a myriad-coloured sky. He tipped his glass back, drained it and stretched his long legs forward on the step. "It is not the fever that you have to worry about."

"Yes," Amos agreed in a small, hushed voice. "I know."

"Anyway," Kyle heaved himself up again and sat with his hands clasped about his knees, "no more of that for the moment. Let's talk instead about Thomas Hungerford."

He had taken home Amos's copy of the statement and read it during the course of the day, having returned this evening to discuss it.

"Did you have time to read it?" Amos asked quickly, more at ease with this topic of conversation than with that of his sister's tragic brainstorm.

"Oh, indeed! I had not imagined that the man would have quite such a dramatic tale to tell, nor so much to expose."

"Neither had I, to be honest. But now I'm convinced that he is telling the truth. Arvind Singh agrees. What do you think?"

Kyle tilted his head to one side. "You believe what Hungerford says? Despite all historical evidence to the contrary?"

"About the killing of Nana Sahib?" Amos hesitated. "Well, I don't know, but. . . ." He repeated to Kyle the rumour that the Maharaja's agent had brought him during the Mutiny. "My father believed passionately that a war should be fought between men, not with women and children. Perhaps it was the Bibighar slaughter that completed his disenchantment with the man who was once his ally. Don't forget, my father had already received that incoherent call for help from his sister. Perhaps he received it too late to do anything about it, perhaps he didn't take it seriously—whatever the reason, he did not answer the call. He must have gone berserk with grief and rage when he heard about the Bibighar massacre. Remember, he truly believed that his sister had perished in it." He raised a questioning eyebrow. "More than enough motive for the murder of the man who had actually ordered the slaughter, wouldn't you say?"

"But, unfortunately, a murder to which there was only one dubious witness!"

"True." Amos refreshed their glasses a last time and tossed the empty bottle far into the river with savage force. "So, at the end of the day, we are exactly where we were before Hungerford arrived. For all his good intentions, his testimony is worthless. It *still* does not prove that my father was innocent of that damned massacre!"

"Well, my friend, if proof of that does exist at all," Kyle said, sharing his bitter disappointment, "it exists with Jasper Pendlebury. Under present circumstances, we might consider that tantamount to not having any proof at all."

Once more a silence descended between them, not a comfortable, companionable silence, but a silence fraught with desolation and foreboding. By tacit agreement, they had not talked at any length of the terrible events of last night. But nevertheless they hovered between them like voracious insects, a lethal swarm buzzing about at the back of both minds. However horrendous the experience might have been, it had to be discussed and disseminated some time or the other. Mention of Jasper Pendlebury now catapulted the entire sequence of events to the forefront.

Amos said quietly, "Tell me everything that happened last night."

Kyle closed his eyes and laid his head back against the wall. "I should have planned it with more care, Amos," he said, once again filled with despair. "It simply got out of hand. I should have seen it coming. I didn't."

"How could you have . . . ?"

Kyle sliced him off with an angry oath. "Don't make excuses for me, I don't deserve them! What happened last night was a human catastrophe, Amos—the start of a chain of events that can neither be repelled nor reversed." For a moment he was silent, struggling to contain his private demons and erase the sordid images that sprang to life behind his closed eyelids. Then, with a mighty effort, he brought himself under control again. "Anyway, it was late," he continued. "My mother was about to put Montague to bed. We were sitting and talking, when Maya suddenly appeared at the door of the room in the tunnel."

"She knew about that room?"

"Oh yes, she knew about it! That she had found out for herself. I looked up and suddenly she was there, with Christian." He squeezed his eyes shut again. "I've never seen anyone looking so bewildered, so unprepared for disaster. She wasted no time on preliminaries. She looked at me and said, *Tell him.* Just like that—*Tell him!*"

"You told him?"

"No. She didn't give me a chance. Before I could say anything, she did."

"Just like that?"

"Yes. Just like that. There was no time to stop her. At first Christian was confused. He couldn't quite grasp what she meant, so she repeated it, slowly and clearly, in terms that not even a child could fail to grasp. As his brain suddenly registered what she was saying, he went wild, like a raging bull, like a suckling tigress whose litter is threatened. He flung himself at her, fastened his hands about her neck and shook her as a game dog shakes a rat, calling her a liar and screaming obscenities."

"Maya didn't fight back?" Amos asked, aghast.

"No. As a matter of fact, she made no effort to defend herself. She merely stood there, like a limp rag doll, with her eyes closed. For all the reaction she showed, Christian could have been invisible. Had we not been able to prise his fingers away from her throat, he would certainly have squeezed the breath out of her."

"He didn't attack you, your mother?"

"He started to turn upon my mother, but then, quite suddenly, his strength ebbed, or maybe his senses returned, and he collapsed. He dropped onto the cot and just sat with his eyes dilated and shocked, staring silently at my mother, at Montague, as if they were apparitions, not truly of this world." A spasm ran through Kyle and he shuddered. "I assure you it was . . . horrible, quite horrible!"

564

"And Maya?"

"Maya continued to stand and watch, very casually stroking her neck, detached from what was happening, absolutely disassociated from her physical surroundings. It was as if she stood there without the faculties of her mind, as if she was being operated like a mechanical toy by some invisible hand behind her back winding a key. There was no expression on her face, her eyes were quite dead. I don't frighten easily, as you know, Amos, but I have to confess that she made my flesh crawl. Then, with Christian just sitting on that cot alternating bewildered glances between my mother and Montague, she simply turned on her heel and walked away, without a word, without even a backward glance."

Amos trembled and hugged himself. "What possessed her to do it, Kyle? How *could* she have done it?"

"She was not aware of anything that she did last night, Amos. As I said, her mind was not in her body. She appeared to be in a trance. Certainly, she has no memory of any of it now."

"You should have followed her," Amos muttered, weak with shock.

"I wanted to, but I couldn't," Kyle explained, the strain even more deeply scored in the lines of his face. "I didn't dare leave my mother alone with Christian. The man was demented, he could easily turn violent again. In any case, I assumed that Maya had returned home. It was only this morning, when I saw her horse on the embankment, that I became alarmed and came here."

"Christian stayed with you for some time?"

"Yes. Once he returned to a state of some sanity, he just broke down. Everything inside him seemed to collapse. He lay down and cried, sobbing his heart out like a child. And later, of course, he demanded answers, explanations, details. He insisted on knowing everything."

"You told him?"

"Yes. There was no point in keeping the rest back. In any case, he would not have accepted less than the entire truth. Ironically enough, what he learnt subsequently seemed to help him regain a sense of perspective, recover at least some of his equilibrium." He shook his head, as if in wonder. "At the same time, the sudden, lifeless calm was unnatural; not only that, it was chilling, even more menacing than his hysteria."

For a long moment neither of them spoke. Then Amos asked again, morose and still confused, "Why did she do it, Kyle? What was the diabolical reasoning behind this act of terrible cruelty?"

"You know the answer as well as I do."

Amos winced. "He rejected her," he said flatly.

"Not quite. A rejection she might have survived," he corrected softly, almost as if talking to himself. "What she could not survive was the alternative I think he offered."

Amos felt his eyelids sting. "But why the cemetery, damn it!" he cried helplessly, "Why *that?*"

"She said she wanted to talk to Joycie."

"But Joycie is dead, for God's sake!"

Kyle looked away, his face drawn with sudden pain. "So, in a way, is your sister."

Amos felt his stomach heave and bile clogged his throat. He couldn't speak. In any case, there was nothing more to say.

The downstairs windows of the house blazed with light. A few carriages lined a side of the driveway and some were parked on the road outside. From the open French windows of the music room, Christian heard sounds of a valiant piano trying to keep pace with a tremulous, off-key soprano demolishing Schubert's *Erlkönig* with commendable relish.

Christian halted uncertainly at the main portals of the house. He had forgotten about his mother's musical evening. To escape the enforced entertainment, it occurred to him, his father might still be at the Treasury. It was an unforeseen prospect, and for a moment, he felt himself sinking, again losing control. But then, in an upsurge of determination, he rallied. No matter. He would see his father wherever he happened to be, he *had* to! He walked round the house into the verandah outside the study, and his heart lurched: the familiar silhouette was outlined clearly against a curtain. He opened the French window and walked into the room.

"Ah, a kindred soul seeks refuge from the German *leider!* Come in, come in. I've been expecting you." His father's greeting was warmly convivial. As always of an evening after a harried day, he was relaxing over a brandy, awaiting the arrival of a freshly filled chillum. "In fact, I. . . ." He stopped and frowned. "Wait a minute, weren't you supposed to dine with us *last* night? I thought you were to leave for Lahore this morning."

Christian slipped into his usual place in a corner of the scuffed leather couch. "Yes."

"But I see that you didn't."

"No. I postponed my departure."

"Oh?"

"I wanted to see you once more before I left."

Sir Jasper peered into his face. "Now that I think of it, your mother did say something about your being out of sorts and that you might leave after a day or two. You are not, I trust?"

"No, I am not out of sorts." His skin was waxen, cold to the touch, but his expression was astonishingly serene. "In fact, I have seldom been as much *in* sorts as I am today." He smiled.

"Good. Well, I can't say that I'm not pleased Ludlow allowed you an extra day in town. Had you come last night I would have hardly had time to talk to you. The Turkish chaps arrived en masse yesterday and I had to prepare for this morning. We were closeted for hours, locked in a most tedious debate about those tariffs I was telling you about the other week. But on the whole, I have to admit, it has been rather a productive day. Finally they had to capitulate, of course."

He related in some detail the tedious debate and his eventual triumph, and Christian listened without interruption. Once the topic was exhausted, Sir Jasper refreshed his glass from a decanter on a silver tray resting at his elbow, and raised a questioning eyebrow at his son. Christian declined with a shake of his head.

"Well, what is it that you wished to see me about?" he asked then, with an indulgent chortle, taking a long sip of his drink. "Nervous about working with Lumsdale, eh? He used to be quite a tartar even at Haileybury, I remember. Once, during an economics tutorial, he. . . ."

Again Christian listened attentively, raising neither comment nor question. When his father had finished the anecdote, Christian said, "No. It is not about Lumsdale."

"Oh? Well, in any case, I have something for you that might ease your way in the Punjab. If you remember, I promised it to you when I first arrived." He got up, and from a drawer of his writing bureau took out a silver mouthpiece meant for a hookah. It was heavily engraved and exquisitely fashioned. "I hope this will come in handy in the Mofussil in pursuance of your more pleasurable duties."

"Thank you." A fleeting look of pain passed over Christian's features as he placed the mouthpiece on the table before him. He did not look at it again.

A knock on the door announced the arrival of the chillum, its softly glowing embers perfuming the air with gossamer spirals of familiar fragrance. After the boy had arranged it to his satisfaction, Sir Jasper picked up the hookah coil, puffed a while and regarded Christian curiously.

"Something troubles you, I can see that. Well, out with it, young man!"

"I wish to inform you that I no longer intend to marry Maya Raventhorne."

At the bald announcement, Sir Jasper's expression underwent a subtle change. It was so minimal as to be almost imperceptible. "Any particular reason for the decision?"

"Yes. She has refused to stay in Lahore as my mistress."

Sir Jasper's eyes narrowed. "You made that proposition to her?"

"Oh yes. That was the idea, wasn't it?"

"How can I say? It was for you to decide."

"Yes, of course," Christian agreed, impassive and unreadable. "It was always for me to decide, wasn't it?" He slid forward in his seat. "For me too today has been a most productive day, Papa. Would you like to know how?"

"If you wish to tell me."

"I spent the morning going through the records of the Corps of Guides."

"Good heavens!" Sir Jasper raised a quizzical eyebrow. "For a worthwhile purpose, I presume?"

"Yes. Very worthwhile. There is no record of any Warren Nesbitt in the Guides, either in the fifties or at any time before or since."

In the act of patting down the tobacco in the chillum with an implement specially designed for the purpose, Sir Jasper's hand briefly stilled; his eyes turned watchful. "I take it there was some further motive behind your investigations?"

"Yes. I wanted to check upon the truth of your story."

"I see." He showed not the slightest hint of embarrassment. "Well, I was merely making a point that needed to be made."

"Oh, I know! You made the point extremely competently. Indeed, it could not have been made better, or with more positive results!"

"I devised the analogy for your own benefit, Christian," Sir Jasper reminded him with a trace of sharpness. "I hope you have the good sense not to doubt that? You know as well as I do that it would have been professionally disastrous for you to pursue your plan to marry the young lady."

"Perhaps. But she *would* have made a damned good mistress, Papa, wouldn't you say?"

Sir Jasper's expression cooled. "I haven't thought much about the matter. And I'm not sure that I care particularly for the drift of this conversation."

"Well, she would have, wouldn't she?" Christian persisted. His eyes glittered like marbles, alive and animated, but his manner remained casual, almost indolent. "After all, she *does* have all the qualifications you consider necessary for a mistress." He raised a hand and started to count off his fingers. "She's Eurasian. Her mother was also a mistress. The girl desperately wants to raise her status by consorting with an Englishman, and, of course, she's very beautiful—aren't those the basic specifications that you mentioned? Why, with a mistress like that, it might even be worth risking a tarbrushed brat or two! What do you say, Papa?"

"I say that you've been drinking," his father said coldly, his lips pursed with distaste. "I suggest that we drop the subject. I find it offensive."

"The subject of Eurasian mistresses, Papa? You find it offensive?" He chuckled under his breath, much in the manner of his father. "A man must do what he must do—isn't that what you've always maintained? So why the sudden coyness?"

For the first time Sir Jasper's eyes showed a spark of anger. "What the devil is wrong with you today, sir? If you have been over-indulging yourself, I suggest that you return to your chummery and sleep off your deplorable condition before you face either Ludlow or, indeed, your mother."

Christian made no move to leave, seemingly untouched by his father's reproof. Instead he made himself marginally more comfortable, stretching his legs out in front of him and folding his arms across his chest.

"Last night I met someone I did not even know existed," he said abruptly. "It came as quite a surprise."

His father's only response was to raise an aloof eyebrow.

"His name is Montague."

"Montague? Who the hell is Montague?"

"Evidently, he's my brother," Christian informed him lightly. "Or rather, my *half*-brother."

There was the hissing sound of a swiftly indrawn breath. Apart from that, Sir Jasper showed no reaction. Neither did he make any comment. Only the wariness returned to his eyes as he held on to his breath. And waited.

"I searched for a resemblance, Papa," Christian continued, using the same conversational tone, "but couldn't see one. In fact, his appearance is rather . . . odd. If you've seen him, you'll know what I mean. You *have* seen him, I take it?"

"No." Sir Jasper exhaled audibly but his voice was level. "Nor do I intend to."

"Oh, I think you should! He's definitely worth a look. His mother, on the other hand. . . ."

"Are you sure you wish to continue with this, Christian?" His father cut him short, his eyes flinty. "It is not a subject devised to give either of us pleasure."

"Yes, I wish to continue," Christian replied softly. "Don't you want to hear about your other son, your other family?"

"No." There were no denials, no outraged protestations, not even alarm, just a sort of guarded indifference.

"But I want to tell you about them," Christian carried on doggedly, determined not to be thwarted. "I was about to say that Montague's mother, unlike Montague, your second son, is *ravishing,* truly a beautiful woman—or, at least, must have been in her younger days, before her . . . accident, when you knew her in Lucknow. I believe she was a dancing girl, a courtesan, at the court of Oudh."

"If there is a point that you wish to make," his father again interrupted brusquely, "make it. As you well know, I detest prevarication."

"You don't deny any of it?"

"No." Sir Jasper looked faintly surprised. "Why should I? It is the truth. She was my mistress in Lucknow many years ago, and yes, she did have this child, I believe. But I have not seen her since then, nor her bastard. I don't really intend to." The timbre of his voice changed; it became even more matter-of-fact. "I don't deny that I would rather you had *not* learnt of all this, Christian. But since you have," he made an offhand gesture, "we might as well clear the air once and for all. In a way, I'm not unrelieved that we have the chance to do so. I suppose this fellow Hawkesworth is behind your sudden enlightenment?"

"You've known him a long time, haven't you?"

"I could hardly avoid knowing him—after all, he is Nafisa's baseborn. But, regardless of your own misplaced admiration, I myself have never liked him."

In fact, the admission was something of an understatement. Sir Jasper had no doubt that it was Hawkesworth who had somehow managed to snatch away that Birkhurst plantation from right under his nose and arrange to have it sold to Raventhorne. The defeat still stung badly. If he had disliked the man earlier, what he felt now was murderous fury, but with practised skill, he concealed the fact from his son. His expression remained unchanged.

"Why didn't you tell me that you knew him?"

"I didn't consider it necessary. It was outside the limits of your concern."

"You dislike him and yet you went out of your way to meet him again when I was in Champaran!"

"Yes, I was curious." Sir Jasper shrugged. "How does a dancing woman's bastard—with no knowledge of who his father was, who takes his name from the fact that he liked *falconry!*—achieve the education and position that he obviously has?" There was not even a flicker of misgiving in his eyes; his control was immaculate. "Was it Lal who told you?"

"Lal?"

"Kyle. Hawkesworth. Whatever he chooses to call himself now."

"No. Kyle did not tell me."

"Then who?"

"It doesn't matter. What matters is that it wasn't *you.*" His voice broke a little but he quickly repaired it, wiping his throbbing forehead with the back of his hand. "You lied to me, Papa. You lied to me all along."

"Come, come, Christian. Concealment of the truth for a salutary reason can hardly be equated with fabrication. Even if you are brash enough to expect that I, your father, would have voluntarily discussed a former mistress with you, surely you don't labour under the misapprehension that I am the first Englishman in India to have had a mistress or, for that matter, the last?"

Christian stared at him, amazed. "You consider the crux here is simply that you had a mistress? You think that I merely question your *morality?* My God, how subtly you divert the issue, Papa, and with what unconcern!"

"Oh, then there is another issue, is there?" Sir Jasper asked sarcastically, even as a gleam of caution appeared in his eyes.

"You tried to kill them!"

"Ah." Perhaps because he knew that it would come sooner or later, Sir Jasper took the charge comfortably in his stride. "That is a lie," he said calmly. "I had nothing to do with her . . . misadventure."

"The midwife lamed her for life, *mutilated* that child! She could never dance again."

"Regretable, yes, but it certainly wasn't my doing! It was my misguided bearer, Wali Khan, who appointed himself protector of my reputation and did what he deemed necessary without either my knowledge or my sanction."

"It was not Wali Khan who engineered the plot," Christian countered thickly, feeling sick. "Henry Lawrence did not tolerate loose living among his officers. Public knowledge of the woman, certainly of that child she bore you, would have put an end to your ambitions for an exemplary career. With so much at stake, I doubt if you would have entrusted your future to the haphazard mercies of a bearer, Papa!"

Sir Jasper suddenly threw up his hands and let go of the tail of his temper. "What is this, sir, an *inquisition?*" he thundered, his cheeks flushed with rage. "How dare you presume that I am accountable to you, Christian? I owe you no explanations. I consider it an impertinence that you should demand them of me and I *forbid* you to discuss the matter further! My private life is *mine,* my own affair."

"You deceived me into believing that mine was *my* affair!"

"You deceived yourself!" Sir Jasper retorted with frigid disdain. "I merely tried to guide you as tactfully as I could, to point you in the right direction."

"You arranged with Ludlow for me to have that posting with Lumsdale!" Sir Jasper started to say something, but Christian stopped him with a gesture. "Don't trouble to deny it, Papa. I know it, I simply know it. I was blind not to have seen it then. It all fitted so neatly, didn't it? The bachelor posting, that mythical Warren Nesbitt, my loathing of Champaran and admiration for Lumsdale. How well you made your calculations and baited your trap—and how well you recognised your son!" He looked up and laughed with a tinge of hysteria. "You manipulated me, Papa, played me like a marionette, and I, mindless fool that I was, pranced and pirouetted in perfect step to the tune that you whistled. I should have known better." He hid his face in his palms. "I should have known *you* better!" He started to cry.

His father watched with acute distaste as huge, dry sobs racked his son's crouched body. "Don't snivel, Christian," he commanded, embarrassed and outraged. "And don't make it sound squalid. It wasn't. I merely acted in your interests, as would any father who loves his son and wants to help him to improve his prospects in life. I got you a posting after your own heart with a man who was a hero to you—and you consider that to be a disfavour?" Incredulous and astonished, he started to laugh.

At the sound, Christian's head jerked up. Roughly, he brushed the tears off his face. "Is that all that you've heard me say, Papa, is that all?" He stared at his father's face, wonderstruck. "The crime that you perpetrated on two innocent human beings to improve your own prospects is of no consequence to you at all? I wonder what Mama. . . ."

"That's *enough,* Christian!" Sir Jasper scythed the rest off with an enraged gesture. "Whatever is between your mother and me is none of your damned business! In any case, I have already told you that I had nothing to do with what happened."

"I don't believe you, Papa," Christian said wearily, his strength again at a dangerously low ebb. "I can never again believe anything that you say." He rose and walked over to the mantelpiece, staring fixedly at a basket of wax fruit under a glass dome. "The posting with Lumsdale is not on merit. I cannot accept it."

"Cannot accept it?" His father was appalled. "Don't be childish, Christian! In the world as it is, this is the way men of substance progress, this is the way events are shaped. One *makes* them happen by recognising one's opportunities, seizing them, moulding them to one's own advantage. Damn it, I increased your chances of promotion in the Civil Service!"

"Yes, but you reduced me as a man," Christian said, his face etched with lines of misery he simply could not hide. "Besides, I no longer belong to the Civil Service. I gave Ludlow my resignation this afternoon."

"What?" Sir Jasper half rose out of his chair, blanching with shock. Nothing that Christian could have said could have horrified him more. "Have you taken total leave of your senses?" He sank back into his seat, for the first time entirely at a loss. "You cut off your nose to spite your face? You throw away your future, the glorious future you have dreamt of, aspired to, for years—in a fit of pique?"

"Pique?" Christian started to laugh. "You don't understand at all, Papa, do you?"

"No, I *don't* understand! I doubt if any sane person would."

"I worshipped the men of the Service," Christian said thickly. "I considered them celestial creatures, saints, martyrs to a cause, infallible men who could do no wrong—*men who could do no wrong, Papa*—all of them cast in your mould! Now, I think of that lame woman and that hideous lump of flesh that is partly mine, and I know that it was all a figment of my imagination, a fantasy. But, frankly, it no longer matters and I no longer care." He walked over to where his father sat and stood above him. "I will not retract my resignation."

"You would accept the word of this . . . this woman and that scurrilous hack against mine?" Sir Jasper asked in stunned disbelief, "against that of your father?"

"Yes."

"It doesn't occur to you that they simply seek to destroy me, to tarnish my reputation out of vengeance? Hawkesworth is nothing but vermin, a petty extortionist, all he wants is money."

"Had that been his motive, he would have exposed you long ago, told me about you in the beginning. He did not."

"Good God. Do you think he has the credibility to expose me? Who would believe the word of that scum against mine, anyway?"

"Perhaps nobody," Christian conceded readily enough. He squared his shoulders and took a deep breath. "I have an appointment to see Lady Ingersoll tomorrow evening," he said tonelessly. "Kyle may not have the credibility to expose you, Papa, but, you see, I do."

Very slowly, inch by robust inch, Sir Jasper's face drained clear of blood. It became a sickly yellow, as if turned to parchment. His knuckles, gripped tight about the arms of his chair, glistened palely, also bereft of blood and translucent. He stared blindly at some indefinable spot in space. For an interminable moment he sat entombed within the sepulchral silence, unable to move, his chest still. Then, a spasm rippled through his frame, and with considerable difficulty, he managed to exhale the air trapped inside his body. He heaved a small sigh and closed his eyes.

"Surely you are not serious, Christian?" he asked, his voice hushed with horror.

"As serious as is attempted murder, Papa."

"Do you know what you will be doing?"

"Yes."

"Without a shred of evidence, you risk making a *fool* of yourself!"

"No more than I already have. And whatever evidence there is will be sufficient to convince Lady Ingersoll."

The deathly quiet in the room thickened, encompassing them both like a fog. With a mighty effort, Sir Jasper stiffened his back to sit up straight and rearrange his features into a mask of impassivity. Lifting the hose, he pulled on it a few times, his lips tight around the mouthpiece.

"There must be *something* I can do to dissuade you from this highly rash escapade?" The nerves of iron were again taut, inflexible, the composure again reinforced with steel.

"Yes. There is."

The metallic eyes gleamed briefly. "Name it!"

"Within the next twenty-four hours you could resign from the Service."

"Resign?" Sir Jasper echoed blankly. He could not have been less comprehending had he been addressed in Swahili. "From the Civil Service?"

"Yes."

Sir Jasper laughed, as much with astonishment as with flaring amusement. He shook his head. "No, Christian. I will not resign from the Civil Service!"

"In that case, nothing." Christian turned towards him, granite-faced. "I have to do this, Papa. I know that I must."

The smile whipped off Sir Jasper's mouth; his slitted eyes showed cold fury. "You would destroy me, my career, your mother, yourself, *every-thing*—for what, Christian? Some esoteric principle, a meaningless ideal, involving those inconsequential half-breeds?"

"Yes."

"What do you think you stand to gain by it?"

"I don't know." Christian lowered his head; he looked wretched. "Peace of mind. Justice. The strength to continue to live with myself. Perhaps a vestige of my self-esteem back. It is only in the fitness of things, Papa. I'm surprised that you, of all people, cannot see it." He realised what he had blurted out and laughed, embittered. "No. Of course you cannot see it. How could you?"

"Think about it, my son." A curious note of urgency had crept into his father's tone. "Think *well* about it. You stand to lose more, much more than I do!"

"I have done nothing but think about it. And I have already lost every-thing that I valued."

"What can I offer you in exchange, Christian? You can have anything you want, *anything!* You want to marry this girl? Very well, I'll arrange with Ludlow to ferret out another posting. I'll speak to him in the morn-ing. If you like, I'll. . . ."

Christian listened carefully, as if mesmerised, swamped by the swift flow of words. Beneath the current he sensed an undertow, a frisson of something, an unfamiliar, unrecognisable note in his father's voice, one that he had never heard before. He stared at his father's features, puzzled, searching his memory to place in perspective the bloodless face, the trans-fixed eyes and alien voice, the diminished form, unable to locate them, all unknown to him, all strangers. He started to fill with pain, a pain so immense, so acute and all pervasive, that it threatened to explode within him, scattering pieces of his body all over the floor, like feathers from an overstuffed cushion. His eyes welled. Within the tightness of his throat, his anguish lay trapped in silence.

His father was pleading with him, *pleading!*

He could not bear it. He felt he would die.

"I had thought that you would make me into a man," he whispered choking, drowning again and unable to save himself. "Now I'm not even sure that you were ever one."

Blinded by tears, Christian ran out of the door into the back garden, suffocated by his need to escape before his spirit surrendered and his anger shrivelled, before he put his arms about his father and told him that he was sorry, that he should erase the past thirty minutes from his mind, that he needed him and loved him more than his life. . . .

The nausea surged upwards from Christian's stomach. As the tremulous notes of an aria from Gounod's *Faust* drifted out of the music-room window and mingled with the moonlight awash over the garden, he staggered to the end of the lawn and was violently sick behind the summerhouse.

"How was the soirée?" Amos asked.

"Grim." Edna laughed. "You should have seen Constance's face during the *leider!* If looks could have killed, Hannah Robinson would have withered into ashes before she even started—or, at least, turned back into a pumpkin!"

Amos volunteered a wan smile. Trying to lighten his mood, Edna chattered on amusingly about the musical evening, recounting her little anecdotes with graphic humour until she forced a laugh or two out of him. Then she sobered and made a wry face.

"But everyone could see that Constance was not herself. She looked dreadful, poor dear, hardly able to pay attention."

"Poor dear?" Recalling his earlier humiliation, Amos gave a snort of derision. "How dare she talk to me the way she did this morning! Who the hell do these Pendleburys think they are, anyway?"

"Don't waste your anger, at least on Constance, darling," Edna beseeched sadly. "Considering everything, what she is more deserving of now is pity." She gave a little shiver and pulled her silk shawl closer about her shoulders.

Amos bent down to pat the head of one of the dogs begging for attention. "Was . . . Christian there?" he asked, not looking at her.

"No. But Constance kept staring at the door. Obviously, she expected him to walk in any moment. He didn't. It was really quite pathetic."

Unable to sleep, sharing a common disquietude, Edna and Amos remained awake till late that night, talking, walking the dogs along the embankment. Kyle had left shortly before eleven, dead on his feet with exhaustion, still profoundly depressed. In spite of his own aching muscles and mental fatigue, Amos found that once again sleep eluded him. Glad of Edna's comforting company, he played desultory games with the dogs, unable to stem the tide of troubling thoughts, relieved to be able to share his unease with someone with such warm understanding of their problems.

So, in a way, is your sister . . .

Maya, dead?

Kyle's terrible words suddenly leapt into his mind again and his heart wrenched with savage pity and pain. He felt his eyes cloud and turned away quickly from Edna. Knowing how much it would distress her, he did not repeat the remark to her.

"She should have gone to America!" he muttered, clenching his fists.

"Yes."

"Had she gone when she should have, none of this would have happened."

"What has happened, has happened, Amos. We can't undo it. Perhaps she will agree to go now." She heaved a sorrowful little sigh. "There certainly isn't much to keep the poor child *here* any longer!"

"But can't you see? Mother won't want to go now!" He could not hide his impatience. "Not until everything else has been resolved—if it ever can be!"

"It's what Olivia lives for, Amos," Edna reminded him gently, understanding his resentment, sympathising with it. "And now, with all this dramatic new evidence in hand, surely it is unreasonable to expect her to abandon everything that she has been fighting for?"

"Oh, I know, I know." He was quick to make amends, ashamed of his churlishness. "It's just that I'm so damn *sick* about it."

"Well, maybe we could find an alternative escort for Maya for her voyage to America. I hear the Lubbocks want to sell out and leave."

"The Lubbocks? I didn't know that."

"Well, I think Marianne has been wanting to leave for a long time. Now, it seems, Grace has finally found herself a young man. He's Indo-Portuguese—like Marianne—a teacher at St. Paul's School in Darjeeling, and he's willing to emigrate with them to America."

"When do they plan to sail?"

"In a month or so, I should imagine. Hal has several prospective buyers lined up for the house and factory. As you know, their furniture business has been booming. Anyway, if Maya agrees, the Lubbocks would make perfect chaperones. And she and Grace do get on well."

"Yes. That might be a solution. We can discuss it with Maya when Mother returns—if Maya is in a fit state of health to travel at all," he muttered gruffly.

"Oh, she'll be as right as *rain*, darling, once she's over this wretched bout!" Edna said brightly, linking her arm through his and giving it an affectionate shake. "Let's at least thank the Lord that it wasn't any worse."

Amos gave her arm a squeeze and released his from it. Picking up the dogs' ball, he tossed it hard towards the top of the lawn as they started to walk back. The dogs sped after it gleefully in a flurry of squeaks and swishing tails.

"It will be worse," he said morosely. "It's not over yet."

It was not yet dawn when Tremaine was roused by the night-chowkidar with a summons from his master: Sir Jasper wished to see him urgently in his study. Fifteen minutes later, grumbling under his breath and still drowsy-eyed, the butler arrived at the study and, following a discreet knock, threw open the door.

The room was in virtual darkness. A solitary paraffin lamp stood spluttering on the bureau in the final throes of extinction. The tortured flame cast grotesque shadows over folders and papers littered across the open flap of the desk. Sir Jasper himself sat dozing noisily in his customary chair with his head resting against a cushion placed behind his neck. The brandy decanter at his elbow was empty; the supper tray that Lady Pendlebury had sent in earlier still lay covered with a white cloth and was obviously untouched. It was evident that Sir Jasper had been up all night working at his papers.

With a cluck of annoyance at the carelessness of the second bearer, who should have cleared away the food before going to bed, Tremaine picked up the tray as quietly as he could. Even so, Sir Jasper's eyes flew open with a start.

"What? Who is it?"

"Tremaine, sir," the butler announced stiffly. "I believe you sent for me?"

"Oh yes, so I did." Sir Jasper blinked a few times, exercising his leaden eyelids, stretched his limbs and yawned at length. "I wonder if you would be good enough to fetch me a fresh towel and some clean clothes, Tremaine. What time is it, anyway?"

"Not yet four o'clock, sir," Tremaine said, making no secret of his disapproval. "What kind of clothes, sir? Formal wear for the office or a pair of pyjamas?"

"Four, is it? I had no idea it was so late—or should I say, so early?" Sir Jasper seemed not to have heard the question and, instead, pointed to the desk. "With all this needing to be done, I confess I rather lost count of the time." He leant back again and sat stroking his chin, submerged in private thought.

Tremaine waited a while, then cleared his throat. "Shall I relight the lamps, sir?"

"Eh? No, that will not be necessary."

"Would *chota hazri* be in order?"

Sir Jasper brushed the offer aside with a shake of his head. "Not now, maybe later. Is her ladyship up yet?"

"Nobody is up yet, sir," Tremaine replied with an aggrieved air.

"Because of the supper party, her ladyship could retire only after midnight." He added pointedly, "Also the staff, sir."

"Is that so?" Not having heard a word, Sir Jasper nodded vaguely. He laid his head back again and stared up at the ceiling. "Shakespeare had it all, didn't he, Tremaine?" he mused. "The best laid plans and so forth."

Never having made the acquaintance of the Bard of Avon, the butler maintained a studied silence.

"You think the fault lies *not* in our stars, Tremaine?"

"I wouldn't know, sir."

"Well, the canny old scribbler certainly seemed to think so."

"I am not conversant with Mr. Shakespeare's writings, sir. I prefer the illustrated pamphlets myself." He again tried a low cough. "Er . . . what kind of clothes would you be requiring for this morning's wear, sir?"

"Fate has a mischievous bent for surprises, Tremaine. One never knows which way it will compel one to turn."

Not a fancier of philosophy either, Tremaine merely tilted his head a little in acknowledgement and cast a surreptitious glance at the clock above the desk. "I daresay not, sir."

"Some of the turns tend to be rather slippery. One has to be careful how one treads. Sometimes, of course, one simply loses one's footing and falls." He intercepted the butler's second look at the clock and slapped his thigh to indicate the end of the discussion.

"Well, Tremaine, time to go to bed, what?"

"I would say so, sir."

"I've left some letters on the table. Remind me to have them delivered in the morning, will you?"

"Certainly, sir. *Chota hazri* at the usual time, sir?"

"Perhaps a half hour later. I intend to indulge myself a little today. The meeting doesn't start until ten."

"Very good, sir."

Sir Jasper struggled out of the chair, raised himself on his toe tips and stretched his arms above his head with another luxurious yawn. "It's good to have all one's senses about one, Tremaine. After all, a man must do what he must, what?"

"Indubitably, sir."

"Well, I didn't sleep at all last night, but I still feel surprisingly spruce, full of energy. Even buoyant, you might say. On second thought, I am inclined to eschew the luxury of sleep to work off some of the high spirits with a brisk walk around the grounds."

Tremaine's heart dipped again. He wondered if his presence might be required during the brisk walk but he did not risk the question.

Sir Jasper slapped a hard hand on the back of his neck to trap a flying insect, but he missed. "Devilish humid tonight, isn't it?" He mopped his face.

"Indeed, sir. One of the worst of the season."

"You know what I *really* feel like tonight—or rather, this morning, Tremaine?"

"No, sir."

Sir Jasper rubbed his palms together in sudden anticipation, his eyes gleaming. "I feel like a swim in the river. Just a quick dip. Quite the night for it, what?"

"A most refreshing idea, sir!" Tremaine endorsed, visibly relieved that his services would not be required. "Will you be gone long, sir? The pantry door is kept locked until the man from the cowshed delivers the milk at half past five. When should I ask the bearer to unlock it, sir?"

"No, I won't be long, maybe half an hour or so. Just long enough to cool down and wash off this pernicious humidity. About the clothes, a pair of cotton trousers and a loose shirt will do. And don't forget the towel. I'll bathe and change again after breakfast before I leave for the office."

"The navy trousers and the striped blue shirt, sir?"

"Yes. Excellent. Just leave the clothes on the embankment wall where I can see them. If her ladyship awakens, tell her I will join her later for breakfast."

"Yes, sir. Her ladyship made an attempt to see you last night, but—" he looked significantly at the hookah—"she changed her mind and said she would wait for you upstairs instead, not knowing, of course, that it would be another working night for you, sir."

"Oh dear." Sir Jasper made a rueful face. "I suppose I should have sent a message up to save her the wait. Anyway, tell her I'll see her at breakfast."

"Grilled kidneys again, sir, with fried toast, tomatoes and three-minute coddled egg?"

It seemed to the butler that Sir Jasper cogitated for an inordinate length of time over giving him an answer to the simple question. But then he smiled and nodded. "Yes, Tremaine, thank you. That would be perfect."

Had he not been so impatient to return to the comfort of his bed for another hour or two of sleep, and had his memory not been quite so sluggish that morning, Tremaine would certainly have remembered something he should have thought of much earlier. As it was, it did not enter his mind until the sun had started its climb above the eastern horizon, and he his ascent up the stairs to deliver Sir Jasper's parting message to his lady wife. According to Lady Pendlebury's ayah, whom he encountered halfway up, the mistress had wakened a few moments ago in a state of extraordinary agitation. She had demanded that her husband be summoned *instantly* from the study, and this, in fact, was the message that she was on her way down to give to the master. It was then, at that precise instant in a lightning flash, that Tremaine remembered what he should have earlier.

He remembered that Sir Jasper did not know how to swim.

CHAPTER

24

A GREAT HUSH DESCENDED over the city.
Like a dark, sodden dome, it pressed down on Calcutta, chilling
bones and nerves, sending people into frightened huddles in
homes and offices, making them peek nervously over their shoulders. As
the wave of arctic shock rippled across the neat, whitewashed bungalows
of the White Town and settled like a pall over the commercial district, all
at once everyone spoke in whispers, walked on tiptoes, shushed grumbling children into sullen quiescence and banished them to their nurseries.
Without a peep of complaint, hostesses hastily called off their forthcoming
burra khanas. Notices were posted about the deferment of sporting fixtures,
weddings, baptisms, confirmations and, indeed, all other occasions for
merriment. In Simla, the Executive Council met in stunned silence, trying
to grapple with the terrible news the urgent telegraph message had
brought from Calcutta. The gymkhana races at Annandale, a performance
of *She Stoops to Conquer* at the Gaiety by the Simla Amateur Dramatic Club
and a costume ball at Peterhof, the viceregal residence, were hastily cancelled. A visibly shaken Lord Mayo and members of his cabinet made
arrangements to return to Calcutta post-haste and a governmental holiday was declared. No one was in the mood for work anyway. Or, indeed,
for jollification. At least, not until the funeral was over.

In any case, where was the time for frivolity? Considering all the extraordinary aspects of the tragedy, there was so much to talk about, so many
mysteries to unravel, such a bewildering spate of rumour to be discussed,
disseminated, scotched or, perhaps, instigated. It seemed that, overnight,
the entire process of governance and domestic activity had come to a virtual standstill in both the imperial capitals of Her Majesty's Eastern
Empire. Taken utterly by surprise, no one could assimilate yet the news

of the tragic drowning accident that had prematurely terminated the life of the popular Finance member.

"I have always maintained that there is a *curse* on this evil land!" Charlotte Anderson whispered tremulously to the group of grey-faced mourners who had gathered at the Pendlebury mansion to record their grief and offer their support to the bereft widow. "And who, pray, amongst us could be more cursed than poor Constance?"

To the sound of muted cheers, she solemnly proclaimed the indefinite postponement of the annual whist drive at the Ballygunge Women's Institute and of the proposed Monsoon Costume Ball in aid of fallen women.

Gossip from the heartland of the Empire arrived at the royal palace in Kirtinagar with remarkable despatch. Immediately, with every other consideration set aside, Olivia cut short her visit and hurried back to Calcutta, instinctively frantic with worry and foreboding. She knew that if the rumours were wild enough as far afield as Kirtinagar, in the city itself they would exceed all bounds of credibility. Like swarms of locusts, they would be buzzing across desks and dinner tables, shops and clubs, down every bazaar lane and gully, picking away at names and reputations with savage tenacity, determined to target and tarnish a convenient scapegoat.

As it happened, everyone did have a different tale to tell, a theory to propound, or a conjecture to offer anyone who cared to listen. No one knew quite what had happened, or when and where and to whom and, for heaven's sake, *why*. But that there was a scandal buried in it all somewhere, nobody doubted for an instant. Neither did anyone doubt that, if one excavated deep enough, long enough, with sufficient persistence and in the right region, one was certain to be rewarded with hidden booty.

The question was where?

About one fact, however, there appeared to be a general consensus: there was definitely some connection between whatever had happened and the scandalous affair between Christian Pendlebury and that Raventhorne girl.

"*Is* there a connection, Amos?"

Riven with pain and anxiety for her much maligned daughter, Olivia put the question bluntly to Amos as soon as she returned.

"Yes, there is." Almost at the end of his tether, Amos confirmed the prevailing suspicions with unhesitating and grim conviction. "There can be no doubt that there is!"

Olivia's mouth turned dry with fear. "*How?*"

Ready to explode with his need to unload the burdens he had been carrying over these past few days that now seemed like an eternity, Amos told his mother everything that had transpired in her absence and why, omitting not a single relevant detail of the horrendous saga.

As his voice trailed away, she groped for a chair and sank into it, utterly overwhelmed.

"All this has been happening and I knew nothing about it?" she cried, still not understanding fully. "I had no *idea* that Kyle's mother was still alive!"

"Neither had I. He brought them from Lucknow—his mother and the child—at about the same time that the Pendleburys arrived."

"Are they still here?"

"No. Kyle has taken them up to the plantation. He felt he could no longer keep them at his premises with safety." He smiled sourly at the irony. "They left early that morning, too early to have received the news of Sir Jasper's death."

"You mean, Kyle doesn't know about it yet?"

"Probably not."

"And . . . Christian?" Thinking of what his wretched plight might be, she dissolved with compassion.

"No one knows where he is. It seems he has vanished altogether."

"But wasn't the funeral arranged for this morning?"

"Yes."

"Surely he was there?"

"I don't know. You'll have to hear about that from Aunt Edna. She's gone to attend the funeral services. From there she plans to go directly to the Pendleburys' with the rest of the mourners."

Too dejected to be able to digest all the answers yet, Olivia held back her remaining questions for the moment, and Amos, sensing his mother's distress, refrained from further comment. Overwrought and profoundly disturbed, she ran up the stairs to be at the bedside of her daughter.

Again she stood and stared down at Maya in dismay, heartsick at how wasted and ill the girl looked as she lay in her bed, unmoving and asleep, oblivious of the finely grinding mills of God around her. Very gently, she loosened the bandage around Maya's neck. The bruises had turned blue and the skin was scored with long red fingernail marks. On the smooth, swanlike neck, as delicate as alabaster, they looked ugly and sinister, and somehow obscene. Olivia was shot through with sudden fury, but then, equally swiftly, the anger died and she filled with anguish. If her daughter was singularly ill-starred, then in what way was this hapless boy any less? Replacing the bandage, she went to the bay window and, no longer able to contain her despair, sat crying softly to herself.

She cannot survive this heritage you have left her, Jai. It corrodes her, muti-lates those she touches. . . .

"It was a most moving occasion," Edna said, when she returned at teatime and joined them later on the back lawn. "They buried him with full state honors—gun salutes, the Last Post, and all the other trimmings. The Queen sent a glowing message of sympathy. The Viceroy and members of his Council could not be back in time for the funeral, of course, but the splendid tribute Lord Mayo sent by telegraph which, I'm told, he composed himself, was read out by the Lieutenant-Governor. The tribute mentioned that, very possibly, India had been deprived of an exemplary future Viceroy. There were nearly a thousand mourners at the cemetery—very impressive and, of course, *most* gratifying for poor Constance, I should imagine."

"And at the house later?" Olivia asked.

"Well, they read out some more of the tributes and condolences that have been pouring in, including another telegraph from Buckingham Palace, this time a personal message to Constance and Christian. The Pendleburys' daughter, who's married and lives in Somerset, sent a wire offering to take the next ship out with her husband if her mother needed her. But she's expecting her first child and Constance will not hear of it." She stopped to dab the corners of her eyes. "Constance bears up well, poor dear. Quite devastated, of course, but—as one would expect her to—facing up to the situation with commendable fortitude."

"And Christian? Was he there?"

Edna shook her head. "Herbert Ludlow says that he has opted out of the Civil Service for, as Christian phrased it, 'personal reasons.' Evidently, he put in his papers before he went to see his father. Herbert couldn't have been more flabbergasted."

"Christian *did* see his father, then!" Amos exclaimed under his breath.

"Oh yes. Sir Jasper's hookah-burdar has confirmed that he was with him for about half an hour on the evening before the . . . accident. That was the last anyone saw of Christian."

"Did he form any impression of what they discussed?"

"The hookah boy? Well, the lad doesn't understand English, but according to what he told Clarence, they didn't play chess, which they usually did. And the tones they used, he said, sounded to him rather less than cordial."

Amos relapsed into glum silence. Olivia busied herself with pouring out a cup of tea for Edna, dropped a sliver of lemon into the golden liquid and added a quarter teaspoon of sugar.

"Clarence Twining has no clues as to where he might be?" Olivia asked, profoundly concerned for the missing boy.

"Rather too many! Some reports have him walking along the Grand Trunk Road heading north, others swear he has made for the Himalayan foothills. One informer insists that he saw him at Princep Ghat, boarding a steam packet on its way down to the estuary. Telegraph messages to police chowkis within a radius of five hundred miles and runners along the Grand Trunk Road have produced more crops of confusion." She chased a minuscule tea leaf around her cup with a spoon. "His absence created quite a furore at the cemetery, I can tell you that. It was the only occasion when Constance almost broke down publicly. She is, of course, *desperately* worried about him."

"I can't see why," Amos said with a spiteful grimace. "She should be relieved that at least he hasn't eloped!"

"Oh, darling, that's unkind."

"He stays away deliberately, can't she see that?" Amos cut Edna short and put down his cup. "He must know by now that his father is dead."

"Well, certainly it would appear so, although, naturally, no one can understand why, least of all his unfortunate mother." Trapping the elusive tea leaf, Edna triumphantly tossed it into the saucer. "And another curious thing: Harriet Ingersoll was saying later at the house that on the day before his father died, Christian had sought to make an appointment with her for the following evening."

Amos's breath caught. "Christian went to meet Lady Ingersoll?"

"No. He never kept the appointment, Lady Ingersoll says. Nor did he send any word of apology. Of course, by then the news was all over town and she was as dreadfully upset about it as everyone else. Under the circumstances, she certainly didn't expect him to keep the appointment. But now that he appears to have vanished, she can't help wondering what it was all about."

"Whatever it was about," Amos said, shaken, "once his father died, it obviously lost its relevance."

No one thought to challenge that.

Sheba arrived to supervise the clearing away of the tea things, and for a while everyone sat nurturing the desolate silence that fell between them. Whatever conversations had taken place between father and son during that last fatal encounter would probably never become common knowledge. In the Raventhorne household, however, there was little doubt as to what had transpired in Sir Jasper's study that significant evening.

"Did you have helpful discussions in Kirtinagar?" Amos asked quickly, anxious not only for information but also to change the subject. "Has the Maharaja arrived at some decision about what is to be done now?"

"Yes, for whatever it might be worth." Olivia shook loose her richly coloured chestnut hair, still dense and glossy and reaching well below her waist, and started to braid it. "Arvind Singh wants to try to reopen the case on the strength of Thomas Hungerford's deposition. He said he would seek an appointment with Arthur Fairfield-Greene, the Home member, as soon as the government settles down again after all this chaos. There is a rumour, he says, that the Viceroy plans to make changes in his Council of Ministers because of the vacancy left by Sir Jasper's death." Her shoulders lifted in a despondent shrug. "The meeting will probably not achieve much, that we already know. But Arvind Singh and Kinjal both feel that we must at least go through the motions."

Had Jasper Pendlebury been in a position to prove his father innocent? Amos again thought of that curious remark Pendlebury had made to Kyle once. He had been sceptical about it then; he still was. He was certain that Pendlebury had been bluffing for his own ends, and Kyle had not been able to convince him otherwise. Knowing that it would unnecessarily disturb his mother, he had not bothered even to mention it to her or, as it happened, to Arvind Singh. Now, of course, there was no point in doing so anyway.

With so much else on his mind, Amos had had hardly any time to think about the details of Thomas Hungerford's statement and to consider all its implications. Nor had he had occasion to discuss them with his mother. But now, with another collision imminent with Arthur Fairfield-Greene, the highly unsympathetic Home member, they talked about it at length, albeit with a mutual lack of enthusiasm.

"Fairfield-Greene is a stubborn, unimaginative old *ass*, dedicated to the sanctity of red tape," Amos concluded with a look of scorn. "However dramatic Hungerford's deposition, he will dismiss it as fiction. Certainly, he will not consider reopening the case on the slender evidence of a man so easily discredited."

Sadly, Olivia agreed.

Late that night, unable to sleep because of a searing headache and plagued by a question that simply would not leave him alone, Amos went into his mother's room to ask for an aspirin tablet. He found her awake, sitting by the window in the dark, wide-eyed and brooding. He swallowed the tablet she offered, then flopped down wearily on the window seat.

"Why did she do it, Mother?"

His thoughts still dwelt on his sister. He had not been able to shake off his persisting sense of horror, still not been able to find the elusive explanation that he searched.

"Why?" Olivia looked out across the dark expanse of the back garden speckled with hesitant moonshine and sighed a little. "Because she is her father's daughter, Amos," she said quietly. "Like him, she has a terrible thirst for revenge. And, like him, she fashions her reprisals very thoroughly."

"Kyle?"

Startled, Olivia almost dropped her embroidery frame as she hurried across the room to Maya's bedside. "What, dear?"

The eyes, open and touched with panic, were sunken deep in skeletal sockets within a tracery of fine red veins set in pallid grey. The fingers, long and thin, scraped at the bedclothes, then clutched the sheet in a tightly knotted fist. Barely audible, the sound she made came from a long way away as she strained to expel it, and the speech, battling with a furry, fallow tongue thick with disuse, was indistinct. For an instant the whispered word trembled in the air, then faded away into silence.

Olivia gently prised open the bunched fingers and pressed the restless hands between her own palms. "Kyle has gone up north to leave his mother at the plantation, dear. I'm not sure when he plans to return."

There was puzzlement in Maya's wide-open eyes as she stared at her mother, but she made no response. Instead, weighted down by sedatives and lack of strength, the eyelids again drooped and the fragile frame, now even more reduced, loosened. The fingers straightened out one by one, then settled into limpness.

Maya did not repeat the name. Drained by the effort of that single word, she slept again.

Indeed, defeated by fever and a mind that appeared to have abandoned her body, she had done little else but sleep over these past days of her strange illness. Whenever her eyes opened, they were sightless and there was no recognition in them. When she heard—if she heard at all—it was without comprehension, for she showed no signs of having understood anything. However, there was little doubt that within the cocoon of her mindless silence, she was consumed by sinister fantasies. The sleep she courted so assiduously was spasmodic and fitful. Weaving in and out of delirium, she frequently tossed and thrashed about, battling secret devils that inhabited her solitary dreamscapes.

"How long will she remain like this?" Olivia asked Dr. Humphries, beside herself with worry. "And why does the fever show no signs of abating?"

"Fever is not a disease, Mrs. Raventhorne, it is merely a symptom." Dr. Humphries stroked his chin and studied his patient with a long, reflective look. "Something happened, didn't it?" Olivia averted her face and he added quickly, "Oh, I'm not interested in all the silly gossip floating around, I'm talking about *these*," he pointed to the marks on Maya's neck. "With very good reason, no doubt, your housekeeper told me they were insect bites," he remarked without rancor. "They're not, of course. My assessment is that she was attacked. Was she?"

Unable to meet his questioning eyes, Olivia merely nodded.

"Well, fortunately for her, the injuries aren't serious. The bruises are already healing with the ointment I recommended, and given time, the scars will disappear." He reassured her with a smile, probing no further. "What troubles me is the havoc her experience might have wrought inside here." He tapped his forehead. "She has suffered grave mental trauma, Mrs. Raventhorne, that much is evident." He laid a comforting hand on her arm. "Don't worry, the physical manifestations of the trauma I will control, that I promise. But it is beyond my capacity to remove the scars from her mind. That will be your responsibility—and, of course, Maya's herself."

The first to agree with the doctor, and most forcefully, was Amos.

"We *have* to get her away from here!" he exploded at the dinner table. "This time, there can be absolutely no argument about it!"

Olivia gave him a look of resignation. "Yes."

"Have you any idea what people are *saying* about her?" His face was dark with anger.

Olivia's pain deepened. "No, but I can imagine."

"Sometimes I feel I should wrench those filthy tongues out from their roots and, by God, some day I will!" He opened his mouth to drive home his point even more strongly, but then, catching the flash of warning in Edna's eye, he shut it again.

"The Lubbocks sail for California before the end of the year, remember?" Edna intervened quickly. "If things work out, Maya could leave with them. And you too, dear, should you be so inclined."

"Yes," Olivia agreed, then added with a despondent smile, "that is, if they are willing to entertain the prospect! They might not be, considering all the unsavoury gossip."

"Well, they are," Amos informed her. "I've already mentioned it and they say they would be delighted to see Maya safely to Grandma Sally's in Sacramento—and you, if you decide to make the trip." The hot colour in his face deepened as he speared a piece of mutton on his plate with savage force. "Fortunately, no one is likely to find out the truth of what happened that night, however extravagant the rumours."

"I suppose so," Olivia sighed. "Anyway, I can't think of anything at the moment except getting Maya back on her feet." A tremble appeared in her voice. "And of going to Cawnpore."

Amos recomposed himself and softened his tone. "Yes, of course."

"There is so much to be done there, Amos, so much!"

"Don't worry, dear," Edna comforted, getting up from her seat and putting her arms about Olivia's shoulders. "We will all be with you. You will not have to suffer that alone."

Olivia looked up at her and smiled and gave her hand a grateful squeeze. "We cannot leave until Dr. Humphries considers Maya fit to travel. I simply cannot *conceive* of letting her remain here now on her own."

"But she sails for America as soon as we return!" Amos insisted with a brisk nod. "It would be cruel to expect her to stay here simply to court more notoriety, more heartache!"

There was no point in disputing that. Nobody did.

That night, wide-eyed and sleepless, Olivia sat down to compose a long, detailed letter to Estelle. Her cousin had been in her mind constantly over these past days during which their lives had again been turned upside down by a turbulent confluence of circumstances. There was much that she needed to tell Estelle, much that she needed to share. Despite their regular correspondence, the thread that bound them was still slender, still tenuous; it was a thread Olivia could not risk breaking. Estelle was as much—perhaps even more—part of everything that had happened as she was. However distanced they might be by their curiously divergent destinies, she could not doubt that her cousin had abiding love for her ill-starred brother and a deep concern for his eventual fate. Therefore, it was only fair that she too should be informed fully of Thomas Hungerford's amazing revelations.

Eventually, Maya's fever broke.

She opened her eyes one grey morning, when the sky was lightly overcast and milky sunshine flickered occasionally through the lacy clouds, and focussed them clearly and steadily on her mother.

"Kyle," she said. "I must see Kyle."

It was the first coherent sentence she had spoken since the start of her illness. Her eyes looked over-bright; the voice was still feeble. But there were few signs of that fog that had obscured her mind with such tenacity and for so long.

Olivia's eyes brimmed. She murmured a prayer of thanksgiving. "Perhaps later, darling," she said, filled with relief and hugging her daughter. "For the time being Dr. Humphries has forbidden you any visitors."

"You don't understand," Maya protested, short of breath and gasping weakly, "I *have* to talk to him now, I *must!*"

Does she remember what happened, or is she still fumbling? Olivia wondered. Either way, she knew, it would be calamitous for Maya to see Kyle just yet. Her mind still teetered precariously on the fine edge of sanity; it would not be able to bear the burden of a memory so fraught with disaster.

"In a day or two," Olivia said firmly. "When you're strong enough to move about."

"Is he back from the plantation?"

Olivia was astonished that she should have been able to retain that little snippet of information. "I don't know. You'll have to ask Amos."

Her mother was lying. That much Maya's mind was clear enough to recognise. She shut her eyes and did not argue.

Behind securely shuttered eyelids, however, her confusions started to unravel, creepingly and painfully, image by image. The sluggish awakening slowly gathered momentum: entangled mirages and kaleidoscopic patterns of the past few days started to resolve themselves into shapes and sounds and sensations. At times her remembrance was faultless, clear as crystal—formations from that night stood out in relief, as sharply etched as with acid. But at other times, the fog persisted—other visions remained maddeningly obscured, as elusive as morning mist, as sepulchral as wraiths. She recognised that her powers of reasoning were impaired, that her tongue was too feeble to obey the commands of a still not fully resuscitated mind, that she was too weak for sustained speech. Therefore, she did not ask questions, nor demand answers. She merely lay with her eyes closed, watching with perplexed fascination as the hazy panorama undulated across her inner vision.

That dark, underworld cavern . . . a pair of demonic eyes in a face of dead white . . . the sounds of madness. Fingers on her neck squeezing the air from her windpipe. . . .

Christian!

Her hand crept fearfully towards her throat, but the scream held within it died, too weak to surface. She turned her face to the wall, shrinking within herself. Behind the privacy of her bedsheet, she wanted desperately to cry. She could not.

That night, late, as the household slept and Sheba lay snoring noisily on the divan by the window, she crept out of bed and, almost fainting from dizziness, groped on all fours for a scrap of paper from the wastepaper basket and a stick of kohl from her cosmetic box on the dressing table. In a shaky, spidery scrawl, scarcely able to grip the implement, she composed a two-word message: *Please come!*

Very early the next morning, when Sheba rose and drowsily plodded off to her own room for her ablutions, she sent the ayah to fetch Abdul Mian. Pressing the note in his hand, she gave him instructions to deliver it to Kyle Hawkesworth at his press. She lay down again, exhausted, and awaited his arrival.

Kyle did not come. Neither did he reply to her note.

The body of Sir Jasper Pendlebury might have been laid to eternal rest, but the gossip mills continued to whir as energetically as ever. There was no doubt that the gruesome death with all its mysterious connotations, coupled with Christian Pendlebury's quite extraordinary (and quite inconsiderate, everyone agreed) disappearance, constituted the juiciest scandal of the decade. As such, it was accorded all the respect that was its due in time, effort and creative endeavour. Nevertheless, as the days passed and the intensity of the shock diminished, the hush that had settled over the town began to lift. People no longer spoke in whispers; once again they moved about their everyday businesses briskly. With the funeral and the memorial service over, even in government offices life started to limp back to normal. One intrepid hostess proceeded with her *burra khana,* then another, and another, and occasions for merriment started to reappear on social calendars.

Hearts, however, continued to bleed for the hapless Constance Pendlebury in her double bereavement. Still dazed and uncomprehending, she nonetheless continued to carry her grief with grace and dignity. Despite the most delicate and discreet questioning by Clarence Twining, she had not been able to assist him in his inquiries, as the popular phrase went. She simply continued to insist that her husband had been murdered, that it was this heathen, cannibal country—this graveyard of the white man— that had conspired to consume him and suck the life blood from his body. She had always known, she maintained, that India would bring them nothing but catastrophe. That she had been proved right seemed to bring her some macabre satisfaction.

The only time Constance Pendlebury stooped to anything as vulgar as overt emotion was when she talked of her absent son. Without mention of Maya Raventhorne by name but by repeated insinuation, she made it clear to Twining that she held the girl responsible for "everything." She had warned her husband again and again; he had refused to take her seriously. Now, he had paid the full price for his indulgence and kindness of heart, and they, she and her son, were left to pick up the pieces.

Eventually, as the long, empty days passed and still no word came from Christian, she took to expressing her grief in the manner that provided her the greatest solace and satisfaction: through her piano. Day after day, and through much of the night, she sat alone playing a repertoire of doleful laments, returning again and again to the Amen theme from the *Requiem* Mozart had composed on his deathbed and not lived long enough to finish.

"It quite gives me the willies," shuddered even her most durable friend and supporter, Charlotte Anderson. "Sometimes I wish the poor pet would at least try something a little more cheering. It can't be *healthy* for her to go on like this."

"Nor for us, dear," Dora Humphries pointed out gloomily with an accompanying shiver.

The McNaughtons, due to sail within the month, suggested that she and her white staff return to England with them. Understandably, perhaps,

Lady Pendlebury declined the well-meaning offer. However abhorrent the country and her circumstances, she said, she simply could not consider leaving until she had news of her son's whereabouts and well-being. To make the interim less intolerable for herself, she announced her intention to hold another musical evening, this time dedicated to the memory of her late husband.

The most determined excavations into the Pendlebury affair had so far produced little that the cognoscenti considered of any significant value. What opened up an entirely new (and quite unexpected) area of investigation, however, was the belated testimony that came from Sir Jasper's butler, Tremaine.

Shattered by his master's demise—and his own unknowing participation in it—the butler had taken to his bed in a state of collapse. Through the rest of the week, he proclaimed himself too sick to talk to Clarence Twining or, indeed, anyone. Haunted by hindsight, he was unable to come to terms with his unwitting acts of omission, which had, in his view, played such a deadly part in compounding the tragedy. He should have awakened Lady Pendlebury and warned her when he went up to fetch Sir Jasper's change of clothing. He should have stood watch on the embankment and made certain that his master was safe when he placed the clothing and towel on the wall as instructed. Most of all, he should have *remembered!*

Constance Pendlebury did not doubt for a moment that her husband's death was an unfortunate accident. Indeed, nobody acquainted with Sir Jasper Pendlebury's hearty appreciation and enjoyment of life could have been expected to believe otherwise.

And nobody would have—had it not been for Tremaine and the letters.

The week passed, but still no word came from Kyle.

Preparations commenced for the all-important journey to Cawnpore. In his immense kindness, Arvind Singh undertook to make the arrangements and laid all his many resources at the family's disposal. Both he and the Maharani were to accompany them on their sorrowful voyage of discovery. The final chapter in the life and death of Jai Raventhorne was at last within their reach. It was inconceivable that the Maharaja and Maharani, such vital components in the Raventhornes' lives, should not be with them when it was eventually opened. As impatient to perform his last duties to his father as he was to renew his acquaintance with his cotton mill—and with Rose Pickford—Amos had already left for Cawnpore with Ranjan Moitra. The rest of them were to follow later, after Arvind Singh had had his meeting with the Home member and as soon as Dr. Humphries pronounced Maya strong enough to undertake the journey.

Helped by the natural wellsprings of youthful resilience, Maya's body continued to heal and, gradually, her physical energies regrouped. But mentally she was still far from well, remaining listless and beset with apathy. Even though allowed out of bed, she lay in her room for hours in the dark with the heavy curtains pulled tight over the windows, troubled by the light, using the gloom to sustain the illusion that she was not part of a world with which she could no longer cope. Her body lived, but she felt as if nothing else within her ever would. She sat for hours gazing into nothingness, prodding herself into feeling, not succeeding.

When she did leave her bed, she took to creeping about the house and garden in diffident silence, her back bent, her eyes darting nervously over her shoulder, as if searching for hidden enemies. She looked pale and wan, a shadow of the spirited girl she once was, her substance gone and only the brittle husk remaining. She talked little, making only necessary responses when addressed. Curled up inside her impenetrable shell, always out of reach, Maya remained entombed in her solitary silence, scarcely aware of the passage of time, but waiting for something, always waiting.

Still Kyle did not come.

Despite her apparent lack of interest in her surroundings and her persistent introversion, Maya sensed that they kept things from her. When she entered a room, talk stopped abruptly; in the overdone heartiness with which they spoke to her, she recognised deception. On occasion, she overheard carelessly dropped phrases, an unwittingly raised voice, furtive whisperings. And, of course, the servants gossiped.

With no more restrictions on visitors, many came: the Lubbocks, women from the Home, including the twins, concerned employees from Trident, Leonard Whitney, the Goswamis with their two daughters. Samir was preparing to sail for England, they told her, finally persuaded to cross the seas in pursuit of his law studies. Had he not come to say goodbye? Well, he surely would!

Everyone spoke with forced jollity, not meeting her eyes, often at a loss for words, their uneasy silences more eloquent than speech. Maya was aware that much had happened during the weeks that she had been ill, but she still asked no questions, dreading the unknown even more than she did that which she now suspected, recognising that there was only one person who would have the courage to tell her the whole, brutal truth.

But from Kyle nothing came, not even a whisper.

During the course of her illness, Grace Lubbock had called often, but using Maya's weakness as an excuse, Olivia had not allowed her in for more than a minute or two. Now that Maya was up and about and a lengthier meeting could not be prevented, Olivia warned Grace against repeating even a word of popular gossip, no matter how much Maya might plead.

This morning when Grace called, Maya was reclining on the chaise-longue in the back garden under the gulmohar, staring abstractedly at a remarkably clear blue sky, listening to the birds, to the sounds of the river, to Abdul Mian offering prayers to Allah for having restored her to health and then telling her about her horses. The strawberry mare had developed a rather nasty ulcer on her right flank, the Marwari foal seemed to be attracting quite a few buyers. One, an English gentleman, had been most keen to make a purchase. Naturally, he had made no commitment, the groom informed her. Master Amos had told him not to until the missy memsahib was better. Morning Mist had been delivered to Mr. Ludlow. . . .

"Oh, my dearest friend," Grace wailed as she flung herself on Maya with a cry. "Why, I can hardly recognise you—how very *changed* you've become!"

"Have I?" Maya made an effort to stretch her lips in a smile. Under tautly stretched skin pallid with neglect, her cheekbones looked even higher and her voice was toneless. She said quickly, "I have scarcely seen you since you returned from Darjeeling. Was your holiday as pleasing as you expected?"

Instantly diverted, Grace clasped her hands together and held them against her heart. "Oh, it was like a dream, Maya, a *dream!*" she breathed, eyes shining. "Alberto is like an ethereal being, a positive. . . ."

"Alberto?"

"Yes." Her eyes flew open wide. "Oh my, hasn't anyone told you? I'm engaged!"

"Engaged?" With superhuman effort, Maya tried to appear interested. "Oh. No, nobody told me. I didn't know. Anyway, tell me what he's like."

"See for yourself!" Opening her gold locket with excited fingers, she displayed a miniature of her Alberto, a cherub-faced young man with plump cheeks, a goatee beard and lively smiling eyes. "He's divine, Maya, simply *divine*. We met at Morning Service at St. Paul's School, where he teaches history. Or, at least, did until a fortnight ago. He's recently resigned his position so that he can come with us to America. Papa wants us to get married in Jackson, Mississippi, where Papa's sister and brother and all the nieces and nephews live. We've never met them, of course." She hesitated a moment, then added cautiously, "I believe that we are to escort you as far as Sacramento?"

"Yes, so I hear." Maya showed no reaction, neither pleasure nor dismay. "That would be nice. Well, what else did you do up in the mountains?"

Grace plunged into raptures about Darjeeling, its wonderful sanatorial virtues, its breathtaking vistas of the Himalayan ranges, of Everest, the highest mountain in the *world*, the dear little cottage they lived in called Ben Nevis, surrounded by green meadows, just like in England, Alberto said—and he should know, having been there and all.

"We went to Tiger's Leap to watch the sun rise on Everest. That's when Alberto proposed. At dawn, imagine!" She giggled. "Oh, it was so unbelievably romantic, Maya. Of course, I accepted *immediately*. See?" She held out a hand and flashed a diamond ring, minuscule, but rather sweet. "It belonged to Alberto's grandmother, who still lives in Lisbon. Oh, I forgot to tell you—his mother's family is Portuguese. His father was English, of course. Alberto himself was born in. . . ."

Grace's words continued to wash over Maya, unheard and unheeded. Fortunately, Grace was far too engrossed in her rapturous account to want more than an occasional monosyllabic response from her friend. Keeping a watchful eye on them both from the verandah, where she sat with Marianne and Edna, Olivia listened for a moment. Then, satisfied, she returned her attention to Marianne's equally ecstatic reports about the sojourn in general and her son-in-law to be in particular.

". . . earrings he gave me for my birthday during the dinner party," Grace was saying. "Mama had arranged it with the mothers of some of the boys at St. Paul's. Well, Papa was going to have that loose stone reset there, but he couldn't find a jeweller competent enough to do it, so he said he'd have it done *here*, where he could be assured of getting a really good job done. But you know Papa"—she bunched her mouth in a little pout—"he still hasn't got round to it! He just hasn't had the time, he says, what with the funeral and everything and all those buyers falling out of the woodwork from morning to night."

Funeral? *Whose funeral?*

Maya did not ask.

With the imperial government now back in harness in Calcutta, Lord Mayo finally settled down to reconstitute his Council of Ministers as necessitated by the passing away of Jasper Pendlebury. The changes, when eventually announced, came not only as a surprise but also as a matter of considerable relief to Arvind Singh. In fact, he was delighted. The responsibility for the enormously sensitive Home affairs department had been taken away from the abrasive Arthur Fairfield-Greene and given to the highly diplomatic and popular present Foreign Secretary, Benjamin Ingersoll.

The Maharaja was well acquainted with Lord and Lady Ingersoll on a personal level. They had been his guests in Kirtinagar some years ago, during a specially prolific duck-shooting season, and he had come to regard them both highly. Not only was Ingersoll an astute administrator and a fair-minded man, he was a thorough gentleman, soft-spoken, easy to communicate with and tolerant of others' points of view even when they conflicted with his own. That he should have to deal with the new Home member rather than the obstreperous Fairfield-Greene in the delicate matter of Jai Raventhorne's derelict file made the prospect not only more pleasant but also more hopeful.

But if news of the appointment was surprising, the communication Arvind Singh received from the new Home member on the day following the announcement was even more so. The copy of Thomas Hungerford's deposition sent to Mr. Fairfield-Greene by His Highness, Lord Ingersoll wrote in a handwritten letter, had now been forwarded to him, and he had read it with interest. In view of the extraordinary nature of the testimony, Lord Ingersoll suggested, it would be advisable to hold the meeting the Maharaja sought in Kirtinagar, rather than in the capital.

Arvind Singh was astounded. Quite obviously, Thomas Hungerford's attestation was being treated with rather more respect by the government than he had anticipated.

He agreed to the suggestion with alacrity.

On the mutually appointed day, Benjamin Ingersoll arrived in Kirtinagar late in the afternoon. With him he brought neither official assistants nor, as was the common practice for travelling dignitaries, a posse of outriders and bodyguards. He came accompanied only by his personal peon and bearer.

He apologised for his delayed arrival, due to paperwork "piled up to the ceiling," as he put it, and added, "Your Highness will also have to forgive the rather unorthodox and presumptuous nature of my request. To be honest, I personally dislike subterfuge, all this cloak and dagger stuff. Goodness knows, we have enough of it in the Foreign Ministry, with the Russians crawling all over Afghanistan! But occasionally one has to bow to the inevitable." He refused to expand on that enigmatic remark, parrying the Maharaja's questions adroitly but with humour. Maintaining a solemn face he observed, "The first lesson we are taught in the Foreign Service, Your Highness, is that no matter of diplomacy, however important, is worth keeping a good malt waiting."

"Point taken, sir!" Arvind Singh laughed as he escorted his guest into his inner sanctum and motioned the two attendants who awaited them to pour out glasses of the excellent Glenmorangie. "But one question before we set aside the subject until later. In a single word, does your lordship believe that Thomas Hungerford is telling the truth?"

Benjamin Ingersoll sipped slowly, with obvious pleasure, and stroked his chin. "You know, Your Highness, I am in the extraordinary position of not knowing how to answer that question! Certainly, there is no single word that could possibly suffice for the purpose. All I can say is that this wretched man has succeeded in opening what our American cousins would call a mighty great can of worms. It will take much more than one word, I'm afraid, to explain the frightful mess the man has created."

"And is that the purpose of your lordship's visit?" Arvind Singh asked lightly. "To clear away this frightful mess?"

"Oh dear me, no!" Lord Ingersoll threw him a smile that was quite disarming. "We politicians *create* messes, Your Highness, not clear them. The purpose of my visit is to try to get at least some of those worms *back* in the damned can and then fit the lid on again as tightly as possible."

Over dinner the conversation remained light and informal. Casting protocol aside, the newly appointed Home member regaled his host with saucy anecdotes and doggerel currently popular in Simla from where he had recently returned. It was only after the meal was over that Lord Ingersoll's lighthearted manner changed and he turned brisk once more. Equally eager to start the discussions, the Maharaja again ushered his guest into the privacy of his inner sanctum—a spacious, graciously appointed chamber in which the centuries merged with ease. The two attendants came in and closed the door securely behind them.

"This man, Thomas Hungerford," Lord Ingersoll tapped the document he held in his hand and got down to business immediately. "May I ask where and how Your Highness managed to find him?"

"He was found in Tunbridge Wells, in England," Arvind Singh replied.

"Evidently, he had been living there with the Findlaters ever since he resigned his commission soon after the Mutiny. The *how* I do not consider relevant to our present discussions—although I can assure you that it took many years of effort since, until recently, the man simply did not wish to be located. What is relevant, however is the position your lordship's government maintains with regard to a deposition that attempts to reverse the course of recorded history."

"Why should Your Highness consider that the British Government cares to maintain any position at all about this?" Benjamin Ingersoll asked with a trace of sharpness.

"Because if it did not," Arvind Singh answered softly, "a newly appointed Home member with paperwork piled up to the ceiling would not have considered it worthwhile to make this cumbersome journey to Kirtinagar."

Benjamin Ingersoll smiled at the Maharaja's remark. About to comment on it, he cast an uncertain glance at the two attendants who stood looking out of the window at the far end of the room. The Maharaja's inner sanctum was a jealously guarded annexe that not even the Maharani was allowed to enter without permission. It was here that sensitive matters of state were discussed and precariously balanced treaties fashioned with visiting rulers. Arvind Singh intercepted Ingersoll's glance and, following a moment's thought, picked up a large, intricately cut glass ashtray reposing on the table before them and dropped it onto the marble floor. It fell with a loud crash and, of course, shattered into a thousand pieces. Neither of the attendants standing by the window turned or, indeed, paid the slightest bit of attention to the calamity.

"I wanted to prove to your lordship that we are perfectly secure where we are," Arvind Singh explained to his startled guest with a bland smile. "Both men are deaf mutes, which is why they have been assigned to these chambers. Not one word of what is said within this room will carry beyond these walls. Your lordship may speak freely."

He walked to the window and touched one of the attendants on the shoulder. Immediately, they both leapt into action and, as silently intructed, started to sweep away the glass.

"By Jove!" Ingersoll exclaimed with a dry laugh. "We could certainly do with one or two of those in our ministry, I can tell you that!" Then, satisfied, he returned to the matter in hand. "I appreciate the point you make, Your Highness, but the fact is that I am here in a strictly private capacity. At the moment, the government has no involvement in the matter."

"At the moment?"

"Yes, at the moment. Precisely that." He folded the document he held in his hand and set it to one side on the table. "As I started to say earlier, even though I abhor excessive circumspection, there are occasions when it becomes a necessary evil. This happens to be such an occasion. Therefore, before I proceed, I would like an undertaking from Your Highness that whatever is revealed this evening will continue to remain between us."

"I regret that I cannot consider such an undertaking until after it has been revealed," Arvind Singh countered. "We have waited many years for all this to be explained, your lordship. Surely it is unfair to impose conditions even before we start?"

While Benjamin Ingersoll mulled over that, the attendants presented an array of liqueurs for his inspection. "Very well then," he finally said, selecting a rather fine Cognac. "In that case, I have no choice but to proceed. I will revive my request later when the reason for it becomes apparent to Your Highness." He took a piece of paper from his pocket and smoothed it out on the table in front of him. "The issues we meet to clarify are so complex that I have been forced to scribble some notes as reminders to myself. As I see it, there are three separate issues involved in this very curious series of events. Let us start with the issue of seventeen July 1857—the day that Hungerford and Findlater chanced upon the body hanging in the clearing near Cawnpore."

Listening with intense attention, Arvind Singh nodded.

"According to his statement, Hungerford deduced that it was Raventhorne who had killed that Eurasian, strung him up and placed his possessions in his pocket in order to establish his own death." He shrugged. "True or not, it appears to fit the rest of his extravagant theory, that much I do concede."

"Your lordship does not find it odd that Havelock should have shown such haste in accepting the decapitated head as that of Raventhorne?"

"No." Somewhat absently, Ingersoll swivelled the glass of brandy he held in his hand. "Hindsight might make it seem so, but I think that he genuinely believed that it was. In any case, Hungerford explains that quite plausibly. The conditions that prevailed *were* exceptional—rampant chaos, revulsion over news of the Bibighar massacre the previous day, an all-pervasive lust for revenge, the terror unleashed by impromptu hanging parties, the decomposed state of the mutilated head, and so on and so forth. At another time, under normal circumstances, Havelock might have looked into the matter more closely. But if he was unduly precipitous, perhaps he had a good reason to be so."

"To strengthen the morale of his own troops and weaken that of the enemy?"

"Precisely. Raventhorne had become something of a folk hero to the rebelling sepoys and to the peasantry. The English troops were exhausted, low in spirits, footsore, stricken with disease and crippled by the intense heat. The capture and summary execution of the man believed to be responsible for the massacre would be received with jubilation by British troops and with dismay by those of the Nana Sahib. If he had any doubts at all, Havelock decided to ignore them, take the risk and seize what he considered to be an excellent opportunity."

"And what if Raventhorne reappeared later and made a laughing-stock of the General? Hungerford suspected that Raventhorne would not, that he wanted it believed that he was dead, but the General did not!"

Ingersoll took a long sip from his glass, visibly appreciating the bouquet and flavour. "Yes, that is what initially puzzled me too—until I went through some of the old despatches. You must remember that the British Army maintained an exceptionally efficient intelligence network, Your Highness, still does, in fact. The despatches indicate that Havelock knew that, by then, Raventhorne was desperately ill, that he suffered from recurrent bouts of high fever, that he had been wounded several times and that he was surviving only through sheer force of will. It was generally believed that he did not have long to live. Also, we must not forget that Raventhorne was a wanted man with a price on his head, living in hiding, hardly given to public appearances. Anyway, Havelock's gamble paid off. No one ever saw Raventhorne again. The men made their depositions, received their reward, promptly resigned their commissions and returned to England to enjoy their booty in Tunbridge Wells, where they jointly purchased a property. As far as the General was concerned, that was the end of the matter."

Arvind Singh raised a questioning eyebrow. "And so, does this bring us to the second issue—the one that is most important to your lordship and, perhaps, potentially to the government?"

"Yes." Ingersoll nodded and smiled. "It does indeed. The issue of what Hungerford *alleges* he saw on the river bank on that night of the seventeenth, the night of the Nana Sahib's stage-managed 'suicide.' The rumour, emanating from Bithoor Palace, that the Nana Sahib had not returned from the river, that he had, in fact, vanished, reached British ears later that night—as, without doubt, it eventually did Your Highness?"

"Yes." Arvind Singh conceded that with a nod. "Right or wrong, I discounted the news immediately. At the time, it seemed too absurd to be believed."

"Your Highness was in good company," Ingersoll said drily. "So did the British generals to whom the rumour was conveyed, one of them being General Havelock. They dismissed it as poppycock. Nobody paid a blind bit of attention to it, and then, when the Nana Sahib reappeared a few days later, it was buried and entirely forgotten."

"And so it would have remained," Arvind Singh murmured with a faintly amused smile, "had Hungerford not decided to go to the river that evening."

"Regrettably, yes." Ingersoll's concurrence was matter-of-fact. "Had the rumour been taken seriously then, and investigated, there would have been no problem. The problem arose because it was *not,* at least, not until later."

"Ah! So a problem had arisen, had it?"

"Oh yes—and it might arise again." Ingersoll gave him a piercing look. "I have to confess, quite frankly, that the first *I* learned of the rumour was from this." He again tapped Hungerford's statement. "I was astonished."

"And your lordship's other reaction—apart from astonishment?"

"That the man lied or, to give him the benefit of the doubt, he misunderstood entirely what his eyes perceived."

"I find it difficult to accept either alternative," Arvind Singh announced bluntly as he rose and started to pace. "Let us, briefly, consider some of the salient facts that history records. Since that night of the seventeenth of July, until his alleged death in the jungles of Nepal in September 'fifty-nine, the Nana Sahib was pursued relentlessly by the British. Yet on no occasion was any British soldier able to observe him from recognisably close quarters. Every British intelligence report about his whereabouts here, there and everywhere was promptly contradicted by another. The Nana Sahib's forces continued to engage in skirmishes with the British, but it was Tantya Tope, the Nana Sahib's general, who fought them. The Nana Sahib himself was never seen on the battlefield, or, for that matter, seen at all! In fact, during the months following July until he fled to Nepal early in 'fifty-nine, nobody knew for certain just where the man was at any given time. Am I right?"

"Certainly. As you say, it is a matter of recorded history."

"Even though the Nana Sahib was a fugitive with a price of ten thousand pounds on his head—double that on Raventhorne's—his elusiveness was not only excessive, it was uncanny. Every movement of his remained cloaked in extraordinary mystery, there appeared to be no material evidence of him at all! Even the spate of appeals he addressed to all and sundry—the British Parliament, Queen Victoria, the Court of Directors of John Company, the Governor-General, even the emperor Napoleon—were composed and written by Tantya Tope, who held the Nana Sahib's seal."

Lord Ingersoll listened in absolute silence, his impassive expression a testament to his long years of training as a diplomat.

"It is true that once he fled to Nepal, the Nana Sahib personally met and spoke to many, including Jung Bahadur, the Nepalese Prime Minister. But historians take much of the information about his stay in Nepal from official British records, as did many English journalists reporting the affair. Even they confess that there was a 'curious fog' over the entire adventure of the Nana Sahib in Nepal."

"But he was accompanied by an entourage, by members of his family, by his coterie of advisers!"

"Yes, and this very trusted coterie comprised the *only* people who knew him by sight. What the Nepalese saw and met and talked to was a man dressed as the Nana Sahib, addressed as the Nana Sahib, treated with the respect due to the Nana Sahib—but not one of them could have sworn that he *was* the Nana Sahib—Dhondu Pant, the Raja of Bithoor, the man who aspired so desperately to be declared the Peshwa like his adoptive father—not one!"

Lord Ingersoll shifted positions and fixed Arvind Singh with a gimlet eye, his fingers pyramided across his chest. "May I ask what exactly is the purpose of this recapitulation, Your Highness?"

Arvind Singh continued to pace. After a brief interval, he resumed in the same level tone: "Your lordship must know that every ruler uses doubles on occasion. For those at a distance and those who do not know the true ruler personally, it is impossible to tell the difference. I myself have practised this innocent deceit with great success when the contingency has arisen. Not one of my own subjects has ever detected the subterfuge." He halted his steps and turned to face his guest. "It was no secret that the Nana Sahib also employed a stable of men who resembled him closely. He, more than most rulers, used them in the interests of survival. And, of course, to confound the English."

The Home member made no comment. He simply listened.

"Colonel Ramsay, the British Resident in Nepal at the time, recorded that even the Nana Sahib's death in the jungle was impossible to establish. There were a dozen different accounts, but no reliable eyewitnesses. As you yourself know, your lordship, to this day people believe that the Nana Sahib is still alive. Each claimant who surfaces is received with total faith until proved an imposter."

Ingersoll raised a sceptical eyebrow. "Your Highness uses circumstantial evidence to suggest that the Nana Sahib was killed on the night of the seventeenth by Jai Raventhorne? That Thomas Hungerford *has* reported accurately what his eyes perceived?"

"I merely suggest that it is not beyond the realms of possibility," Arvind Singh amended. "Naturally, news of the death and that nascent whisper would have been immediately suppressed by the Bithoor coterie, and the services of a double used without hesitation. I agree that the ploy was hasty and crude, but—if my theory is correct—it succeeded. And," he smiled with some complacency, "it certainly confounded the English!"

The Home member straightened in his seat and voiced an amiable laugh. "Well, I have to admit that it is an amusing thesis, Your Highness. Largely fanciful, of course, but indubitably entertaining!"

"Is it, your lordship? Sometimes I wonder."

For a moment Ingersoll made no response. He sipped the final drops from his glass and, hastily, the watching attendant sprang forward to replenish it. When the Home member spoke again, it was in an entirely different tone and there was not a trace of amusement on his face.

"No man in his right senses could possibly accept as anything other than imaginative fiction," he said slowly and solemnly, "a premise such as Your Highness has just propounded. Indeed, I myself would be inclined to dismiss it instantly, were it not for one rather disturbing factor."

"That factor being?"

Ingersoll stared hard into his glass. "After reading Hungerford's statement, I naturally embarked upon a thorough search of the military records of that precise day, July seventeen." He paused. "I found no mention in any despatch of the rumour of the Nana Sahib's death. None at all! I discerned only one veiled phrase in an obscure file that could have been an oblique reference to it, nothing more. Had I not been looking for mention of that rumour, I would certainly have missed it."

"The rumour was never recorded in any despatch?"

"Either that, or"—he took a deep breath—"and I say this in the strictest confidence, Your Highness, the pertinent despatches were subsequently removed. The can of worms that I mentioned refers to this aspect of the case. If there ever was such a rumour—and Your Highness confirms that there was—then it appears to be one of the best kept secrets of the Mutiny."

Arvind Singh's eyes gleamed. "But there must also be a reason for the *English* to court such secrecy."

"Yes. There must." Ingersoll said just that, no more.

During the mutually troubled silence that fell between them, they avoided each other's eyes, lost in separate thoughts. It was Ingersoll who finally broke the silence. "Tell me, does Your Highness honestly believe that this supposition could be true beyond each and every reasonable doubt?"

The Maharaja reflected, his gaze fixed to the intricate design on the lush Persian carpet under his feet. Then he smiled enigmatically and spread his hands. "Who can say, your lordship? In all honesty, all that can be said is that we don't know, we simply don't know. And we will never know." He shrugged. "We have to accept that the mystery surrounding the Nana Sahib's death will never be satisfactorily resolved. There will always be a question mark against that—and that question mark, too, history will record. It *could* have happened the way Hungerford describes. But did it?"

Ingersoll nodded in tacit agreement and glanced at his pocket watch. It was well past midnight. It was obvious that both men were tired. Despite Arvind Singh's raging impatience, he bowed to the Home member's request that the rest of the discussion be deferred to the morning.

In the morning, Arvind Singh knew, they would finally discuss the one issue that still remained, the issue most vital to himself and to the Raventhorne family. They would talk of Jai Raventhorne—and his connection with the events that took place on 16 July 1857, the day of the Bibighar massacre.

CHAPTER

25

THE ROOM AT THE END of the tunnel was deserted.
Maya placed her flickering lantern in a corner of the floor, then watched fearfully as a grotesque shadow ballet sprang to life around her on the high, bare walls. On a window sill lay a child's broken rattle and a sprinkling of dead flower petals. There were few other reminders that the room had ever contained human presence. The string cot and the slatted wooden "cage" were gone, as were the neatly ranged Urdu books, the musical instruments, ankle-bells, toys and all the other flotsam and jetsam of everyday occupation. The rough-hewn walls and floor of the cavernous subterranean tomb seemed to her like sentinels, silent witnesses to whatever calamities she had caused to unleash in the entrails of this stark, secret underworld. A faint, cloyingly sweet fragrance of attar-of-roses hovered above her in the moist air.

Because of Maya's commendable physical recovery, Sheba no longer slept in her room; it had not been difficult to slip away without being seen. The prospect of a return to the tunnel terrified Maya—as much as did the brutal penance of a memory restored. Perversely, she could not bear the torment of not knowing, of never knowing! Torn between her two nightmares, she had finally made her choice. She had gathered up her diminished resources and, goaded by hidden forces, ventured forth once more, one last time, into this eerie nether region. She saw now that Kyle would not come to her; perhaps he had gone away again. The thought filled her with dismay. He was the only one she could talk to, the only one who could understand. They were, after all, inextricably bound in the same conspiracy.

She walked aimlessly around the room, running her palms over the corrugated surface of the walls, drawing a fingernail across the brickwork.

The very silence promoted involuntary mental evocations, adding to the limited patchwork of her remembered imagery. The longer she lingered, the deeper her mind penetrated into reality, the prancing shadows exacerbating her imagination and accelerating her fears.

Somewhere behind her she heard a hollow sound, a footfall. She felt ice creep through her veins, a renewed surge of panic.

Kyle . . . ?

"There is nothing left for you here." He stood in the doorway behind her. "Why did you come?"

She spun round with a gasp, part in relief, part with a sense of entrapment. "Why did you not?"

"There was no point. What more is there to be said?"

"There *is* more to be said!"

"Not now, later perhaps."

"No!" She took time to steady her breath. "There will be no later. I heard it said that you are going away soon. When you return, we would have left for Cawnpore. Or America." The tremble in her knees compounded, but there was no place to sit. "There is something more to be said, Kyle— I need to know what happened!"

He raised a mild eyebrow. "And you don't?"

"Not everything. There are still vacant spaces in my memory. No one can fill them except you."

"It might be best to let the spaces remain as they are, Maya."

"No, I cannot!"

He walked into the denuded room and leaned his shoulder against a wall so that he faced her. "What is done is done. Memory will not undo it, no matter how detailed."

"We shared something, Kyle, you and I," she pleaded, feeling the first flutters of panic. "Neither of us can ever be the same again. It seems to have changed everything in my life, perhaps yours too. I *have* to know what it was!"

"Ask Amos."

"Even Amos keeps it from me! Surely you must see that to be at peace, I need to be told everything?"

"What you really need is reassurance," he said, unmoved. "You want me to help you wash away your guilt, tell you that it doesn't matter, that it was all right. Well, I cannot."

"Guilt?" she frowned. "You are wrong, Kyle. I feel no guilt. I feel . . . nothing. That is what is so frightening. No guilt, no remorse, no anger, no grief." She looked at him in puzzlement. "Don't you think that I should feel *something?*"

"You want me to devise a penance for you, is that it?"

"No. I am able to devise my own penance—but I cannot until I learn the extent of the crime." Her nails cut deep into her palms as she clenched her hands by her sides. "Don't mock me, Kyle. Whatever I deserve, it is not that."

"Mock you?" He considered that a moment, then laughed. "I can hardly claim to be in a position to mock you!" His expression changed; he heaved a sigh of surrender. "Very well, what is it that you want me to tell you?"

Her knees threatened to buckle. She walked to the window and gently brushed aside the dead petals and the rattle. Hitching herself up, she perched on the ledge and folded her hands in her lap.

"There was a funeral."

"Yes."

"Who died?" She felt a flicker of fear, a minimal loss of breath, as she waited for his response.

"Sir Jasper Pendlebury."

"Oh." She released her breath.

"You didn't know that he had died?"

"No. Yes. I don't know. I knew *somebody* had."

She gave such little evidence of emotion that he was again scornful. "A doctored memory? How convenient."

"Convenient?" There was a time when she might have been enraged by his remark, wounded even, but she had lost the capacity for that. "No. On the contrary, it is inconvenient not to know," she explained patiently.

"Even though it makes ugly hearing?"

"It is still my right to hear it, Kyle." She spoke with detachment. Only her heart beat like a kettledrum, but that he could not hear.

She could see the effort with which he argued, out of habit, nothing more. He rubbed the nape of his neck with the back of one hand and his eyes looked raw. She had never before seen him so fatigued.

"All right, what else?"

"Everything. Tell me everything."

When he had finished, she stared in turn at each of the walls, impassive. She had the illusion that they moved inwards, that they closed in on her. For an instant she could not breathe. But then the illusion passed. She slipped down from the window sill and walked away from him, into the passageway and out through the grilled aperture into the open. There, under the vast expanse of eternity, she turned her face up and filled her lungs with air, savouring the taste of night on her tongue, the touch of the moon on her cheeks. It had not rained all day; the rock ledge was bone-dry. She sat down, cuddling her knees against her chin, staring out across the gaunt outlines of the masts in the distant dockyard. Without turning her face, she knew that he had joined her.

"I killed him, Kyle."

He swung his legs over the ledge and sat down some feet away from her. He did not discount her claim.

"I killed without a trace of blood," she said, a first tinge of bitterness fouling her mouth. "I was a good pupil."

"Oh yes, that you were!" He picked up a stone from the ledge and, with savage force, flung it down the embankment. "If you must know what we truly shared," he said, his own bitterness spilling over, "it was that. The honours are equally divided between us. Therefore, if you hoped that I would wipe clean your slate, I cannot—any more than I can my own."

She hardly heard him, lost in enumerating her own discoveries to herself. "I wounded your mother, I had no right to. It was not my secret to reveal. I betrayed her, Kyle. And you."

"Don't worry, she understands your compulsions better than most," he observed with sour humour. "She bears you no grudge."

"He need not have died."

"Don't expect me to share in the mourning," he said crisply. "I regret the way it happened, but that is all."

They sat in taut silence, lost within their own inner spaces, thinking the same thoughts without voicing them. Down by the riverside, a shadowy figure crept from boulder to boulder, a scavenger looking for snails and frogs hiding in residual pools under rockfaces. Maya finally excavated the name she had tucked away deep in a remote fold of her consciousness.

"And . . . ?" When the moment came, she could not say it.

He understood anyway. "Christian?"

A spasm rippled down her spine. She lowered her head.

"Vanished in some unknown limbo, poor devil. Gone to earth carrying *his* compulsions with him."

"Where?"

"Who knows? Somewhere. The world is a big place."

"They have not been able to find him?"

"He chooses not to be found."

"Could he also be dead?"

"Perhaps. Or worse. Death is an easy escape."

"Worse?"

"He has to learn to live with himself again. Like you. Like me."

There were so many questions she wanted to ask about Christian, so much she wanted to know, but she did not have the words. Or the courage. Above the bitterness she felt something, a pinprick, an echo of an ache, nothing more. She turned away to rest her other cheek on her knee so that he could not see her face, or recognise her need. As always, he had assessed her correctly; it *was* reassurance she sought. In the arid immensity of her mind, from amidst the desolation, she wanted to reach out to him, to beg for his help, but her pride would not let her. In any case, he appeared to have forgotten her existence.

"They are seduced by the songs of the Siren," he murmured to himself, squinting upwards, far removed from her. "They pursue haunting melodies, try to catch a sound, a vision, a fragrance. They cannot. The path is slippery, they are inadequately shod. And the Siren destroys without mercy."

She did not need to ask to whom he referred. Christian's face, blurred and disfigured, floated across her eyes like a passing cloud, a wisp of mist. Then it merged with the night and simply disappeared.

"They live in the illusion that they can trap the soul of India, tame it. They cannot." His voice was touched with despair. "They see India as a physical entity, the colour pink of their maps. It is not. India is an abstraction, a concept, a feeling, no more, no less. Like the Siren, it cannot be tamed, nor learned, nor *changed*. It can only be sensed—and for this they lack the equipment." He turned to her in sudden anger. "Do you understand?"

"No."

The point of the pin again pricked. Before it could dig deeper, she stifled the pain and chased it back against the distant frontiers of her mind. She asked quickly, "What will you do on the plantation? Where will you start?"

"Start?" His reverie snapped with the question. "We will start with the land."

"You will sow crops?"

"Yes, that, and allot land to those who have none. A man without land is a man without a soul."

"But it will take time for the crops to grow. What will people eat until then?"

"They are used to eating little. They will survive." He shrugged. "And the soil of Bengal is generous. If treated well, it rewards with abundance. It allows a man to live with dignity, with self-esteem. My mother wants to start a school."

"Where?"

"In one of the sheds of the indigo factory. Or, perhaps, under the shade of a generous tree."

"Will you live there always?"

"I don't know. Always is a long time."

"Some day will you think of it as home?"

"Home? Forever a place where one is not!" He laughed, amused by her naïveté. "Perhaps. Stranger things have happened in the pursuit of that pot of gold at the end of a rainbow."

"But you said Eurasians *have* no home! They belong in those spaces between the keys of a piano, the black and the white—or hang upside down in dark crevices like bats!"

He was taken aback that she should remember. "Well, that I suppose, is the paradox, isn't it?"

"The paradox?"

"One must learn to live on the treadmill. But that is precisely what one can never learn!"

She sighed. "It will not be easy, what you want to do."

"Easy? You expect anything worthwhile to be easy?" He lay back and crossed his hands beneath his head, his eyes far away among the distant galaxies. "There comes a time when one tires of destruction, one seeks another direction, an axis around which to revolve. Everyone needs a focus. In building something, anything, a future, one locates that focus. And hard work leaves little spare energy for the self-satisfaction of hate. No, it will not be easy."

"And this?" She waved at the dark, sombre building of his press. "You leave all this behind?"

"Yes. Grinstead and some of the other lads want to continue to run it.

Will the foreigner let them?" He grimaced. "I don't know, but they have my blessings."

She pushed a pebble around with the tip of a finger. "In all this that you want to do, will you succeed?"

"Succeed?" He shrugged uncaringly. "I don't know. Maybe, maybe not. Either way, it will not be in my lifetime." There was a curious shine in his eyes, perhaps only a reflection of the stars he gazed up at, but the radiance seemed to illuminate his skin from within. "No grand projections, Maya," he breathed with muted passion, "just modest hopes, some attainable, others not. Perhaps the hopes are hollow, like our lives, but perhaps they are not." He rolled over on his side and looked at her, smiling, without evidence of hostility, his face aglow, his teeth white and even. "Small dreams, Maya, for small people."

She listened to him intently, astonished that his heart should be so evident in his eyes. She struggled to comprehend what he said, but the world he talked of meant nothing to her; she could not identify with it. Yet, as she stared at him, absorbing what he said with an impersonal sense of wonderment, something stirred in the pit of her stomach, a curious sensation, not uncomfortable, just unfamiliar, something she had not felt before. She searched hard to put a name to it, and then did. Unbelievably, it was *envy!*

From across the river came the sound of singing, of laughter, of a rhythmic beat of the double-sided drum carried over on the wind. Someone was getting married in a shanty beside the docks.

She forgot her pride and asked, "Why did I do it, Kyle?"

"Ah! So it *is* reassurance you need, after all!"

"Yes." There was no point in denying it. "That and understanding. Why am I like this?" She again felt estranged from reality, engulfed by a curious sense of disorientation. "They say my father had a canker in his soul—do I too?"

"Whatever his sins, his virtues too are visited upon you."

"What virtues?"

"Why ask me?" he said, not angry, just weary. "Look to where the answers lie, within yourself."

"I need help to find them."

"I cannot help you any more than you can help me, Maya. We have to negotiate separate rapids in separate canoes. We strike out for different shores."

She felt bereft at his analogy; it sounded like an abandonment. She couldn't bear to think of it. "After we return from Cawnpore," she said quickly, her chin once more held high, "I will leave for America. Perhaps Mother will come too."

"So I hear."

"You are right, Kyle—there is nothing left for me here. There never was." Her mouth twisted in a smile of faint defiance. "They say America is a new world."

"You think this new world will give you what you want?"

"I don't know what I want."

"A rich, white-skinned husband? Acceptance in a community?" He laughed, again harsh. "And then? Some day you will produce a coffee-coloured brat, the colour of your father's mother, the colour of India. Then what?"

"Then?" She gave a hard little laugh. "Then I might as well return and seek work at the Golden Behind! I wouldn't be much good for anything else, would I?"

He rose so abruptly that she almost jumped. "You make me *sick*," he spat at her, all at once infuriated. "You and your mealy-mouthed self-pity! The only infinitive you conjugate in your endless pursuit of self-interest is *to want*. Do you ever consider anyone or anything in your trivial existence besides yourself and your own over-indulgences? Have you ever cared to spare a useful thought for the rest of mankind?" He paused to curse generously under his breath. "That you are arrogant and spoilt, I have always known, but I had never thought of you as a damned *coward!*"

She blinked, winded by the storm of condemnation. "You despise me," she said quietly, hiding behind a defiant smile.

"I despise people like you—over-pampered, ungrateful, greedy for self-gratification. People who orbit about their solar selves like parasitical planets. I despise the breed you symbolise, the takers of the world. You take of the sun and the sea and the air and all this, all *this,* and give nothing in return."

"I can hardly cure the world's ills!"

"No, but you can cure"—he stared at the scavenger further down on the embankment—"*his.* Those with neither past nor future and barely a present. Do you feel no responsibility at all to humanity?"

She stood up, humiliated, her anger starting to stir. "If humanity cannot accept me, it has no right to need me," she said coldly.

"A convenient shelter behind which to hide from reality!"

She fixed him with a frosty smile. "And what about you, Kyle? That settlement that you build, that ghetto for Eurasians—what is that for if not to escape from reality? The world, *this* world, doesn't accept you either, and so you seek a refuge, make a virtue of convenience. And what better place to hide a leaf than in a forest?"

In the pale moonlight his face looked shocked. For a moment he stared at her, his temper dying. He asked, "Is that all that this is to you, a ghetto, an escape?" Before she could say anything, he answered himself. "Well, perhaps you are right," he conceded, deflated. "I should be the last person to castigate you, to pass judgement. Perhaps the sordid truth is that we both try to escape, both chase after rainbows. In our own ways, I suppose, we are the same, both cowards. You seek the sanctuary of your new world, I of mine."

How deftly he had bound them together in yet another conspiracy! She saw now that she had been wrong to expect help from him.

"We have nothing in common, Kyle!" she corrected him with a stony stare, "except this . . . this hideous experience. You see your future here, I don't. I could never live here again."

"Because you feel ashamed? Guilty? Because you believe you can never face anyone again?"

She evaded his question. "Because I have no roots here."

"You have no roots anywhere!"

"In America, eventually, they will grow, flourish!"

"Roots grow not from the soil but from the heart."

"I don't *belong* here!"

"Nor will you anywhere—unless you accept who you are."

"Who *am* I?"

"You are *you*. Unique. One of a kind. No other human being in the world is like you. Isn't that enough, for God's sake? Amos asks for no more, why do you?"

"Amos *chooses* to have roots here."

"Because he recognizes and respects himself, because he does not question who he is, he simply accepts with grace."

"Well, I cannot," she said flatly. "I will not!" Her eyes started to sting; she bit hard on a lip. "It's not fair, not fair!"

"No one has ever claimed that life is *fair*. What you want is a label, a stamp, a brand on the haunches. Is that important?"

"*Yes!* Had I had that, I might not have. . . ." She cut herself off before she could say more.

"Don't try to blame the universe for what happened." He tossed his hands up in the air, then ran impatient fingers through his hair to try to calm himself. "Anyway, it *has* happened, Maya. It cannot be erased. Neither anger nor self-pity is going to change it, or," he added rather more gently, "help you to heal."

"Then what is?" she cried, the pain reviving.

"Another orbit around another axis, maybe." He started to add something to that, then changed his mind. "That is for you to decide," he concluded curtly instead. "I cannot advise you."

"I have already decided."

"And what if you're wrong? What if you look back with regret and want to return?"

She turned her back on him and strolled to the edge of the outcrop, gazing out across the river, pewter-coloured in the night light. When she returned, her eyes were once again cool and undisturbed. "No, Kyle," she said calmly, "I will not look back. Nor will I ever return."

"Then why the hell are you crying?"

She put a hand up to her cheek and was astonished to find that it was wet. She had not known that she cried. Roughly she brushed away the tears and walked away from him.

She left him where he stood. True to her word, she did not look back.

That night, all night long, and for the first time in an eternity of darkness, Maya thought of Christian. She thought of his shattered life, and of her own, stretching ahead like an endless grey, wintry road leading nowhere. Emotion uncoiled; she was swamped with pain. She could not bear it.

Finally, finally, she wept.

Both Arvind Singh and his guest had slept well. They had savoured the delights of an early morning stroll in the palace park and enjoyed a hearty open-air breakfast by the lake. Lord Ingersoll had been much amused by the virtuoso dance performed with great disdain for their benefit by an imperious peacock, indeed, quite entranced by his exquisitely coloured raiment. Then, refreshed in mind and body, they once again made their way to the Maharaja's private chambers, impatient to resume the unfinished discussion of the previous night.

"Before we proceed further," Lord Ingersoll said as they seated themselves in the comfortable alcove with the fringed punkas swinging in perfect rhythm above their heads, "there is something that I would like to point out to Your Highness. What we talked about yesterday was mostly conjecture. What I am about to reveal today is not. It is fact, authenticated fact." His face was without expression, but there was a rare spark in his watery blue eyes.

During three decades of rulership and dealing with the British, Arvind Singh too had mastered the art of the phlegmatic. He showed no reaction but merely inclined his head.

Without further preamble, Lord Ingersoll plunged straight into the heart of the matter. "I should imagine Your Highness was aware at the time that Raventhorne had become disenchanted with the Nana Sahib and his methods," he said, not as a question but as a statement.

"Yes. I was aware of it. Jai mentioned it the last time we met sometime in May, here in Kirtinagar. He had envisaged an honourable fight between men. He was bitterly opposed to the rampant killing of civilians, and particularly to the forthcoming siege of the Cawnpore entrenchment. He said he was sick of all the senseless slaughter on both sides."

"Yes, that is precisely what attracted the attention of Lawrence."

"Sir Henry Lawrence?"

"Yes."

Ingersoll broke off to accept the welcome cups of coffee the attendants presented. They sipped a while in silence and then Ingersoll resumed, impatient to continue.

"When the Mutiny first erupted in Meerut, Henry Lawrence was the Chief Commissioner of Oudh, stationed in Lucknow. He had recently been promoted to Brigadier-General and given full military powers. From intelligence reports, Lawrence had learned of Raventhorne's disillusionment with his erstwhile ally. Lawrence was a man of rigid self-righteousness, equally appalled by the carnage on both sides. In a gesture of some boldness, he sent a covert message to Raventhorne suggesting a meeting to initiate a discussion with the Nana Sahib. Raventhorne agreed. With a price on his head, Raventhorne naturally asked for safe passage to be guaranteed. He also stipulated that he would speak only to Lawrence, that he should come accompanied by only one aide, and that the army should not in any way be involved. Lawrence consented to the conditions. It was to be a secret rendezvous in a forest on the outskirts of Lucknow on Tuesday, June twenty-three."

An involuntary muscle started to twitch in the Maharaja's right temple. He had known nothing of this; he listened in spellbound silence.

"By now, Raventhorne was an extremely sick man, plagued by constant fever. Somehow, over a night and a day, he made the journey from Cawnpore to Lucknow. Once he reached Lucknow, however, he collapsed and was forced to go into solitary hiding in the jungle. On June twenty-three, accompanied by only one aide, Lawrence went to the place chosen for the secret rendezvous. Raventhorne was not there. Lawrence went again on the following day and then on every day until June twenty-nine. There was still no sign of Raventhorne. The following day, June thirty, Lawrence could not go. The Lucknow Residency was surrounded and Lawrence was besieged. He was not to emerge again."

"The meeting never took place?" Arvind Singh interjected.

Ingersoll shook his head. "It could not, but Raventhorne was not aware of that. Crippled with sickness and lying alone in that dense jungle, Raventhorne was as unaware of the siege as he was of the fact that, on July four, Henry Lawrence had succumbed to the injuries sustained during the bombardment." Ingersoll paused and gave Arvind Singh a look of inquiry.

"No, no more questions. Not yet. Pray continue."

"Realising that the siege of the Residency would be long and that he might not survive it," the Home member resumed, "Lawrence managed to smuggle a hasty message to his aide who, through sheer chance, was not among those besieged. He instructed the man to keep a watch on the rendezvous point every day until Raventhorne appeared—as he was convinced he would. The aide did as instructed, loyally and conscientiously, continuing his daily visits even after Lawrence had been killed. Then one day, Raventhorne *did* appear, desperately weak, only just able to stand on his feet. It was from the aide that Raventhorne now heard everything for the first time: about the siege of the Residency, Lawrence's death, the evacuation of the Cawnpore entrenchment, the treachery and slaughter of the evacuees—including his sister and her son—at the Satichowra Ghat. He went insane with rage, unable to think of anything but revenge. Without pausing further, he flung himself on his horse and raced back to Cawnpore, once again riding like fury." Ingersoll drained his coffee cup and, with a motion, declined another. "The day on which the aide finally met Raventhorne in Lucknow was a Thursday. The date was the sixteenth of July."

The Home member's voice trailed away, but the date continued to reverberate in the air between them. Arvind Singh was stunned. For a few seconds he struggled to speak. "In that case"—he swallowed hard—"Raventhorne could not *possibly* have covered the fifty-odd miles between Lucknow and Cawnpore to be at the Bibighar on the same day, the day of the massacre!"

"Precisely."

By tacit consent, it seemed, the two men allowed the tension-charged silence between them to expand. Then Arvind Singh asked, his voice still hushed, "How does your lordship come to know all this?"

"From an unimpeachable source."

"Am I permitted to know the name of that unimpeachable source?"

"Yes." Ingersoll hesitated, then added, "But not yet, Your Highness. First I must revert briefly to the matter that we discussed yesterday—that of Thomas Hungerford's statement." Normally a soft-spoken man, Ingersoll hardened his tone perceptibly. "I have to point out to Your Highness that *under no circumstances whatsoever* can that statement ever be made public."

With the monsoon clouds now on the run, it was a warm morning. Both men were informally dressed, but the humidity had made patches of sweat on both their coats. As Ingersoll dabbed his forehead with a handkerchief, the Maharaja gave a signal to the attendants for further refreshments. Ingersoll accepted the tankard of chilled beer offered to him with visible relief.

"Because it would greatly embarrass the British Government!" Arvind Singh's eyes gleamed. He was now finding it difficult to contain his simmering anger.

"Embarrass?" Ingersoll shrugged, then laughed a little. "All governments, including mine and, no doubt, yours, Your Highness, have thick hides. Fielding embarrassments is their stock in trade. No, if Hungerford's statement is made public, it would inflict far worse consequences on my government. In fact, that can of worms would be all over Parliament!" He leant forward, his expression intense. "Those despatches were abstracted from the archives for good reason—and I speak to you very frankly now, Your Highness. It is very likely that, during the tail end of the Mutiny while English forces still fought the Nana Sahib, that rumour somehow resurfaced. Suddenly, it might have become evident that no one, at least no *English* soldier, had laid eyes on the Nana Sahib's face since mid-July. Some perceptive English officer might have made bold to ask, what if the Nana Sahib *had* died that night on the river?"

Ingersoll sat back again. "As Your Highness can imagine, terror must have struck the hearts of the high brass at the prospect of such an event, however far-fetched it might have seemed. What if the rumour reached Whitehall and, horror of horrors, the Opposition? The Press? The great British public? What if it became known that the British Army in India was fighting someone rumoured to be dead? That young British soldiers were laying down their lives doing battle with a fake, an imposter? Even a sane Opposition would have gone mad at such a prospect. Ours, bless its heart, has always been rabid. Now it would have simply gone berserk. Believe me, we would have had our own version of the Mutiny in England!"

He raised a thin smile. "The British Press and public have always been fascinated by the charismatic and elusive Nana Sahib. They still are. Hardly a month goes by, even now, without some highly fanciful theory about him propounded in print to boost circulations." He added with grim emphasis, "What applied *then*, also applies today. If made public, Hungerford's statement would *still* create havoc. Perhaps now Your Highness can understand why I chose to come here rather than discuss such a volatile matter in town where every wall has more ears than a damned field of corn!"

Arvind Singh had listened wordlessly to the recitation. Now, he rose abruptly and went to stand by the large, ornate fireplace, his back to his guest. He was exceedingly angry.

"All these years it has been known to the British Government, and within their means to prove it, that Jai Raventhorne was innocent! Yet the injustice was perpetuated?"

"It has not been known, Your Highness, nor has it been within our means to prove it."

Arvind Singh spun round to face Ingersoll, his eyes narrowed and incensed. "Well, it is known now! Therefore, I insist that your lordship reveal to me the name of Henry Lawrence's aide—no doubt your unimpeachable source—who met Raventhorne on the day of the Bibighar massacre!"

"Yes, of course," Lord Ingersoll said with a resigned sigh. "His name was Jasper Pendlebury."

Arvind Singh battled with his astonishment, then flushed. "Jasper Pendlebury chose to hold this information secret rather than clear the name of a man unjustly accused and condemned?"

"Yes, perhaps understandably so." Ingersoll scratched the tip of his nose with a tentative finger. "For one, since he believed that Raventhorne had been caught and executed in Cawnpore, he decided to let sleeping dogs lie. For another, he did not wish to give away a secret that belonged to Henry Lawrence, one that he had been urged to maintain. And thirdly, as far as Pendlebury was concerned, Raventhorne was still the enemy. In warfare there is no room for concessions as, no doubt, Your Highness would be the first to concede."

Arvind Singh's jaw was set in a hard, determined line. "Nevertheless, Raventhorne *is* innocent, Pendlebury *is* dead, and dead men tell no tales," he said icily. "Therefore, I consider that the government has a bounden duty to reopen Jai Raventhorne's file for a fair and frank re-examination."

Lord Ingersoll made a wry face. "I doubt if that will be possible, Your Highness."

"Why ever not?"

"Lord Mayo might be an Irishman and as obdurate as they come, but even he cannot fail to recognise a can of worms when he sees one! Once he has read Hungerford's deposition, he would have to be mad to agree to reopen Raventhorne's file."

The Maharaja stared at him unbelievingly. "Are you saying, your lordship, that the British will continue to pillory a man even after it is known that he is not guilty? That there is no way in which his innocence can be publicly established and acknowledged?" He was cold with outrage and restrained himself with visible effort. "If that is the case, your lordship, I regret that I will have no choice but to make it my pleasure to scatter that much feared can of worms wherever I am able to!"

"What would that gain Your Highness?" Ingersoll asked mildly.

"Satisfaction, *considerable* satisfaction, I assure you."

"But it would not prove Jai Raventhorne innocent."

"Jasper Pendlebury's death has ensured that nothing now will, your lordship." Arvind Singh retorted harshly.

Lord Ingersoll rose to his feet and went to join the Maharaja near the fireplace. From the breast pocket of his coat he withdrew an envelope and placed it on the mantelpiece.

"As it happens, there is still something that will," he said, his tone equable. "Your Highness will find much in this that will be of particular interest."

The envelope was addressed to Lady Harriet Ingersoll. Inside were several sheets of paper crowded with handwriting. Arvind Singh carried the letter to his mahogany desk set in a corner near the window. One of the attendants sprang forward and handed him a brocade case, from which the Maharaja extracted a pair of gold-rimmed half-moon spectacles. While the Home member sat in silence in the alcove and waited patiently, Arvind Singh perused the lengthy letter with infinite concentration. It recounted in somewhat greater detail and with extreme clarity precisely the events that Lord Ingersoll had related to him that very morning. It was an extraordinary document, a complete confirmation of everything that had been said earlier, a vindication in black and white of his much maligned dead friend. The signature at the bottom of the last page was that of Jasper Pendlebury. It had been written on the eve of his death.

For full five minutes after the Maharaja had finished reading, there was silence in the room. Too stunned to speak for a while, Arvind Singh sat back and stared sightlessly out of the window. In his inner vision, Jai Raventhorne's long-gone face rose again and again as he struggled to control his emotions and put his rampaging thoughts back into some form of order. He could not hide the fact that he was profoundly moved.

"So you see, Your Highness, sometimes dead men *do* tell tales!" Ingersoll said gently.

Arvind Singh agreed with a mute nod. There was a slight tremble in his fingers as he replaced the letter in its envelope. He crossed the room and rejoined the Home member in the alcove.

"The letter reached my wife only a week ago," Lord Ingersoll explained. "It seems that Sir Jasper wrote several letters the night before he decided to take his own life—for what reason, we will never know. This and the others were found in Jasper's desk in the study by an assistant from the Treasury who came to sift through official papers kept at the house. It seems that the butler had put them away that night as instructed by Jasper and, in his subsequent state of shock, forgotten all about them. I believe there were letters also for Pendlebury's wife and son, and a copy of his last testament and will."

"But after having remained silent for so long," Arvind Singh asked, puzzled, "why should he have suddenly decided to write this letter at all?"

Ingersoll's shoulders lifted in a minimal shrug. "Strange things can happen to men's minds when they stare death in the face, Your Highness," he mused. "Who knows what impulses passed through Jasper's during his final hours—or, indeed, what provided the trigger for them? Maybe he simply wanted to make his peace with his Maker."

"And your lordship believes that this is true, even though there can be no corroboration?"

"Yes. It is generally believed that a man on the threshhold of death rarely lies. Courts of law are inclined to accept even uncorroborated dying declarations as the truth—*Propter mortis causa,* you know, 'in expectation of death.' And Jasper had no more axes to grind, poor devil."

Arvind Singh returned the envelope to Ingersoll. "May I ask what your lordship intends to do with this letter?" he asked, his eyes glinting and alert.

Ingersoll replaced the envelope in his breast pocket. His own eyes twinkled a little. "I'm sure Your Highness has already calculated the answer to that," he suggested lightly.

Arvind Singh raised a caustic eyebrow. "A trade?"

"Yes, a trade, Your Highness." Ingersoll's smile widened, but it remained bland.

"With the government's involvement?"

"No. As I mentioned earlier, officially the government cannot be involved."

Arvind Singh caught the subtle inflection. "And unofficially?"

"Unofficially, we have an option. But that is conditional."

"The condition being?"

"That all existing copies of Thomas Hungerford's affidavit be handed over to me, as also the man's address in Burdwan."

"For what purpose?" Arvind Singh asked sharply.

"Merely to keep an eye on him, I assure you. Our trade would be futile if the man simply went and repeated it all again."

"The poor man will probably be dead within the month." Arvind Singh's smile was still tight. "How unfair that he will have died without ever learning of his inadvertent importance to the mighty British Government! Anyway, to return to the matter of the trade—what would be your lordship's contribution?"

"Once I have all the documents, my wife will leave for England with Jasper Pendlebury's letter. In view of this fresh and incontrovertible evidence, she will beseech Her Majesty to issue a proclamation declaring Jai Raventhorne innocent of any involvement in the Bibighar massacre."

"And if Her Majesty is not willing to do so?"

"My wife is a very determined and persuasive woman, Your Highness," Ingersoll remarked with a wry grin, "as I know to my cost! She usually achieves what she sets out to do. And, of course, Her Majesty looks upon her with favour."

"Lady Ingersoll is prepared to undertake such a mission?"

"Yes. She has great compassion and concern for the Eurasian community. She considers that it deserves better than what we have been able to give it and, of course, there are many of us who endorse her opinion. Having met the Raventhorne family that night at the Pendleburys' and been charmed by them, she is, in fact, eager to do whatever she can in the matter. You see, Your Highness," he pointed out quietly, "we must not forget that Jasper sent that letter to my wife for a purpose. A purpose Harriet now considers it her bounden duty to fulfil."

Arvind Singh reflected for a moment, then nodded in agreement. "And, in all this, what would be the attitude of the government?"

"Once the Viceroy and the Secretary of State for India see Hungerford's statement and assess all the disastrous implications of an inadvertent disclosure, I can assure you neither will be inclined to make a fuss. To ensure that they do not will be my responsibility."

Arvind Singh was still not entirely mollified. Unable to sit, he leapt to his feet and started to pace. "But then the truth about Jai's death will always remain obscured! It will always be believed that it was he who was hanged that day in the clearing like a common criminal—that is what I find difficult to stomach!"

"On the other hand, it will, at least, remove the stigma from the Raventhorne name. Under these bizarre circumstances, Your Highness, surely what I offer is the best option available?"

"An option with no explanations, no admission of error, no apologies for the suffering caused by that error!" He continued to walk up and down the length of the room, his hands plucking restlessly at each other behind his back.

Ingersoll laughed. "Come, come, Maharaja Sahib," he said, reverting to the more informal form of address, his tone persuasive. "To expect a government, especially a colonial one, to offer explanations in its defence or make admissions of error—or, indeed, apologies—is scarcely reasonable. All we can hope for is that a sympathetic, highly literate bureaucrat is called upon to compose Her Majesty's proclamation. Bureaucrats can be remarkably manipulative with language. Many have a positive genius for using the same words for both revelation and concealment, and, indeed, for making a single innocuous phrase acquire a dozen simultaneous meanings. What is hinted at between the lines is often more eloquent than what is stated."

Ingersoll joined the Maharaja as he paced, forcing him to halt his footsteps. "Surely, half a biscuit is better than none, Maharaja Sahib," he pointed out with all the coercive skill at his disposal, "particularly since we both know that there is no chance of ever acquiring the other half. As you have seen better than anyone else, the Raventhornes have had more than their fair share of mental torment. It is time now to end it. The trade I offer may not be perfect, but all things considered, it is as fair an exchange as I can make. I implore you to accept it."

Arvind Singh walked over to his desk and stood staring down at something, motionless and unspeaking. Then he ran the back of his hand across his eyes and nodded slowly. "Yes," he said with some sadness as he pulled in a deep breath. "Yes, I suppose it is. The final decision to accept or reject, however, cannot be mine. It can only come from Jai Raventhorne's family."

"Your Highness will put it to them as soon as might be conveniently possible?" Lord Ingersoll urged anxiously.

"Oh indeed, I will place the matter before them tomorrow. As it happens, the Maharani and I leave for Calcutta in the morning on our way to Cawnpore to search for Jai's grave according to Hungerford's directions. I will make it my duty to apprise the family in all detail, not only of these astounding revelations but also of the suggested bargain."

"Your Highness will advise them to accept my offer, assure them that it is an equitable exchange?"

Arvind Singh did not speak for a while, then he sighed. "Whatever has come has come thirteen years too late, but I suppose we should be grateful that at least it *has* come!" There was lingering sorrow in his face. "Yes. I will advise them to accept your lordship's offer."

It was again the month of October.

The auspicious season during which Hindus prepare to pay homage to the Mother Goddess Durga and her incarnations, Lakshmi and Kali, was a season of ritual and revelry. The rains were over; the countryside wore a green mantle, presaging fruit and fecundity. If in the Western hemisphere the season turned the foliage to russet and gold before stealing it away altogether for winter, to the tropics it brought abundance. Nature's vibrant canvases were alive with colour, its forests resonant with birdsong. Clouds of butterflies exploded over delicately perfumed gardens and parks, the lime green of the paddy fields so brilliant that it stung the eyes. Breathless with anticipation, people waited impatiently for the festivities to begin, humming as they worked, preparing to expend precious savings on new clothes and gifts and mind-cleansing obeisance. In the lanes of Kumarthuli, tucked into the bosom of Calcutta, fingers of potters and sculptors flew frantically over shapeless lumps of clay to fashion them magically into the images of divinity. It was during this season that commercial establishments set aside old ledgers and turned to fresh pages, the traditional symbol of a new beginning.

For the Raventhorne family, too, the season marked a new beginning.

The past few weeks spent in Cawnpore had brought both torment and deliverance. Their long, painful quest was over: thirteen years of anger and heartbreak had finally come to an end. Thomas Hungerford's impromptu map had proved adequate. Considering the lapse of years, it was indeed commendably accurate. Even so, it had taken a week to find the banyan tree in a dense forest made more lush by the rains. The passage of time and the assault of the elements had eroded the carvings on the main trunk and obscured them with lichen, but eventually they had discovered Hungerford's hastily engraved inscription:

And by its side, near the roots of the tree, a gentle mound overgrown with moss, a mere ripple in the surface of the earth, waiting patiently to be discovered and claimed. On the grave, mildewed and eaten away by termites and barely holding together, were the remains of the rough cross Hungerford had fashioned out of branches.

Jai Raventhorne's final resting place!

It seemed ironic that so simple an epitaph and so modest a grave in this tranquil niche of some distant, undisturbed forest should mark the passing of a life as complex and turbulent as that of Jai Raventhorne. At the same time it seemed fitting, a hard-earned reward of eternal peace. Olivia wept quietly. Crowding memories of yesteryears returned; they consoled even as they convulsed, reviving a sense of loss once again insurmountable. By her side were her children, mourning with her in silence, awestruck and moved beyond words at the realisation of this extraordinary myth about a man they barely remembered.

Even those who had never known Jai Raventhorne shared in the tears: Edna Chalcott, David and Adelaide Pickford, and their daughter Rose. Others, bound by a common thread of love and remembrance, were the intimate handful who had held Jai Raventhorne dear, those whose lives he had touched and, perhaps, added meaning to: Arvind Singh, Kinjal, Ranjan Moitra.

Throughout the long journey north, Olivia had wondered in a state of high nervousness just how Estelle had received the detailed letter she had written to her before leaving for Cawnpore, relating Thomas Hungerford's shocking revelations. Could the resurrections have been too painful for her cousin to absorb? Would they, perhaps, have driven her back into the fragile security of the cocoon she had fashioned to insulate herself from her agonising memories?

Olivia need not have worried. To her great joy, when they arrived in Cawnpore, a letter from Estelle awaited her at the Pickfords'. Not only had her cousin delivered the letter in person and revived her acquaintanceship with Rose and Adelaide, she had expressed a fervent wish to be included in the search for the grave, however lengthy and arduous that hurtful exploration might prove to be. True to her word, she had hurried to the family's side as soon as she received news of their arrival in Cawnpore, and had remained with them throughout their stay, mourning for the brother she had loved deeply and still cherished. Overwhelmed by the reunion with so many from a past she had denied for so long, heartbroken that it should be in such sorrowful circumstances, she had sobbed uncontrollably when the grave was eventually located. That she suffered profoundly, still unable to bring herself to share her horrendous remembrances, was evident. But it was also evident that she endured her inner torment with remarkable courage.

Amos had arranged for the grave to be cemented and covered with a slab of plain white marble. It was inscribed with the same modest epitaph that Hungerford had devised, an appropriate tribute to a man who despised extravagance. Each of them had planted a favourite bush about the grave, some sweet-scented, others heavy with blossom, yet others simply eternal and evergreen.

For Olivia it had been an extraordinary feeling to have Jai so close, to touch the soil with which he had merged. She had felt his presence in the air, all around, everywhere, sensed his joy that they were, at last, reunited, separated now only by that fragile heartbeat that divides the dead from the living. . . .

Amos had remained behind in Cawnpore with Ranjan Moitra to tackle the manifold problems they now faced in reactivating the defunct cotton mill. Adamant that he would not declare his feelings to either Rose or her parents until the Queen's proclamation became a reality and his father was publicly accepted as innocent of any complicity in the Bibighar massacre, he nevertheless displayed a sense of joy Olivia had not known in him ever before, not even as a carefree child in Hawaii. That Rose—as quietly and completely in love with him as he was with her—would agree to become his wife whenever he asked her, and that her parents would give them their blessings, Olivia already sensed. She was happy for Amos, delighted with his choice of a bride, but at the same time, filled with melancholy that the radical change in his life would mark the closing of yet another chapter in hers. The melancholy was compounded by the fact that, over the years, her quest to vindicate Jai Raventhorne had become a habit, an all-consuming obsession. Without it now, she felt a curious kind of inner vacancy. She returned to Calcutta with an undoubted sense of deliverance, of jubilation and gratitude. But, inevitably, with all that also came a vast emptiness.

"How do I fill all these hours of the day?" she asked Edna on the first day of their return home. "With what do I occupy my mind?"

"Once you reach Sacramento, you can leave that to your stepmother to decide," Edna advised. "Sally will make sure you have so much to do, there will be no time to worry about an unoccupied mind!"

"I wish I could go with you to the Nilgiri Hills," Olivia said wistfully, harking back to their long-planned holiday.

Edna sighed. "Yes. I wish you could, dear."

"I'll miss you, you know."

"I'll miss you, too."

It was a season of farewells also for many others. Samir Goswami had sailed for England while they were in Cawnpore. Abala came bubbling with the news, bearing an enormous basket of fruits and sweets. Before Samir left, she told them, they had celebrated his engagement with great aplomb to a Brahmin girl of sixteen. The marriage would take place when he returned home next year for a holiday. The girl had been selected by her eldest sister-in-law, Sarala, Abala said. She was much relieved, she added, that the horoscopes of the couple had matched perfectly, ensuring them sons, prosperity and a happy life together.

"But I thought all you social reformists were dead against the use of horoscopes as a matter of principle, Abala," Olivia exclaimed with a laugh.

Abala's plump cheeks turned red. "Whatever one's private beliefs," she murmured, confused and abashed, "one sometimes has to bow to the wishes of the elders."

It was a social hypocrisy rampant among alleged social "reformers." Maya listened to it in silence and without comment.

Lady Ingersoll had finally persuaded Constance Pendlebury to return to England with her, and they too had sailed. Tremaine, still decimated by guilt, had needed no persuasion to leave with them, but much to Lady Pendlebury's chagrin, Monsieur Pierre had elected to remain behind in India. The inducement to end a long bachelorhood had been provided by the delectable M'amselle Corinne. The couple had decided to settle in the French possession of Chandernagore as partners in the bride's mother's thriving kitchenware business.

That Constance Pendlebury had finally received a letter from Christian was known to her friends. The contents of the letter were not. Tight-lipped but still determinedly protective of her son, she indicated only that he had suffered a grave and prolonged illness soon after leaving station. It was this that had prevented him from maintaining contact with her over these past weeks. If anyone doubted her explanation, certainly no one had the courage to question it openly.

Despite her secret hurt at Christian's unforgivable behaviour, however, Lady Pendlebury remained privately convinced that it was the intolerably evil vibrations this wretched country exuded that had instigated Christian's temporary insanity. In her mind there was not a vestige of doubt that once he tired of his aimless wanderings, he would return to the fold, ready to settle down in England and resume his rightful position in society. Content in this belief, Lady Pendlebury had already set her sights on a certain target and activated her brain into devising precisely how it was to be achieved. If she used her influence with politically eminent friends, she decided, she was sure to secure a satisfactory post for Christian in Whitehall. As a young baronet with a newly inherited title and fortune, he would be much in demand, both professionally and personally. In fact, as soon as she reached England, she determined to resume her earlier discussions with the Derbyshire Worthingtons about their second daughter, Lucy, the one who sang like a lark and was due to be presented early in the summer. . . .

As to what her husband had revealed to her in his final letter, no one even dared to ask about that. And certainly, Constance Pendlebury herself volunteered not a wisp of information. Pale-faced but characteristically serene, she merely went about the business of winding up her household in stoic silence, letting everyone draw whatever conclusions they pleased.

Among the expatriate community, the McNaughtons had left for home under rather mysterious circumstances. Ostensibly, they were returning to celebrate their daughter's forthcoming nuptials. Secretly, however, it was whispered that Nemesis had finally overtaken Bruce McNaughton and—many maintained—not a moment too soon. Through the good offices of some anonymous informant, it was rumoured, the Lieutenant-

Governor had been caught red-handed accepting a handsome bribe from a local contractor in exchange for various favours granted vis-à-vis the new road being laid between Dharamtala and Baghbazaar. Apparently, someone had sent an unsigned letter to the Viceroy's Secretariat acquainting His Excellency with all pertinent details of McNaughton's profitable personal "arrangement" with the contractor. Being a man of strict principles, Lord Mayo had ordered immediate surveillance, and McNaughton had been trapped with his trousers down, so to speak. In the interests of the morale of the Civil Service, however, he had been allowed to "resign" on grounds of "ill health," but no one was fooled by the euphemism. So far, the identity of the secret informant had not been discovered; whoever he was, there was no doubt that there were many who blessed him.

While some prepared to leave for homes across various seas, others, eager and excited, arrived in droves, bright-eyed and expectant, in search of swift fame and fortune or merely English husbands. Unaware of both the lethal climate in Calcutta and the intangible predators lurking in the shadows of this brooding, baleful subcontinent, they appeared blissfully content simply to be avoiding another punitive English winter.

There was further news, some heartening, some saddening. Sarojini's father and his brother had been judged guilty and sentenced to four years of rigorous imprisonment. A message, brought by a neighbour from Burdwan, informed Olivia that Hungerford was dead. He had passed away peacefully in the arms of a loving mother, who blessed the Raventhornes many times over for their generosity to her. A telegraph from Alistair in England conveyed the news that he had arrived safely in Farrowsham following a comfortable voyage. Both he and his grandmother were well, the telegraph said. Lady Birkhurst sent her love. So did Alistair!

"You didn't have anything to do with McNaughton's rather abrupt departure from our midst, did you?" Olivia asked Leonard Whitney when he called on her and Maya following their return to station.

"Me?" Whitney's expression went blank as he met Olivia's eyes squarely. "No, Mrs. Raventhorne."

"But then, who else could possibly have known the precise location and time of Sir Bruce's clandestine meeting with the contractor?" Olivia persisted, her eyes twinkling.

Whitney's face remained determinedly impassive. "Regrettably, I am not in a position to pronounce opinion on whatever possibilities existed, Mrs. Raventhorne," he informed her primly.

"Aren't you?" Olivia smiled and let it go at that. She was well aware that whatever Whitney was in a position to pronounce opinion on he would take to the grave with him. "Anyway, tell me how the project for the new settlement has been progressing."

Whitney immediately waxed eloquent. "Well, ever since we announced the project," he said, once again buoyant, "people have been flocking to us, eager not only to stake claims to plots of land but also to help in whatever way they can. The caravans moving north are endless, and believe it or not, donations are simply pouring in."

"Donations?" Olivia asked, surprised. "Who from?"

Whitney voiced one of his rare chuckles. "Well, many are sent anonymously, probably from 'interested' parties such as Douglas Hooper. I should imagine he's overjoyed at finally ridding himself of that woman and her brood in Molunga."

Help had indeed come from several surprising quarters. Before she sailed for England, Lady Ingersoll had sent a charming letter and a handsome sum of money as a personal contribution. Obviously urged by her, several others had done likewise. Lord Ingersoll had promised assistance in unravelling bureaucratic knots. Two or three builders had offered free expertise, wholesale suppliers building materials at cost prices, and an elderly Welsh doctor retired in Patna had come forward to set up a free dispensary in the new settlement.

"Lady Ingersoll and some other English residents are under the impression that the scheme was Jasper Pendlebury's brainchild." Whitney shrugged. "Well, what does it matter anyway? Kyle doesn't care who gets the credit as long as the project becomes a workable reality." He himself, he added with a modest blush, would remain in Calcutta for the time being, since he had been selected as administrator of the marine school project on the *Ganga*—or rather, the S.S. *Jai Raventhorne*. "Amos is most determined that the institution should get off to a good start."

"As I'm sure it will with you at the helm." Olivia knew already about Whitney's appointment to the high post and was pleased about it. "And Kyle and his mother—are they both well?"

"So I hear, although the going is fairly hard. She is very keen to start this school as soon as possible."

"And the press? Are the boys running it in accordance with Kyle's own high standards? I must say, I haven't seen a copy of *Equality* this week, have you, dear?"

Maya shook her head.

Whitney's face fell. "You haven't heard?" he cried, all at once distressed. Apparently, during their absence in Cawnpore and Kyle's at the plantation, the press had been smashed to pieces and then torched.

"Oh dear God!" Olivia was horrified. "Was anyone hurt? Any of those young boys at the premises?"

"Thankfully, no. They suffered only minor burns and abrasions, but they were lucky to escape with their lives. The assault was mounted in the middle of the night by a gang of unidentifiable men wearing masks. They were obviously professional rogues, used to working fast. Within minutes, they had demolished everything—the printing machinery, the stocks, much of the furniture. And then they set it all alight."

"The books?" Maya's involuntary question escaped before she could stop it.

"Charred beyond redemption," Whitney said unhappily. "Everything else Kyle will take in his stride, but those books . . . the collection was the joy of his life, the only possession he truly valued."

"None of it could be salvaged?"

"The boys did their best but could save only a fraction of what was there. Kyle is the only one who can determine the extent of the loss. He's due to return in a day or two."

"Who could have done such a terrible thing, anyway?" Olivia asked. "Has Clarence Twining made any arrests?"

Sadly, Whitney shook his head. "There are many here who hate both Kyle and his paper, and everything they stand for. It could have been anyone."

Maya asked no more questions, but she accelerated her preparations for the journey to America.

The month in Cawnpore had been a sobering time for Maya. It had offered her a chance to think, to untangle her confusions, to rearrange her thoughts. To start to heal. She had spent long hours by her father's grave, trying to picture him in her mind, trying to understand his curious motivations in order to better understand her own. The change of environment had brought a touch of pink to her cheeks, a faint sparkle to her eyes. The return of energy was apparent in her gait, in the greater confidence of her manner. Evidence of her scars remained, would always remain, but the pain was no longer intolerable, her inner wounds no longer raw. She prayed for Christian, for his future, for the miracle of a fresh beginning for him, too. She prayed that some day he could come to terms with himself and find whatever it was that he sought.

As she herself was so desperately trying to do. . . .

Kinjal had remained behind in Calcutta at their Kalighat house to be able to spend a final few days with Olivia before she sailed for San Francisco. But as the day of departure approached, she noticed that Olivia was turning visibly morose, always on the verge of venturing some heartfelt pronouncement, never quite managing to make it.

"Why don't you simply say it, my dear?" Kinjal suggested bluntly one afternoon as they sat in Olivia's upstairs parlour. "It's been hovering on the tip of your tongue for so long, you might as well spit it out!"

Continually taking clothes from one trunk and putting them into another, then mindlessly reversing the process, Olivia suddenly banged down the lid of a trunk and sat on it. "You know what I'm trying to say!"

"Yes. You don't want to leave at all. Isn't that it?"

Olivia nodded, pulled up her knees and hugged them tight, swaying back and forth on the trunk. "Everything I love remains here, Kinjal, rooted in this soil, this once alien soil that I have now made my own. Even Jai. . . ." Her throat tightened. "Now that I have found him again, how can I abandon him to lie there alone, in that anonymous forest where he has languished, forgotten, over all these dreadful years?"

"The change would be good for you," Kinjal pointed out. "Besides, you can always return after a year."

"A year? So much is to happen in a year, Kinjal!" Olivia looked even more distraught. "Amos starts a new enterprise in Cawnpore, which means he will have to set up house, prepare his new home to receive a bride. Before that happens, I would so like to travel south with Edna to see the Nilgiri Hills—and I have so many plans for the Home now that we have the extra space in the annexe. I want to start adult literacy classes for the women who can't read or write, train those who can to teach, perhaps finance them to start elementary schools. I've ordered one of these brand new mechanical writing machines from America and that means that I will have to learn how to use it so that I can instruct the others . . . and Estelle, my darling, ill-starred Estelle, now almost returned to me, *almost.* . . ." She spread her hands helplessly, "You saw how warm and loving she was in Cawnpore, how much like her old self again. We *need* each other, Kinjal! If I belong anywhere now it is here, with Jai, with this earth that nurtured him and still gives him refuge, with my beloved cousin. It is Maya who so passionately yearns for a new world. For me there can only be the old world, Kinjal, this battered, woebegone one!"

"I accept what you say, my dear, but Maya also needs you, perhaps more now than ever before, considering everything that has happened."

"Oh, I know, I know. That is precisely what is tearing me apart, Kinjal— I simply don't know what to do!"

Kinjal's eyes softened; how well she understood her friend's continuing dilemma. Over the past twenty-three years, Olivia had had a strangely paradoxical relationship with India, part hate, part love. Even now, she was torn between the two. Kinjal offered no solution, aware that when a solution did arrive, it would have to come from Olivia herself. Surprisingly, however, when it did come, it came from Maya.

"If you would like to stay behind, Mother," she said, quite unexpectedly at breakfast one morning a week before the sailing date, "I would be perfectly happy to go on my own with the Lubbocks."

Considerably taken aback, Olivia nevertheless grabbed the straw her daughter offered, with painful eagerness. "Would you, darling, *would* you truly?"

"Yes, of course I would, Mother."

"But if I back out now, your grandma Sally would be dreadfully disappointed!" Olivia wailed. "She's been so looking forward to seeing me!"

"Don't worry, Mother," Maya reassured her. "I'll try my best to make amends on your behalf. Besides, I'm sure Grandma would understand."

Anxiously, Olivia scanned her daughter's face as she tried to read behind the blankness, but as always, Maya's expression was ungiving.

Three days remained before the embarkation. Almost hysterical with excitement, Grace Lubbock was in and out of the house bearing various tidings, mostly about her much cherished Alberto, matching plans with Maya, wildly impatient to be away. Neatly stacked baggage stood in the Raventhornes' hallway waiting to be despatched to the hold of the Trident clipper now being loaded and provisioned at the wharf. Sheba's enormous excitement had gradually waned, as had the glitter of the shining new world of America. Now, with departure imminent, the housekeeper seemed permanently dissolved in tears, devastated at having to leave behind places and people she loved. In her state of mental distress, she fussed around in a daze, making a mess of the labels, amending lists, leaving the packing and insurance agents tearing their hair as they made valiant attempts to meet her endless and often contradictory demands.

For Maya herself, there now remained nothing to do. Possessed by disturbing moods, she wandered about the house and stables on her own, buried in private thought, edgy and directionless, as if a part of herself was lost and she was unable to find it. She could not stop thinking of Kyle, of their last meeting, of those premises now wrecked and gone forever. Every word that he had uttered that night seemed to have burrowed its way from her ear into her brain like a noisome maggot, gnawing away at her peace of mind from within. When she was awake, she heard his voice reverberate in her mind; when she slept, he returned to scurry about on the fringes of her dreams, infecting them with panic. She hated having him with her always, day and night, wherever she went. Try as she might, she simply could not rid herself of the haunting spectre of this strange man who afflicted her so greatly.

From within the mists of her endless introspections, however, something did finally emerge to clarify at least part of her inner confusions. She had been considerably discomfitted by the discovery that she envied Kyle Hawkesworth. Now she knew precisely why she did so.

It was late afternoon. The waters of the river were slowly turning yellow, speckled with pink and orange from the western sky. From the hutments alongside the distant wharf, spirals of smoke curled up in the air as a dozen charcoal stoves were fanned into life for the evening meal. Soon, the western horizon would be ablaze with another glorious sunset.

Maya slowly and carefully picked a path up the familiar embankment. This, she knew, was truly the last time she would come here. She would not pass this way again.

Even though the fire had occurred many days ago, the trenchant smell of burning still lingered in the air, filling the nostrils with unpleasantness. From a familiar vantage point she peered down at the ledge below. The entrance to the tunnel was blocked with rubble; in a grotesque mess of stone and mud, what had been the roof of the tunnel had collapsed inwards, forming a deep crevasse in the earth. She strolled up the slope, past the skeletal hulk of what had once been the press. The back door into the compound of the house hung limply on jagged hinges, the wooden panels charred beyond redemption. The surround of the wall was thick with soot and had crumbled in several places. What used to be the courtyard was now a wasteland of blackened bricks and ash, the house itself a hollow shell with gaping windows and a sagging roof.

Standing in what was once a doorway, Maya surveyed the scene before her in a state of shock. The study next to the parlour was a travesty. The desk, cupboards and bookcases sprawled across the debris in a grotesque tableau were all in various stages of disintegration. It was such a horrific sight that, briefly, her mind went blank; she could not recall why she had come. As she regrouped her senses, she started to fill with rage at the unspeakable act of vindictiveness. But then, quickly, she discarded the anger and steeled herself. This had to be positively her very last visit here. If she weakened now, she would be lost.

Her searching gaze finally located Kyle in a far corner of the devastation. He was on his hands and knees, rummaging among the charred remains. Deep in concentration, he did not hear her approach. She stood and watched him for a while—darting eyes, frantic fingers, the bronzed, sun-weathered face ravaged with anguish. The tip of her shoe struck against something and he looked up.

"I'll find some of it, I'm sure," he muttered, accepting her presence without question, unsurprised that she should be there. *"All* of it could not have vanished!"

"What?"

"Omar Khayyám. *The Rubáiyát."*

"Have you recovered any of it?"

"Only the cover and the flyleaf." He pointed to a pile of salvaged pages stacked over some assorted folders he had obviously also managed to rescue. His hands, she noticed, were calloused and stained, the fingernails black. "Some of the volumes were leather-bound. Leather doesn't burn as well as paper. Or, at least, it burns slower." He picked up something, a metal object, twisted into the strangest shape. "The cylinder from one of the printing machines," he explained, tossing it over his shoulder. "I was going to get rid of it anyway."

She walked over and, getting down on her hands and knees, also started to rummage. He did not stop her.

"Who was responsible for all this?" she asked, her anger well hidden.

"Who knows?" He sat back a moment, thinking, a curious expression on his face. "Perhaps a hand reaching out from beyond the grave!"

She shivered and gave him a questioning look, but he did not explain.

"It was her jewels that sustained the press, you know. She insisted."

"Joycie?"

"Yes. She wanted to repay my mother."

"Your mother gave her shelter when the nawab threw her out?"

He nodded. "In Lucknow. My mother took care of the jewellery for her. They threatened her, came looking for it—the nawab's family, that is—but my mother had hidden it well. They never found any of it. It was rightfully hers."

"Joycie financed the magazine?"

"Partly, yes. She said it gave her pleasure."

Maya surveyed the havoc. "Will you stay and revive it?"

He turned his face away from her and shrugged. "Grinstead and the boys want to. I wish them well, but I personally have no stomach for a revival. This belonged to yesterday. I have tomorrow to consider."

There was sudden pain in his face, as if he mourned a loved one mauled beyond recognition. She quickly lowered her eyes and continued her search.

"Ah!" He pounced on something and extracted it triumphantly from

624

under a pile of blackened bricks, then rubbed it clean against his trousers. "Thomas Paine. *The Age of Reason*. The final pages with only the corners gone." He added the sheets to the pile by his side. "Have you read it?"

"No."

"You should. It is magnificent. Maybe the rest is also somewhere around here."

He spoke with an effort, the enthusiasm forced, the pain scored too deep in the lines of his face not to betray him. Oddly enough, it hurt her to see him so vulnerable, so much at a loss, scrounging amid the ruins of an intrepid enterprise that was once so arrogant, so defiantly rebellious. Now he seemed drained, undefended against the terrible hate of society, no longer a victor, simply another victim. She had not seen him with his life force at such a low ebb; it disturbed her to look at him. Walking up to the skeleton of one of the bookcases, she started to go through some more salvaged pages he had stored on that half-charred shelf. The leaves on top came from *Don Quixote*, she noticed, the middle chapters.

"We went to Cawnpore."

"I know."

"My father was innocent."

"That I have always known."

"I didn't. I thought he was guilty, and I hated him for it. I hated the shame, the sniggers, the whispered remarks and looks of revulsion." She shuddered in vehement remembrance. "I hated what he had made me—a half-caste, an *outcast!* I hated him for never going away. More than that"— her tone went flat—"I hated him for making *them* hate me."

He sat back, his arms draped around his knees, head tilted to a side. "And now?"

"Now?" There was a shine of tears in the corners of her eyes. She snapped them shut so that he would not see them—or discern the embryo thought forming inside her mind. "Now, I don't know. I'm sick of hating, of being hated—so damned sick of it!"

"So much hate, so much wasted passion!"

To whom did his murmured remark refer—to her alone or to them both? She did not ask. Instead, she again busied herself scrambling through the debris. What she had just told him, she had never before said to anyone. It astonished her that she should have said it to Kyle, that she should communicate with him on such an intensely private level. She ventured a sidelong glance at him, but he was again lost in his hopeless quest, his fingers and eyes boring into the detritus that half buried his boots.

"It was a long journey," she said.

"Long? To Cawnpore and back?"

"No, not that. . . ." She faltered.

In terms of distance, the journey to her father's grave was hardly long— but then, not every journey can be measured in geographical miles. During the past weeks she had travelled extraordinarily far, beyond space, into infinity, within and around herself, and she had emerged on the other side with startling new perspectives. But all this, of course, she could not tell him. He would only laugh. She contented herself with an evasion.

"What I meant was that there are some journeys that seem longer than they really are."

"A letter awaited me here from Christian."

He said it quite suddenly, without warning, and Maya's stomach somersaulted. She remained silent.

"He is living in a monastery somewhere in the mountains. He didn't say where."

"Is he . . . well?"

"As well as he can ever be." He arranged some more sheets of singed paper neatly on the precious pile. "He lives with the torment of an incurable guilt. Always will, he writes. But, he says, he could not have done otherwise. Apparently, the monks are kind and wise. They teach him to recognise the curious equations of life, and the even more curious devices of the mind with which to accept them."

"He does not think of returning to England?"

"Perhaps some day he will. He neither accepts nor discounts the possibility. He is learning, he says, how to live one day at a time."

She buried her face in a relatively unharmed section of the *Panchatantra* fables, pretending to browse. "Does he mention . . . me?" she asked casually.

"No." He picked up another few leaves of some charred book and dusted them. "Nor his father."

"Oh."

Then, before the unwanted topic could be explored further, she hastily handed him a packet that she had brought with her.

"What is this?"

"Books, crayons, pencils, some slates and chalk. For the school—the school that your mother has started." His surprise showed in his eyes, wide and puzzled. He merely nodded and put the packet by his side.

"Is this why you came?"

"Partly. I came to apologise for what I said the other day. I didn't mean it."

"Why not? It was true."

"No, it was unjust. You do what you do out of selflessness. That I know. It is I who run away." She again felt bitterness sting the back of her throat. "What you say is true—I want to hide, I cannot face anyone. It would be hypocritical to deny it. Foolishly, I tried to attain that which for me is unattainable and beyond my reach."

"An identity? A label? That brand on the haunches?" He brushed it all away with a gesture. "To want those is a natural part of human desire, a congenital arrogance—evidence of the great herd instinct, if you like. The human race has an inborn capacity to pretend not to see itself as it truly is, only as it would like to be."

"But isn't that hypocritical?"

"In the final analyses, I suppose, we are *all* hypocrites of one kind or another."

She sat back unheeding of the mess, drifting away, high up above the

land and river, wafting into a private trance. Within her swirled a confluence of emotions: amorphous thoughts, still nascent, drifted across her
mind, solidified and, all at once, took shape. They were disturbing
thoughts but, amazingly, she was not disturbed. She knew that she was
losing her grip, weakening, but the very weakness was too strong to resist.
She heard a voice say something, an alien voice she did not recognise.

"I want to go with you when you return."

It shocked her that that alien voice should be her own! Was she quite
mad?

Kyle's groping hands stilled. "What?"

The voice, rebellious and unheeding, strengthened, and without con-
sciously intending to, she persisted in her madness. "I said, take me with
you."

He stared in mystification. "Where?"

"To the plantation."

"To the plantation?" He broke into a disbelieving laugh. "You want to
go to the *plantation!* To a Eurasian ghetto filled with destitutes? Tut, tut!
What do we come down to!"

"There is more than one kind of destitution." She stopped. She could
not explain to him what she meant, expose to him that deep inner hunger
of an undernourished mind, of a life vacant and unfulfilled and without
direction. "That too I should not have said," she said, sidestepping an
explanation. "I merely exercised my own bitterness on you. I'm sorry."

"Well, what *is* this, then"—he was withering in his scepticism—"an
answer to a clarion call, to some mysterious inner challenge—or just
another fleeting fancy, because it is alluringly different?"

"Whichever you choose to believe."

"And your new world, abandoned even before a taste?"

"There can be more than one new world."

"Not this one, not the plantation!" He was vastly amused. "Besides, we
have our fill of lame ducks at the moment. We certainly don't need any
more."

"You don't consider that I can pull my weight as well as anybody?" she
asked sharply.

"Since you ask, no. You simply don't have the resources."

She was incensed by his condescension, by the supercilious dismissal.
"I am capable of work," she retorted, "as capable as you or any of the
others."

"Capable of living out in the open? Under canvas? Of satisfying your
appetite with a handful of puffed rice, raw chillies and onions? Of carrying
buckets of water over a mile, washing once every three days?" He snorted.
"You wouldn't survive there for five minutes, and you'd only end up
being a damned nuisance. *You* were the one who said it will not be easy.
Well, it isn't."

"Yes, and *you* were the one who said nothing worthwhile ever is!"

"What can you do, for heaven's sake?" he said in disgust. "You can't
even *cook!*"

"No, but I can look after horses better than most."

"Without grooms at your beck and call? I doubt if your equestrian talents encompass the complex art of clearing dung."

"Well, they do," she snapped, her eyes gleaming. "That too I can do better than most, I assure you. And, talking of resources, I do happen to have one that you don't."

"Oh? What, pray?"

"Money!"

"Money!" He lifted a scoffing eyebrow. "You think money can buy you anything you want?"

"No, but at the moment it can certainly buy you everything *you* want!"

"To flaunt money," he said contemptuously, "is snobbery of the most despicable order!"

"And to *sneer* at it is a juvenile affectation!"

He flung up his hands. "All right, so you want to go to the plantation to help keep the township free of dung. Is that about the extent of it?"

"No." She responded with assumed calm, privately furious at her curious compulsion to earn his approval, relieved that he could not see it. "If you really wish to know, I would like to help your mother build that school and dedicate it to my father." He sat back heavily, winded. She had the satisfaction of seeing that the flicker in his eyes was no longer one of amusement. "I can hardly believe that even you would be unthinking enough to turn down such an offer."

He scratched his nose with a blackened fingernail, still nonplussed. "And is that the only reason for this extraordinarily selfless decision?"

Selfless? If he only knew how selfish it really was. . . .

"No. There are others."

"Such as?"

"It doesn't matter. All I know is that that *is* what I want."

"A month ago you didn't know what you wanted!"

"That was a month ago. I do now."

A focus!

He stood up, put his hands on his hips and frowned. "You don't seem to understand what it's like out there," he said, still irate and impatient with her persistence. "These are not elegant people, people who adorn drawing rooms, or your romantic vision of the noble poor, destitute but dignified, proud in their poverty. Many out there are the dregs of humanity, dragged off the gullies, out of the gutters, unfortunate wretches with neither grace nor grammar. Most of them are illiterate, some have never washed, never used a comb or a cake of soap or sat at a table to eat. They crawl with lice and grime. They would *repel* you." He was starting to look helpless. "How would you tolerate them?"

"Your mother tolerates them. There must be others like her." She found a leather cover with two or three pages still intact inside, Plato's *Dialogues*. Dusting it well against the side of her riding skirt, she handed it to him.

"The secret of survival, Maya, is compromise—something you have never learned."

"Well, you know that I am good pupil," she reminded him. "While the school is being built and if your mother agrees, we could compromise by starting classes under a tree."

He raked his hair with both hands, harsh in his exasperation. "Is this the penance you have devised for yourself?" he asked, again, mocking. "Sackcloth and ashes amid the great unwashed hordes of this world?"

She felt the heat rise in her chest and climb to her head. His sarcasm was insufferable!

"It's not a penance, Kyle," she said, enraged and yet desperate for him to understand, frustrated that he could not. "Can't you see, it's a"—she almost said "need," but then amended it—"a choice."

He sat down, draped his arms about his knees, and studied her through narrowed eyes not entirely hostile. "It takes time to learn to heal, Maya, to start afresh." His tone was suddenly less abrasive. "There are no easy solutions, no instant remedies. If it is merely a fantasy that you chase, the reality will be unbearable."

Her mouth quivered. "The reality is already unbearable!"

Something in his face softened. "Go to America, Maya," he sighed. "That is where your future lies. You will not be able either to endure or to accept the . . . indelicacy of this other life. It will be a waste of time. And the work will be backbreaking."

"I have the time. And I have a strong back."

"And the perseverance to see it through?"

She got up and stared through the gaping hole that used to be the window, out into the radiance of the western horizon. It glowed with colour. "I don't know, Kyle, any more than you know whether your project will succeed. I am not sure that the assessment I have made of my capacities and powers of endurance. . . ."

"And limitations!"

"Yes, all right, limitations too, is accurate. But wouldn't it be a tragedy never to have tried to find out?" Why, she wondered, was he so dead against her going to the plantation? Did he truly consider her incompetent, or was there another reason? She spun around to face him. "Don't you see? I want to be a *part* of it," she began passionately, then bit back the rest in rising despair.

"Part of *what*, for heaven's sake?"

A dream, that small dream. . . .

Oh God, couldn't he *see* how much she envied him that? But how could she tell him? It would sound fanciful and childish, and he would be even more scathing.

"Of . . . something, perhaps just a delusion," she said slowly. "You wouldn't understand."

"A delusion." He sat silently for a while, abstracted, shuffling the sheets he held in his hand, lost within himself. "You know, sometimes I too wonder if I'm not deluding myself," he mused. "I wonder if what I want to devise is indeed a paradise—or merely the illusion of one, an expression of my own need. Is it truly a rainbow that I so nobly seek to bring within the reach of the unfortunate Eurasian, or, like Christian's father, do I simply strive to secure my own future?" He squeezed his eyes shut. "Christ, I wish I could be sure of my own motives!"

And she? Was she sure of hers? "What difference does it make *why* one does anything," she cried, "as long as one does it?"

"It makes a difference to have motives that are suspect. You said yourself the other day. . . ."

"What I said was out of spite. I have already apologised for it. You pursue a dream, a small dream, a 'rainbow,' as you call it. What could be suspect about that?"

He gave a hollow laugh. "Only fools chase after rainbows! Does anyone know where a rainbow begins? Or, for that matter, ends?"

He put down the papers he held, restless and full of self-doubt, once again at a loss and not quite knowing what to do to reassure himself. His dispiritedness, the despondently fumbling hands and bleakly staring eyes, the undertones of defeat, were unfamiliar to her. They revived the strange ache in her heart. Uncoiling a wispy skein of memory, she daringly allowed herself to look at him again through the distorting mists of adolescence as she had once done many years ago on the *Ganga*, when he had appeared to her like a god, omniscient and invincible. It was an impromptu figment of a childish imagination, she saw that now. He was neither invincible nor divine, merely a fallible, immensely careworn human, trying vainly to grapple with what he had called the curious equations of life.

As they all did!

She looked beyond that, letting her inner gaze wander over the many unexplored aspects of his enigmatic personality. She saw now how devastated he too was by the terrible succession of events of the past weeks during which they had both learned the true meaning of grief—and guilt, oh yes, that more than anything else! She saw how severely depleted they had left his confidence, and how tormenting were his proliferating uncertainties and dissatisfactions with himself. Like her, he too struggled to steady himself, to secure slipping footholds and regain precarious balances. And like her, he too maintained a facade merely as a protective device fashioned to conceal a soft underbelly, vulnerable and unshielded. In the virulence of the past weeks, they had both sustained mortal wounds, unable to come to terms with the terrifying ugliness that had invaded their lives. She could understand his self-questioning well; in it she heard echoes of her own.

Somewhere within her a chord stirred. She filled with slow, tremulous wonder. Perhaps what Kyle had said was true: perhaps they *were* kindred spirits after all, bound by that inescapable commonality she had fought so hard to deny. But would it ever be possible to bridge the divide of antagonism that had kept them on such implacably divergent paths for so long?

"It doesn't really matter, you know," she said gently.

He raised his eyes, still darkly troubled. "What doesn't?"

"Where a rainbow begins or ends. Isn't it enough that a rainbow *is* . . . ?"

He showed no reaction, merely sat with his head down, staring at the ground. He appeared not to have heard her. But then he gave a minimal nod and looked up. "Yes," he said, rewarding her with a surprised smile.

"I daresay you're right." He got up, dusted his trousers and walked away so that his back was towards her. "Tell me honestly," he said entirely without warning, not turning to look at her, *"did* you love Christian?"

She went still, disconcerted by a return to the subject. Then she strolled over to the shelving and carefully arranged an almost complete book of miraculously unscathed epic poems on top of the growing pile of excavated papers and folders.

"Is it always necessary for love to be a component of a marriage?"

He spun around, his stare hard. "I wouldn't know. I was hoping you would enlighten me!"

"Well, it isn't." She matched his stare, not letting her own waver. "Since honesty appears to be the order of the day, I too have a question for you. Tell me, *honestly*—what was the true reason you set out to destroy Chester Maynard and his relationship with me?"

He cocked his head to a side. "You can't guess?"

"If I could, I wouldn't be asking."

He walked across to the remains of the bookcase, rummaged among the salvaged folders, and pulled one out. From within its covers he withdrew an untidy handful of papers and, flicking through them, extracted what he sought. The sheet, once white, was now brown with smoke and badly singed. Wordlessly, he handed it to her.

"What is it?"

"Read it."

Not much remained legible, but there was enough to show that the paper was the copy of a certificate confirming a marriage between Chester Bolton Maynard and one Elspeth Agnes Fullerton. The ceremony had been solemnised more than five years earlier in a village church near Doncaster, England.

Maya went rigid, her face like a mask. "Where did you get this?"

"I have my sources."

"Why did you not show it to me earlier?"

"Would you have thanked me if I had?"

She turned away from him and closed her eyes, shaken and sick with humiliation. For a while she stood in silence, staring incredulously at the certificate she held in her hand. Then, with slow, deliberate movements, she tore it into a hundred small pieces and broadcast them into the wind out of the gaping window. They wafted away like a cloud of brown butterflies, coming to rest finally in the obscurity of the dust.

Kyle had gone to such excessive lengths for her salvation? Why . . . ? She was again torn and unexpectedly moved, waiting for some minimal explanation of his intent in doing so, but he remained stubbornly unforthcoming. She did not begrudge him his reticence. Whatever his compulsions, it was unlikely that he would reveal himself sufficiently to share them with her.

"When do we leave for the plantation?" she asked evenly.

He threw her a curious look, then shrugged. "You truly want to go?" He made no reference to the certificate.

"Yes."

"Does your mother know about this?"

"Not yet. I intend to tell her tonight."

"And Amos?"

"He arrives tomorrow from Cawnpore to see us off. He doesn't know, of course, that we've changed our plans. I'll tell him when he comes."

"He won't like it."

"That's *his* problem, not mine!"

He took a short stroll around the perimeter of the littered floor, agitated and uncomfortable, one hand massaging the back of his neck as if to pummel out the tensions. "Do you promise not to be a nuisance?" he demanded abruptly.

"A nuisance?" She gave him a sidelong look, nervously excited that the prospect of her being on the plantation should discomfit him so much. "No, of course I won't be!"

"And you promise to do exactly as told?"

She contented herself with a meek nod.

"And to stay well out of my way?"

"If you stay well out of mine."

"Naturally! I will have better things to do than waste time in bickering with you."

"Likewise."

"There will be no special comforts devised for your benefit," he growled. "I doubt if you will find *anything* there to please you, anything at all!"

Nothing . . . ?

An unbidden thought, swift and vaporous as a transient cloud, sped across her mind and then again vanished over the horizon of her consciousness. She felt his troubled stare on her, watchful and questioning, and knew that he had already sensed the thought. "I understand," she said quickly, reddening. "I have no preconceived expectations."

"Good. Just as long as you understand where we both stand."

"I do, I assure you."

"And for God's sake, don't come whining to me with complaints when your lily-white hands start to blister!"

"They won't blister."

"No?" He flung up his own with a muted curse, then thrust them forward for inspection, calloused palms up. "See these? That's what you're likely to end up with too!"

"Really?" She gave his hands a cursory glance, then ran a casual fingertip across the roughness. "Well, obviously your skin is too soft, Kyle," she suggested with immense satisfaction, even as her eyes began to smile. "What you need to do is *toughen* it."

Sharing in the remembrance, he had the grace to blush. For a moment he fingered his chin, lost for words. Then, conceding defeat with a mighty sigh, he started to laugh.